# THE
# LUMINOUS
# NOVEL

# THE LUMINOUS NOVEL

*Mario Levrero*

Translated by Annie McDermott

SHEFFIELD – LONDON – NEW YORK

First published in 2021 by And Other Stories
Sheffield – London – New York
www.andotherstories.org

9 8 7 6 5 4 3 2 1

ISBN: 9781913505011
eBook ISBN: 9781913505028

Editor: Lizzie Davis; Copy-editor: Bella Bosworth; Proofreader: Sarah Terry; Typeset in Monotype Bembo Book and Verlag by Tetragon, London; Cover Design: Steven Marsden; Printed and bound on acid-free, age-resistant Munken Premium by CPI Limited, Croydon, UK.

Quotations from the following sources gratefully acknowledged: Rosa Chacel, *Obra completa vol. 9: Diarios*; Somerset Maugham, 'The Lotus Eater'; Somerset Maugham, *The Moon and Sixpence*; Saint Teresa of Avila, *The Interior Castle (*or *The Mansions)*; Thomas Bernhard, *Old Masters*; lyrics from 'Yo en mi casa y ella en el bar' by Los Náufragos; Constantine P. Cavafy, 'The City', translated by Lawrence Durrell; William S. Burroughs, *The Place of Dead Roads*; JD Salinger, *Seymour: An Introduction*; lyrics from 'El monito' by Julio de Caro. Whilst all attempts have been made to find the copyright holders of quoted passages and secure permission where relevant, the publishers would welcome approaches in the case of omission.

This book has been selected to receive financial assistance from English PEN's PEN Translates programme, supported by Arts Council England. English PEN exists to promote literature and our understanding of it, to uphold writers' freedoms around the world, to campaign against the persecution and imprisonment of writers for stating their views, and to promote the friendly co-operation of writers and the free exchange of ideas. www.englishpen.org

And Other Stories gratefully acknowledge that our work is supported using public funding by Arts Council England.

# ACKNOWLEDGEMENTS

To the Powers that allowed me to have luminous experiences.

To the John Simon Guggenheim Foundation.

To all those who agreed to feature as characters in the 'Diary of the Grant', especially Chl.

To the guinea-pig readers who helped me edit the 'Diary', especially Eduardo Abel Giménez, Carmen Simón, Mónica Suárez and Fernanda Trías.

To the people who encouraged me to apply for the Guggenheim grant, in particular Malaro Díaz, Hugo Verani, Julio Ortega, Fernando Burgos and Rómulo Cosse; and to Mariana Urti, an impeccable secretary throughout all the paperwork from the Foundation.

M. L.

Any people or institutions who feel affected or injured by the opinions expressed in this book should understand that these opinions are nothing but the ravings of a senile mind.

M. L.

# CONTENTS

# HISTORICAL PREFACE
# TO THE LUMINOUS NOVEL

I'm not sure what exactly the origin was, the initial impulse that led me to attempt the luminous novel, although the beginning of the first chapter says expressly that the impulse arose from an obsessive image, and the image is clear enough to allow the reader to believe this statement. I myself ought to believe it unreservedly, because I have a very strong memory of both the image and its obsessive quality, or at least its recurrence over a long enough period to have suggested the idea of obsession.

My doubts relate more to the fact that now, when I look back on that time, another completely different image occurs to me as the source of that impulse; and judging by this image, the initial impulse arose from a conversation I had with a friend. I'd told this friend about an experience of mine that had been extremely transcendental, and I'd told him how difficult it would be to turn it into a story. According to my theory, there are some extraordinary experiences that can't be written about without becoming denatured; it's impossible to set them down on paper. My friend insisted that if I wrote it just as I'd told it that night, I'd have a beautiful story; and that not only would I be able to write it, but that writing it was my duty.

In fact, these two images don't contradict one another, and they're even both supported by an attentive reading of the first lines of that first chapter – an attentive reading that I undertook just now, before beginning this paragraph. It seems that the opening of the novel contains both elements, but they don't mix, because I didn't yet know, when I started to write, that I was writing about that transcendental experience itself. I talk about the obsessive image, which relates to a particular arrangement of the items I need for writing, and later, separately, I talk about a parallel desire to record certain experiences I describe as 'luminous'. It takes me a few more lines to wonder if what I'd started writing because of the first impulse wasn't actually that other text I'd been wanting to write. But there's no mention of my friend, which strikes me as unfair – although he's no longer my friend, and from what I've heard is going around the place bad-mouthing me. It's very likely that at that moment I'd completely forgotten my friend's suggestion, authorisation or demand, and was quite convinced that writing that story was something I wanted to do.

I find it surprising that now, after all this time, I can see the cause-and-effect relationship so clearly: my friend encouraged me to write a story I knew would be impossible to write, and he imposed it on me as a duty; that imposition remained, working away in the shadows, rejected outright by the consciousness, and eventually it began to emerge in the form of that obsessive image – and all the while it was cunningly erasing its tracks, because impositions invariably generate resistance. To remove that resistance, the imposition coming from outside me disguised itself as a desire coming from within. Although, of course, the desire already existed, since something had made me tell my friend the story I told him; maybe on some secret, subtle level I knew my friend would find a way of obliging me to do what I thought was impossible. I thought it was impossible then and I think it's impossible now. It being impossible wasn't reason enough not to do it, as I knew full well, but the prospect of attempting the impossible made me feel very lazy.


Maybe my friend was right, but for me things are never straightforward. Now I see myself, in my imagination disguised as a memory, simply writing the story I'd recounted to my friend, exactly the way I'd recounted it, and watching it fail; I see myself ripping to shreds the five or six pages the story would have taken up, and this could even be a genuine memory because I have a sense of having written that story once before, though there's no longer any trace of it among my papers. And that's where the obsessive image must have come from, showing me the way to arrange myself in order to write it successfully, and it's also where the desire to write it must have come from, only by then it was transformed into a desire to write about other transcendental experiences, laying them out like a staircase in order to reach the story I wanted to write, or felt I should write, the one I might have written and destroyed. What I mean is that probably, deep down, I understood that the failure of my story was due to the lack of anything around it, the lack of any context to set it off, or of a particular atmosphere created by a vast array of images and words, which could reinforce the effect the anecdote was meant to have on the reader.

This was how I came to make life difficult for myself, because that context, that atmosphere and all those images and words were carrying me in unexpected – though very logical – directions. These processes are explained brilliantly in *The Interior Castle* by Santa Teresa of Ávila, my patron saint, but obviously it's not enough for anyone to have the processes explained: you have to experience them for yourself. Experiencing these processes is how you learn about them, but it's also how you make mistakes and lose your way. I think that in the chapters I've retained of the 'luminous novel', the way is lost at the very beginning, and those five lengthy chapters are nothing but an energetic attempt to find it again. An energetic attempt, yes, and even a worthy one, especially if we consider the circumstances that accompanied it, surrounded it, and eventually left it mutilated.

The thing is, I had to be mutilated as well, and I was. Most of the actions that shaped the circumstances of my beginning the luminous novel had to do with my then-future gallbladder operation. Once I'd accepted that the operation was inevitable, the first thing I did was talk to the surgeon about postponing it for as long as possible, and I managed to get an extension of a few months. In those months, I finished four books I'd been putting off for a considerable time, and I also launched myself into the furious writing of those chapters of the luminous novel. It was clear I was very afraid of dying in the operation, and I always knew that writing that luminous novel was an attempt to exorcise my fear of death. I also tried to exorcise my fear of pain, but I didn't manage. I was more successful with my fear of death. I can't claim to have gone calmly into the operating theatre, because I was still very frightened of the pain, but the idea of death no longer scared me after I'd written those first five chapters (which actually turned out to be seven). My fear of death comes back every now and then, especially when I'm enjoying myself, but I went into the gallbladder operation, in that respect, with my head held high. At the same time, the idea of death had been a useful incentive to work, against the clock, like a thing possessed. I was able to put my affairs in order, or at least to put my writing in order while disregarding everything else. It was during that time that I accumulated a debt, which for me was considerable, and that debt was what then took me to Buenos Aires, to work.

The definitive mutilation didn't come, then, on the day of the operation, but the operation itself was a significant mutilation, since I was left without a gallbladder, and worst of all I ended up secretly convinced I'd been castrated. A long time afterwards I freed myself from this secret conviction – and at the same time, the secret stopped being a secret – in a dream. In this dream, the doctor who'd sent me to the surgeon returned my gallbladder to me in perfect condition, inside a jar. The gallbladder, whose real form I've never known, in the dream looked a lot like male genitalia. Things had come full circle.


At first, I did everything I could to avoid having the operation. The doctors were categorical, but then doctors are always categorical, especially surgeons, and everyone knows that surgeons are paid a lot of money for operations. I once read something about this by Bernard Shaw, with which I fully agreed: he said it was absurd that the person who decides whether or not an operation is advisable is none other than the surgeon who'll be paid a hefty sum to carry it out. But the truth is that I was suffering more and more often from gallbladder infections, which left me feverish and worried about dangerous after-effects. Eventually, the message reached me by means of a book – it's astonishing how every time I'm facing a difficult problem, the information I need appears at exactly the right moment. I was browsing through some books, as I often am, in search of detective novels, on the sale tables outside a bookshop on Avenida 18 de Julio. Suddenly a title caught my eye, seeming to twinkle in the light: DON'T OPERATE UNNECESSARILY, the book was called, and if it wasn't called that it was called something very similar. It wasn't cheap, and I didn't have much money at the time. All the way home, I was weighing up whether or not I should buy it. Buying new books (this was a new book, even though it was on one of the sale tables), and, what's more, books that don't belong to the detective-novel genre, is a long way from my usual principles and habits, not to mention my economic capacity. But I was still thinking about the book when I got home. The next day it was the same. In the end I made up my mind, went back to the bookshop and picked the book up again, but it occurred to me that I didn't necessarily need to buy it. I looked at the contents page and saw there was a chapter devoted to the gallbladder. The rest of the book didn't interest me. It wasn't a very long chapter. I'm an extremely fast reader. Glancing over my shoulder and seeing no shop assistants paying much attention to what I was doing, I nonchalantly opened the book, like someone flicking through the pages whilst deciding whether or not to buy it, and turned to the first page of that chapter. Everything was resolved in the first few lines. The chapter began by saying that gallbladder operations are some of the only operations that really are necessary. Then it gave some advice about not operating if you don't want to – different methods of attempting a neural control of the bile ducts, to let gallstones come and go at will without getting blocked in the sphincter of the duct, and other things like that – but it concluded by saying that having gallbladder trouble is like having a ticking time bomb inside you that could explode at any moment and require an urgent operation – which, of course, is hardly the safest kind. I closed the book, left it in its place on the sale table and went home pondering my acceptance, which was already a done deed.

I wrote that luminous novel by hand, and when I finished a chapter I typed it up on my typewriter, making minor changes and corrections in the process. One chapter was originally written on the typewriter. And there was one chapter I didn't think was very good and destroyed, but, as the reader who gets that far will see, I soon have regrets and include a summary of it in the replacement chapter; I must only have destroyed the copy, though, because I evidently then retype the original and put it back where it was. But I also kept the summary in the chapter that followed, which complicated the numbering of the chapters. I'm not entirely sure at what stage in the interminable edits the five surviving chapters ended up in the form they're in today (the two destroyed chapters disappeared without trace); I was carrying this truncated novel around for sixteen years, and every so often I'd embark on a new set of corrections that added or removed things.

In the year 2000 I received a grant from the Guggenheim Foundation to carry out a final edit of those five chapters and write the nine chapters necessary to finish the project. The edit was completed, but the new chapters weren't written, and the comings and goings of the year I spent enjoying the grant are written up in the prologue to this book. During that period, which lasted from July 2000 to June 2001, all I managed to produce was a story called 'First Communion', which almost became the sixth chapter of the luminous novel but didn't quite: I'd changed my style by then, and many of my views had changed as well, so I kept it as a stand-alone story. It continues the luminous novel, in a sense, but it certainly doesn't complete it. The prologue, too, the 'Diary of the Grant', could be seen as a continuation of the luminous novel, though only in terms of the subject matter.

I thought about collecting all the related material together in this book, and including my *Diary of a Swine* and *Empty Words* alongside it, since these texts are also, in a sense, a continuation of the luminous novel. But that struck me as excessive, and in the end I decided to focus exclusively on unpublished texts. It's still lacking – it will probably forever be lacking – the series of chapters that weren't written, among them the retelling of the story I told my friend, which gave rise to the luminous novel.

I was right: the task was and is impossible. There are some things that can't be written about. This whole book is the testimony of a monumental failure. The system of creating an environment for each luminous event I wanted to describe took me down dark and even sinister paths. In the process, I underwent countless moments of catharsis, recovered many fragments of myself that had been buried in my unconscious and managed to do some of the crying I should have done long ago, and it was without doubt a significant experience. Even now, I find the text moving and therapeutic to read. But the luminous events, once written down, cease to be luminous; they disappoint, they sound trivial. They're out of reach of literature, or at least of my literature.

I believe, ultimately, that the only light to be found in these pages is the light that the reader will give them.

M. L., 27 AUGUST 1999 – 27 OCTOBER 2002

# PROLOGUE

*Diary of the Grant*

# AUGUST 2000

Here begins the 'Diary of the Grant'. I've been trying to do something like this for months now, but systematically avoiding making a start. The aim is to set the writing in motion, no matter what it's about, and keep it up until I've got into the habit. I have to associate the computer with writing. The most-used program needs to be Word. This will mean taking apart a series of cybernetic habits that have consumed me for the past five years, though I shouldn't think of it as taking anything apart, but rather as putting this together. Every day, every day, even if it's only a line to say I don't feel like writing anything, or I don't have time, or to make any other excuse. But it has to be every day.

I almost certainly won't manage. Experience has taught me that. And yet I find myself hoping things will be different this time, because the grant is involved. I've already been sent the first half of the money, which will be enough to keep me until the end of the year in a reasonable life of leisure. As soon as I knew for certain I was getting the grant this year, I began more or less clearing my schedule, getting rid of some things altogether and spacing others out, so as to leave very few days each month when I have any commitments at all. You see, a life of leisure takes time to arrange. It doesn't come about just like that, from one moment to the next, simply because you have nothing to do. At the moment my instinct is to fill every gap, devoting all my free time to stupid, pointless activities, because, almost without realising it, I have become like those people I always look down on: intensely afraid of my own selfhood, of being alone with nothing to do, of the ghosts in the basement pushing at the trapdoor, eager to poke their heads out and give me a fright.

One of the first things I did with this half of the grant money was buy myself a pair of armchairs. In my apartment it used to be completely impossible to sit down and rest; for years now I've had my living space set up like an office. Desks, tables, uncomfortable chairs, everything there to encourage work – or playing on the computer, which is a kind of work.

I had the electrician come and change the position of the plug sockets so I could move the computer out of sight, out of the central area of the apartment; I'm typing this now in a little room by the bedroom, and in the central area, where the computer used to be, there's now a strange armchair, very soft and springy, its fabric a lovely greyish blue. The two or three times I've sat in it, I've fallen asleep. You relax, you can't help but relax, and then, if you're at all sleep-deprived, before you know it you're dead to the world and dreaming. But this armchair is another thing I've been avoiding. As for the second one, I haven't sat in it at all yet, except to try it out. It's the kind known as a *bergère*, with a tall, rather hard back that makes it just right for reading. I only really intended to buy one armchair, but when I was testing them both out in the furniture shop, switching back and forth between the two, I realised it wouldn't be that simple. One chair was perfect for reading; the other was perfect for resting and relaxing. In one, you can't possibly read: it gets uncomfortable and your back ends up crooked and sore. In the other, you can't possibly relax: the hard backrest means you have to sit up straight and pay attention, which makes it ideal if you want to read. For many years now, I've only ever read at mealtimes, or in bed, or in the bathroom. Admittedly, I've also been steering clear of this armchair. But its time will come, just as the time for this diary has come.

I was able to begin it today thanks to my friend Paty. Some time ago I told her about Rosa Chacel, whom I discovered by chance at a second-hand book sale. I thought *Memoirs of Leticia Valle* was an extraordinary novel and lent it to all my witch friends, because I was in no doubt whatsoever that Doña Rosa was a genuine witch, in the good sense of the word. Paty is one of my witch friends, and of course she loved it. In return, a few days ago she left me a Rosa Chacel book I hadn't heard of with the caretaker downstairs, *Money Box: The Way There*. It's the first part of an intimate diary (if you can call it that, since Doña Rosa Chacel doesn't give away many intimate details), the second part of which is called *Money Box: The Way Back*. Paty emailed to explain that she'd sent me the book to help with the grant, since Rosa also received a Guggenheim fellowship at one point and all the ins and outs of the experience are recounted in the diary. In fact, even before reaching the part about the grant, which comes halfway through the book (and I have most of the second half yet to read), I noticed that this diary was inspiring me and making me want to write myself. I'm amazed at how much Rosa and I have in common. Impressions, feelings, ideas, phobias, discomforts; all very similar. She must have been an insufferable old woman. There's a photo of her on the back cover; she looks surprisingly similar to Adalgissa (I've never known how to spell that name; I think there's an H in there somewhere. Perhaps: Adalghissa), whom we used to call 'the fat aunt' when I was a boy. She was actually my great-aunt, the sister of my maternal grandfather. But the difference between Rosa and the fat aunt is the way they look at you; although Rosa's eyes are partly hidden by her round spectacles and slightly drooping eyelids, you can see the powerful intelligence of the brain behind them. The fat aunt, in contrast, was not very intelligent.

SATURDAY 5, 18:02

Today I woke up filled with enthusiasm about this diary, very keen to get started and thinking of all kinds of things I wanted to discuss; however, it's now six in the evening and I'm waiting for a friend, who'll be ringing the doorbell at any moment, and until a minute ago I hadn't written a single word. Instead, I've been playing a card game called Golf on the computer. I think food is what always leads me astray; today it was breakfast, but I realised last night that it's often after my dinner-lunch that my flights into alienation really take hold. As soon as the digestive process begins, my conscious, volitional self evaporates to make way for that rebellious escapist who wants nothing more than to fall into a trance over absolutely anything at all. It's definitely worse at night; I can't do anything to stop it, and it goes on almost until dawn.

Today I also woke up determined not to reread what I write here, or at least not very often, so this diary really is a diary and not a novel; that is, to remove the need for continuity. I realised straight away that it will still be a novel, though, whether I like it or not, because these days a novel is practically anything you can put between a front and back cover.

There goes the lift. Now the bell. My friend is here.

SATURDAY 5, 22:28

My friend came, my friend left, I played a round of Golf, had lunch-dinner, and then for the first time I sat down to digest my meal in one of the armchairs. Every other time I've tried this armchair out I've fallen asleep. Today was almost no exception, but I just about managed to stay awake. I listened to D'Arienzo butchering a few tangos on Radio Clarín, from fairly far away because I still haven't arranged things so I can have the record player in the new living room. As I sat there I remembered a dream I had this morning, and the memory of the dream made me do something I've been senselessly putting off for about a month: telephone my recently widowed friend Jorge. I think calling him is so hard because of how painful I find the memory of my friend Elisa, his dead wife, even though I have evidence that she's perfectly content where she is now; after all, it's well known that the pain we feel at other people's deaths comes from the implicit reference they make to our own, although why the idea of one's own death has to be so frightening is something I still haven't got to the bottom of. In my case it probably relates to my fear of the unknown, of finding myself deprived of all the reference points I so rely on. Dying must be like leaving the house, something I find it increasingly difficult to do, but without the hope of ever returning home. Perhaps, in my unconscious, the image forms of my dead self as a kind of rootless and disconsolate ghost who can't find anywhere it belongs, just as

I haven't found anywhere I belong in life. Since non-existence alone can't frighten us because there would be nothing there to frighten, it might be that we're scared of death because we see it as another birth; and indeed, faced with the prospect of being born a second time, well might we clasp our heads in our hands and cry, 'Oh, no! Not again!' Not that I have any great complaints about life; far from it. I just wish I hadn't always suffered from such a terror of the unexpected and the unknown, all the time, even when I've had no real reason to think there's anything nasty in store.

I spoke to my friend. Among other things, we said we'd meet up in about a week's time, since for me the week beginning tomorrow is already looking quite complicated. So is the week after, in fact, because I keep complicating it by arranging to meet up with people; for example, I spoke to Julia yesterday, and we also agreed to see each other that week. Julia is an old friend, though not as old as me, and needless to say, that isn't her real name.

I can't remember exactly what was going on with my friend Jorge in the dream; I know we were talking, sitting together in a semi-enclosed space a bit like the structure we used to call 'the gazebo' when I was a child, which was attached to the house my grandparents had by the seaside. The roof looked like it was made of branches – living branches, I mean, still part of the tree – and the walls were also formed of a kind of vegetation, though I seem to remember there being some mesh there as well, like chicken wire. There were two ways in: one, a kind of narrow door by the boundary separating my grandparents' land from the neighbours' (this door may just have been a hole in that wall of foliage that we – that is, my cousins and I, skinny children who could slip through all kinds of unlikely apertures – had forced open), and the other broader, almost the width of the gazebo itself, on the left, like an extension of the side of the house. What a terrible description; I'm sure it's completely impossible to understand.

SUNDAY 6, 00:09

I was interrupted by a minor incident caused by the strange behaviour of a program I made on the computer (in Visual Basic, to be precise) to monitor when I take my medication (for the curious reader: I'm taking antihypertensives, in the form of half a 20-milligram tablet twice a day; and antidepressants, in the form of one 150-milligram tablet every day. I started taking the antidepressants a month ago, not because I thought I needed to take antidepressants, but because they were widely advertised as a major help with giving up smoking. I haven't stopped smoking, at least not yet, but I have discovered that I needed to take antidepressants because I was depressed and didn't realise it). The program closed, disappeared from sight and uninstalled itself without completing its function. And it's a good thing it did all that then, when I was alert and able to see what had happened. I checked through the program and found the error: as usual, the computer was right and I was wrong. I think I've fixed it now, but I'll only know for sure tomorrow evening, because I don't want to go changing the clock on the computer.

But I wanted, and still want, to write about the dream involving my friend Jorge, which took place somewhere similar to that gazebo from my childhood, though it wasn't exactly the same. As I said, we were sitting and chatting about something, I don't know what. There was another character: a naughty child, a mixture of various characters who either are children or suffer from infantilism, since at times he seemed like the embodiment of my old friend Ricardo, that diminutive individual who was the inspiration for Tinker in my novel *Nick Carter*. Anyway, this boy in my dream, among other annoying things, had thrown a key ring full of keys over his shoulder into an expanse of nothing but sand and weeds: a gratuitous, unjustifiable act of rebellion. Worst of all was the fact that, originally, the person who threw the keys had been me. Then I split off into an adult who was horrified at this child's behaviour. I must have created the child character to hide the fact it had been me all along. At some point later on I thought about looking for the keys, but I don't remember doing it; I do remember how lazy I felt at the thought, knowing that they wouldn't be easy to find, half-buried in the sand and hidden by the weeds. However, not long afterwards I had the keys in my possession. When that child character threw them away, I wondered how he'd manage to get back into the house. I suppose that was part of my strategy of dissimulation. I'm glad I got them back, because they had a strong sexual symbolism. When I got them back, or realised I'd got them back, they were already in my pocket; I took them out and examined them carefully. I was surprised to see there were various keys, a considerable number; the key ring divided them into two groups, one of which was like an extension of the other, connected to it by a little chain. There was also a strip of dark-green paper, attached to the key ring without any purpose I was able to work out.

The presence of my friend Jorge in that dream made me decide to telephone him, and I'm glad I did, because it was one of the things I'd been putting off indefinitely for no valid reason.

The other thing I've been putting off, and which I continue putting off, at least so far, is shaving. My beard is far too bushy and my mouth fills up with bristles when I eat, which I find intolerable. But I don't just want to trim it, because then it would look too neat, too intentional, when in fact letting my beard grow this long wasn't a deliberate choice; I simply let a lot more time pass than I should have done without shaving. By now it would be very difficult, very arduous, to get rid of my beard, and my face would be left itchy, red and burning until at least the next day. But I have to do it. And I will. Very soon.

SUNDAY 6, 17:20

Absolutely zero interest in writing today. I woke up already feeling a bit crooked, i.e. with that unsteadiness I'd forgotten about and which must therefore relate to my blood pressure, since it went away when I started taking the medication last month. Why it came back today in spite of the medication I have no idea, unless it's something to do with my routine. My doctor told me not to take the tablets in the early hours of the morning; I'm supposed to take them by midnight at the latest. But this means I can't space them out enough; there's meant to be twelve hours between them. My plan is to take the first at eleven in the morning and the second at eleven at night. But I'm never awake at eleven in the morning, so I normally end up taking the first at two or three in the afternoon. The next one then gets pushed back to 11.30 p.m., or midnight, but that leaves a gap of more than twelve hours until the next: fifteen or sixteen hours even, which could be why it doesn't have the same effect. I'll have to think about going to bed earlier . . . ha.

Well, I'm still crooked and I don't feel like writing. Chl will be here soon (which is a whole other story that 'isn't for telling here', as Rosa Chacel says in her diary every so often, always leaving you wanting to know more); she's bringing me a pea stew she made at home. Chl makes wonderful stews, but she says this one didn't turn out very well; apparently the peas are a bit hard. Still, I'll have to eat it anyway, because for too many days I've been living on meat alone (and tomatoes with garlic); the diet doesn't bother me as such, but all the meat is a bit frightening.

MONDAY 7, 02:31

Today it's still yesterday. By which I mean that the day I began on Sunday still isn't over, even though the date has changed. I have no idea how to sort out the chaos of my sleeping hours. A few days ago my doctor offered to put me in touch with her colleague, a psychiatrist who specialises in treating addictions and other behavioural disorders from a behaviourist approach. I thought this sounded interesting, since at sixty years old I'm not sure I have the energy for any more of the psychoanalytical approach, which, what's more, was no help at all with this particular disorder a few years ago (though it was very helpful in other ways). This psychiatrist also had the advantage of being contactable via email; one of the major obstacles created by my disrupted sleeping hours is the difficulty in communicating with people at what they consider a reasonable time. I wrote to him, briefly explaining this difficulty and requesting an appointment some time after 7 p.m., the later the better. He answered right away; when I woke up the next day and began my routine by checking my email folders, the reply was already there. He told me, very politely, that his last appointment slot was at 6.30 p.m., and offered me some dates in the near future. I didn't like the way he presented his schedule as something preordained, as if he were explaining a genetic characteristic that no one in their right mind would expect him to be able to change. As if he'd said: 'I have one leg shorter than the other.' Or could it be that his own behavioural disorders cause him similar difficulties to the ones mine cause me? And if so, have his behaviourist techniques not helped him to correct those disorders?

But there was more: he explained that he was attaching some .doc files to his email with forms for me to fill in before our first meeting, so he could 'get on with the diagnosis'. I didn't like the sound of this either. I can't get used to the idea of someone reaching a diagnosis without having had any direct personal contact with their patient whatsoever. I don't want to be categorised like that, and to encounter someone when I go along for the first appointment who's already formed an idea of what I'm like, an idea that won't easily change. The doctor would see his diagnosis and not the person I am.

I read the questionnaires, and while I was reading them I composed my responses in my head. The questions addressed a multitude of personal topics and referred to my life history from birth to the present day. Each one had only a limited space for the answer, and yet each one deserved a response that was almost infinitely long, or at least spanning a volume or more, and not the slim ones either. For example: your relationship and its problems. Which relationship? All of them? Wow . . . Please describe in five lines the problems with every relationship you've ever had. He might as well have set the questionnaire out as one of those multiple-choice exams. There were also questions about professional matters: how do I get on with my bosses, with my subordinates, etc. Bosses? Does anyone have a boss in this world? And subordinates? God forbid. In other words, I saw how the whole thing was shaping up: therapy for builders, office workers and executives. If you don't fit into one of those categories, it's because you're mad. There must be something wrong with you if you're a free person.

The questions were very well formulated. As I answered them in my head I saw my whole life parading past me at full speed, and plenty of things popped up here and there to explain why I have the disorders I do. After the initial shock, I realised that the things I'm fighting against as if they were disorders, without managing to overcome them, are not in fact disorders at all but admirable solutions I've been devising, unconsciously, in order to get by. This is an excellent definition of my disorders: they're the result of all that's happened in my life, and more than that they're the price of my freedom. Two plus two equals four. Thank you, Doctor. I replied to him, explaining that our schedules were incompatible but that he'd nevertheless helped me a great deal with his questionnaires, which may not have resolved my behavioural disorders but which had at least made me feel more tolerant of them. That doesn't mean I won't go on trying to correct them, at least in part. I'm not asking to start going to bed at midnight and getting up at eight; I'd be happy with getting up at eleven and going to bed whenever I do. And, speaking of which, it's now three in the morning. I should probably stop writing, turn the computer off and begin my bedtime routine before I get engrossed in something stupid all over again and the next thing I know it it's gone eight.


But I wanted to say that Chl's stew is delicious. I'd rather she gave me sexual satisfaction like she used to, but no, she gives me stew. Well, she also gives me good company and plenty of affection for a few hours each week, so I can't complain. Today we went for a walk and stopped in a *boliche* for a coffee. I hadn't left the house in days and was feeling a bit light-headed. Going out helped; I made slow progress, but on the way home the unsteadiness left me and I stopped feeling crooked. In fact, I felt good. I almost let out a few whoops of contentment right there in the street. Afterwards, Chl took a bus home, and I went back to my apartment and played Golf and had another plate of stew. Luckily, and thanks to Chl, the day turned out all right. It stopped seeming so grey and infected, and I stopped feeling at odds with myself. If only there'd also been some sex . . .


I still don't understand why I threw the keys away in my dream and then got them back again. This dream is part of a long series that began when I started taking the antidepressants; they're all seaside-town dreams and happen in similar places, always at night, and always surrounded by vegetation. In one of them I even found myself driving a car with total competence, though a few manoeuvres I made left me worried I couldn't control it – especially when I challenged some friends in another car to a race to wherever we were going. I got there first, of course, but I have no idea why I challenged them like that, let alone why I was driving a car. I don't even know how to start an engine.

MONDAY 7, 16:58

I just came across these lines in the book by Doña Rosa Chacel (or should I call her Aunt Rosa?), about a certain source of suffering in her life:

> I try hard to overcome it through narcotics: films and books. How well I understand people who turn to drugs! These ones I use seem harmless, but they're not. That is, as soon as one uses them to that end, they turn out to be as destructive as the others, because the destructive thing is removing oneself from reality. It doesn't matter what poison we use to numb the senses: the effect of numbing them is the same.

Replace 'films' with 'the computer' and they could be my own words.

In this part of the book, Aunt Rosa has begun talking a lot about her dreams; and, as if I were going through a parallel process, I came across the lines quoted above just after beginning the day with some reflections on my own dream (the one about the boy throwing the keys away). In the interpretation that eventually occurred to me, you can see the connection with the topic 'drugs'.

In one back and forth in my reflections, it suddenly struck me that the child's intention when he throws the keys away is to make it difficult for himself to return. I think about it in the dream: 'How's he going to get back in later?' And now I see that the keys are the keys in more than one sense of the word, and that on throwing them away my intention is to hide them – but not too much. It's more about slowing things down; concealing them for a bit but not losing them completely.

This means that the keys to my unwanted behaviours, such as my addiction to drugs like the computer and books, are there, almost in sight, but the small and tiresome task still remains of hunting for them in the sand, among some tufts of grass. In the dream I get the keys back, but then I examine them as if I didn't quite recognise them.

I think the meanings are nice and clear. Now that I'm proposing a 'return' to myself and my writing, and resuming a novel I left unfinished more than fifteen years ago, the dream tells me I won't be able to manage it without the keys to myself, which I myself had hidden. I didn't hide them very well – I didn't bury them in the unconscious – but I'll have to dig for a while in the subconscious sand before they appear, and then, when they do appear, I'll have to do a bit more work to untangle them.

## TUESDAY 8, 04:54

I'll be brief: today (I mean yesterday and what we've had of today so far, of course; my day) was long and difficult. It's almost five, I'd already turned the computer off when I remembered about this diary and turned it back on again, and meanwhile my waist hurts and the garlic is repeating on me. I spent most of the day playing Golf, believe it or not. I think I've explained before that it's a kind of solitaire. And worst of all it's a mindless game, almost entirely down to chance. On average, you win about one round in every hundred. I also did some inappropriate things that I don't want to write about here (including making some improvements to a recent program of mine in Visual Basic). So I'm still hiding the keys, the keys to myself; I'm still putting off confronting the thing that will allow me to do what I want to do.

Today I woke up crooked again; that is, insecure and somehow unstable. I called my doctor and she came to see me – a spontaneous offer on her part. But she didn't find my blood pressure too outrageously high, and she also carried out several very funny neurological tests; I myself added the standing on one leg test, which is used for proving you're not drunk. It could be the stuffy, stormy weather; it could be a particular strain of flu everyone's getting this year. It could be a problem with my right ear, which is blocked. And it could also be simple madness. Or not so simple, come to that. Good grief.

Later on, my daughter came. In this 'Diary of the Grant' I should record that I'd put aside a tiny portion of the money for her, and she was coming to collect it. She happened to turn up with her current partner, whom I hadn't met before. He seemed like a very odd person. I don't mean he seemed particularly bad or unpleasant, just odd. My daughter's almost at the end of her pregnancy. My fifth grandchild. Good Lord.

According to her, my cousin Pocho cured his high blood pressure by eating garlic. I started eating garlic a few months ago, a little each day, and it's become a kind of vice or compulsion. It could be that my body sensed it needed garlic. Now I'm going to carry on eating it, safe in the knowledge of its therapeutic qualities. Maybe I should eat more: an entire clove per day. But my stomach has never been good with garlic, which is why I went most of my life without eating it. And now perhaps it's too late.

I'm still encountering strange similarities between Aunt Rosa and myself. I'm not sure how we can have so much in common, when our personalities are completely different and even opposed. Maybe we only overlap on a particular, somewhat mystical or magical plane. In the diary of hers that I'm reading, and that led me to start a diary of my own, among the countless trivial details there are a few reflections that leave me speechless. For example, something I began writing once and stopped, about the relationship between sex, eroticism and mysticism. Anyway, my waist is killing me. I'm going to bed. Tomorrow I have work. This is a week of work, in fact: workshops on Tuesday, Thursday and Friday, 'live', and on Tuesday and Wednesday virtually. Shit.

TUESDAY 8, 23:42

Just to record that Flaco has died. I was woken by the telephone at who knows what time of the morning; it went to answerphone and I could hear Lilí's voice, as strident as usual, or more strident than usual, demanding I pick up. I took no notice, of course, and tried to go back to sleep, but I didn't quite manage, and nor did I manage to wake up.

I don't know how long afterwards the phone rang again, and I heard Lilí's voice again, and this time I did pick up because I was feeling more awake and I could tell it was important. She said she had bad news, and I thought: 'Ruben.' But no, it was Flaco. Completely unexpected.

Now, luckily, I'm able to recover my thoughts from before the shock. In that half-awake state, I saw that my mind had been working away mysteriously as I slept, and now it was delivering an answer. The phrase appeared in my mind: 'Key number one: my mother's death.' And indeed, that must be one of the keys the child threw into the sand in my dream a few days ago. I found that death very painful for many reasons; it filled me with guilt and fear for a long while afterwards, years, even, though in bursts rather than all the time. Fortunately, in a therapeutic setting, I managed to get back the memory of my mother as she was in life, and of many of her good qualities. I was glad, and said to the therapist: 'I've stopped seeing my mother as a pile of bones, and now I can feel her living presence within me.' Then I had a few relapses, during one of which I was able to talk to Chl about it all, and the next day my mother had completely vanished from my thoughts. It was a great relief. Still, the topic was never really closed, and today something made me see that. I began thinking about how much I missed my mother, or a mother, because for many years she was the person who enabled me to 'reset', as it were; when I felt overwhelmed for some reason, or I couldn't see a way forward, or I had something to sort out, I'd go and visit her in her seaside town and stay for as long as I needed to, usually a week. The first thing I did was go to sleep; even if it was early in the afternoon, I still went to sleep, at least for a couple of hours. I put my need for sleep down to the bus journey, but that wasn't it; I'd simply been sleeping badly for days and days, and the protective presence of my mother allowed me to relax and sink into a deep slumber. I'd emerge from those two or more hours of sleep as if I'd been drugged, with my brain completely muddled, and then, very gradually, I'd begin the exchange of news with my mother. Often I had to slow her down so she didn't come out with all her information at once. I'd sleep a lot over the following days as well, and then the point would come when I wanted to return to my Montevideo apartment, and off I'd go. It's years since I've had anyone to look after my sleep like that. And not only my sleep, but also my food; I had nothing to do and nothing to worry about when I was there, beyond eating and sleeping. That's exactly what I need right now. I've been needing it for a long time, but only today do I see and feel it so clearly: I have no way of resetting because I'm always meant to be doing something. And the point is: I'm not sleeping well, and I haven't slept well for ages. Trying to relax doesn't work for me either; I can't control my mind. I don't know where I'd get a mother from at my age, but I could at least try; someone to watch over me while I sleep and provide me with food for a few days is just what I need for this 'return to myself' that I'm trying to bring about.

In the afternoon I went to do, or attempt to do, some shopping. I wanted a couple of little round metal tables to put next to the armchairs, for example. It's not that I'm getting addicted to buying this sort of thing for the house; it's necessary, as is the floor lamp I didn't manage to find today. The idea is to set the place up for reading and relaxing, and for reading I need a suitable light source. The floor lamps in the shops are very expensive, but they're also very low. I need something a little higher, because I have to use a very bright light, and if it's too close my head gets hot and I start feeling unwell. A light that's too concentrated and too white on the paper is no good either; it affects my eyes. I need something very similar to the main light, but a little closer to me and a little less diffuse. Well, that doesn't exist, so I'll have to invent something as usual; my solutions are generally effective, but most of the time they're not very aesthetically pleasing and look like signs of eccentricity. They're not, though; they're the practical solutions of a poor man who has to work with what he's got.

Oh, and: I'm not feeling anything. About Flaco's death, I mean, but also in general. A few hours ago I started to worry about this lack of emotion, of any hint of feeling at all: this nothing. It means I've gone back to my usual tactics; submerging, burying anything I don't like deep under the surface and pretending it doesn't exist. There's always a high price to pay. But I don't know how to summon the emotions.

THURSDAY 10, 02:13

Just showing my face in this diary. A strange day; not a bad one, but I don't really know what I did. Yes, I remember I had to go up the stairs (four floors) because the lift was being repaired. I'd gone to convert some dollars to get a bit of small change, and on the way I paid my phone bill. The tables I bought were delivered from the Bazar Mitre. I felt a bit worried when I saw them. Metal, black, low, to go next to each armchair. For my ashtray, book, glasses and coffee. Am I becoming frivolous? Have I been spared from frivolity for all these years simply because I was poor? But no, I don't want to worry about that. The tables were necessary, just as the armchairs were necessary. I'm beginning to think about myself, though it's a bit late in the day for that. About the return, the return to myself. To what I was before the computer came along. Before Colonia, before Buenos Aires. I think this is how I'll gain access to the luminous novel, if such a thing is even possible. A few months ago, during the summer, before hearing back about the grant application, I had to use the I Ching for the first time in twenty-five years. I was plunged into a terrible confusion about what I should do, torn between carrying on as I was and trying to go back to what I used to be. Sometimes I thought trying to go back would only make things worse (and maybe I was right). Anyway, the I Ching never fails; it answered me with a hexagram called 'The Return', told me I'd come into a considerable fortune and showed me the right approach (though now I've forgotten what it was) (I'll check).

I checked. The only line that suggests danger is the sixth, which shows the subject confused by the idea of the return. Precisely the state I was in. In other words, at that very moment I stopped being confused and decided to return, nobly, like the subject of the fifth line. The process that produced this hexagram also produced another complementary one, thanks to a moving line. The complementary hexagram was called 'The Joyous'. All this made me think I was going to get the grant.

Anyway, it wouldn't do to become frivolous. I won't buy any more tables. I think I have almost all the furniture I need now, though there's still something missing. I'm not sure what. A shelf of some kind, somewhere convenient to store the things that are currently spread across all the tables and flat surfaces in the apartment. And maybe in the summer I ought to install air conditioning; I wouldn't go through what I went through last summer again for anything. People say it was unusually hot, but I think things can only get worse. We're all going to die burnt to a crisp. If you ask me, the Earth is heating up much faster than people say it is, and they're not telling us because they don't want us to panic. Every year it's worse. The summer that's just gone almost sent me over the edge. Complete annihilation. All I did was escape and escape and escape endlessly into the computer.

What else happened today? Ah yes, yoga class. Half an hour, because the teacher was late. Since we only had half an hour, she tried to cram in too many exercises and made me do them too quickly. By the end I was exhausted. Now I'm tired and I'm going to sleep. I fell asleep in the armchair earlier, with a full stomach. Now I can go to bed. Exceptional: it's just gone two in the morning.

I was forgetting to mention that I've also been sorting out the virtual workshop yesterday and today. And now I remember, too, that when I was out I went to the bookshop across the road to ask them to order some books by Rosa Chacel. I finished *Money Box: The Way There* and thought it was wonderful. The other day, I was searching for Doña Rosa online; 365 results that included her name appeared, but not one of them had any useful information, whether biographical or bibliographical. If the bookshop can't get hold of anything by her, I'll see if Marcial can send me something from Spain. I find it inexplicable how much I identify with this writer. Everything suggests I shouldn't: the century, the culture, the interests (at least, the visible ones), the personality, the gender. And yet I'm drawn to her not because she's so different to me, but because she's the same. I identify with her. I want to know more about her and read more of her work. All of it, if possible. It's ages since I've been this excited about an author.

Because I'd finished that book and didn't have anything else I felt like reading, I went to the second-hand bookstall on the corner of my road and, after looking through everything, found eight little detective novels from the Rastros series. Forty-eight pesos. They're probably awful, but I'm going to read every single one. The first one I chose has a promising title (goddamn it): *Everyone Must Die*. I didn't choose it for the title, though, but because it's the earliest of the set of eight, in a series that got worse and worse as it went on. I saw the title after I'd already chosen it on the basis of its number.

It was freezing at the bookstall. When I was leaving, I asked the bookseller: 'How do you put up with the cold?' He smiled and answered right away: 'Oh, I put up with it. It's the customers who don't.' And he made a sweeping gesture towards the deserted tables. 'You looked through everything, but other people aren't like that; they don't stick around.'


It's gone three in the morning. And tomorrow I need to be up early: I've got a workshop at 4.30 p.m. I hope I have time for breakfast.

FRIDAY 11, 04:14

Every other Thursday I have an intense day of writing workshops: session one, 4.30 p.m.; session two, 8.15 p.m. This is Uruguay, so the four-thirty workshop starts closer to five, and today there was a lot to read, so we didn't finish until a quarter to seven. A gap of an hour and a half before the beginning of the next workshop; and I have to wash the coffee cups and the glasses, have my lunch-dinner, order the shopping from the supermarket, telephone Chl, make another batch of coffee, brush my teeth . . .

Working with these groups always wears me out. It's now almost half past four in the morning, and I'm shattered. I need to make a final effort and go to bed. My back's aching. My back's been aching for days. Ever since I began this diary, I think. The two may or may not be connected.

I like my students, I like the workshop. I wouldn't want to do it every day . . . Twice a month is all right. Usually it's once a week, but this year I had to change it because of the grant. I need free time. I still haven't managed to get much of it. I'm still running away from the vague anxiety I feel whenever there's any leisure on the horizon. It's horrible, that vague anxiety.

There's not much else you can say about a working day.

SATURDAY 12, 03:55

I'm exhausted. Today, the editing workshop; it's only four students, and only one workshop, today (yesterday), i.e. Friday; and yet it takes more energy than the two workshops yesterday (Thursday), where there are more students. It's true that my tiredness has been building up since yesterday; but still, in the editing workshop, I have to exercise a lot of sensitivity, with my ears, eyes and mind fully alert. I won't deny that I enjoy it, but it leaves me exhausted, and that always has unpleasant consequences; any slight progress I've made with my sleeping hours, late-night meals and everything else is cancelled out. What's the name of the guy who had to push a rock up a hill? I don't have a single functioning neurone left.

He was called . . .

I went to get a cigarette. Ninety minutes without smoking: not bad. But I was playing Golf. Sisyphus. He was called Sisyphus. I remembered while I was getting the cigarette.

.   .   .

Mario Levrero

Working days: luckily they're over. Now I have a clear, free week ahead. Only to an extent, though, since a lot of people are coming to see me. Always this habit of having visitors one at a time. Why not have several in one go? It's never occurred to me before. But they won't like it. Everyone wants the same thing: the private, confidential chat. They talk about what's going on with them. If there's someone else there too they won't talk. There's also Chl, who doesn't want to see anyone; when she visits, it has to be exclusive. It's the same with Julia, I suppose; she says she only wants to listen to me talk. Not because of my voice, but because of what I say – or so she believes. She has an incredible memory; most women have that kind of memory, which records and keeps to hand even the most minor details. Yesterday, Julia told me over the phone that a girlfriend of mine once married another guy, and I sent her a Paco Ibáñez CD as a present. I'd scratched out all the other tracks with a knife so that it only played one: the one where he sings the Quevedo poem about Lord Money being a powerful gentleman – 'Poderoso caballero es don Dinero' and all that. I heard the story as if for the first time. Then I thought I could remember it, but at this stage in life it's impossible to know what I really remember and what I just believe I do. As Julia was telling me the story I was forming the images in my head, and later I didn't know if I was remembering something that really happened or just those recent images. It's the same with everyday events. I think: 'I'm going to do such-and-such a thing,' which is then registered with total precision in my memory, in full detail, just as if I'd done it. Then I realise that no, I didn't do anything, I just imagined it. It must come down to my habit of thinking in images. Which means I'm never sure of anything. Medication, for example. I think about taking a tablet, and it's as if I've already taken it. I made a program on the computer that reminds me, with a little beep, when I have to take each tablet, and it goes on beeping until I take it and click a button that says 'Medicine taken'. When I click that button, the beeping stops, the visual information is no longer displayed, and a note is added to a file with the name of the medication and the day and time it was taken. Even so . . . sometimes I press that button before I take the tablet, and then get distracted when I'm about to take it and end up doing other things instead. Later the doubts creep in, and that's why I've had to get used to keeping another record, on paper, of the number of tablets I've taken; that way, by counting the ones I have left, and knowing how many I started out with in total, I know whether I've taken one or not.

I ought to get my visitors used to coming at the same time. Although I don't think I could get used to it myself. If there are three of us rather than two, any sort of depth would be lost. It's only natural. And when there's no depth I feel awkward. Except with Chl, who spends most of the time chatting away about trivial things. She does it on purpose, because she thinks she shouldn't be so deep all the time, that it's not good for a person. She's right. So she talks about trivial things and I listen with rapt attention, because I like her very much, whatever she does and whatever she says. And then I also talk about trivial things, and it really is a way of relaxing. Of course, afterwards I have to throw myself into some complicated program on the computer, because my mind flounders if it's not doing something complicated. The mind is like a set of teeth that has to be chewing all the time.

Within a fortnight, then, I'll have my period of leisure, or of the pursuit of leisure. I hope I manage it more fully than I did last week. I think I've made some progress, and this diary is itself a sign of progress. I might not be writing anything worthwhile, but I'm writing, I'm at least moving my fingers over the keyboard and worrying a little about the coherence of the discourse, though I'm not paying any attention to the form. I'm writing more or less what comes to mind (which can be written down). I'm a long way from being able to confront my grant project; I don't even want to think about that, not yet. I want to come to it naturally. Through my leisure time. Through a genuine need to write it.

SUNDAY 13, 05:35

Look at that, it's half past five in the morning. A terrible day, really awful, whichever way you look at it. Some extremely irritating digestive upsets; I'm worried because I think the antidepressants are poisoning me. Cold weather. I didn't go out today either. Frustrations with the program in Visual Basic: I wanted to improve my medication reminders, and I didn't succeed. Lots of time on the computer, working on the program and playing games. Brief visit from my doctor: at least my blood pressure is finally normal. Visit from Chl; for a moment it seemed the heavens were about to open, but no. I need to stop hoping, but I can't. It's the way I am. And the most annoying thing of all is that the most annoying thing of all is my frustration with the program in Visual Basic.

MONDAY 14, 03:03

Now we're into 14 August, that cursed date. It's always a tough day to get through. I hope it's less painful this year.

My previous day: Sunday, brightened up in the evening by Chl and her stew and her *milanesas*, and her patience in taking me out for a walk and a coffee nearby. The woman's a saint. It's very strange, this business with Chl. I can't decide what her role is: girlfriend, daughter, sister, friend? Not a lover any more, but in a way, yes, a lover as well.

But I don't feel like writing anything else; it's 14 August. One 14 August, my father died. Twenty years later, on another 14 August, my mother died.

TUESDAY 15, 05:53

The fourteenth is over, thanks to the dialogue with the computer and thanks to Chl. I finally figured out how to do that procedure in Visual Basic that hadn't been working. I spent all day on it, but now it's almost perfect. It still has one tiny defect . . . which I don't know if I'll be able to fix. The funny thing is that this procedure isn't an important part of the program; the program still worked, even with this imperfection, and besides, it's not something that's used very much, if at all. Now it's still imperfect, because it has this defect, and I won't be able to rest until I can fix it properly. It's almost six in the morning. The sun's coming up, or maybe it's up already. It was a rainy day, absolutely disgusting. I didn't leave the house. You could say it was a lost day, but I have yet to find out what a gained day would be.

WEDNESDAY 16, 01:10

Today, a visit from my recently widowed friend. Terrible anguish (on his part), which I absorbed patiently over the course of a few hours. Many things rising to the surface. At times, old-people conversation: illnesses, fears, real and imaginary ailments. He brought me a present; a good-sized photo in a frame showing Avenida 18 de Julio and the London-Paris building, where my father worked for most of his life. Lots of people on the pavements and even in the street; the odd few vehicles, Fords by the looks of it, the square ones. I imagine it was taken in the 1930s, maybe before. The men are wearing hats.

Exquisite (as Archie Goodwin would say in the Rex Stout books, in Macho Quevedo's translation), that stew of Chl's. I've just tried it for the first time, since the *milanesas* yesterday made me forget all about it. Even so, after the plate of stew today, a *milanesa. Milanesas*: something I've never known how to make, much as people have tried to teach me. They always and invariably turn out wrong. The breadcrumbs come off the meat when I fry them.

I woke up extremely late (Chl on the phone, exhorting me very charmingly to reach out my hand and pick up the receiver; I didn't answer. I couldn't. She tried again a bit later, and that time I was able to get out of bed). I woke up with a very clear, simple idea of how to fix the procedure that yesterday seemed so difficult, or impossible, to perfect. But I couldn't get to the computer all day, not until after my lunch-dinner. Then I finished it off in the space of half an hour. Impeccable.

And the grant? I imagine some impertinent reader, the sort there inevitably is, will be thinking: 'Did they give this guy a load of cash just so he could play Golf (and Minesweeper – a new habit) and entertain himself with Visual Basic? Outrageous. And he calls it a "diary of the grant".' Reader, relax. It will take me a while to change my ways. Just today, when I was nodding off in front of the computer after finishing that program, I had to send out the evaluations for the virtual workshop, as I do every Wednesday in the early hours. The 'real' workshop last week drew me out of my incipient leisure time, or at least the vague anxiety that precedes it, and afterwards I didn't sit back down in the armchair; I ended up glued to the computer for all these days. I can't help it. Today I feel like I'm getting closer. Besides, Visual Basic is a bridge leading back to my lost self; when I feel the need to write programs, it's because I'm detaching myself from the games. After some satisfactory programming, writing seems more within reach; I'm in a better position to do it. As I noticed some time ago, the language of programming seems to be a necessary transition point between a state of what you might call dependency and one of greater mental freedom. In programming there's a lot of space for creativity; it's not like a game, where you're a passive, almost idiotic instrument, moving senselessly and more or less mechanically, guided only by conditioned reflexes. Still, games and programming are both ways of escaping the vague anxiety; the programming absorbs my mind even more than the games do, and often, like yesterday, I'm still thinking about how to solve a problem by the time I get into bed, and I turn it over in my mind while I sleep; it's as if through these problems I set myself I can even rein in my dreams. Whatever it is, when the cycle's complete I feel much more prepared to continue my pursuit of leisure time, to get through the vague anxiety. I think about having workshops again next week, and I want to postpone them, even though they're enjoyable. I'm worried about never escaping this Sisyphean game; the rock being pushed up the hill and the rock rolling back to the bottom, over and over again, over and over again. And this week I didn't leave much room for manoeuvre; as I've already mentioned, I'm expecting visitors, one per day. That's something I really should cut down. I'll try to make this the last week in which I spend my free time socialising, at least as intensively as this. Much as it frightens me, I need to win back my solitude – if I really do want to go on with the novel, that is. But at the back of my mind there's a conviction that I'll manage, and almost certainly within the time frame.

As per my original plan, I haven't reread what I've written in this diary so far. But I'm very curious, and I suspect I might change my plan at any moment.

Virtual workshop: one exercise I've devised asks the students to choose an object that's fairly complicated but not very large (during the in-person workshops I suggest a small handmade wooden box, which a girl gave me a long time ago, as a possible object; the box has things stuck to the lid, like screws, a ring, etc.). The exercise involves sitting comfortably and taking some time to handle the object, familiarising yourself with it by touch and paying no attention to what it looks like. The task then is to write a description of the object based on these tactile impressions. My students have chosen all kinds of objects in their time, but never anything like what this particular student chose, a girl who writes very enthusiastically and very well, with plenty of imagination and sensitivity, and whose exercise I read and evaluated today: her object of choice was a penis, and her text included a description of it becoming erect. It's incredible how, with this topic, she managed to write a beautiful, delicate and even poetic text. My students never cease to amaze me.

The Word 2000 spellchecker has some very strange characteristics. Try as I might to master it, I find it completely impossible. It often doesn't recognise words related to sex, like for example 'penis', which was marked as unrecognised when I spellchecked this page just now before saving. Nor does it accept 'tits' or 'orgasm', and the strangest thing of all is that, if I try to add the word to the dictionary, it tells me it can't be done because the dictionary's full. Which isn't true, because then a different word it doesn't know appears immediately afterwards, and I can add that to the dictionary with no trouble at all. Stranger still is that it allows me to add some other words, like 'fanny'.

I didn't shave today either.

## THURSDAY 17, 01:44

A difficult day, with weak muscles and, in the afternoon, a terrible cramp in my right arm. I put it down to the medication, but my doctor says it's not that. According to her: probable psychological causes + lack of exercise + bad posture at the computer (and spending too much time with my arm outstretched to move the mouse). She might be right, but I wasn't 100 per cent convinced. I generally react to medication in strange ways, especially if I take it the way I am at the moment, i.e. regularly and for an extended period of time. I'm now definitely allergic to aspirin, and I'm getting there with the intestinal antiseptics as well; I have to miss one in every two because otherwise I have an allergic reaction. Of course, there are also sound psychological reasons for my mental state to be manifesting in physical ways, especially in relation to a few people having died recently, and my friend's visit yesterday, and our conversation about illness and death.

It all began when I woke up; I had a pain in my left hip, perhaps because of the way I'd slept, lying on my left side and with my hip bone pushing my flesh into the mattress, which is made of rubber and therefore fairly hard; but it could also have been what people call an 'articular' pain. That thought sent me over to the exercise bike, which I hadn't touched in far too long. When I tried to get going, the bicycle felt very heavy (which might have been accurate, since the tape that regulates the tension and apparent weight seemed to make a louder noise than usual when I braked), but it was also hard to move the handlebars, which are naturally very 'heavy' (a series of pistons produce the 'weight' by means of the air that's compressed when you move them). Anyway, the point is that I couldn't do much exercise because I got tired very quickly. I gave up. The cramp I got a few hours later could also have come from the effort I put into moving the handlebars. But the really worrying thing is definitely my lack of energy. After breakfast I went to the pharmacy to have my blood pressure checked, and it was more or less fine; at least, it wasn't too low, which I'd thought it might be. My doctor came over in the evening anyway. Since she found my blood pressure normal, she said I could halve the amount of medication I'm taking for a few days and see what happens. My yoga teacher had come before that; I didn't want to take the class, because my muscles were feeling so weak. And then, just as she was about to leave, after chatting for a while, I got that horrible, excruciating and thoroughly alarming cramp. My teacher attributed it to the medication, which, according to her, uses up a lot of potassium, so that you need to take extra potassium to make up for it (my doctor says this isn't true any more; that medicine these days doesn't have that side effect). My teacher was on her way out when I began complaining and voicing my distress; fortunately it was my right arm, since if it had been my left the panic would have been too much for me. She decided then to do a mini reiki session, and applied her hands to the painful area. I don't know if it was the effect of the reiki or if the cramp had run its course of its own accord, but the pain gradually subsided. It felt like a battle between the yoga teacher and the pain. The pain would try to advance, then it would stop, then retreat, and then it would gather its strength for a new offensive; but in the end it began to give way, and when it wanted to come back it didn't quite manage; it just made a few half-hearted attempts. Finally it disappeared once and for all, though it left that part of my bicep feeling tender.

That, plus some more errands I did around six in the afternoon (I bought, among other things, toner for the printer and a different brand of yoghurt), and another telephone call from Felipe, listing the books he's going to lend me, then the usual phone conversations with Chl, and that was my day. And a bit of playing on the computer, of course, but nothing major.

Going out to run the errands made me feel good. I need many more outings like that. It was possible because yesterday I went to bed earlier and went to sleep earlier and so today I was able to get up earlier; you could still see a bit of sun by the time I went out. I didn't enjoy it as much as I'd hoped because I was in a hurry; my doctor was due to arrive soon (although she then postponed her visit until the evening) and I had to get home quickly. When I went past a bookshop on Avenida 18 de Julio, near my house, my eye was drawn almost automatically to a pile of books with a sign on top saying '10 pesos' (around a dollar), and the first one I saw was by John le Carré, new and in a nice edition. I thought a customer must have put it there by mistake after rummaging around elsewhere in the shop, but, intrigued, I retraced my steps, went over to the book and picked it up: the same price was written in pencil on the first page. I entered the bookshop and approached the counter, which was at the far end. I asked the cashier whether it was possible that the book cost just ten pesos, and she answered unenthusiastically: 'It's possible.' A chubby girl, apparently disillusioned with life and in particular with her job, this last point being entirely reasonable on her part. I bought the book, and then I lent it to my doctor. I hope she brings it back, because I want to read it too. Le Carré isn't one of my favourites, but he's good, very good. The book is called *Smiley's People*, and I'm not certain I haven't read it before. It doesn't matter, though: even if I have read it, I forgot all about it a long time ago.

And no, I didn't shave.

SATURDAY 19, 04:27

Tired, with no desire to write. Julia's visit in the afternoon; strong emotions. Chl, in the evening. The same. I was left overexcited and had to play on the computer, then I answered a long and very well-constructed list of questions from an Argentinian reader who wants to publish my responses. Today I continued my intensive socialising; first Felipe, who brought me some books, then Gabriel, to discuss literature and life, and then Chl, to eat. A very active day, too, with a few changes around the house, as if the momentum of the move is returning slowly after stalling more than a year ago, when Chl went on her trip. I'll have to explain that further, because sometimes I forget the fateful repercussions of that trip. But not today; I'm tired, jotting things down for no apparent reason, but I must do it. I want to read this diary. I'm still holding out. Needless to say, I didn't shave today either. But I did arrange for the two pairs of sandals to be mended, which I've been putting off for more than a year (since the fateful trip, etc.). Maybe the antidepressants I'm taking to help me stop smoking, which aren't helping me stop smoking, are doing me good. Livening me up a bit.

I also want to make a note, before I forget again, and for when I read back over this diary, that I need to discuss pornography. I once wrote that I detested it, which was true; but now I've accrued something of a collection of pornographic photos, so I really ought to explain myself (have my tastes changed? Be patient, reader; I can't discuss anything effectively today. It's all notes, notes).

Chl woke me from a deep and dream-filled sleep around midday, precisely to tell me about a dream of her own, which she left recorded on the answerphone because I didn't have the strength to pick up. Maybe it was telepathic jealousy that made her call, because she woke me from a dream in which I was feeling very much in love with a woman. She was an unusually attractive woman, though not eye-catching; an ordinary housewife, though something about her made her terribly attractive to me. I was in her house, and she lived with her husband, a pleasant but rather distant character, neither controlling nor communicative. When I realised the unbearable love I felt for this woman, her husband was in the back garden; I approached her and said: 'I have to tell you something. I admire you—' 'And you love me,' she broke in, finishing my sentence. She took it all quite naturally and didn't ascribe it much importance. That's when the sound of the telephone wakes me up, and I try to cling onto the feeling, so necessary, so immensely necessary. It's been such a long time since I felt anything at all, and the slight ache from the feeling of love is like a treasure. I wanted to hold onto it, to hold onto it forever, but I could feel it dissolving; soon I couldn't recall the image or the psychological presence of that extraordinary woman, and eventually everything was lost, except the memory of that small fragment of a dream that had been much, much longer.

## SUNDAY 20, 00:55

As I write this, Chl is asleep in my bed; this hasn't happened for months. I'm waiting until I've digested my last meal of the day, and then I'll go to bed myself. Even when she's asleep she doesn't lose track of time, and if I'm not by her side at a reasonable hour she doesn't like it, which might be one of the reasons she stopped sleeping here. In other words, I can't delay too much; it's still a reasonable hour for now, but soon it'll stop being one. There won't be any sex, of course, but there will be that pleasant sensation of not being alone, and of being in the best possible company; fortunately, at my age, my sexual urges are fairly limited, and it's not too difficult to go without.

She'd already fallen asleep when the sound of the telephone woke her. I answered; I don't really know why, because I never answer the phone when I have guests, but I did. Chl was probably annoyed because I shut the door to speak; she'll think I didn't want her to hear me, and in a way that's true, though I didn't close the door for that reason but rather because I didn't want to disturb her with the conversation, if there was going to be any conversation. And there was; it was none other than Julia, worried she'd left a bad impression on her last visit, during which she severely questioned my current lifestyle. She called me, among other things, a robot. She's completely right, and I told her so. I wasn't annoyed by what she said, because in a sense it's a confirmation of what I think myself, and discussing the matter with someone else, someone as well intentioned as Julia, helps me a lot. It seems more and more obvious that if I don't manage even a slight return to the person I used to be, the novel won't get finished.

Last night, and when I got up today, I mean immediately after getting up, without having had breakfast, without even having got dressed, I made a macro (a Macro?) in Word that lets me — as usual, at the press of a button — collect all the files that make up this diary, however many there are, into a single file (called 'master document').

Creating this procedure is a sign that I'm becoming increasingly interested in reading what I've written here, and that I'm getting ready to print it, since I try not to read on the screen, which is bad for the eyes and doesn't provide the same kind of reading experience as letters printed on white paper.

Why on earth did I eat so much? The digestion is still going on, laboriously and very slowly, as usual. I hope this isn't a bad experience for Chl, that it doesn't put her off sleeping here again.

This afternoon we went for a walk, though it looked like a storm was brewing; a boiling hot day, like summer (and the caretaker turned the heating on anyway; even now that it's off again, the apartment is still revoltingly stuffy). We didn't go very far because walking was such hard work, but we managed to see two exhibitions, one of which was a truly awful one in the Subte; the other, in the MAC, included some interesting things and one spectacular thing: a drawing in charcoal and some sort of colour, of a staircase going down (I realise staircases don't go up or down, and that instead you can use them to go either up or down, but in that drawing the staircase is *going down*). The artist was Espínola Gómez. And when we were leaving we saw him – Espínola – talking to a lady. I wanted to say hello, to express in some way how much I'd admired that drawing, but my shyness held me back. Actually, I think it was both our shynesses combined, Chl's and my own, that held me back; if I'd been by myself I might have done it, since I do lots of things like that these days. But Chl is very shy, self-effacing even, and she might have felt awkward if I'd tried to communicate with the maestro, or at least that's what I was afraid of. So I hesitated, and we left in silence.

Needless to say, I didn't shave today either.

SUNDAY 20, 16:29

It was the same all night long. A very peculiar thing: I kept dreaming I was awake, feeling fully aware of my body lying in bed, the contact of my body with the mattress and the weight of the duvet making my legs uncomfortable, the presence of Chl to my right, the noises from the street, the summery heat of these stormy days . . . until all of a sudden I'd hear Chl's voice: 'You're snoring' – and I'd wake up, surprised, very surprised indeed that it was possible for me to snore while I was awake and not realise it. Then, in the morning, I finally fell into a deep sleep, and of course when I woke up I saw that Chl had left, silently, as she usually does. I phoned to apologise for keeping her awake with my snoring, but she assured me she'd slept perfectly well and that those interruptions in her sleep hadn't disturbed her at all. However, she's feeling depressed and has muscle pain.

Dreaming I'm awake, as I discovered some time ago, seems to be a normal part of my entry into sleep. It could well be that my resistance to falling asleep, which lasts into the early hours of the morning, is still there even once I'm lying in bed with the light out, so that 'sleep' itself, so to speak, tricks me into thinking I'm awake in order to make me fall asleep. I discovered this mechanism through various chance interruptions in the process, but I never believed it could go on for so long; it seemed more like an ingenious way of moving me from wakefulness to sleep, and that when 'sleep' noticed I'd dozed off it would abandon the ruse and begin to produce less realistic dreams. Now I suspect that what happened last night was that my sleep never got any deeper because I was aware of Chl by my side, and therefore afraid of falling into a deeper sleep and snoring; she hates it when I snore. Meaning that 'sleep' had to prolong its tricks so I could rest, even if I didn't manage to sleep deeply.

Today, Sunday, is the beginning of my week 'of work'. Yesterday was the end of my week 'of leisure', which appears to have been wasted because I made such intensive use of it to see friends and sort out various practical matters, steering clear of the vague anxiety but also of any kind of genuine leisure. But I don't think it was a waste, because it all worked in favour, it seems to me, of what I'm calling 'my return' – especially seeing Julia. In every conversation I have with Julia, even in some phone conversations, I learn things about my past that I'd completely forgotten. Julia's memory is unaltered, at least when it comes to details like these. For example, I don't have the slightest recollection of anything that's ever happened with Julia outside my apartment, except for one time when we went to a seaside town, and another time when we went to a different seaside town. But then I learn that we also went to the house of some friends, and that Julia's daughter came too. Sometimes when people tell me one of these stories from my past it sounds familiar, and I gradually recover some of the images, at least, or an impression that yes, it happened; but I don't have any memory whatsoever of that visit. I have no idea why I've erased it so meticulously, but it could be that an infinite number of things have been erased from my brain in the same way, perhaps simply because of the deaths of groups of neurones, and certainly because of a lack of mnemotechnic practice. Julia seems to live buried in the past, constantly reliving everything that's ever happened to her. I don't think I have the mental capacity to relive things like that. Sometimes, but very rarely, I try to relive a particular part of my life; the one I feel drawn to most often, though still very infrequently, is my Buenos Aires period. I try to remember my walks through the streets, and I try to remember the street names. It's hard work, and I can almost never do it as well as I'd like.

Now I ought to confront the vague anxiety, but I also need to tidy up my computer. I'm extremely behind with the regular cleaning of files, and the email programs, for example, have become slow to open and close because I've accumulated so many messages. I need to compress the emails and save them onto disks, and then delete them from the hard drive. The same goes for other groups of files that are accumulating unnecessarily and slowing all the processes down.

It's that or the vague anxiety.


MONDAY 21, 04:47

Here I am at five o'clock on Monday morning, coming to the end of my Sunday. Always the same nocturnal addiction. Always unshaven. But today it struck me that I might be putting off shaving because I can't remember ever having had a beard this long, or at least this white, and I thought I'd like to have my photo taken with it before

I shave. So now at least I have an excuse for not shaving: I'm waiting for Juan Ignacio to come and take a photo of me. I spoke to
his mother – my doctor, that is – tonight, who by the way found
my blood pressure perfectly normal (14/8), despite having halved
my dose of antihypertensives, and despite the fact I'm putting a bit
of salt on my tomatoes (I hope she took my blood pressure right).
I was saying that I have an excuse, but I don't know who I'm meant
to be making excuses to, since most people I know think the beard
really suits me and I shouldn't shave it off; the women are all unani-
mous on that count. The excuse must be for myself. Maybe also for
the readers of this diary. I'm embarrassed about deciding to shave
and then not doing it. And I decided to shave because my beard is
annoying me, and my moustache is also annoying me, since it gets
in my mouth when I eat. And when I drink yoghurt. My beard
ends up streaming with yoghurt. And I've noticed that people who
don't know me look at me with a certain distaste, because my beard
is very untidy. And since I don't dress very well, and my clothes are
a bit ragged and grubby, I think the overall impression is that of an
old beggar. Buying the armchairs was fun, for example: the shop
assistants weren't particularly keen at first. I must have looked like a
homeless guy, pretending to test out the armchairs when really he
just wanted somewhere comfortable to sit. But be that as it may, the
fact of deciding to shave and then not actually doing it makes me feel
uncomfortably powerless, as do these all-nighters and my addiction
to things on the computer. What's more, I never even decided to
grow this beard; I simply went on and on not shaving, out of the
same feeling of apathy or whatever it is, or because there's always
something more interesting to do. It's an unplanned beard; unculti-
vated, unlooked-after. And I've also acquired the habit of rummaging
around in it with my fingers; if I'm talking to someone, for example,
my fingers will be poking out here and there among the hairs the
whole time. It's a very pleasing thing to do, because it feels as if I'm
stroking a woman's pubis. But the fact that said pubis happens to be
on my own chin makes it a rather suspicious habit, at least to my
mind. Is this why I'm not shaving? Is it a kind of auto-eroticism?
The lack of feeling in the hairs is a point in my favour, because the

sensation of stroking something that's not part of you makes it more excusable. It makes it a kind of contraband auto-eroticism. I should think about this more carefully. But I won't.

Today my contact with Chl was exclusively telephonic. She stayed at home, depressed and with muscle pain, reading in bed. When we talk on the phone she falls into these long silences, which I call 'the plates shifting'. It's not the least bit entertaining, but it's hard to say goodbye and hang up because I feel she needs that form of communication; although she doesn't speak, she's communicating her unease to me, sharing it, by means of those silences. I try to be patient. I even find it moving. When she gets depressed she seems very fragile, and somehow it does me good that she calls me, if only to communicate her silence, and that she needs to share her abysses with me.

I was having a bit of a tidy-up of the files on the computer, particularly in the email programs. Now they're much nimbler, opening and closing immediately. But I need to keep cleaning the hard drive; there's loads and loads of rubbish.

MONDAY 21, 21:15

Waiting for Chl, though she's not definitely coming. It's stormy outside. I can see the lightning through the window. I remembered noticing a few days ago that Chl was looking at me strangely; it was as if she hated me, which sometimes happens when she's depressed. It's not that she hates me personally; it's a generic hatred of the world in general and human beings in particular. Often, in those states, she goes quiet, and it's obvious she's holding things back that she ought to say out loud; sometimes I'm able to make her speak, though often I'm not, and it turns out she's bearing unjustified grudges. I point out that they're unjustified, that she's misinterpreted some word or gesture, and then she laughs and relaxes, and feels better. This time she wasn't especially depressed, but she was quiet, with that strange look in her eye, and with all the appearance of having something to say and not saying it. I asked her if it was a look of hatred.

'No,' she answered, very decisively. And after a pause, she added: 'It's a calculating look. I was wondering if you were a good idea.'

MONDAY 21, 22:28

I broke off because Chl arrived. Now she's gone. It seems very significant that I began writing knowing I was almost certainly going to be interrupted. I don't remember doing anything like that in many, many years. It would be excellent if I were losing my phobia of interruptions, which has led me to put off writing – and ultimately never to write – entire novels. I'm seeing it as a good omen, or at least an important precedent.

So, Chl had said: 'It's a calculating look. I was wondering if you were a good idea,' and I burst out laughing. Of course I'm not a good idea, and I'm glad she's begun to realise as much. It must be one of the results of the therapy.

When our relationship began, I took for granted that it wouldn't last long. She warned me that, in her previous relationships, the day had always come when she woke up and felt as if the relationship had absolutely nothing to do with her, at which point she ended it abruptly. I prepared myself for that. But I didn't prepare for what actually happened; this gradual cooling of the relationship in strictly sexual terms, but nothing more; we still see each other regularly and talk on the phone several times a day, and when we're together I can feel the great affection she has for me. It's strange, very strange, and I don't know how to deal with it. Sometimes I despair and think: 'It's over; we can't go on like this,' but they're momentary wobbles that I regret after a few minutes. I know I'd miss her very much and that everything would be far more difficult without that affection, without that generally cheerful and vivacious presence which time and again has turned a dark day into a happy one. Nevertheless, things are moving towards a separation; and they'll carry on doing so as long as the therapy continues to work. But I don't want to keep preparing myself for a future which, experience suggests, never turns out the way you expect. Better just to let things happen.

TUESDAY 22, 17:11

Big news. Two tangos I didn't know with Pugliese, on Radio Clarín, and one was even instrumental. I didn't catch the title, but I heard the name of the composer: Ruggiero. Have they updated their music collection?

Today I woke up later than ever; technically I was woken up by Chl with her usual phone call, but for some reason (I always suspect sexual escapades) she didn't ring until 3.30 p.m.

Even so, I stayed in bed a bit longer. It's still raining. I can still hear the sound of distant thunder. I was deep in a disturbing dream; not a nightmare, but one of those maddening dreams where nothing is ever resolved, full of trivial details and at the same time with a terrible weight of meaning.

A long, long dream, in what I call 'real time', built on minutiae; I always forget those plots, the way I forget everyday occurrences, as if they weren't worth filing away in my memory. At one point I had a conversation with a young man who could have been Juan Ignacio, about undertaking some kind of action, making something happen, but then I found that the bulb in a floor lamp was broken; broken, not burnt out, as if someone had smashed it. I was very annoyed, because it meant someone had broken it and left it like that. The lamp hadn't changed shape, it hadn't exploded or shattered, but part of the glass was missing. And there were problems of some kind, I don't know what, with another sort of light, which stopped us carrying out our plans. This left me feeling indignant and disheartened.

Then I was in the street, still with the young man nearby, and there were lots of people getting ready for a car journey. My parents were among them; I knew this even though I couldn't see them and wasn't sure exactly where they were. Some neighbours had offered to drive us. The journey, according to a map I consulted, was fairly long; we had to cover around two hundred miles. The name of a seaside town – La Paloma – was hanging in the air, but I'm not sure if we were starting there and had to go back to Montevideo or vice versa, or if we had to go to both places. The street was in a city I didn't recognise, but wherever it was, I was settled there; I had a house, or at least I lived in a house where my things also were. This collective house move wasn't a surprise, but I wasn't prepared for it either, as if no one had told me exactly when it was scheduled to take place. I realised I hadn't packed my suitcases or anything, and suddenly I remembered I had some jars in the freezer containing something medicinal, something I needed. I asked the youth to run and get them while I tried to work out which vehicle I was meant to travel in. I went over to a dark-coloured truck, which was full up and had its doors shut; a round-faced boy I recognised was sitting on the back seat, between some other people. I asked him something. He gave an unsatisfactory answer. In the end I thought I'd better go by bus, since I couldn't find a single car with people I knew in it and a space reserved for me. The neighbours organising the move were an elderly, Jewish-looking couple. They seemed very keen to get going right away. The youth who had supposedly gone to look for the jars didn't come back. I wondered which bus to take, what time it would come, where I should wait for it. That's when the phone woke me up.

For some reason, I associated this dream with one I had many years ago, whose crystal-clear meaning I was unable to see until my therapist explained it to me (some kind of party in my old apartment on Calle Soriano; loads of people milling around in the corridors and bunches of flowers all over the place; there were some men at the door who'd brought some circular flower arrangements and wanted to hang them on the landing. I moved among the people in my apartment and nobody paid me any attention; it was as if they couldn't see me. I spoke to them and they didn't answer, but not in an aggressive way; they simply ignored me. My therapist made me see that it was my funeral).

Considering that I associated today's dream with that other, older dream, maybe the 'travellers' in it are travellers heading towards death. I can't see my parents because they're dead. I need to join them . . . but I'm not ready.

I think the novel I'm trying to finish because of the grant was originally written to exorcise my fear of death. And now comes this string of deaths among my friends. The topic is in the air . . .

WEDNESDAY 23, 03:42

A working day; one private student, then the evaluations for the virtual workshop. I think it's stopped raining; the streets look dry, but it's still cloudy. I hope I manage to leave the house tomorrow. I haven't been out for days. I hope I can get to bed a bit earlier, too . . . On Thursday I have workshops all day, starting at 4.30 p.m. Tomorrow is Wednesday.

I'm going to stop saying I haven't shaved (but it's true, I haven't shaved). At the very least, I can say I still haven't had the photo taken.

Today my cigarette intake rose a bit. The effect of this medication, the antidepressant, is strange: first it doesn't seem to do anything whatsoever, then suddenly one day there's a considerable drop in my cigarette intake, and another day I can't taste cigarettes at all and smoking is profoundly unsatisfying; then my intake rises again, but it doesn't seem to reach the same levels as before. We'll see what happens on Thursday; it'll definitely go up a lot, because of the workshops. Working is very bad for me. Though in another sense it's good for me.

Chl is still making progress with her therapy; it's interesting to see how she's opening up to topics that she used to be very closed to. These days she talks easily about things that were once completely off limits, or too painful to address. She told me on the phone that today she attacked the therapist (attacked him verbally, that is). A positive development. But then she regretted it, or at least she was worried about it. She feels sorry for people too easily. She always puts herself in the other person's place and suffers over things they probably don't care about at all.

As for me, I was left stewless and *milanesa*-less because of her depression at the weekend. But she gave me a slice of a spinach and ricotta pie she'd bought; really good, really well made, with a really good flavour.

I played lots of card games, both last night and today, though less so today. Last night I spent hours playing a game called Pipe Dream, which involves building a pipe out of separate pieces that appear one by one, and all the while the water is travelling through it. You have to make as long a pipe as you can before the water spills out of the end.

It's a bit like Tetris. Now I'm going to play some more, trying not to fall into a trance, and soon I'll go to bed. It's almost four.

WEDNESDAY 23, 06:12

I don't know if any readers take an interest in the date and time markers at the top of each section of this diary; when I read other people's diaries, it's as if those markers don't exist. Still, the time on this particular page shows that the sun's about to come up, or is already coming up. I've turned on the computer, which I turned off a few minutes ago after playing and playing that stupid Pipe Dream game like a fool until I ended up with cramp in my arm and hand. But I didn't want to go to bed without recording the thoughts that engulfed me as soon as I turned the computer off and dragged myself into the kitchen to make a coffee – an essential preparatory stage every time I go to bed – because it occurs to me that those very thoughts might be what I was trying to escape when I started playing on the computer in the first place.

I know they don't have any scientific validity, but things like this, like the thing I'm about to describe, seem convincing to me, especially when they're more the general rule than the exception; they happen to me very, very frequently, and they leave me feeling deeply uneasy, whether I like it or not.

It turned out that the student who came today, or rather yesterday, the 'private student' I mentioned a few hours ago, had brought along her attempt at the task I'd set the previous fortnight. The task was to write down the story of a dream, simply and with no literary pretensions, and then, in the second stage, to try to write a story based on that dream, removing any signs that it was a dream and presenting it to the reader as a realistic story. Or indeed coherent, rather than realistic. It could be a fantasy story, if it follows the rules of fantasy. It's not important to tell the story of the whole dream, either; you could even write a story based on associations produced by the dream, beginning from an image or scene, but above all trying to recreate the atmosphere of the dream, focusing on what it's like rather than what happens.

And so my student brings me an account of her dream, not a very recent dream but not from very long ago either, and then attempts to make it into a story as per the assignment. She doesn't manage, because she sticks to the plot of the dream too closely and simply retells it with more details; it's fairly well written, but she doesn't get rid of the signs that it's a dream. This, however, doesn't matter to what I'm going to say next. In my student's dream, she walked through a graveyard, entered a house, looked at a few things, and then went home. There she found her family all together, talking about her – saying bad things about her. Then she notices they've messed up her bookshelves and gets annoyed. She storms back to where her family are and tells them off; she shouts at them and even grabs one of her brothers by the collar and gives him a shake. No one responds; they ignore her; they all look like sleepwalkers. The last sentence of the story says that she couldn't bear the situation, and 'I disappeared'.

I pointed out the obvious fact, which is that in the dream she'd died and become a ghost. She hadn't realised this; at the time, not even her therapist had interpreted the dream that way. I told my student about the dream that I, coincidentally, had written about today, involving my wake, and suggested she turn her text into a ghost story told from the point of view of the ghost. It's not an original idea; it's been done before, probably more times than I'm aware of, but in this case it seems to be the most authentic way of telling the story. She was very impressed. And so was I.

As always in these situations, I wonder: did I remember that dream of mine (about my wake) because of a genuine association with the dream I had this morning, or did I telepathically pick up on the essence of the story my student had written? But in this particular case, the association is more direct, more powerful. I'm almost certain it's that. I can't prove it, but, as I was saying, these things happen time and again, to the extent that I can never tell whether what I'm thinking, or what occurs to me, has arisen from within my own mind, or if it comes from elsewhere, from another mind. And so I find myself thinking again about the boundaries of the self, and the tangibility of what we call the 'individual'. I remember a quotation I read a while ago, which was attributed to Einstein (I'm quoting from memory, of course): 'Seeing ourselves as separate individuals is nothing but an optical illusion.'

THURSDAY 24, 03:43

I was sitting in the armchair, the one for lounging in, after my dinner-lunch, when I began to feel an overwhelming need to go and play games on the computer. 'I mustn't do it,' I told myself. 'Why do I think these things are necessary?' I tried to resist. Then I had a sudden realisation; 'Goddammit,' I said out loud, and I got up and came to sit at the computer and played Pipe Dream followed by Golf. What I'd realised was that the vague anxiety was about to make an appearance, and that I couldn't devote myself to exploring it because the process would inevitably be interrupted tomorrow (today), workshop day. I like my workshops and I'm very fond of my students, but that's not the problem; the problem is being interrupted while I'm in the process of exploring the vague anxiety. The other day I proved I can write if I want to, even when I know I'm going to be interrupted. I can write this diary, at least, since I don't have to concentrate too hard on it; I barely use any imagination, and the writing follows the largely erratic comings and goings of my thoughts. Maybe if I tried to write a story or a novel it would be different, and the fear of being interrupted would hold me back completely. Anyway, the point is that it's impossible to explore the vague anxiety if there's any threat of being interrupted, let alone if I'm certain that an interruption will definitely come – and a prolonged interruption at that, since I have two workshops and they take me all day. This is the moment in the Sisyphean process when my rock inevitably goes rolling down the hill. Tomorrow (today), i.e. Thursday, workshops; and the day after I'll be tired and overexcited, with the unconscious up to its usual tricks, and there'll be no space for the vague anxiety; Saturday will be about the same, alleviated by the likely presence of Chl, though that presence is, ultimately, another interruption, and to hell with the vague anxiety. That's why I swore out loud and sat down at the computer, resigned. By then I knew what was going to happen, though I didn't think it would be so extreme: I was playing for about four hours. Pipe Dream, as I've discovered, is a dangerous game, because it's so exciting; it's a game of speed, against the clock; the water comes oozing down the unfinished pipe, and you have to do your best to make the pipe longer, and sometimes you don't find the right piece in time and you lose. This means that the muscles in my arm and hand that operate the mouse become far too tense, which probably also raises my blood pressure. I noticed this and switched to playing Golf, which is more relaxed because there's no time limit, but it's still a stupid game, completely stupid. Although it takes a certain amount of reasoning, the result is always down to chance, and at the end of the day it's no different to tossing a coin in the air and betting on one of the sides. And my arm still ends up bothering me, because I play automatically and fall into a trance, forgetting to relax my muscles. Sometimes I remember and relax them momentarily, but then a few minutes later I'm tense again and haven't even realised. And so the hours pass, and all the while I'm thinking, 'I mustn't play any more, I mustn't play any more, it's tiring me out, it's idiotic,' but on and on I go. No doubt I've undone all the positive effects of my yoga class, which was excellent today, though my teacher's face was swollen because she has an infected molar.

Before my yoga class, after getting up very late and having break-fast and doing the things I had to do, and while the maid, who comes on Wednesdays, was here, I also played some games, and that's how I ended up not going shopping. There are lots of things I need from the supermarket, but when I finally came to my senses the teacher was ringing the doorbell and I couldn't even put an order in over the phone. Once again, my sleeping hours are making life very difficult. Tomorrow I have to be up early, i.e. no later than 2 p.m. I'm going to request a wake-up call from the phone company, and Chl's going to ring me as well, which is more effective because she talks and shouts into the answerphone until I pick up, if I'm in a fit state to pick up. But because she sometimes forgets to wake me, and after all, she's under no obligation to do so, I make use of the wake-up call service and programme two calls, half an hour apart, because the first one only registers faintly, distantly, or I don't hear it at all; and yet, even if I don't hear it, something within me does, because I always hear the second one, meaning that some part of me is awake by then. Anyway, tomorrow, or rather today, I'll have to hurry if I want to be ready when it's time to open the door at four thirty; sometimes I end up having everything arranged with just seconds to spare, and there have been times when I've been late and had to sort out the living room in front of one of my students. It's not a big problem, but I don't like them seeing me do it. It's about image, I think; as if I were afraid they'd lose respect for me.

Today I left Pablo a message and he called me after my yoga class. He told me about a lot of what happened to him in Mexico, in relation to Flaco's funeral. I learnt things I would never have suspected, like for example that Flaco was very sentimental (his son's word) and had a big box where he carefully stored all his children's letters and other reminders of them, including school exercise books and things like that; and all in perfect order, meaning that as well as being sentimental, Flaco was very orderly. He didn't seem it at all. He also kept my letters (which ones? I don't remember writing any letters to Mexico, or maybe I do, once) and copies of the letters he sent me (again, what letters? Has my memory devoured those as well? But I'm almost certain that there wasn't more than one letter from him in all the many years he spent there). Pablo also gave me a more accurate account of his death; a death foretold, what's more, first because his doctorly instinct wasn't mistaken, and second because he seems to have made a fairly conscious decision to consider his life over, as did my other friend who recently passed away. Not long before it happened, Flaco had put some of his affairs in order, for instance by increasing his insurance premium in favour of his Mexican children; and, what's more, he'd announced that he was going to die. And apparently he didn't go to bed that night, as I'd been told, but sat down in an armchair instead. He said to a neighbour that it looked like a heart attack because he could feel a tingling in his left hand, and that there was no point calling the emergency services; he'd prefer to carry on chatting with her, or rather listening to her talk. It was in this armchair, and not in bed as I'd previously heard, that he drank his little glass of brandy, and that was where he stayed. It's very good that Pablo and his siblings resolved to go to Mexico as soon as they heard about his death; as I told Pablo, that's the sort of thing I never do, ever, and then afterwards I pay a terrible price. They experienced a funeral with mariachis singing. They saw their father's students crying their hearts out, and all in all, they returned to Montevideo with a far more positive image of their father. Still, Pablo is upset, and shaken. I remembered the death of my father, which happened when I was about the age Pablo is now, and I remember that I was much more frightened than I was sad. Sadness about death is something I don't really understand; or rather, I understand that it's sadness for oneself and not for the dead person, whom there's no reason to feel sorry for – it's sadness about what you no longer have, about the things you didn't say or do, about real or imaginary guilt. And the fear – as I decided to explain to Pablo, believing it might do him good to think about it a little – was because while my father had been alive, in a magical way he'd served as a kind of shield protecting me from my own death. He was the one who had to deal with death, not me. And as soon as he wasn't around any more, I was left face to face with that good lady. Without a shield.

And then my friend who lives in Chicago rang; she's visiting Montevideo and has brought me some chocolates. She has a migraine, she's had it for days, and on top of that she's been bitten by a tick. I'm seeing her on Friday afternoon. Then Julia called and explained at great length all the discoveries she's made about herself through spending time with me; amazing lucidity for a woman who's normally all over the place. Her explanations included a difficult confession, something that upset her modesty, but she went ahead with it anyway, and afterwards she was in very high spirits. I wonder how this friendship of ours will turn out; it's moving a lot of things in both of us. I don't think there's much chance of resuming our old romantic past. What's more, I don't think a sexual relationship with a woman of that age would work very well. I wouldn't work very well, I mean. I've always been attracted to women who are younger than me, and now I'm attracted to women who are a *lot* younger than me, which is why I don't think the diagnosis of arteriosclerosis is entirely mistaken.

I've been forgetting to mention something that I don't want to lose sight of. I was too lazy to turn the computer on again yesterday, after I'd already turned it back on once to write something or other and then turned it off again, but I would have liked to make a note then. For the second time, I heard the tango 'Derecho Viejo' by the Julio De Caro orchestra on Radio Clarín. Who knows where they found that record; it's extremely rare, and I was completely unaware of its existence. Don Julio De Caro, whom as a teenager I had the honour of meeting in person when he was passing through Montevideo on his honeymoon. He'd married a woman who was very, very fat, and a similar age to him. I don't know how old Don Julio would have been then, but I don't think he can have been less than sixty. A charming man, and a musical genius. According to the experts – and it's easy to verify this by looking at his discography – De Caro invented tango, or tango as we know it today. Just as Gardel showed how to sing tango as it's sung today. De Caro and his sextet showed how to play the tango of the Guardia Nueva; they paved the way for Pugliese and Troilo and even Piazzolla, and all the others. My first contact with De Caro was in the Tristán Narvaja market. As a boy of fifteen I used to go there and look for old records, the old shellac 78s, and sometimes I found marvellous things. On one of those occasions, I found a record called 'El Monito' – the little monkey – by the De Caro sextet. The man at the stall played it on a gramophone and made me listen; I was instantly transfixed. That tango, that sextet, made me feel something I'd never felt before. It has exactly the same effect today. It's a kind of extreme nostalgia for something I've never experienced, the sort of nostalgia that sends you into violent fits of sobbing, and yet paradoxically it's also joyous. Like some other records, 'El Monito' included a few words, a dialogue as crazy as the sextet's crazy bohemia, and this was my first encounter with surrealism. 'Monito, do you want some coffee?' said a voice, maybe the voice of Don Julio himself. 'No,' the little monkey replied. 'Why not?' the first voice asked immediately. 'Because my shoes have fallen apart,' the second answered.

Well, they played 'Derecho Viejo' on Radio Clarín. The first time I heard it I couldn't believe my ears; I didn't know which orchestra it was. Initially I thought of Osvaldo Fresedo, because I could hear a harp, or a vibraphone, but then all kinds of wind instruments came in, a clarinet or oboe by the sounds of it, and almost certainly a trumpet, plus lots of strings. The speed wasn't very typical of Fresedo, either, and nor was the energy, or – I can't think of a better way to put it – the balls. It was strange and powerful, very powerful. I would never have dreamed it was De Caro, because I'm not a big fan of De Caro's orchestra; it seems too formal, it's missing the light-hearted, playful and terribly nostalgic madness of the sextet. But this orchestra, weighty as it was, had much of the sextet's agility and feel. Suddenly, almost in the final bars, I heard a sound that couldn't be anything other than the 'De Caro sound'; a way of striking up with a phrase, something sudden and violent, with those scraping strings, which I'd only ever heard in De Caro. In spite of being alone, I exclaimed: 'De Caro!' – a few seconds before the announcer said the same thing, though without my surprise or excitement. I heard it again last night. It's a freak of nature, a carnival, a pastiche, a *murga* . . . I don't know what it is, but it's magnificent. I've never heard a tango like it. When was it recorded? Are there other tangos played in the same style? Where were – where are – those records? (A little earlier, they'd played something horrible by Juan de Dios Filiberto. Another string orchestra . . . but so stupidly absurd, so cheaply pretentious; such bad taste, such paucity, such lack of imagination.)

And it was gone seven in the morning, I think, when they played a tango by an orchestra which at some moments sounded sublime. Charlo was singing, a young Charlo, meaning that it must have been Canaro. But a musical Canaro, with none of his usual stiffness and heaviness. And towards the end, a surprise: a violin that could be none other than Cayetano Puglisi. No one but Puglisi could achieve that quality, for which the only possible word is 'sublime'. I often listen to D'Arienzo only to see if there's a little phrase, at least, of Puglisi – who, as they say, had it and never let it go; and when that violin comes in, D'Arienzo is erased and everything is magical for an instant.

FRIDAY 25, 06:20

And just like that, it's almost 7 a.m. I knew this would happen. The workshop. All day long, the workshop. It was satisfying; my students are excellent. But it tires me out, it tires me out and then afterwards I don't want to go to sleep for hours and hours. At least I wasn't messing around with games; I was working intensively on a macro – or Macro – in this very program, Word, considerably improving on what I did the other day, with the aim of putting together a master document for this diary. I also, before that, printed out everything I'd written until yesterday, which must mean I've made up my mind to read it. I haven't read it yet. I'm curious. I want to know if there's anything interesting here, anything that might be interesting to a reader other than myself. Why? It's not that I want to pull the wool over the Guggenheim Foundation's eyes and present them with this diary instead of the project; what's more, the Foundation have expressly stated that they don't want me to present them with anything. They just want to know what I've spent their money on when it comes to the end of the year. And what's even more, I WANT to finish the project; it's just that I haven't yet reached that point, and I still have a long way to go, I think, before I do; but when I get there, and get there I shall, I'll do the work quickly and well. I believe in myself. I just have to stop putting off the act of confronting and overcoming the vague anxiety, overcoming it and reaching my life of leisure; it's all as simple as that. As simple and as painful. Dear reader: never dream of mixing your writing and your life. Or rather, do; you'll have your fair share of suffering, but you'll give something of yourself, which is ultimately the only thing that matters. I'm not interested in novelists who grind out their four-hundred-page doorstoppers with the help of index cards and a disciplined imagination; the only information they transmit is empty, sad, depressing. And deceitful, since it comes disguised as naturalism. Like the famous Flaubert. Pah.

I'm amazed this country isn't overrun with writers. Many of my students write far better than I do. And yet they don't keep up a constant output, they don't make the things they write into books, they're not interested in being published, they don't want to be writers. They're happy to share their experiences with the other students in the workshop by reading out their texts. They all have other work. No one wants a life of starvation or poverty. They're probably right. It's a shame things have to be this way, that it's impossible to get by as a writer here with any dignity at all. Meanwhile, my own publishing project has stalled. I don't know what the problem is; it's just not going anywhere. I ought to take charge of it personally, but I don't want to; I don't want to acquire a single complication. At least, not in the year of the grant. I need to arrive at full-time leisure, which I still can't bring myself to do, but I need to. And now I need to go to bed, because in a few hours my friend who lives in Chicago is coming to see me. Chl's also coming, and she says she's made me some *milanesas*.

SATURDAY 26, 07:24

Just look at the time. I'm off to bed right this minute. I'll explain later.

SUNDAY 27, 05:51

The rock goes on rolling down the hill. I didn't recover after the workshop on Thursday, and now we're into Sunday and it's almost six in the morning. On Friday, a national holiday, I got up at around 5 p.m.; at half past six, my friend from Chicago was due to arrive. She came on time and began telling her anecdotes one after another, while I gradually fell into a trance. Her stories are very vivid and at times very entertaining; it's a shame she never manages to write them down, even though she'd be perfectly capable of it. At 11.30 p.m. I started feeling ill, as if I was going to faint, and all of a sudden I realised I hadn't had lunch; I'd only eaten an apple while my friend was eating some pork ribs and potatoes I'd given her. When I got up with great urgency to prepare a tomato with garlic and bread as quickly as I could, and leave a steak out to defrost, I realised I'd also been completely oblivious, until that moment, to the fact that my bladder was about to burst. As I ate the tomato, and then the steak, and then drank a coffee, my friend carried on with anecdote after anecdote. She left at half past one in the morning, and I suddenly felt emptied of myself. I hurried to the computer and played and played until who knows what time, and of course on Saturday I got up late again, and now here I am at six in the morning, and soon I'll go to bed and then get up very late all over again. This can't go on; somehow or other I have to find the way back, if not to normality then at least to a reasonable schedule. Luckily Chl came today, and not only did she bring me *milanesas* but she also joined me for a walk, and for something to eat in a bar on 18 de Julio. I hadn't left the house in a week and it felt good to be out, like my blood was circulating again. After eating, we went to check the sale table in the Feria del Libro bookshop and found a few interesting things. We walked home as well, very tired by then; the weather is horribly humid. Chl's young, but she got tired, too, because she'd done a lot of walking already, making the most of the sunny afternoon that I completely missed. She thought about staying the night, but in the end she went home. I didn't insist that she stayed, partly because I know it's totally pointless; when she makes a decision, it's very difficult, impossible even, to change her mind. And partly because I know that if by some strange twist of fate I do convince her and she decides to stay after all, she'll most likely end up in a bad mood. Last Saturday she stayed the night of her own accord, but even though it had been her choice she was in a bad mood when she arrived; I'm sure she forced herself to spend the night, and that was what put her in a bad mood. She forced herself because she wants to overcome her phobias, or at least the behaviours she thinks are irrational, but she shouldn't force herself, because irrationality has its reasons, and as long as you don't uncover them, and sometimes even if you do, irrationality goes on doing its thing one way or another. She tried to convince me that tomorrow she really would spend the night, but I asked her not to make any promises. If she comes, and stays over, wonderful, but she shouldn't feel obliged, because today she was exuberant, cheerful, beautiful, I'd almost even say happy, and it would make me sad to see her depressed tomorrow, or in a bad mood, because of something to do with me.

I asked Chl to read what I've written of this diary so far. The other night I printed it out, read part of it and got quite bored because it's so fresh in my mind and everything in it feels far too familiar; I wanted a second opinion, to see whether it's worth carrying on with. It's true that Chl is also implicated, as a character in the diary, so her judgement won't be entirely objective, but she's a good reader and very balanced in her assessments, and I thought she'd make an effort at objectivity.

And she's completely frank, too; she'd never twist her opinion just to please me, because she knows things like that don't end well. In short, she read it and found it interesting; I heard her laugh in a few places, which is a good sign. Her opinion has encouraged me to continue and leave my own assessment until later on, when I can read it with more distance, and when I've forgotten a bit of what I've written.

I ought to record at least a few of my friend from Chicago's anecdotes (the poisoned tick, the real-estate business), but they wouldn't be as funny because I can't tell stories the way she does, and the comedy is mostly in the way they're told. Anyway, I have my own way of being funny, but I use it for my own things. I'm very jealous of a writer like W. Somerset Maugham, whose *The Razor's Edge* I'm currently reading. He can retell stories he's heard in great detail, and he can even imagine those details, invent them, using some story sketched out by a friend as a starting point. He's an excellent writer, though for some reason underrated. I used to underrate him myself, in fact, perhaps because he was too successful, and because his narrative style is fairly unassuming. I remember at home we used to have several of his books, which were fashionable when I was a child or a teenager, and I even came across copies of those same books in my bookselling days, though I never once decided to read them. And it's very likely that if I had read them back then, they wouldn't have interested me at all. When you're young and inexperienced, you look for dramatic plots in books, just as you do in films. With time, you come to see that the plot has no importance at all; and that the style, the way the story is told, is everything. Because of this I can watch the same film or read the same book innumerable times, even a detective novel whose ending I remember perfectly. All I'd read by Maugham was *Ashenden*. I read it for the first time when I was in Buenos Aires and as a result of my interest in spy novels – an interest that Graham Greene in particular had awakened. I found the book entertaining, but very inferior to Greene. Then I read it again a few years later, not many, and found it a bit more interesting. And very recently I read it again, and I liked it even more. It made me want to try Maugham's other books. Now I'm enjoying *The Razor's Edge* enormously; a book that's been so underrated, and so unfairly, for so many years. I suppose I'll have the same experience with countless other things. It's difficult to spot one's own prejudices, which take root in the mind in a strange and inexplicable way, accompanied by a certain sense of superiority. Those dwarves settle in like absurd dictators, and we accept them like revealed truths. Very rarely, because of some accident or chance occurrence, we find we have to reconsider a prejudice, argue with ourselves about it, lift a corner of the veil and peer through the gap at how things really are. In those cases, it's possible to uproot them. But the others are still there, out of sight, carrying us foolishly in all the wrong directions.

What I'm saying is that I'd like to write with the same serene pleasure as Somerset Maugham.

MONDAY 28, 05:56

Without touching the ground. It's always six in the morning. At least I've cut my nails (my fingernails) and washed the dishes, which had formed a disgusting pile. A rainy day, as usual. Chl didn't come, though I could tell from her voice over the phone that she was still in a good mood despite the rain. I thought about lots of things I wanted to write in this diary, but I didn't write anything. I spent all day distracting myself with the computer. A new program I downloaded from the internet; something I'd been searching for unsuccessfully for months, and the one I found is pretty good. No new emails, except for a couple of exercises from students. Not that I write to anyone myself, of course. Dozens of unanswered emails. Today was the beginning of my week of leisure, but there was no leisure; as you can see, I'm on the run from the vague anxiety. My friend from Chicago took some photos of me on Friday. If they come out, they'll be horrible, with flash. Yesterday Chl told me my beard has been longer than this before and just as white, and showed me a magazine that had published the photos. But I was much fatter then. A fat man with a beard and a thin man with a beard are very different things. Still, I didn't shave, in spite of the photos and Chl's demonstration. My back hurts.

TUESDAY 29, 00:23

Today I put a few blank sheets of paper in a pile on the dining-room table, along with a pen. I turned the computer off and went to the dentist, intending not to turn the computer back on for the rest of the day and to write my diary on those sheets of paper. I came back from the dentist ravenously hungry. Chl arrived as I was making dinner and sat with me while I ate. Maybe because I was hungry, or because I got cold when I went out, or both, or something else I'm unaware of, I was . . . not exactly in a bad mood, but distant and not very polite, as if the most important part of me was elsewhere. I don't mean I was rude to her, but I wasn't nice to her either. When she left, I turned the computer on and played Golf. Now I'm writing on the computer. The sheets of paper remain blank.

The truth is, I'm still feeling strange. Is the unpleasant effect of the antidepressants finally kicking in? My previous experiences with other antidepressants tell me this is very likely, that I need to be on my guard. Even if these are a new kind . . . My previous experiences led, at one point, after a few weeks, to my beginning to feel a kind of separation or otherness, like I was splitting in two. I stopped taking them right away and didn't try them again for years. I'd be very annoyed if I had to give these ones up, because they've definitely done me good over the almost two months I've been taking them, and the original purpose – the anti-cigarette effect – remains the same. Even if I haven't stopped smoking, my relationship with cigarettes has clearly changed. On many days I've smoked less than usual, and on some days much less. It seems there's a general downward trend, and it's not impossible that one day I might be able to reach zero cigarettes, or perhaps a more reasonable number like four or five per day. Now that I think about it, it's not just today I've been feeling strange; it's a process that began some days ago, when my will disappeared almost entirely, and, as this diary records, or should record, since then I've been surrendering too much to the games on the computer and going to bed later and later: the opposite to before. Unless there's something else, something I'm still not aware of. Maybe there were a lot of those rainy days, when I didn't go out; today the sun was shining, albeit in a pale and watery way, and the cold was extreme. I felt fine when I was outside; the cold didn't bother me, my lungs didn't feel under attack and, most importantly, I didn't have those terrible pains in my chest. The absence of those pains confirms my diagnosis of gastric reflux, because when I went to the dentist today I hadn't eaten anything since breakfast. I had breakfast at around 4.30 p.m. and left for the dentist at a quarter to eight.


I have a debt to this diary, or rather to myself, which I'm finding difficult to pay, more out of laziness than embarrassment. I realise I can't go on talking about my computer addiction, especially the games and the VB programming, without also mentioning the time I spend online searching for pornography. I feel particularly uncomfortable because some years ago I wrote in a book: 'I detest pornography,' and I feel even more uncomfortable when I think that someone might remember that statement and assume I was lying when I said it. I need, then, to explain that I wasn't lying, and I also need to stop hiding this facet of my addictions; hiding it is an attempt to disguise the fact that my behaviour contradicts that statement. When I wrote what I wrote, my words were an accurate reflection of my thoughts and feelings. It's not that nowadays I feel or think exactly the opposite, or that old age has loosened my strict morals, or that I've gone completely senile (although we can't entirely rule that out). As for the strict morals, I've never had any, at least not when it comes to sex. My rejection was purely and exclusively visceral, an immediate feeling of repugnance, with no intellectual or moral filters.

Some time after I wrote that about pornography came the beginning of my video phase, my video addiction, which intensified when I stopped smoking around 1993. During that period I watched a few porn videos and found that my feelings of revulsion had softened somewhat, though I still had to close my eyes during certain scenes. Around the same time I read something by D.H. Lawrence on the subject and felt I agreed completely with the essence of his thought: the detestable thing about pornography is that it degrades human beings, stripping them of all spirituality and turning them into material objects to be manipulated. Those are my words, not Lawrence's, but it's what I remember having understood.

I didn't persevere much with the porn videos, though I did become a fan of one particular actress, who had an ample bosom and a very sweet expression and seemed utterly different to all the other women in those films. Her way of acting, of being fully present in the scenes, however lubricious, in a sense contradicted Lawrence's thought and my own. She never lost her humanity or the presence of that spirit which can be glimpsed in people's eyes. But she didn't feature in very many films, so I soon lost interest.

Then came the computer, the internet and email; the end of 1995. As soon as I was able to surf the Web I set about looking for photographs of naked women, and I became an enthusiastic collector. In the process I often stumbled onto porn sites, where I looked through lots of photos without adding them to my collection; I only kept a small number, a very small number, because they contained extraordinary women. Since you can't conduct a search for naked women without inevitably ending up on porn sites, it could be that I've now encountered so many of these scenes that I'm getting used to them, becoming immune, considerably diluting my initial distaste. But, strangely, my feelings of distaste and disgust came back, and come back, in full force at the sight of some scenes, the kind that very much do match what I've called 'Lawrence's thought'. Often the woman is objectified, turned into a thing to be manipulated, and that kind of scene still makes me feel repelled, disgusted and angry.

Japanese girls were my great discovery. As well as their intrinsic qualities, they often have great artists working on their behalf, who not only avoid reducing them to objects with no spirit, but also enhance everything charming about them.

When I'd amassed a collection of around a thousand photos, I suspended my costly internet searches and forgot about the whole thing for a long time; rarely, if ever, did I look back at the photos stored on the disks. I think I found searching for them more exciting than looking at them, and, to be honest, something very similar is happening to me now.

I still need to write about my relapse in 1999, but I'm tired of writing and I'm going to play a bit of Golf, if the reader will permit me.

## TUESDAY 29, 05:58

Yes, once again it's six in the morning. But at least I didn't go on the internet. I wonder what I have been doing all this time.

## TUESDAY 29, 19:22

I still haven't started writing by hand. I just deleted all the games from the hard drive, after copying them onto ZIP disks first. I can play them from a ZIP disk, and I definitely will, but the disks aren't stored anywhere near the computer. In fact, they're in another room. Which means that when I want to play, I have to overcome my laziness and get out of my chair, and experience suggests that my laziness is generally more powerful than my habit of playing games. Although that's not exactly it; really, what happens is that I often play because I have the game to hand, and if I don't have it to hand I can reflect, ask myself if I really want to play a game or if I'm giving in to an automatic reflex. Because the computer generates automatic reflexes; it's an automaton, and if you spend too much time around automata, after a while you become one yourself. A robot, as Julia quite rightly called me. Speaking of Julia, I haven't heard from her for a few days. I'd call her if my hours weren't so out of kilter that I can only make phone calls at very inappropriate times. When I've finally finished whatever I'm doing and am free to communicate with people, everyone's asleep.

I didn't write any more about pornography yesterday. I felt far too lazy, and today I realise why: because it's a very complicated subject, and will involve me doing some historical research and remembering some things I'd rather not remember. I don't think it's a suitable topic for a diary, but it's part of the current contents of my mind, and I have to address it, whether it's suitable or not. I have to address it, I realise, because it's bound up in this laborious journey towards my 'return', and maybe it's pointless to wait for the vague anxiety, which has already come and gone; it seems I've now entered the realm of specific anxieties, and this is a case of specific anxiety, which is why I need to make the effort to discuss it. Objective: clear a path towards my life of leisure and the novel I want to write, which currently seems very far away.

TUESDAY 29, 19:45

Yes, it's definitely a difficult subject. I broke off to make a coffee, and while I was in the kitchen I did some work in the dairy industry. I'm making my own yoghurt, and it was time to unplug the yoghurt-maker and pour the contents of each glass into a jar. I've been making yoghurt since last week, when I discovered that the cause of my gastrointestinal troubles was the low-fat natural yoghurt made by a very well-known brand. It was probably full of E. coli or something similar. This happens every so often; a variation in the quality of the yoghurt, which at times I think is due to in-house sabotage. Sometimes it's the taste, which reminds me of the smell of mothballs, and sometimes it's that it's extremely sour. Sometimes it's wonderful; there's nothing like the taste of natural yoghurt. But I can't find other brands that suit me; they all contain sugar or sweeteners or pieces of fruit or artificial flavourings. There's one other brand, which comes in large glass jars, and it's a good natural yoghurt; however, I think they use ascorbic acid as a preservative, or at least it tastes like they do. That would normally be fine because it's vitamin C, but as it happens, synthetic vitamin C gives me haemorrhoids. So I decided to make my own yoghurt, at least for the time being, while I wait for the well-known brand to stop causing me trouble. I ought to make a complaint, but I'm not the sort of person who does that. Besides, I might be wrong. I should ask a laboratory to analyse the yoghurt, but I wouldn't know where to start. I expect if I was right and the yoghurt really was contaminated, it would be public knowledge; there are plenty of very enterprising people out there who take charge of these things. They go to the doctor, track the origins of their digestive disorders, make complaints and so on. But it's not my style. My style is making my own yoghurt. The first batch didn't go well at all, since I used a yoghurt that tasted of vanilla and artificial sweeteners as a base. It was disgusting. My yoghurt turned out marginally less disgusting and I was able to drink it; but it didn't taste good. From that first batch of home-made yoghurt I made another, which went a bit better, because there was only a slight trace of the vanilla flavouring left; but the consistency wasn't so good; it was too runny. I could drink it fine, though, and last night I began the process of making a third batch, which I imagine will turn out perfectly. I still haven't tasted it, because I don't like drinking yoghurt at this time of day, and besides, it's still warm.

Back to the difficult subject . . . My relapse into searching for pornography last year, I mean. I'll need to go back to some earlier events. Towards the end of May '98, I met Chl, and then, around the middle of July, our romantic relationship began. This made the atmosphere in the house where I was living unbearable, because the woman who at the time was my wife didn't look kindly on this new relationship, even though by that point she and I were merely living under the same roof and our relationship had ended around two years before. Little by little a kind of war was gathering force, becoming more and more terrible, erupting into torturous everyday scenes, and in the end there was nothing for it but to move in with some friends who knew about the situation and had invited me to stay. I planned to be in that house for ten days; I didn't leave for six months.

I've skimmed over what I called that 'kind of war' because it affects the privacy of another person, my ex-wife, with whom these days I have a very good friendship. It took me a lot of work to get to this stage, but I think it was worth it, because despite the various ways she's incompatible with me when it comes to life as a couple, she's a wonderful woman. I don't want to go into my own suffering in those months, either, which was made bearable only by the magic of Chl; I'll simply say that one fine day I realised my ex-wife was right to be hurt, and I put a stop to all our arguments and waited for time to soothe her pain and heal the wound. This realisation came to me by means of a dream, which I can't remember very well right now.

(I went to look in my dream files, and luckily I found it. I'll take the liberty of copying it out here. The date is 28 July 1998, meaning I had this realisation before moving out, and I was mistaken when I thought it was afterwards; I should say, then, that this realisation didn't help me avoid the war.)

'I come running into a very large room where several women can be seen lying on the floor, on mattresses with white sheets, although they're not fully covered and their bare legs are in view. There are three to my right, near the entrance, and I pass them quickly; in front of me is a fourth woman, in the same position, only in the middle of the room and not with her head by a wall like the others. I'm running along, carefree, and I think I jump over this fourth woman so I can carry on going, but then comes one of those inexplicable things that happen in dreams, perhaps a slip of the mind, because I don't actually jump and instead I pause one step away from the woman and see that she has a big lump on one leg, as if she's been horribly injured. Strangely, this lump is rectangular in shape; it looks like a brick. She speaks to me; she said I did it to her when I ran past. I'm taken aback, because I didn't even realise I'd touched her and hadn't felt a thing, but she insists. She tells me I hurt her head, too, and points to a place near her eyes and the bridge of her nose. "They had to operate," she said, and I was stunned. She explains, or rather I'm somehow able to visualise, that she'd had to have a kind of round, grey stone removed which had been lodged in the place she was pointing to.

'I wake up and immediately understand that the woman is [my ex-wife], and that the unconscious is showing me how I really injured her with my careless, hurried crashing around (and indeed, the way I came into the room backs up the idea of a "crash"). It also makes particular reference, I think, to psychological damage, rather than just momentary emotional upsets.

'That woman in the dream made me understand that I'd hurt her because she spoke calmly and didn't try to blame me; her way of speaking was purely informative, and even friendly. There was no emphasis of any kind, nothing that could have seemed like an accusation. She allowed the information to speak for itself, and me to be the judge of my own behaviour, leaving me with no opportunity or reason to be defensive. As a result, the feeling of regret generated by the dream is still with me, and it's taking a long time to dissolve.'


Then I moved into my friends' house and stayed for six months. Now I'm going to have lunch. To be continued.

WEDNESDAY 30, 23:30

Half past eleven at night, and I'm tired. I'm not going to bed because I have a full stomach. My full stomach could be what's making me tired; I often find myself feeling sleepy after my lunch-dinner these days. I should have more meals throughout the day, and lighter ones. I might also be particularly sleepy today because I had a yoga class; although really it wasn't exactly a yoga class, since there was a bit of witchcraft mixed in as well. My yoga teacher sometimes behaves like a kind of healer; this time it was because I shocked her with a description of my deranged sleeping hours. Yesterday, by which I mean today, I went to sleep at ten in the morning. It's madness, completely ridiculous. I stayed up reading in order to finish the last, or what I think is the last, Hannibal Lecter novel. I find it odd that a character like him is a kind of hero for me. It must be because he eats the really bad people, the ones you spend the whole novel hating. When these people – generally smug, corrupt, good-for-nothing bureaucrats – appear, I think: 'Please let Doctor Lecter eat this one,' and he never disappoints. I also find it strange that I can read something so full of gruesome, horrifying scenes so calmly, when I normally find that sort of thing deeply upsetting; I couldn't handle Ellroy, for example. He made me feel intensely, physically sick to my stomach, and psychologically sick as well, for days afterwards. I swore I'd never read him again. It's a shame, because Ellroy writes very well and is very talented; a shame he's a genuine psychopath who uses his talent to spread his horrible illness. Consuming one of his novels is like swallowing a bucketful of shit. Harris, however – the creator of Doctor Lecter – doesn't have the same effect on me. The scenes are gruesome but less believable, less vivid; the tone of it all verges on the comical, as in the Tom and Jerry films. Jerry can blow the cat to smithereens with a firecracker, but you laugh, you don't feel any pain. It's not quite like that with Harris's novels, but it's similar; the unreality is too blatant.

And before that, I was online looking for more material, thanks to a very interesting recent discovery. There are web pages devoted to women with particularly well-developed breasts, and best of all they offer fairly long videos, of several megabytes each. I don't want to spend too much on my phone bill, but this month I've been very restrained. I made a program that shows me, whenever I connect to the internet, how much I've spent so far and the projected cost for the whole month, and over the past few months I've managed to stick to the limits I set myself. Since we're in the last days of the month, I can spend a bit more without the predicted total cost changing too much, and yesterday I took full advantage of this. Still, I don't download the longest videos and instead look for more moderate ones. In general, the free samples of porn videos are less than 200K, which means they only last a few seconds. But that's where my other recent discovery comes in: among those sites full of sizeable busts, I found an advert for a site that lets you edit videos, and yesterday, as well as browsing the internet, and before I turned my attentions to Doctor Lecter, I used the program to stick some shorter, fragmentary videos together to make longer ones. With the same program, I was able to modify a few videos, making my own montage; I deleted some parts and moved others around, to end up with videos that were better put together from an artistic point of view, and, why not, from an erotic point of view as well. After all these procedures I ended up more or less falling for a beautiful stripper, who not only has reasonably generous breasts, but also beautiful facial features and an intelligent gaze. I highlight these virtues because women with ample bosoms, at least the ones I've been able to download from the internet, most of the time are real monsters; their breasts are monstrously large, bordering on the unpleasant or even laughable, their faces are ugly, and there isn't the slightest glint of intelligence in their eyes. Despite the abundance of videos, there aren't many I'm interested in downloading, and even among the ones I've downloaded there isn't much beauty to speak of; I downloaded them more as curiosities. But that stripper is something else. I feel a real affection for her. You could even say I love her.

I know I didn't finish my story about Chl, which was where the explanation of my relapse into searching for pornography began, but the topic upset me a little and I think I should continue more slowly. I'll return to it, of course, because it's necessary; but not today. Speaking of Chl, yesterday she didn't come to see me, and I went to her house instead. She didn't come today either. She's having problems at home that I shouldn't go into here so as not to make her family easily identifiable, but these problems are why she decided to stay at home yesterday. I went over in the evening and sat drinking coffee with her while she had her dinner. Then I came back to do some work. Although it's my week of leisure, on Tuesday nights I still have to send out evaluations and new assignments for the virtual workshop. There aren't many students left, so it's not much work, but it gave me an excuse to stay awake until the crack of dawn, since whenever I work I have to reward myself with some fun afterwards. This isn't something I apply deliberately, like a system, but it's what always happens. There's an utterly unhinged creature inside me that knows no limits, and few things excite it more than work. Doing some work sends it into a frenzy, and then it spends hours rolling around in whatever fun it can find. Taking the games off the hard drive helped me to avoid playing those games, but I played at other things instead, like searching the internet and editing videos. Well, it's a step up from the robotic games I was playing before. I hope I can keep those under control. And I hope I can get to sleep as soon as I've finished digesting my food. By the way: what I'm trying to digest is an exquisite plate of stew; I came back from Chl's house last night with a Tupperware container full of pea stew, a real delight. I still have some *milanesas* in the freezer, too. What more could I ask for?

# SEPTEMBER 2000

FRIDAY 1, 03:50

Phew. I've just finished editing two email interviews I was asked to complete urgently (by two different places). The muscles in my back and neck are stiff. My doctor came and found my blood pressure had stabilised. She wants to reduce it a little more (it's currently at 15/9), so I have to take an extra half-pill three days a week. Chl didn't come; I'll probably see her tomorrow. But I'm still eating her stew. And thinking about her *milanesas*, which I have in the freezer. And, yes, I'm also thinking about her.

SATURDAY 2, 02:19

Dear Mr Guggenheim, I'm afraid you have wasted your money on this grant you so generously awarded me. My intentions were good, but I just don't know what's become of them. Two months have passed, July and August, and all I've done so far is buy those armchairs (which I'm not using) and fix the shower (which I'm not using either). I've spent the rest of the time playing on the computer. I can't even keep this diary of the grant up the way I'm supposed to; you'll have noticed by now how I leave topics in suspense and never manage to return to them. Well, I just wanted to let you know. Best wishes, and regards to Mrs Guggenheim.


A terrible day. I got up extremely late; it was 6 p.m. by the time I'd finished breakfast. My head was aching and I was in a foul mood.

I didn't leave the house. I think Chl's stew is attacking my liver; maybe there's too much oil in it. Today I gave the stew a miss and had a *milanesa* instead; they also have oil in them, but so far I don't think it's caused me any problems. Chl came and had a plate of stew. We were going to go to the Feria del Libro; today's the first day of their annual sale, and although it gets worse every year, I always hope for a return to form. But it got late and we didn't go. Chl looked so beautiful. She's always beautiful, but today she was luminous, like in her best times, even though some things had happened to upset her and she'd been crying. After she left, I went online and downloaded a few films with fake lesbians in them.

SATURDAY 2, 03.15

Very good; ever since I stopped writing in this diary earlier today, I've been correcting the macro I made recently that's meant to collect all the files of this diary into a single master document. It was working very well until the month changed. Today is the first of September, or rather yesterday was, and most of my programs run into problems when there's a change of month, or year, or century. I have to adjust them, make them more general, predict all the possible variations. In this case, the macro had been putting all the files in perfect date order, thanks to the fact their file names contained both the date and the time; but what my program had really been telling it to do was to order them not by date but from lowest to highest. And when the month changed, 1 September ended up before 8 August, for example, since one is lower than eight. So I had to change that instruction and tell it to order them by date, which turned out to be no easy task. But I managed, and that made me happy. It was the second happy moment of the day; the first, of course, was when I was contemplating Chl's radiant beauty.

Since getting up, I've been avoiding the task I set myself of recording my dreams. I don't know why I'm avoiding it, but I am. Now it's time:

Yesterday (when I was awake) I got an email from Marcial. I'd asked him for information about Rosa Chacel, and I'd also asked him to send me her books. For now he's just sent some information, and very good information too; an article I could have found online myself if I'd known how to search for it. I used AltaVista and he used Google, and he found interesting biographical details. In other words, it made no difference, in this instance, that Marcial is living in Spain.

I found the article quite moving. It's written very lovingly by someone called Federico Jiménez Losantos, who admires Doña Rosa as much as I do, or perhaps even more, since he seems to be familiar with all her work, whereas I've only had a few glimpses. It was very pleasing to see that Jiménez used the same word as I did in this diary to describe Doña Rosa: insufferable. It was also strange to find other things I have in common with Doña Rosa: like me, she used to worry about her weight, because, also like me, she ate like a horse. I think she used to drink as well, which is a habit I haven't fallen into, thank God (and thanks, too, to my father, who instilled in me from a very young age his hatred and disapproval of drunks). And another habit of hers that I share: she was apparently a fanatical reader of detective novels.

The article also mentions the fact that Doña Rosa's husband, the Timo who often appears in her diary, was a 'notable painter', and that, although in her diary Doña Rosa seems to look down on him somewhat, he was a kind of hero and saved a large collection of famous paintings, among them works by Velázquez, during the Spanish Civil War.

As a result of this article, I dreamed about meeting them both. In my dream, Timo, or rather Timoteo Pérez Rubio, had a shop of some kind or other; probably a bookshop, but that detail has been erased. I talked to him for a long time, and he was extremely polite and even affectionate towards me. He had the mark of a gentleman, and his manners showed impeccable style. I wish I could remember more details. Then I found myself face to face with Doña Rosa, and we spoke. She had a very strong, clear presence and didn't look much like my aunt Adalghissa. It's true she was also rather plump, if not obese, and around the same height as my aunt, but her presence was different and much more solid, revealing an immense inner strength. I felt emotional speaking with her, probably remembering what the article had said about her being overlooked and badly treated by the literary crowd, in Spain but also elsewhere. At one point I said, 'Rosa, please: don't ever stop writing, no matter what happens, not for anything in the world.' The words came from deep in my soul, and I spoke them very emphatically. Then I said something about us, the accursed writers (though not in those words; I don't remember the phrase I used, but I do remember what I meant, and the pain I was feeling), and I began to cry uncontrollably, unconsolably. I woke up with that ache in my soul, an ache of pity for Doña Rosa, and for all the writers who've suffered at the hands of the establishment – and, of course, for myself.

I had another revealing dream, in which I was drinking from one of the breasts of a woman I know and am not going to name, or, if I wasn't drinking from it, I was at least kissing it enthusiastically. This woman is unquestionably a maternal figure for me, and this explains my monumental disorders of recent times: I'm going through a terrible regression; I'm living life as my baby-self.

Yes, this situation arose, or if it had already arisen, it at least continued to develop (although I've been through these phases at various points in my life, this one seems very difficult to get out of, and I'm not even sure if I'll manage); it arose, I was saying, during that stay in my friends' house, which began in October 1998. And now that I've reached this point, which is where I need to resume the interrupted story, I'll stop writing for today. I can't face it; not now.

SATURDAY 2, 04:04

Well, I had to correct the macro again because there was an error (it put the dates in order fine, but it took no notice of the different times attached to each date). Now it seems to be working well, but my good mood was ruined, and it's got late again, and I'm going to go to bed feeling, if not frustrated or dissatisfied, then at least a bit ill at ease with myself.

SUNDAY 3, 00:09

Chl's here again, asleep in my bed, so I can't let the computer distract me for much longer. I haven't been able to sort my sleeping hours out at all, but after a conversation with my doctor I've decided to come at the problem via one of its possible origins, which is food. Perhaps if I eat little and often rather than filling up on big meals, my sleep patterns will change. I remembered the ideas of my first therapist, who thought that an individual person's rhythm was determined by the cycle of fasting and eating. The three dimensions of the being were formed, as far as I remember, by two vectors that ran through this rhythm, which was represented by a vertical line: the physical vector and the significative vector. An interesting theory, to say the least.

I went to the Feria del Libro with Chl and we found a few things, nothing very important for the most part, though there was one VERY important thing, and it's thanks to Chl that I found it; the book wasn't on sale, but I bought it anyway. It's what seems to be one of Rosa Chacel's most acclaimed works, *The Maravillas District*. I'm currently reading a novel I bought days ago, very cheap, by Wilkie Collins: *The Law and the Lady*. I'd never even heard of it before, but I started it today and couldn't put it down; what a marvellous writer. Some of the passages are strikingly fresh, and what's more the whole thing is told so capably that you stay interested page after page. If Chl's arrival hadn't interrupted me, I'd have finished it by now. But luckily she did interrupt me, and she took me out for a walk, and we bought those books, and now I'm not going to sleep alone.

SUNDAY 3, 00:56

Unbelievable: there were still errors in the macro I was working on yesterday. It's odd how a process can work correctly without revealing the slightest imperfection, and then, bang, at a given moment, due to certain unforeseen circumstances, up crops a terrible error. The only way to be sure a procedure works, especially when it relates to time, is to test it and test it and test it, and even then . . .

SUNDAY 3, 19:03

A slight variation in my robotic existence. Thanks to Chl, of course, who directly or indirectly is always organising my life. Last night she stayed over, and I went to join her in bed at three in the morning, i.e. about four hours earlier than what's recently become my usual bedtime. Beforehand, to help me sleep, I'd taken two small doses of Valium. I read a few pages of my book, and then suddenly Chl informed me that I was asleep. The book hadn't fallen from my hands, but I'd been sound asleep and dreaming. She noticed because she was still awake. Awake and furious. Nothing upsets her more than some part of herself not doing what it's supposed to, and her intention of sleeping here is almost always sabotaged, one way or another, by some force within her. I asked if she missed her own home and she said she did. Then I fell asleep, but as usual I was dreaming about being awake. I'm awake, using the time to do some relaxation exercises and some thinking, and having a lovely time, when I hear Chl's voice: 'You're snoring.' This happened three or four more times throughout the night. Chl didn't sleep a wink. I never once fell into a deep sleep, because every time I started snoring Chl woke me up. I did everything I could not to snore; I got into a position that allowed the air to travel through my nose and internal airways as easily as possible, and I said to myself over and over again: 'I will not snore.' Then I'd start trying to think of a topic that would distract me from the fact that there, next to me, was the adorable body of the most beautiful woman in the world, since I couldn't even touch her (she didn't so much as let me look when she undressed for bed); that's how things are, and I need to respect them. So there I was, trying to think of a distracting topic, and I'd go on thinking until once again I found I'd been snoring. And so it went on, until six in the morning. Then Chl got up and left. I stayed in bed a bit longer, but I was hungry, and eventually the hunger stopped me sleeping, even though now I could snore and snore to my heart's content, and I got up as well. Seven thirty. A real record. I called Chl at home to make sure she'd got back OK, and she answered politely and affectionately. Then I made breakfast, and while the water was boiling for the tea I plugged the yoghurt-maker back in. I'd unplugged it before going to bed, because for some reason I get nervous leaving it on. However, the yoghurt looked like it was ready, and I tried a bit from one of the glasses. Excellent: my best result so far, thanks to the fact I mixed the yoghurt I've been reusing with another yoghurt I bought for that purpose. It's a Brazilian yoghurt made from lactic-acid bacteria and with a Japanese name; they sell it in very small 80-gram bottles, and it seems you take it like medicine. Unfortunately it comes with added sugar and a horrible artificial flavour, something undefinable with a vague hint of chocolate, and very average chocolate at that. However, it didn't change the flavour of my yoghurt, which currently tastes exactly like natural yoghurt, and it gave it the perfect consistency. It's runny but not watery; that is, it's solid like a jelly at first, but when you give it a stir it turns to liquid without going lumpy or curdled. I ended up having two glasses, and then I waited for the unpleasant after-effects, but they didn't come. As I was having breakfast I read the Leo Bruce book I'd started in bed; a very entertaining detective novel. I noticed out of the corner of my eye that it was a sunny day, very pleasant by the looks of things, and made a mental note to consider going out to run some errands before midday. When I finished my breakfast I realised my plan of going to the supermarket would be unattainable, because it was Sunday, and that supermarket closes on Sundays. Then it occurred to me that another supermarket, on 18 de Julio, might be open, and I was glad to have an excuse to go out on this sunny day. But first I turned on the computer, checked my email, read something someone had sent me, and then had the idea of searching for a few games which, as I discovered yesterday, I hadn't deleted from the hard drive, so as to put them on a ZIP disk and then delete them. I found them, transferred them to the ZIP and then had to check, from the ZIP, that they worked. They did. I spent a couple of hours playing them, in a trance, practically asleep. With one thing and another, it was midday by the time I left the house. Outside, there were all the indications of a sunny Sunday. It was a bit chilly in the shade, but when I was walking across the square in the sun it felt warm. It was as if spring was already here, though I had to put my hat on to protect my bald head from the cold. At that moment, the Sunday feeling took hold of me and I had an urge to visit the Tristán

Narvaja market. It wasn't a bad time to go and look at the books; the booksellers normally stay until around two in the afternoon, or at least they used to. And there are the second-hand bookshops that overlook the market, as well, which open on Sunday mornings. I was very tempted, but a brief analysis of my strength levels changed my mind. In truth, I was barely even awake. I was having to walk very carefully and I realised I was attracting attention, not only thanks to my beard. I must have looked a sorry sight, walking more slowly than ever and with a certain hesitation in my step, and with that bodily stiffness you get when your spine hasn't rested properly. But the main thing attracting people's attention was presumably my facial expression, not because of my beard but because of the look in my eye, I think, since it made two different ladies do a nervous double take within the space of a few minutes – first one, then the other not long afterwards. They came walking calmly towards me and their gaze fell naturally on the part of their surroundings made up of me, and then they carried on looking around automatically until something set off an alarm in their brain. Suddenly, the head spins back the way it came and the lady stares into my face again, consciously this time, before turning away once more. I made them start, is I believe the expression. But start what, I don't know.

The question of the market resolved, then, in the negative, I continued on my way and reached the supermarket, bought the things I'd been planning to buy and a few things I hadn't, like a little tube of PVA glue that had disappeared from my shopping list a while ago by accident, and some baguettes that turned out to be exquisite. I didn't find a single pharmacy open where I could ask about the price of some medication I'm running out of; other than that, my trip was a success. By the time I got home I was already hungry. I'm still trying to bring my rhythm back to normal by spacing my meals out more reasonably, and I'd had a very light breakfast. I decided on the stew, half a portion. Since it was midday rather than midnight and I wasn't going to eat much, I hoped it wouldn't do me any harm. The results of the experiment couldn't be measured appropriately, however, because as soon as I'd finished eating, smoked a cigarette and drunk a coffee, I sat down in the relaxing armchair, propped my feet up on one arm of the reading armchair, and fell into a very deep sleep. I was woken up by the need to urinate. My arms had gone numb and my legs were aching; it was hard work unfolding myself and getting out of the armchair. I went to the bathroom without managing to open my eyes fully, and from there I went straight to bed. I didn't undress. I got in between the sheets without lowering the blinds, which was a mistake, because the light tortured my eyes. My eyes had been worrying me during my midday walk, since the right one was sore and I couldn't see very well in general; there were brief bursts of time in which everything suddenly went blurry. Of course, I'm not used to being in the sun; my eyes have grown accustomed to artificial light, and who knows if I'll ever be able to see properly in the sun again. I hope I can one day; it's very nice to walk around when there's still natural light in the sky. But as I was saying, the light was torturing my eyes and I didn't have the strength to get up and lower the blinds; what I did was put my woolly hat on and jam it as far down onto my head as I could, until the brim was covering my eyes. It didn't give me complete darkness, but it was enough to stop my eyes complaining. And I slept, until not long ago; I slept like a log, like a stone. I don't remember dreaming. Needless to say, the stew didn't entirely agree with me, and now I have a horrible taste in my mouth. But it would be the same with anything I'd eaten, since lying flat upsets my digestion. And so my experiment failed.

Speaking of eating, now I'm hungry again. I'll go for a *milanesa* this time. And a tomato with garlic.

MONDAY 4, 02:21

New developments: I'm writing by hand. Meaning that I didn't press a button in Word to add the date and time, and instead I added them myself. I worked the date out, and to find the time I looked at a clock on the wall that's not very accurate. I took a minute off the time it showed; bear this detail in mind.

This means that the computer's off and I'm about to go to bed. I've stuck reasonably well to my decision to divide up my meals, and now my stomach is reasonably full.

After dinner I sat down at the computer to carry on with this diary, planning to begin, directly and without further ado, the story I still need to tell about my relapse in 1998. I was about to open Word when I said, 'Shit,' because I could feel my momentum being drawn perversely off course. Instead of Word, I opened a card game I'd copied onto the ZIP (FreeCell) (the advantage of FreeCell is that you can always complete it if you think it through; it's not like Golf or Solitaire or other card games, which are based on luck and often frustrate your best efforts). I played three rounds. I won all three. There are seven games recorded, and I've won 100 per cent of them. These statistics will always show a 100 per cent success rate, because whenever I lose a game I reset them and start again from zero.

As I was playing the third game, I could feel the depraved urge to search for online pornography taking hold. I checked my special program and it told me the projected cost for September is 50 per cent higher than the limit I've set myself. But this didn't stop me opening Netscape and wasting an hour and a half downloading some not very satisfying videos. Then I got hungry again and turned off the computer. I had a cup of tea with two slices of toast and two biscuits with cheese and ricotta. I began another detective novel, something by John D. MacDonald, with Travis McGee as the protagonist. It looks like one of the good ones.

And here I am, bringing my day to a close. Not long ago I took 2.5mg of Valium, and while I was reading I began nodding off. Now I'm going to take another 2.5mg.

It's obvious I'm avoiding writing about the period that began in October 1998. Presumably because it's so painful. I won't force myself; I'll keep it in mind, in a peripheral sort of way, as if I'm watching it out of the corner of my eye so as not to lose sight of it. But I won't go into it properly, not yet.

TUESDAY 5, 04:45

Dear Mr Guggenheim, I hope you're aware of my efforts, as recorded in this diary, to improve my bad habits, at least some of them, and at least to the extent that these habits prevent me from devoting myself fully to this project of writing the novel you have so generously financed. You will have seen, sir, that I'm doing all that's humanly possible, but I'm forever crashing into the pile of rubble that I myself once tipped into my path. I need to remove all of that rubble before I can carry on; I'm telling you this because I know myself, and I know only too well that I can't arrive at inspiration any other way. You see, the inspiration I need for this novel isn't any old inspiration, but a particular sort, bound to events that lie buried in my memory and which I have no choice but to revive if my continuation of the novel is to be genuine and not a mere simulacrum. I don't want to fall back on my trade. I don't want to impersonate myself. I don't want to pick the novel up where I left it sixteen years ago and carry on as if nothing had happened. I've changed. My points of view have changed. My memory has changed, and it's almost certainly altered the facts. I remember well, I'd almost say perfectly well, aside from inevitable minor variations – because the memory is dynamic and creative and, as I've said many times, it adds and removes plenty of things of its own accord – I remember well, as I was saying, the events I want to describe. I even have a few pages written, though they took a lot of work. I wrote them last year, when I still didn't know whether or not you were going to award me this grant. The events are present in those pages, but they're not alive. I write what I can remember, what I think I can remember, but it's no more than information stored in the part of the memory that stores information. When I was writing, my feelings were nowhere to be seen. There were none of those things people call 'experiences'. There was no inspiration. And so there was no style. And so those pages were fraudulent. I might still use them when the time comes, because they're just a few pages and they don't address the most important part of what I want to write; maybe it's impossible – impossible for me, I mean – to write them any better. But I don't want to carry on that way. I want to *feel*, I want to *see* the scenes I'm describing. And for that, Mr Guggenheim, I need to use this diary to find the way back through my emotions, first reviving events that are more recent; fresher, even. And since I'm going round and round in circles, I can't do it. Just like I can't go to bed any earlier or get up any earlier. You'll tell me: use part of the grant money to see a psychotherapist. And you're right; but I tried that, I really did, and I think I've already described what happened in this diary; the problem was that I didn't find the right therapist. Still, you're right; maybe I should persevere. In my experience, therapy actually blocks the literary impulse, at least in its early stages. It could be a long journey. Maybe there's no other way. To begin with, I'd need to find a therapist prepared to see me in the evenings. Then I'd need to pay them, and pay them an excessive amount, because psychotherapy is a luxury. I'd have to go without some of the things I want to buy with your money, Mr Guggenheim, such as the air-conditioning units that will save me from spending this coming summer the way I spent the last; that summer was what plunged me into my bad habits once and for all. I almost wanted to die. Summer has always been difficult for me, and every year it gets worse; I expect I grow more sensitive to the weather the older I get, because I have fewer defences against it. What's more, the weather, as you will have noticed, becomes objectively a little less tolerable every year. The earth is getting hotter and hotter, and one day it's going to explode. I'm sure the official figures shared with the public are doctored; I think the warming process is happening much faster than we're told it is. The air-conditioning units don't make things any better; in fact, I'm sure they make the climate considerably worse. But that's what people are like; everyone thinks of themselves, and as for the Earth, the future – not our problem. Ordinary citizens can't do anything about issues like that. They just have to put up with them. My grandchildren will probably end up frying like potatoes in a pan of boiling oil, but there's nothing I can do about it, and I'm going to buy those air-conditioning units that will make my summer marginally less miserable. It's either that or psychotherapy. What would you do, sir, in my place? Although I imagine it would be difficult for you to put yourself in my place, not for want of good intentions but for cultural reasons. You probably can't imagine what it's like to live in the underdeveloped world. Some things may be simply inconceivable to you.

Well, I won't bother you any more with this chatter. I just wanted to inform you that I haven't forgotten my obligations to you for an instant, and that I'm doing everything I can to bring my project to fruition.

Regards to Mrs Guggenheim.

WEDNESDAY 6, 04:41

A working week. Tuesday. The day my student comes and the day of the virtual workshop. My student didn't come; I rushed home for no reason after returning the cheese. I returned the cheese because instead of maturing it had coagulated. I don't know exactly what that process is called, but for me it's coagulation. Rather than getting softer, the cheese goes hard, like plastic, and produces a really horrific sensation in the teeth when it's chewed. All the nerves in the body squirm, like when someone runs a fingernail down a blackboard. It's as if the teeth come loose in the gums. The shop assistant who'd sold it to me, a woman who's not exactly young and seems rather slow on the uptake, didn't listen to what I told her. 'Did you keep it in the fridge?' 'No, I didn't put it in the fridge until yesterday. It was out of the fridge for four days, and it was releasing whey for two.' 'That's it. You shouldn't have put it in the fridge.' 'I didn't put it in the fridge.' 'But if you give it a little brush, like this' – and she showed me the part of the rind that was covered in mould. 'It's coagulated. You can't eat it.' But it was no use, she kept going on about the brush and how I shouldn't have put it in the fridge. She wanted me to take it home with me and brush it. 'You've lost a customer,' I said, and left in a rage, leaving them the cheese as a present. Let them chew it, if they can. I tried to maintain my dignity as I was leaving, but you could see I was furious because I got into a muddle with the glass door, pulling and pushing without managing to open it. Then I pushed the other door too hard, which made a terrible racket, but at last I was out. They must have thought I'd made all the noise on purpose, to show how angry I was. But I didn't want to look angry; I wanted to look dignified.

Yesterday the dentist postponed my appointment, and today my student couldn't make it. I still had work to do for the virtual workshop, but I spent most of the time playing card games, moving files to the ZIPs and doing a bit of cleaning and tidying, though only on the computer. The kitchen, meanwhile, is a disaster; I've run out of clean plates and cutlery. If the maid doesn't come tomorrow – and she definitely won't, the way things are going this week – I'll have to roll up my sleeves and wash them myself. It'll give me a sore back. I bet my yoga teacher doesn't come tomorrow either. I'll still have the workshop on Thursday, though; the students can't all fail to turn up. There are loads of them. It would be too much of a coincidence.

Unfortunately, I didn't use the time to try achieving any leisure. Chl didn't come; or rather, she called in briefly in the afternoon, on matters of interest to her. She's more determined by the day when it comes to giving up on sex; not only with me, she says, but with all men. She hasn't said anything about women.

I got tired early, before midnight, but I held out. I had to prepare for the virtual workshop. But I would have held out anyway, even if I hadn't had to work. I don't know why; I still can't quite accept that I'm incapable of doing a simple thing like turning off the computer and getting into bed. It doesn't matter whether or not I sleep; the important thing is to get into bed. But I don't do it. I'm a strange person. Today I thought I might actually be experiencing a serious psychosis, because I'm still losing weight, and I think I remember that losing weight can be a symptom of psychosis. If we add to that my behavioural disorders, especially in relation to sleep, the picture isn't very encouraging. It's odd, because I can think clearly. I might also be losing weight because of a terrible illness. My back still hurts, at the base of my right lung.

So today I didn't make any progress either, of any kind; I couldn't even stop the shop swindling me over the cheese. And the checkout girl in the supermarket where I buy mineral water, when I went to the checkout and asked her to charge me for twelve bottles and then send them to my apartment, made me go and get a bottle from the fridges at the back to show her. It's the first time I've had to do that. I complained. I said: 'Before, when you liked me more, you'd jump over the counter and get it yourself.' But she must have been tired, because now she's the only checkout girl and works all day from the morning. That's what she said. Anyway, today I have a clear impression that nobody loves me.

## WEDNESDAY 6, 17:43

Just as I foresaw, the maid didn't come. She left a message on the answerphone this morning, which I heard in my sleep but without understanding who was calling or why; I thought it was Julia, who often leaves messages in the morning even though she knows I won't listen to them until the afternoon, because she says if she doesn't call at that time she loses heart and ends up not calling at all. The message is always the same: 'Call me when you can.' The maid's messages, meanwhile, are always incomplete because she starts talking while the welcome message is still playing, before the beep that indicates when it's time to speak. So I only ever receive the ends of her messages; but they're enough. She's not coming, and that's that.

I'm in what's known as a 'period of centrifugation'. Something intangible inside me is pushing people away. There are also periods when the opposite happens; periods of centripetalism, when no one will leave me alone and I can't cope with seeing people. You have to be patient and wait for things to change. You also have to be patient and roll up your sleeves and wash the dishes.

I found some mysterious spots of blood on one of my pillows. Not the pillow I laid my head on to sleep, strangely enough, but a big one from the top of the pile of pillows I arrange when I read and then move aside when I go to sleep. I connected those little spots of blood to some horribly itchy skin behind my right ear, in the little hollow that forms next to the lobe, where the ear meets the head. The skin there always flakes in a way I put down to psoriasis, and it's always slightly irritated. Now it looks like my psoriasis is cured; a couple of months or so ago, it almost entirely disappeared from my forehead. It was a gradual process, and Chl was devastated. She loved the dry skin on my forehead, and used to spend ages detaching the flakes with her fingernails and hunting for others among the remaining hair on the back and sides of my head. Her posture was identical to that of a female monkey picking lice off her husband. The most astonishing thing was the almost mystical concentration I could see in her eyes as she stood facing me, peeling the flakes off my forehead. That was in the early stages of our relationship; later she became more confident, and one day I saw her surreptitiously slip a little flake of dried skin into her mouth. I reprimanded her severely; I couldn't believe she'd do something so disgusting. I explained that those flakes of skin were a breeding ground for mites and who knows what else, but there was nothing to be done. She's a fan of what she calls peelings; she loves the taste and she loves how they crunch between her teeth. In the end I got used to seeing her collect and eat my peelings like someone picking grapes off a bunch. Then the peelings grew scarcer, and now they've completely disappeared. I'm always waiting for a new cycle to begin, but by this point it seems the psoriasis isn't coming back. However, that eczema, or whatever it is, keeps on turning up behind my ears. And last night it was itching terribly, and I couldn't wake up enough to apply any iodine or ointment, or anything else soothing. Curiously, when I did wake up, and it was the afternoon by then, the itching had completely stopped. I still haven't checked whether the spots of blood on the pillow came from there, and I'm not sure I can see in the mirror what exactly is going on behind my right ear.

Maybe the blood is part of a process I've been attributing to the antidepressants; a kind of drying-out of the skin in a few places, a few parts of my body with no special significance, like my big toe or the joint at the base of my right thumb. And on one side of my face, near my left eye. The skin in those places suddenly broke and a drop of blood came out. Then there was nothing left but some almost invisible scars.

WEDNESDAY 6, 21:11

> The will needs obstacles in order to exercise its power; when it is never thwarted, when no effort is needed to achieve one's desires, because one has placed one's desires only in the things that can be obtained by stretching out one's hand, the will grows impotent. If you walk on a level all the time the muscles you need to climb a mountain will atrophy. These reflections are trite, but there they are.

This quotation is from a book by Maugham that Chl lent me, which I started yesterday and finished today. It's called *The Mixture as Before*, and the story the quotation comes from is called 'The Lotus Eater' (and I couldn't work out why) (I just looked it up in the dictionary, and it turns out that 'lotus eater' refers to a member of a particular African people who feed on lotuses. Perhaps, then, the quotation explains the title: the lotus eater need only stretch out a hand in order to eat).

This quotation, as well as fitting me like a glove, shows exactly what W. Somerset Maugham is like: he's intelligent and educated enough to know when one of his observations is trite, but that doesn't mean he leaves it out. You could say that most of his literary output is trite, or perhaps trivial or even frivolous, but I think what saves it is this way he has of splitting in two, of giving an ironic running commentary on himself that creates a kind of negative of his stories. In this book, the stories are almost all well written and entertaining; there are only two or three which don't work, and they're the ones where he's clearly trying to make things up. Maugham is a great observer, but he doesn't know how to invent things; at least, that's the impression I get based on the few examples I've seen of his writing.

I started *The Maravillas District* not long ago. I picked it up because I'd run out of detective novels and I'd run out of Maugham and, although I wanted to carry on avoiding things that might be capable of elevating my spirit, I suddenly made up my mind to begin it. My God, what an absolute marvel! I was hooked from the very first lines. Such freshness, such control of the language, such psychological intuition, such capacity for ultra-subtle observation, such insight; such a joy to read. The language is so rich that I had to look four words up in the dictionary; they're not unusual words, but part of what would have been the typical Spanish of her time. When it comes to language, and, why not, when it comes to literature, too, Rosa Chacel makes me feel like a kind of deformed dwarf.

To return to the Maugham quotation at the top of this page: it explains the whole mystery of my abnormal behaviour. I've lost my willpower because I haven't been using it. Because I don't want anything other than what I have within arm's reach. And to think how hard I've worked to become this way, to achieve this total lack of inconvenient desires! And then I've had the good luck, or the bad luck, to have almost all, if not all, of my important desires granted. I had to wait years, in some cases, but I don't think any of them let me down. In other words, I don't want much, but when I want something I get it. With no effort. And the word 'effort' is key here: I've developed a kind of contempt, or lack of respect, for the things you obtain through effort. I feel that if I have to put effort into something, it can't possibly be for me. That by putting in effort I'm somehow working against Nature and the correct order of the Cosmos. And after all, I may well be right. It's just that over the years, this philosophy has been making my willpower weaker and weaker until it's almost completely disappeared; and this 'almost' is very slight, very slight indeed. I still have the dregs of my willpower left, as far as I can tell, meaning I can face the outside world when there's no way around it, for example when it comes to the inescapable need to earn a living, which fell upon me like a curse last summer. I made an effort and achieved more than enough, but then the grant came along and showed that all my efforts had been pointless anyway, a product of my lack of faith in that Providence which never leaves me wanting. And whenever I try to think of an example of a time that I've made an effort, a negative example occurs to me. It seems I'd always have been much better off not bothering.

The problem is that now I'm powerless over myself, ruled by that child or baby who wants only to be entertained by whatever he has to hand, especially if it's inside the computer. In this case, I think a minimal use of willpower is required. It wouldn't make sense, I realise now, to take a violent stand against the habits that will be the toughest to beat; a more reasonable plan would be to practise using my willpower in smaller ways, to curb my smaller childish desires. Maybe then my willpower will grow stronger and I'll be able to confront the most difficult things. I'm not trying to do anything huge. I just want to get my sleeping hours back to normal so I can be more active when I'm awake, walking around outside at appropriate times of the day, that sort of thing. It's not much, and yet it's more difficult than climbing a mountain.

I'll try to start right now. By washing the dishes.

THURSDAY 7, 20:18

The centrifugation continues. Today, Thursday, only three students came to the 4.30 p.m. workshop. Two told me they weren't coming. I didn't even hear from the others. I know it's miserable weather, with storms and drizzle, but I refuse to believe the centrifugation isn't real. Now, having started writing this at 8.18 p.m., I'm waiting for the students who come for the 8.15 p.m. workshop. No one's ever very punctual, and I've heard from at least one student that she's definitely coming (and from another that she's not), but we'll see. We'll see how many turn up. It's not a very big group at the best of times.

Yesterday, before washing the dishes, I played a few rounds of FreeCell. I played some today, too, and I'm on twenty-six wins (with a 100 per cent success rate), having reset the statistics a lot in recent days. But twenty-six is a record. Then I began washing the dishes, and I made a great discovery. But there goes the lift; a student must be on the way up, so I'll have to stop.

FRIDAY 8, 05:01

A few students came. They read some excellent pieces. All of them write better than I do; it's very gratifying. Although it's a shame none of them want to be professional writers: they seem happy enough just writing for the workshop. Oh well. I can't do anything about that.

As usual, workshop, Sisyphus, the rock rumbling down the hill, etc. It's 5 a.m. I played lots of games of FreeCell; I'm not on 100 per cent any more, but I'm still on a respectable 95 per cent; two games lost out of forty-four. Not bad, but what does it matter. I also went online. Japanese girls. Porn videos. Telephone bill costs. But the monthly prediction didn't go up too much because I've kept myself perfectly in check over the past few days. It's a little bit high, but it'll go down again. Last month, my telephone bill went down overall. And it'll carry on going down. I think.

I mustn't forget about the discovery I made last night while I was washing the dishes. I won't be able to describe it very well now because

I'm tired and my eyes are watering. Too much staring at the screen. But I'll try to get something down, so I don't forget.

First I tidied the plates, cutlery and other bits and pieces into a washing-up bowl, to get them out of the sink and make the job easier. While I was trying to tidy up, I began to feel a very pleasant sensation. I'd turned the computer off and my mind was on other things. Thoughts began to appear; my thoughts, or maybe they weren't mine, but the point is that they were human. Memories, reflections. And while I was engrossed in the task of washing the cutlery and then the plastic containers and then the plates, I made my discovery: namely that this, and nothing else, was the leisure I needed. I realised that leisure doesn't have to mean sitting in an armchair and waiting tensely for the vague anxiety to come. That the vague anxiety will come of its own accord, when it has to, if it has to. I'd been trying to impose a particular state of mind on myself, and that's where I was going wrong. It's fine to sit in one armchair to rest or in another armchair to read, when you feel like it, when it's necessary. But if you do it out of duty, in order to begin a project like the one covered by this grant, it's not leisure. It's not even the pursuit of leisure. Rather, the pursuit of leisure turns into work, or indeed business, and business is the very opposite of leisure. Many years ago, a friend pointed out that the word 'business' is actually referring to being busy, to busy-ness. Leisure, i.e. not being busy, isn't what I thought it was – to be honest, I didn't think much about what it was, I just went on behaving in that misguided way. What I mean is that leisure doesn't have its own substance, it's not an end in itself. It's nothing: leisure is an attitude of the soul, and it can accompany any kind of activity. It's not the contemplation of the void, let alone the void itself; you could say it's a way of being. Sitting in an armchair doing nothing isn't necessarily leisure, and washing the dishes can be leisure, if you have the right attitude. The right attitude, when it comes to washing the dishes, is washing the dishes as if it were the most important thing in the world. Not as if it were; *it is* the most important thing, like anything else I might have been doing at that moment, and it's leisure insofar as what I'm doing leaves my mind clear and unattached, unattached to anything other than my contemplation of the thing I'm doing. And that thing shouldn't be done for the purpose of any kind of business, because that ruins everything. I wash the dishes without wanting to be doing anything else, taking my time. And after washing the dishes I get the little yoghurt jars ready and plug in the yoghurt-maker. It's the kind of thing I always do, only at that moment I was being leisurely about it, because my mind wasn't on any kind of business, because I didn't want to be doing anything else instead, because I was having fun doing what I was doing. That's leisure, or at least it's the leisure I need. My workshops aren't leisure because their purpose relates to business, however enjoyable they might be and however much they move my spirit. They're an activity with a timetable and a purpose. They're not leisure, and they always upset my nerves. Last night, however, washing the dishes brought peace to my spirit and showed me the path to follow. And I'll try to follow it.

I went to bed relatively early after that, but I couldn't get to sleep until the usual time. It doesn't matter; I rested, I read, I turned the light off, I carried on resting, and today I was up in time to do the things I needed to do before the first workshop.


This Rosa Chacel book is a bit disappointing. Not disappointing, exactly, because it's wonderful; there's plenty of substance to it and I'm enjoying it a lot. But there's something that hasn't worked, something forced, something that isn't quite her. Now and then, passages remind me of *Memoirs of Leticia Valle* and *Since Dawn*; the obviously autobiographical passages, I mean. But she muddies the plot with philosophical digressions, or with a narrative style that's a bit too symbolic or poetic or something, I don't know. She also writes in the first person, from the point of view of various different characters, but they all sound the same, they're all Doña Rosa. I would have much preferred a linear and fully autobiographical novel, and by that I don't mean historically accurate, so much as just Doña Rosa speaking, writing as the girl she once was and never completely left behind; her systems of thought, her way of seeing the world, her depth, her mystique, her playfulness. All of which are present in this novel, but in a tangled and needlessly complicated way. And the whole thing plays out on a very profound level, with no respite; constant analysis of things, points of view, the interrelations between objects and people. It's fine, everything's very elegant, so elegant, so delicate and deep, but the way it develops is a bit overwhelming. So much so that today, faced with the prospect of the workshop, I had to cut my reading of it, the way you might cut one drink with another, and so I started one of the wonderful little novels Jean Ray used to write to scare himself, to get his own adrenaline running. Ghosts and other macabre things, but it's almost like a cartoon; nothing too nerve-wracking.

Reading isn't necessarily leisure. Whereas going for a walk, even if it's with the aim of doing some shopping, can be leisure – if you have the right attitude. I must remember this. I must remember this.


Postscript: I just ran the spellchecker in Word, and it told me the word 'Joyce' wasn't in the dictionary. It offered to change it, among other things, to José.

### SATURDAY 9, 05:07

A bad day, very bad indeed. Friday. Nothing to do; wet and stormy. I'm on FreeCell number eighty-five. And I've stayed at 95 per cent, with only four losses. But my eyes are ruined. And the muscles in my arm and back are killing me. I had an image of the workshop, the workshops on Thursdays, as a stone hitting water at speed, sending out ripples that upset the surface for days. Sometimes I think it's more like a stone shattering a pane of glass, but that vision is too dramatic. I certainly end up in pieces. I don't really understand why.

Chl came in the evening and brought me some food. She got caught in the storm and arrived sopping wet and in tears, but she soon cheered up. She was adorable, and I could feel my emotions and desires stirring dangerously. After she left I carried on playing FreeCell. Game after game. I can't get out of this cycle. As I've said before, I woke up crooked and I was crooked all day long. I'll have to accept that this is how things are. It's strange not to be able to change them.

It could be that this extremely odd situation with Chl is a way of punishing me for adoring her. I adored her religiously. I think I still adore her, only without realising it; I've completely blocked all awareness of my emotions. Today a bit of the barricade came loose and I could feel the presence of something very powerful in my chest. It must be a bad thing to adore a human being as if they're a god. The gods will get annoyed.

I was saying, then, a while ago, almost at the beginning of this diary, that I moved into the house of some friends for ten days and stayed there for six months. During that time I tried to look for an apartment, but it wasn't easy. I flicked through the paper that listed apartments for rent and felt terribly depressed; I couldn't read it, I didn't have the strength. When Chl came along I'd been living with the woman who was then my wife for ten years, and although the last few had been very, very hard and we were no longer strictly a couple, just living together, and although at first the separation felt like a relief, like being set free, I still went through a kind of prolonged mourning period. I couldn't deal with the situation; I couldn't set myself in motion. I had some savings in the bank and I could see them disappearing by the day; this made me panic, and the panic paralysed me even more. On top of that, the situation in my friends' house was very complex. My friend was sick, and he still is, in what now seems to be the terminal phase. His wife was in a state of extreme agitation; unable to accept my friend's illness, and at the same time suddenly faced with an onslaught of practical matters she knew nothing about. She slowly began to sort through the piles of papers and work out what was going on with things, with the household accounts; what was going on was that they were very complicated. It was an enormous house with a lot of outgoings, and you also had to take into consideration the salaries and other movements of money that I didn't trouble myself to learn about, though I did help her with the paperwork every now and then. I also helped by listening to her talk, and I began to worry about her family's problems as well as my own. And the children's problems, too. Although the children didn't live there, they were frequent visitors and I had a lot of conversations with one of them. And most of all I felt like I was suspended in mid-air, without my things, without my books, with almost nothing of my own, and I've always been very dependent on my habitat. My bedroom was tiny, and the bed inside it was tiny; I had to learn to sleep with my head resting on one arm, because there weren't enough pillows and I got gastric reflux. Eventually I realised I was going to end up staying there much longer than planned, and my friends and I agreed that I'd pay a bit of rent and they'd give me a room where I could put my computer. Until then I'd been using their computer, but I didn't have access to my programs or files – my memory, in other words. It took a long time to get the room ready. There were also maids in the house, sometimes one and sometimes two, which meant I had almost nowhere to go during the day other than into the computer; first my friends', and then mine once it was set up. That's when I first became addicted to playing card games, and I began staying awake until the early hours, far later than any normal person would. As if I only felt at home during the night. Though I still wasn't at home. Sometimes I was left by myself and had to look after the house. If my friends were going away for a few days and I was in the house alone, on those days I wouldn't go to sleep until eight in the morning. I couldn't; I was on the alert all night, keeping watch. These altered sleeping hours of mine made apartment-hunting more and more difficult; my ex-wife helped, and sometimes Chl helped as well. All the ones I managed to go and see were terrible; some thoroughly miserable apartments. It looked like I'd have to consider paying more rent; to do that I'd have to start working intensively, and I knew I'd be able to, but it would take time, some months of being settled in my new place, before I could start. Then the summer came around, and for me every summer is like death. I realised I wouldn't be able to rent anywhere until the autumn, and I would have been too weak to deal with moving anyway. In summer, my thoughts become muddled and I spend the whole time trying to escape my body. It's because of the heat, but it's more than that as well; there's something really deadly about the summer, something that makes me feel hopeless and depressed, that wrings out my nerves, constantly, one by one.

Twice a week, on average, I took a taxi and went to see Chl. Back then, we still used to make love. Sometimes she'd come and see me at my friends' house and we'd go for a walk. Even in summer, her presence was a tonic; she gave me strength, life, energy. Thinking about her was all that got me through that terrible period.

SUNDAY 10, 03:26

What could have been the blackest day of the year, saved at the last minute, as always, by Chl. Yesterday one of my teeth started hurting, on the right side of my mouth. It could be that I have a cavity, or a receding gum, but most of all I'm certain there's a tightness originating in my neck or even my spine, perhaps as a result of my back pain. This is probably all caused by my posture at the computer and the tension in my right arm when I use the mouse. Before going to bed I applied some acupressure. There's a particular part of the thumb, almost where the nail begins, on the inside, i.e. the side closest to the rest of the hand. You have to press on that point with the nail of the opposite thumb, or of any other finger, even the index finger of the same hand, and if the pain can be alleviated it will be. It worked for me, which seems to confirm my theory about the tightness, because while you're pressing down with the nail, whether you like it or not, you're concentrating and making an effort to get better, and that may well release the tension.

I read for an hour before going to sleep (another Jean Ray book, and now I've run out; today I carried on cutting my reading of Doña Rosa, but with Henry James stories. He writes so well, that man, even if I don't always understand exactly what he's trying to say). I was reading in an odd position, and the pain came back. I used my nail again and it must have gone away, because I fell asleep.

I woke up at around 1 p.m. needing to urinate, and when I came out of the bathroom I remembered my doctor saying she'd slide a pack of antihypertensives under the door for me. And there they were. I took half a tablet as instructed and went back to bed. I fell asleep right away. Later I had to get up to urinate again, after which I went back to bed and slept some more. At one point my doctor left a message on the answerphone, a bit long for my tastes, but I couldn't get up and listen to what she was saying. I slept on. And I dreamed, among countless other tedious, complicated, troublesome, sticky things (just like the weather; the storm's still here, and the humidity, the heat, the rain, the sudden cold spells; seriously crappy weather), I dreamed I needed to urinate and was looking for a bathroom. I found one that, as always in my dreams, wasn't completely private: it had a glass wall. The glass was thick, but you could still more or less see through it. My grandmother was on the other side, in what looked like a dining room. The bathroom was full of objects blocking the way to the toilet, and for some reason, perhaps because I felt more protected from onlookers there than by the toilet, I began to pee into a baby's pram, or, more specifically, onto a big white cushion inside a baby's pram. But I didn't finish and I wasn't satisfied; I also felt bad about getting the pillow wet and reproached myself severely. I wondered what I could do to put things right, but nothing occurred to me. Maybe it would dry, I thought, but deep down I knew it wouldn't. My grandmother was definitely going to find out, and I had no way of justifying my behaviour. Later on, I was speaking to my grandmother and she told me I owed her some money, somewhere in the region of two hundred pesos. 'I'll pay you now,' I said, reaching into my pocket, but then I realised I didn't have any money, only pieces of paper. I saw that these pieces of paper were IOUs, or something like that, each for a different amount, and if I put them all together I'd be able to pay her. I was pleased with this solution, but then I realised the papers weren't actually money; they were just pieces of paper, though they had different amounts written on them. I woke up once more to go to the bathroom. The telephone rang again before that, and I heard my daughter's voice saying she'd given birth to a baby girl. I didn't have the strength to answer. In the end I got out of bed at 6 p.m. with my tooth hurting and my body a wreck, all twisted this way and that, and in a foul mood. I moved about the apartment trying to find a comfortable position, but it was hopeless. Then I began my usual routine: computer, breakfast, medication, coffee, bathroom . . . As soon as I'd got up, Chl called to tell me off for not calling her. She was in a terrible mood as well, and demanding attention. I explained that I was having a really, really bad day, so she wouldn't unload any more onto me; I even described my dream about my grandmother. Then I told her I'd become a grandfather for the fifth time, and she wanted to know the details. I said I hadn't even listened to my daughter's message properly yet. 'And instead of listening to it you're doing what?' she asked rudely. 'Talking to you, for God's sake,' I answered.

After breakfast I called my daughter and she told me the details: María de los Ángeles, born on the sixth of this month at four in the morning, weighing seven and a half pounds, a painful birth (two hours of pain). The first girl in my series of grandchildren. I hope the procession doesn't get much longer.

Then I felt curious about the message from my doctor. To be honest, I didn't want to listen to any messages or hear anything about the world, but something told me this was no ordinary message. I played it. It mentioned the medication, but it also talked about the pansies she'd left me. A chill ran down my spine. I went to the door, looked outside, and there it was: a white nylon bag containing yes sir yes sir three pots full of plants and flowers. Cursing, I put them outside on the balcony, where they'll wither and die. I hate the way living, sentient beings are treated like this. I ought to give my doctor a dozen monkeys as a gift and see how she likes looking after them. Chl was due to arrive at any moment, and I was going to have to explain the presence of those flowers. She's jealous of my doctor, especially because my doctor, besides being my doctor, is also my ex-wife. Chl doesn't like it at all that I'm still friends with her and still see her. I think there's a secret, silent war between the two of them, and I'm caught in the middle of it. Yesterday Chl left her tights, with the ends of them wet from the rain, hanging over a chair in the middle of the living room, in full view of anyone who came to visit me. I have to spend all my time looking out for these things. Luckily, when Chl came, if she noticed the pots of pansies on the balcony she didn't mention it. I don't think she saw them, but she'll see them eventually. Women. Even a goddess like Chl has that rotten side they all have, where jealousy festers.

With plenty of misgivings and very little enthusiasm, we finally set off on our Saturday walk: Feria del Libro and *boliche*. The rain had stopped and didn't seem about to start again, at least not immediately.

The streets were packed; you almost never see as many people as there were today. At some points it was even difficult to walk. It was also difficult to walk because the ground was wet and slippery. Before going out, I had to return to my fingernail treatment for the toothache. Since it didn't fully work I took an analgesic, which I'd been hoping to avoid because I never know what I might turn out to be allergic to. I have allergic reactions to almost all medication, especially aspirin.

I bought *America* by Kafka again; thirty-five pesos. The Emecé edition, in pretty good condition. I might want to read it again soon. I haven't gone back to it since I read it for the first time in 1966 and it inspired me to become a writer. Every time I put my library together I buy it again, and then I always end up lending it to someone and losing it. But this book should never be absent from my shelves, and just yesterday I noticed I didn't have it. Chl bought the exact same edition last week. Today she found *The Great Wall of China*.

In the bar, I was tucking into a delicious filled croissant, accompanied by an exquisite espresso. Chl was having a hot sandwich and a cortado. She mentioned our mutual friend X, saying she'd seen her recently. This person had an illness that affected the lower end of her digestive tube, so to speak. 'Is she completely cured now?' I asked, and then, to my cost, I took a spectacular bite of my croissant; anxious as I am, I always stuff my mouth with too much food. 'Cured of what?' Chl asked, distracted. Unable to speak because my mouth was too full, I stretched out my left arm, with the palm upturned, in a gesture not lacking in elegance, reminiscent of certain sorts of statue, and without thinking, without thinking at all, I gave my answer by making a very slight – but very suggestive – movement with one finger. No one who witnessed the scene (and in fact it was witnessed by many pairs of eyes, since the bar was full) would have suspected this movement of the slightest indecency, but to those in the know, it could only have meant sticking a finger up somebody's bottom. I hadn't meant to do it, and so far so good; I went on placidly chewing the substantial wad of croissant in my mouth, and then suddenly I noticed Chl. Perhaps because she'd realised with a start the only possible response to her question, or perhaps because she'd interpreted my gesture perfectly, her eyes were bulging and she'd clasped a hand over her mouth. She closed her eyes, or half closed them, so her eyeballs didn't actually escape, and began to tremble, convulsively and silently, in the throes of uncontainable mirth. When I saw her I realised what my gesture had meant, and the absurdity of her absent-minded question and the whole situation, and started to giggle uncontrollably myself. What a nightmare. It was like walking along a tightrope whilst juggling six oranges. We were in a public place; I couldn't let out my thunderous guffaws. What's more, my mouth was still full of chewed-up croissant. I had to laugh silently, and at the same time try to breathe and not choke on the croissant. All my insides were shaking in terrible spasms and my face was turning red, a really deep red. I panicked to think I might be on the verge of a heart attack or a stroke. My blood pressure, I guessed, must have risen to somewhere above 20/14. When I looked at Chl she was getting more and more hysterical, laughing like I'd never seen her laugh before, and this set me off all over again. There seemed to be no way for the scene to end; it went on and on, while I felt the snot about to burst from my nose and tried to contain a fit of coughing. Breathing; breathing is key. After a long time, when she was finally able to speak, Chl told me I was moaning, making a kind of 'Aaaaaaahhhh' noise, but trying to hold it in at the same time so people didn't look. I pulled one serviette after another out of the dispenser and used them to dry my eyes and, while I was at it, surreptitiously, my nostrils. I dropped each balled-up serviette onto the floor before pulling out the next. I was very careful not to look around; who knows what the other people there would have thought of our scene, but I had a feeling everyone was looking at us. I considered spitting the croissant out into a serviette, but I didn't dare. And we went on setting each other off until little by little the spasms began to die down, and the subsequent outbreaks became gradually more sporadic. I managed a brief interval of solemnity during which I was able to swallow the croissant with no repercussions, to my immense relief. Then the attacks of hysterical laughter came back, begun by one of us or the other, but we pulled ourselves together and eventually broke the cycle by not mentioning the matter, and above all not thinking about it. I said something inane about a bar across the road which had closed its doors for good, Chl said we'd talked about it already some time ago, and that's how we eventually got back to normal. It goes without saying that my tooth stopped hurting altogether and the tension and aches in my body lessened considerably.

'Well,' I said to her on the way home, as we were passing the Palacio Salvo, 'we had our orgasms after all.'

I just ran the spellchecker in Word, and it wanted me to change 'aspirin' to 'Aspirin'. I know it should be capitalised, but it still looks wrong to me. I can never write 'Xerox', 'Hoover' or 'Kleenex', either. I have my minor disagreements with the linguistic authorities.

I just ran the spellchecker again, and it seems these days you don't write 'Xerox' or 'Hoover'; it suggested 'xerox' and 'hoover' instead. It didn't say anything about 'Kleenex', though.

## SUNDAY 10, 18:31

Of course: I knew something was missing. Mosquitoes. One woke me up at five on the dot this afternoon by biting my right forearm. The storm is still going on. Rain, then drizzle, then nothing; and distant thunder that hasn't stopped for days. It's hot. And on top of everything else, the heating's at full blast. Mosquitoes. Toothache. Damn it all.

## MONDAY 11, 01:57

I'm writing by hand again, testing out a Rotring pen Chl gave me. I saw her using it yesterday and was struck by its unusual appearance; it didn't look like an ordinary ballpoint. She let me have a look and I saw the brand was Rotring; just a few days ago I was thinking about buying one, though not a disposable one because I didn't know they existed. The thing is, for some reason I don't find my normal pen very comfortable to use, and what's more I remembered that the luminous novel, which thanks to the grant I'm trying to get back afloat, was written with a pen that used Indian ink, not a Rotring but a Staedtler, 'on very high-quality paper'. I'm not using high-quality paper now, but rather the remains of some fanfold paper with those holes down the sides; my new printer takes ordinary paper. I hate the holes down the sides, but I hate tearing them off even more, so I leave them on. But this isn't the luminous novel. Anyway, Chl left me the pen. Now, as I write, I can see it has a few defects. The ink is very runny, for one thing; it looks like Indian ink, but it doesn't have that slight stickiness Indian ink has, which slows the writing down a little. I miss that stickiness; it's as if I needed something to hold me back slightly when I write, to give me a bit longer to think through what I'm writing, or about what I'm writing. Secondly, and this may be closely related to the previous point, the tip of the pen is very large, which means that the line it produces is too thick. If I had better handwriting, this could be an advantage, or at least not such a disadvantage. But the appalling state of my current handwriting, after years of not practising (see *Empty Words*), is made even worse by the thickness of the line, which makes the writing, and especially reading the writing, more confusing. I hope I'll be able to decipher this scrawl. Thirdly, the body of the pen is a very thin cylinder, very small in diameter, perhaps a quarter of an inch. I'd prefer it a bit thicker and more substantial. Maybe I could solve this by wrapping something around the cylinder to thicken it up. Because it's so thin, I bunch my fingers together too much when I hold it, which makes my muscles ache. Although I might just be out of practice. I've never learnt the right way to hold a pencil or a pen. I don't know how to rest it on the middle finger in an elegant, relaxed way; instead, all my fingers, or four of them at least, end up bunched around the cylinder, gripping it as if it were trying to escape. I'll have to check whether this pen comes with a finer nib; not much finer, but something like one or two points less. This one has a letter F on it, which might indicate the thickness of the line.

That's enough about that for today, and enough writing by hand as well. It would do me good to take up those handwriting exercises again. The mouse has completely ruined my hand.

MONDAY 11, 04:56

And now, cold and fog.

TUESDAY 12, 03:46

Good Lord. Fourth day of toothache; I went to the dentist this evening but came back in pain. It all began in what I learnt today is the lower right canine; that was on Friday afternoon. On Saturday it got more intense, and one of my upper teeth, or molars, almost symmetrical with the other, started hurting as well. When the acupressure stopped working I turned to Dorixina, which meant I was able to sleep. On Sunday, the storm and the central heating didn't help matters, and my bad mood, irritability and listlessness rapidly worsened. Today the pain came back again as I was having breakfast. Luckily the storm had gone and the weather was fairly good, although there was an icy wind blowing when I was coming back from the dentist in the evening, especially in the square and around my apartment. I managed to have a shower before breakfast; it's been a very, very long time since I last did that. And before I went to the dentist I cut my toenails, some of which were protruding by almost half an inch. Is my psychosis cured? By no means. Sometimes I shower, when I feel unbearably dirty and showering is inevitable, and that's what happened today. As for cutting my toenails, it would simply have become impossible to walk if I hadn't. When I was in the shower, I moved my foot and it hit the side of the tub. Agony: I didn't hit it hard at all, but my longest toenail took the impact. So there was nothing else for it. Now I notice my fingernails have grown again, too, and it's difficult to type; I'm making lots of mistakes because my fingernails keep hitting the wrong keys (and the keyboard is terrible too; I urgently need a new one).

It turned out to be two cavities, one on the top and one on the bottom. Since my dentist never does more than one job at a time, today he cleared the cavity in the bottom tooth, which I thought would make the biggest difference to my suffering, and put in a filling. It's a bad place for a filling; he told me it could easily come off. He also told me not to chew anything for two hours. I'd gone to the dentist with nothing in my stomach but my breakfast, which I'd eaten when I got up; in other words, my stomach was empty. Not eating is how I avoid the attacks of reflux I get when I'm out, but today I didn't factor in the anaesthetic, let alone the filling. I left the dentist at 10 p.m., and

I couldn't eat anything until midnight. Fortunately I had the remains of some long-life milk in the fridge, left over from when I was making yoghurt; it wasn't much, and skimmed milk doesn't exactly fill you up, but that glass made the wait until midnight slightly less fraught. My doctor came while I was waiting. Unsurprisingly, my blood pressure was a bit high: 18. But the minimum, 9, was fairly reasonable, so I wasn't worried. I expect being on edge from the pain raises my blood pressure.

There was another piece of bad news before breakfast, too: the living-room shutters wouldn't roll up. It seems the spring that collects the tape at the bottom when you raise the shutters has broken or come off. The room with the computer in it has broken shutters, too, so I phoned the shutter man, or whatever you call the person who fixes shutters. I think he's coming tomorrow, but it's not definite. When I got back from the dentist, I had some more news: an answerphone message from the caretaker, saying I hadn't given her enough money for the rent because this month the maintenance fees have risen by a ludicrous amount. I expect they're swindling me, but with my altered sleeping hours I can't investigate. Both my bottom tooth and my top tooth need to have crowns put on. Dentist, shutters, maintenance fees: you do the maths. The money from the grant will go up in smoke at this rate.

### WEDNESDAY 13, 04:54

Cold, grey weather; toothache; analgesics attacking my stomach; no sign of the shutter men. You get the idea. Chl was very affectionate, though. The little angel.

### WEDNESDAY 13, 17:28

I dreamed that the president died. I hope it was only a symbolic dream, and not a premonition (the last thing we need now is for the mafia to come back). I was on my way to visit his wife, who received me in a small room I couldn't see in much detail; I was sitting very comfortably and she was on my left, perhaps at a little desk. She was a fairly young woman, around forty, and I think she was a friend of 'my family';

we spoke without any formality. She'd inherited the presidency; in my dream there was no such thing as a vice-president. She said she was finding it difficult to accept her new circumstances, though she wasn't dramatic about it, and at that moment she didn't seem to be feeling any pressure or stress; she chatted away quite calmly, as if she had all the time in the world. At one point I lent her some money; two thousand and something pesos, which I took out of my pocket and handed to her. The 'and something' consisted of a few hundred, two or three, which appeared to be represented by some lightweight oblong stones, like those synthetic pumice stones for removing dry skin from your hands and feet. They were a pale, sandy colour and no larger than the notes, and probably a fair bit smaller.

I woke up, and when I went back to sleep I had a semi-conscious continuation of the dream, in which I returned, after some prudent amount of time, to collect the debt. Since the woman wasn't there, I looked through her desk drawers and took the money myself, though I felt a bit guilty about it.

After that I had another very important dream; so important I couldn't remember it afterwards. As soon as I woke up, my famous dream-erasing mechanism whirred into motion, and my mental search for the dream was obstructed by music and songs. All I was able to get back was a single scene or section of the plot, a kind of finale or synthesis of the whole dream. It was about some sort of lawsuit, something that had to be completed within a specific time frame, and a woman who was suspiciously similar to my doctor intervened to falsify a document, or rather to remove some piece of evidence from a file. At the last minute, at the last second, when the time was about to run out, I managed to put back at least part of the evidence, which I can only describe as resembling a little ball of chewed-up bread.

THURSDAY 14, 02:23

The shutter men didn't show up today either, and I didn't call them. Maybe tomorrow. And my friend H didn't come, though we'd agreed over email to meet at 8 p.m. I had an excellent yoga class; it helped me relax my back, shoulders, neck and jaw, which thanks to the computer and my aching molars had become unbelievably tense. The same two teeth, the top one and the bottom one, are still taking it in turns to hurt, though the bottom one supposedly doesn't have a cavity any more and has a filling instead. The good thing is that they never hurt at the same time. The top one hurts when I drink something hot, or eat something hot, and sometimes for no reason at all. It hurts a lot and then, just like that, the pain vanishes. The bottom one, or indeed the lower right canine, can go ages without bothering me at all, and then suddenly I'll feel a sharp, stabbing pain. Then it fades. Even so, I had to take some Dorixina; I tried my best to avoid it, but at one point when the pain was particularly bad I caved in.

I'm still cutting my reading of Doña Rosa Chacel; now with Beckett, and a book about Beckett, an essay that includes some biographical notes. I found it very interesting, even though essays normally annoy me. But then, I was extremely curious about Beckett, and this book shed light on a few things. I'd already read a really hilarious short story of his called 'First Love', and now I'm reading some other stories. Beckett can always make me roar with laughter. I know, of course, that his work isn't only about humour, and in fact one of my disagreements with the author of the book relates to that. The author doesn't like it when people look for particular philosophical meanings in Beckett and interpret his work in those terms; I'm entirely with him there. I too think that Art, in general, shouldn't be judged on its content. But the author, a German, goes a bit far in claiming that the meaning isn't important *at all*. He's guided in part by what Beckett himself says, but everyone knows that authors never tell the whole truth about their work, often because they don't know it. What I'm trying to say about my disagreement with the German is this: OK, Beckett doesn't build his work around any meaning or message or ideology, and that's how Art should be. Great. But my disagreement lies in the fact that having a character called Godot is not the same as having a character called something else. This Godot has a meaning, which evidently relates to God. I agree that this doesn't explain the work, and nor does it give the work its power or justify its existence; but let's not deny that there are *also* meanings in the work. What's important about literature doesn't derive from its meanings, but that's not to say the meanings don't exist or don't matter. I've often said and written: 'If I wanted to convey an ideological message, I'd write a pamphlet,' or something to that effect. But that doesn't mean my writing doesn't express ideas, or that those ideas aren't worth mentioning.

My dream about the president's wife has been on my mind all day. It's very interesting. On the one hand, I fear the president's death might represent the definitive disappearance, or at least the concealment, of a superego-like part of myself that allows me to maintain some sort of order in my life; I'm worried that without it I'll descend very quickly into madness. But my yoga teacher, when I told her about the dream, pointed out that you should never underestimate a woman's powers of organisation. It's true. The dream could also represent a readjustment of the Anima, my feminine side, as it gets ready to take over the organisation of my life. I'm not afraid of turning gay. On the contrary; the more I think about it, the more I think handing over control to a feminine part of myself could yield positive results. We'll see.

On another level of interpretation, the woman could be the Virgin Mary. This makes a lot of sense, because the continuation of the luminous novel I'm trying to bring about would begin with a chapter featuring Mary as the main character. In this reading of the dream, the money I lent her would have to be seen as the repayment of a debt, and my debt would consist of writing that chapter. I began it last year, as I've said, but I was feeling uninspired, I was feeling very uninspired. Maybe now, with that woman as president, the inspiration will come.

FRIDAY 15, 03:35

Chl has always been very beautiful, but today in particular she was radiating a kind of infinite beauty. I think she's in love (not with me, of course). She denies it. But . . .

Since coming back from the dentist I haven't been in pain any more, even though he couldn't work out exactly where the pain was coming from or why. Maybe the canine was giving off harmful vapours that affected the other teeth; now he's filled it properly and put a crown on it. We'll see what happens. It's strange for my mouth not to be hurting at all; only a week ago, the pain had me in a constant state of agitation. Now maybe I can start concentrating on what really matters.

Before going to the dentist, I spent some time on a new VB program. I finished it when I got home; there wasn't much left to do. It worked like a charm. And it's very useful. It's a program for renaming groups of files. I'm pleased with it, and doubly pleased because I think my interest in programming is a step up from my interest in playing stupid card games. Today I didn't play a single one. Maybe I'll play a few now . . . but I'm not sure.

SATURDAY 16, 02:13

As I was saying, the money I had in the bank was running out, and soon I'd have to start using what I'd put aside for the initial moving costs. I'd looked around a bit by myself, and more often with the help of my ex-wife, who, after a few fraught months, was gradually agreeing to resume our friendship, although there were still a few rough patches to come. About once a week she drove me to see different apartments she thought looked suitable. Unfortunately, they didn't look suitable to me. They looked gloomy and horrible, and the moment I stepped inside, or even when I saw them from the street, I could tell I'd feel trapped and claustrophobic in any of them. There's a particular building style that you see all over the place, and that isn't very old, where the apartments are small and narrow with bad ventilation. They have low ceilings, and if there's a corridor at all you brush the walls on either side with your shoulders as you walk down it. The walls are thin and they vibrate when cars go past, and you can hear the noises your neighbours make far too clearly. Sometimes I didn't even go up to look at them; I didn't even get out of the car. 'No, no, no,' I kept saying, and my ex-wife ended up convinced I didn't want to move out at all and would rather have gone on living with my friends. But I did want to move; every day I felt more stifled in that house, every day I missed having my own space and my own things, every day I spent more time escaping into those stupid digital card games and staying awake later and later, almost until sunrise. Which only made things more difficult. But then one day, Chl told me she'd seen a 'FOR RENT' sign in the Old Town, on the very building I'm living in now. It had the advantage of being an old building, with solid walls and reasonably high ceilings, and the rents in this area are more affordable than in the other parts of the centre I'd been looking in. All along I'd been wanting to get as close as possible to the area I'd lived in for thirty-eight years, and this apartment wasn't far away. Chl had also phoned to check what amenities were included, and the price, and everything matched what I wanted. So I set myself in motion, snatched victory from the jaws of defeat – as people used to say – and with my faith in Chl's instincts and intelligence, I decided to go and see it, almost certain I was going to take it. And take it I did; from the moment the caretaker, a very agreeable lady, opened the door to apartment number seven on the fourth floor – from that moment on, from my first glimpse of the spacious living room, I knew it was just what I'd been looking for.

It was April by then, and I'd begun my writing workshops – well, one of them – in my old secretary's house. She'd got married, was no longer my secretary and was about to move away from the capital, but she very kindly offered to organise my workshops for me the way she had in previous years, and she said I could begin one of them in her house. The others would begin in May, by which time I should have moved, and I'd made a plan that involved doing twice as much work as in previous years, since now I had to pay the rent and cover various costs I hadn't had before. Everything was arranged against the clock, and it was a stroke of luck that I found the right place to move into when I did. I rented the apartment, then, with my ex-wife as my guarantor, and I'll always be grateful to her for that. Chl found me some old furniture to add to what little I already had, and at the end of April, if I remember correctly, I started the move, and by the first few days of May the workshops were happening in my new apartment. Meanwhile, the move was still going on. I had the good sense to do it in stages, the most urgent things first and then the rest – with 'the rest' including none other than my books – but it was still exhausting, because of all the work and because of my nerves. Nothing destroys my nerves more than having to do things at particular times, and waiting for the workmen who were going to move my stuff and the others who were looking after who knows what extra bits and pieces was torture. At the same time, I had to explore my new neighbourhood to find out where I could buy food and everything else I needed. It's not a neighbourhood with much in the way of shops – useful shops for everyday items, I mean. There's no shortage of antique shops and art galleries and places that provide services to offices, and other things like that.

During that stay with my generous friends, I travelled by taxi like never before, mostly to visit Chl. After I moved, the journeys became less frequent, because Chl very often came to see me and sometimes even spent the night, and I began to hope we might live together one day. I think that period was the high point of our relationship, and I – I, at least – experienced moments of intense happiness. I got on with the workshops cheerfully; two every Thursday and one every Friday. By the time Saturday came around I was exhausted; the workshops always left me in a state of great mental excitement, and when each day's work was over, I'd stay awake for hours on end. One of the first things to be set up properly in the new apartment, with the help of an electrician, was of course the computer. And when workshop days were over, I used to sink back into those games I'd got into the habit of playing at my friends' house. Still, everything was more or less under control, especially because of the fulfilling relationship with Chl, which gave me strength and resolve, and because I had to keep up a constant stream of productive activity, dealing with the move-related problems that went on cropping up on a daily basis for quite some time.

The date I moved was 27 or 28 April; I spent May settling in, running the workshops from my apartment and spending all that wonderful time with Chl, at my place or hers. Just one month later, in June, if I remember correctly, came the collapse.


The shutter man came today, without his partner. He did a good job, and both sets of shutters are now working again. He didn't charge too much or take too long. Maybe my centrifugation is weakening, since he made it to my apartment in the end, and another visit that was arranged days ago didn't fail me either: Paty, my ex-student who sent me the Rosa Chacel book that made me start this diary. Chl didn't come, though: she says she went to the cinema with a friend. I don't believe her; I still think she's in love, with another man of course. She said I could call her friend and ask her, but everyone knows that women . . . anyway, I don't want to go on about it. I'm jealous, perhaps unfairly, in fact definitely unfairly, because even if there is another man, I'm not with Chl any more and she has every right, etc. It's just that I don't like being lied to, as the old joke goes. But this has a lot to do with the story I was telling, and I find it as painful as I find that story, so I'm going to stop writing immediately.

SATURDAY 16, 05:48

Did you see what just happened? There I was playing FreeCell and now it's six in the morning.

My friend emailed me the photos she'd taken; now I can shave, though I don't know what for exactly. The photos show quite clearly that I'm an old man 'on the way out'. It's not even the beard, to be honest; it's the skin, the look in my eye, the reddish tinge of my face, the curvature of my spine. What you'd call an old dodderer. A Beckett character.

I'm doing the right thing by playing FreeCell. What other options do I have?

Strangely, I look a lot like Onetti, though I've never looked the slightest bit like him before. Onetti in his final years, in bed. I ought to be in bed too, but I don't have anyone to look after me. So every day I get up – at great cost to myself, yes, but I get up – among other things, because I'm hungry.

SATURDAY 16, 19:00

Forty games of FreeCell, and I've won 100 per cent. I think it's the first time I've kept this up for a whole forty games. A few days ago

I finished a run of 100, winning 95 per cent, and then I reset the statistics and started again a few times because I kept losing very early in the run and sending the percentage down to below 95, which for some reason I find unacceptable. I think I use these card games not only as an anaesthetic but as a barometer. If I don't fall into a trance, or if I don't fall into the bad sort of trance, if I use my brain rather than functioning automatically, I'm unlikely to lose. However, when I play out of sheer desperation, I immediately fall into a destructive loop and lose one in three, or one in five or six, and sometimes I get stuck on one that I can't seem to complete however many times I try, until suddenly a simple solution occurs to me. So I'm taking this current percentage as a sign that something within me is working a bit better. But I might be wrong . . .

I'm waiting for Chl to arrive so we can go for our Saturday walk. The painful things I wrote yesterday, not yesterday but in the early hours of today, the story of my move and even the effect of those photos of me I was sent via email, had me thinking hard about Chl and my relationship with her. I'll have to write about that – when I'm strong enough. Meanwhile, I read *Wittgenstein's Nephew*, a short book by Bernhard that Chl bought recently and said I could borrow for a few days, but only a few days, because she's constantly rereading it. It's not amazing; true, some parts are extraordinary, really masterful, and it's written with Bernhard's characteristic truth and sincerity, which make his work so moving and somehow so vast. But I think it's one of the last things he wrote, and you can sense a kind of wornness to it; a kind of exhaustion, perhaps. Until about halfway through I was finding it difficult to persevere, in contrast to most books by Bernhard, which have quite the opposite effect: they're impossible to put down, even for a moment, because of the hypnotic power of his crazy, and I mean really crazy, style. In this book, however, that power, at least in the first half, is reduced, weakened, and his style seems more like an imitation of his style, as if this book should have been written in a different style and he didn't realise. Then come a few memorable passages which made me laugh out loud, for example when he and his friend Paul Wittgenstein are trawling through one city after another, covering miles and miles, hunting for a copy of the *Neue Zürcher Zeitung*. There was an article in it that Bernhard was keen to read. Every time he mentions the paper, and he mentions it on practically every line for many lines, he says *Neue Zürcher Zeitung* in full, instead of saying the newspaper or the *Zeitung* or any other simpler way of putting it; no, he repeats it again and again, in his finest obsessive style, as if wanting to leave the reader in no doubt whatsoever about what he means. Really wonderful.

I read it after finishing some Beckett stories, along with two short plays, one of which was entirely in mime. I still have *Molloy* and *Malone Dies* left to reread, but I switched to Bernhard and recently tried to carry on with Rosa Chacel, which is becoming more and more difficult. What a mistake it was, this book, *The Maravillas District*, and to make matters worse it seems to be the first volume of a trilogy, meaning that when I get hold of the other two I'll have to choke them down as well. I hope they're more appetising than this one. Too many soliloquies from different characters, and you have to guess who it is that's soliloquising, which you sometimes only manage many paragraphs later. Too many exclamation marks and question marks, too many ellipses, too many digressions about things that aren't always interesting. Why am I still reading it? Because of my love for Doña Rosa, and also because amidst all the confusion and all the verbosity I'm finding so hollow (even though it's not; it's not hollow at all, it just hasn't worked), among all the boring bits, here and there you come across a real gem; sometimes a casual observation that perfectly matches an observation of my own which it took me a long time to arrive at, certain shared inner experiences that I don't usually find in other books or other people. Anyway, I'm reading it half out of obligation and half out of curiosity, without enjoying it much; or in sudden bursts, enjoying it immensely. The worst thing about the book is the way the action is constantly interrupted by those pointless, unnecessary, artificial-feeling switches in narrator, even though the voice always sounds the same.

.   .   .

After I moved house, just like after I arrived in Buenos Aires in 1985, I began obsessively reading detective novels. I read EVERYTHING on my shelves . . . Chl's arrived; I can hear the door opening.

SUNDAY 17, 04:16

This Saturday ritual is very satisfying; I found three books by Maugham I didn't know about and one by Len Deighton I hadn't read, and which I've now started, cutting my reading of poor old Rosa Chacel once again. If you ask me, Deighton's better than le Carré when it comes to spy novels. They have some things in common (the bureaucracy of espionage, for example), but Deighton is much more entertaining. Then a delicious croissant and a delicious coffee in our usual *boliche*. And, most importantly, spending time with Chl, who's passing through what looks like the best phase of her life, though she doesn't seem to realise it; that time in a woman's life when she's at her most beautiful and seductive, still very young but with a hint of maturity. In the *boliche* we talked almost exclusively about Wittgenstein's nephew and Thomas Bernhard, whom she admires perhaps a little too fervently. I share her admiration to an extent, but I'm not as fanatical. At one point I had to say, 'I hope that after I die, somewhere in the world two people like us sit in a *boliche* and talk about me like this.' That way of living on through art. It was as if Bernhard were there, sitting at the table with us; it was even a bit alarming, because we agreed he must have been an insufferable man (more insufferable than Rosa Chacel), and perhaps even frightening.

But Chl didn't spend the night as planned; when it was time to go to bed, she went home. That's fine; after seeing myself in those photos, I understand perfectly.

When she left, I plunged headlong into my addictions. FreeCell (my percentage dropped, I should say, to 96 per cent. I had a feeling that would happen even before I started playing) (because every time Chl leaves, something inside me snaps and I play for the sake of playing, so as not to feel what I have inside me, but I don't concentrate on the game) (once, at the beginning of our relationship, she took me for a drive. Eventually the outing came to an end and it was time to go our separate ways, and the moment I realised I had to get out of the car, it was as if I'd been kicked by a horse. As if I had a horse inside my chest and it had kicked me hard in the chest from there, or as if a ghostly invisible hand had reached through my flesh and bone and into my chest and yanked out whatever was in there with a single movement. I yelped loudly in surprise and pain, a terrible spiritual pain that was physical as well. This hasn't happened again, because now I'm on the alert and able to control it, or repress it, or control or repress my awareness of what's happening inside me. Nevertheless, the effect is always devastating, as if Chl's a part of me and whenever we're separated a piece of my body is being pulled off) (which is one way of understanding that episode I called 'the collapse', and why I'm explaining it now so casually, so nonchalantly, without really realising what I'm saying. Only a month after I moved into my new apartment, Chl decided to go on a trip. It was an opportunity she obviously couldn't turn down; it would have been foolish. I knew I'd miss her, but as usual I suppressed my emotions and pretended I didn't mind. She was going to be away a long time. Over a month. As soon as she left I started going downhill, and I've been going downhill ever since. I've always known I have an abandonment complex, and I'm well aware of the causes; not for nothing have I been through several bouts of psychotherapy. But I've never been cured, and under the circumstances, having just moved house and with the stress of all that change, and after those six months in my friends' house, including one torturous summer, and gripped by panic about my responsibilities in this new life . . . And you have to consider that for many years I'd barely had an official existence. I didn't pay rent, I had nothing to my name, I had no responsibilities as such; if I worked I could put most of what I earned in the bank, and if I chose to I could stop working for as long as I liked, because my basic necessities were covered and I wasn't interested in going around buying things. I paid for my vices, and beyond that I've always been very poor. Anyway, as I was saying: considering the circumstances, the changes in my life, the new responsibilities, and the feeling of being a stranger in my new home and my new neighbourhood, it's understandable that the sense of abandonment caused by Chl's trip was crushing, overwhelming. I resumed my desperate card games on the computer, I put the move on hold halfway through – everything stayed where it was, piled up on the floor any old how – and it remains unfinished to this day. I still haven't 'moved into' my new apartment, I haven't made it a home; it's just a place for working in that I'm only now trying to change – hence the armchairs. In fact, you could say that my whole life was put on hold, in a sense, as if it had been put between parentheses. Chl hadn't been gone long when I returned to my old habit, which I'd given up, of searching for erotic images online. That gradually turned into an acceptance of pornographic images; I ventured beyond my usual tastes and boundaries, and one day I found myself examining some photos with interest even though I'd ended up in a place where there was plenty more going on besides naked women. Initially I saved the images as what are known as thumbnails, which are very small versions of the photos, the ones you have to click on if you want to see them full-size and then download them onto the computer's hard drive. Then I began to save a lot of the larger photos too).

Writing in brackets makes me nervous, probably because I'm scared of forgetting to close them – not that it really matters – so I'm carrying on outside the brackets with the topic from inside them. At one point I analysed my situation; I asked myself why I was behaving like that, and why I didn't find pornography disgusting the way I used to. As I thought about it, it slowly dawned on me that searching for those photos was a masochistic way of expressing my jealousy; jealousy I wasn't aware of, but that was very much there nevertheless, stealthily working away at me. Those crude photographs, then, were representations of my secret innermost thoughts – images of Chl being taken in a thousand ways by a thousand foreign men. It was painful, of course; but I needed to feel that pain precisely because I hadn't been feeling it, and I was hypnotised, night after night, by that slow movement of bytes from a remote computer to my own. I still hadn't bought my new computer, which has a much faster modem, and I was spending a fortune on my telephone connection. This was bad for me for lots of reasons, most of all because it meant I had to sit and wait while the images passed slowly onto my computer, and all the while I was seeing what I didn't want to see, the representations of the images that were hidden in my mind. I also realised why I don't find pornography disgusting any more; I realised it by chance, when I came across a few pornographic photos with captions somewhere, a sort of photo story, and it struck me that the words alongside the pictures still did seem repellent and disgusting, hateful even, and they made me feel deeply uncomfortable. I discovered then that what gives the images a perverse sort of significance is none other than the words, the tool I work with. The images themselves, with a few exceptions (when they show something really horrible, for example when the woman is positioned in such a way that she seems to be completely under the man's, or men's, control), the images themselves, the images of normal sexual acts – and normal, to me, includes various positions and even what people call oral sex – are actually beautiful and don't disgust me at all. I can't stand the sight of sperm, though, especially when it's used aggressively against the woman, for example splattering her face. But on the whole I find the images completely acceptable. However, a single written word can transform an image that seems innocent or beautiful into a despicable perversion.

Words . . .


MONDAY 18, 01:53


I'm writing by hand, aiming to make it legible. It seems easier this time, though I haven't practised since that first day with the Rotring. Sometimes you practise things in your head, unconsciously, and that intangible practice often counts.

I turned the computer off some time ago; I don't know where I found the strength. I wavered for a few minutes before I made up my mind, thinking about all the things I could do on it, such as writing this diary and sending some long-overdue replies to emails; many people will be wondering what's become of me. But I held firm and turned it off. Now I just hope the tiny monster that lives somewhere in my head, or my gut, doesn't make me turn it back on.

I know, I know; I shouldn't divide myself in two like this, trying to find someone to blame ('The cat broke the vase, Mum'); I need to accept that the person who decides to play games and stay up until dawn is me and no one else. But I find it hard to believe my brain could be so obtuse; there *must* be some unconscious formation controlling my life. Of course, if there is, it would mean the unconscious formation has grown stronger at the expense of my own self, and even somehow with its tacit permission (or rather – so as not to go on dissociating myself from myself and multiplying my fragments – with *my* tacit permission).

The thing is, my current abnormal situation didn't come about overnight; it's been developing and evolving for years – in a way, ever since I was born. At least, I have a vivid memory of when I was very young, around seven or eight, or maybe less, which shows quite clearly that I was making use of self-hypnosis and trance states even then. This memory, which I may already have described elsewhere, and if I have the reader will have to put up with it, because this is my diary and I'll write whatever I want, and right now I want to write about that early experience. This memory, I was saying, shows me going on a long-distance bus journey without any of my family, which in itself was very unusual. I'm sure my mother bombarded the guard and a fair few of the passengers with instructions, but still, it's strange that she sent me by myself. It wasn't a particularly long journey, but nor was it particularly short; nowadays, you could do it by car in around thirty or forty minutes, but the buses were slower back then. The seaside town I was being sent to was, and still is, called Costa Azul. All I remember from the journey is that when I realised I was alone on the bus I felt scared, but I soon found a secret technique that helped me to travel more calmly. Instead of looking at the urban, and suburban, landscape outside, I focused on a spot very close to the bus, a strip of tarmac on the road, and probably also the pavement. I watched the fuzzy, monotonous blur pass before my eyes, a greyish mass that didn't mean anything. And then I thought, and I remember this like it was yesterday: 'Everything comes eventually in this life, and the end of this journey will also come.' A moment later, almost as soon as I'd finished thinking these words, the journey was over. Magically. I recognised the familiar landscape I'd seen so many times before when travelling with my grandparents or parents, and I saw that the house was just a few blocks away, on the corner – the house with the gazebo. And my grandparents were waiting for me in the doorway, or at least I think they were, because all I remember of that journey is the moment when I discovered, amazed, that time had shrunk to nothing. I don't know where those self-hypnosis skills came from, but evidently, long before I'd heard the word, and long before my therapist recommended the self-hypnosis exercise in Laurence Sparks' book, I was already an expert. Although who knows what my technique was on that occasion.

And the addictions I'm wrestling with at the moment are addictions to that very trance state; to that way of shrinking time so it passes without my feeling any pain. But that's also how my life is slipping away from me; how my lifetime ends up transformed into non-time, a kind of zero time.

MONDAY 18, 02:32

While Chl was away, then, things went from bad to worse. Put simply, I felt abandoned, like that time on the long-distance bus, and in much more pain than I knew how to deal with, so I turned to my usual defence systems. When she came home, I thought things would go back to normal and we'd carry on as before. I asked her to stay over every night for a period of at least ten nights, thinking her presence in my bed would be much more appealing than anything the computer had to offer. But I was wrong, because I hadn't taken the feelings I'd been hiding into account. She did as I asked, coming to my apartment religiously on each and every one of the agreed nights. But the poison that had invaded my spirit was still doing its work, and, perhaps as a kind of revenge on her for abandoning me, I kept her waiting (even when she was asleep she was waiting for me, and she moaned in her sleep when she sensed I wasn't with her) and carried on playing my stupid computer games until three or four in the morning. I think those days sowed the seeds of the current situation with Chl. She must have felt let down, and even badly treated, as indeed she was. I'd like to say: not by me, but by the cursed force that controls me. But I won't say that. Anyway, when those nights came to an end, she went back to sleeping in her own house, and she hardly slept here at all after that. Our sex life also began to deteriorate. It's possible, it occurs to me now, though this isn't something I can confirm, or deny, but it's possible I was also using sex aggressively at that time; and she, as an extraordinarily sensitive, perceptive woman, couldn't help but notice and resent this. It began, if I'm not mistaken, with a pregnancy scare, though until then she'd managed all that perfectly through calculations based on the dates of her menstrual cycle. She made me start using condoms, contrivances I detest, even on days when it was clearly unnecessary. There was no rupture, no sudden change, but she grew more and more distant until one day she decided to end our relationship – though only the sexual part of it. Not only did our relationship go on uninterrupted in all other respects, but it actually became more devoted and, in a way, more intimate; fraternal, even, and far more than just a friendship. I gradually resigned myself to this, and stopped hoping on a conscious level that our relationship would go back to being complete. But, as I've begun to realise over the past few days, on a less conscious level I'm still clinging to that hope, which shouldn't be called a hope but rather a dream, a fantasy, and my addictions and all-nighters are my way of waiting for her, waiting until she comes back to me with all her being and all the passionate love for me she once had. And how, what's more, can I convince this dream of mine that it's futile, if we see each other almost every day and she's always so affectionate towards me? Still, only by quashing this ridiculous dream will I begin to fight back against my madness.

MONDAY 18, 03:00

So now you see, Mr Guggenheim: I'm working hard on the disruptive factors in my life, which are keeping me from confronting the grant project freely and directly. Since the material I need to cover in order to finish the project is based on my life and experiences, if I don't clear the path, I'll never be able to reach it. And you'll no doubt appreciate that the emotional and existential problems I'm trying to solve are very delicate, very delicate indeed. Each one of these sessions with myself leaves me exhausted, and if I were a drunkard I'd say: exhausted and thirsty, really thirsty.

MONDAY 18, 03:10

Farewell, Chl, my lover.
Hello, Chl, my sister.

TUESDAY 19, 04:40

Writing in Word.

I went to the dentist today, but he didn't solve the problem. My tooth still hurts – when it touches hot water, or cold water, or food, or even cold air if I go outside and open my mouth. Today all he did was take a mould of the tooth. Now I can't go back again for a week, not until next Monday, because this is my week of work. So I have to carry on living in fear and, now and then, in despair.

Some of my teeth, of the few I have left, are in a terrible state. My dentist says it's not all his fault, and that I'm partly to blame because I grind my teeth. It's true, I do grind my teeth, especially when I'm asleep.

My FreeCell success rate dropped to 95 per cent. Still acceptable. Eighty games won out of eighty-four.

Yesterday I finished the Len Deighton book and today I started the Maugham.

TUESDAY 19, 05:57

Back on 96 per cent. Ninety-two games won out of ninety-six.

WEDNESDAY 20, 04:44

Just checking in with the dear diary. I had to do a few things for the virtual workshop and I'm tired. I wanted to talk about my return to the dentist yesterday, and other things as well, but I can't do it now.

THURSDAY 21, 04:49

Yes, I definitely find it hard to write in this diary during my week of work. Not because the work is particularly intense; I think I've said before that I now have one student on Tuesdays, along with the virtual workshop, then two workshops on Thursdays, and this Friday I have another, on editing, which takes place once a month. Two workshops in a day is too many. It'll be five hours' work in total, but it's work that takes a lot of concentration, and something else, too, that I don't know how to describe. I could say 'dedication'; yes, I could say that.

Anyway, I'm not going to write what I promised to write, not now (about the return to the dentist; I hope I don't forget), because I'm not feeling inspired. I don't want to write anything. I'm only writing these lines because I have to. Enough.

SATURDAY 23, 18:31

This really won't be easy to explain. Last night, or rather early this morning, while I was getting ready for bed – I was at the stage of changing my clothes, which is the most arduous part – a phrase came back to me that I read a very, very long time ago, in a *Selections from Reader's Digest*. It stuck in my mind, and I've thought about it often over the years, always in similar situations. I'm not exaggerating when I say that I first came across this phrase thirty years ago, and in fact that probably still comes up short; it could well be forty years or more. Something tells me I was extremely young at the time. I can never remember the exact words, but I remember the concept very clearly. Last night, the phrase appeared as something along the lines of: 'People say that to strengthen the will we need to do at least two things every day that we don't want to do. I stick rigorously to this rule: every day I go to bed and I get up.'

I realised at the last minute that I didn't have a single book on the go (aside from the Rosa Chacel, which I'm still putting off). I'd just finished a pretty insipid book, *Ah King*, the worst one I've read so far by Somerset Maugham. Before that I read *Six Stories Written in the First Person Singular*, also by him, which was much more interesting and entertaining, and *Semmelweis*, by Céline. I went to my library and took a long time to choose; I even thought about picking up this week's *Búsqueda*, but I was worried the political news would overexcite me or give me frightening dreams. In the end I opted for another Somerset

Maugham: *Pride*, an awful translation for something that was once called *The Moon and Sixpence*, in a horrible Plaza edition with tiny print. I realise I decide the order in which I read books based on the size of the print, leaving the ones with small print until last. I got into bed and began reading *Pride*. When I reached the sixth page of text, which was the eighth page of the book, to my immense surprise I came across the following paragraph:

> I forget who it was that recommended men for their soul's good to do each day *two things* they disliked: it was a wise man, and it is a precept that I have followed scrupulously; for every day I have got up and I have gone to bed.

This hard-to-explain occurrence may have been responsible for some very disturbing dreams I had this morning.

### SUNDAY 24, 06:37

It's got to this time in the morning and all I've done is mess around. I wanted to write about my dreams, but I also didn't want to. There's one in particular that, more than disgusting, I find extremely confusing; it seems completely unhinged, but at the same time, something tells me there's an important message to be found in that ignominious image, deeply embarrassing as it is. I can't decipher it, and I've been avoiding this diary all day because I need to write about the dream and I don't dare. Now I'm very, very tired, my back's aching and my eyes are completely ruined, thanks to the screen. I successfully finished a program in Visual Basic: it allows me to search for any word or phrase across all text files (not in the .docs, alas, because they're not text files and there's no way to access them with VB) (but it's very useful anyway). Really the program was finished yesterday, but today I woke up with an urge to add another procedure. It took me a long time, but in the end it turned out beautifully. When the search is complete, it makes an amusing noise. If it finds the series of words it's looking for, it makes another noise: a kind of soft, dull thud. And now I'm going to bed.

SUNDAY 24, 19:25

I'm writing by hand, with the new pen Chl brought me a few days ago. It's another Rotring, only with a thicker body and a finer point – in other words, it meets my requirements perfectly, and it's a pleasure to write with.

The book *Pride* is really confusing me, because it's 'inspired' by the life of Gauguin, but the central character is an Englishman called Strickland. I have no idea which details are genuinely biographical and which ones Maugham has made up or borrowed from elsewhere. It's an interesting read, like almost everything by Maugham, and as usual it's only interesting up to a point. This deliberate mediocrity is one of Maugham's virtues. His reflections always verge on the trivial, and yet they're also timely and exact. This book, like many of his others, is written in the first person, by a writer, but I don't know to what extent the writer is him. When he talks about other people he's very astute; but when he talks to other people, he often sounds like an idiot. There's a strange split, as if his social being, which comes out in the dialogue, were a mask that had nothing at all to do with the writer telling the story.

It's a terrible edition. Luckily the translation isn't completely dire, though of course it could be better. But the publisher seems to have cut a lot of corners: the ink is very uneven, for example, which, combined with the small print, makes it hard work for the reader. There are also a lot of mistakes. The most notable is one that I find completely bewildering, because I can't imagine what caused it. On page 135, it says:

I couldn't believe my heyes.

I couldn't believe mine when I saw that H; how it could have appeared there is an unfathomable mystery to me. On both typewriters and typesetting machines, or whatever they're called, the H is a long way from the E, so it's not as if they hit the wrong key. The translator couldn't possibly have made that mistake, any more than the printer could have done; and no editor, however careless, would have let it through.

MONDAY 25, 03:55

I've finally shaved. It's all thanks to my determination not to turn the computer on today – or at least not first thing. I got up late. It was grey and rainy outside, just like yesterday; not heavy rain but intermittent drizzle, and absolutely freezing. Chl and I couldn't go for a walk today or yesterday; yesterday we were put off by the cold, but we were even more put off by the celebratory atmosphere outside, and the knowledge that the bookshop would be shut because of the national holiday. Chl is in one of those phases of her therapy in which the unconscious uses up a huge amount of energy, and as a result she doesn't feel like doing anything (she's a brilliant patient, incidentally; it's incredible to see the progress she's making, step by step).

As for my own lack of energy, it could also be down to the medication, and especially, I think, the antihypertensives. The same goes for the pain in my back and my waist.

Anyway, as I was saying: I got up late, and when Chl arrived I'd only just finished my breakfast. We sat around being bored together for a long while, and in the end she went home earlier than expected because she wanted to read in bed. By the time she called to say she'd got back safe and sound, the shaving process was well under way; I'd removed as much as I could with the scissors and used up the first disposable razor. After I finished, I ate a plate of the lentils Chl had brought me, and a tomato with garlic. Then came the coffee, by which stage I was feeling a bit edgy from the lack of computer time, so I turned it on, and I've been here more or less non-stop until now. I visited some porn sites on the internet that I hadn't been to for days and found lots of excellent photos of Japanese girls. Excellent photos and very beautiful, very attractive girls. Later I corrected the Visual Basic program that reads me the title of whichever CD-ROM is in the drive, and lets me change it for a different one if it's not the one I want, or start it up if it is. While I was at it, I found Gauguin on Encarta and confirmed that most of Maugham's novel is made up. It's strange how he left some details of Gauguin's life unchanged, such as him leaving his wife and children, and his time in Tahiti. But even in that part things happen differently. I also read up on Maugham.

I hardly learnt anything new, except for the dates of his birth and death. He had a long life, that man.

After mentioning my lack of energy, I was immediately distracted by other things and forgot to add that I had a go on the exercise bike today and was utterly exhausted in no time. For one thing, the bicycle is objectively 'heavier' (I can tell by the noise it makes, and the way the belt rubs against the disc as it spins); I expect the cold makes the mechanism tighter than usual. But I also don't have much muscle strength, or much energy in general. Maybe I'm low on potassium.

Once, when I raised the blind in my bedroom, I noticed there was a dead pigeon on a flat roof very close to this building. I saw it again more recently, and on that second occasion, I saw the dead bird's partner standing motionless a few feet from the body as if she were at a funeral, with her back to me and her eyes fixed on the corpse. Or who knows where she was looking, in fact, because when pigeons want to look at something in front of them they turn their heads to one side as if they're cross-eyed. But in this case, her beak was pointing straight at the middle of the dead body. Today I saw her again; it looks like what I've read about pigeons grieving is true. But today's scene also had its dramatic moments. Without knowing if this reflects the reality of the situation, I'm going to designate the pigeon that's still alive 'the widow', assuming the corpse is a male. When I saw the dead pigeon for the first time, I found myself pondering the possible causes of his death. I couldn't imagine what had befallen him, there on the third floor, on a flat roof no one would be likely to visit since there's nothing on it; no plants, no string for hanging up washing, nothing. I expect people go up there when the water tank needs cleaning, and that's it. The pigeon is lying near the middle of the roof, which is a rectangular space of about five hundred square feet, whose longest edges run parallel to this building. The widow was standing stock-still in the same place as the other day; I have no idea how long she'll be there. It's a few days since I last looked out of that window at a reasonable time, but she doesn't appear to be going anywhere. Although I suppose at night she goes somewhere suitable to sleep.

I wondered what pigeons know about death. At one point I had a sense that the widow wasn't so much mourning as waiting, as if she thought what had happened to the pigeon could be reversed. My suspicions were confirmed, in a way, when the wind started to blow. The widow got excited because it looked like the corpse was stirring; the wing that was outstretched, as if it had fallen there, began to move in a kind of flapping motion. The widow abandoned her pose and started pacing nervously up and down, though she didn't move any closer to the corpse. She simply walked back and forth in a straight line, shaking her head and looking concerned. When the wind dropped, she returned to her waiting. This happened again, two or three times, with every fresh gust of wind. I kept putting off my breakfast, fascinated by the scene. Then my memory presented me with the key to this tragedy: I suddenly recalled that a few months ago I'd seen a different incomprehensible scene unfold outside my window. On a balcony of the hotel opposite, on a higher floor than my apartment, I'd seen a man, who was neither young nor thin, absorbed in a strange pursuit. The hotel is no longer in use; it's closed down, and the building is very dilapidated. There are no windows or blinds, and one of the openings that lead onto the balconies doesn't even have a door. On the floor below there's always a little window lit up at night; I don't know who lives there, or even if they're legal residents. Now and then I've seen someone, someone younger and thinner than the other person, drinking *mate* on the balcony of the floor level with this one. In the strange scene my memory presented me with, the man who was neither young nor thin was firing stones from a catapult, aiming at the street corner diagonally across from the hotel. The man noticed me at the window and launched several stones one after another, apparently at random, and then vanished into the hotel. I thought he'd found a catapult in the street and couldn't resist trying a few shots. But today I realised something else was going on: that man hated pigeons, and had made the catapult himself in order to kill every single one that came within range. It seems implausible, but I'm sure it's what happened. I hope the widow is spared.

While I was still at my window, engrossed in the scene, I noticed a male pigeon had flown over and landed on the flat roof near the bereaved wife, and was now performing a vigorous little courtship dance. The widow was incensed. She responded extremely violently, spreading her wings and advancing upon her seducer with her beak open and ready for use. The male pigeon beat a hasty retreat. The widow was left tapping out a kind of enraged jig on the railings, where the fury of the chase had carried her. She strutted desperately up and down, up and down along the railings, winding back on herself over and over in a crazy, incomplete way. It was like a typical courtship dance only done wrong somehow, cut short, angry, with her head shaking from side to side and an air of real desolation. It was clear she couldn't contain her grief; she didn't know what to do with it.

Then she calmed down and returned to her post a yard or two away from the dead bird. A light drizzle began to fall and she held out for as long as she could, but then it got heavier and she flew away.

MONDAY 25, 17:46

I'm writing in Word.

When I raised the blinds today there was no sign of the widow. Later I noticed a bird perched on the railings, but I think it was a different one. It was probably male, because it looked bigger, and it seemed to have more white feathers than the widow.

As for the dream I didn't write about the other day, I don't think I'm going to write about it at all. My unconscious seems reluctant to expose itself like that, and I have no reason to use violence on myself; I've used too much of it already in the course of my life. Better to live in peace. I can write about today's dream instead, however, in which I was looking for Jorge Batlle so I could pay back some money I owed him; a hundred pesos or a hundred dollars, I wasn't sure which. At various points I was holding the money, a banknote I remember as sometimes red and sometimes green. It wasn't folded; it looked new, stiff, as if fresh from the mint, like the hundred-dollar notes that come out of ATMs. But in the dream Jorge Batlle was the president's son, not the president. Although I couldn't find him and therefore didn't see him, I could picture him; I imagined him as a young man, a boy. He lived with his parents, and I went to look for him in their building. I was a bit worried about ringing the bell and interrupting the president in the middle of something important, but before I reached the door, I saw a very luxurious car pulling out of the garage; when the car came towards me, I signalled for it to stop and walked over. There was a man in the back seat whom I initially thought looked like Jorge Batlle, but when the window was lowered I realised it wasn't him. He said he was the secretary and his boss was busy, I don't know where or with what. I showed him the banknote and told him I wanted to settle a debt, but I didn't give it to him and he didn't suggest it. Then there's a gap, after which I reappear on my way into a building that might have been the president's house. I hear an elderly man, probably the president, addressing me from upstairs; the irritable voice shouts for me to come up, saying he's waiting for me. I'm sure he's confusing me with someone else, and I explain, almost shouting myself, that I'm Jorge Varlotta. Then he answers, in a less irritable voice, that there are clean sheets in the cupboard. He assumes that, considering the time (in the early hours, probably), all I can do is go to bed, and he's right.

WEDNESDAY 27, 03:57

Today I don't feel like writing. I'm low on energy and a bit fidgety and uncomfortable, perhaps because for some reason I got up before I'd had eight hours of sleep. I spent a bit of time reading this diary; I'm going slowly, because it's tiring. I don't know if it's tiring because it's badly written or because it's my diary and my brain has to work harder than it would if it had been written by someone else. But even if it is badly written, I think it's an interesting read. I'll have to edit the style a bit, give it some substance; it covers so many different topics, and sometimes I try to say too much in a single sentence. And because it only talks about trivial things, if the style doesn't draw people in there'll be nothing going for it. Who knows what I'll do; nothing, for now, besides carry on, one way or another.

THURSDAY 28, 06:03

I'm writing by hand.

I just got up to have a coffee. This may be hard to believe, but last night I went to bed at 11 p.m. I felt sleepy after I ate and dozed off in the armchair for lazing in. The phone woke me up (Chl, of course), and after talking for a bit, I said to myself: why not go to bed right now? There was plenty to do – I'd collected the dishes that needed washing and left them soaking in soapy water; yesterday, i.e. Wednesday, the maid didn't come, which wasn't surprising (she never comes when the kitchen is in chaos) (the woman evidently has extrasensory perception); I had to make some yoghurt (the last batch turned out splendidly, so much so that I soon polished it off); I had to wait until half past eleven to take the antihypertensives; I had to write this diary, which has been semi-abandoned; and I won't even go into all the things I had to do on the computer. But I was determined. I switched the computer off, took my medication, drank my usual coffee and got into bed. I finished my book (*The Theatre of Memory* by Pablo de Santis), which was excellent. After turning out the light I lay awake for a long time, but then, inevitably, every so often I was jolted back to consciousness by a lion's roar: I'd been snoring. I wasn't awake, in other words, but dreaming I was awake. At four I got up to go to the bathroom (damn those antihypertensives) and had a cigarette, the tenth of the day. Then I got back into bed, but I don't think I slept any more after that. Still, I didn't let the time go to waste; I decided to practise using my memory, inspired by the book I'd just read. I made a mental visit to my old apartment on Calle Soriano, and as soon as I began visualising some of the rooms, who should appear but ZZ (a girl I knew some years ago). She'd been almost completely erased from my memory, which strikes me as very suspicious. So completely erased, in fact, that even now I can't picture her face. The closest I got was the memory of a photo of her I'd kept somewhere, and which I found a few months ago. But I only remembered the photo, and not the face in the photo; just a few blurred features. I couldn't remember her voice, either. But I could remember the things she did, some of which were very memorable, like her acrobatic little dance when, in the days after my gallbladder operation, I used to wake her up at dawn to ask for some tea and toast. I'm not sure why I had to wake her up at that time. It could have been part of the post-operative diet; or, more likely, it was because the wound was infected, meaning I was almost certainly taking antibiotics, and antibiotics disagree with me if I take them on an empty stomach. Anyway, ZZ woke up, or didn't wake up, in her usual excellent mood, which wasn't at all her usual mood once she was actually awake. But it was more than a matter of moods: I'd say she was another woman entirely, a real delight. Very nice and very funny – and very polite and happy. She'd wake up straight away with her eyes closed or half-closed; I was always surprised, when I roused her and said it was time for some tea, to see how she'd leap up, with no delay or time to adjust, and be in the kitchen like a shot. When everything was ready, she'd appear holding a tray with the tea, the toast and whatever there was to put on it, perhaps ham or some kind of jam. She brought it over to my bed, or rather my mattress, because in the time after the operation I didn't sleep in the bed but to one side of it, on a mattress on the floor. I don't know why I did that either. Perhaps I didn't want her to catch the infection from my wound; or, more likely, because immediately after the operation, as far as I remember, I couldn't stand having anyone less than two or three feet away from me. It made me panic. Either I was afraid they'd brush against my wound or I was simply hypersensitive in the extreme and the mere presence of another person nearby was painful. ZZ, then, brought the tray over to my mattress, and instead of handing it to me right away, she invariably did a strange and wonderful dance I find it impossible to describe. It looked a lot like she was making a kind of ritual offering, the parody of a sacrifice to a god, or paying homage to a king or a sultan. At the same time, it was comical and affectionate in a way I've only seen in the dances of Laurel and Hardy. The first time she did it I thought it would be a disaster; the tray shook from side to side, the tea threatened to spill or even slide off the tray entirely, cup and all, because the movements were fast and looked out of control, and the tray didn't even stay horizontal. To my surprise, however, not a single drop was spilled, and I realised she was in a trance, almost sleepwalking, and that the Unconscious was making those movements with the wisdom that only the Unconscious has. The ceremony was repeated every morning without fail, and there was never the slightest incident. Not a single drop made it out of the cup, not even when ZZ leant forward, her legs crossed, in a final reverent sweeping motion, and placed the tray elegantly into my lap.

FRIDAY 29, 03:38

A whole day spent programming. Uncalled for. Inappropriate. Inadequate. This won't do.

SATURDAY 30, 04:23

I should be in bed by now, because today I was 'up early', and it felt good to be out and about at a more respectable time. I got up at 12.30 p.m., a real record. I doubt I'll be up so early tomorrow – or indeed today, after I've been to sleep – because what with one thing and another I lost track of time, and now here I am. On the plus side, I haven't played any card games, and I didn't play any yesterday either. The nice weather helps, though it's not nice weather exactly, so much as a possible storm on the way. Apparently it's going to rain tomorrow.

I was up so early I caught the weather report on SODRE, the national radio station. You get some interesting information at the beginning, but then time passes and the woman carries on talking, and when I realised I was hearing her read out a list of the minimum temperature and the maximum temperature in every single one of the country's nineteen departments, I switched to cassette mode and listened to a tape of Piazzolla. Before that, I'd been looking for alternatives to Radio Clarín, as I have been for a few days now; since I read the Bernhard book, to be precise, which passed some – but only some – of his passion for classical music on to me. I don't have much on cassette, so the only option is SODRE. There's also a radio station called Classic, which I've been assured has almost no adverts, but it's on FM and my radio doesn't have an aerial, though it must be around somewhere, so it doesn't sound right. Besides, Classic *does* have adverts, as I've now heard for myself, and they're the sort that most get on my nerves; typical FM radio ads, with slimy presenters speaking in seductive, hypnotic tones. I won't have my unconscious infiltrated by that rubbish; no, sir.

A new advert they're running on Radio Clarín, for a kind of *mate* leaves, did as much as Bernhard to send me elsewhere. It has a horrible jingle, so ugly and inane that you lose the will to live, and sung by some unfortunates who make a living from enthusiastic renditions of that sort of trash. I've made a note of the brand in order to sabotage it; sadly I haven't been able to drink *mate* for years, ever since my aforementioned gallbladder trouble, but I can try to ensure that everyone I know steers clear of it. Anyway, I switched over to SODRE, and my apartment began filling up with strange sounds. I remembered my stay in my friends' house; unfortunately, my breakfast time there coincided with the time when my friend usually listened to SODRE, which was also the time when SODRE invariably played bleak, oppressive orchestral music. My breakfasts were tense and dramatic. My friend would come in holding the transistor radio, blasting it out at full volume, and sometimes he'd put it down near me and then wander away. I didn't want to turn it off because I assumed he was somewhere in the vicinity, listening, and that just because I couldn't see him from the kitchen it didn't mean he wasn't there. But often it did mean that, and I'd realise too late that my friend had disappeared, and sometimes even gone out, leaving me at the mercy of that depressing hullaballoo. These days I bring it on myself, but I don't have the radio as loud, for one thing, and besides, what with the adverts on Clarín and the folklore on Clarín and even most of the tangos on Clarín, I find the depressing music a little more bearable. And I don't have many other options, so I put up with it. Occasionally they play some baroque; not often enough for my liking, because I could spend all day listening to that quite contentedly. They also play pieces by Uruguayan composers and other little-known (to me) Latin Americans, and sometimes they even play a bit of Villa-Lobos, which is always enjoyable. Now and then you hear some very peculiar noises on those programmes, contemporary music whose only aim seems to be to alter your nervous system, but that makes a nice change as well. The one thing I can't tolerate is opera. And the thing I find most difficult to tolerate is orchestral music. I used to be mystified by the strange phenomenon of symphonies; I could never work out what the point of them was. A friend from Buenos Aires explained it to me once: orchestral music began when the time of kings' and queens' courts ended. It's a product of the Republic, in other words, and they have to play loudly and make plenty of noise to reach the large gatherings of people, since playing for the king in a little room and playing in a concert hall or out in the open are very different things. Naturally, the quality of the music also declined so the general public could understand it, or believe they understood it. They're essentially very simple musical forms, whose only merit is how loud they are. There are exceptions, as always; I'm a fan of *The Rite of Spring*, which, though not quite a symphony, uses all the resources of big orchestras and makes as much noise as possible. But it's creative, joyous, full of imagination and colour, not like Beethoven's clumsy crashing around, which has always reminded me of a child banging a drum at siesta time. All his music has the simple-mindedness, childish persistence and arrogance of military marches. It *is* military music, or militaristic music. Inextricably linked to Napoleon and other brutal types.

Mozart is something else. Even his most rabble-rousing works retain something of the qualities of chamber music, its freshness and imagination.

All that just to explain how today I came to be listening to the weather report, which had me on the verge of hysteria.


The widow hasn't come back. Her mourning must be over, if she really was in mourning. The dead pigeon looks less like a pigeon after all the rain, wind and sun, and more like a small heap of dark-coloured rags. Now that the sun's out, and the landscape has lost its homogeneous grey colour after days and days and days, I can see a stone on the flat roof, maybe a piece of gravel or a pebble. It's near the railings on the side facing the hotel, and the street's fairly narrow . . . in other words, it's a 'catapult's throw' away from the hotel. Judging by where it is now, it was shot from the hotel in a straight line, hit the pigeon that was on the railings and knocked it backwards onto the flat roof, a few feet from the railings. The dead pigeon is almost perfectly in line with the stone, and the place where the stone was presumably fired from the catapult.

Strangely enough, there's also a clothes peg on the flat roof. There's no washing line, as I said before, but there's a clothes peg. It's fairly empty other than that, except for the dead pigeon and the odd few feathers that have come loose from the body and ended up scattered on the ground nearby. I suppose an infinite number of tiny predators are already hard at work on the body, and that more feathers will come loose and be carried away by the wind, eventually leaving nothing but a pigeon skeleton on the roof – but I don't know if things really happen that way. Maybe there are reasons why it would be impossible for all the feathers to come out, and instead the corpse will retain the vague form of a pigeon with feathers for as long as it can, as long as no one goes onto the roof and takes it away.

My back started hurting when I was out. I noticed that my eyesight's in a very bad way, too. I don't know if the sunnier weather will be good for my eyes or not, but its first effect has been to show me the calamitous state they're in. And I realised I don't know how to walk down the street any more; I'm uncoordinated and slow to react to things. Except for my Saturdays with Chl, it's a long time since I've ventured any further afield than the couple of blocks to the supermarket.

I decided to carry out a mental examination of the pain in my back and trace its path, and I noticed straight away that my centre of balance when I walk is closer to my throat than to my pelvis, where it should be. As a result, my shoulders are too high and do lots of pointless extra work, and they also tilt forwards, which makes me stoop. It's as if I went around dangling from a hook that's attached somewhere around my upper vertebrae. So I focused on lowering my centre of gravity and relaxing my shoulders. It made a big difference: the pain vanished immediately, and I found myself walking more confidently. Later, back home, I noticed I'm forever stooping and hunching my shoulders here as well, even without my phobia of the street as an excuse. It's as if when I get up from the computer my body stays in the same position, specifically the position I'm in when I type. All afternoon and evening, I've been making sure I check my shoulders every so often and lower them if they're hunched. This has been working well, but they always go back to the forbidden position in the end. If only I could keep this in mind long enough to fix it once and for all. When I was working at the computer earlier, and when I went online for a while (no interesting findings, by the way), making the most of the fact it's the last day of the month and I won't go over my limit by more than four or five pesos, yes, even when I was sitting at the computer I remembered to keep an eye on my shoulders and lower them whenever I caught them tensing up. I also hunch, I realised this evening, when I read at mealtimes, which I invariably do. Since my eyesight's bad I wear reading glasses, and they only work for very short distances. The book gets in the way if it's too close, so instead of moving the book closer to me I move my head closer to the book, and this brings my shoulders forwards and upwards and makes me hunch. Lots of bad habits to address, but it has to be done, because when my spine gets twisted it affects my head and distorts my spatial and cenesthetic awareness, and this gives my brain the impression that I'm constantly about to fall over. It tries to correct the data but doesn't always get it right, which is why I walk everywhere so tentatively. That tightness in my back also makes me tighten my neck and clench my jaw, which in turn causes the deafness in my right ear and damages the teeth on the right side of my mouth. My neck crunches every time I turn my head.

# OCTOBER 2000

SUNDAY 1, 01:32

A horrible Saturday (and now it's Sunday). Stuffy weather, a storm brewing. I woke up with all my vertebrae stuck together and my whole body in pain, and I could feel a cold and a migraine coming on. The only good thing about the immediate aftermath of waking up was finding that the yoghurt I'd left overnight had come out perfectly. After that, nothing: mind gone, reading, computer (unproductive use, but not games), bad mood, until Chl arrived. She wasn't feeling good either but she made a huge effort to be pleasant, which by the way she managed 100 per cent. She also brought some lentil stew. Last night she gave me some *milanesas* to take home when I left her house. I'd said I wasn't going to go and see her, but when she called after her therapy there was something unusual in her voice and I could tell she'd been crying. So I thought I should go and keep her company for a bit, and it was worth my while. Today, by which I mean yesterday, after hours and hours of doing nothing, we went to look at the reduced-price books and then to the *boliche*. I thought, 'Please let there not be any more Maugham books. I'm sick of him, but if there's one I haven't read I'll have to buy it and read it, and I really am sick of him,' and as soon as we arrived Chl pounced on a book and presented it to me triumphantly: Maugham, something by him I hadn't heard of. I bought it, of course. I also bought three short books by Edgar Wallace. I've been saying bad things about him recently, but since I'd run out of unread detective novels it seemed like a good idea to stock up. I also bought a book by Chesterton; I've read it before, more than once, but I can't remember anything about it. It seems to contain four short novels or long short stories, collected under the title *Four Faultless Felons*. A dreadful Plaza edition, one of the old ones, with small print and uneven ink; it doesn't even have a contents page. But I couldn't resist, especially because I'm reading another book by Chesterton at the moment, one Chl bought a few weeks ago, *The Man Who Knew Too Much*, which I've also read once before, or more than once, though I don't remember much about it. And it's very entertaining. That was it: slim pickings. When Chl left I remembered that my body was in pain, that I could feel a cold and a migraine coming on and that my mind was gone. But I didn't play any card games. Since I'd been so well behaved with my internet use in September, reducing my bill by a third, and since this is a new month and everything's back to zero again, after midnight I went online. Not only was there nothing interesting to be found, but Netscape also performed a strange operation and stopped working. I had to open Explorer, which I don't like, and since it's not configured properly it filled up with cookies. I was going round in circles for half an hour, and eventually I gave up and shut everything down. Now I'm going to have a cup of tea, and then hopefully get an early night.

MONDAY 2, 03:30

I'm writing by hand, and only to stick to my resolution of writing a few lines every day. Yesterday, or rather the day before yesterday, I finished reading what I've written of this diary so far. I have to say, the more recent parts are a little more sophisticated; they make for more enjoyable reading and come a bit closer to what you might call literary language.

Another day of muscle pain and distraction, or rather what my doctor, who called in late last night, described as [a word I can't remember right now, a synonym of 'splitting'; she used a more technical psychiatric term]. Chl came before that. Her PMT was in overdrive, but she's always a delight. Today her radiant beauty was enhanced by two equally delightful Tupperware containers full of *milanesas*. My freezer is packed: bread, *milanesas*, stew. What more could I ask for in life?

But now I'm rambling. I'll just mention that the computer was turned on for most of the day. I didn't receive a single email. I turned one of my Visual Basic programs into another, which will tell me whenever I'm straying from the schedule I set myself for using the computer. Because today I woke up furious at my addiction; I'd gone to bed furious the night before and I woke up furious after spending the small hours, and much of the morning, dreaming – and thinking – about a program that would close Windows at a specified time. In the end I opted for a less aggressive system, because having Windows close automatically after a series of strict, draconian warnings has never helped me much; in situations like that, I generally rebel. This program, which is very advanced, will simply show me a little box with a friendly reminder that I'm trying to detox. I'm not sure if it'll work, but I owe it to myself to try. I'm still doing everything I can, as with the difficult, even arduous task of paying attention to my shoulders. Every now and then I remember and lower them to their natural position. Yesterday, or rather today, I was able to go to sleep without the back and kidney pain of recent days. The body responds quickly, and very positively, to the slightest effort to improve.

Anyway, this stuffy, humid weather is to blame for my muscle pain and general discomfort. They say tomorrow the storm will finally come.

FRIDAY 6, 22:48

I won't explain why I haven't come near this diary in so long, because I don't know the reason myself. The truth is, I stopped writing the day after the night I finished reading what I'd written so far. Maybe reading it all through like that put me off; not because I think nothing written here is worth reading, or because I think the narrative only very rarely reaches an acceptable standard – I never had high hopes about that – but rather, perhaps, because of the thought of the huge number of pages I've accumulated, and which I now need to work on, neatening some sections up and developing others, making edits and cuts and additions. And I don't really feel like doing all that.

I do, however, want to record my efforts to escape my computer addiction and improve my sleep patterns. Today I turned the computer off at 7 p.m. In the six days of October so far, on average I've used it for a little more than three hours a day, whereas in previous months it was never under five and a half. But that average of three and a bit hours will keep going down, because now I've finished the program that's taken up the most screen time in recent days – the very program, in fact, that will tell me when it's time to turn off the computer, based on the day and the circumstances. Today I got up at 2 p.m., which, after a Thursday of workshops, is enormous progress. We'll see how things develop. At the moment I'm having severe withdrawal symptoms. Sometimes I feel very weak, and I can't think clearly at all.

SUNDAY 8, 04:11

I went over the limit with the computer, but it was a Saturday (now it's Sunday) and on Saturdays and Sundays I'm more lenient. The fact is, there were about a thousand things I was desperate to do on the computer. That's OK. Tomorrow, or rather today, Sunday, I need to turn it off at 5 p.m. It'll be tough . . . but I have to persevere with this for a while, until the habit fades.

The Saturday ritual took place at the usual time, or indeed slightly before the usual time, because I've gained some extra waking hours now that I'm getting up a bit earlier. Not much earlier, but enough to be able to see the sun and notice the difference between this month and the previous ones. Sometimes I can't believe how long I spent locked in that prison.

Yesterday (Friday, I mean) I had time to phone my cousin; he left me an answerphone message about ten days ago, and I hadn't been able to get to the phone at a reasonable hour to call him back. And you need plenty of time to spare if you want to talk to my cousin; he doesn't share my phobia of telephones in the slightest and can rabbit on for hours, the way women do. When you try to suggest that you're busy and need to hang up, he works in yet more topics of conversation. Ever since we were much younger, he's been introducing me to his friends by saying, 'This is my crazy cousin,' and I introduce him in turn with exactly the same words. Although we're very different in lots of ways, I'm sure we have a very similar psychological make-up. For now, what differentiates us is what you might call our awareness of the illness; my cousin almost completely lacks that awareness, and is convinced his problems are caused by things that have nothing to do with him, such as the situation in the country, and perhaps a set of circumstances that have come together by chance just to annoy him. I'm aware of what's wrong with me and I fight against it – unsuccessfully, most of the time, though with the odd transient or temporary victory. But I carry on being aware of it, even if I can't overcome it. I wonder how long this awareness will last, and these partial victories which, though fleeting, let me keep doing what I need to do to survive. It's very likely that before too long I'll find myself with no solution, restricting myself more and more by the day, and without a clue where my problems come from.

And now I'm in the midst of this battle against my computer addiction. My theory is that if I can gradually beat the habit, I'll recover some of my faculties, and more importantly my waking hours – productive waking hours, I mean, at times of the day when I can share them with other people.

## MONDAY 9, 00:20

I managed to update my schedule for the week, print it out and turn the computer off again; eight minutes in total. While I was at it, I checked the graph of my screen time; it's still a bit high for my liking, but it's dropped considerably, from five hours a day to three hours and fifty-six minutes, so four. Come to think of it, I wonder if this program, which I made myself, has an error in the process it uses to calculate the average. We're eight days into October, and if my average is four hours a day, the total number of hours should be thirty-two. However, quickly adding up the number of hours each day gave me a total of twenty-four, which should mean an average of three hours a day rather than four. And now here I am, writing about the world of the computer as a way of overcoming my withdrawal symptoms. The world of the computer is even appearing in my dreams; before waking up this afternoon, I dreamed repeatedly about a particular operation in Visual Basic. It involved one line of a program that was meant to delete a file when I ran it. But the line contained a contradiction, because right there within it was a command to recreate the same file. I ran that line, or that program which consisted of a single line, over and over again, and I was always amazed when nothing changed. I couldn't find where in that line the second command was, the one which invalidated the first. I realise now that, in the dream, I wasn't trying to change the line because deep down I wasn't sure if I really wanted to delete the file, and I'd probably added the second command just in case I regretted what the first command had done. This is surely a sign from the highest part of my unconscious, showing me that my ambivalence about something is making me ineffective or, worse, making me waste my energy repeating, over and over, some contradictory actions that don't change anything, don't lead anywhere and are therefore completely pointless. I'll sit down and have a go at analysing this message soon. But now I want to talk about another repetitive dream, or fragment of a dream, which I had before the one I've just described. I was working in what looked like a kind of laboratory (there were lots of tiled walls and glass doors), doing a not particularly important job; perhaps I was an errand boy or lab assistant. At one point, my boss, a man in a lab coat to my left, whom I couldn't identify or even see clearly, passed me a little tray and told me to take it to . . . I don't know where, another part of the same building. The tray (or round plate, perhaps) had some square slices of bread on it, like bread for sandwiches with the crusts removed (I don't know how many slices there were, but I think it was more than one, or only one but accompanied by other things). One of the slices, if there were more than one, had a kind of cream spread on it, or something that might have been ricotta. I walked down a corridor with the plate or tray, and then suddenly, for no discernible reason and with no right to do so, I grabbed the slice of bread with the spread on it and greedily wolfed it down. Immediately afterwards it somehow came to my knowledge, whether from the taste or because someone told me, that what was on the bread wasn't cream or ricotta but a bacterial culture. I was disconcerted. I didn't understand why I'd eaten it, and for a few seconds I worried I was infected with what might turn out to be a horrible disease, but then I reassured myself by reasoning, not entirely convincingly, that my gastric juices would soon take care of the germs, dissolving them with no trouble at all. And then the whole scene was repeated, and once again I ate the bread. With every repetition of the scene, my feeling of disgust increased.

I'm finding this Rotring I refilled yesterday quite difficult to write with.

## MONDAY 9, 01:07

I took the Rotring apart again, thinking I'd add a few drops of alcohol to the ink. When I'd dismantled it, I saw it was almost empty, meaning I didn't refill it with enough ink last night. So I added a few drops of alcohol using a cotton bud, and then I added some more ink. When I'd screwed the end with the metal nib back on, a few drops of ink came out and stained my left hand, but not my jumper. While I was doing all that, I realised that in the drawer where I keep the Rotring ink I still have the Staedtler I used to write the 'luminous novel'. It's incredible how these items of stationery have survived so many losses, so many moves, so many ruptures – so many lives lived, in short. The same goes for my texts. Writing and writing implements are evidently the only things I look after. In terms of my texts, all I've lost are a few I wrote during that stay with my friends, or on the days I spent at Chl's house. I'm particularly annoyed to have lost the account of a dream which wove together many of the key elements from that period. But I'm not sure these pages are really lost. I have a feeling they might turn up at any moment, when I'm looking for something else.

And what did I achieve by refilling the Rotring? Nothing to speak of. I managed to write the date and time fluently, impeccably, but that was it. Then it started to work the same way it always has done, or perhaps less well. I've asked Chl to buy me a new one. I don't want to use the Staedtler; I remember only too well all the trouble it caused me, how I was forever having to take it apart and clean it, and how an extremely fine needle inside the metal nib – which was obviously what allowed it to write at all – invariably used to get bent.

I refuse to go on writing with this crap.

MONDAY 9, 04:57

It's very simple: the contradictory line of the program (in my dream) was none other than a cybernetic representation, a cybernetic metaphor, for what I've been calling 'Sisyphus'. I haven't been thinking about it all this time; I only remembered now, while I was cleaning my teeth before bed. This very day, I started tidying up some books and magazines that were covering most of the floor in my library, and among many other things I found a bound collection, and one loose edition, of *Little Lulu*, and started reading them all. I also found lots of the puzzle magazines I worked on as editor-in-chief. In a special edition of one, there was a photo of me, the owners and all my contributors. And there were also photos of some of the freelance contributors, many of whom I'd recruited from among the readers. And in one *Humor & Juegos* magazine, I came across a puzzle I'd been telling Chl about a few hours ago – 'The Disappearing Chinaman', actually called 'Get Off the Earth', by Sam Loyd. Tomorrow I'll scan it and try to make it work. It's not easy to figure out the trick; if you turn one disc a certain number of degrees over the other, just twelve of the original thirteen Chinamen are left.

I'm writing in green ink that's too runny, and my handwriting's very misshapen because I'm writing so fast. But it's better than that pen I refilled, which, what's more, I've now thrown away.


PS: I'm trying to say that the dream is showing me I've got a contradictory 'line' in my mind, which makes me take a step back whenever I take a step forward. I need to look into this further.


TUESDAY 10, 01:03

I'm bored. It's embarrassing to admit it, to admit it to myself, but it's true. I've never been able to understand people who get bored, and I always wind them up by saying it only happens to boring people. But today it's happened to me. Maybe I'm a boring person. For five years I've been building this deadly trap for myself, transferring my interests one by one into that miraculous machine. Now it has almost my whole life inside it, and now it's switched off. Since yesterday, Monday, at 6.30 p.m. (yes, I went a few minutes over the limit, but there were reasons for that; I had to prepare a printout of some graphs to show my doctor, graphs and other data that ultimately led to a break in the use of the antidepressants in my treatment, because they haven't caused any significant reduction in my daily intake of cigarettes) (17.3, compared to 19 in the months prior to the treatment) (approximately 2 per cent, after two and a half months) (it's true there are other advantages to the treatment, which I won't go into here, but I think my doctor's decision is the right one) (on a separate point, my blood pressure seems to have remained stable: 14/8).

As I was saying, I'm bored, and now seems like a good time to analyse this condition a little. The boredom is mixed with something stronger, something that hits me every so often like a gust of wind and brings with it a kind of panic or extreme desolation; as if everything were going to lose all meaning from one moment to the next. At those times, my eyes drift towards where the computer is. I can't see the computer, because there's a wall in the way, but I'm in no doubt about the intention behind that movement because, as well as my eyes moving, something moves within my chest. It's similar to that feeling of being torn apart I once had when I was getting out of Chl's car. Less extreme than that, needless to say, but painful nonetheless. At the same time, I notice that most of my thoughts are still drawn to the computer, to the language of programming, and more generally to anything with the slightest relation to the machine. So far I've resisted the urge to turn it on, though I have good reasons to do so (various practical matters); I decided it could wait until later, in the permitted time window (from eight in the morning until midnight; tomorrow, because it's Tuesday and I have the virtual workshop, I allow myself more time, as I do on Saturdays).

I wouldn't say I regret this pathological relationship I've entered into with the computer. I do, however, think this kind of relationship has more than served its purpose by now, and it's time to change it for another. Unfortunately, it seems impossible to detach myself from the computer completely, to go without it from now on. That would also be a silly thing to do. I have no reason to cut myself off from my email correspondents, no reason to return to writing laboriously on a mechanical typewriter, no reason to go through the onerous process of making carbon copies every time I change something, or – my God, the very idea! – to deprive myself of that magnificent cornucopia of nude Japanese girls. Or to deprive myself of an electronic secretary that never fails to remind me of what I have to do and when I've arranged to see my friends. I must, however, discipline all the things that have disciplined me so effectively, and overpower the force that has overpowered me.

Here I am, then, bored, like any office worker on a day off; my once splendid inner world seems empty. Not a hint of the spirit; not a hint of an image; no hope of relaxing, of enjoying the sensation of being in touch with myself, of feeling as if 'the spirit of the mind' is linked to the 'spirit of the body and now they cannot be separated' (Tao Te Ching). That reassuring warmth of the self. I lost all these faculties years ago; now, if I try to get them back, either I'm seized with anxiety or I fall asleep.

But I'll have to persevere. Perhaps I won't succeed today, or tomorrow, or the next day, but eventually I'll get there. All thanks to Mr Guggenheim, whose generosity has allowed me to embark on this adventure, this rescue mission. I wasn't planning it when I applied for the grant; back then I didn't know I'd lost anything. Only now do I realise the full extent of the catastrophe. Which, as I said, didn't begin yesterday, or five or even ten years ago. Meaning that if it can be cured, this cure won't come today, or tomorrow, or the day after.


WEDNESDAY 11, 02:12

I have a new Rotring, or rather two new Rotrings. I reached the place that sells them just in time; it was about to close, but I made it. And then I went to the barbershop, which by some miracle was also open, and had my hair cut, since it was getting absurdly long. My beard's already grown back, of course. And my nails. You can't keep on top of everything at once. I got up, and before I'd even washed my face, got dressed or had breakfast, I turned on the computer and dealt with a few practical matters, which I had reminders about all over my screen (bits of paper stuck on with Scotch removable magic tape), and I also checked my email and replied to the things I absolutely couldn't put off. No games or distractions, no trance. I also confirmed that the procedure for calculating my average hours of screen time was working perfectly; who knows what happened when it calculated four hours that time, who knows what was going wrong, but the current correct average is two hours and thirty-four minutes per day, almost exactly what I thought it would be. My average screen time per day has gone down by half. I don't think I need to worry about reducing it any further; if everything carries on like this, the average will fall a little more, but that's not my aim. I think an average of two and a half hours is good going, at least at this stage. If I can keep it up then I'll decide later, based on how I feel and how much I reasonably need to use the computer, if I need to cut down any more.

Today, contrary to my expectations, I didn't manage to type up a single line of this diary, and now I'm a few days behind. But its time will come, I'm sure. I couldn't fit it in today because I decided to go for a walk before it got dark instead. I ate all my meals calmly, reading as usual: my breakfast, my lunch-dinner, or almost-dinner, and my actual dinner. That meant a lot of time stolen from the computer, and I'm surprised by how relaxed I feel about it. Chl also came for her visit. When there was an hour to go before midnight, which is switching-off time, I made my actual dinner, and by the time I got to the computer there were only fifteen minutes left. Among other things, I dealt with the virtual workshop and prepared the menu of virtual workshop options for the people who've finished the first course. All that made me over-run a bit, and then, I confess, I let myself get sidetracked and fell into a trance. My transgression lasted until 1.15 a.m. The night, the early hours, is always the most difficult time; at night my willpower is weaker than ever and disappears very easily. A transgression of not much more than an hour, though still a transgression, is also a big step forward. For years I've found it impossible to turn the computer off at night, and often I've stayed in a trance until after the sun's come up. I'm enjoying getting back a few hours of natural light and overcoming the difficulties I'd been having (stupid difficulties, perhaps, but insurmountable until a few days ago) with buying things I need, like the pens, or getting my hair cut. Some satisfying things happened yesterday too: I made it to the second-hand bookstall on the corner in time, which I've only managed on three or four occasions in the past year. I found two Colette novels and a horrible novel by Edgar Wallace; horrible or not, I raced through it yesterday from cover to cover. I was suffering from severe withdrawal symptoms and it was a blessing to have something really, genuinely silly to distract me. I've looked down on Edgar Wallace my whole life, and in the past month I've read four or five of his books. Because I've never taken him seriously before, they're all new to me.

The real surprise when it comes to my recent reading was *Sivainvi* (an awful Spanish translation of *VALIS*), a novel by Philip K. Dick. In it, Dick combines science fiction with autobiographical details that are clearly real, and it's less a novel than a philosophical-religious treatise of the first order. I was surprised to find that several of Dick's experiences resemble things that have happened to me, although in his case the experiences went much, much further. Still, some of his conclusions are similar to mine, although there, too, he goes much further than I do. I'm infinitely glad never to have tried drugs of any kind (except for some authorised ones, like tobacco). I don't think I would have survived experiences as extreme as Philip Dick's. Although neither did he, I suppose. Anyway, it's very enjoyable to read things which, in a sense, put one's own madness into perspective.

By the way: today I didn't feel any bad effects from skipping the antidepressants. The plan is to take them every other day for a while, but if I carry on without any upsets I may well start forgetting to take them at all, especially because my program that tells me what day and time to take them isn't capable, because I didn't think about this when I made it, of reminding me to take something every other day.

I've written a lot with this pen now. It's very smooth. A pleasure to write with.


WEDNESDAY 11, 17:15

Since the very early days of my computer addiction, I've been convinced that my dialogue with the machine is, deep down, a narcissistic monologue. A way of looking at myself in the mirror. This diary is also a kind of narcissistic monologue, though in my opinion it doesn't have the same pathological connotations as my dialogue with the computer. I don't mean it doesn't have any pathological connotations at all, but it also has a few positive effects that somehow balance things out. In my dialogue with the computer, however – in that it's compulsive in nature – there are practically no positive aspects that could work as a counterweight.

This is on my mind because last night, or rather early this morning, with the computer turned off and my diaristic duties complete, instead of going to bed I found myself drawn to the magazine *Cruzadas*. Over the past few days I've been organising my library, which I think means I'm finally 'taking possession' of this apartment, a year and a half after moving in; that is, over these days I've resumed the moving-in process that was put on hold by Chl's trip. And so all these books and magazines have been appearing, among them a huge collection of science magazines (mostly Spanish editions of *Scientific American*, which Gandolfo left me when he went to Buenos Aires; they were really fascinating, but I stopped reading them when the monologue-dialogue with the computer began to swallow me up) and some copies, supposedly duplicates, of the magazines I was in charge of during my Buenos Aires office-work adventure. Including, of course, *Cruzadas*, which was practically my own personal creation. A couple of nights ago I picked up a copy and tried to solve some of the puzzles, which made me feel faintly anxious for reasons it's not difficult to identify. I left huge pieces of myself in that magazine over the three years. And not just in the magazine, but in the city as well. The whole Buenos Aires package threatened to come crashing down and squash me, just like the Montevidean package in Buenos Aires and Colonia, and even in Montevideo itself, where I still can't bring myself to venture beyond a few familiar and carefully defined routes. Yesterday I found a photo of my contributors, the owners and me in a special edition of *Cruzadas*, and a series of photos of the freelancers. It was chilling to realise that some of them are now dead. And many are buried in my memory.

Early this morning, then, instead of going to bed, I thought I'd have a quick look through some issues of *Cruzadas*. I did a couple of crosswords, and then turned almost automatically to the letters to the editor. But the issue was from a time when I no longer dealt with the letters. That didn't do it for me, so I looked for the bound collection. I came across one of the letters I'd written myself, and there I stayed, locked in the cycle, in the narcissistic monologue, and unable to get out. I read, one by one, all the pages of all the letters to the editor with responses written by me, and then I found another volume of the collection . . . and so it went on, until seven in the morning. When I emerged from my trance I realised that the sun was already most of the way up, poking out from one side of the Palacio Salvo. And that I'd left all the living-room lights on. And that I'd been on my feet for hours, with my back all twisted, in the worst possible reading position, completely engrossed in the hidden past that was gradually coming into view. I was remembering every single reader (especially the women) with whom I'd exchanged letters, and the physical environment in which I'd spent my working hours. I even found a letter from a reader who'd included a few paragraphs in code at the end, a message with the letters swapped, something like CBJHF XFR. And I found my response, in the same code. What did those cryptograms mean? I decided to solve them, and some time later I was able to read what the reader had written, as well as my reply.

That whole section of my past is a cryptogram I need to decipher. The narcissistic monologue is working on a higher level. I mustn't condemn it or reject it as pure pathology, because there are many different routes back to where I need to go. And I mustn't forget that where there's no narcissism there can be no art, and no artist.

WEDNESDAY 11, 21:11

On the roof next door, the pigeon's corpse has been getting flatter and more misshapen in the rain, wind and sun, and perhaps also with the passing of time. A couple of days ago, looking over from my bedroom window, I wondered if I would have guessed it had once been a pigeon if I hadn't seen it before, in its original form. Other pigeons, however, seem to recognise it immediately. I haven't seen any more visitors to the roof since I last mentioned the dead pigeon in this diary; what I did see,

not without some alarm, was a pigeon perched on the railings facing
the hotel, more or less exactly where the deceased pigeon must have
been when it was struck down. But there's been no sign of the widow,
or of any other pigeons in the vicinity of the corpse. That's why I was
surprised this afternoon, when I lifted the blinds, to see that another
pigeon had appeared. I didn't think it was the widow, though it was a
similar dark colour, a blackish shade of grey – as you'd expect from a
widow. But this pigeon looked bigger, which probably meant it was
male rather than female, although, when it comes to these things, all
I have to go on is conjecture and extrapolation. And I was even more
surprised when this presumed male pigeon suddenly broke out into
a frenzied courtship dance around the corpse. I'd just got dressed and
hadn't had any breakfast; I was keen to have some and get on with my
day, since my monumental all-nighter meant I'd woken up very late
and had a lot to do before it was time to turn the computer off (6.15
p.m.) and start my yoga class (7 p.m.). But I couldn't stop watching
the strange spectacle of what I believed was a male pigeon, courting
what I believed was another male pigeon, who was, let's not forget,
dead and decomposing. The suitor's little dance was brief and violent,
as if prompted by uncontrollable sexual passion; but then, faced with
the immobility of the object of desire, the lack of any response, he
broke off abruptly and seemed plunged into a terrible confusion.
An occasional light breeze fluttered a feather here and there, on the
corpse and on the paving stones where a few were scattered, small and
white. That movement seemed to be the main cause of the suitor's
confusion, since although it wasn't the ideal response it was at least
a sign of activity, and therefore, he must have thought, of life. And
so, faced with this dilemma, all the suitor could do was walk up and
down, like someone pacing nervously to and fro with his hands clasped
behind his back, his mind working keenly to solve some urgent problem or reach a decision. Up and down he walked, and then suddenly
he jumped onto the dead pigeon like someone climbing onto a small
promontory, the better to survey the landscape. He walked around
on top of the body, turning in circles, pirouetting, stamping his feet.
Then he hopped back down onto the paving stones and walked a bit
more, shaking his head slightly the whole time as if to express serious

doubt, a total inability to believe what was happening. A gust of wind, a slight ripple of feathers and the suitor was up once again, stamping his feet, turning in circles, until suddenly, with his back to me, still on top of the corpse, he made a few frantic movements of copulation. He must have reached orgasm almost immediately, because he quickly detached himself from what had once been the object of his desire and flew away. I thought: 'Now this poor dead pigeon has seen it all.' I also thought: 'Please don't let that happen to me when I die.'

I took a long time making breakfast and had just got everything ready when I realised I'd forgotten something, I don't remember what, and went back to the bedroom. I couldn't help glancing out of the window at the sunny evening and, my God, what do I see but the necrophiliac male pigeon back for more. This time he was less frantic, though still confused and hesitant. He walked around the corpse, walked over the top of it, stamped on it; all more sedately than before, but the ritual was the same. Then he climbed down from the dead pigeon and stood to one side of it. He pecked among the feathers on his chest, and then pecked at the feathers of the corpse, probably on its wing, which is still lying outstretched. A small white feather appeared in the live pigeon's beak. The operation was repeated various times. For a second I thought maybe he'd started eating the corpse, but then I realised that wasn't what was going on, or at least it didn't seem to be. Another little white feather appeared in his beak. Then, I don't know in what order, he walked around the body, stood on top of it, strode around a bit more up there and then got back down and stood next to it again. In the meantime, another, considerably bigger and more aggressive male pigeon arrived, whiter and with iridescent blue-green feathers around its neck (a kind of pigeon that for some reason I dislike more than all the others), and began its own courtship dance. The previous suitor beat a hasty retreat. The new male was left in charge of the situation, but he wasn't interested in the corpse; the object of his desire was clearly the other male pigeon, if he really was a male pigeon, because by this point in proceedings I'd stopped understanding or trying to understand or believing I understood what was happening. The supposed male took a few turns around the roof and left. I went to have my breakfast, feeling a little queasy.

THURSDAY 12, 02:55

The bookbinder. Now it comes back to me. If I'm not mistaken, the *Cruzadas* magazines that had me on my feet all yesterday morning were bound (in four volumes with twenty issues in each) by a bookbinder in the city of Colonia. And if I'm not mistaken here either, his surname was Saavedra. At least, I remember associating it with *Don Quixote* at the time, and it seems unlikely he was called Cervantes. Or Alonso, or Quijano. It must have been Saavedra. When I dropped the collection of magazines off, my heart in my mouth, I told him that under no circumstances was he to guillotine them – a reprehensible practice among bookbinders. It's not often, at least in this part of the world, that two issues of a magazine are exactly the same size or have the same margins. Perhaps things are different these days, with technological progress (so-called technological progress, Bernhard would say), but when I was at *Cruzadas* that kind of precision was by no means to be expected. What's more, the first issues of the magazine were decidedly bigger; not until issue fourteen (and I joined the publishing company when they were preparing issue thirteen) did the owners realise that if they reduced the size slightly, they could save a lot of paper and also print two issues simultaneously, which was another considerable saving. It was an economically sound decision, but a catastrophic one in terms of the quality of the magazine. Those missing square inches meant we had to make the games and the font size smaller, leaving everything much more cluttered and awkward. Before, a standard crossword, with clues, would take up one page, whereas after the size changed it took up a page and a bit. To return to the bookbinder: when I told him not to guillotine the magazines, he looked disapproving and protested. I told him it was a crucial point and not up for negotiation; I didn't want guillotined magazines. If he didn't think he could do the work perfectly under such conditions, I'd take the magazines back home with me. But as for guillotining them: certainly not. Finally we reached an agreement and I left them with him.

He guillotined them. Not only were the issues before number fourteen horrifically mutilated, but plenty more had incomplete pages, sliced up in absurd and unnecessary ways. I felt enormously sad. It was a real crime, and completely stupid. There was no way I could build up the same collection again. It would have to stay like that. And stay like that it did. I could gladly have strangled that bookbinder, but sometimes the law isn't fair.

Saavedra, I think he was called.

THURSDAY 12, 18:18

I'm writing in Word while I wait for Julia to arrive, and unfortunately I have no time to do justice to a topic so extremely, immeasurably important as the dream I had this morning, or the other, less important topic of the recent developments in the pigeon saga.

I dreamed about a DOS program, which is easily explained by the fact I was thinking about it when I fell asleep. I'd had a strange bout of insomnia, even though it was late, and was feeling restless and a little on edge, so I decided to think about something computer-related. My topic of choice was a program I've acquired that removes unnecessary files, and is meant to work in DOS and not Windows. In the dream, I ran a line of the program and somehow the program told me that, before continuing, I had to go to the far end of an empty plot of land, something like the garden of the house I lived in for two years in Colonia. But it wasn't very clear where the far end was, and my vision was restricted (for example, I couldn't see the whole of a very large tree, only part of it, and I couldn't see where it ended on either side). In that garden there was a kind of work surface, presumably set up against the far side, with a machine on top that may have been the computer. Before I reached it, I came to a bushy tree, a pine; I could only see the bottom part, and in particular one branch that was much larger than the others. This branch extended from the tree towards what could have been the other end of the plot of land. It was around six to ten feet long and emerged from the trunk at a height of about five feet, or a little more, and then sloped smoothly down until it almost touched the grass that carpeted the ground. That part of the pine tree, and that branch in particular, were at the centre of some feverish, noisy activity; insects and vermin coming and going, a constant industrious buzzing. There were birds there as well, at least two; one had a red breast, or was entirely red, with very thin feathers arranged like pins in a pincushion, though much closer together. It had a fairly small body, and it seemed benevolent. In the dream I knew the name of this type of bird, which wasn't a robin. The branch stretched towards what I saw as the front, and to the left. On the ground, near the end of the branch, was another dark-coloured bird, which I vaguely identify as a quail, although I think quails are normally bigger. When it saw me, the bird moved, running a little way as if getting ready to take off, but then it stopped and remained in a rather threatening pose, waiting to see what I did next. I could see plenty of insects and flies coming and going, too; perhaps also honeybees and bumblebees, and some biggish white insects that crawled up and down the trunk and along the branch; and some ants, of course. I thought I could make out some slightly larger insects scuttling around in the grass, too. Something told me the place was dangerous, especially because of that quail-like bird. It seemed wise not to keep walking in that direction and to instead take a detour to get back to the computer. A lot more happened in the dream, both before and after this, but I don't remember any of it. I woke up to go to the bathroom (I'd taken a second half-dose of antihypertensives the evening before), and my mood was somewhere between frightened and happy. 'This is none other than Life itself,' I thought, feeling that my abstinence from the computer was beginning to derobotise me. And then I thought: 'Life is always dangerous.'

When I woke up again, after some other dreams I don't remember very clearly, featuring a woman of considerable erotic appeal who lived in an apartment and a fat, old Jewish man who wanted that apartment for himself, or who was the landlord; when I woke up, as I was saying, I thought about the tree dream again. The visual and auditory images were very powerful, as was the feeling it gave me, that mixture of elation and fear. When I got up some time later, a deeper and more mysterious interpretation occurred to me. I went to get the Bible, turned to Genesis, and read:

3:22–24. And the Lord God said, Behold, the man is become as one of us, to know good and evil; and now, lest he put forth his hand, and take also of the tree of life, and eat, and live forever: Therefore the Lord God sent him forth from the garden of Eden, to till the ground from whence he was taken. So he drove out the man; and he placed east of the garden of Eden Cherubims, and a flaming sword which turned every way, to keep the way of the tree of life.

Those birds in the dream could well have been two cherubim, and the long branch teeming with life the flaming sword. They achieved their mission of keeping me away from the tree, at least.

## THURSDAY 12, 19:18

Computer off (on the Thursdays when I don't have workshops, the limit is 7 p.m., but today I switched it off at six forty-five because my friend was due to arrive at any moment, although incidentally she still isn't here. And fifty minutes is a long time to be late by, even in this country).

Pigeons: today I raised the blinds and didn't see anything unusual, but a while ago, at around 5.30 p.m., when I was in a hurry to leave and changing out of my sandals and into my shoes, I saw the blackish pigeon, the necrophiliac from yesterday, appear. He repeated most of the same rituals as last time, though with no visible erotic connotations. He was calmer, but looked worried and rather unsure of himself the whole time. He strutted around, stood on the corpse's chest and walked in circles in both directions, then paused on the head and pecked at the chest, pulling out some little white feathers. Maybe he was eating something, I don't know. Then he stood on its chest again but with his back to me (he has a little white mark, perhaps a sticking-out feather, where the ends of his dark wings meet when they're folded). I couldn't see exactly what he was doing, but his movements suggested he was pecking the dead pigeon in the head. Maybe he was trying to bring it back to life with beak-to-beak resuscitation. Maybe he was eating it. Maybe he was eating the little creatures that are no doubt swarming around in its feathers. Who knows; but he was pecking away for a long time without stopping, and with great dedication. Then he got down and stood next to the corpse, on one of the paving stones, not doing anything, completely motionless. I stopped watching at that point and went to get on with my day. I wonder if that dark-coloured pigeon is the one I originally called 'the widow', only older; it's entirely possible she was a young pigeon back then, still at an age where she was growing. Or maybe I thought she was smaller than she was. I wonder if it's male or female, and I wonder what sex the corpse is. Everything seemed so clear until the presumed male pigeon with the iridescent neck came along yesterday and messed up all my interpretations. Do you get homosexual pigeons? How do pigeons work out the sex of other pigeons? When you're as ignorant as I am, it's unwise to draw conclusions about the phenomena you observe.

My original aim in going out was to find some good-quality corn oil (Argentinian, or failing that Brazilian), because I think the kind I'm using is what's making me so sleepy immediately after my lunch-dinner. If I eat just one *milanesa*, it's fine, but if I eat a *milanesa* and a salad (and I always put a lot of oil on salads), then I'm seized by an almost insurmountable tiredness. I generally have a longish nap in one of the armchairs. I'm suspicious of the oil. It may be Argentinian, but it still passes through the hands of a Uruguayan oil company, and it occurs to me that it might undergo some kind of modification, some kind of adulteration, in the process. I get this idea from an experience I had many years ago, when I was consumed by tiredness in the afternoons, after a lunch which, in those days, I used to eat at a fairly conventional hour. A friend of mine saw a bottle of the oil I was using on the table and said, 'You're going to kill yourself. You can't use Uruguayan oil.' I followed his advice and set about sourcing some Argentinian corn oil, and have never used anything else since. I've annoyed plenty of travelling friends over the years by asking them to bring me oil. But it's worked, because I've had no more trouble with that post-lunch somnolence until now. Today, then, I went to a shop not far from here which claims to sell imported 'delicacies'; but that claim seems to be a thing of the past, because I found largely the same products you'd find anywhere else. The corn oil they sell there is the same one I'm using. They didn't have any exotic brands of coffee, either.

On the way home, although I was in a rush, I had an urge to stop by the second-hand bookstall. I think my telepathic connection is now reaching too many minds, because both times I've felt that urge I've found books the seller knows I'm interested in (namely detective novels from the Rastros series; that's the only thing he knows about my tastes at the moment, but on those two occasions he didn't fail me). My friend is here!

SATURDAY 14, 02:15

An exhausting day. Action-packed. Every part of my body is in pain, but it was worth it.

1) I got up at an almost reasonable hour.

2) I turned the computer on, loaded my email and made a few practical notes in the relevant programs.

3) I read a detective novel over breakfast (the second of the Rastros books I bought; both terrible) and went through my usual routines.

4) I looked out of the window; nothing interesting taking place on the flat roof next door.

5) I let myself be seduced by the computer for seventy minutes. I stuck videos together and moved files onto the ZIP disks. Meanwhile, I thought about all the things I had to do and summoned up my courage; I think I started playing on the computer because of my phobias, since the things I had to do would have to be done outside the house.

6) I went to the ATM and withdrew two hundred of Mr Guggenheim's dollars.

7) I went to the currency exchange and changed the two hundred dollars.

8) Without going back home, I took a taxi to the corner of Juncal and Sarandí. I went to a furniture shop (where they sell cheap and thoroughly average furniture; Chl found me the address, and even a card showing the prices of the shelving units I wanted to buy).

9) I looked at the shelves. I didn't like them. I bought them anyway. I left a small deposit so they'd keep them aside for me, and they promised to deliver them to my apartment by 7 p.m.

10) I strolled another couple of blocks, in the mood to carry on walking and looking for things I needed. Ideally I would have walked all the way home, because I felt disoriented and slow-witted in the street and wanted to push myself, but the maid was at home doing an extra bit of work, a deep clean of one room, which is something I try to have done twice a month. I had to get back before she left so I could pay her. I could have paid her before going out, but I didn't because I would have had to hurry back anyway, for a dentist's appointment at 8 p.m. And I wanted to have something to eat before going to the dentist, because he was definitely going to give me an anaesthetic, and who knew how long I'd have to wait to eat again after that.

11) I took a taxi home. The driver was very young and talked nineteen to the dozen, comparing how much gets done in other countries with how slowly things move here: buildings that have been unfinished for years, etc. He had a long, thick pencil protruding from his right ear (to clarify: not actually sticking out of his ear, but rather resting in the place where his ear met his head, and held there by the top part of his ear).

12) I got home and found everything in order, and no messages on the answerphone.

13) I telephoned through an order to the supermarket.

14) I began preparing my lunch: a *milanesa* from the freezer (there aren't many left, and Chl won't make me any more for a while), heated up in the microwave, and a tomato, carrot, onion and garlic salad (poor dentist; he'll have to put up with it).

15) I called the supermarket again after noticing I only had one carrot left. They still hadn't set off for my apartment with the order, so they added the carrots to it.

16) I had lunch, and started the third Rastros book (I bought six in total). It was a lunch-elevenses, at around 6 p.m.

17) I paid the maid, and she left.

18) The boy from the supermarket came: Fernando, musician and reader of *Quixote*. The order arrived fine, except for the biscuits. Some are always broken, even though I specifically ask them to choose whole ones. Four packs of cigarettes: the 12

October holiday is happening on Monday the sixteenth this year.

19) At 7.03 p.m. I phoned the furniture shop. They told me the shelving units were on their way. I said I hoped they'd be here by seven thirty, because I had to go out. They told me they were definitely about to arrive. But I still had to wait a bit longer.

20) The four shelving units arrived. They were brought round by the owner of the shop himself, or at least the same person who sold them to me. I said he could just leave them there, piled up in the living room, and later I'd arrange them how I wanted them. He insisted good-humouredly on doing it himself. I said my plans for them were a bit complicated; he replied that even so, he'd paid for parking and wasn't in a hurry. I thanked him, adding that I appreciated his help because I have a hernia and am meant to avoid certain kinds of activity. The technical term is 'eventration', but most people don't know what that is, and besides, it's almost the same thing as a hernia: a piece of intestine trying to get out of the body. The man arranged all four shelving units perfectly, even the two that went in a little room that's awkward to reach. I paid him; he refused to accept the small amount of change as a tip, and left.

21) Wishing I had time to put things on the shelves, I cleaned my teeth and set off for the dentist. It was already very late: seven fifty. I took a taxi from the corner of Juncal and Sarandí, but first I had to walk one block along the pedestrianised bit of Sarandí, which the Council's henchmen were filling up with pots of earth, squares of turf, and various bucolic structures that even included small palm trees. The Council's only concern seems to be blocking pedestrians' way. They've covered the street in rocks that destroy the pavement and trip you up every couple of steps. You have to watch your feet the whole time you're walking. They've put huge palm trees <u>in the middle</u> of the street. On the pavements, in the pedestrianised area and even in the Plaza Matriz, cyclists pass by with impunity, some at a considerable speed. From time to time there are clowns juggling, plus very strange characters who paint themselves white and stay perfectly still so people think they're

statues, a crazy saxophonist with a shaved head who plays disconnected fragments of unidentifiable tunes, and tables to sit at, and carts selling ice creams, and advertising posters. It's a terrible sacrifice having to walk through the Old Town. Aside from all the camp decorations, there are crooked or missing paving stones, which, combined with the very narrow pavements, are enough to bring anyone to the brink of panic or despair.

22) I arrived on time for my dentist's appointment and went up to his surgery. The tune his bell played was unusually fast, as if it had been sped up. Sometimes it plays 'Happy Birthday to You'. There was someone inside, and someone else in the waiting room. The dentist looked pale and seemed to have lost a few pounds. He explained later that he'd had an extremely tough week and on some nights had only slept a couple of hours. He's trying to get into the film industry by making videos.

The television was on at top volume, and showing adverts. I smiled beatifically and asked the man sitting opposite if he was watching something. He replied that he'd been watching the news, but that I was welcome to change the channel to whatever I liked. I said that actually I'd been thinking of turning the TV off altogether. This gave rise to a conversation on the matter, in which we practically had to shout at each other to be heard over the adverts. I didn't know how to turn the volume down. I only know one button on televisions: the one that turns them off. The man facing me was young and friendly, and wearing glasses. I didn't manage to follow all his arguments; he launched into various topics with great zeal, but then seemed disconcerted by his own enthusiasm and wrapped them up quickly, without proper conclusions. The adverts finished and the news report came back on. Horrible stuff, as usual. The threat of a war breaking out somewhere. A policeman with a black hood over his head hitting a civilian on the head with considerable dedication (and an equally considerable stick). Once, when I was alone in the waiting room, I let myself be tempted by a documentary about monkeys, but it turned out to be a segment on cannibalism. A gang of enormous monkeys stole a newborn baby monkey from its mother and ate it raw. A close-up of a monkey sucking on a bone with genuine relish. I had nightmares for weeks. I suppose now I'll have nightmares about hooded men beating me violently about the head.

After the weather report, I felt I was within my rights to turn the damn thing off. The man didn't object. 'What a relief!' I exclaimed inadvertently when silence fell.

Right away, there came a frantic knocking at the door that separates the waiting room from the rest of the house. The dentist's children, no doubt; kids missing their father. The dentist came out of the surgery and went into his house, mumbling something inaudible. I looked at the time. Chl would be at my apartment soon. She was going to make me a spinach and ricotta pie with some spinach the maid had brought me. When the dentist came back through on the way to his surgery, I told him I was off, and please could he go down and open the door for me. 'Is it eight already?' he asked. 'It's half past eight,' I answered, though really it was only twenty past.

23) I decided to walk home, and be ready to call a taxi at the first sign of those symptoms that I call gastric reflux and my doctor calls angina.

24) I didn't have any trouble. Since it was early, I called in at a supermarket on Calle San José to look for Argentinian corn oil. They didn't have any, but I found a little bottle of cider vinegar they don't have at my usual supermarket. I had to wait a while at the checkout because both cashiers were having problems of some kind; returns, that sort of thing.

25) I walked up to Avenida 18 de Julio and then back a few yards towards another supermarket. They had a brand of Argentinian corn oil I didn't recognise. I bought it. I also bought some Colombian coffee and low-salt ricotta. Luckily, the express checkout lanes were free. The others had sizeable queues, which must be because Monday is a holiday. Everyone's stockpiling, like me.

26) There's nothing else to report about my journey home, except that I had to walk back down that pedestrianised street, which is like a labyrinth or an obstacle course. The workmen were still

there, arranging the squares of turf and generally adding to the obstructions erected by the Council in any way they could.

27) Chl still hadn't arrived, but I wasn't waiting long. She was surprised to see the shelving units; she never dreamed I'd get to the shop in time to buy them one day. I asked her to drill a few holes in the bottom of one of them, for the telephone and answerphone cables, since the main purpose of that particular shelving unit is to free the desk of the telephone and all its accoutrements. The holes she drilled were perfect, just like her, and just like everything she does.

28) We had some coffee. I told her about my tree-of-life dream. These days she no longer goes into detail about her therapy; she just said she'd had a good session.

29) I walked Chl to the bus stop. A drunk man had stationed himself on the opposite pavement, a pitiful and ridiculous sight. He shouted a few things. Then he began to direct, by means of wild gesticulations, a woman who was trying to park a very large, long car. The drunk man, tall and ridiculous, made puppet-like movements as he lurched from side to side. At one point he seemed about to fall over and end up under the wheels. His pathetic and potentially dangerous presence must have been making the woman nervous, and she kept edging the vehicle forwards and backwards without managing to park properly. Then I thought she'd decided to give up and drive away, but no; she reversed again, and the drunk man, still ridiculous, once again narrowly missed being run over. Eventually it was all resolved, though I'd been distracted by Chl by then and didn't see what the woman did, and nor did I see her get out of the car. The drunk man was still staggering around on the corner. Chl got on her bus, telling me to take care on my way home. Before that, she let me kiss her, though only on the cheek. I headed for the corner, planning to cross the road, but then I noticed the drunk man looking at me from the other side, and I saw he was going the same way as me. Instead of crossing there I carried on in the same direction and onto Bartolomé Mitre. On the next pavement I decided to cross over to the other side at last, because the drunk man had stayed

on his corner, without stepping into the road or crossing over like me. I carried on down Bartolomé Mitre towards Sarandí with a funny feeling in my back, as if the drunk man were following me, though I didn't want to turn around or walk any faster. In spite of Chl's concerns, I reasoned, the drunk man couldn't be dangerous. He'd never build up enough speed to reach me; I always walk very slowly, it's true, but he wastes a lot of time moving from side to side and even stumbling backwards in an effort to keep his balance, and what's more, if he did catch up with me and try to attack, I could simply push him away. Unless he was pretending, he was very, very, very drunk. And to suspect him of pretending would be to read rather too much into the whole thing.

30) I got back home with nothing further to report, except for the mortifying sight of the camp, gay, kitsch – or a mixture of all three – scene the Council has been rigging up in the pedestrianised area. I started defrosting a bit of lentil stew; it was a little late for a heavy meal, but when I passed one of the new *boliches* on Bartolomé Mitre I caught the aroma of pasta and sauce. This gave me an irresistible craving for something with sauce, and the quickest option was to defrost the lentils.

31) Chl called to say she'd arrived home safe and sound.

32) I ate the small portion of lentils and still felt hungry. I prepared a tomato with grated carrot and garlic and then poured on some of the new vinegar and the new oil. I ate it, and it didn't make me sleepy. This doesn't prove anything definitively, though, because I was still on a high from the new shelves.

33) I had a quick rest in the armchair without dozing off, and then got up to start work on the shelving units and everything else. My God! The things I did. I even moved the desk and the record player, and dismantled one of the tables and took it into the little back room. I worked and worked. By the end my hands were black and I was hot, exhausted and aching all over – I still am – but I couldn't stop until I'd managed to impose at least a general sort of order on things, not in terms of details but in the overall picture. I think my apartment is shaping up just right – just right, that is, for me and my requirements.

34) I'm writing this at the desk, and not at the table as usual. The desk is now in the living room, under the clock (it's four in the morning already!), and it's completely clear; the only things on it now are these sheets of paper and this Rotring. All the rubbish that used to cover it has moved to the new shelves.

35) I'm going to have a couple of biscuits and a coffee, and then go to bed.

MONDAY 16, 00:44

After my hyperactive Friday, it was always going to be a slow weekend. I got up too early on Saturday (not in terms of the time, but because I didn't sleep for as long as I needed to; I was still excited after my hyperactivity, and the pain in the muscles that had been moving in unusual ways added to the insomnia). Really I just got up to go to the bathroom, thinking I'd go back to bed afterwards, but some cursed thing – I don't remember what – caught my attention, and I ended up spiralling into one pointless activity after another. I turned the computer on and got dressed . . . but I didn't wake up properly all day. Chl came. She wasn't feeling very energetic either, and after a while we began to give up on the idea of going out; it was cold, and the cold did nothing to perk me up. Chl made a spinach and ricotta pie and we ate it together. But before that, while she was busy in the kitchen, I fell asleep in one of the armchairs. In fact, it was Chl's idea, and she even turned the light out for me. When it was time for her to go, I insisted she call a taxi. I didn't want to walk to the bus stop with her; I didn't feel like going out.

We didn't go out on Sunday either. Chl came back and I bored her; I noticed her sighing with boredom and sneaking regular glances at her watch, waiting for a time when she could leave without giving the impression she was trying to escape. This time I went with her to the bus stop. While there, I remembered that the drunk man had been wearing a hat with ear flaps, or something like that, which made his performance all the more grotesque.

In the early hours of the morning, I went on a computer binge. Turning it off at midnight was out of the question; I'd begun some work organising my files at a quarter to twelve. I didn't stop until almost four in the morning. Fortunately, today I saw that my average is still going down: two and a quarter hours per day. And I did some useful things as well, such as testing out that DOS program I downloaded from the internet. Lots of error messages came up (I need to adapt the program to my computer's configuration), but it carried on working and didn't cause any upsets, and it successfully deleted hundreds of completely useless temporary files. I manually deleted another lot of useless temporary files, which were in a folder the program hadn't found, and I also deleted the whole Netscape cache. It was striking how the computer's behaviour immediately changed; it became more agile, files and programs opened more quickly, and even the images on the monitor seemed sharper. I don't understand why the workings of the computer are affected by an overloaded hard drive, but they are. A few years ago I had a similar experience with my old computer.

Today, as requested, Chl brought me a CD-ROM containing the telephone directory. I wanted to see it in action so I could decide whether or not to buy it. It wasn't easy to install; I don't know why it takes so long. After a while it told me it couldn't begin the installation proper – it had only been installing who knows what extra elements it needed for the installation – because the screen had to be configured differently. I configured it the way the program wanted me to and it looked a total mess, with everything ridiculously small. I tried installing the program again and had to start the whole thing from scratch; a waste of time and yet more time. Finally it agreed to begin the installation proper. At one point it told me that to complete the process I should remove all the disks in the disk drives. I removed the only one there was, which was the CD with the program on it, and it told me to put it back because it couldn't work without it. What a thoroughly idiotic, slow and useless installation process. The program itself is no better; it's too inflexible, for one thing, and visually it's very unappealing. Worse, at the bottom of the screen there's an advert about advertising in the directory, and worse still, it's an animated advert that annoys you continuously. As if the disk were being given away for free, when in fact not only is the disk not free but it's very expensive for what it is. I entered my name to see if it would reveal my telephone number – which shouldn't appear in the directory because I pay for it not to – or at least the number of my cousin, which does appear in the directory. Nothing came up: the whole section with the white background remained blank. I entered Chl's surname and it was the same. I thought it might be because I'd personalised my Windows colour scheme; perhaps they'd put the results in white text on a white background and that was why nothing showed up. But there's no way to change the colours in the program; you can't even highlight the text with the mouse so it appears in negative, and nor can you copy it. Then I thought no more about it and hit uninstall. That didn't work very well either, because it left remains of the program on my computer, which I then had to delete manually. The famous Uruguayan software industry . . . what absolute crap. Modestly, I should add that my own programs, though simpler and less ambitious, are much better designed and made, whichever way you look at them. I configured the Windows screen so it returned to how it used to be, and luckily it worked. Everything was back to normal.

Meanwhile, there's a new edition of the telephone directory available, but to get a copy (of one of the old doorstoppers, not the software) you have to fill in a form and go to one of a particular set of supermarkets. There's no other way of getting hold of a directory, and none of the supermarkets on the list is anywhere nearby. The previous delivery method was perfectly simple; you could pay twenty pesos and then pick the directory up from one of many different places, several of which were very close to where I lived. The current method is free . . . not counting the cost of the taxi, which I'd estimate to be around seventy pesos for a trip to the nearest supermarket. And you have to leave your personal details in the hands of certain supermarket chains, which surely means you'll be bombarded by advertising, including those awful answerphone messages. Bad times, my friend.

As I saw on my way back from the bus stop, the fancy little islands of fancy grass and fancy palm trees the Council has set up all along the pedestrianised street now have garish advertising posters stuck to them. The final straw! This city has turned into a nightmare, with the streets and even the buses filled with ads and *cumbia* music; at weekends you can't walk down 18 de Julio without being deafened by loudspeakers. There are even loudspeakers attached to one of the Council buses, which is parked on the corner of Río Negro and 18 de Julio. Who knows what its cultural mission is, but the speaker emits some really hideous tunes. Once I even thought I heard political messages in the lyrics, but I couldn't be sure.

MONDAY 16, 03:39

I'm in my pyjamas, but just as I was getting into bed, I suddenly remembered the source of all the current changes in my life, the ones I'm trying to bring about and stick to. This diary has helped me to reflect and remember; until now I've never had a clear sense of the events leading up to the current situation with Chl, let alone the ways I was responsible for what happened. It only became clear when I wrote the whole story down (so slowly, and so painfully). And I realised that my computer addiction and other unhelpful behaviour patterns were a way of expressing my sense of abandonment. On the one hand, yes, I was trying to run away from my pain; but on the other, crucially, I was pushing things to extremes because I wanted <u>someone</u> to set me limits. I realised I was behaving the way badly adjusted children do, children whose parents don't know how to set them limits, or don't want to, or have no interest in doing so. They push things further and further, and every step is a cry for attention. Then I said to myself: as long as my transgressions only affect me, <u>nobody</u>'s going to set me any limits. Not only was my behaviour inappropriate, but it was useless at what it was trying to achieve; my actions were doomed to failure in every sense. The hole I was digging was becoming deeper and deeper, and by then it was almost impossible to get out. In the end I decided that if a part of me was demanding limits, I'd try to set some myself; I'd listen to my demands insofar as they were reasonable and fair, but fight energetically to stop them escalating into that nebulous infinity. Limits. Strict, precise. But necessary.

On Saturday I lost control and relapsed for a few hours, but on the whole my plan is working. Maybe I'll need to make some adjustments, loosen the odd screw that's too tight, but I'll be careful. It's not easy, none of this process is easy. But there's no other way.

MONDAY 16, 20:05

Things didn't stay the way they were. I just turned the computer on to see if I ever wrote up a very important dream I had – about the computer and my addiction, in fact – thinking I didn't and I should. And now I find that Word isn't working properly. Installing and, perhaps more to the point, uninstalling that infernal telephone directory software seems to have made some of my files disappear. While it was uninstalling, the program told me there were some .dll files, the kind which are usually shared, and which weren't attached to a particular program, and asked if I wanted to delete them or keep them. I told it to keep them, just in case, but I have a feeling it deleted them regardless. Anyway, now I can't do anything in Word without a message appearing every few seconds to tell me it can't access the library of .dlls. This isn't something I can solve on my own. I need the person who sold me the computer and installed the programs, and that person is very difficult to pin down. I didn't notice if the old version of Word was still working. In a way it would be a relief if it is, though not a particularly big one. That damn software from the phone company. It behaves the way some viruses do.

TUESDAY 17, 05:10

Mosquitoes. Just as I was dozing off. Luckily I managed to spot one of them at an accessible height on the wall above the headboard and take it out with a well-aimed sandal. Since I was up, I made a trip to the bathroom. There was another one in there, near the ceiling, and it was huge. I found the Flit and sent a cloud in its direction. It fell to the floor immediately and started rolling around. I stamped on it, just in case. Then I gave in to the fear, which was perhaps a mistake, and went on spraying little clouds of Flit here and there in the apartment. Now I'm a long way from the smell. I think I was awake all night. I lit a cigarette. The Flit was a bad idea; the smell will stay in the air for ages, and it'll give me respiratory problems. As will the cigarette.

Maybe I should read the second chapter of the last of the six detective novels I bought the other day. I had enough willpower to put it down after the first chapter and turn out the light, in spite of the cliffhanger the authors always put in the last line of each chapter. Before that, I read a fairly recent issue of *Búsqueda* from cover to cover.

The first chapter of the novel took me back in time. I'd read it before, when I was at secondary school. I tried to remember whether I'd been in the first, second, third or fourth form. My reference point was a particular French teacher. I'd asked him about the meaning of '*loup garou*' after class one day, since at the time I was obsessed with that term. I knew it meant werewolf, but I was interested in the literal translation of '*garou*'. He couldn't tell me. He knew what it was, but he couldn't think of the equivalent in Spanish. Or rather, he said he knew what it was but he obviously didn't, as I realise now that I've found '*garou*' in the dictionary. At the very least, he could have said it was a plant. I might, I thought, be able to use that teacher to work out what year it had been; I was almost certain that in the first form at that school, when I was twelve, our French teacher had been a woman, the wonderful *Madame* . . . (her surname was pronounced 'sha-*bo*', but I never saw it written down; it could have been Chabot or Chaveax or some other variation). She wasn't a young woman but she was very cheerful, good-humoured and funny. Her voice was deep, but not manly, more as if her throat had been ravaged by tobacco, though I don't remember seeing her smoke. I've just remembered something surprising that happened in one of her classes: I turned up for a lesson without having so much as opened my French book since the last one, and this woman called me up to the front of the class. Not wanting to say, 'I haven't studied,' I went down the wooden steps (the classroom had a tiered floor so the students at the back could see properly, or perhaps so they could be seen. I was quite tall and sat in one of the back rows – the seats were allocated according to height, with the shortest at the front). So down I went to the blackboard, my spirits very low, thinking I had no way of escaping a low grade and the embarrassment of being told off in front of the whole class. The teacher almost never got straight to the point; she liked to chat, philosophise, tell stories. She began directing the preamble of a question at me, but then got caught up in another exciting topic and carried on talking. I had no idea what she was talking about because I was so focused on my terror, unable to relax, waiting for the guillotine blade to drop. And the woman talked and talked, and the question didn't come. And the most extraordinary thing of all was that it never did. When she'd finished talking she picked up her book, and while she was looking for my name, she told me to sit back down. As I made my way back up the steps to my seat, disconcerted, I heard her exclaim enthusiastically that these students were exceptional, a real delight, that she could call on them at any moment and know they'd have the lesson learnt. I hadn't even opened my mouth.

It occurs to me now that perhaps this woman, who was quite the psychologist, had sensed my terror, and went on talking like that as a kind of diversionary tactic; maybe she feigned distraction, not wanting to humiliate me in front of the class, since, after all, I was a good student. It's possible; but until this very moment I thought she simply got distracted.

On reaching this point in my reflections this evening, I wondered when we could possibly have had a male French teacher, if I recall having had the same teacher every year. And then it came to me: the Frenchman was in fact a drawing teacher. Why did I ask him rather than the French teacher? Perhaps because we only took French in the first and second forms, and perhaps we had that drawing teacher in the third form. If that's the case, if these suppositions are correct, then I read that detective novel when I was fourteen years old.

TUESDAY 17, 12:53

This is just to record that yesterday, Monday, 16 October, was a sad and rainy national holiday. In this country, 12 October is sometimes celebrated on 16 October. The ends and beginnings of centuries and millennia are also celebrated a year in advance. The next 2 November will fall on 6 November. I don't know when the next 25 December will be, but there's not long to go.

My doctor came (blood pressure relatively stable) and we talked about how unbelievably short the year 2000 has felt. Could the earth be turning more quickly these days?

My week of work is beginning.

WEDNESDAY 18, 05:02

Today, or rather yesterday, Tuesday, I had work; just a couple of hours with my private student, but enough that later on I plunged headlong into messing around on the computer. Not only did I go well over the time limit, but I was at it for so long that I got hungry. Only now, a few minutes ago, was I able to detach myself from the damn machine and hastily fill up on bread, biscuits and ricotta. I have an uncomfortable night's sleep ahead of me – if my stomach will even let me sleep, that is. Oh well . . . and tomorrow, Thursday, I'm working all day: two workshops.

I saw no new developments on the flat roof next door for a few days, and I thought the story of the dead bird had come to an end. This afternoon, however, before breakfast, while I was changing my sandals by the window (swapping the sandals with no strap at the back, which I wear when I get up, for sandals with straps above the heel, which are more secure for walking in); this afternoon, as I was saying, I saw the widow arrive, if it really was the widow, if there was ever really a widow. I didn't recognise her at first, because I could only see her head-on, and from that angle she looked completely black. And perhaps an even darker shade than before, because it was a cloudy day. She also looked different to the first time I saw her; bigger, more like the pigeon I've seen recently engaging in necrophiliac activities. I'm now almost certain she's the same one, and that she's grown, or got fatter; it wouldn't make sense to think in terms of two different pigeons who look very similar, and who both seem worried about the dead pigeon. She looked so black today that it was as if she'd come dressed in mourning. Or as if she were an envoy from the kingdom of darkness. A funereal pigeon, an appropriate kind to be stationed there, next to the dead bird. She was calm, composed, moving her head a little from side to side as if keeping watch. I was feeling impatient because I wanted to get on with my breakfast; it's very tiresome the way these birds put on their show just as I'm about to eat. I'd even poured the tea, which was going cold on the living-room table. I was about to abandon my espionage when she moved, and started walking slowly in circles. I thought she was going to begin the courtship ritual, but she didn't. She paced up and down a little and then hopped onto the corpse, first the tail and then the chest. I thought she was going to start pecking the dead bird, but she didn't do that either. She did the last thing I was expecting: hopped back onto the paving stones and sat down. She sat down. I mean: she didn't stay standing with her legs upright, but rather adopted the posture of a broody hen, as if she were sitting on some eggs, with her legs hidden under her body and her chest resting on the paving stones. And there she stayed. By this point I'd got onto the exercise bike and was pedalling slowly, wanting to do something productive while I waited to see what the widow was up to. I carried on pedalling for a bit, and the widow didn't move. It looked like a cosy family scene. There was something quite moving about the way the widow had settled herself there; something snug and affectionate, and homelike, or nest-like. All it needed was for her to start knitting.

Before the widow arrived, I noticed the dead pigeon was shaped like a pigeon again. I don't know if it was the rain or the wind, or the widow's fiddling, pecking and stamping, but the fact is that although it was still a bit flat, squashed-looking and lacking in volume, it was recognisable as bird and pigeon once more. The left wing, which had been lying by its side, was now outstretched, or at least apart from the body, and you could see its wing-like quality. The tail was fanned out, too. And lots of little white feathers on its chest seemed to be fluffed up in different positions, giving the flattened body an illusion of volume. The head is still out of sight; from where I am, it looks like the bird doesn't have one. I left the widow there, incubating her imaginary orphans, and went to have breakfast. When I looked again, she was gone. Later she came back and perched on the railings very close to my window; it was almost sunset, and I knew that if I waited a few minutes I'd see her leave. I was patient and waited, though it was getting a bit late and I had to go shopping. I wasn't waiting long. She shook herself abruptly, scratched around a bit in the feathers on her chest, and then, without a backward glance at the deceased, flew off to that mysterious place where pigeons go at nightfall.

## THURSDAY 19, 03:20

My stomach didn't stop me sleeping soundly, despite my fears, and I woke up feeling well rested. And then I felt well tired again, thanks to my yoga class. Lately, my yoga classes have been leaving me weak and exhausted. Chl was marvellous, and very affectionate. She also brought two kilograms of *milanesas*. She made conversation with me for a while, and eventually managed to perk me up a bit. Now I'm reasonably awake, but I'd rather be sleepy because I'm about to go to bed. I'm tired. The weather helps: it's humid, and the temperature is reminding me that summer's not far away. I'll have to sort out some air conditioning; I have serious reservations, but however harmful some of its effects are, I need protection against the cruel summer months. I don't want to have to escape my body as intensively as I did last summer; I don't want to go back to being an automaton under the computer's spell (today – yesterday – I turned it off at 6.15 p.m.) (then I turned it on again for a few minutes to check something important, but I resisted the temptation to keep using it) (today, Thursday, workshop day, there are no limits – at least not until midnight – but I'm worried I'll carry on until long past midnight; a predictable after-effect of the workshop, though I'm not entirely sure why) (in spite of my transgression yesterday, my average is still very good: two hours and seventeen minutes per day).

And that's all. I read an Edgar Wallace book, the last one I had left: *White Face*, better than most of the others. I got hold of three more Rastros, none of which look very appealing. Luckily Chl brought me the latest *Búsqueda*; she says it's very juicy. Political gossip, that sort of thing.

No news from the flat roof next door.

Mosquitoes: there were two in the bathroom. No bigger than a chihuahua, as Chandler might have said. It's a good thing they appeared now; I sprayed some Flit, but I'm making sure I don't breathe it in, and I think it's already dispersed. The joys of hot weather.

SATURDAY 21, 18:11

I'm writing in Word 6.0 because there's something wrong with Word 2000. It's a result of installing and uninstalling the telephone directory program, which is essentially a virus fabricated by the state. Last night I spent hours hard at work with Patricia, the systems engineer, but we couldn't solve the problem. I'll have to uninstall the whole of Office 2000 and then reinstall it; quite an ordeal. It seems hard to believe, but you can't install and uninstall Word in isolation. The whole of Microsoft is very promiscuous; each program is mixed up in all the others. Word 2000 is also a real step backwards compared to Word 6.0: slower, clunkier and more complicated. Whereas 6.0 is agile and quick. Why do I use 2000, then? For reasons of compatibility: I can't process other people's files in 6.0, and 2000 also has the advantage of allowing long file names, longer than eight letters, and I need file names of more than eight letters for this diary. I had to alter a few macros and make some more in 6.0 to manage the diary, but still, when 2000 is fixed, if it's ever fixed, I'll have to convert the files manually.

Last night, as I said, we were working at the computer for hours – although really it's Patricia who does the work. All I do is watch, and make a suggestion every now and then that generally doesn't work. As well as trying to fix Word, she gave me a few Windows files I needed that hadn't been installed before, and information about some other problems. She also brought me a new keyboard, a really good one, very smooth. Now I can write much more quickly, and I make fewer mistakes. The keyboard I had before was terrible. I paid seventeen dollars for the new one, and it was worth it. In fact, I would happily have paid even more, but Patricia doesn't need to know that.

You'll notice that this page of the diary is even less interesting, if such a thing is possible, than the previous pages. It's just because I'm testing out the new keyboard and seeing how things work in 6.0. I still have to type up everything I've written by hand, pages and pages, but I won't do it today: I'm waiting for Chl, and we're going to attempt our Saturday ritual. In spite of the heat. Thirty degrees, she told me over the phone. A storm brewing, humidity and at the same time blazing sunshine. At least the sun's about to go down.

A more interesting topic, though also a slightly cruel and heartless one, is my discovery of the dead pigeon's symbolic charge. I'll try not to forget about it, much as I might like to, and discuss it further as soon as I can.

SUNDAY 22, 01:27

More practice with my wonderful new keyboard on this stormy Sunday morning. I'm allowed to work out of hours; yesterday, Saturday, I barely managed to do anything on the computer before Chl arrived; and when she left, and I sat down to do a bit of work, I answered the phone thinking it would be Chl but it wasn't. It was Julia, sounding very worked up, and with an enormous number of things to tell me. I felt it would have been disloyal to cut her off, and besides, she was saying interesting things, so I postponed my computer work and gave her my full attention. Then I got hungry . . . Anyway, the point is that I'm allowed to do some work out of hours, especially on something like this diary, which isn't exactly a game.

SUNDAY 22, 02:13

What I meant to say was that the Saturday ritual underwent a slight variation: we came home by taxi. I insisted on it, because on the way there we'd seen yes sir yes sir three violent muggings in less than ten minutes, all involving the same characters (the same thieves, I mean, not the same victims), on 18 de Julio, where there were hordes of people walking along and no police in sight for blocks and blocks. We were sitting ducks. Chl got very nervous; I'm not entirely sure why. She says it's because she was worried about her purse being stolen, but

I know she doesn't carry anything valuable in her purse, so anyone who made the mistake of robbing her would toss it aside in disappointment a short distance from the crime scene. Now that I think about it, there could be another, more logical reason, which is the fear of getting caught up in some violence, of falling victim to an act of aggression. I find that easier to understand. It's not a nice experience. Maybe she was also worried that if anyone was aggressive towards us, I would have reacted violently myself and ended up getting hurt – a possibility that would only ever have occurred to Chl, at least the part about my response. My usual response is to do nothing, remaining calm and ostentatiously serene about the whole thing, and then perhaps have a breakdown a few days later, as I did when a burglar broke in to our house in Colonia. The second mugging involved not only the two thieves from the first one, but also a boy on a motorcycle; the two original thieves tossed him the fruits of their labours before running away. Then we saw a fourth character one block ahead of them, who whistled to indicate that some police officers were in sight. As you can see, they were surprisingly organised, a real gang; the whole thing was very well orchestrated. Maybe there were a few more of them scattered around the area. Luckily, when we saw the third mugging we stopped in the middle of the street, and from there we saw a friend coming towards us, or more specifically a good friend of Chl's and an acquaintance of mine; a big man, tall and broad, who was quite happy to accompany us to the entrance of the Feria del Libro. Chl walked between us, clutching her purse, like the cheese in a sandwich. After the bookshop (where there was nothing interesting, of course) we went to the usual *boliche*. There, we discussed very important things that had nothing to do with the muggings, and Chl calmed down a lot, enough to question whether we really needed to take a taxi back. I held firm, however, because today Chl was depressed and hypersensitive, and any nasty incident would have left her in a very delicate condition, if not a dangerous one.

The topic of the dead pigeon as a symbol still needs to be addressed. I should explain to the reader, or remind them if they already know, that a few years ago I wrote a text called *Diary of a Swine*. I wrote it in Buenos Aires. My initial impulse had been to continue the 'luminous novel' (take note of that detail, because the luminous novel – or rather, its completion – is the project covered by this grant), and as soon as I sat down to write it, I began having problems with birds. First, a baby pigeon fell into the narrow back garden of my ground-floor apartment, and when it managed to fly away another one fell in, not a pigeon this time but a baby sparrow, and the presence of those fallen birds became the main focus of what I was writing, which by then was almost a minute-by-minute account of the events unfolding in my back garden. I realised that this bird-based epiphany was symbolic; sometimes so-called objective reality takes on a strong symbolic charge. And I realised that somehow, by starting to write, I'd set those events in motion. I still haven't changed my mind after all this time, though I'd like to add for the record that I don't think you could call it a miracle. A little magical, perhaps, if we understand magic as a technique that can be explained. The Unconscious can do all kinds of things our poor conscious self would never dream were possible.

And now, as I begin the project of continuing the luminous novel, and even receive a grant that means I can devote all my time to the task, lo and behold: more strange bird-related occurrences. A dead bird appears, then the possible widow appears and behaves very oddly. Might this, I've been thinking recently, be a symbol as well? A symbol of my dead spirit, which no widow (my conscious self, let's say) will be able to revive in spite of her best efforts. If this is the case, Mr Guggenheim can give up on the idea that his grant will produce the expected results.

This is sad, but it makes sense. Why should I only be on the lookout for encouraging symbols? It's very worrying to think about my spirit being dead – at least, the spirit that led me to begin the luminous novel in 1984. The thing is, I still haven't managed to get anywhere near it, or even feel a hint of its presence. It's true that I've seen, and am still seeing, some extremely interesting results when it comes to my memory and handling my emotions – and that, for example, I'm even managing to carry on with the interrupted house move and gradually take possession of my home. What's more, I've now amassed nearly all the paraphernalia I need for the project (the only thing missing, I think, is the air-conditioning unit, as the heat today reminded me). I even have a new keyboard. I have two Rotring pens. And I have twelve completely clear days each fortnight. In that sense, I couldn't ask for more. But my spirit . . .

Come on, dead pigeon, get up and fly.

SUNDAY 22, 17:06

In the early hours of the morning, as I was brushing my teeth before going to sleep, I made an important decision: on the first of December, I'll begin work on the project. If my spirit is still dead, I'll be patient; I'll write with what I am now. The formal unity will suffer, and the results will probably be pretty dismal, but this project needs to be finished, no matter what. There are important things to say. It'll be a shame if they're not said in quite the right way, but still, they need to be written down.

In three minutes' time I'm going to turn this computer off. I would have liked to finish and send out the menu of options for the students carrying on with the virtual workshop, and I'm also very behind on my emails. However, I need to stay strong and stick to my abstinence regime; the computer has been used too much over the past couple of days, albeit for reasons beyond my control . . . Well, there goes the tune that announces the end of the computer session. So long!

TUESDAY 24, 00:33

I'm in one of those boring transition periods; there's nothing interesting to say. Even the books I'm yet to read (the ones I have to hand, I mean) look horribly dull. I'm all ready to go to bed; who knows what time I'll manage to sleep, but getting into bed is the only thing left for me to do. Everything's so boring that today the dentist cancelled on me, and so did my doctor. I didn't even have the excitement of someone sticking a needle into my gum, or of watching the movements of that other needle, the one on the machine for measuring my blood pressure.

I'd requested a wake-up call from the telephone company for eleven in the morning. I heard the phone ring but I didn't get up until twelve thirty – which is a step in the right direction, at any rate. I'm going to persevere with the eleven o'clock wake-up calls from now on. The time will come, I suppose, when the habit gives way to boredom and my sleeping hours become more normal. I can't think of any other way to do it. I'm amazed, incidentally, that I'm still managing to turn the computer off at a quarter past six every evening. Tomorrow, or rather today, I'll be able to use it until midnight with no restrictions; let's hope I can concentrate on my emails. I have no idea how my son's doing, or almost anyone else. I haven't typed up all these handwritten pages, either, and there are so many of them now. Today I focused on improving my medicinal memo program, and now it also tells me when to take the medication I take every other day. In the morning I thought of a way of doing it, and when I got up I did it. Word 2000 still isn't working, and Patricia hasn't come. Chl didn't come either, because my doctor was due to visit and they give each other a wide berth. I dozed off in the armchair after lunch. I do that every day now. It's a bit frightening, and I can't think of an explanation. It's not the oil, or at least not that brand of it, because now I'm using another brand. Unless it's some kind of brain disorder (which is what I'm frightened of), the only other avenue to explore is the bread. I wonder if the flour they use in this bakery has too much bromate in it, more than the permitted amount. It's hard for me to cut down on bread, but tomorrow, or rather today, I'll have a go and see what happens. I've already ruled out the oil, meat, tomatoes and garlic. Oh . . . the coffee's another possibility, but I very much doubt it's that, since I drink several cups a day and only fall asleep after my lunch-dinner. The investigations continue.

Surprisingly, today (yesterday) it was very cold. Ever since the early hours of the morning. I even had to sleep with the gas heater on. And outside, in the evening, the weather was harsh and wintery.

TUESDAY 24, 15:02

I fixed Word 2000!!!!!!

Before going to sleep it occurred to me that if there were communication problems with the macro system in Word 2000, there must also be problems in PowerPoint, since they both use the same Visual Basic library. I opened PowerPoint and asked it to load a particular template that contained macros, and hey presto: a little box popped up to say it couldn't load because a certain .dll file was missing. And unlike Word 2000, PowerPoint informed me in that little box what the missing .dll was. I looked for it in the set-up program, and there it was. Then I copied it to Windows/System and PowerPoint started working again, and now Word is working too. I did a better job than Patricia. I'm feeling thoroughly pleased with myself. What's more, today I got up at eleven thirty.

WEDNESDAY 25, 15:49

Word 2000.

I've been neglecting this diary, I know. I'm still in the difficult transition phase, but yesterday I had a very active day. It's funny how setting strict limits on my computer use has led to my gradually recovering skills I used to have, and how getting closer to respectable sleeping hours is helping me to achieve things I used to find impossible. For example, yesterday I managed to do several things involving the shops that close at 6 p.m. here in the Old Town, such as buying a special kind of light bulb that's sold just around the corner from my apartment but is nevertheless completely inaccessible to me most of the time, or picking up a few things I needed from the hardware shop. Yesterday I successfully returned a Chinese-made portable lamp with an extendible arm, which had solved the problem of my lack of reading light for the armchair. I bought it the day before yesterday, and it turned out to be missing some parts (two springs, a screw and a nut). I managed to exchange it but it wasn't easy, not because the people in the shop weren't cooperative but because all the others they had were in the same miserable condition: dented, scratched or with missing parts. Finally one appeared that looked OK. It's red rather than white, which I would have preferred, but it doesn't look too bad, and as I said, it solves the problem. And it solves it very economically, too; these portable lamps cost around 50 per cent of what a floor lamp would cost, and a floor lamp wouldn't have solved the problem so perfectly. Admittedly, these Chinese products don't last; I'll need to be careful with it, but if it breaks in a way that's impossible to fix, I'll buy another one: simple as that. Then I bought two light bulbs, a kind you can't get in supermarkets; they're not easy to find, and I'm lucky they sell them here on the corner. The bulbs that are sold en masse in supermarkets don't last nearly as long, and some of them explode instead of simply burning out. I've often narrowly escaped being hit by a piece of one, because they go flying like cannonballs. They're made in Brazil in the name of a prestigious international brand. The ones I bought today are European and high-voltage, so they can cope with the sudden jumps in voltage you always get in this country. Then I went to the hardware shop and bought two screws with two nuts each, and a gimlet (that's what the salesman told me those things that make holes for normal screws to go into are called), and a little screwdriver to replace the one I generally use to clean the mouse and which is now very old, and a tube of glue. To buy the glue I had to give them my name, address and ID card number, so now I've been logged as an addict. Then I went to the bookstall on the corner, but I didn't find anything new; and on the way home I went into a nearby second-hand bookshop I'd never been into before – I spotted some detective novels in the window a few days ago. The atmosphere inside was a lot like my old bookshop, which gave me a bit of a funny feeling. I saw myself in the figure of the veteran bookseller, gloomy, depressive, putting up with the conversation of those ever-present customers who flick through the books and don't buy them and make you listen to their stories. The customer of the moment was an old man who'd got in my way minutes before when I was walking down the street, because he had a dog on a lead, and the dog, a white monstrosity with curly fur and pompoms, decided to take a shit in the middle of the narrow pavement. The old man muttered something but obeyed his dog and stood there waiting, obliging me to step into the road. Now that same man with that same dog was leafing through the books and chatting away to the long-suffering bookseller. I didn't find anything new in the way of detective novels there, either, so I went home. Although I was hungry, I was eager to put into practice my idea of fixing the phone upright to make more space on the shelf. I made a hole with the new gimlet, put the screw through with one nut on this side, and put the other nut on the other side. I placed the screw at the right height and cut off what was left with a small saw, which was a more onerous task than I'd imagined: those screws are harder than they look, and it was also an awkward position for working in. Then I repeated the operation with the other screw, lower down, so the telephone would be held firmly in place by the two devices it has for that very purpose. After testing it out and giving it a few tugs, I deemed it solidly attached and felt extremely pleased with myself, because although the reader may not believe this – or, more likely, may find it ridiculous – until a few days ago, and for a period of several years, it would have been impossible for me to do a job like that. I'd developed a growing irritation with everything that couldn't be done at the click of a mouse, and this made my hands incredibly clumsy; what's more, it would never even have occurred to me to do a thing like change the position of the telephone, and if it did occur to me, I'd blithely put it off until some remote point in the future. I'm not saying I'm completely cured of this shameful incapacity, which I brought upon myself and cultivated almost lovingly for years, but I am saying that I'm achieving things now that would have been unimaginable until a few days ago. I don't want to think about everything I still have to do; it's not very therapeutic to go around focusing on your failings. Now I have proof that when I manage to surrender completely to those dreadful feelings of boredom, the positive activity comes about by itself, like a natural protest from the body, like a natural and logical consequence. It's worthwhile reaching boredom, the rock bottom of boredom, because that's where the right impulses begin.

And speaking of boredom, once I'd finished the collection of detective novels I'd picked up, and after reading some other boring things, I went back to Doña Rosa. I'm reaching the end of her horrible book. I can't just give up on it, out of respect for such a wonderful writer as her, and also because, although it's awkwardly put together, many parts of it, considered in isolation, contain real gems of observation, insight, logic and wisdom, and exemplary use of language. The huge mistake is in the conception of the novel as a whole. Doña Rosa must have been trying to fit into some trend or other; her autobiographical writing never hides her desperate longing for recognition and a place in Spanish literature. Naively, she believed merit alone would be enough, unaware that in literary careers, as in all careers, everything is primarily a question of politics, or nepotism. Rosa Chacel's talent and nature should have made her remain in obscurity out of choice, dedicated to developing her writing simply out of a spiritual or vital need, but that wasn't what happened. And that must be what led to freakish creations like *The Maravillas District*.

THURSDAY 26, 03:03

Rotring.

Yes, I should be in bed. It's got a bit late, but not because of the computer. Today was more relaxed than yesterday, but still interesting – except for my journey back from the dentist in the evening. The same thing happened as last time, which I promised to write about then, but I don't think I did in the end. That time I thought one cause of my discomfort was having to go past my old apartment. But today I took a different route, and I was still gripped by that uneasy feeling, that paralysing pain. There's one thing linking this time and last time: on both occasions, I set off with a full stomach. Very full. Both times I went by taxi and then decided not to come back by taxi, perhaps because I don't walk much and I should, and the weather today was just right for walking. When I feel the first symptoms – a twinge, a hint of the pain to come – I ought to stop and wait for a taxi, but for some reason I don't. I think it's always the same process, the same chain of reasoning: 'No, it won't happen this time. It's just because I'm scared, it's all in my head. If I keep my back straight, if I lower my shoulders, if I relax and slow down, it'll be fine.' Later, when it's clear that the pain really has set in, I still don't stop and wait for a taxi. I think: 'It's just a few blocks. Maybe if I'm sitting in a taxi it'll be worse. It's easier for me to relax when I'm walking, so my stomach will loosen up and let out the gases that are causing it all.' I swallow an antacid tablet; this sometimes works, though it takes a while. Today I only had one tablet left; it's better to take two or three. But I only had one and it didn't do a thing, either straight away or later. It was really awful. I had to stop every so often, although stopping doesn't help and in fact makes me anxious, because it means it'll take me longer to get home, and getting home is, without question, the only thing that puts an end to the problem once and for all. I reach my building, go up in the lift, open the door to my apartment, and then immediately relax and burp. The pain vanishes as if by magic. Well, that's what happened today, but the walk back to my apartment was torture. I thought: 'I'm going to drop dead at any moment.' They're the symptoms of a heart attack, including the pain in my arms. Even breathing is painful; the air hurts as it passes into my lungs, as if it's a corrosive substance.

I'd been home for less than an hour when my doctor turned up; not because I'd called her about this discomfort, but because that was what we'd agreed. The moment she arrived I asked her to take my blood pressure and pulse, thinking that if she's right (which is likely, though I don't want to admit it) and this is a problem with my coronary arteries, my pulse would be very different to usual, and so would my blood pressure. My pulse was a little faster, but no more so than my usual smoker's tachycardia; I'd just had a cigarette, I was on edge because of my recent discomfort, and the very fact of someone taking my pulse makes it speed up. My blood pressure was normal. Still, later on, before she left, I asked my doctor to take my pulse again, and it had gone down from 96 to 80, as I expected. I think the problem, which always arises when I'm in the process of digesting my food, is caused by my digestive tract contracting and pushing air towards the eventration. The eventration is a result of the operation I had on my gallbladder sixteen years ago, and it involves a piece of intestine escaping through a hole in my insides around four or five inches above my belly button. My phobia of going out makes my muscles contract, and the intestine, that little bubble that comes into view, pushing out my jumper, inflates and inflates, and it hurts the sides of the hole it's trying to escape through. That in turn sends the pain spreading out in all directions, especially towards my chest and back; the vertebrae in the middle of my back are the ones that suffer the most. That's my theory; I hope I'm right. If one of these days I suddenly float into view with a little harp in my hand, I'll know I was wrong and the person who was right was my doctor.

I have two visitors scheduled for tomorrow, or rather today, Thursday; Felipe in the afternoon, with a new delivery of books to lend me, and Malalo in the evening. Malalo is my biologist friend who lives in the US, the husband of the friend I've referred to in this diary as a resident of Chicago.

The interesting thing about the day, aside from a good conversation with my doctor, was the arrival of various pieces of news in my email inbox, which has been very quiet lately because I haven't been replying to anyone. Today's emails included a few from the students in the virtual workshop, responding to my proposals for how to continue it. Last night, one of them sent me an email containing a virus. Although really it was the virus itself that sent the email, and not him. It's the fourth time I've had it; a real epidemic. It's called Win32.MTX. Luckily it didn't affect me: I was suspicious of the executable file, so I ran the antivirus, and the antivirus deleted it. Receiving viruses always leaves me overexcited. Last night I couldn't sleep because I was so worked up. It's strange, but that's how it is. As if I don't trust the antivirus to get rid of them for good.

The other interesting thing about the day was doing a small series of manual jobs. I put a portable lamp I'd taken apart back together and attached another portable lamp to one of the shelving units in my library, where yesterday I'd been adjusting the shelves to create a space where I can comfortably make use of the fat dictionaries. This portable lamp will shine a light onto the dictionaries. It will shine it, but it's not shining it yet, because today I only attached it to the shelf; I still need to install the electrical part, or rather change the electrical installation, because it has a very short flex and the plug socket is slightly too far away. I also want to attach a switch to one leg of the shelving unit. I need to look in the box full of electrical things to see if I have the necessary items and buy them if I don't. I really enjoy,

I'm really enjoying, doing these sorts of tasks. Please, God, don't let me relapse into my computer addiction.

And now I'm going to bed, and maybe to sleep.

FRIDAY 27, 03:42

Rain, rain and more rain. Today I only went as far as the corner of my road, to buy cigarettes, and to the pharmacy next door. I ordered the other things I needed from the supermarket by phone, not so much because I didn't want to go out – it wasn't raining at that point, although the air was very humid – as because I didn't have time. I'd got my appointments muddled up. I forgot about Julia, but luckily she had the good sense to leave me an answerphone message in the morning, letting me know that she hadn't forgotten and would be arriving at 6 p.m. This had me thoroughly confused, because 6 p.m. was more or less when Felipe was coming with the books. It's not strictly true that I'd forgotten Julia; the last time we saw each other, a fortnight ago, as I was accompanying her down to the ground floor in the lift, we agreed to meet again today. When I got back to my apartment I should have written the appointment in my calendar immediately, but of course the computer was off, as per my new routine, and so I didn't write it anywhere. It's an important distinction: I didn't forget about Julia, I just forgot to make a note of when she was coming. Fortunately, I managed to sort things out with Felipe and no one got annoyed. Julia brought me a beautiful little plant as a present, really beautiful, and I've put it on this desk. What's more, she gave it to me unconditionally, making clear that I could pass it on to someone else if for any reason I didn't want to look after it. But I'm not going to give it away for the time being. I don't know why I like this plant so much. It's a strange plant and I don't remember its name. It consists of various stems emerging from a log; according to Julia, the log wasn't originally part of the plant, and she grafted the whole arrangement together herself. Each of the five stems has about five or six long leaves sprouting out of the end of it, like the corolla of a flower. However, the leaves aren't all alike: the ones that make up half the circle are smaller than the ones that make up the other half, and not even the leaves in each half are exactly the same size, but rather they form a kind of gradient. One of the five stems is very, very small, and the leaves, of which I think there are six, are minuscule. This fragment of a plant is beginning to put down roots; for now it's in a plastic pot with some water.

As I was saying, I had to explain the situation to Julia over the phone and ask her to accept an end time of 8 p.m. for our meeting. Because that's when Malalo was coming. She didn't object. And she stuck religiously to the schedule we agreed. When she left, I realised I was in a similar state to after my yoga classes. During some sections of the conversation, which was essentially a meandering sort of monologue, as usual, I realised I was in a slight trance. She has a very pleasant voice and speaks softly, and the difficulty she has in telling stories in a linear way means your mind begins to wander. Now, in the early morning, I'm still feeling the effects: I'm very sleepy and, as I said, tired in that strange way I am after yoga classes.

Malalo stayed a long time as well, over three and a half hours. A different sort of conversation, more demanding, with lots of scientific information and other interesting subject matter. Malalo is a biologist, a geneticist, and I like him because he talks about his work at a level I can understand, but without cheapening it; as if he knew exactly how knowledgeable and interested I am, he discusses scientific matters in a way I'm perfectly able to follow, though not without an intense intellectual and mnemonic effort. You can see he's a born teacher. Chl had promised to come and meet him; he even brought a bar of fancy chocolate for her. But as I feared, at the last minute, Chl found some excuse and didn't come. As a poor substitute, I showed him the photos. It was Malalo who introduced me to the Guggenheim Foundation for the first time, in 1978. I think he liked sitting in one of the armchairs I'd bought with the grant money. And now I can't write any more; I'm falling asleep.

SATURDAY 28, 00:57

Over the past few days, this diary has turned into a record of minor personal triumphs, which is a horrendously boring thing. The personal triumphs are good in a way, because a record of feelings of guilt and incredibly low self-esteem would be not only boring, but also depressing and pointless. Still, enough is enough. I don't think I should carry on with this sort of writing. I'm going to wait until I have something to say, something with a minimal amount of plot, and then try to do it justice.

I'm reading an old Burroughs book, *Junkie*. A remarkable writer; concise, direct, weighty. I also finished a very strange book, very strange indeed; the story of a Russian pilgrim in pursuit of constant prayer. This book, which is by an anonymous author, plays an important role in *Franny and Zooey*, by Salinger, and my yoga teacher miraculously found it in a second-hand bookshop on a weekend trip to Buenos Aires. It's also excellently written, in spite of all the religious quotations. Felipe brought *Junkie* round today, along with lots of other books, all of which look very promising. I'm going to go to bed early, right now, to read, and try to sleep.

SATURDAY 28, 02:31

I forgot – but I had to get up to heat some water for the hot-water bottle for my feet, which seems hard to believe at the end of October. But as I was saying, I forgot to record that a day or two ago I finished *The Maravillas District*, by Rosa Chacel. I couldn't tell you what happens in it, exactly, if anything happens at all, or who the protagonist is, if there even is one, and all the characters, male and female, seemed to merge into one. It's part of a trilogy . . . one day I'm going to come across the other two volumes, and I'm going to suffer through them – if they continue in the same vein – and yet I'll find it impossible not to read them, because of this business of sympathy, or empathy, or identification.

MONDAY 30, 16:50

Word 2000.

I've been getting up late for two days now and I'm worried I'm slid-ing back into my cycle of all-nighters, though I could also be sleeping more because of the gas heater. It's been alarmingly cold over the past few days; Saturday was bitter and wintery. When I went to bed I had to turn the heater on and adjust it so it didn't cut out so often, because the cold air was hurting my nose when I breathed in and making me cough. I didn't have it on as high last night, but it still, I think, had a negative effect on the oxygen levels in the room, and that makes me need more sleep – as I know from experience. Last night, there were also psychological factors at play, because Chl was having one of her depressive episodes, and although I didn't exactly catch the depression from her, I couldn't help but end up in an unpleasant, uncomfortable, apprehensive mood. Things got worse when she called me on arriving home and said she'd seen a violent incident in the street while she was on the bus; her voice sounded very quiet. I also took the violent incident on board, mentally adding it to the string of muggings one after another last Saturday; the safety margin in this part of the city centre is almost non-existent. I suppose the state being unable to defend its citizens is a small step up from the state attacking its citizens, as it did during the dictatorship years, but the jittery feeling we live with is certainly very similar.

All these factors, plus a few more (the series of recent deaths among my friends and acquaintances, for example) gave me dreams that, though not entirely unpleasant in and of themselves, were unpleasantly difficult to extricate myself from as I was regaining consciousness. I couldn't escape them, and I returned to them over and over again, remembering different parts and even making up new parts, at a mental frequency that was neither deep sleep nor total awakeness; a kind of intermediary state. I spent over an hour listening to the bells on the Cathedral clock (or on a different cathedral clock, since my theory is that the bells I usually hear are somewhere else, closer to my apartment) chime every fifteen minutes, noticing how time was passing at what seemed like a fantastical speed. When I finally dragged myself out of bed, my mind was still foggy, and it hasn't become any less foggy since, as you can probably tell from the way I've written this page.

The main dream included various events; one of them, the one that took up the most narrative 'time', related to a string of deaths that all followed a common pattern, like the work of a serial killer, though they weren't murders. One of the deaths seems to map onto the death of a childhood friend of mine; the others, two or three or four of them, are more abstract, perhaps different versions of the same death. My role in the dream was that of a detective, but a psychological detective; I was establishing a clear list of similarities between one death and the others. Among the common factors was the existence of a love affair. I wish I could be more specific, but that's all the information I have. Towards the end of the dream I was explaining, or trying to explain, with some agitation, my ideas about these deaths to a friend (I believe it was Álvaro Buela), but he thought I was wrong and completely dismissed my conjectures. Earlier in the dream, there was a very vivid image of me picking up a coin with a symbol of death on one of its faces. They were divinatory coins, like a tarot of coins, and the one I was picking out of an enormous pile referred quite unmistakably to death. In another part of the dream, I was in bed with Chl (at points it could have been another woman, but mostly it was Chl) and we were getting ready to have sex. I was explaining something to her in technical terms, to counter some objections she was raising, or her slightly frightened attitude. I don't remember if the sexual act was consummated or not; I suspect it was, but the scenes have been suppressed. Towards the end of the dream, after the person I think must have been Álvaro had dismissed my conjectures, we both went into a shop, or a kind of small bar, staffed by a very unusual man, unusual in ways I can't explain right now. I wanted to buy some cigarettes, but this seemed like a complicated thing to achieve; the man said he couldn't sell me two packs, because the law restricted sales to one pack per person. However, there was another way of buying cigarettes, and Álvaro did it this other way and was given a nylon bag containing three bread rolls, yellowish like corn bread, in the shape of cubes. I was handed something similar, though I'd been expecting a pack of cigarettes; or rather, the pack of cigarettes I'd been expecting actually consisted of this thing they were giving me. I had fewer bread rolls in my bag, I forget whether it was one or two, although later I found myself with three as well. Each of the rolls was spread with a sticky yellow substance, like honey, which made them cling to the bag and got all over your hands if you touched them. I tried to juggle it all without dirtying my hands, and that's when the stickiness of the dream began, or became more pronounced. Then came the repetitions of scenes from the dream, the returns to previous scenes, and the not being able to get out, or wake up.

MONDAY 30, 19:58

Rotring.

Another factor has just come into play, which seems to be crucially important to the genesis of my sticky dreams. As I was getting ready to go out and run an errand, noticing how the violence in the streets is affecting my agoraphobia – something I noticed even more clearly once I left the apartment – it suddenly struck me, almost like a revelation or a discovery, that the bookseller on Paseo Policía Vieja had got hold of some more detective novels from the Rastros series. It also struck me that this paranormal knowledge of mine must have shaped some aspects of my dream; that the information had somehow been woven into the more strictly symbolic materials of the unconscious. So I changed my plans: instead of going straight to the supermarket on 18 de Julio, I'd stop by the bookstall first, and if there was anything new – which there certainly would be – I'd take the books home and then go out again, so as not to have too many things to carry. As it is, I'm already too clumsy to navigate the supermarket with the items I'm buying clutched under my arm or in my hands. I hate using trolleys – they make me even clumsier. I don't even know if that supermarket has trolleys; the truth is, I've never checked, and the truth is also that I've never had a woman or child crash into me with a trolley there, which is what always happens in other supermarkets.

I was disappointed when I got to the bookstall, because at first glance there didn't seem to be anything new; when there are Rastros books the bookseller tends to put them at the front, with their covers facing onto Calle Sarandí. But I did my usual circuit, and of course, when I arrived at the detective-novel section, there they were. I saw about five I was interested in, as many as there were deaths in my dream; or perhaps four, if we rule out one that had no front cover, and whose missing cover the bookseller had replaced with a different back cover from who knows where. I didn't think I should have to pay the same for the book with no cover as for the others, and I asked the book-seller how much it would cost. 'Five pesos,' he said. They usually cost fifteen, so that seemed fine. However, when I went to pay it all came to forty-five pesos rather than sixty-five; for some unknown reason the others had been reduced from fifteen pesos to ten.

Two of the titles were relevant to my dream, and to the other contents of my mind when I woke up, as you can see from the pre-vious page of this diary, where I recorded the details. The book with two back covers is called *Robbery Unpunished*, which relates it to the violent scene Chl described last night over the phone. And the other significant title is *Death Was a Wedding Guest* (which relates this book to the detail that in my dream every death was linked to a love affair). I can't see any connection between the remaining three and the dream. And I'm glad, because they could have been behind some very nasty stories: *Build My Gallows High*, *The Glass Tomb* and *Crime Aboard*. This last one has a beautiful cover, showing the figure of a skeleton sitting in a boat, rowing.

I don't expect anyone to accept my parapsychological explanations blindly, and I don't want to imply that I think they're definitely correct. They seem very convincing to me, but then I'm also the only person who was inside my head, or so I hope, at the time of the revelation, so I can't expect my own conviction to be universally shared.

Bad luck, Truman Capote (*The Dogs Bark*) (it's a wonderful book, entertaining and a pleasure to read). I'm going to make a start on the Rastros right now.

TUESDAY 31, 03:23

I shouldn't be up at this time, but the fact is I had a computer relapse. In my unrestricted time. I feel a bit guilty, even though I know that doesn't achieve anything. When I make a mistake I feel like everything's falling apart, but it isn't necessarily. The computer is not exactly heroin or cocaine. I've been reading *Junkie* by Burroughs (yes, I'm in a run of homosexual authors) (you don't notice it with Burroughs, though he declares it explicitly; whereas with Capote you do, however much he tries to hide it). The Burroughs book is one of the most convincing arguments against drugs I've come across, precisely because it's not an argument but a cold, objective account. Drugs like that, and the computer, when you're an addict, have the power to steal your whole life away from you. You live for the drug, and there's very little space for anything else. Burroughs makes it quite clear that drugs don't bring you pleasure. The computer does (or I think it does). Hard drugs must work like that other drug, tobacco. I don't find smoking pleasurable, but not smoking when you desperately want a cigarette is very unpleasant indeed. The tobacco alleviates the unpleasantness of the lack of tobacco, and that's it. Doing things on the computer, however, although it's as unreal as the world of drugs, is positively pleasurable. Not doing things on the computer is also unpleasant, but, unlike with tobacco, the unpleasantness is linked to the need to escape some uncomfortable feeling related to my life rather than to the computer; and it's perfectly possible to resist the urge to use the computer, with no more dramatic consequences than a bit of boredom or self-loathing. And there are plenty of ways around that, and no way around the unpleasantness caused by a lack of tobacco.

It wasn't needing to escape myself that made me relapse today, but needing to feel something good. It was a tough day, psychologically speaking. My confused mental state lasted until now, distancing me from the rest of the world and even from myself. It was a kind of indifference, interrupted only by a sense of wonder at the paranormal phenomena connected to my dream. Wonder at having brushed against that world whose dimensions are normally invisible to us, and in spite of the negative effects. In the evening I made another discovery, this one a posteriori. When I began telling my doctor, who came to see me (blood pressure normal, 14/8), the story of the Rastros title linked to the dream, I was amazed to discover another link, which I hadn't noticed before. This paranormal business goes much deeper than I thought. In the afternoon, hunting for an expression that would convey the nature of those coins with meanings, I wrote that they were a 'tarot of coins'. And I picked a coin out of the pile with the sign of death on it. This relates to a thought I had the day before yesterday, in the kitchen. I remembered that when Ruben Kanalenstein did a tarot reading for me a few years ago in Buenos Aires, the death card came up, and he explained that the true meaning of the death card wasn't death itself, pure and simple, but rather the kind of death that lies in routine, in repeating the same things every day. I applied the image to the last years of my life and saw that, yes, my routine was indeed a kind of death. Very well: nothing out of the ordinary so far. That thought I had in the kitchen produced – among other things, I'm sure – the image of the tarot-coins. Today, however, when I went out to the bookstall, what's the first thing I see when I set foot on the pavement, after closing the door to my building, but the great big belly of Kanalenstein? He was standing in the entrance to a hotel a couple of steps away from my building.

Of course, it's true that I ran into him around ten days ago on Sarandí, almost at the crossing with Juncal, and he told me he was in a hotel . . . the name of which I then couldn't remember. One day I even looked it up in the telephone directory; he'd said the hotel was on Bartolomé Mitre, the very street I live on, but I couldn't find any hotels with names that sounded like the one he'd told me. And then I forgot all about it.

When I saw him today I couldn't believe he was living so nearby; I'm not sure I've ever even seen that hotel before, with its very narrow entrance, although I walk past its door almost every day. I really am very absent-minded and unobservant.

Anyway, the point is that you could easily interpret the reference to Kanalenstein and his tarot in my dream as an image produced by the thought I had in the kitchen. Less easy to interpret, however, is the fact that today I saw Kanalenstein himself just as I was on my way to the bookstall, where I was about to come across something else that appeared in my dream. Kanalenstein was only there for a few minutes, while he waited for his wife to come out of the hotel. I could easily have left my building a little before or a little after and not have seen him at all. The way these things occurred, squashed into a tiny portion of space-time – the encounter with Kanalenstein, the books – allows me to think that the dream was a premonition, a way of mentally skipping forward in time. It's happened to me before, sometimes more clearly and more dramatically. This instance leaves some room for doubt, but I have no doubt. There are other, additional factors I find convincing, such as my unusual psychological state, or, more objectively, the behaviour of the bookseller. He's a man of few words, and he doesn't normally show any signs of warmth. I've been a customer of his for years, since before my time in Buenos Aires, and when I started visiting his stall again, nothing had changed; the man had aged a little, but everything else about him was the same. Today, however, as well as charging me ten pesos for books he'd recently charged me fifteen for, when I was leaving, he launched into an unstoppable stream of eloquence. As if during that telepathic encounter we'd become friends. I find this the most persuasive factor, but I'm persuaded by the whole thing, the whole paranormal package.

After giving me my change, and when I'd already said goodbye (for the first time . . .), he said, apropos of nothing:

'Just last night they started showing a series of old horror films on cable. Must be because of Day of the Dead.' I didn't know people celebrated Day of the Dead these days, but it looks like they do: in the supermarket later, a girl dressed as a witch offered me a sweet, as a promotion for something or other. 'They showed loads, from the forties, really old ones. Some had Boris Karloff in them. *Frankenstein's Bride*, for example. And another really, really old one, with' – and here he said a name I don't remember – 'who was Charles Laughton's wife. She played Mary Shelley, the author of *Frankenstein*.'

I said I didn't have a television set because I hate television, but that maybe it would be worth buying one now that you can watch this kind of thing on cable.

'Well . . . if you like old films,' he said.

'I can't stand the normal channels,' I told him. 'They show terrible stuff.'

'The adverts are the worst,' he replied. 'I once almost smashed my head open because of an advert. It sent me to sleep and I fell over. Not forwards, either, but to one side. Hit my head on the bricks of the fireplace – it could have killed me.'

'Well, adverts don't send me to sleep. Just the opposite: they make me so furious I can't sleep at all.'

'They send me to sleep. When I'm watching a film I'm wide awake, but then they cut to the adverts and I start nodding off.'

I'd already said goodbye two or three times, in the middle of this conversation, which had a bit more to it than it does in this account, but he kept drawing me back in with more stories. In the end I had to start walking away and leave him talking to himself, because it was getting late.

TUESDAY 31, 16:31

Reading a book with two back covers is a vaguely disconcerting experience. Especially if it's a book in the Rastros series, which I know well and have been devouring since I was ten or twelve years old. The back covers are much more eye-catching and easily identifiable than the front covers: 'RASTROS Collection' is emblazoned across them in big red letters, above a list of the last nineteen titles published, including the title of the book whose back cover it is, plus the title of the next book to come out, in black letters, all on a garish yellow background and surrounded by a blue frame about half an inch thick. As if that weren't enough, at the bottom there's a red blob meant to look like a wax seal, displaying the name of the publisher: 'ACME [*sic*] Agency.' For fifty years, I've been accustomed to seeing a Rastros back cover as a Rastros back cover, and now, in the unusual situation of encountering a book like this, with two back covers, every time I pick it up to carry on reading, the first thing I do is turn it over, thinking it's face down on the table, only to be confronted by the very same sight, a back cover that's more or less identical. And so I always end up opening the book upside down. Luckily I've finished it now. It wasn't bad at all. The hundredth in the series; I'd never read it before.

# NOVEMBER 2000

Well, well, well, well, well, well, well . . . If anyone's paying attention to the dates at the top of each entry, they'll notice I haven't written anything in this diary for a very long time. Why? Because I had an absolutely shocking computer addiction relapse. This is an attempt to get back into the habit of writing this diary, even if I only manage the date.

My relapse began with that dream involving the tarot and the detective novels. At first I thought it was the dream that caused the relapse, but now I've changed my mind. I think what really led to the relapse was how ruthless I was with myself during my period of abstinence, shutting down the computer at 6 p.m. every day. This created a build-up of pressure in the unconscious, and my dream's flight into the future was in fact a consequence of that, a way for the unconscious to protect itself from the inevitable relapse it saw on the horizon. I think it's as if that extraordinary force we all have inside us had decided: 'Things are about to get tough around here. Let's see if there's anything I can do to protect this poor self from suffering . . .' and popped out to look for some detective novels. In that glimpse of the immediate future, my unconscious caught sight of Kanalenstein in the hotel doorway and thought it might as well give me the message about death from the tarot, reminding me in the process that routine is a kind of death.

It's also possible that the unconscious influenced the mind of someone at the Feria del Libro, because the following Saturday I came
across some Rastros books there for the first time. Very cheap, as
well: three pesos each. There were five of them . . . With those and
the five I'd picked up round the corner from my apartment, I had
enough detective novels to last me ten days. Eleven, if you count the
one a student gave me at the workshop on Thursday; a novel by Erle
Stanley Gardner no less, one of the Perry Mason ones, which I've read
before but didn't have in my collection. (My collection is limited to
Gardner and Rex Stout.)

Detective novels and the computer, then. Full-time. Twice now
I've hit ten hours on the computer. Until the day before yesterday,
I'd been averaging almost seven hours a day. Compared to the two
and a half I was on by the end of October . . . Oh well, yesterday the
average started going down again; but slowly, very slowly.

Just today I wondered whether everything I'm going through is a sign
that this project is too much for me, that I'm in no fit state to complete
it. At the very least, it's clear that if I want to recover my impulse from
1984, financial assistance won't be enough.

Now I have another kind of assistance. My sculptor friend has
finally agreed to sell me a piece of hers called *Book*. I've been after that
sculpture for about a year now, ever since I saw it in an exhibition.
I asked my friend not to sell it to anyone else until I knew whether
or not I was getting the grant. Then I did get the grant, but she still
wouldn't agree to sell it to me. She had other possible buyers, and
could charge them an amount much closer to its real value . . . if it's
even possible to talk about its real value; as far as I'm concerned, its
value is infinite. The sculpture is a masterpiece, and I decided I couldn't
possibly complete my project if I didn't have it here in my apartment.
I'm not normally someone who goes around buying sculptures; most
of the time all I buy is food and the odd bit of stationery or computer
equipment. But in this case it seemed essential; having that sculpture
in my apartment was, I thought, and still think, more than necessary
if I was going to make any progress with the project. As far as I'm

concerned, that sculpture <u>is</u> my book. And now that it's finished, it's the book I want to finish myself.

My friend eventually brought me the sculpture, and for an almost nominal price – really it was a gift. I couldn't persuade her to accept anything closer to what she could have charged the other possible buyers. And there it is, looking a little cramped in its new surroundings, because my apartment has very few walls and plenty of doors and windows. It should really have a whole room to itself, so it can shine with all its presence. It's a book, a luminous novel.

I was very pleased to hear the sculptor recognise that it's a good piece of work. It's the first time I've ever heard her speak highly of something she's made. She never appreciates her own work, or indeed her own person. She's shy, self-effacing. I think she has an inferiority complex. But this time she recognised that she'd made something worthwhile.

And so my week of work begins. Lots of work; my private student on Tuesday, and the virtual workshop on Wednesday, when the students are going to start a Course Two that I haven't yet prepared. On Wednesday I have to send them the first assignment . . . And there's the odd new Course One student, as well. On Thursday, two face-to-face workshops. On Friday, the editing workshop that happens once a month, and that didn't happen last month because the students couldn't make it. An intense week. Meanwhile, I'm trying to get over my relapse, to return to slightly more normal activities. I won't enforce such strict limits with the computer this time, but I definitely need some boundaries in place. Less dramatic ones, perhaps, but boundaries all the same. I can't go on like this.

The dead pigeon is still a dead pigeon. By which I mean it's still shaped like a pigeon. It's flat, and its white breast is dishevelled, perhaps bloodstained, but it's kept most of its feathers and continues to be more or less the same shape. I find such permanence surprising. Don't rats eat dead pigeons? Doesn't the flesh decompose? Or maybe the flesh has already decomposed and the feathers are attached to the bones, which stops them blowing away in the wind and leaving the skeleton I was expecting.

I haven't seen the widow again.

I went to see Chl today. Not a good idea: I didn't realise I was in such a bad way, and once I got there, all I could do was bore her because I was incapable of opening my mouth. I spent the whole time staring into space. Who knows what was wrong with me. Maybe I'm getting my sex drive back, and my sudden decline is caused by trying to suppress it. Trying to be polite and not molest Chl. I don't know; it feels like the beginnings of the flu, which personally I've always confused with symptoms of schizophrenia, and there must be a reason for it.

To return to the original topic, now that I've mentioned the flu: I was also wondering about the relationship between my regressions and the reading of detective novels. I don't know which comes first, which is cause and which effect; but I remembered my Buenos Aires period, and the afternoon when, after work, I went as usual to the second-hand bookshop that had just opened on Corrientes, and found a delivery of detective novels from the Séptimo Círculo series, new arrivals, at fifty cents apiece. I bought them all, and then on the way back to my apartment, laden with bags of books, I began to feel the first symptoms of the flu. The first symptoms of illness in my time in Buenos Aires. When I had just arrived in the city, as I think I've already said, all the bookshops were offering deals on the Club del Misterio series, those ones made to look like the old pulp paperbacks. Three for a peso, and then, a few days later, five for a peso. I bought them and read them from time to time, and that helped me through the early stages of my adaptation, of my fictitious hyperadaptation. But when I got hold of those Séptimo Círculo books, the situation was very different. I was nearing the end of my days as an office worker, though I didn't know it then – I still hadn't let myself think about it clearly. So I don't know if it was the flu that made me want to lie in bed reading all those dozens of detective novels I'd bought, or whether, again, the unconscious could tell there was a crisis on the way and was sorting me out some entertainment. If I'm not mistaken, before returning to my apartment I also purchased a bed, on the condition that it was delivered immediately because I didn't feel well and wanted to lie down. The bed I had was broken and tied together with string, but then the string had broken as well. It came as part of a ridiculously cheap set of bedroom furniture; as with everything else I bought in Buenos Aires, including the fridge, I paid as little as possible for it, thinking that if it lasted six months I'd have got my money's worth. I had the first bed for two years. The second, the one I bought on the way home when I felt myself coming down with flu, I'm still using today.

That bout of flu was the beginning of my realisation: I couldn't go on with the office job; something within me was angrily demanding freedom. That's why I don't know what comes first, the chicken or the egg. I don't know if detective novels provoke crises or impending crises require detective novels for me to get through them. I think the second option is more likely.

MONDAY 13, 21:06

When I said the sculpture was my book, that wasn't exactly what I meant. It may have come across right, but I didn't explain it right. The sculpture isn't my book, any more than it could be any one book in particular. It's simple, white and pure, potent and luminous. This is something you can never achieve with literature. And, more specifically, my soul lacks the virtues of my sculptor friend's soul, so that even if literature were able to achieve such luminosity, I myself could never do it.

MONDAY 20, 19:58

Rotring.

Today I'm feeling extremely weak, most of all mentally. So much so that I put off going to the dentist, despite the important work I need to have done. It could be the effect of some new medication, which I used to take in the form of herbs and had to abandon because it was making me confused. I've been trying it in tablet form for a few days, but now I've stopped. My doctor will be here soon; it's days since I last saw her. Perhaps I'll have to go back to the antidepressants, especially since when I stopped taking them it affected my smoking: I started smoking more, and my cough came back.

In the past few days, two phenomena have occurred; the one today, in fact, related to my doctor. These phenomena are obviously caused by a weakening of the self, and although there's nothing dangerous about them as such, they're an alarming symptom.

A few hours ago, in the kitchen, I suddenly thought about Katia. I haven't heard from her for a long time. Ever since she published her book, several months back, I've had the feeling she's been avoiding me. We haven't been able to agree on a date to meet in person, and nor has she sent me her book by any means, and I've hardly had any emails from her. Meanwhile she's been giving me plenty of publicity in interviews, including on television, so it's not as if she has any particular animosity towards me. This afternoon, I thought about emailing her to try to find out what's going on and why she hasn't sent me her book or written to me. A few minutes later, while I still had Katia on my mind, my doctor left a message on the answerphone. I was so surprised I couldn't lift the receiver and speak to her directly, because the message was about . . . Katia. Apparently Katia had emailed my doctor to say she'd received an electronic virus from her computer. In other words, my doctor read the email and thought about calling me for advice on viruses and antivirus programs, and I picked up on this thought of hers, though only enough to see the image of Katia. I wonder how many more people will invade my mind before the end of the day (and the night! And tomorrow morning!), as if it were the easiest thing in the world.

THURSDAY 23, 19:36

I've just typed up in Word some pages of this diary that I wrote with a Rotring about a month ago; they included an immensely detailed and extremely boring account of an attack of pain I had in the street. I had another of those attacks yesterday evening, fortunately in the presence of my doctor. We'd gone for a coffee in a café in Pocitos, and before going into the café we decided to walk a few blocks, because the breeze was very pleasant and we'd both been inside all day. We crossed onto the *rambla* surrounded by a sea of cars all tearing along at Rambla-de-Pocitos speed, and I expect the sudden switch from my protective isolation to this wild environment set off my phobic mechanisms. It's also true that I'd eaten not long before. We followed the *rambla* along the coast, and after two or three hundred yards I felt the pain threatening to take hold. I suggested we turn back, and then, pointing to my eventration, which is where the discomfort originates, told my doctor I was about to have one of my famous attacks. The pain was getting more acute and soon it was climbing up my chest, following the exact path of my coronary arteries. My doctor watched closely, concerned, but she soon realised my problem was that I was panicking. Later, after I'd made a quick recovery and we were sitting in the café, she told me my body was expressing, quite clearly, the panic I was suffering from (but not feeling). Finally, she ruled out once and for all the idea that it's a heart problem, and accepted my much-repeated diagnosis of phobia + contractions of the digestive tract. Which can only be good news for me.

MONDAY 27, 00:26

Imagine for a moment, if you will, that you grow flowers for a living, and suddenly you inherit a chain of supermarkets. You have no interest in supermarkets and know nothing about them. You'd be quite content to collect the considerable profits every so often and spend them as you see fit, whilst continuing to devote your days to growing flowers, which is your main interest in life. However, the moment comes when you're seized by curiosity, or perhaps by fear. Since you know nothing about supermarkets, you could easily be exploited, robbed or deceived by the people running the businesses that legally belong to you. Or perhaps it just gives you a strange feeling, collecting all that money as if it's growing on trees, and you think you ought to do something in return. Whatever it is, you gradually take more of an interest in the business, and suddenly you're completely absorbed in a mass of information that your brain needs to process: organisational diagrams, recruitment of personnel, the legs of the cashiers in their nylon tights, the price of tea leaves and toothpaste, the names and surnames of your immediate colleagues, etc. Little by little, you realise you actually find it interesting, and that after all, it's not without its creative side. Ideas occur to you, and you start experimenting with this, that and the other. You find that making certain intelligent changes allows you to increase your profits, and that other changes mean you make a loss. The whole thing is turning into a game you can't stop thinking about, and one day you realise you've completely abandoned the flowers. You think about them rather wistfully, and even a little guiltily, because you feel like you're betraying your true calling in life. However, you're trapped in a system, and although no one's stopping you leaving, you can't do it. You've probably become addicted to the intense cerebral activity, so different to the leisurely activity of growing flowers. Your whole life has changed beyond recognition. You're not the person you used to be, but neither are you anyone else. You feel possessed by a conflict, or inhabited by something slightly alien to you.

I'm trying to explain, by means of these images, what's happening to me with the computer. Although I bought it rather than inheriting it, and although it doesn't bring me any tangible material reward, my fascination with the cerebral activity I've been engaged in ever since I began using it is exactly like what I describe above in relation to the supermarkets.

I'm possessed by a system. I feel alien to myself. And yet I'm the same person. I want to break free, but at the same time I don't; I have a deeper desire to do exactly the opposite. To be honest, it's as if instead of inheriting a chain of supermarkets I'd inherited a chain of brothels. The pleasure I get from exploring the computer is very intense. I don't know how to escape it.

.   .   .

Meanwhile, D-Day is approaching. The first of December, when, as I've written in this diary and as I've decided, definitively and irrevocably, I need to begin the grant project. Since making that decision I've barely written a word in this diary; I haven't been able to get the computer off my mind for a moment, not even when I'm asleep. I've become a man possessed. This is the first time in almost a month that I'm writing in this diary at length. And I have a much more delicate activity ahead of me, since the grant project is so ambitious. It doesn't just mean sitting down and typing for a certain number of hours each day, but rather, as I think these pages have made clear, going through a psychological process I've been calling a 'return'. And I've never been further from returning than I am now.

But I'm going to do it. Today I realised, when I happened to catch sight of a calendar, that the first of December is a Friday. A very appropriate day, because Friday is the day of Venus, and also the day of the Virgin – the day of the transcendental feminine. And my project is aiming towards just that; or at least, it's the first topic I need to address when I begin what will be chapter six of the 'luminous novel'. Which so far, in the five chapters written in 1984, has done nothing to deserve such a name.

For the whole of this month, which is now almost over, instead of focusing on what I want to achieve on that Friday, 1 December, all I've done is bury my head in the hidden workings of the computer and Windows 95. I've discovered the Registry and how to operate it. I've had resounding successes in mastering aspects of the machine that until now I've been unable to control. I've defeated several of Bill Gates's most monstrous impositions. I've acquired, by means of the internet, a series of programs ('utilities') which allow me to manage these things. And which then, of course, manage me, because everything you add to the computer gives you vastly more to learn and involves a great deal of extra hassle. Here I am, studying this and that like a madman and moving bits and pieces around, and everything I do, everything that will supposedly make a whole swathe of operations infinitely easier, in fact forces me to work exponentially harder and more assiduously just to stay afloat. The hard drive is filling up with rubbish, and as for my brain, I don't even want to think about it. And the whole thing is beautifully unreal. A world enclosed, or almost enclosed. Virtual reality.

And the dead pigeon is still there, dead and not visibly altered. There have been some new developments on the scene, however; two or three days ago, several young pigeons appeared which looked a lot like the widow; and the widow appeared with a new husband. All this couple do is scratch around in their feathers, not each other's feathers but their own. They ended up making me nervous; I felt like I was being pecked all over my body, after watching their endless scratching. They don't approach the deceased, but they don't keep very far away from him either; they perch on the railings, almost directly in front of my window. That's where they scratch. The young ones arrived afterwards, three of them, or at least that's how many I saw. They and their mother all look very alike, with shiny, smooth feathers. Today one of them was scared of flying. His brothers and sisters had flown off with no trouble, but he stayed where he was on the railings, buffeted by the odd gust of wind, and trembling, but not from the cold. He kept making as if to take off, with incipient movements of his wings that never got beyond incipience. The poor thing was obviously terrified and distressed. Suddenly, along came the father, or at least the husband of the mother, and he took a very high-handed approach. He advanced energetically towards the younger pigeon and practically pushed him with his chest. The poor young pigeon stamped his feet a bit and began edging away, but then he ran out of railings; he was cornered against a wall, and in the end he made up his mind and flew away. It wasn't a perfect flight, but he did it. The father immediately flew off in the other direction.

A few days ago, or perhaps a few weeks ago, I'd been disconcerted by the widow when she perched on the railings, in the same place where just now the young one was being frightened by his father, and then sat down abruptly as if she were sitting on some eggs, with her body puffed out and her feathers all ruffled, exactly like a broody hen. It would seem she's been brooding for real in a nest somewhere, judging by the unexpected arrival of those young pigeons. But she hasn't forgotten her late husband, and so she left her nest for a bit and came to keep him company. Not by his side, like before, but a little way off, though still with him in sight. It could be that this is all an arbitrary fabrication of my reasoning, but it's how the events unfolded and it's how I'm describing them now.

I just ran the Word 2000 spellchecker. It didn't recognise the word 'brothel'. Nor did it recognise 'incipience', but it seems to be right on that count because it's not in the dictionary. Still, it must exist.

### WEDNESDAY 29, 15:53

Have the celestial powers finally decided to step in and give me a shake? We're getting very close to D-Day. And the fact is that today was no ordinary day, to put it lightly.

My deep sleep was disturbed after just five hours by a persistent, insolent and urgent meowing. It was coming from right outside one of the three windows that make up the half hexagon at the front of my bedroom, on the other side of the blinds. Only cats are capable of that sort of insistence. Could I say that I'd fallen asleep thinking about a cat, and that a few hours before, in the street, on seeing an ungainly dog with big ears, I'd been immediately struck by the guilty memory of another dog? I know dogs and cats are different things, but the point is that yesterday, in the street, I saw a very comical dog, the kind that walk as if they're on stilts, as if their long legs are going to snap at any moment, and they criss-cross them clumsily as they go, or move them in a rather haphazard way. The dog also had extremely long, droopy brown ears, which almost trailed along the ground and were connected by a fold of skin on the top of its head, as if it were wearing one of those hats with ear flaps and the ear flaps weren't tied

under the chin, or in this case the snout, but flopping down loose.
This dog instantly reminded me of another dog back in Piriapolis,
some thirty-five years ago – it was the legs and ears that did it, since
the dog from before was white with black spots rather than purplish
brown like the one yesterday. But they both loped along in the same
awkward way, dragging their enormous ears, and they both had the
same naive, almost dopey and therefore contented expression. Of all
the images my memory could have shown me, as usual it chose the
most unfortunate: the look of surprise on the face of the dog from
years ago, when, ready to withstand, out of love, heroically, the jug
of cold water hitting his loins, he instead received a jug of boiling
water I'd been patiently heating up in the kitchen. At four or five in
the morning. I regretted it right away, because the effects were horrific.
The poor creature writhed around, squealing in a wild, high-pitched
lament, and it broke my heart. The animal had been howling insistently
under my bedroom window – the reader will notice the connection
with the cat today – and I was going mad with rage and exhaustion.
I don't know if the female dog in heat he was after was inside my
house; if so, the best thing to do would have been to let her out. The
problem was that the dog was tied up during the day and then, for
some mysterious reason – since he was too stupid and trusting to be a
good guard dog – his owners let him loose at night. The female dog
was out and about all day, peddling her wares with whoever took her
fancy, meaning that at night she probably preferred to sleep. Or she'd
gone on one of her rampages, because among other things she was the
leader of a gang of stray dogs that went off and killed a sheep every
now and then, as I gathered from stories I picked up here and there
and my own observations of the behaviour of that dog, who seemed
more like a fox. She wasn't my dog, but she lived in my house. She was
taken in or simply accepted by a woman I was living with at the time.
Then the woman left and the dog stayed put, but that's another story.


And at night, before going to sleep, I remembered another time I'd
mistreated an animal. It was in my early childhood, and I was almost
more of an accomplice, since the idea of mistreating the cat came,

I remember, or want to remember, from my friend Sussy. Sussy was three years old at this point and I was five or six. She had a lovely little black cat called Bijou, very nice and friendly. For some reason, one day we decided to throw stones at this cat, and we had great fun chasing after him and pelting him with whatever we had to hand. It became a habit. Most of the time, the poor animal ended up taking refuge in a pile of chopped firewood leaning against a shed at the far end of my neighbours' large field, since we couldn't follow him in there. After a few days the cat disappeared, I think for good. I remembered that as I was falling asleep.

I was woken up, then, by today's cat, at a highly inappropriate hour. It's still an inappropriate hour for me, because even now I'm half asleep (at 4.19 p.m.), and it looks like I'll be half asleep all day. I think it was 1.30 p.m. or thereabouts when that creature woke me up. I hadn't got to sleep until gone eight in the morning. The likelihood of being woken up by a cat meowing under your window is normally very small when you live on the fourth floor, but, as I think I've already said in this diary, my neighbours are the proud owners of two female cats, and one of them regularly goes prowling around the cornices of the building in search of a boyfriend or some other kind of victim, such as a mouse or a bird. I thought that longed-for boyfriend had finally appeared and that as a result I'd have no peace or rest for a very long time. The calls were so urgent and imperious that I had to make up my mind to act; I struggled out of bed and dragged myself over to one of the windows, opened it and raised the blind. There was the cat, meowing with her mouth wide open. I knocked on the glass repeatedly, without the slightest success. When I opened the window the cat tried to slip inside; I shouted at her very rudely and slammed it shut, but she was unperturbed and carried on opening her mouth and calling out as if nothing had happened. I was beginning to despair. She ran a few yards away and then began to trace a path around all the windows of my apartment, walking along each of the parapets and the two balconies. When she was a long way from my bedroom I went back to bed. The cat and her meows soon came nearer again, and again I got out of bed, this time ready for a fight. Remembering my experience with the dog, I resolved to be less cruel. I went to my desk drawer and took out a rubber-bulb syringe, the kind that's normally used for enemas, though I use it to blow the dust off delicate pieces of machinery. In the bathroom, I filled the bulb with water and then went back to the cat's window of choice, which is the closest one to the neighbours' balcony, wondering why she was so determined to torment me from that particular window. I opened the blind and saw her whiskers. Then I fired a jet of water through a chink in the slats. The cat took a step back, moving out of my reach, but didn't stop meowing. At that point, my doorbell rang. I thought the neighbours had noticed the drama and were coming round to have a word, but when I went to the door there was no one there. The person was ringing from the street, and so it wouldn't make sense for it to be the neighbours, or anything to do with the cat. 'A bad day,' I thought. 'A very bad day.' I went to the other window and was just raising the blind when I heard the neighbour's voice, his or hers, I'm not sure which, saying something like could I pass them the cat please, since she was hurt and couldn't jump. So it wasn't about a lover at all. I put my trousers and sandals on, then went back and opened the door to my apartment. The door opposite was ajar. I waited. The neighbour emerged, in black socks and no shoes, but fully dressed other than that. He apologised and I invited him in, and set about raising blinds. The cat was nowhere to be seen. Absolute silence. Empty balconies. The neighbour went back to his apartment, to see if the cat had decided to jump after all and was already back home. She hadn't. The neighbour peered out of each window again and finally found her on one of the other balconies, obviously frightened, perhaps by the water I'd sprayed at her, or perhaps by her owner's voice; I don't know what kind of a relationship they have. Anyway, he found her and took her away, and I went back to bed. The doorbell rang. Several times. I was hungry. I remembered I'd sent out a few feelers by email and was waiting for some replies. A clumsy lucidity filled me, clumsy but lucidity none-theless, and I decided to give up on my day of rest.

.    .    .

Later, as I was making breakfast, the phone rang. Around two in the afternoon. I thought of Chl and was about to pick up, but stopped myself just in case. It rang five times and then the answerphone clicked into action. The person hung up.

A few minutes later, the doorbell again. Someone is looking for me, for me or Doctor Turcio, which is the name displayed next to my doorbell downstairs. Someone who doesn't know me very well, because if they knew me, they wouldn't do it at this time of day, or hang up when they heard the answerphone.

The whole way through my breakfast, though I didn't notice at the time, some music playing on SODRE was making me feel uneasy. I realised it was the source of my discomfort when I finished my breakfast and sat down in the reading armchair to drink a coffee. An epileptic-sounding pianist was bashing away at his instrument as if trying to wind his parents up at siesta time. He was accompanied by some string instruments, which were equally manic and unhinged. 'Beethoven,' I thought. It might as well have been. According to the presenter, it was a trio called Arpas. Harps! Good grief. A moment later, the presenter's voice gave me a fleeting hope: 'Erik Satie,' she said, and my mood lifted. Good, I thought, something cheerful at last. Then the presenter dashed my hopes: 'Soprano,' she added, and I turned the radio off.

In other words, there's nothing good in the air, or on the air. Except for the possibility I mentioned at the beginning of this diary entry, namely that the gods have decided to needle me and keep me awake.

# DECEMBER 2000

Almost five hours have passed since the beginning of D-Day. Needless to say, I still haven't begun my work. Yesterday, Thursday, I had a workshop, after which I raced over to the computer to release all the tension, and now here I am, on Friday, 1 December, at almost five in the morning, remembering my commitment. I expect tomorrow, or rather today, when I wake up, I'll gradually get down to it.

FRIDAY 1, 20:06

In the early hours of this morning, I began my work at what I think is the beginning: by reading my patron saint. Before that, I read a few incredible pages of Bernhard, from his book *Old Masters*. He found a way of saying the things that can't be said, and he piles searing truths one on top of another, though in such a repetitive and exaggerated way that the effect ends up being explosively comical.

My patron saint, Santa Teresa, didn't let me down. I turned to her now because I've been keeping *The Interior Castle* next to my own books for years, and in my most productive period, reading even a few pages of it would have me shooting off to start writing myself – so much so that I never got very far with the book. I don't think I made it past the first chapter. It used to fill me with tremendous psychological excitement. She's a truly great writer, extraordinarily powerful. You begin reading, and in no time you can feel the enormous amount of energy contained in the fabric of her words – energy and reality, of course.

I don't react now the way I did a few years ago; these days I'm insulated by a thick protective layer. Still, I found the very beginning of the book profoundly moving; I would have written the words myself, today, in this diary, if I were capable of it:

Rarely has obedience laid upon me so difficult a task as this of writing about prayer; for one reason, because I do not feel that God has given me either the power or the desire for it, besides which, during the last three months I have suffered from noises and a great weakness in my head that have made it painful for me to write even on necessary business.

However, as I know the power obedience has of making things easy which seem impossible, my will submits with a good grace, although nature seems greatly distressed, for God has not given me such strength as to bear, without repugnance, the constant struggle against illness while performing many different duties. May He, Who has helped me in other more difficult matters, aid me with His grace in this, for I trust in His mercy. I think I have but little to say that has not already been put forth in my other works written under obedience; in fact, I fear this will be but repetition of them. I am like a parrot which has learnt to talk; only knowing what it has been taught or has heard, it repeats the same thing over and over again. If God wishes me to write anything new, He will teach it me, or bring back to my memory what I have said elsewhere. I should be content even with this, for as I am very forgetful, I should be glad to be able to recall some of the matters about which people say I have spoken well, lest they should be altogether lost. If our Lord will not even grant me this, still, if I weary my brains and increase my headache by striving to obey, I shall gain in merit, though my words should be useless to any one. So I begin this work [. . .]

### SATURDAY 2, 02:29

I reread the very small number of pages I wrote back in January, and which might be the beginning of my project – the second part of the 'luminous novel', that is. They're not bad. But nor are they particularly good, at least not as a continuation, since there are marked differences in the style and focus. Still, I think it's all I can manage for the moment, and if I try to begin another way it won't go any better. I don't want to copy myself in 1984; the only definitive value these things can have is their authenticity. So yes, I think I'll use those pages and carry on with my project from there. All I did today (yesterday, Friday, and in the early hours of today, Saturday) was read a bit more of my patron saint and revise those pages. I found it difficult to begin work on them; I feel consumed by a mortal heaviness, an infinite clumsiness, when I think about moving that material around. It's what Santa Teresa calls 'the natural'. That crazy natural that's been driving me crazy for so long, and I don't have many tools left for dealing with it. Well, at least today I managed to sideline the computer for quite some time – except, that is, for the legitimate use of Word for all this.


Over the past few weeks, when I've gone to bed in the early hours of the morning, the sun has already been up. It comes up very early these days, but admittedly I've also been going to bed very late. Before going to bed I sit for a while in the reading armchair, letting my horribly twisted muscles relax after their stiffness at the computer, and muttering self-critical things. I look out of the window at the splendour of the heavens. Once, I was lucky enough to witness an incredible spectacle, before a very stormy day, when the storm still hadn't made up its mind and a timid sun was emerging where the sun normally emerges. The spectacle involved some impressive banks of greyish and even black clouds gradually gathering at different heights in the sky, trying to form a roof over the entire city. There must have been a huge amount of smog in each of them, because I can't imagine how they could have been so black if not for the soot. Who knows where they came from; our city produces all kinds of crap, but I don't think our industry is active enough to fill the clouds with that much smog. The most attractive thing about the spectacle was its air of unreality; it made you think of a sky painted by Disney Studios. The blocks of cloud were rounded and rather spongy, but I'm not sure exactly what it was that produced the Disney effect. Perhaps it was the way the fluffy shapes looked deceptively saintly, as if wanting to disguise their lethal contents. Whatever it was, the spectacle was wonderfully enjoyable to watch; there's something fascinating about reality when it doesn't look real. When a sky looks like a painted canvas, it gives you the shivers in a different way to any other kind of experience. Even the most perfectly made work of art always has something that exposes it as a work of art, such as the frame around a painting.

And these absurd bedtimes allowed me to follow the pigeon family's activities for a few days. I couldn't work out exactly how big the family was, because sometimes there seemed to be an outsider hanging around too. The outsider was tolerated for the most part, though not very enthusiastically, like one of those uncles who turn up uninvited and you can't very well ask to leave. I think there are three young pigeons. I saw two of them pestering the mother, trying to get food from her beak, exactly like chicks and nothing like the teenagers they really are. I also noticed how the father, or the head of the family, would sometimes put up with them and sometimes, in an unexpected and apparently unjustified outburst, give them a shove with his chest to make them fly away. Fortunately they've stopped scratching themselves, or at least they're not doing it as frenetically as before; there was one day when the five of them stood in a line and rooted around in their feathers for ages without stopping. They must live in a nest full of lice, I thought. Another day I saw the couple picking lice off each other, in a rare moment of tenderness. It's a tense family; never for a moment do those birds seem to relax. They move around, they walk up and down on the railings, and even when they're not moving they look nervous, as if they're expecting something unpleasant to happen. And the fact remains that always, a few yards away, lying on the roof, is the corpse of the female pigeon's late husband. Nobody pays attention to it any more, it seems, though somehow one of them always has it in view; at least, there's always an eye turned in that direction. I haven't seen them for a few days now because I'm going to bed slightly earlier. I'm not going to sleep any earlier, but I'm going to bed earlier. Only slightly: when you can't yet see the sun but the sky's already fairly light. Sometimes I do go to sleep earlier, it's true, but only to be woken up by a mosquito or, inevitably, by the need to urinate. The antihypertensives are still having that effect, and it looks like I'll have to live with it until the end of my days. I tried not taking them when my blood pressure had more or less stabilised and the figures were normal, but it soon went up again. Now I'm in a phase of high blood pressure. I have an electric device in my apartment for measuring it, and the results might be different because it's me doing the measuring. It still excites me a little, and scares me a little, every time the sleeve inflates and tightens around my arm.

Yesterday morning's mosquito bit me on the knee, through the sheet. It swelled up enormously, almost like a second knee. When I turned the light on the mosquito was nowhere to be seen, so I couldn't squash it and decorate the wall with more of my blood. I had to spray some Flit, which I could feel poisoning me immediately. I got up and stuck my head out of the window. The sun was already shining. Today my whole respiratory system is protesting; the combination of Flit and cigarettes is making my poor lungs despair.

My sculptor friend was walking down a street in my neighbourhood, the Old Town, somewhat distracted. A man, whose appearance she didn't register, was going in the opposite direction. When they were almost next to each other, he swerved slightly, just enough to give her a surprise kick on the ankle. Her sandal went flying. The man didn't stop, or even say anything; he just carried on walking, impassive. She was left with a nasty bruise. Montevideo in the year 2000.

MONDAY 4, 01:49

It was eight in the morning yesterday, Sunday, and I hadn't finished my Saturday. I was lying in bed, reading some fascinating information I'd found online about the Windows Registry. When I reached a particular sentence, I had a sudden revelation, and I got out of bed and turned the computer back on. The information was nothing new, but it had never occurred to me before: I could configure Windows for a second user, or rather for myself with another personality. Then I felt frightened because I realised I'd taken another step, and a serious one at that, towards total splitting, though I don't see any other symptoms for the moment. Anyway: now, when I turn the computer on, it asks me who I am – well, in a manner of speaking. Really what it does is show me some initials in a box and wait for me to say that I do want to use that configuration, by clicking OK, or to change those initials for others, and open Windows as a different user. One of those users, the new one, is the writer. His desktop is relatively clear of toys and games, and there's an eye-catching icon that lets you open Word straight away. The idea is to avoid easy temptations. It's true that I can still access any program I want while in that configuration, but it takes a bit more effort – which, I imagine, will give me time to think better of it. Let's hope it works.

Configuring those users and dealing with some complications that arose meant it got later than ever, and by the time I went to sleep it was gone 10 a.m. Absolutely ludicrous. Today I didn't wake up until after 5 p.m. Once I'd had breakfast I corrected a few things in the configuration and then embarked on an extremely painstaking electrical task. It took me about a year to realise I didn't need to put up with the scanner running a test every time I started or restarted Windows, a test which drags on unbearably considering my limited time at the computer. The infernal contraption has no off button, and according to the manual, if you want to turn it off you simply have to unplug it. But my sockets are in inconvenient places, by the skirting board under the computer table. So I looked through all the junk I've been accumulating in boxes over the years and found a switch for turning a lamp on and off, and a suitable cable, and a pair of connectors, male and female, and used it all to create a kind of extension, though it's more of an intermediary, one end of which is attached to the switch. Every stage was a lot of work, from the planning to the eventual use of masking tape to attach the switch and the scanner plug to a metal bar that runs horizontally along the underside of the computer table. My sight gets noticeably worse by the day, and my fingers are extremely clumsy, so fiddling with the tiny screws and the rest of it was torture. I was sweating by the end, but I did it. Now Windows loads in half the time. There's still room for improvement; I could do a bit of work on two or three of my own programs, which open when I start up but don't always need to, to make them only open in certain situations.

But the scanner is a real nightmare. It's on the same line as the printer, and I discovered just now, when I went to print my schedule for the week ahead, that the printer doesn't work when the scanner is unplugged.

## TUESDAY 5, 00:02

In the early hours of yesterday morning, I began. Although really I should say 'I continued', since I've decided to use the small amount I wrote in January too. It's been happening for a while now that when I get into bed, I work on the text in my head, or rather I work on the images, or the mood, of what I want to write, and often I find myself mentally putting it into words. Early yesterday morning I was outlining yet again how I'd continue the story I began in January, when I saw quite clearly that I was going round in circles and getting nowhere; that I was forever thinking, 'I'll write it tomorrow,' the way you might think about beginning a diet or a plan to quit smoking. But today I said: 'Tomorrow doesn't exist and it never will. The project won't happen at this rate. I need to write down what I'm thinking this instant, because when I wake up tomorrow I'll get tangled up in the thousand things I get tangled up in every day and the text will go on being postponed until it's time to go to bed and . . . ' And although I was already wearing the clothes I sleep in, I turned the computer on – configured to the user who's a writer – and started to type. I don't know how it turned out, but when I went to bed seventy minutes later I'd stopped feeling guilty.

The end of the story – the 'luminous' part itself – is yet to be written, though there are plenty of other events I could write about too. The end of the story was left for 'today', or rather yesterday's 'tomorrow', and today I feel particularly nervous for superstitious reasons. Superstition, I know full well, is an invention of people with no religion; it's about submitting to a kind of higher law, even if that law has been created by people themselves. I realise I'm always very alert to 'signs' and often make the mistake of thinking that completely unrelated things are connected, seeing one as a 'sign' of the other. Today, for example, the day I was meant to reach the main part of my story, the computer monitor exploded. It left me in a state of shock. And I immediately took it as a 'sign': from an invisible, higher place, I was being told not to write that part of the story. I was being told to abandon the project.

Since the monitor's guarantee expired a few days ago (the manufacturers calculated it perfectly), I had to buy a new one. By the time it had finished burning (it was a proper explosion, like a gunshot, accompanied by a flash like a small bolt of lightning), the new one was already being installed. The image quality isn't the same as it was on my old monitor; it's worse. All the colours, especially the light ones, are perforated with little black spots. I called Patricia straight away, since she sold me the new monitor and installed it, and an argument ensued. She says this monitor is better than the one I used to have; I think it looks worse and refuse to put up with it. She's agreed to investigate, in case it's a question of hardware or software, but it will have to wait until tomorrow – and because I've paid for the monitor already, I doubt tomorrow will bring any solutions.

And so a distance has arisen between me and the computer. Only just now did I manage to sit down and try to type this diary entry. I kept coming over and sitting at the computer, but there was nothing I wanted to do on it. I checked my email for no reason. I had a kind of computer craving, but with the shock of the explosion, the possibility it was a 'sign' and my frustration with those little black dots on the screen, I found myself completely devoid of cybernetic impulses. Even now I'm not working happily; I feel uncomfortable and irritated.

On an intellectual level, I have a deep contempt for superstitions (not so much for superstitious people, because plenty of my friends are superstitious and I like them too much to be contemptuous), and when I catch myself deferring to them I don't hesitate to extend that contempt to myself. However, also on an intellectual level, I've learnt to respect them. I know they're a substitute for organised religion, and I use that term in the broadest sense, to cover not only religion but also its many substitutes, which can include politics, football or any other kind of partisanhood (a word that isn't accepted by any of my dictionaries). Unlike with jealousy, which is another part of myself that I abhor, I respect and try to pay attention to my superstition when it makes itself known. Although I very much doubt that not doing so could offend some higher being, it seems obvious that it would offend some lower being, which lives inside me and with which I'm obliged to coexist. So I've been mulling over this business of the sign in relation to my project, and I think I'm going to opt for a compromise, namely: continuing to write as if I hadn't received any signs, but at the same time being on the lookout for further signs that might support the first. I could write something, for example, and keep it but not publish it. I could even delete the files, if it came to that. But I'm not going to stop writing until it's clearer whether there really is some invisible being who'd prefer me not to write and, if its existence is in fact confirmed, until it's clearer what kind of being this invisible being might be.

### TUESDAY 5, 03:31

I should probably be working on the continuation of the project right now, but while I was drinking my night-time cup of tea, and perhaps because I'd been reading a very interesting book by a neurologist (*The Man Who Mistook His Wife for a Hat*, by Oliver Sacks), I had a sudden powerful memory of a recurring phenomenon; not frequently recurring, especially not in these more peaceful years of my life, but something that recurs, or recurred, always the same way, in different circumstances. This phenomenon could be described as a state of mind, and it can only come about if a particular kind of situation arises. And although it's distressing in many ways, at the same time it's accompanied by an atmosphere I'd almost call artistic, and therefore pleasurable.

The catalyst is always my arrival in an unfamiliar place, and an essential condition is that I'm going to spend some minimal amount of time there, at least a few hours and ideally a few days. It could be a hotel, or better still a roadside inn, with a more intimate feel than a hotel; it could also be a hospital or a sanatorium, where I need to focus on or be attentive to the development of a relative or close friend's illness. It could also be the house of some people I don't know very well, which I might be visiting, for example, with someone who does know them. Anyway, in situations like this, the first thing I do is develop a strange kind of nostalgia, a nostalgia for something completely unfamiliar to me. It's not curiosity in the usual sense, by which I mean that I'm not interested in learning details about the people. But there's a kind of global curiosity, so to speak; curiosity about the workings of a whole system of interpersonal relations, but also about details, though not just any details, and a curiosity about the history, or rather the present-day stories that mingle together in the place. For example, if I spend a few days at a hotel in a seaside town, at some point I'll discover the activity of some ants and become profoundly, genuinely, passionately interested in where these ants have come from and where they're going. In the same way, if anyone from that place discusses personal details with anyone else, or asks about their family, using specific names, in no time I'll be eavesdropping on their conversation, trying not so much to keep hold of the details as to produce a sort of sketch, something like a series of threads or invisible lines that turn into a single line connecting the person who's talking and the people and places they're talking about; and I attempt to put together a kind of diagram of the speaker's life based on those small snippets of information. I don't manage, of course, and nor is it possible to manage just like that, so I get upset. It gives me that feeling of yearning for something lost, for a world where I'll never set foot.

In larger places, for example Piriapolis, where I lived for a few months and where I've been spending relatively long stretches of time for many years, that curiosity doesn't arise. Although I have the inter-relations of countless people displayed before my eyes, they interest me so little that I never remember them, and, while everyone thinks that surely I know so-and-so is the wife of so-and-so, I'd probably be surprised if they told me. I don't particularly notice my surroundings. In contrast, when it comes to my closest neighbours, the ones who live on either side of me, I'm enthralled by the most trivial details. But it's not the curiosity of a gossiping old lady; I don't really care if that man who lives with that woman is her husband, concubine, brother, husband, uncle or friend, and nor do I care where he works or how much he earns. What I do care about is where he works as a physical place, or rather the imaginary line this man might trace when he leaves home and goes to work. And the fragments of information they let slip during conversations, preferably with other people. It's a bit like the attitude of a thief or a spy, but I don't think it's the result of a perversion; when they speak to me directly I'm obliged to pay specific attention, to show I'm listening and to say something every so often, and this interrupts my artistic fabulations, if that's what you'd call them. These characters I come across now and then at the tables of the bars along the *rambla* . . . for me, the fragments of their conversations are gold dust. They chatter away freely, speaking almost in code about things that seem completely foreign to me, but I collect these fragments day after day and try desperately to make them into a painting, a story, a whole of some kind. That is: the overriding feeling is one of incompleteness. If I could gather all the information, if I could piece the whole narrative together, I'd lose interest right then and there, and of course I'd forget the whole story – because what matters to me is the discovery, the process of solving the jigsaw. Something like what happens to me these days with the computer and the infinite world of elements it contains, and which I can access, just as I can the interrelations between its parts.

TUESDAY 5, 06:12

Rotring.

I'm about to go to bed, but what I was writing earlier just came back to me and I realised I didn't explain it very well, partly because I don't understand it very well myself. I should have said that those attitudes and curiosities of mine were never conscious; what I'm writing now is what I'm discovering now, as I think back over those scenes, which are all infused with a very particular mood. I look at the images that arise and wonder what I'm feeling, why I'm so anxious, what's going on in my mind – and then these answers come.

Just now I was thinking how this anxiety relating to a kind of nostalgia or longing for unfamiliar things is due mainly to the fact that I'm only in the place for a <u>limited period</u>. It's about knowing

I don't have time to integrate, to belong to that place and those people; I arrive somewhere, in other words, and I'm already saying goodbye, I'm longing for it in advance. I'm already leaving, already incomplete. It must be one of the most powerful reasons why I hate travelling: because that feeling makes me a stranger everywhere I go. Sometimes even in my own home, but that's another story.

## WEDNESDAY 6, 04:22

While I was asleep this morning, my friend Inés left me an answer-phone message. I can call her by her real name because I understand that what a person dreams about doesn't compromise the person who appears in the dream. I had a dream about Inés, an erotic dream. When the telephone rang it barely woke me up; I didn't hear the words of the message, but I realised it was her. I have a feeling I then slept for a lot longer and dreamed about other things before I dreamed about her, but only a feeling; the feeling of time passing, nothing more.

The message, which I listened to later, said she couldn't come and visit me this afternoon as we'd agreed. In my dream, she did visit. The house I was in wasn't where I live now. In the first image I remember, we were in a corridor that led to a room further on and then continued towards the back of the house; I could see the door to the room up ahead, but I couldn't see what there was at the end of the corridor. Inés seemed worried or anxious, as if she wanted to say something but it wasn't the right moment. Then she said there was still a long time to go, or something like that. I began to suspect what was happening and tried to help things along a bit, making myself more accessible. Then she walked over, put her arms around me and asked directly: 'When are we going to sleep together?' 'Right away,' I responded breezily, but the truth is I had my doubts. There were other people in the apartment, although I wasn't sure who they were, and I was also meeting Chl the next day, and I felt a kind of anticipatory guilt about my infidelity (much as Chl, in 'real life', has stripped me of all hope and often says I should try to form relationships with other women). I also felt rather confused by the idea of sleeping with Inés and not continuing the relationship with her afterwards; the presence of Chl was very dominant, and the possibility of entering into a romantic relationship with Inés seemed unacceptable to me; one way or another I was with Chl (which is something I still feel, consciously, in my waking hours). Then I find myself with Inés in a big, spacious room containing a huge bed. She had put on some highly appropriate sky-blue pyjamas, which suited her very well. I'm fairly sure this room we were in was my grandparents' bedroom, where I often slept in the early years of my life.

We were embracing, standing next to the bed, when I noticed that at the foot of the bed was a group of people, a whole family, plus a kind of salesman or estate agent, a man who looked like he was good at making money. His eyes were twinkling and he was holding a notebook or a plan of the house. There was an older, rather corpulent man; a woman I couldn't clearly make out, evidently his wife; and a girl, or young woman, in a blue dress. They were all very stocky, even the girl. And they were all looking at something to the left of me, in the distance, I don't know what, while the supposed estate agent was talking and apparently setting out reasons why the couple should buy the house – or at least, that's how I interpreted the scene. They seemed not to notice our presence, but they were looking very hard at that point to my left and were obviously aware that Inés and I had been about to have sex. They were pretending not to know. After putting up with that situation for a while, and probably as a result of a gesture from Inés, of irritation or despair, I was suddenly furious and strode over to confront them. I told them emphatically that this was a private place and they had no right to be there, that it was outrageous for them to have come into the room without knocking and that they should get out immediately. They started to leave without protesting, though also without much enthusiasm, and as the last of them, which was the salesman, was leaving, he turned back to say something. I shouted in his face: 'Insolent louts!' and slammed the door.

But the doors didn't have keys, and there were two doors, in two different walls, one opposite us and one to the right (which wasn't the case in my grandparents' bedroom, where there was only the one opposite). Then comes a gap in the narrative, during which we must have made love, because when I return to my dream Inés and I are walking down the street together; I was feeling light-hearted and content, and I put my arm around her shoulders, a way of walking that made it clear we were a couple. I began to get nervous again because I didn't know how to explain to Inés that we had to leave things there, that I was with another woman; I didn't want to hurt her, and the relationship with her was proving most satisfactory, but from my point of view it was completely impossible, completely inappropriate, and completely unthinkable and out of the question. At the same time I was sad, since, for me, ending this relationship would be a real loss – but I was feeling more and more nervous because people could see us, and many of our acquaintances might get the false impression that we were a couple. The longer we went on like that, I thought, the more difficult it would become to set things straight.

We reached a very wide avenue, and I had to restrain Inés when she tried to cross it under circumstances that could have been dangerous. I checked carefully that no cars were coming before crossing with her and arriving at a kind of large flower bed, which I can't visualise or describe very well. Further into that flower bed was a small structure, and in the top section of that structure was a window, or a very low balcony; whatever it was, someone we knew (someone we knew in the dream) was leaning out of it and waving at us happily, and, as far as I could tell, he approved of the fact we'd finally got together. This character was more Inés's friend than mine; he could have been one of her colleagues. The structure looked precarious somehow; I think it was made of logs, and had probably been erected as part of a celebration. There was something political in the air, perhaps related to the Council, and definitely related to the left.

This dream, which I enjoyed because of the erotic elements and despite the anxieties, could well be a product of the antidepressants, which I started taking again three days ago. And the fact I had a shower when I got up today is definitely thanks to the antidepressants. I hadn't showered for ages; the thought hadn't even occurred to me.

Speaking of which, today I realised that I tend to suppress a lot of my impulses because of a hyperawareness of my energy levels. It takes me just a fraction of a second to measure, in some mysterious way, the amount of energy available to me, and then decide if I 'want' or 'don't want' to do a particular thing at that moment. Most of the time, I put the thing off, postponing it until an unspecified future point. This must be part, I think, of a very deep depression. It's strange to live for years in a very deep depression without realising, though I realise the moment I poke my head out a little way, like today for example. Today I made decisions very quickly, but I noticed I was oscillating between bursts of energy and paralysing tiredness. After doing something I'd sit back down in the armchair, but I didn't spend much time sitting down; something else would occur to me and I'd spring up in a single motion, with what you might even call agility. I'd do whatever it was that had prompted me to get up, and then I'd sit back down again. That happened several times. It was, I thought, as if the drug was battling against the depression, with one winning one minute and the other the next.

THURSDAY 7, 04:30

More computer-related catastrophes, now in terms of software. I don't remember if I've written here about the monitor exploding and being replaced with another monitor that's no good, followed by another one that's no good either. And now, while waiting to sort out the monitor, I've started having problems with the software – of which some of the more serious, I have to confess, were caused by me. To cut a long story short, a series of errors that had been building up for a long time culminated in ALL the programs I've made in Visual Basic being deleted. Fortunately, most of the project files were saved. I was able to reconstruct almost everything, but it took a lot of work, on a sweltering hot night, and now I'm shattered.

FRIDAY 8, 02:40

After endless years of preaching in the desert, of being shunned and vilified for certain views I hold, at last I've found a twin soul. I refer you to page eighty of *Old Masters*, an uncategorisable book by Thomas

Bernhard, translated into Spanish by Miguel Sáenz and published in Barcelona in 1991 by Editorial Alianza Tres:

> Take Beethoven, the permanently depressive, the state artist, the total state composer: the people admire him, but basically Beethoven is an utterly repulsive phenomenon, everything about Beethoven is more or less comical, a comical helplessness is what we continually hear when we are listening to Beethoven: the rancour, the titanic, the marching-tune dull-wittedness even in his chamber music. When we hear Beethoven's music we hear more noise than music, the state-dulled march of the notes, Reger said.

FRIDAY 8, 04:30

I'm very tired. The computer in general, and Windows 95 in particular, are still making life difficult. This needs to stop RIGHT NOW. But I'm still waiting for Patricia and her solutions for this monitor, which is lopsided and looks like it's had holes pecked out of it; a ridiculous screen. It's hot. It's stormy. It almost feels like summer. The holidays are coming. Already there are fireworks and drunk people all over the place. Summertime in Uruguay.

I'm going to bed, exhausted. It's a pity, because I have lots of things to write about.

SATURDAY 9, 05:35

The business of my disappearing programs is still causing all kinds of problems. Some of the ones I reconstructed by means of their project files have slight errors. It's a terrible hassle and it's left me unable to do anything else.

Yesterday, when I closed this diary before going to bed, I realised there are problems with how it's being saved, and that created a great deal of extra work – which, what's more, I still haven't finished. It's all too much for me.


And the month started a week ago. I should be spending all my time on the novel. But I haven't seen any new signs . . . I don't know what I'm supposed to be doing.


And then there are the plants. And the ants.

SUNDAY 10, 04:17

Rotring.

*The Goalie's Anxiety at the Penalty Kick* (which some translations call something slightly different, though I prefer this title) is a book by Peter Handke, an Austrian who's a long way from being a Bernhard, though also a long way from the sweeping picture Bernhard paints of his fellow countrymen, i.e. he doesn't seem to be an idiot. The person who does seem to be an idiot is the man who wrote the introduction, a certain Javier Tomeo. I saw the book at the bookstall on the corner around ten days ago, and it appealed to me because of some resonance or other that never quite turned into a memory. A nicely made book, a hardback in good condition, with a glossy dust jacket. The marked price was ninety pesos, which seemed about right, if rather high for that street stall. More like the price of a new book, though new books are even more expensive. Anyway, I didn't want to spend ninety pesos on the book. I asked the bookseller how much it was just in case, because sometimes the prices written in the books are still there from when they were new, and the real price, now that they're second-hand, is different. He said he'd give it to me for seventy. I put it back and told him I'd wait for him to try selling it a few more times, in case it got a bit tattered and the price went down.

Last Friday, after paying the electricity, gas and telephone bills, I decided to stop by the bookstall. I was thinking about this book, and I also wanted to see if any new detective novels had turned up, though I was sure there'd be no new Rastros books because I hadn't received any telepathic signals. There was nothing new, and the Handke book was in the same place as before. I opened it and saw it still said ninety pesos. 'I was hoping you'd have reduced it,' I said to the man. 'If I reduced it for you . . .' he responded. 'How much did I say? Fifty?' I wasn't about to correct him, so I kept quiet. 'Well then, I'll let you have it for forty.' Even fifty would have been reasonable, and perhaps I would have paid that, but I'd had forty pesos in mind all along as the ideal price, so I was happy (as I write this there are a pair of ants walking along my desk. I'm scared of accidentally squashing them every time I move this block of paper. I'm still writing on part of a ream of fanfold).

I learnt from the inside cover that the novel had been made into a film by Wim Wenders. I'd like to see it, because if it's done well it could be very interesting, visually I mean. Especially if the narrative intention has been respected.

On principle, I never read the introduction to a book before I read the book itself, and recently I've been trying not even to read the blurb, especially if they're books published in Spain, because Spanish publishers have a real passion for telling the reader everything important that's going to happen in the story. The pinnacle of this, as I think I've said before, is a Nero Wolfe novel, where the murderer's identity is actually revealed on the front cover of the book. This introduction is no exception, and I've never been more grateful to my principles; if I'd read it first, it would have completely ruined the experience. But I'm glad I read it after finishing the novel, because it turns out to be very funny indeed. The introducer begins by saying it's a difficult book to understand, goes on to say that he doesn't understand it himself, and then ends by saying that he doesn't even understand the title. Which is very surprising, because even I understood the title. Even me, and I never normally pay attention to subtleties like that. But just as the book's coming to an end, one character tells a brief story that explains the title, and then, almost at the very end, the protagonist repeats exactly the same story, though changing the context, and then you realise once again what the title means. It's simple and unequivocal. But the writer of the introduction didn't understand it.

Nor did he understand the novel, and what's more he doesn't seem to realise that novels aren't meant to be understood. He's disconcerted by the protagonist's attitude and turns to psychology, telling a kind of criminological parable to explain to the reader why it's not possible to label the protagonist with such-and-such a mental illness . . . He's quite hilarious, this gentleman turning his hand to introductions. The really serious, unforgivable thing, however, is that the introduction tells the story of the novel from start to finish, at some points in minute detail. If the author was hoping to surprise the reader with a shock revelation (of which there are several), Señor Javier Tomeo decided not to allow it. This situation is perhaps more serious than the situation with the Spanish introduction to my novel *The City*, in which there are no shock revelations, but in which the reader might be interested to discover for themselves what they feel when reading certain passages, or see for themselves how the plot develops. Señor Muñoz Molina decided to spare the reader all that hard work, even though he isn't just any old introduction-writer but a notable author himself. It seems it's nothing to do with these gentlemen personally, but rather a kind of unwritten Spanish rule. You rewrite the novel in the introduction. Fortunately, things might be changing, because for the publication of my novel *The Place*, Marcial Souto got hold of a very worthy man called Julio Llamazares, who says he hates introductions, and who doesn't give much away or interfere at all in the reader's conversation with the book.

I can't see the two ants any more. I got distracted and now they've gone.

SUNDAY 10, 04:39

At least I'm now fairly up to date with the things that needed doing on the computer, though not entirely, because I still need to clean the small disks. But everything had become too slow and perilous, so I cleared my email programs and saved the emails onto disks, cleared the ZIP disk I use to save the backups from each day, and backed up ALL my texts, including this diary and the whole of Visual Basic; in other words, the foundations of my existence. I also played some games for a bit, I confess. And as for the grant project, I didn't even go near it.

SUNDAY 10, 05:10

I found myself wondering whether, when these people try to <u>under-stand</u> a work of art, it's because they think they understand the Universe. Which is really pathetic. If they didn't think they understood the Universe as a whole, why would they demand explanations from one of its parts? Or, put another way: based on what reference for understanding, within what parameters, do people want to understand a work of art? What's the perfectly intelligible model with which to compare it?

SUNDAY 10, 05:17

But this business of the introduction made me lose sight of the most important thing about the novel, which is exactly what the introducer didn't see. The protagonist seems to have a fragmented perception of reality. He's mentally ill, if you like. But the most striking thing about the text isn't the behaviour and fragmented perception of the protagonist, but the fact that the omniscient narrator – the narrator who records the actions and perceptions and thoughts of Bloch, the protagonist – seems to suffer from the same condition. Because the story he tells is fragmented, his perceptions of Bloch's actions are fragmented and have the same strange selectivity as Bloch's own perceptions. So we're faced with two characters who suffer from the same condition, though we don't know if the narrator is really a character or if it's the author who suffers from the same condition as Bloch. I'm inclined to think that the omniscient narrator is a character created by the author, but one who isn't exactly a fabrication, who didn't come out of nowhere; rather, that the author has tendencies that allow him to construct this character who tells the story, and, in addition, the protagonist, Bloch.

One possible reading of the book is that it's written by Bloch himself, that he has a split personality.

SUNDAY 10, 06:15

Rotring.

The little plant Julia gave me has just lost another stem. The smallest one was the first to fall, and it came as a real shock. There'd been nothing to suggest that one of those young stems might drop off, just like that. The leaves hadn't lost any of their colour or firmness. I phoned Julia and told her there'd been a tragedy. She was alarmed, but then, when she found out what had happened, she took the news calmly and told me that yes, these plants do that and she doesn't know why. It's the same with the ones she has. I asked her if it wasn't perhaps time to transfer it to a pot of soil, since it was still feeding on water alone, and she said it definitely was. That very day I put it in some soil, which was no easy task. I had to clean a plant pot that had been out on the balcony, exposed to pigeons and other sources of grime. There was no longer anything inside it, except for a few little ants. That plant pot had previously housed a horrible herb I once took it upon myself to plant in Colonia; really it was very beautiful and elegant-looking, but at certain times of the year, and perhaps rather too often, it gave off a horrible stench, like rotting meat, or at least like meat that's gone off. Whilst cleaning the plant pot, I remembered the way Pongo the dog smelled at certain times of the year, when he came back from his rampages around Colonia (whatever became of Pongo the dog?). I used to imagine him rolling around perversely in the flesh of rotting animals he found here and there, but when I discovered the properties of that herb, I realised it would make much more sense for him simply to have passed through places where that herb grew in abundance. Of course, there was still something perverse about it, because he must have liked the smell or he wouldn't have been in those places. And almost as proof of the rivalry between dogs and cats, I could see that the neighbours' cat hated the herb, and this cat was the one who decided to set about destroying it, over a period of weeks and months, until the poor thing was no longer even trying to stay alive. The plant pot was taken over by grasses that no one watered, and which eventually dried out. But perhaps cats and dogs aren't total opposites; perhaps the cat destroyed it out of love, because she was fond of it, and maybe she tore it down so she could eat it. I wish I'd paid more attention to the facts at the time; now I have no hope of finding out how much truth there is in these disquisitions.

Someone will be wondering why I kept that herb for so many years, and why I always had it with me when it was alive. The answer is that I've never personally dealt with my house moves, of which there have been a few, and the people in charge of moving my things inevitably brought the pot with that herb in it to wherever we were moving. When I finally ended up living by myself, the person who took charge of that move thought the herb belonged to me and sent it to my new apartment, along with other pots containing other plants I'd once looked after, although by then I didn't want to have plants, because here, in this apartment, there's no suitable place for them, and I don't like seeing them suffer. I had them put where I thought they'd suffer the least, i.e. on the balcony, the living-room balcony, and there they were exposed to the sun, rain, wind and cold and all the rest of it, without anybody worrying about them. It's possible I was cruel, but the truth is I could hardly look after myself, and perhaps not even that. Perhaps not even that.

A few days ago, my doctor sent me a 'money plant'. She'd asked if I wanted it, reminding me it was mine, and told me it was blooming splendidly and that she knew how much I liked those plants (which in Buenos Aires I'd grown in large quantities). I reminded her in turn that the plant she was offering me was the descendant of a mother plant, or rather a great-grandmother plant or something even more remote, which my mother herself had given me, although I don't remember what the occasion was; perhaps it had been when I said goodbye to her before going to live in Colonia. Yes, it must have been then, around 1989. Well, when the plant arrived I put it on my desk, by the plant from Julia that was still in a little bowl of water, and I got the impression that it was making Julia's plant jealous. Hers is an extremely sensitive plant, and now I'm going to bed. I hope I can carry on with this topic when I get up. I hope I don't get abducted by the computer.

MONDAY 11, 01:09

The computer captured me briefly, but I still have time to escape; it's not very late, and so far I haven't done anything too stupid. I've

stuck to cleaning some floppy disks and finishing the backup I started
yesterday. I also typed up some pages of this diary I'd written by hand.
I'm very behind with that, but gradually I'm getting there. All I have
left to type up are the first twelve days of October (I'm going through
the pages in reverse order, because I always pick up the first piece
of paper I see, which is the most recent), but as it happens, in those
twelve days, I wrote like a man possessed. I must have been almost
manic. Compared to my usual state, I mean. I have no reference points
any more; I can see now that I was seriously depressed for years, but
it was a depression that went with the flow and I didn't have a bad
time. And I only notice when the antidepressants begin to take effect,
a cumulative effect that isn't visible at first, and I think: 'I was really
sick,' and feel quite astonished. It seems I only notice my depression
as it manifests in my strange behaviour, which could, now that I think
about it, be the depression's way of making sure I *don't* notice it and start
trying to fight back. I know this is all a bit roundabout, but perhaps
the essence of what I'm saying comes across; I can't put it any better
right now. The fact is that knowing I don't know when I'm depressed
doesn't tell me whether I'm depressed or not. Ideally I'd ask a doctor,
but doctors, and especially psychiatrists, terrify me. I've had very bad
experiences with some of them, like the stupid one who did nothing
but give me a different kind of medication each week, to see if any of
them did the trick, and whose only achievement was poisoning me.
It's true that I have my doctor, but since there's a friendship there she
can't be my psychiatrist, and although she agrees to prescribe me or
procure me certain medication for free, it's always after a long debate
about the pros and the cons, and at the end of the day it feels more
like I'm medicating myself. By which I mean that she doesn't exert all
her medical authority over me, precisely because she isn't my doctor,
or at least not my psychiatric doctor.


But I was supposed to be carrying on with the topic of plants; only
now I don't feel like it, or rather, it's no longer at the forefront of my
mind. I want to record that today almost all the other stems fell off,
except for one, which looks to be in a very bad way. The plant has

ceased to exist, in other words, and perhaps putting it in the soil only hastened the process. I said before that it's a very sensitive plant, I now recall, and it was definitely jealous of the other plant, the money plant I was given. Maybe that's what made it ill. The proof of its sensitivity came one time when I wasn't feeling well at all, and the health of the plant, still in its little bowl of water, declined noticeably, leaving me very worried about it. It was a day when I had markedly low energy levels. When I felt better, the plant got better too. And then I noticed how well it looked on workshop days, as if happy to be around so many people.

TUESDAY 19, 00:36

A long time has passed, I think. It's not that I've been busy with the grant project; far from it. Lots of things have happened and I've been meaning to write them down, but for one reason or another I haven't done it. These things probably won't be of the slightest interest to any eventual readers, but they're of interest to me, and to the structure of this diary, so I'll try to write them down, at least briefly, as they come back to me, perhaps not in a precise chronological order.

At the end of October I made the mistake of spacing out my anti-depressants and eventually giving them up altogether, since they weren't fulfilling their purpose of helping me to quit smoking, or at least to considerably reduce my cigarette intake. That sent me into a relapse that lasted all of November and is very much still going on, though it looks like it's calming down a bit.

The pigeon family seems to have fallen apart. The young ones left many days ago to live their own independent lives, and for a while the couple could be seen alone, in their usual place on the railings of the flat roof next door. But soon they stopped coming together. Sometimes the male pigeon would show up and sometimes the female, and then I didn't see either of them again. Maybe, once the children were grown-up, the widow saw no reason to carry on living with that male pigeon who probably wasn't their father. The father of her children is still dead, lying motionless on the flat roof, and more alone now than ever. Other pigeons come and go from the railings, always different ones, and none of them take any interest in him. That corpse is beginning to get on my nerves. It's the first thing I see, or the first thing I look at, whenever I open my bedroom blinds. It's too conspicuous to ignore. And it's an ominous presence; it seems very out of place in the urban landscape of historic little streets running down to the port.

The computer, working in league with its accessories, began a rebellion that's still going on. First came the explosion of the monitor. It was like the signal for everything else to start acting up. The most recent thing is the printer, which didn't tell me it was running out of black ink. By the time it told me, it had already run out, and it was jammed. It's a printer that uses two toner cartridges, one for colour ink and one for black. You'd think that if the black ink ran out it would be able to print in colour, but no; the printer is still jammed and there's no persuading it to use the colour ink. It wouldn't be so serious if I were getting up at a reasonable hour these days, but by the time I'm in a fit state to go out, the places that sell toner cartridges are closed. I asked Patricia; she doesn't have any. She says she'll get hold of some, but she never does. I also asked her for a mouse, another of the implements that have started causing trouble, and she brought me one, but there was something wrong with it. Patricia says I have bad luck. The new monitor still isn't working properly, and she's going to bring me another; at least, that's what she says, but she hasn't so far. Today she told me that everything will be resolved on Thursday. The only good news I have to record in relation to the computer is that, on the advice of Patricia's husband, I had her put in a new RAM memory card. Now I have 64 megs instead of 32, and it's made a huge difference. More speed in various operations, and it even seems that Windows Explorer freezes less than before. I can also open several programs at once without being told there isn't enough memory, and without them slowing down. I got hold of a kind of manual, which is very interesting and can be downloaded online, about how to use the Windows Registry. I learnt a lot, but some of the author's advice ('tips') doesn't work. I wrote to the author and he hasn't replied. I also wrote to a company that installs air-conditioning units, and they haven't replied either.

The little plant Julia gave me is now completely dead.

Chl dreamed, a few days ago, that she was travelling on a bus driven by her therapist. I was the conductor. I wasn't at all pleased by this secondary role, but I realised the therapist had managed to win her over, which is necessary for therapy. I've suggested to Chl myself that her relationship with me might hold her back, as far as her therapy is concerned, because I could see the transference wasn't working and I always appeared in her dreams in the most important role. But I didn't like it one bit, and I liked the next part of the dream even less: the people travelling on the bus gradually got off, and Chl stayed on; then the therapist and I, the driver and the conductor, got off, and she stayed on, and the bus kept going. After that she faced a series of difficulties, fears and anxieties, but in the end she made it home and felt good. I'm happy for her, but not for myself, and as far as I'm concerned the therapist can drop dead. One thing's for certain: Chl is going to push me out of her life. I knew it was going to happen, but it still hurts. Perhaps it'll do me good, and help me get out of this emotional labyrinth. I'm surrounded by women who love and pursue me, but I'm tied to little Chl, even though we're not together any more. Now she's going to be away for a long time. We'll see each other sporadically, but these sporadic visits won't bring me any relief. I'm going to suffer. I'm suffering already.

WEDNESDAY 20, 03:02

On Sunday I had the visit from Flora. I wasn't expecting her to come, since I thought she'd only promised to visit me because of a maternal command. Her mother is my friend from Chicago, and I know she goes out of her way to impose this sort of obligation on people. Plus, on another of her trips here, Flora stood me up. And nor was I sure whether, even if she did turn up, we'd have much to say to each other, since her interests and experiences seem so different from my own. And yet she stayed for four and a half hours. It wasn't until 1.30 a.m. that I deposited her in a taxi.

Flora, or rather that name, which her parents decided to give her shortly before she was born, was what caused me to write a novel called *Fauna*, over twenty years ago. I don't remember if Flora has read this novel. It bears no direct relation to her, of course, but I think I'd be interested in reading a novel that had been inspired in some way by me.

A few hours ago I had a secret fit of jealousy. I knew Chl was having some friends over and that this was why she didn't come and see me today, but, as usual, she denied it, and I distracted myself with the computer. I was on the point of sinking into an interminable series of mindless activities on the machine when I felt – when thank God I was able to feel – a pang of jealousy in my chest, and I realised I was putting out another edition of the same old story. Then I phoned her and made some joke about it. I didn't feel much better, but at least I managed to escape from the trap, which could have had me hypnotised until sunrise. There's still a hint of that unpleasant sensation in my solar plexus, but in spite of the unpleasantness, and how stupid it makes me feel, I'm trying to hold onto it, or at least not to forget about it while it's there. It's good to feel something, even if it's only that.

WEDNESDAY 20, 15:43

Yesterday, during a friendly chat with my friend Felipe (who'd come with his regular delivery of books to lend me), he mentioned that I was 'fairly autistic'. I agreed without giving it much thought, but today I remembered the expression and realised that I'd always seen autism in absolute terms; either you are or you aren't. The 'fairly' struck me as a good diagnostic discovery. I'd say I'm 70 or 80 per cent autistic. And with the remaining percentage I get by pretty well.

WEDNESDAY 20, 18:02

I've just got in. A hectic day. Chl took me to see a special chair for using with the computer, which isn't cheap, but which, according to her, will solve all the problems in my life. The chair I'm using now could send me toppling over backwards at any moment. Still, I have to wait about a week for them to deliver the new one, which will let me adjust the height of the seat, among other things. On the way back, I called in at the pharmacy for some antacids. Then, just as I was putting the key in the lock of the door to my building, telepathic inspiration struck: 'There are new books at the bookstall.' I went to see. And of course, there was a new Rastros. Well, a very old Rastros, but it had only just arrived. I'd never seen it before; it's a difficult one to get hold of. Its back cover is missing and has been replaced by a cutting from a magazine that shows a comical face. The novel is none other than *Red Harvest*, by Hammett. I've read it several times, of course, but I've never seen this edition before; it's probably the first edition in Spanish (1945). Hammett wasn't famous among intellectuals back then, and so *Red Harvest* ended up in the lowly Rastros series. *The Dain Curse* is also in the catalogue, though I've never come across that either.

Yoga class soon. Then new things for the computer (apparently I'm being brought the monitor, the mouse and the toner cartridge). This could interfere with my doctor's visit, which is scheduled for 9.30 p.m., since the computer people are always horribly late. Because of all this, I won't see Chl today, though she'd been planning to come. I did see her just now, it's true, but in her hard-working young woman persona, pressed for time, wearing dark glasses; it was as if I hadn't seen her at all.

SUNDAY 24, 06:05

I'm writing by hand, in natural light. I spent all of Saturday meaning to record a disturbing dream I had. Finally, once Chl had left and I was by myself again, I went to the computer intending to do it. But instead, I downloaded two programs a few megabytes each in size, one of which a friend sent me and the other of which I expressly looked for online. And only now, six hours later, have I turned the computer off. Without writing about the dream. Instead I was exploring the new programs.

The dream: I was going to urinate and I noticed a considerable crack in my penis. On the glans. Like a non-painful wound, with jagged edges, resembling the earth when it cracks open during an earthquake, reducing my penis to a third of its thickness. The crack ran along the very tip, perpendicular to the urethra. As I said, it didn't hurt, and there was nothing to suggest it was an injury, strictly speaking; it was as if the flesh had come apart quite easily, with no blood, as part of a natural process. I vaguely understood that I couldn't have sexual relations with anyone while I was in this state, because then I really would get an excruciating and traumatic injury. I also thought vaguely that perhaps it could be sorted out with surgery or some other medical procedure. But at that moment my mind was busy with other things, I don't know what, and the problem of my penis was working away in the background, coming to the fore from time to time but never seeming like a priority, although it was clearly worrying me and making me profoundly nervous.

The need to urinate was coming back, and becoming quite pressing (I really did need to urinate; it wasn't an invention of the dream). I went into a bathroom, which then turned out not to be a bathroom, and I found myself a long way off the floor, standing on something like the blade of a wooden fan, similar to an aeroplane propeller. From there I was peeing downwards, and although I had the end of my penis between my fingers, I was trying to run my other hand down the whole length of it, but this turned out to be very difficult because it was so long, almost like a hosepipe hanging down to my left.

Underneath, also to my left but very far away, because it was an extremely long room, were some beds with people asleep in them. I knew they were women. One of the women, as I imagined or knew, since I couldn't see anyone in the pervasive darkness, was my mother.

Yes, I know: castration, or the threat of castration, as a punishment for the Oedipus complex. But this interpretation fails to explain what I was feeling at the time, and I don't understand why I had such excessively long genitalia.

SUNDAY 24, 17:13

Strange, very fat pigeons, on the railings of the flat roof next door. Yesterday: a bird whose head was completely white, except for two black circles into which its black eyes disappeared. It looked like a skull. The body was mostly white, with a few black patches. It stood directly opposite me and plucked a few little white feathers from its chest. Today: a bird whose head was completely black. Abnormally fat, like the one yesterday.

SUNDAY 24, 18:00

For some days now I've been thinking, and what's more, there are notes all over the place reminding me – on the computer, on little cards by the phone – about calling my recently widowed friend Jorge. Now I want to record the dream I had as a result, among other things, of my worries about him. Though not without first explaining that the frame of a wooden chair is destroying my back, because yesterday I finally, and deliberately, broke my computer chair once and for all; I removed the backrest, which was threatening to break my neck. Whenever I tried to lean back, the backrest would give way a little too much, throwing the chair off balance, and I felt like I was going to fall over backwards. So I manoeuvred the backrest to and fro until I broke the wrought-iron tube that held it up. I was left with a nice stool which has no backrest, but which after a while gives me backache. So I've started using this chair instead, with the frame that digs into my back somewhere around my thoracic vertebrae. Now I'm going to try sticking the backrest I broke off the other chair onto this one, to see if things improve.

I didn't need to stick it; resting it on the seat of the chair was enough to improve things considerably.

Today's dream: (oh! An image from a dream I had yesterday just appeared to me, which I'd forgotten about; it's from the last section of a long dream, perhaps the same dream as the crack in my penis: there was a small animal somewhere, perhaps a mouse, which for some reason was important to the events taking place, and I'm damned if I remember what they were; someone picks the animal up, and it's not a mouse any more, or whatever it used to be, and instead it's a little black cat. The cat is talking in a reedy voice; it speaks slowly and in well-structured sentences. I look at the person with the cat in his hands and see that he's moving the lips imperceptibly. 'A ventriloquist!' I exclaim, and he smiles. This person looks very familiar, very familiar indeed, although I can't say exactly who he is. He has a European air about him, and very regular and pleasant features, which I'd almost say were feminine, but it's not the joker-style gay character who sometimes appears in my dreams, though it could have been one of his disguises). Anyway, the dream, today's:

I'm worried because I need to phone my friend Jorge. I don't do it because I can't think how to do it, because he's the one I need to speak to and I'm not sure if he's at home, and besides, even if he is there, his wife's more likely to pick up (his wife is my childhood friend, the one who died this year) (of course, in the dream she's still alive). And I don't want to talk to his wife, because it turns out we'd been lovers for a while (only in the past invented by the dream, I should clarify) and I'd left her, presumably because the situation made me feel immensely guilty. At one point I see her, at home, with her children (who are alive and well, and still very young, as they were in the period corresponding to my 'golden age', during those wonderful times in their house in Villa Argentina). I see her looking abandoned, worried because I've disappeared from her life, and those images also make me feel guilty. There was more, much more than this in the dream (an erotic feeling, among other things), but now I don't remember anything else.


It must be the continuation of the previous dream, since, as I was saying, castration is punishment for the Oedipus complex, and in this dream, my friend certainly represents a maternal image. It seems the unconscious is trying to help me out of this cesspit I'm currently in. I have the key: the fucking resurgent Oedipus complex, the cause of everything bad in my life (and also, unfortunately, of everything good). But I'm not doing anything with the key. I hope the unconscious carries on helping me.

·   ·   ·

(The Word spellchecker still doesn't accept the word 'penis', and it still won't let me add it to the custom dictionary. However, it allowed me to add 'fucking'.)

I'm going to call my friend right away. I promise. Soon. Any minute now.

### MONDAY 25, 03:16

Here I am, messing around on the computer. I keep thinking of plenty of things to write, but I don't write them. I still haven't started, or rather continued, the project; so far I've only written a page. I promised to work on it full-time from the first of December.

Merry Christmas.

### MONDAY 25, 06:58

Rotring.

I'm still up, at seven in the morning. I'll have to go to sleep with those pinpricks of sun on my eyelids – the rays that filter through the mended shutters.

And after all, I was thinking just now as I waited for my coffee to heat up, if I've gone over to live in the world of the computer, it's because there's almost no other world possible for me. Where else could I go, what else could I do? What other chance do I have of intelligent conversation? And affection. Distant, distorted by the words (and even the sounds) that transcribe it, but there nevertheless, within arm's reach. Chl went to have Christmas Eve with her family. That's OK: she still spends too much time with this boring old man. Today, Monday, Christmas Day, I'll see her, I think, and then from tomorrow I won't see her very much. As a precaution, I asked my old friend M to take me for a walk every now and then as an act of charity. We went on our first walk on Friday, calling in at the *boliche* halfway. From home to Calle Ejido and from Calle Ejido back home, all straight along 18 de Julio. It was satisfying, or at least I thought so. We're going for another walk this week. And today (yesterday) I called my friend Jorge, whom I'll see tomorrow, Tuesday. So there are other sources of affection in my life. But this Christmas night, what else was I going to do besides converse with the computer? True, I spent a while sitting in the darkness in silence, or the relative silence of tonight, a silence broken by firecrackers and bottle rockets. During that time, I managed to relax a little. I didn't feel bad. The anxiety didn't come. But what did come after a while was an urge to go back to the computer. To use my brain. While the brainless throw their firecrackers around in the streets, releasing all the aggression they've built up over a year of wretched slavery.

The world of the computer has already been very much invaded by the wretched, and the cheaper things get, the more wretched it becomes. Not because the poor are necessarily wretched (though they often are, sometimes even as much as the rich), but because cunning people will use the wonders of technology to further brutalise the poor, the kind of poor who live in tin shacks with television antennae on the roof. And in doing so, they, i.e. 'the powerful people', also brutalise themselves. They've always been brutes, in one sense, and now they'll become even more brutal, thanks to technology. The internet will leave the cultural sphere where it began once and for all, and will instead be under the control of businesses and states. But even so, the structure of the computer, and the intelligence of the human race who made it work, will always be there. It will always be a world to be untangled, a world you can converse with, because it must necessarily be governed by logic. Without logic, the machine doesn't work. Even if the person using it isn't logical. These days a drooling football fan can press a few buttons and get a few results. Soon he'll be able to do a lot more, with even less intellectual effort. Nevertheless, there may always be a few individuals who'd rather converse with the inner workings of an operating system on Christmas Eve, indifferent to the firecrackers and drunken revels. Of course I find this solitude somewhat painful; things could easily have been another way. Of course I submerge myself in the world of the computer to numb the pain, which is more nostalgia than pain, or a kind of nostalgia, the kind you find in tangos, which doesn't need to relate to a concrete fact or a real-life experience. Nostalgia for what a race, or a country, could have been. Ah, people . . .

FRIDAY 29, 00:49

For the past few days, I've been completely submerged in computer-related things. Except yesterday, Thursday, which for me is still going on, when it seemed – it seemed, at least – that the antidepressants were beginning to take effect. Whatever it was, I was feeling more lucid than usual, more able to exercise my willpower, and the computer was turned off for most of the day. But the computer issues were on my mind just the same, however hard I tried to concentrate on what I wanted to write in this diary, and of course on the grant project. Practical tasks, including going to the dentist – which has to happen on Thursdays because two Mondays in a row are holidays – helped me to think about other things, though not the things I wanted, and still want, to think about. It's as if the computer were the devil himself. I read somewhere about a rabbi from the United States who says the devil can – and indeed often does – inhabit computers. It's strange that the solution he proposes, in addition to exorcisms, is sending the computer to the repair shop to be taken apart. As if, when you put it back together, the devil couldn't slip back inside.

Today I took delivery of the deluxe chair Chl made me buy. It's not that she forced me to buy it, but she convinced me. I'm more comfortable than I was in the old chair that broke, but I still haven't managed to train it to do what I want. I think something's wrong with the controls for the backrest. I'll have to look into it. Meanwhile, I'm sitting a bit higher up than usual, which makes using the keyboard easier; I can see I'm making fewer typing errors. There's no neat way of saying 'typing errors' in Spanish. I say *'errores de tipeo'*, but the word *'tipeo'* doesn't really exist. There's only *'tipiadora'*, which can mean either a typewriter or a female typist. You'd think we'd have the word *'tipiador'*, too, for a male typist, but no. And nor do we have the verb '*tipiar*', for 'to type'. It's a funny old world.

I've just raised the seat a little more and lowered the armrests; this seems to be an even better position if I want to type, or '*tipiar*'. But the seat doesn't stay in the highest possible position; when I sit down, it sinks considerably. In one sense this is probably a good thing, because otherwise my feet would hardly touch the floor. But it would be interesting to know what it's like to type from up there. Still, I'm very high up even now.

My computer-related occupations and preoccupations are making me feel like one of those people I've always rather looked down on, or perhaps never understood: people who buy a car and then spend all their time taking it to pieces, putting it back together, replacing its various parts, washing it with a hose, polishing it with a cloth and talking about it at length. I try not to talk too much about the computer, because I can see that the people I'm talking to, most of whom are women, get bored immediately. They do more than get bored, in fact: they get annoyed and start hating me. They announce that they don't understand a word I'm saying, even though I use ordinary language, nothing technical, and in my opinion I explain things with total clarity. I think it's more that they're not listening properly, like Chl when I start telling a joke. The moment she realises it's a joke, she switches off. She stops following. When it's over she doesn't laugh, or understand why I find it funny. And yet she's capable of understanding perfectly well and laughing at more subtly funny stories, as long as they're not in the form of jokes. I've concluded that Chl, like many, many women, intuitively captures the psychological significance of the system of telling jokes and realises that it's actually a form of disguised sexual penetration. Laughter is the equivalent of an orgasm. When a man tells another man a joke, he's exercising his right to sublimated homosexual desire, which is of one of the few such rights that are socially acceptable. This is what I think, and it sounds very convincing to me. It's highly probable that women who shut themselves off from jokes also shut themselves off (one way or another) from sexual penetration. By 'one way or another', I mean they shut themselves off both in the sense of closing their legs, and in the sense of not participating in the sexual act or reaching orgasm, even when they open them. That's why they don't laugh at jokes. Not because they don't understand, but because they understand all too well. I like this theory of mine.

As I was saying, I've started feeling rather too similar to those men who fuss over their cars. I've spent days and days, weeks, maybe months, maybe years, absorbed in dismantling and reassembling my computer, not its physical parts but its intellectual components. When it comes to the physical parts I tend to be more conservative, sticking to the same model for as long as I can, until it stops being compatible and I can no longer communicate with the rest of the world to a reasonable extent. The same goes for the operating system: I kept Windows 3.1 (so solid, so reliable!) for as long as I could, and when I had to update it, I chose Windows 95 (much more unreliable) even though everyone else had 98 (more unreliable still) and 2000 was about to come out, if it hadn't already. It looks like now I'll have to update this operating system, because the monitor can't be fixed. It's been replaced three times now, and I always get the same grid of black dots and the letters look like they've had their edges trimmed off. Apparently, getting a more recent version of Windows could solve this. We'll see; it'll be traumatic, whatever happens. Not until a few days ago, after having had it for a year, did I manage to get the screen looking just how I want it. I mean the screen when it's almost empty, with no programs open; what's known as the desktop. I normally have it completely black, because I've realised black doesn't hurt my eyes so much.

Through all this work of studying and trying to make changes to the computer, and creating programs that can automate all kinds of things, I've discovered, in recent days, that I have a real talent for stealing.

I am, essentially, a thief; and I enjoy it enormously. It all began when a friend, whom I'm not going to name, was kind enough to give me a CD-ROM with some stolen programs on it, among them a program containing codes that allow you to steal many more programs in turn. The manufacturers make a program available, which you can download from the internet, and they let you use it for a certain time so you can see what it's like. Then you have to 'register', which involves paying some money. In exchange for this money, the manufacturers send you a code, or codes – a series of numbers and/or letters – which you enter into the relevant box in the program. You're then allowed to use the program indefinitely. The property you acquire, so to speak, is the right of use. The stolen program that helps you steal other programs contains many of these codes, and when you use the correct code in the program you want to steal, you end up with a relative right of use; and sometimes not so relative, but just a right, plain and simple. It's a relative right when as part of the code you have to add the name of a user who isn't you; it's the name used by someone who bought the program once and then decided to share it with the world. That's how I come to have programs registered in other people's names or pseudonyms, including some women's names.

The point is that, at the moment of entering the code and clicking the button to complete the registration, my heart pounds nervously, rather like when the roulette ball is getting ready to stop and you've made a substantial bet; and when clicking the button results in a little box that thanks you and confirms that the program has been registered, you feel, I don't know, an almost orgasmic sense of relief, a rush of pleasure that's ephemeral but very intense, and most of all very unusual; something I couldn't bring about in any other way.

The material benefits aren't very large. Most of the programs I steal are worth between five and forty dollars; the forty-dollar ones are very complex, made by big companies, and it's difficult to find codes for them because the versions are constantly being updated, and with them the codes; what's more, of those sophisticated programs, there aren't many that interest me. I'm not, then, stealing for primarily financial reasons. Stealing makes my life easier, since I don't have a valid credit card to use online, and even if I did I might not want to use it; it's a dangerous thing to do. Most of the times I've been sent money by post it's been stolen, so I also prefer not to send money by post. A long time ago, a friend of mine who sold newspapers, and who was himself a friend of one of the postmen who used to work in my old neighbourhood, told me how he watched with his own eyes as his friend the postman rummaged around in the sack full of letters, took out an envelope, said, 'There's definitely cash in this one,' and then opened it and produced a banknote. The man had developed a special gift, and it looks like he's not the only one. Cheques used to get stolen in Buenos Aires as well. It doesn't matter if they're not cheques payable to the bearer; there's always someone who buys them and some way of cashing them.

When I was a recent initiate in the world of email and the internet, I looked for and eventually found a program that would let me dial up automatically to get online. It wasn't easy to connect back then; sometimes you had to dial and dial, and the lines were always busy. The automatic dialler could go through as many as two hundred unanswered calls before it was able to connect. Finding that automatic dialler was a great relief, and I wasted no time in automating the entire process: when I turned on the computer and Windows started up, the dialler appeared and began to dial. In the meantime, the dialler itself launched my email program and a program called Trumpet, which looked after the interface between the telephone modem that responded and the modem of my computer (protocols). All this has been simplified, and hidden, in Windows 95, and as a result something has been gained, and, as usual, something has been lost. The losses include the Trumpet control panel, which showed the result of each of the operations between one machine and the other on a little screen; and I personally have lost access to the dialling from a program I made myself, because I have no idea how to get at those hidden mechanisms.

But that dialling program had one flaw: if you didn't register, which cost around twenty dollars, when it started up a small box appeared showing a countdown from 10 to 0. You had to wait for it to finish, then click a button to get rid of the box and carry on using the program. The box also reminded you that you weren't registered, and that you urgently needed to register in order to carry on using the program. That annoyed me beyond words, because it was a flaw in my perfectly automated process. If I turned the computer on and went to have breakfast, for example, it wasn't enough to listen out for the piercing sound I'd assigned to the dialler, which alerted me when the connection had been successful; instead, I had to stay nearby, waiting for the program to appear, and the box to appear, and for it to count all the way down, and then click that famous button, so the whole thing would carry on the way it was supposed to.

The manufacturer was a Texan man, and he turned out not to be particularly nice. I wrote him a very interesting, entertaining, agreeable email, explaining the difficulties I had in getting to the post office because of my advanced years, and how people here steal any money you post anyway, and how I was poor and didn't have a credit card; and I offered to send him some amusing stories in exchange for the codes that would get rid of that damn box. The whole thing was a huge effort because my English isn't very good, and back then it was even worse (because now the internet has made me practise a lot). But I couldn't soften his hard Texan heart; he responded briefly, coldly, and even went so far as to say that whenever he gave things away, people forgot to say thank you. As if that man had ever given anything away. In an attempt to win him over to humanity a little, I wrote back, thanking him for having replied, and ended up repeating 'thank you' in a sarcastic-sounding way. I was very frustrated, and obsessed with finding a solution. There was no similar program online; nothing matched what I was looking for. I tried making a dialler myself, but I didn't have Visual Basic back then, and nor did I know enough to be able to do it.

One warm, muggy summer evening, I felt a strange need to lie down and have a siesta, which was a habit I'd lost ever since a certain woman who lived with me had come out as utterly against my doing it, for psychological reasons there's no need to go into here. That day I felt an overwhelming desire to lie down, and I fell into a very deep sleep.

I dreamed I was in Texas, at the home of the program manufacturer. I didn't get a good look at the house from outside, but it seemed to be fairly modest, not a cottage but something along those lines, very homely and unpretentious. His wife, a mature woman, opened the door; I didn't get a good look at her either, but there was a strong domestic and even maternal air about her. She was wearing an apron and took me through to the kitchen. As she poured me a coffee, she explained that her husband was asleep and it would be a shame to wake him. I felt very comfortable in that kitchen, chatting to the woman.

When I woke up, very muddled, I had an idea fixed in my mind that sent me straight over to the computer like a robot. I opened XTree Gold, a DOS program that was an antique even in that early Windows era, but which I still have and still sometimes use, and that program let me see the inner workings of the dialler. The dialling program was written in a language more cryptic than Chinese, since it didn't even use ideograms; but XTree would show you, on one side of the screen, once you'd carried out certain operations, the intelligible words that formed, if they formed. That's where I found those infernal words from the box; the demand that I register, the whole spiel. Then I did something I've never managed since, which was use the 'editor' mode of XTree, and DELETE the contents of that box. Every other time I've tried things like that the effects have been disastrous, and I invariably end up with the screen frozen and the computer paralysed, and need to turn it off and then on again, sometimes losing a valuable program in the process. But that day, when I was in a trance, connected through the dream to the mind of the Texan, it worked. Sweating, sweating with nerves, I closed XTree and opened the dialler. The dreaded box didn't appear. And the program calmly began doing its job, just the way I wanted. And it went on calmly doing its job, just the way I wanted, for years, until I got a newer version of Windows and didn't need it any more.

That was my first theft.

I'm not trying to justify myself. I don't know exactly what the law is in this country, but when people sell you hardware it comes with stolen software on it (translation: when you buy a computer it normally comes with a stolen operating system, and a few programs – also stolen – thrown in for good measure). It's very common practice and nobody seems particularly shocked. Very well; even so, I don't feel I have the right to be a thief. I don't like being called a thief, by other people or myself. I see thieves as reprehensible types, whether they're poor or rich. Lately I've been asking myself: would I burgle a house? Certainly not. If I knew how to do it, would I make fraudulent bank transfers to myself? It depends; perhaps, if I was assured of total and absolute impunity. That is, I wouldn't have a moral objection, as long as I knew the person the other account belonged to was dishonest. A dictator, for example, or an ex-dictator, who keeps his money in Switzerland. In fact, I think it's a shame I don't have anywhere near the technical ability I'd need for something like that. It would be a lot of fun, if nothing else.

I think I'm not strictly a thief; I don't have the right mindset for it. So why do I steal programs?

In response to that, I'd say that I don't steal programs, but rather the right to use them. The program isn't a physical thing; it's information, a kind of information, just as one of my novels is a kind of information. It doesn't bother me if one person lends another a book I've written, and if that borrowed book is passed around many more people; on the contrary, it's a practice I approve of and try to encourage. In the same way, it doesn't bother me if people make photocopies of my books. I'm even tempted to publish my books online, so they can be downloaded for free. It bothers me if a publisher steals from me, and they do, often, as they do from all writers, one way or another.

Conclusion: the copyright, which is ultimately what you pay for when you use a program, is completely non-existent. For a theft to have occurred, someone has to have taken possession of a physical object that isn't theirs. Or they need to derive material benefit from another person's work. For example, if you buy one of my books, copy it and then print a load of copies to sell, you're stealing from me. You wouldn't be stealing from me if you printed a load of copies and gave them away.

When I 'steal' a program I'm exercising my right to culture, which isn't anyone's private property. The programs I 'steal' don't earn me any money; on the contrary, they make me waste time. I don't derive any material benefit from them. Culture, the product of intelligence and sensibility, is something that should circulate freely, with no charge; it can't be anyone's private property, because the mind isn't anyone's private property. If I was able to read in the mind of an unknown Texan a procedure that let me use his program, that means something. If I write a story and then destroy it because I feel like it's not 'mine' (and a long time afterwards I find material proof that it wasn't 'mine'), that means something. A text I've written isn't 'mine' because I own it; it's 'mine' in the way a child might be 'mine'.

We ought to find a system that would allow writers to survive without needing to traffic in copyright; we ought to destroy this rotten system of blood-sucking publishers, of books as objects, of penalties for photocopying or pirating work. It's true: a writer who hits on something that matches popular taste can get rich overnight (unlikely in this country, of course), and writers of software even more so. But as we all know, becoming rich like that is also a way of becoming poor, and anyway, if people want to be part of that system, fine, I'll leave them to it.

I have no idea how to solve the problem of artists and writers of software (who are artists too, in their way), but the solution won't come from the percentages charged for copyright.

# JANUARY 2001

Since I haven't touched this diary for many, many days now – although, as usual, I haven't once stopped thinking about it – events have been accumulating, filling my memory to overflowing; and the memories that remain have probably lost whatever interest or emotional charge they had at the time they were formed, or shortly afterwards, which is when I should have been writing them down; and whatever wording I imagined I'd use to record them has certainly been lost as well. Meaning that now, when I try to return to them, the same thing will happen as is happening, or would be happening, with the grant project: they'll turn into a kind of fraudulent literature.

The most transcendental event was, beyond the shadow of a doubt, the death of my friend Ruben – the friend whose house I stayed in during the terrible transition period that led to my current way of life. He died last Tuesday or Wednesday. The telephone rang; I was sitting near it, in the reading armchair, and I didn't move. It was the height of the brutal summer heat, and the ceiling fan was completely incapable of creating any movement in the air. Instead, it seemed the thick, damp, sticky atmosphere was going to clog up the blades of the fan, jam the motor and make the whole thing explode. The answerphone started up, and I heard the voice of my friend, Ruben's wife. From the way she said the first two words, I knew what the news was going to be. Of course, I had to get out of the armchair and answer the call, but although I got up, all I did was stand there, frozen, next to the phone. My friend said that if I wanted to call her, I could reach her on such-and-such a number. 'I'll let the news sink in first,' I thought, 'and then I'll phone.' I did call my doctor right away, though, to pass on the message, since she never fails to be there for people on momentous social occasions, whether happy or tragic – something I'm always deeply envious of, because on such occasions I never fail to be elsewhere and afterwards I always feel bad. But some things are more powerful than the will, and in my particular case, the things that are more powerful than my will have become overwhelmingly and terrifyingly numerous. For example, my cousin Pocho rang a few days ago to tell me that our aunt Celia had been hit by a falling piece of roofing at the grand old age of ninety and seemed to be in a very bad way. I took a few days to get in touch with my cousin Pocho, and I certainly didn't call my aunt Celia, and nor did I learn any more about the situation, and then one day, wracked with guilt, I unleashed a tirade of imprecations against my aunt and made an unimpeachably reasonable assessment of why it was just fine for me not to have called or visited her. Maybe I'll discuss this matter in more detail later on.

As for my friend, the recent widow, I called her a few hours later. The news still hadn't sunk in, but I felt able to talk to her. She was no longer where she said she'd be; I reached an answerphone with a message in a voice I didn't recognise, though it wasn't completely unfamiliar; I expect it was one of her children. I left a message that probably made no sense, because all I did was mumble a few innocuous words and then hang up. The next day I didn't call my friend at home, thinking it would disturb her in the midst of all the funeral arrangements and relatives paying respects; so I called her the day after and disturbed her then, because she was about to fall asleep. But at least I'd made contact, which was what I'd been finding so hard.

Not until last night, or rather early this morning, did I see any sign that the news was sinking in. My friend appeared to me in different phases of our long friendship, good times and bad – and we've been through both together, in considerable quantities. I felt myself reliving the rages he could always provoke in me, and that I could always provoke in him, as well as the happy times, especially those marked by laughter, because the rock upon which our friendship was founded, back when we were in secondary school, was our sense of humour. Ruben, Jorge (my recently widowed friend) and I formed, at one point in our teenage years, a trio that was like a kind of machine for producing comic effects, which sometimes had an artistic element, but were mostly just brief outbursts of energy and life.

As I was saying, this isn't coming out right. Besides, I'm tired.

SATURDAY 6, 18:49

At last. It started raining, a little while ago. Heavily. And thundering. We didn't go for a walk today either, of course; it had been N's turn to escort the geriatric this time. I don't remember if I mentioned my walks with M in this diary; but with N, due to the weather or personal circumstances, I still have yet to begin them. Never mind: it's raining, it's cooling down a little, and happiness is returning to the city.

(Another inexplicable facet of the Word spellchecker's behaviour: it doesn't accept N as a single letter, whether or not it's followed by a dot, and it won't let me add it to the dictionary. Curiously, in this case, the spellchecker highlights M as an error, and suggests changing it to one of a series of possibilities, and the first of these possibilities is . . . N. I agree to this change, and then everything carries on as normal.)

SATURDAY 6, 21:04

Unfortunately, as everyone knows, the joys of this world are generally fleeting. Some time ago now, the thunder faded into the distance, the pouring rain thinned to a miserable drizzle and the cool breeze vanished completely, with the air, once again, taking on the texture of that greasy sponge which has been torturing us for too many days. At this point I should perhaps include some strong words about a gentleman called K, but I won't, solely for legal reasons. I do, however, think I'm at liberty to say that I have several very strong words in mind which I'd like to use about this man, whose behaviour I find abhorrent and inexplicable. He appeared in my life, to my great misfortune, as a result of a circular I sent round on one particularly hot night, to various companies that specialise in air conditioning. Admittedly, I deserve some strong words as well, and I haven't hesitated to apply them to myself mentally throughout this period. The thing is, I've been thinking about air conditioning for months, and in September I added it to my calendar as an urgent and essential item; every day, at a given time, a reminder to request some quotes flashed up on my screen. Did I do it? Not in September, or October, or November, and not in the first half of December. Why not? I've been giving this question some very serious thought in recent days. Economics may have played a role, but I'm not sure it was the deciding factor. The very day I heard I'd been awarded the grant, my mind formulated this thought, clearly and resolutely: 'I won't go through another summer like the last.' Last summer I was on the brink of irreversible madness. I find the weather in summer more unbearable by the year, and there was no reason to expect this summer to be any different. It certainly pains me to spend Mr Guggenheim's money on home comforts, but equally, cool air in summer is more than a home comfort; in my case, it's a matter of mental health, and health in general, because once I've been paralysed by the heat and the humid weather in this city, I can no longer think straight, or even move; my body seizes up, and I find myself faced with the likely risk of very serious illness. But there was another factor which combined with the economic one to make my decision more difficult: the fear that an air-conditioning unit wouldn't be the right solution, because my respiratory problems might keep me from using it. I didn't know how it would affect me, and to be honest I still don't. Those two factors, according to the results of my ruminations during those terrible days, were combined with a third, which was vaguer and more difficult to analyse, and could be defined as a slightly magical expectation that this summer would be more benign than the previous ones. Or something more magical still, and perhaps more psychotic than magical: the notion that if I don't think about a troublesome issue, it will somehow sort itself out. Or, if you like, an outright denial of the situation – as with my friend's death, which is still sinking in very slowly, very slowly indeed, while I refrain from doing the necessary things like going to the vigil, and to the funeral, and participating socially in all those activities that must have been invented for a reason. I simply distract myself on the computer and let reality take its course elsewhere, a long way away from me. Yes, it's very likely that my fear of summer made me deny the obvious fact that summer was going to come and make my life a misery, as it has been doing for the past few days. Finally I made up my mind and sent a tentative email to one of the air-conditioning companies, and was left waiting for a response that didn't come. This led to my delaying things for a few more days, during which time the heat was getting worse and the whole situation was becoming very dramatic, until at last, on that desperate, sweltering night, I reached for the telephone directory and looked for the names of all the companies that published an email address. Why an email address and not a phone number? For one thing, because my sleep patterns were still altered and, by the time I was in a fit state to speak on the phone, the shops had lowered their shutters. I have the same problem with bakeries. In the end, I sent that email to four different companies, and at dawn the next day the heat filled me with a psychic agitation that kept me awake until the late morning. I went to bed at about 8 a.m., but I didn't sleep. The phone rang at nine, and I heard the voice of a secretary responding to my email. I got up and called back on the number she'd left, establishing that precious contact I needed in order to receive a visit from a technician, who would have to assess my requirements and decide what kind of unit would be best for me. The technician promised to call one day the following week; I wasn't overjoyed at that, but I thought it was reasonable, since I'd sent the email on Thursday night, and by then it was Friday morning, and the following Monday was a holiday: the first day of the new millennium, to be precise. All very bad planning on my part, revealing my total lack of practical sense.

Some time later, when I woke up after six or eight hours of sleep, I found another message on my answerphone; Mr K, calling back on behalf of a different one of the air-conditioning companies that had received my circular (and that night I received an email from a third company; the fourth never made itself known). I called this Mr K on his mobile and he told me, very kindly and with great conviction, that on Tuesday, the first working day of the following week, he'd be outside my building and ringing the bell at 5 p.m. on the dot. He sounded so definite that I believed him, and I put up with the weather throughout that interminable weekend, clinging to the hope that the problem would soon be solved. On Tuesday, incredibly, Mr K was ringing the doorbell at ten to five in the afternoon.

SUNDAY 7, 05:15

. . . Mr K, then, was ringing the doorbell at ten to five on Tuesday afternoon, and he even apologised for arriving before the agreed time. He turned out to be an elegant man, a bit of a silver fox; greying hair, at least as far as I remember, and well dressed, with something playboy-like in his way of moving through the world. He also turned out to be straightforward and efficient; there was no charade of measuring the spaces, and nor did he deliver a pre-prepared speech about the advantages of the product he wanted to sell. He swiftly explained what he thought I'd need, told me the price, gave me a leaflet, wrote the quote on a form – and when I say he wasted no time, I don't mean he gave the impression of being rushed or uncomfortable; on the contrary, he sat in one of my armchairs, cool as a cucumber, and it was more like being visited by a friend than by a salesman. The quote turned out to be a lot higher than I was expecting. It wasn't completely crazy, but it made me start doubting again, though I'd have preferred to make a decision straight away because I didn't think the competitors' prices would be very different. After all, the spaces I want to cool down in my apartment are fairly large, and there are several of them. While I was thinking about all this, I suddenly remembered the advice of my dentist, who had said I should buy a portable unit. I'd heard bad things about portable air-conditioning units, but my dentist had said good things, and I respect his opinion. In fact, just yesterday I learnt why people have said bad things to me about those units; I'll try to tell that story later on.

It's 5.30 a.m. and I'm writing this a little out of obligation, so as not to leave the topic unfinished, but the thing is, when I decided to take a break from what I was writing in the last diary entry and relax a bit by playing on the computer, the computer began to do wild and incomprehensible things. I gave it a run for its money, managing to format the wrong ZIP disk – I thought I was formatting a different one that had been causing me problems – which meant I lost all the backups from the past month and a half, and I don't want to think about what else. The computer had already, without my assistance, deleted around six hundred photos of nude females, of which – after considerable effort – I managed to rescue some 120. So my rest break descended into nothing but loss, and left me far more exhausted than if I'd carried on writing this diary.

So, I mentioned portable air-conditioning units to that gentleman, never imagining the effect my words would have: he threw out his arms with enthusiasm and declared emphatically and joyfully that I'd had a very good idea, an excellent idea. He gave me full assurance that the portable units his company sold had the same advantages as the usual, non-portable units, and that I'd easily adapt to the minor inconveniences of using one (moving it from room to room, which doesn't sound especially complicated until you learn that you also have to move a small compressor, which is attached to the unit by a tube a few feet long, and also to place this compressor outside the apartment, on a windowsill or balcony). And this option would save me two thirds of the price originally quoted. I told him that even if I bought two portable units, so I wasn't forever dragging them from one place to another, I'd still save money.

'Buy one for now,' he advised, 'and see how you go. You can always get a second one later if you need to' – in other words, exactly the opposite of the overbearing salesman who wants to maximise his commission at all costs.

I said I'd think about it for a very short time, and that I'd call him the following day without fail. As I was accompanying him down in the lift, I remembered an experience I'd had a few years before, with a different kind of air-conditioning unit I tried to buy from the same company. I told Mr K that they had once missed out on a sale by demanding I show up in person to make the payment. Mr K responded that times change, and this had probably happened some years ago. I said it hadn't been so very many years ago, no more than three or four. He looked amazed that the company he worked for could have been so senselessly bureaucratic.

'Anyway,' he added, 'if there are any issues, I'll bring it round myself.'

And off he went, as cheerfully as he'd come, leaving me relieved to have such a serious problem so very, very close to being resolved. It was scorching; absolutely scorching. But already this bothered me less, because there's nothing like hope for getting you through hard times with less heartache.

To cut a long story short: I asked Chl's advice, and she said that of course I should buy it, which was all I needed to make my decision. The next day I called Mr K on his mobile phone and asked him a couple of things that had occurred to me about how the units work. He answered my questions, and then immediately said he had to go and would call me back very soon, when he had time to talk. I waited. And he didn't call. The next day, which was Thursday, the weather was hotter than I have words to describe, and the first thing I did after getting up, even before turning on the computer or anything else, was call Mr K on his mobile. I don't know where on earth he was; he answered edgily, over some background noise that suggested he was in the street or another very crowded place. I told him he'd forgotten about me, and that I was waiting for the unit.

'I'll bring it round tomorrow,' he said. 'Right now I don't have a car and I'm very tied up.'

'Listen, I'm in hell here. Please do everything possible to get it to me today.'

'Let's see . . . I'll sort it out at the end of the day, if I can.'

At a quarter to seven I called him again. Now he was in the office. He said he'd just arrived. And that he'd send it round the next morning without fail. I asked him why not now. He said he didn't have the car. I said: 'Why not use a removal van?' He said: 'The thing is, it's getting late and the sales department is closed.' Two different excuses: a bad sign. Mr K was beginning to seem suspicious. In the end I told him I'd leave the money with the caretaker, and they could ring for the caretaker when they arrived. He said that suited him. 'It'll be with you tomorrow morning,' were his final words.

I took the money downstairs and left it with the caretaker. I asked her to bring the unit up when it arrived, and to ring the bell a lot, then maybe I'd wake up and manage to make the unit work – though I already suspected it wouldn't be as easy as all that; a plug wouldn't work in the sockets I have, or something like that. But the hope of putting an end to that inferno still shone. I went to sleep early and imagined myself the next morning, struggling to prise my eyes open when the caretaker rang the bell, and I saw myself changing the underpants I sleep in for some shorts, in case the caretaker was still there outside when I got up. On Friday I woke up bathed in sweat, feeling like I was being asphyxiated. I hadn't heard the bell, but I don't normally hear the bell when I'm asleep; still, I had a vague sense that something wasn't right. I put on the shorts and slowly walked down to the building entrance. Through the glass doors of the little booth, there was nothing to be seen. And there was nothing that afternoon, either. I didn't call Mr K again, and nor do I plan to. I began a frantic search, before breakfast and before turning on the computer, even before having my yoghurt and antihypertensive tablet; I called a number of shops which sell domestic appliances, and that was how I found out that those units don't exist, that they've run out, that everyone's trying to get hold of one in the dark days of this heatwave. Some people I spoke to said they'd have a look and call me back, but no one did. Mid-afternoon, after breakfast, on the phone to someone about a different problem (the computer – bah), I learn that one particular homeware shop is selling them, and for half the price Mr K offered me. I found the number of this shop in the directory, called, and a shop assistant answered. I asked if they had one of those units. She said they'd bought in twenty and sold fifteen, and at that very moment they were selling more; she told me to wait on the line while she checked whether there were any left. She returned before long. There was one left. I thought: my luck's about to change. I asked for the details, and she went on very politely to tell me the make, the price, how it worked . . . In relation to this last point, I heard her say, among a whole host of other things, something about how it could work with either water or ice. My mind went blank for a few moments and then I asked her if she could please explain about the water and the ice.

'Well,' she said, 'if you want cold air, you put in water, and if you want even colder air, you put in ice.'

Put in ice? Put in?

'Tell me,' I stammered, 'I don't understand these things at all, but I've heard about the thousands of BTUs these units have . . . '

'Well, no; this isn't air conditioning as such. It's a simulation.'

A simulation.

OK. Thank you very much. You've been very helpful.

I thought about taking ice out of the freezer and putting it in a bucket next to an ordinary fan. Every half an hour. I also thought how another way of cooling the place down is to have someone blow on your neck.

That's when I lost hope. The next day, Saturday, was a holiday: Epiphany. And now we're into the early hours of Sunday. The sun's already up, and I still haven't been to bed. And the temperature's beginning to rise. There was a bit of a breeze in the past few hours; I wouldn't say it cooled down, but at least you could breathe. Now, it seems, the whole thing's starting again. And tomorrow will be Monday and I'll be back to square one, hoping the fixed units don't run out as well.

SUNDAY 7, 06:30

But I was distracted from the heat for a few hours on Friday night, thanks to a visitor I had. A woman, relatively young, whom I didn't know personally. I knew something about her literary style, and I was afraid I'd find myself face to face with one of those domineering female types. But she didn't resemble her literary style, which as a style is excellent but in real life would be difficult to take. On the contrary, she turned out to be extremely pleasant and an excellent conversationalist, very intelligent, and very well informed about a range of topics that interest me too. We talked and talked.

When it was time for her to go, she got up very unwillingly and began gathering her things, but she also announced that she didn't want to leave. That she'd never leave, were I think her exact words. I didn't see it as a sexual proposition at the time, and perhaps it wasn't one, because there'd been nothing of that sort in our conversation so far. I replied that if she hadn't decided to leave of her own accord I would have had to throw her out; it was time for my addictions, and I really didn't think I could stand to be away from the computer for much longer. And then, when we were downstairs, standing by the door to the street, which I'd even got as far as opening, I moved my cheek towards her for that brief brush we call a kiss and she hugged me; she hugged me with both arms, and made it clear by means of an invisible language that I should hug her too, and so I did, with both arms, and she pressed her whole body against me, squeezing me tight, and I squeezed her. She stepped back just as I was feeling the stirrings of an erection. It was a very nice goodbye. I wouldn't say she's 'my type', although my tastes are very broad. It's not that she's ugly or that there's anything to dislike about her; she simply doesn't fit the psychological or physical profile of a woman I'd have sexual relations with. And besides, there's Chl. Well, there isn't really; she's abandoned me again, this time for a fortnight. But she still exists; and when we hugged the day before she left, the hug made me cry. She felt so much like flesh of my flesh, and the separation was so painful, as if I'd cut myself open. The hug from my visitor was very nice, almost an antidote to the hug from Chl, because it left me feeling nothing but happiness. I won't pine for that woman, and it doesn't hurt when she leaves. But it was a good hug, and I feel very grateful.

MONDAY 8, 04:16

The greeny-blue-grey armchair, for resting in, is the armchair I hardly ever use. Visitors choose it, not for itself, but because the other one has something almost majestic about it, throne-like even, and, no doubt out of good manners, they leave that one for me. I don't sit in the resting armchair when I'm alone, either, because when I sit down it's in order to read, and the majestic armchair is the reading armchair, the one that makes you sit up straight. And as I explain these details I can't help but reach the conclusion that I never rest, I never waste time on pure leisure. I waste time horrendously, of course, on my unproductive activities, activities that go nowhere; but for the past six months or thereabouts, which is how long I've owned the armchairs, I haven't achieved my objective of resting. I either play on the computer or read; if I'm not doing those things, I'm running errands or going to the dentist or busy with other minor obligations. But what I'd begun to say, or rather, what I wanted to begin to write, was something else. I wanted to write that a while ago I sat in the greeny-grey-etc. armchair, with the light off, and watched, fascinated, as the clouds blew past. The clouds form a roof over the city, a roof that doesn't let the humidity evaporate, and although that roof travels at a considerable speed up there, it seems like it never ends, and never will end. It runs from the *rambla* towards the bay. The clouds are white and they look like smoke, white smoke, because they have a tendency to disintegrate, although they never fully do, and there are holes in them that gradually change shape, as if some parts of a cloud move at a different speed to others. These holes, through which you can see a dark sky, constantly threaten to give the cloud the form of a skull; but I was watching for a long time, and the threat never materialised. Other holes come along and almost do the same, and they don't manage either. I'm glad, because signs from the sky are always frightening, and besides, I already have too much death in my midst. There aren't many of us left.

MONDAY 8, 04:40

When it comes to the flat roof next door, I have to say that I don't look at it much these days, because I generally leave the blind down as a barrier against the heat – which, needless to say, makes no difference whatsoever. At one point in the first day of the new millennium, I raised the blind and saw that next to the dead pigeon's head was a small object I couldn't identify, something yellow and cylindrical. I could only assume it was the remains of one of those flying rockets. Some days later, the object was gone, and in its place, now perfectly distinguishable, were the remains of a firecracker. A long, yellowish stick, speckled with black, emerging from a tube that might have been pink, and which corresponded to the part of the artefact where the powder goes.

The remains of two flying objects, very close together, almost touching; one the product of a mindless evil act, and the other too.

As for the widow, I forget whether I've already said this, but I stopped seeing so much of her, and never saw her again in the company of that male pigeon who acted as the father of her children. I didn't see her children again either. But then she reappeared, on the railings, once more in the pose of a broody hen. This time she was with another male pigeon, who was nothing like his predecessor; very fat and very ugly, with an entirely black head and eyes I remember as bright and yellowish. The widow stayed quite still while her current companion scratched around in his feathers at great speed. He pecked at his chest, at one wing and then the other, never once breaking off from his feverish activity. His movements must have been infectious, because the widow gradually began to scratch at the tuft of little white feathers visible between the tips of her folded wings; and then she got up from her seated position in order to reach other areas with her beak, and soon the two birds were driving me mad with their frenzied scratching. My body felt pecked-at all over and I looked away.

MONDAY 8, 18:45

I'm writing this by the faint light of the sky, which is still filtering in through the window, and, of course, I'm writing by hand. I should be on my way to a friend's house right now; she's gone away for a few days and asked me to water her plants and keep a general eye on her apartment while she's gone. But the day had different plans for me, and right now I'm opting for docile resignation. I woke up feeling compelled to solve the problem of the air conditioning; before going to bed, I'd resolved to cut all contact with Mr K, ask the caretaker to give back the money I'd left with her for the unit, call another company and begin the whole process again. Fortunately, once I was up I found the weather a great deal more benign than in recent days. But something was wrong with me, though I couldn't work out what, and I ended up hovering by the phone without being able to bring myself to call anyone. I decided to wait until after breakfast; sometimes breakfast clears my head a bit.

After breakfast I was still in a hesitant mood, and it didn't take me long to discover the cause, or one of the causes: today turned out to be one of those days when, due to a build-up of side effects from the antidepressants, perhaps combined with other things, my digestive system encounters serious problems. I won't go into the gory details, but I will say that problems of this kind often take up several hours of my time and require almost infinite patience. When I emerged from the bathroom I had a brief moment of respite; I knew it would only be a moment, but I made the most of it to call the air-conditioning company, the same one whose salesman, or technician, had rung me last week and been so patient and polite, trying to persuade me out of buying a portable unit (if only I'd listened). I got in touch with this man, then, explaining the situation and saying I was interested in starting again. He agreed to come over tomorrow, Tuesday, and when the moment came to set the exact time for the visit, he asked me to give him fifteen or twenty minutes to finish a meeting he was in the middle of – and which I'd interrupted – because he didn't have his diary to hand. I called the caretaker and told her I'd given up on buying the portable unit, and that she wasn't to accept it on the off-chance it was delivered. She said she'd bring me up the envelope with the money, as well as a sheet of paper with the bill for this month's maintenance costs. A minute later I saw the envelope and the paper, which the caretaker had slipped under my door. She almost got stuck in the lift on her way down, because a minute after that the power cut out, just as I was heading over to the computer to record the return of the money and also my spending for the month (which is still very high!!). At first I thought the computer had simply switched itself off, in one of those typical Windows upsets, but then I realised the whole apartment was affected. I called the caretaker again to ask if there was any maintenance work being done in the building, and she said there wasn't, and that the power cut was affecting at least the whole block. I unplugged the fridge. The power came back for half a minute; enough time to reset the clock on the microwave, and then *ciao*, it was gone again. I sat down to await the call from Mr L, salesman or technician from the air-conditioning company. I tried to relax in the greeny-blue-grey armchair, and meanwhile my intestines were beginning to feel a bit ropey again. But I couldn't take any notice of that; the answerphone had no power, and the call I was waiting for seemed absolutely crucial, so I decided to think about something else and carry on waiting whilst at the same time trying not to wait; the thought occurred to me once again that I had to water my friend's plants, but I brushed it aside; I was aware of my left ear stretching longingly in the direction of the telephone and attempted to bring it back to its usual place. 'No waiting; just relaxing,' I repeated to myself, not always to much effect. Fifteen minutes went by and then twenty minutes went by and that's when the phone rang. At the second ring I was already by its side, clutching the receiver. And the call was cut off. I stayed where I was, waiting for the next attempt, but there wasn't one. I wanted to return to my state of non-waiting in the armchair, but first I had to light a cigarette. I paced anxiously to and fro, trying to tire out my nerves. Eventually I sat down and stubbed out the remains of my cigarette in the ashtray. I waited ten more minutes. My intestinal trouble was becoming impossible to ignore. I got out of the armchair again and dialled the number of Mr L's company. The noise of sirens of various kinds floated in from the street; they came and went, as if there were some kind of civil unrest out there. The company didn't pick up, either directly or through the answerphone that's always on. I thought: 'They've got a power cut too, and the phone system must be down.' I hung up. Later I learnt that the power cut had affected the whole country, hard as that is to believe.

I lit the end of a candle, left over from a previous power cut, and stuck it in a clean ashtray. I carried the lit candle to the bathroom, resigned to facing the second phase of my martyrdom – damn those antidepressants – while trying to shake from my mind the uncomfortable notion that I was falling prey to the shadowy machinations of even more shadowy powers.

I feel more like a Beckett character by the day.

THURSDAY 11, 00:40

Toothache in one tooth, caused by the dentist. A repair that affected the workings of the prosthesis and, more generally, of my entire mouth. It's not the first time. He says this is the problem with jacket crowns when there's a prosthesis installed, which seems reasonable to me. What seems less reasonable is that every time I chew, I feel a horrible pain and need to take sedatives. He couldn't see me today, so I have to wait until tomorrow, and it's not even certain that the problem will be sorted out then (he needs to file down the crown and the hooks of the prosthesis until they fit together properly), and next week he's going on holiday, along with everyone else in this city except me (Rosa, the caretaker, is also going away; last year, her time off caused me various problems, because the good lady normally takes care of a lot of things on my behalf). Well, Chl's gone . . . I haven't seen her for a whole week. Last night, or rather this morning, I dreamed about her. It was horrible, really painful; she was rejecting me, not with her usual gentleness and affection but quite scornfully, almost as if she hated me. I felt very hurt and humiliated. The thing is, yesterday I had another unsettling crisis of jealousy, mixed with my usual crisis of abandonment, simply because she didn't answer when I called her mobile. Having no control over her actions at any given moment is enough to send me mad. I'm not remotely justified in this, of course. Sometimes I think I really hate myself.

And today I discovered another unfortunate side of myself, though for some reason it was more of a joyous discovery. I think I know why. I'd gone to the supermarket on 18 de Julio; I forced myself to go, want-ing to give myself a reason to leave the house (my lady companions have also disappeared for the time being, after our failed attempts during the heatwave) (today it was, and is, cooler, and at points it was even cold). The sudden change in the weather caused the usual problems, most of all a kind of extreme distraction and a frightening sluggish-ness in my mental processes, particularly my short-term memory, and as a result I found myself doing a series of absurd things that went nowhere, like somersaults in the void; I'd set off for some part of the apartment, and when I got there I'd find I didn't know why. I also had my famous reversal of brain hemispheres, which makes me look to my right for what's on my left, and vice versa. To say I felt clumsy and demotivated would be an understatement. I also made a dubious business decision; another technician from another company came to see me, and I proposed another solution, involving a substitute for the portable air conditioner that's impossible to get hold of; according to my calculations, my solution would cost twice what the portable unit would have cost, but it would be closer to what I need, based on my experiences during the heatwave. Even so, it would still be just two thirds of the price of the original solution, which involved installing a single very powerful unit in the biggest room. My solution places a small unit here in the computer room, and another small one in the room next door, where the armchairs are, which is next to this room but not connected to it. I'd leave out the biggest room, which after all I'm only using as a dining room for the moment, while the workshop's on holiday. But it turned out that with the prices inflated by VAT and the doubled cost of the installation, which is very expensive, I ended up at more or less the original price – with the emphasis perhaps on the *more* – i.e. triple the cost of the portable unit. This means spending precisely all the money from Mr Guggenheim I have left in the bank, and it also means a cold sweat trickling down my back and the hairs at the nape of my neck standing on end when I think that if, for some unforeseen reason, the other half of the money doesn't arrive, I'll be ruined in no time. I know I'll be ruined eventually, and have to sleep in the street and all that, but I wasn't expecting it to happen quite so soon. The Foundation supposedly paid the money into the bank in the USA on the third, so it should be with me any day now. Supposedly.

I took the gamble. I told the man, Mr L, that yes, I'd like to go ahead. The installation starts on Friday. It will be finished on Saturday. Which is my fault, since I won't let them work in the morning; otherwise, it would all be over in a day. Tomorrow they're coming to take a deposit, and on Monday they'll come for the rest. Since I still have the dollars at home which I'd set aside for the portable unit that never came, I'll be left with a small amount in the bank which will just – just – cover February's rent and maintenance costs. As for food, I'll have to work something out. If Mr Guggenheim fails me. If he doesn't, my heart rate will go back to normal for a few more months. I'll hold onto the next lot of money; there won't be any more major purchases. I have the armchairs, I have the shelves, and soon, I hope, I'll have the air conditioning.

As I was saying, I'd made myself go out, setting the supermarket as my objective. There were things I genuinely needed: fresh yoghurt and fresh ricotta, neither of which I could find in my usual supermarket. Not that the other one's a great deal further away; it's just a few extra blocks, but in the wrong direction, since you have the problem of crossing the Plaza Independencia. It's torturous in winter because of the permanent icy wind, and in summer because of the ray of sunshine that descends vertically onto the top of your head. Today was the ideal day to walk across it, weather-wise, though there are other factors that make it tiring and disheartening even to consider that route. One such factor is the appalling funerary monument to Artigas, the 'liberator', which the military dictators were so kind as to deposit right in the middle of the square. It's a ludicrous burial mound, dark and pretentious, towering and absurd, in what used to be a pleasant spot. Only soldiers could mess things up so spectacularly. I've always thought they did it to make sure the old man is definitely dead and under control. That to stop him escaping they've given him a permanent armed guard, right there on the steps leading down to those depths to which I, of course, have never descended. Inevitably, then, to think of crossing the square is to think of encountering that eyesore. And what's more, it's dangerous, because people can hide behind it and jump out at you as you're walking past the pyramid. That's another thing that makes crossing the square so unappealing: the risk of being mugged. The whole area, which includes the square and the blocks of 18 de Julio that come after it, is a kind of no-man's-land where violent incidents take place very frequently, and with impunity. Once I was mugged on the corner of 18 de Julio and Andes, next to the chorizo van, in plain sight of all the people eating chorizo. A friend who works near there told me that from time to time he sees chases and shootings. And there never seem to be any police around.

Now I'm reaching the supermarket. I go inside. I drift around like a sleepwalker, still gripped by that uncomfortable or distracted feeling, something that's like dizziness but isn't quite dizziness, and, little red basket in hand, I move very slowly and laboriously through the obstacles scattered in my path, towards the far end, behind everything else, off in the distance, where they keep the yoghurt, and the cheese. The salt-free biscuits are near there too, and the coffee and sliced bread; my usual purchases. I thought there'd be no salt-free cheese, and there wasn't any. I also thought there'd be some fresh yoghurt, and there wasn't any. I did find some yoghurt that was almost fresh, and I found the biscuits, and the sliced bread, and the fresh ricotta. I sleepwalked back to the checkouts near the entrance, though my return journey was more complicated because I'd forgotten the biscuits and had to go back. I paid at the checkout and added extra bags to the heavier shopping, which the cashier had wisely distributed across three separate bags. I put the receipt into one of the bags and headed for the exit. Before the exit, there's a stall selling meals and ice cream. Various metal tubs are laid out, within arm's reach, filled with ice cream in magnificent colours; it's difficult to walk past without being tempted, but since I had a toothache and my hands were entirely taken up with shopping bags, I was able to resist the temptation with no trouble at all – or that temptation, at least. I had to resist another one as well, only because of the total impossibility of succumbing to it; if there'd been the slightest chance of succumbing, the toothache and shopping bags wouldn't have held me back for a second. Because standing facing the tubs of ice cream, next to a woman who could have been either her mother or her grandmother and waiting for the attendant to serve her, was a young woman. The moment I saw her, the problem with my brain hemispheres instantly vanished; it was a shock, a bolt from the blue. It's been a long time, a really long time, aeons, since I was last so bowled over by a woman's presence. Something about my relationship with Chl makes it impossible; perhaps an automatic comparison means I dismiss everything inferior to Chl immediately, in a subliminal way, and since there's nothing superior, or even on the same level, everything is dismissed automatically with no trouble at all, and often without my realising.

But what was it about this girl that brought on such an immediate rush of desire? I have no idea. She was standing very straight and completely motionless, facing the tubs, her posture perhaps determined by shyness or mistrust. Because the girl looked like she was from the countryside; from the mountains, I'd even say, if there were any mountains in Uruguay. As did the old woman, her mother or grand-mother, who was standing nearby and fumbling with some money or who knows what else inside an enormous handbag. They both had the same air of extreme poverty, even deprivation, although the girl's clothes were fairly new and of decent quality. She was wearing jeans and a light-coloured sweater. The front of the sweater was elevated propitiously by some hard, or rather firm, breasts, not very sizeable but attractive, yes, for some reason attractive; perhaps because of the way they pushed the sweater straight upwards, as if they were pointing upwards themselves; you could imagine the nipples aimed almost at the ceiling. The girl would have been, I don't know, I can never tell how old people are, but I think she would have been between fourteen and sixteen years old. And yet she behaved as if she were younger, with that stiffness, that dependence on the old lady still rooting around in her handbag. The girl had her eyes fixed straight ahead and her gaze was guarded, or rather it was as if she were hiding a second gaze underneath. There was something stupid about her expression, but it was a proud kind of stupidity and suggested she was extremely ignorant as well as not very clever. But something beneath this gaze slightly refuted what I've just said; not about the pride, but about the stupidity and the dis-tance she put between herself and the world; as if she were watching everything out of the corner of her eye, amazed; as if she were delib-erately avoiding looking around so as not to be amazed, because she'd realised that what she saw would amaze her. My God, I don't know how to explain it. She wasn't ugly. But she wasn't very beautiful either. I don't have a clue what it was I found so attractive, but I was violently attracted to her nonetheless. I could even pick up the scent of her, not because she smelled bad but because I'm sensitive and have a powerful imagination; she smelled of the countryside, of sunshine and dried grass. When I passed nearby, I stared at her with all the enormous eyes at my disposal. When I reached the exit, I turned back for another look. My God! I wanted that girl so much! I spent the whole walk home thinking about her, imagining different scenarios, those erotic fantasies

I've always looked down on and never let myself indulge in. I gradually realised that my desire for her was violent, and a desire for violence rather than sex, or violent sex, at any rate. I didn't imagine myself seducing her so much as forcing myself on her. Taming her, like an animal. That was it: she was a dumb beast and wouldn't understand any language other than brutality. But there was a lot more inside me than this. At one point I imagined I was a feudal lord, saying to the old lady: 'I shall take your daughter away,' and the old lady had no choice but to hand her over. The thought of being alone in a large room with the girl drove me crazy. I wanted to make the struggle last forever, because she wouldn't give in just like that; I had to make her, I had to fight, and she'd fight back, biting and kicking. I'd have to hit her and dominate her, I'd have to rip off her clothes. Oh, my God, my God. And all in silence, without a word; with nothing, perhaps, but moans. I couldn't picture her naked; my mind lingered on the struggle, or the point before the struggle: the moment she found herself shut inside the room with me alone, preparing for a defence that she knew would ultimately be futile. I'm sure she wouldn't alter her gaze, her shyness that looked like pride or distance; that in the end, whatever I did, I would never reach her real gaze, and that this would be her triumph, and my defeat.

THURSDAY 11, 03:11

I meant to say that despite the discovery of the sadistic feudal lord living inside me (who knows how long he's been there), it was a joyous experience, because, my God, Chl's spell was broken, if only for a moment, and I was able to feel a fervent desire for another woman. So there's a glimmer of hope. Because it means I might feel desire for another woman again; another, more accessible woman. And that it's still possible a new romantic adventure will bring me back to earth. Even if it's not for very long.

FRIDAY 12, 02:25

Rotring. Computer off, and I have to go to bed early because I have to get up early. I slept very badly in the small hours of this morning, waking up several times because my tooth hurt. I had to take some sedatives, and getting out of bed was a struggle; luckily no one (not the electrician, the person collecting the money for the air conditioners or the computer technician) arrived on time, and the day gradually started to come together, although the pain never disappeared. In the evening I went to the dentist, and he fiddled and polished away until he managed a union of teeth and prosthesis that seemed to cause no further suffering. But I can't be certain, because the tooth is still sore; there's considerable swelling at the base, and there's trauma. The worst part is that tomorrow, or rather today, Friday, is the last day before the dentist goes on holiday, meaning that if the pain doesn't stop, I'll have to find a way to go and see him this afternoon, although I have no idea how, because at 2 p.m. the air conditioning is supposedly being installed, and then the electrician will come, and I doubt the work will be finished in time for me to get to my appointment, because the dentist told me that 7 p.m. was the latest I could possibly arrive.

On one of the occasions when I managed to stay asleep for any time at all, I had an important dream about a woman. This woman bore some resemblance to Ginebra, whom I expect I'll see this evening, or one of these days. It wasn't quite her, however, because the woman in the dream was a possible woman, and Ginebra, for various reasons, is not. True, Ginebra has appeared more than once in very important dreams of mine; I think she's the most perfect representation of the Jungian Anima that my unconscious could ever find. As such, she's featured in a number of dreams with erotic aspects, but faced with the physical person, that eroticism disappears completely. It's the exact opposite of what happened to me yesterday with the country girl in the supermarket: only her physical presence could inspire that extraordinary burst of passion; since then, I haven't been able to piece together her face, or her expression, or anything else, in my memory, and the only thing she makes me feel now that she's no longer here is bewilderment at the way I reacted.

I'm not sure if I've recorded anywhere, or at least not in this diary, the full story of a dream I had about Ginebra two or three years ago, with all its fascinating ramifications. I'll see if I have anything written down about it; maybe an email, which is a very difficult thing to search my files for. Yes, I emailed Ginebra to tell her all about the dream, but later the dream had some ramifications that affected various other people, and that's what I'm most interested in recording.

I don't have any details about today's Ginebra dream, which is a shame, because I know there was a lot to it. My abuse of the computer screen has left me with no imagination, no capacity to form images, and this means I forget most of my dreams.

But I'm only here to record the fact I dreamed about Ginebra, and, more importantly, to note down an observation that occurred to me just now, when I remembered about my dream, though not the details of it: that something within me is opening up when it comes to women. I think I'm going to meet someone, because I can tell that inside I'm preparing for it. Who knows when she'll appear, and under what circumstances. However forewarned I am, it'll take me by surprise, as it always does.

FRIDAY 12, 02:50

Rotring.

A reminder popped up in my calendar, telling me to withdraw some money from the bank to pay for the air conditioners. The person won't come to collect the money until Monday, but since I don't trust cash machines (or their human equivalents) (or myself) I like to do these things in plenty of time, just in case – especially because, given the current situation with my sleeping hours, reaching the bank before closing time and doing all the paperwork, which often involves a considerable wait, appears to be beyond my capabilities. I called the automated bank services to find out about the state of my savings account; the second half of the money from Mr Guggenheim still hasn't arrived. Once I'd taken the money I needed out of the ATM, which I did at the end of the afternoon, I only had enough left in my account to cover next month's rent.

Chl called today, in the afternoon. She sounds different, happy in a serene sort of way and more sure of herself. Not only is she not doing her normal job, which drives her crazy, but she's even working on something she really enjoys. I hope she notices the difference for herself and decides to carry on with the work that suits her better. Whenever I explain this to her, over and over again, in different ways, she gets annoyed. Now, perhaps, this experience will make her see things more clearly.

I'm expecting her in three or four days.

SATURDAY 13, 04:02

HA HA HA!

I have defeated summer! The air conditioning is installed. To celebrate, I had half a glass of wine. I'm drunk.

SATURDAY 13, 20:45

My walks with M have a dreamlike feel. I'm not sure if this is provided by M, because the three or four walks we've been on have taken place under similar circumstances; I think they were all on Fridays, and more than one happened very close to a major holiday, such as Christmas or the New Year, when the city takes on a dreamlike feel of its own accord. But really, I think Montevideo always has a certain dreamlikeness to it, though in my walks with M it's more pronounced, or my mood makes me more inclined to notice that particular aspect. In fact, more than dreamlike, Montevideo has become nightmarish, and it's not only the Council that's to blame. What with the growing numbers of Koreans and marginal people of all kinds, and the constant threat of immediate violence, and the ridiculous noise levels (and the Council is very much to blame for those; or it's complicit, or it turns a blind eye), and something hard to define in the demeanour of the people in the street; yes, it's a permanent nightmare. Like all old people, I long for a past I think was better, and yet it wasn't better, just different. Fortunately, I have various texts I wrote in previous decades which meticulously describe the nightmarish character of the city back then; it's just that now the nightmare is different, and some elements have changed. It wasn't better before, not definitively. I just had ways of protecting myself from it; I was stronger, or rather younger. And perhaps nightmarishness is a quality that all cities share, and can't help but share; it's part of the very idea of a city.

Yesterday, the workmen I was expecting at 2 p.m., and on whose account I'd got up so ludicrously early, didn't appear until four. Still, they finished at a reasonable time, which left me reasonably free at a convenient time to go for a walk with M. We followed our usual route until a little past Calle Ejido. We went into a couple of *boliches* but walked straight out again because of the unbearable noise (one or more TV sets with the volume turned up, forcing everyone to shout) and in the end we sat down at one of the tables on the pavement outside La Pasiva. We went inside first to see what it was like, but it was not only noisy but also infernally hot, and as if that wasn't enough, sitting just two steps away from me was none other than T. T is an old friend; I haven't seen her for about twenty years, luckily, and for about twenty years, I've been avoiding her like the plague. There was a time when, driven by a particular kind of madness, she began wildly disseminating all kinds of gossip, and everyone she knew, myself included, ended up falling out with each other. The gossip was chosen really maliciously and it wasn't always based on fact, though it invariably originated from some germ of true information, which was generally distorted. If, for example, in a conversation with T, it occurred to me to make some humorous comment about X, T would be off like a shot to see X and tell them I'd said such-and-such a thing; a word or an ironic phrase, perhaps said with great affection or sympathy for X, would be transformed into something serious and disapproving, perhaps accusatory, and carefully extracted from its context, so that it became a terrible insult. In the same way, I heard unbearable characterisations of myself, constructed by X, Y and Z, and always in the distorted version of T. Consequently, our little family of friends began to suffer a string of incomprehensible upsets, because we didn't always realise T was involved. Often the victim of the calumny simply cut all contact and maintained an injured silence, and it wasn't easy to get to the bottom of what was going on. And now there was T, older and plumper, with a bovine gaze that had lost all the charm it once had. I spun around violently, strode out onto the pavement and looked for a table where I'd feel safe from the risk of being recognised by T – much to the amusement of M, who didn't understand why I'd made such a swift exit. I explained. The table I'd chosen wasn't completely out of T's line of vision, but I realised she'd be unlikely to spot me with my Father Christmas beard and the other changes the years have wrought; what's more, she never took her eyes off the people she was with, two or three women, I think, as if hypnotised by the thrilling conversation they were having. I imagined, I couldn't help but imagine, some of the topics of that conversation. Meanwhile, on the pavement, the nightmare had taken the form of a very old man clutching a guitar and singing (so to speak), first a little waltz, and then a tango. I caught a few snatches of lyrics that helped me recognise them. As for the notes he was attempting to extract from the guitar, not one bore the slightest relation to any kind of melody or harmony. He was using the guitar more like a percussion instrument, hitting all the strings at random with his rhythmic slapping. And the voice . . . all that was left of the old man's voice was a pathetic squeak, and needless to say, it was completely tuneless and lacking intonation. I feel sorry for people like that, and I was ready to give him a few coins when he came over to our table. But he didn't come over to anyone's table at any point in the whole half hour we were sitting there; he went on singing and battering his guitar, and as soon as he finished one song he launched straight into the next. As if he was only trying to express himself.

I forget precisely which songs I heard him singing, or rather deduced he was singing, but none of them were very well-known or predictable choices, and nor did they stand out for any particular merit. The old man had his own personal way of selecting his repertoire, shaped by who knows what kind of life. How I wish I knew these things, but alas, they'll go on living within me as unsolved mysteries.


(The word 'dreamlikeness' doesn't exist, it seems; not only does Word tell me this, but so do all the dictionaries I own.)

SATURDAY 13, 21:31

During that walk with M – and in a betrayal of Chl, in a way, because it meant incorporating part of the ritual I share with her – I picked up three detective novels from the sale table at the Feria del Libro. They weren't cheap, but they were affordable, especially because two of them will fill gaps in my collection: I found a Perry Mason one, no less, and another by Carter Dickson that's very difficult to get hold of. There was also one by Ellery Queen, which is normally impossible to find – the last in the series featuring Drury Lane, originally published under the pseudonym Barnaby Ross – but I didn't buy it. It wasn't in brilliant condition and I have no desire to reread it, even though I've only read it once, forty-odd years ago, or perhaps fifty, because, due to various peculiarities, I can remember perfectly who the murderer is and even the main clue that gives him away. And besides, although as a teenager I was a fan of Ellery Queen, these days I find him very hard to read. His style is atrocious.

I've already finished the Perry Mason book. Now I'm going to start the Carter Dickson. I should go back to the Feria del Libro more often, because that new section of second-hand detective novels, and high-quality ones at that, could bring some more surprises.

MONDAY 15, 03:07

Today, or rather yesterday, Sunday, Chl made a surprise appearance. She'd had to return home sooner than planned for personal reasons, and she called me right away. I was asleep and vaguely heard what she was recording on the answerphone; when I woke up at 2 p.m. I'd forgotten about the call, and it was a surprise to find a message waiting for me. I listened to it, but then I went back to bed. I'd only got up to go to the bathroom and drink a bit of water. Chl called again later, and that time I picked up. I spoke to her and asked her to go on talking until I was fully awake. It was three in the afternoon. She promised to come over in an hour. I hurried to make a start on my day.

Later on, we were sitting in the armchairs, facing each other. I started to feel ill. Dizzy, and with hot flushes in spite of the air conditioning.

Then I tried to relax, and my arms started moving by themselves in vaguely restrained spasms. I looked at Chl and couldn't quite recognise her, couldn't quite receive her. I'd clearly done everything I could to forget about her entirely, so as not to suffer while she was away. Her presence shook me up from head to toe.

All of a sudden I jolted forwards inadvertently, my arms still jolting around as well, and a strangled cry emerged from deep in my chest. Chl was scared. Evidently I'm a hysteric. But it did me good; from then on, once my arms had waved around a bit more in slightly calmer spasms until eventually falling still, I felt better. And I could see Chl better, as if with that cry I'd let her inside me again. It never ceases to amaze me, much as these things happen again and again, how close my connection is with this woman.

She seems more mature and self-confident, just as she sounded on the phone. The change won't necessarily last, since when her holidays are over and this other work she's been doing finishes and she goes back to her old work . . . I hope she can make some changes in her life, using the way she's feeling now to reaffirm who she really is.

TUESDAY 16, 16:42

The blasted bureaucrats have caught me; damn them to hell. Today, which for some reason is a day of heroic acts, I got up at midday and had a shower. After going through my routines, I called the electricity board to request what they call an 'electricity-supply upgrade'. To that end, I have two certificates from the company that sold me the air conditioners; due to some strange agreement, the electricity board charges far less for the power upgrade if you have those certificates. I need to increase my electricity supply because if the boiler's on I can't use the microwave, and now I can't use the air conditioners either; the fuse blows and then the computer switches off, among other things. Anyway, a helpful lady on the phone told me I had to do the paperwork in person. This is because of the certificates – you can't send them by post. Nor can I have someone else go in my place. I checked, with the same lady, where the nearest electricity board office is (it's on Calle Mercedes, between Paraguay and Ibicuy, if that's still what those streets are called), and when it's open to the public (9 a.m. to 5 p.m.). Very well; it had just gone 3 p.m., so I decided to embark on the adventure. At four on the dot, I phoned for a taxi; the temperature outside is really horrendous. I arrived at the electricity board office easily enough, except for the suffocating heat. Inside, it was cool. The receptionist, a paradigmatic figure in the world of Latin American bureaucracy, gave me some instructions and a little piece of paper with a number on it. I went up the stairs to a landing and waited to be called. I wasn't waiting long. For some reason, the people in possession of the eight numbers before mine had all vanished, as if by magic. I sat down at a desk, and the official took the envelope containing the certificates. I removed my ID card from my pocket and passed it to her. It gave her a bit of a shock.

'This ID is out of date!' she exclaimed, looking more horrified than I thought was entirely warranted.

I tried to look astonished, even though I knew full well it was out of date. I frowned at the ID card she'd thrust under my nose and murmured, 'November . . . '

'November '99!' she cried, still in a tone that would have been warranted if, for example, I had deposited a jar full of shit on her desk, or suggested I sodomise her.

She carried on, in a slightly more normal tone:

'First, you'll have to renew your ID, or at least bring something to prove you've started the process.'

A piece of paper, in other words. Pieces of paper; the world of bureaucracy. Why do these people want my ID to be up to date? Can't they see I'm the same person? (Well, perhaps not. I have a beard these days, and I'm eleven years older) (but why couldn't it be done over the phone? And why the hell does it matter if I'm the same person the ID card is for or not? All they have to do is replace a fuse whose actual value is five dollars with another whose actual value is five dollars and fifty cents, and charge me somewhere between fifty and two hundred dollars for the privilege, and on top of that they want me to come and see them personally, and have an up-to-date ID.)

Well. On the way home, by taxi again, I stopped off at the book-stall; I knew there'd be something there. Two detective novels from the Séptimo Círculo series. Thirty pesos each, plus forty on the taxis: a hundred exactly. Spending a hundred pesos was all I achieved by getting up at midday.

And now comes my battle with the branch of bureaucracy that has to renew my ID. We'll see what they come up with. The office is just around the corner from my apartment, but there are always terrible queues outside the door, under a sign that says something like 'IT IS NOT NECESSARY TO QUEUE'. A good start. I also know they give the numbers out at an impossible time, 5 a.m. I believe, and then you have to go back at the time they tell you, on the day they tell you, and queue underneath that sign.

TUESDAY 16, 21:35

And I know what will happen: when I go to renew my ID, those other bureaucrats will demand to see my voting card. Then they'll see that I didn't vote in the last Council elections (and even if I'd wanted to vote, there was no one to vote for, for God's sake) (besides, it was cold and rainy that day, and I got up at 6 p.m.). Then they're going to say: oh, first you have to go to the Electoral Court (or wherever I have to go) and pay the fine, then get another number and queue up under the sign again, and bring proof you've paid the fine, and then we'll renew your ID card.

Meanwhile, I need to keep turning off the boiler and/or the air conditioners and/or the computer whenever I want to use the microwave. Damn everyone to hell.

THURSDAY 18, 01:18

The day had hardly begun when I found myself on the brink of a nervous crisis. Whenever the Adinet email software does anything, the computer freezes; I had to restart it more times than I can remember. And then the magnetic fuse that cuts off the current in the WHOLE of my apartment began tripping, and so of course the computer switched off as well. In this stifling heat, I was left without air conditioning every few minutes. I didn't have a clue what was happening, and I called Ulises, the electrician. He's the electrician we always used in Colonia, and by a happy chance I heard that he's now in Montevideo. He came round the day the air conditioners were installed to get a sense of the problems I wanted to sort out. We decided to wait until I'd received the electricity-supply upgrade, so we could do the work knowing how much electricity I had available. After yesterday's bureaucratic adventures, it seemed the electricity-supply upgrade would be forever out of reach. The faces of the electricity-board people appeared before me from time to time, like ghosts. Especially the receptionist, whose face, and posture, were those of a broken woman. All those years spent doing the work of bureaucracy had taken their toll – and it looked like there'd been plenty of years, too, filled with all the vices attached to her job: stress and disappointment, yes, but also a kind of malicious sharpness, of being constantly on the lookout for opportunities to exert the slightest bit of power. When I arrived, she was in conversation with a woman. Soon, though, I realised it wasn't a conversation, and in fact the receptionist was applying a very sophisticated form of torture. The moment she saw me arrive and stand in front of the desk, she sent the woman away with some final instructions, and while the woman was leaving with her own quota of stress, the employee turned to face me, practically licking her lips, like a vampire who spots a demijohn of fresh blood on the way over. Unfortunately for her, my business was very simple, and there was nothing she could get her teeth into. She just applied a bit of pressure by asking me if I was the account-holder with the electricity board, hoping I'd say no, but I said yes, leaving her with no further options besides giving me a number and telling me to go up the stairs I could see to my left.

Today, then, I called Ulises without feeling at all hopeful, because everything was going badly, very badly indeed. But he was at home, and said he'd be with me at around 6 p.m. Which he was. And he solved everything within a few minutes. He simply replaced the fuse that kept tripping with another that had a higher capacity. Now I just have to see if this fuse does its job. Its job is to trip when there's a power surge or short circuit, so the fuse on the meter doesn't go.

The fuse on the meter is in the caretaker's apartment. When the fuse on the meter tripped early one morning, shortly after I'd moved in, I had no way of getting the power back on and went to bed with gritted teeth, leaving all the things I'd been doing on the computer half-finished. Before going to sleep, I read a bit with a torch, which is always an unpleasant experience. The next day I wasted no time in asking Luis, my old electrician, to come and sort it out. I had to request an electricity-supply upgrade, but fortunately I could do it over the phone because there were no certificates to complicate matters. And they charged me a huge amount. But until now I've been secure in the knowledge that the fuse won't trip. Now I have my doubts, because the fuse Ulises installed in my apartment has exactly the same capacity as the fuse downstairs, in the caretaker's apartment, so I'm not sure it'll stop the fuse downstairs from tripping. Meanwhile, for the first time, I've been able to enjoy having all the appliances and all the lights in my apartment turned on at once, without anything tripping. I turned the boiler on, began cooking a thick steak in the microwave, used the toaster, started up the two air-conditioning units . . . and everything was fine.

I'm crossing my fingers.

Before the electrician came, I went down to buy some cigarettes and post a couple of letters at the pharmacy, since in this country you take your letters to the pharmacy rather than the post office, though I haven't yet seen any postmen delivering medicines. In the pharmacy, making neighbourly small talk, I complained to the pharmacist about my trials and tribulations at the hands of bureaucracy. When she heard I had to renew my ID, she offered to get me a number, by some method she knows about and I don't – which would be wonderful because, as I think I've mentioned, the numbers are given out at about 5 a.m., and there are terrible queues, and not always enough numbers to go round. Now I have to be on the alert; if the kind-hearted pharmacist tells me they're expecting me at such-and-such an hour to undergo the humiliations that precede the handing over of a new ID card, I need to be there on time. I want to shave, because I'd rather not have a beard on my ID card. Maybe I'll do it now.

God bless Ulises.

FRIDAY 19, 03:32

Incredible: the pharmacist got me a number so I can renew my ID. The first of February, at five in the afternoon. I could begin the paperwork with the electricity board (the 'electricity-supply upgrade') today if I liked. I don't think I will; the weather's dreadful. Rain, drizzle and that damp heat that wraps itself around you and smothers you (not right now, though; at this time of night it's fairly cool). Still, in my apartment I've even been cold at points; the air conditioners are doing an excellent job. The moment I stop paying attention, I start shivering. I don't know what the temperature was today; the air conditioners created a pleasant climate when it was twenty-three degrees outside and even twenty-four, which under other circumstances would have seemed intolerably hot. Ulises came back and carried on with the bits and pieces I'd asked him to do. Just now I realised he'd made a couple of slip-ups; I hope he fixes them tomorrow. I won't retract my blessing for the time being; all the electrical appliances are still merrily humming away. According to Ulises, I don't need to do the paperwork and get the electricity-supply upgrade, but I think I'm going to anyway. When the caretaker isn't here and the fuse on the meter is left inaccessible, I still feel slightly afraid that something I do might leave me with no electricity until the next day. Sometimes the fuse trips when a bulb blows. And what if the fuse lets the short circuit reach the meter? People who operate primarily during the small hours need to keep a close eye on these things. The precautions have to be taken to almost pathological extremes.

FRIDAY 19, 19:50

> *She goes out at night*
> *and sleeps through the day,*
> *She's a philosophy*
> *student, they say . . .*

I got that song stuck in my head when I went to the supermarket an hour ago to do my shopping. Three or four old-timers, one with white hair, plus an ambiguous character who looked a bit like a punk, martyring everyone's eardrums on the pavement of Sarandí, opposite the square, to one side of the bar that has tables outside, in the Plaza Matriz itself. The tables were filled with happy customers, and there were even a few people, some of whom were in suits and carrying briefcases, and none of whom were young, standing in the street, listening to <u>that</u>. Everywhere you go, the Council is imposing the same particular style on Montevideo, especially along this 'Old Town route', and it's very hard to swallow. Until that point I'd been feeling vaguely uneasy, which I put down to the sudden change of temperature (it had dropped by a few degrees); but by the time I went outside the weather had become ambiguous, which upsets my nerves even more: a few gusts of cool, almost cold air, which are enveloped every step of the way in a kind of invisible, muggy mist, a summery condensation that's typical of the current weather in this city. To think that I fled Colonia because of weather like this, and after a few years the weather's catching up with me, as if that infernal city is following me wherever I go – which reminds me once again of that poem by Cavafy I discovered one day, in Colonia in fact, in a book by Lawrence Durrell.

I read it in Spanish as a re-retranslation, but nevertheless, the meaning that came across still sends a shiver down my spine:

> *You tell yourself: I'll be gone*
> *To some other land, some other sea,*
> *To a city lovelier far than this*
> *Could ever have been or hoped to be —*
> *Where every step now tightens the noose:*
> *A heart in a body buried and out of use:*
> *How long, how long must I be here*
> *Confined among these dreary purlieus*
> *Of the common mind? Wherever now I look*
> *Black ruins of my life rise into view.*
> *So many years have I been here*
> *Spending and squandering, and nothing gained.*
> *There's no new land, my friend, no*

*New sea; for the city will follow you,*
*In the same streets you'll wander endlessly,*
*The same mental suburbs slip from youth to age,*
*In the same house go white at last —*
*The city is a cage.*
*No other places, always this*
*Your earthly landfall, and no ship exists*
*To take you from yourself. Ah! don't you see*
*Just as you've ruined your life in this*
*One plot of ground you've ruined its worth*
*Everywhere now — over the whole earth?*

My indecipherable unease began turning into grumpiness after that, and now I can safely say I'm feeling grumpy. It didn't help when M phoned to tell me she couldn't come for a walk today; she proposed putting it off until tomorrow. She left a message and insisted I call her; I called several times but she didn't pick up. I wasn't sure whether to go out alone or stay in. I really wanted to go to the Feria del Libro and look at the detective novel section. But at the same time I was hungry. While I was waiting for the boy from the supermarket, who was meant to arrive 'in ten minutes' with my shopping, I began preparing a light lunch-dinner: bread with tomato and garlic. The boy didn't show up, and I couldn't stop eating the tomato. That's put paid to my Feria del Libro trip, at least while the food going round and round in my stomach puts me at risk of having one of those panic attacks brought on by my digestive tract. I telephoned the supermarket; everyone there thought my order had already been delivered. Apologies. 'He's setting off now.' Eventually he arrived. Now I'm writing by hand. The computer's turned off and I don't want to turn it on again. Something's going wrong and I don't know if it's Adinet or my modem, or both. Patricia has to come and investigate, and put in a new video card to see if that solves the problem with the monitor once and for all, and while she's at it she's going to install the latest version of Windows. This will cause more problems, I'm sure, because a few programs will stop working and I'll have to adapt a new operating system to fit my needs all over again, which is a process similar to training a temperamental colt. But Patricia's not coming today, and these things have been pushed back until next week. Meanwhile, I'm feeling rather detached from the computer, which would be good news if I'd started feeling attached to something more important instead; but as it is, there's only my grumpiness.

SATURDAY 20, 03:37

Rotring.

I did go out in the end, by myself; I went to the Feria del Libro and came back with four detective novels. I hadn't even heard of one of them, though it's by a writer I collect. Another is that Ellery Queen book, *Drury Lane's Last Case*. It was still there and I decided to go ahead and buy it, in spite of everything. After all, when I'm in one of these extended phases in which I want to read detective novels more than any other kind of book, my thinking is: better to have something not very good to read than to have nothing at all. Addictions are like that, and you can end up suffering terrible humiliations out of desperation for the drug. I'll end up reading Agatha Christie one day, I know it.

On the way there, I felt that pain I get in the street threatening to take hold. This time I reacted quickly, chewing an antacid tablet before the process reached the acute stage. When the threat didn't go away, I chewed a second tablet. I managed to burp a little, too, which seemed encouraging. At the same time, I tried to relax my shoulders and shift my centre of gravity towards my pelvis, and to relax my legs and feet so they grew heavier and made me feel more secure. Still, the threat didn't go away; it didn't advance, but it didn't retreat either. I tried to distract myself by looking around at the things and the people. I went into a couple of bookshops I passed, which have awful sale tables. In one square there was a loudspeaker, advertising something. In another square, a band playing some Latin American music; I think they were Bolivian. They were pretty good, and what they were doing was less offensive than the other things you hear, but I still don't know why we have to put up with them. We have concert halls and other enclosed spaces for a reason. There's no need to turn the streets into places of psychological torture; people have no choice but to walk down them, and if they don't want to hear a particular kind of music, or advertising, they have to grin and bear it. The noise in this city is reaching excruciating levels. So is the bad taste.

On the corner of 18 de Julio and Julio Herrera y Obes, one of the traffic lights makes an electronic beeping noise when the green light means you can cross Julio Herrera y Obes. Supposedly, when it doesn't beep, it's because the green light means you can cross 18 de Julio. I, and other people I've discussed the matter with, think they've installed this system to help blind people. But first of all, they could have installed a kind of signal that doesn't disturb people's minds the way that insistent and infuriating beeping does; some sign in Braille or any other silent code. And the most extraordinary thing is that this help for the blind, if that's what it is, only exists on that corner, suggesting that blind people can only cross 18 de Julio where it meets Julio Herrera y Obes. On the other street crossings of Montevideo, blind people have to fend for themselves. What's more, I've never seen a single blind person crossing there. You'd think they'd have installed the system on that corner after carrying out a statistical study and finding that it's blind people's crossing of choice, but if anyone blind has ever crossed the road there, it would be news to me, and to everyone I know. The whole thing's as ridiculous as the bells the Council hung up in a few different streets at Christmas, for example outside the door to my building. A green ribbon that's meant to look like a pine branch crosses the street from pavement to pavement, and in the middle there's a red ribbon tied neatly in a bow, and next to it a plastic bell that's supposed to look like metal. Decorations in poor taste on a street with cracked paving stones, dog shit on the pavement and all kinds of other dirt and grime.

Since the threat remained – and as well as the discomfort around the eventration, I could feel the aching in my arms that seems to come from my bones, and in my back, which was still trying to hunch – I took a quarter of a Valium 10, which I always carry in my trouser pocket, like a talisman. I did this just as the uphill part of 18 de Julio ended and I was on the flat again, which always helps; and the threat soon dissipated. The rest of my walk to the bookshop was very pleasant, and the walk home was even better, since I was cheerfully carrying the bag with the four books in it.

Then, back at home, I had more trouble with the computer. It's in a bad way, a very bad way. As I write this, the hard drive is completing a process of defragmentation, which takes a long time. Before that, I scanned the whole hard drive with the antivirus. There were no viruses. There's just an unreliable operating system: Windows 98.

SATURDAY 20, 20:36

I'm writing by hand, and not because the computer is switched off, or because I feel any profound need to write by hand, but because the computer is busy. It's almost done, but it's been busy for hours; this morning I fell into the trap of the new DEFRAG that comes with Windows 98. In previous versions of Windows, I'd run the DEFRAG and everything would be resolved in a matter of minutes. Although, I realise now, it wouldn't be resolved particularly WELL. This time, I started the process in the early hours of the morning and it worked away for ages and ages without finishing so much as 10 per cent of the job. But even so, when I paused the process and opened a few programs to see if things were working, lo and behold, they were working far better than before.

When I understood, after a long wait, that this Windows 98 DEFRAG was very different to the previous ones and taking considerably more time, I turned everything off and went to sleep. First, though, I put a little sign on the screen to remind me that today I needed to run the DEFRAG defrag until it was 100 per cent complete. And that's what I did.

Now, after who knows how many hours of continuous work, the DEFRAG procedure is reaching 100 per cent. I think it's taken around four hours. I tried to distract myself in the meantime and do the things I needed to do, like having breakfast and reading my detective novels, but my curiosity about the procedure kept getting the better of me and I spent a long time watching how it worked in a kind of trance, trying to understand exactly what the program was doing. But in fact, like everything made by Microsoft, it's a very cryptic program and doesn't give much useful information away.

SATURDAY 20, 21:12

I went to check on the computer. The process was 95 per cent complete. Now it's on 97 per cent. This program reminds me of Sancho Panza and his story about the goats who needed to be transported in a boat, one at a time, to the other side of the river. If he was interrupted, he couldn't carry on with the story and had to start all over again. If you interrupt the defrag, it, too, has to start all over again.

Well, I suppose it will have finished by now. I'm going to take a look at the results.

SUNDAY 21, 01:14

In Word, long after the DEFRAG.

Writing every day about events that have just taken place is a mistake. For the most part, the interesting things surface in my memory the following day, or several days later, if at all. Writing things down immediately means I have a record, but it's difficult to convey the reality of what happened because there's been no development; the information you present is raw, bare and lifeless, and worst of all you don't realise it, because when you write, and when you reread what's just been written, what you're really reading is what you have in your head rather than what's on the page (or the screen). If you read the same thing again some time later, you probably won't have the slightest clue what you were trying to say; unless the event has been branded on your memory for reasons of its own, those lines won't manage to bring it back, and you won't understand why you wrote them in the first place. And readers who aren't you will understand even less.

This line of thinking stems from the fact that today I recalled a snapshot of the walk I went on yesterday. I thought I'd transcribed the main points of it, but it turns out I'd skipped over the most transcendental part, and that was what came back to me today. It was an encounter with a girl. I was going along 18 de Julio, as usual, and I don't remember how far down I was; it probably wasn't far from that square, Plaza del Entrevero. I was feeling a bit worried about the pain threatening to set in. Suddenly, I saw a very pretty, friendly-looking girl approaching from my right. She was carrying some enormous rolls of cardboard under one arm, and perhaps more in her hands. She saw me and smiled, and made a small movement towards me. I felt as if the heavens were opening; a smile like that was exactly what I needed on my solitary walk, and for one crazy, out-of-my-mind moment I was expecting a marvellous proposition ('Could you hold my breasts while I sort out these rolls of cardboard?' – to paraphrase Woody Allen), or at least a minimal opening to a friendly chat that would pave the way for a proposition of my own. But in fact, what she said was: 'Would you like a poster?' My heart sank; I said no, too quickly, and she bounded over to another guy who was coming up behind me and asked him: 'Would you like a poster?' I didn't hear what he said, and I didn't care; I was too busy giving myself a few mental kicks on the behind. First of all, I'd missed the opportunity for a brief conversation. 'A poster of what?' I could have enquired, which would also have circumvented the curiosity I later felt. I'm still wondering what image or what words that poster had on it. It was huge, made of cardboard that wasn't very thick, or perhaps a special kind of paper, but whatever it was, it was definitely good quality. I also wonder if she was selling them or giving them away; it seemed more like a gift than a transaction somehow. Maybe the poster was a photo of her. My God, I'm such a joyless idiot. And then I complain about the sterility of my walks. All I was thinking at the time was how uncomfortable it would be to go all the way to the Feria del Libro, and back down 18 de Julio to my apartment, with that enormous roll of cardboard under my arm.

SUNDAY 21, 16:57

I haven't had breakfast yet, but I feel compelled to record this in the diary: another death in my group of friends. This time it was Tuli. He was on my mind a fair bit last night; Lilí, who gave me the news just now, must have been thinking about telling me. Strangely, I wasn't thinking of Tuli as the protagonist of any funereal news; I simply remembered him, and how I hadn't paid him for some bed sheets I bought from him about twenty years ago. Nor had I paid back the money I borrowed from him once, or perhaps twice, for my electricity bill. I thought, a little jokingly, though I meant it: 'It would be good if I paid him back now.' I didn't know it was too late.

Since people need to be told about these things, I tried to make a mental list of friends who'd known Tuli, but the only person I thought it was up to me to inform was my friend in Chicago. I sent her an email, in which, as I was searching for a way to deliver the news, an image appeared that I'm very fond of:

> Since you haven't said anything to me, maybe you don't know; he died last Thursday and I've just found out from Lilí, who always passes on this sort of news. I'm sure you knew him because he went to your house, at least once; he came with me to a party of yours, and we brought packets of some kind of food with us. I announced us over the intercom as 'Mr Laurel and Mr Hardy', because at that moment I felt like we were a comedy double act. His name was Tuli, or Natalio.

WEDNESDAY 24, 18:48

'Everything is double.' The powerful conclusion of the dream I had a few hours ago.

The plot is fairly complex and confusing, and the dream-erasing mechanism that springs into action the moment I wake up, or start waking up, has done its work; as a result, it's hard to put together a clear narrative. Always the same irritating phrases: 'it was as if', 'it seemed', 'although it could also have been'.

There was a man who had made, or wanted to make, a film; he'd already made something, because the first thing I remember from the dream is a film showing the San Antonio hill in Piriapolis looking completely different to usual. It was entirely covered in buildings of all kinds, a city on a slope, haphazard and tangled the way our cities generally are. The winding road up to the top wove in between the buildings. The little city was bright and multicoloured, with whites and hot pinks particularly prevalent. At the beginning of the film, a lorry was driving along the road to the summit. There was a loud-speaker attached to it (or perhaps it was a voice coming from off-screen, though the vehicle could be glimpsed every so often through gaps in the buildings. It was less a lorry than a small, dark-blue car. It was night-time). The booming voice that could be heard was talking ironically about the virtues of this new, civilised hill, and the irony extended to the way the voice delivered its message as if it were a TV commercial, in the syrupy, deceitful style of all self-respecting advertisements.

As I saw these images I had a few brief thoughts, such as, 'I didn't know Piriapolis had changed so much'; then I started to doubt the veracity of the images: 'It could be a trick.' Later on, Tola Invernizzi, from one end of a counter or bar somewhere, made his only interven-tion in the dream to confirm that it was indeed just a model.

Then I found myself involved somehow in the cinematographic project, and the man who was going to direct the film assigned me some production tasks. This man, whom I can't identify or associate with anyone I know, was what you'd call 'solid', both physically and in the impression he gave of self-assurance and competence. He wasn't a giant like Tola, but he was fairly tall, and broad-shouldered, you could say, though not 'stocky', for which he would have needed a few extra pounds. His age is also difficult to pin down; he was neither very young nor very old, perhaps around thirty-five or forty. There was some sort of complicated paperwork involved, which was taking a long time, several days. And there was also an episode I can't remember, which reinforced the conclusion of the dream.

This man appeared at one point and said he'd just sorted everything out with a telephone call. I asked him why he'd assigned me that task, if he had such a simple solution himself. He was disconcerted; he didn't know what to say, and looked bewildered. To that, I added the other piece of information I can't remember, and the two versions of Piriapolis, the one with the real hill and the one with the model of the hill, and exclaimed: 'But everything is double!' and around me the various shadowy characters present looked solemn, absorbing what I'd said, and then nodded their heads, telling me I was right.

WEDNESDAY 24, 19:57

I had to rush to leave the house before the currency exchange closed. I didn't manage yesterday, and ended up owing the supermarket money. What's more, the lady who does the cleaning came today and I didn't have any Uruguayan money to give her. I also wanted to rush so I could reach the bookstall in time. All this rushing around is due to the fact that, for some reason, I'm going to sleep every day at such inappropriate times as 8 a.m. Reaching the bookstall was important because I <u>knew</u> there were some new arrivals. I've known for a few days, but whether because of the rain, which makes both the bookseller and his books disappear, or for reasons of my own, I haven't made it to those tables in the street. Today I did make it, after speculating during my journey to the currency exchange, and from there to the bookstall, about what kinds of books I'd find; it seemed impossible to say. They weren't Rastros, of course; I wasn't even sure they were detective novels. But there was something, there was something.

When I got there, I was bitterly disappointed; despite the fact that, according to my calculations, there was still another half hour to go before the bookseller packed up, the stall was empty and the tables were bare, or almost bare. There was just one pile of books in the middle of the longest table, and a little crate on the pavement containing a few not very good books and some bits and pieces for the bookseller's use. I stood there for a few seconds, waiting for the bookseller to come and finish packing up, to take that little pile of books and the crate to wherever it is he takes things when he leaves, but there was no sign of him. I walked around mindlessly for a bit and then headed towards the corner. Before giving up completely I glanced back at the side street, and at last I saw the man. I gesticulated, Italian-style, in a way that could have meant something like, '*Ma cosa è . . .* ' or, 'Why have you already upped sticks?' and he responded by pointing at his left wrist, where presumably there was meant to be a watch. I walked towards him, he walked towards me, and when we were closer together he explained: 'I close at six this month.' And then: 'I've got some detective novels.' 'Do you?' I asked, delighted, both because he had some and because it meant my telepathic reception hadn't been mistaken.

'I'll bring them over,' he said. And he went through a door. A few moments later, he came back with a little pile of books. He put them on an empty table and I looked through them one by one. No, nothing I was after. Either I had them already or they didn't interest me. 'I've got some more,' he said, 'but I couldn't find them. I just grabbed the ones I had to hand.' I thanked him and said I'd try to come back earlier tomorrow. But I was pleased nonetheless; even if I'm not interested in the novels I haven't yet seen, I am interested in these confirmations of my telepathic connections. The bookseller sees detective novels and thinks of me. And I receive the message. What's the purpose of all this? There isn't one. But it's real.

THURSDAY 25, 05:35

Rotring.

I'm off to bed, feeling immensely satisfied. And excited, too, I'd even say. It was an uphill battle, but for the second time in as long as I've owned a computer, I managed to modify a program. I know it's very boring to read about these sorts of details – the sorts I've gone rather overboard with in this diary – so I'll skip them for the benefit of the hypothetical reader. I'll merely record that this program did something annoying every time I used it, and, what's more, I use it a great deal. It's an excellent program, but the manufacturers are very interfering and controlling, and even arrogant. After putting up with these humiliations for a few years, in different updated versions of the program I obtained to meet the changing system requirements, and after managing to eliminate, one way or another, some of the nuisances it caused me, today I confronted the last of those nuisances; and, after trying other kinds of solutions that ended up causing other nuisances, I decided to open the program in an editor and see what I could do. First I copied it, just in case I ruined everything. And it's a good job I did, because before solving the problem, I did in fact ruin everything horribly a couple of times. Then I looked through the jumble of strange symbols for words that would orientate me, and I found some. And I started deleting things, here and there, this and that; I made those two failed attempts, but on the third attempt

I succeeded. Adrenaline was coursing through me. It was a thrilling adventure. And, as always with these victories, I felt dazed for a long time afterwards, not quite believing what had happened. I tested it a few times, and it worked. I turned the computer off and then on again, because sometimes changes and their consequences only take effect when you restart Windows. It still worked. Finally, I made a copy of the program and saved it, with a note that it's a corrected version, so that if for some reason the program changes or gets lost, I won't have to go through the whole process again.

I'm hoping to return to this diary and organise its contents a bit. I've now collated and printed the first two months, August and September. I'm very keen to read them through calmly and make notes, corrections, changes, additions. It would also be good to start feeling more motivated about the project. I added a new section the other day, and I'd like to carry on.

Chl goes away again tomorrow morning, for a few days. This will make it easier for me to get on with the things I have to do, if I can get past the initial pain of the separation; because after all, it's one separation in a week, unlike normally when there's a separation almost every day. That, I think, destabilises me more. And without changing the subject – later it will become clear why not – I'll quickly mention that I'd like to include a few comments on a book by Burroughs in this diary, and transcribe a few surprising passages.

SATURDAY 27, 03:32

Yesterday, Friday, I managed to reach the bookstall before 6 p.m., and before the coming storm made the bookseller pack up, though when I got there it looked like he'd already made a few moves in that direction. Not a brilliant harvest; a Chandler, which, of course, I've read a thousand times before but didn't have in my library, and a short book by Kenneth Fearing, a detective novel with some literary pretensions. While I was there, I picked up a couple of *Selections from Reader's Digest*, from thirty or forty years ago; I don't really know why, but it's the sort of thing I do (perhaps I'm preparing for a transition from detective novels to something lighter, something that makes it easier for me to interrupt my reading). I did, however, glean some interesting information.

The other day, a competitor had appeared on the side street. The bookseller explained that the owner of that stall, who wasn't there at the time, was someone I identified, at first only hazily but then very clearly, as a young guy who'd developed the bad habit of manhandling the books in the bookshop I used to have, many years ago. I'd run into him at the Tristán Narvaja market a few years before; he'd set up a kind of bookshop in a building that faced right onto the market. It was a good spot for a bookshop, although the appearance of the shop itself, which wasn't much more than a long, narrow corridor, and the appearance (and contents) of the books, made it seem more reminiscent of a rubbish tip than a bookshop. In fact, I'd been planning to walk straight past it when the young man called me over (he can't be that young, thinking about it now, though he looks it): 'Hey, Guardia Nueva!' (Guardia Nueva was the name of my bookshop.) We chatted for a bit and, out of respect for an old customer, I went inside and looked at all the books, one by one, though without touching them.

'But he doesn't have that shop any more,' the bookseller on the corner of my road continued. 'He gave everything away because the end of the world was coming.'

'What do you mean?' I asked, like an idiot, because I couldn't believe my ears.

'Yes, he gave everything away because the end of the world was coming, and now he's got nothing left. The end of the world didn't come after all, so he has to start again.'

Absolutely extraordinary. But that was the time before; yesterday, Friday, what I gleaned was different. I don't know how this man waited thirty years to tell me what he told me yesterday: that he'd once bought a large number of books from me.

'You had a bookshop, right? Guardia Nueva. New Guard. Or was it Old Guard? No, Guardia Nueva, that's right. And I made a big purchase from you one day. But that night everything was stolen. I had a shop on the corner of Mercedes and Paraguay, and I had to leave it and go back to Ruben.'

Ruben was one of the first people, or perhaps the very first, in the second-hand book exchange business.

'Is Ruben still alive?' I thought to ask.

'Ruben died last year. Or the year before, I forget. But he spent the end of his life taking tablets.'

I didn't want to hear any more about that. But the point is that this man, the bookseller on the corner of my road, has known me for years and years, which explains, although 'explains' isn't quite the right word, why we have this telepathic link.

So now I know I have two old customers for neighbours. I know about the end of the world, and I know that.

TUESDAY 30, 20:23

Scanned fragments of *The Place of Dead Roads*, by William Burroughs. I think these fragments justify the book's existence. I was quite taken aback when I read this passage; later I'll try to explain why.

The phenomenon of phantom sexual partners was of particular interest to him since he had experienced some extremely vivid encounters. He surmised that such occurrences are much more frequent than is generally supposed: people are reluctant to discuss the matter for fear of being thought insane, as they were reluctant to make such an admission in the Middle Ages for fear of the Inquisition. He knew that the succubi and incubi of medieval legend were *actual beings* and he felt sure that these creatures were still in operation. [. . .] The evil reputation of phantom partners probably derived largely from Christian prejudice, but Kim surmised that these creatures were of many varieties and some were malignant, others harmless or beneficial. He observed that some were seemingly dead people, others living people known to the uh visitor, in other cases unknown. He checked where possible to find out if at the time of such visitations the uh beneficiary was aware of the encounter. In some cases not at all. In others partially aware. [. . .] He concluded that the phenomenon was related to astral projection but not identical with it since astral projection was usually not sexual or tactile. He decided to call these beings by the general name of 'familiars' [. . .] His studies and personal encounters convinced him that these familiars were semicorporeal. They could be both visible and tactile. They had the power to appear and disappear [. . .] and now the boy was slowly melting into him or rather Kim was entering the boy's body feeling down into the toes and the fingers pulling the boy in further and further and then there was a fluid click as their spines merged in an ecstasy that was almost painful, a sweet toothache pain [. . .] and Kim was alone or rather Toby was all the way in him [. . .] Kim concluded that the creature was simply composed of less dense matter than a human. For this reason interpenetration was possible.

TUESDAY 30, 20:58

After *Junkie* I wanted to read more by Burroughs; Felipe lent me another two of his books, but not without warning me that they were very different to *Junkie*; he wasn't sure if I'd like them. Felipe knows about my prejudices towards homosexual authors, which aren't in fact prejudices but aesthetic judgements; and it's true that when I began *The Place of Dead Roads* I found that, unlike in *Junkie*, the topic of homosexuality was front and centre. What's more, the book is the complete opposite of *Junkie*'s narrative rigour, and I almost gave up on it. But there's something special about Burroughs that made me continue reading, thoroughly perplexed at my own behaviour, because I didn't understand what secret reasons I could have for reading this book. In fact, that was two weeks ago, and I still have a few pages left. It's not an easy or satisfying read, and yet I found it impossible to abandon completely, though I had to intersperse it with a veritable legion of detective novels. What's more, the homosexual fantasies and enormous quantity of morbid, grotesque expressions and descriptions didn't bother me, and I still don't understand why not. For some reason, Burroughs is incapable of offending me.

It was only when I reached page 230-something of the book that I came across the passage I quoted above, and it struck me that the whole book was a kind of packaging riddled with nonsense so as to disguise that passage as just another nonsensical flourish. But I know there's nothing nonsensical about what's written there. Perhaps a few of the interpretations or embellishments of the facts could be challenged, but I have no doubt whatsoever that the author really experienced the basic situation he describes. And I know this because the same thing happened to me.

From that passage onwards, I started to think quite seriously that everything in Burroughs' work that looks like drug-induced fantasy isn't necessarily so; and I started to think about how some drug addicts, like him and like Philip Dick (and perhaps like me, though with a few obvious differences), don't owe their work to drugs, but rather that drugs offer them the escape they need in order to live with the way they naturally perceive the universe, which is so different or so far removed from the way most people perceive it. It's not easy to live under the weight of these perceptions, intellections and/or intuitions. That's what makes the drugs necessary, and not the other way round.


Early one morning, towards the beginning of my relationship with Chl, around two and a half years ago, I'd gone to bed, but I wasn't asleep. I wasn't entirely awake either; I was in what you might call an alpha state, passing from wakefulness into sleep. It was around 4 a.m. As I remember it, my bedroom light was still on, which is strange because I never try to sleep before turning out the light. Perhaps, then, I wasn't quite falling asleep; perhaps I'd been reading, and put the book down in order to turn out the light and go to sleep. I can't be sure. I don't remember exactly how it began, either. All I know is that I felt as if I'd been invaded by a strange presence; I could feel myself being caressed from within, as if someone had got inside my body and was lavishing love and caresses on me from there. At first I was scared. I thought it was a heart attack or a stroke, and that maybe I was going to die. Which wasn't a completely crazy idea, because there seemed to be a kind of super-energy running through my whole body, a powerful pressure in my arteries, something I could feel bubbling up inside me and surging around my body inexhaustibly. I soon decided the experience was far too pleasant and transcendental to be interrupted; I didn't call for help, either from my wife, who was asleep in the next room, or from the emergency services I could have reached via the phone on my bedside table. I stayed very still, trying to breathe slowly and surrender to the infinite pleasure of those caresses, and thinking that if it all had to end in death, it had been worth being born just so I could live through that moment, even if there was nothing else in my life to justify it.

A few months later, a routine medical check-up revealed what appeared to be heart-attack scar tissue. I never looked into exactly what had happened in my heart to cause those signals on the electrocardiogram; it might, according to a cardiologist friend of mine to whom I described the experience via email, have been heart-attack scar tissue, but it also might not have. The fact is, when they told me about that supposed scarring, my mind leapt back to the experience that night, an experience of phantasmagorical, or indeed spiritual, love. But a spirituality very closely linked to the flesh.

WEDNESDAY 31, 01:29

I'll carry on with the topic that arose thanks to Burroughs. The day after that extraordinary experience, I saw Chl and briefly described what had happened. She told me she'd woken up at around 4 a.m. the night before, and that she'd thought about me, about caressing me and kissing me and making love to me.

I didn't believe her, but I didn't not believe her either. I wished I hadn't mentioned the feeling of being caressed, because she could have made her story up based on what I told her. But subsequent events made me believe her. A few days later, for the first time in my life, and I hope also the last, I saw a ghost. It gave me a horrible fright. It was two in the morning and I was standing in my bedroom, still dressed, with the door ajar. Through the gap I saw a strange figure coming swiftly and very silently down the corridor. This figure didn't look like any of the people in the house – my wife or her son, that is. It was small, and feminine, though I don't know what made me think that, since all I could see was a dark shape, with no details, like a shadow. It was walking in a peculiar way, almost floating, and at the same time looking for all the world like someone trying not to be noticed, slightly bent over, as if crouching down, and travelling at considerable speed. The ghost didn't come into my bedroom; it turned left, where the corridor turns a corner, and carried on, as if heading for the bedroom of my ex-wife or her son. I felt the palpitations of fear and desperation, as if I couldn't contain or process the terror in my mind; I'm not sure why, but supernatural occurrences have always frightened me. I summoned up my courage and decided to investigate. First I peered into my wife's room, where she was sleeping with her bedside lamp switched on. She was definitely asleep, and she wouldn't have had time to get into bed and pretend to be asleep if it had been her floating down the corridor. I knew it hadn't been her, of course, but I wanted to be absolutely sure. Then I headed for her son's room, thinking he might have smuggled his girlfriend into the house and that they might now be in bed together, but that was a ludicrous idea. The actions I had to rule out, on the part of both mother and son, wouldn't have fit with their psychological profiles in the slightest. Besides, her son was snoring peacefully in his bed and there was no girlfriend in sight, either under the bed or hidden in the bathroom, which I of course checked. The idea that I'd seen a ghost had me in a state of shock, and it took me a long time to calm my thoughts and the pounding of my heart.

The next day, Chl told me she'd had a very intense dream about my wife's son. I deduced, then, that it had been her I'd seen moving down the corridor in the direction of his room, but I was still dubious, because I'd never had an experience like that before, or believed such a thing could be possible. Nor had I ever had hallucinations, and I didn't like the idea that that was what this had been.

No doubt Chl was worried about how my relationship with her had affected my family, and was trying to find a way of calming the tensions stirred up by that relationship's unexpected beginning; at no point had I kept it secret, because for a long time I'd felt completely separate from my wife and believed I had every right to do as I pleased. The situation meant our family was in a constant state of stress, with frequent violent outbursts from one or another of us. And this, as I understand it, was how Chl came to continue, and fortunately conclude, her series of ethereal visits to the house. I was in my bedroom, once again at that time in the early morning when everyone else is asleep and I'm about to go to bed myself, when I heard my wife calling me. I went into her room and found her half asleep, and sleep made her voice sound furry when she spoke. 'There was a girl,' she said. 'I didn't dream it, she was there, leaning on the door frame. She gave me something, some papers, and she spoke to me. Then she disappeared.' I didn't mention this to Chl the next day, but I asked her if she'd had any dreams the night before. 'Oh, yes, this time I dreamed I was talking to your wife for hours.'

I never found an explanation for these phenomena, other than the usual parapsychological explanation: that it's possible to pick up on a thought in someone else's mind and somatise it somehow. With the first phenomenon, the somatisation was that surge of energy and pressure that ran through my body, causing me infinite pleasure. Fine. In the second instance, rather than a somatisation, my reading of the other person's thoughts led my unconscious to show them to me by means of a hallucination. It wasn't a hallucination as such, but it came about through the same mechanism as hallucinations, which let you see things that aren't there. But the third instance, which affected another person, seemed too much. Surely there was something else going on.

Burroughs' explanation isn't exactly an explanation, but it comes closer to the true nature of these phenomena. I can connect it, now, to my conclusion in the dream I had recently: 'Everything is double.' Yes, it seems people have 'astral' doubles, or whatever you want to call them, though Burroughs, as we've seen, distinguishes between astral phenomena and these other, more tangible, and you might even say more material, phenomena.

> Kim concluded that the creature was simply composed of less dense matter than a human.

I think this is a human phenomenon, and that Chl, despite looking very much like a goddess, is human. But if we accept that 'everything is double', any one of us might have a part of ourselves that's composed of 'less dense matter'. I like the 'matter' part, because the first of these phenomena was, for me, undeniably material. The matter may have been in the form of energy, but that doesn't mean it wasn't matter.

Needless to say, I'll never learn the truth about these strange and perturbing things. Not in this life, anyway.

WEDNESDAY 31, 22:11

I've had the flu for three days. I can tell I'm feverish during the night, because my dreams are muddled and I wake up with cracked lips. My body's aching all over. I took my temperature just now: 37.6. It's very annoying, because I feel even more idiotic than usual. There's almost nothing I'm capable of doing, or want to do. So I read detective novels.

Tomorrow I have to be round the corner from my house at 5 p.m. to get my new ID card. A real epopee. (According to the dictionary, 'a series of glorious deeds, worthy of being sung of in an epic poem'. Maybe I should have said 'odyssey'.)

# FEBRUARY 2001

## THURSDAY 1, 20:14

I got the new ID card.

## FRIDAY 2, 02:27

I had time to learn the sign off by heart, but just in case, when I finally emerged from that hellhole, I copied it down on a piece of paper (the '− NOT BEFORE −' is written in red letters):

DO NOT QUEUE
UNNECESSARILY
IF YOU PRESENT YOURSELF
AT THE TIME
INDICATED ON THE
TICKET
**−NOT BEFORE −**
YOU WILL ENTER
WITHOUT DELAY

That's the sign I saw whenever I walked along the opposite pavement, and I'd noticed that under the sign and in the area around it there was always an impressive crowd of people, most of whom were queueing. I put it down to people's mentality; to the ancestral tradition of queueing that we Uruguayans share. But knowing what I do about bureaucracy, I didn't fancy my chances. I tried to reassure myself that my piece of paper said quite clearly: 5 p.m., and warned me that it was pointless to arrive earlier, and even allowed a half-hour grace period. Since I live about four steps away from the place, I left with eight minutes to go. I paid a quick visit to the pharmacist on the way, since I knew she was worried about whether I'd manage to get out of bed in time, and arrived with two minutes to spare. There were a fair few people there, but, ever the optimist, I assumed many them were waiting for later times. I saw a queue to the left and joined the end of it. I asked, just in case, 'Is this for the five o'clock people?' The friendly brunette said it was. But a young man further ahead in the queue corrected her: 'The four-forty people are just about to go in.' I didn't think there was much point in my being in the queue, and it occurred to me to let the doorman know I was there and that I had an appointment for 5 p.m., to see what he said. I moved closer. There was a big group of people near the door, some of whom were harassing the doorman. Suddenly he shouted to the public as a whole: 'Is there anyone left for four forty?' So the young man was right. And there were a few people left for four forty; they joined the others, who were pouring through the doors in droves. I could see that the inside of the building was full. I'd thought that if they assigned me a time of five o'clock, I would simply turn up at five and find them awaiting me with open arms. But no. They'd assigned five o'clock to lots of people, rather like my dentist does. I began to understand something of the mechanics of it: now they were attending to the four-twenty people, and meanwhile they were letting the four-forty people go in. When they let us five o'clock people in at twenty past five, they'd be beginning to attend to the four-forty lot. This meant I had time to go back home, twiddle my thumbs, smoke, go to the bathroom, read the Ellery Queen novel I'd left midway through, or do any other activity more interesting than standing there on the narrow pavement with this motley crowd, assailed now and then by the abominable perfumes of some of the women. Luckily, most people were from the so-called lower classes, and the perfumes those women were wearing weren't the most abominable; the most abominable ones are the most expensive, sticky and penetrating. These were unpleasant, but not unbearable. Then there were the exhaust fumes from the cars which now and then formed a traffic jam on that narrow little street called Rincón; at points I was afraid of being poisoned. But the traffic jams didn't last long, and about a minute or two after each one it was possible to breathe less polluted air again. Why didn't I go back home? Because my reasoning had been logical reasoning, and in bureaucracy the usual logic we're all familiar with doesn't exist. I was almost certainly right about how it all worked, but there's always the risk of a sudden outbreak of arbitrariness, such as a person sticking their head out of the building and calling my name. And if I wasn't there, all would be lost. So I steeled myself for a twenty-minute wait in the street, with the wild hope that there would be enough seats to go round once I was inside. Because who would think it a good idea to schedule more people than there were seats for? But the fact is that I was only able to sit down once it was all over, almost two hours later, and I was able to sit down for the three-minute wait before they called me over to a window to receive my ID and then sent me out into the street and the fresh air.

So there I stayed, trying to entertain myself by watching the people, and trying to overhear snatches of conversation. But there wasn't anything interesting going on. Every now and then I reread the sign and tried to memorise it. Then I began trying to remember it without looking, but I never got it quite right. There's something so quintessentially bureaucratic about bureaucratic language that non-bureaucratic people find it very hard to imitate, or even remember.

DO NOT QUEUE
UNNECESSARILY
IF YOU PRESENT YOURSELF
AT THE TIME
INDICATED ON THE
TICKET
—NOT BEFORE —
YOU WILL ENTER
WITHOUT DELAY

It really is a perfect text. Impossible to fault. The right words in the right order. No; I could never have managed a thing like that myself.

.    .    .

At 5.20 p.m., just as I thought, the doorman announced: 'Five o'clock people, queue up on this side, single file.' ('This side' was to the right, or rather, the opposite side from the people who'd been queueing since long before I arrived). I joined the end of the queue on the right; it wasn't clear exactly where the end was, because there was a woman in a purple dress, plump but not unattractive, and then space for two or three people, and then a miserable-looking old woman leaning against the wall, and then an old lady and a child sitting on the steps of a house, eating ice creams. I asked the miserable-looking old woman if this was the queue for five o'clock, and she told me she wasn't queueing. I went up to the woman in the purple dress and asked her the same thing; 'No,' she replied, 'this is the queue for five twenty.' Eventually I found the queue for five o'clock, which wasn't very large or well organised, near the main steps, and put the same question to a burly, bald man in white overalls, who would be my point of reference from then on. He confirmed that yes, it was the queue for five o'clock. I had to work hard to make sure no one got in between that man and me, because there were plenty of people hanging around who weren't in any kind of queue and were looking for an opportunity to slip in. Finally I reached the doorman, showed him my number and he let me through, after advising me to follow the man in white. I followed the man in white on a very strange, slow route, first down a narrow passageway formed by a wall on the left and a low barrier on the right. When, after a considerable time, we reached the end of that passageway, we were funnelled into another passageway, which was joined to the previous one, this time with the same barrier as before on the right, and on the left a row of cubicles containing computers that nobody was using. In other words, this part of the route went in the opposite direction, towards the street. This section was slower. Finally, when we reached the end of the passage, we found ourselves back where we'd entered the building, very close to the doorman, but now we had to walk in the original direction again, away from the street – 'boustrophedon' is, I think, the name for this pattern. I remembered the mazes for rats in those lab tests. From where I was, I could see that the huge space was packed full of people. There were a few seats, more than thirty, I guessed, all occupied, but there were people on foot spilling out in all directions. Still on the right, after the seats, there was a line of desks with letters and booths with numbers. The letters went from A to F, and the numbers I could see, from 7 to 9. Then I saw that further ahead, hanging on a long L-shaped counter, were the lower numbers, white on a blue background, and that the 1 said 'RENEWALS'. I had to get all the way over there to begin the process. But to the right, on the desks, were two small, important-looking signs, also in white on a blue background, which said something to the effect that we had to read and check all the information carefully before . . . and you couldn't see the rest, because it was covered by the comical plume of an enormous Christmas wreath. The second sign said exactly the same thing, and another comical plume of the wreath was covering the rest. A Christmas wreath on 1 February. Covering up important information.

I'm bored of writing about this now, and I'm tired; I think I'll go to bed. Besides, there aren't any major developments left to mention, except for the exhausting wait, always on foot, surrounded by a perspiring mass of bodies, which was without doubt responsible for the horrible expression on my face in the photo on my ID card.

SATURDAY 3, 20:48

Many years ago, I heard a dentist relative of mine expound the theory that the flu can last for three, seven or twenty-one days. The numbers are too cabbalistic to be very trustworthy, but it's true that for me personally, over the years, this theory has worked fairly well. I'm on the sixth day of this bout of flu, and I hope it goes away tomorrow because I'm fed up with it, and the thought of spending another two weeks in this state is very depressing. The worst part is not being able to leave the house; not because going out brings me any great joy, but because being cooped up at home for an extended period makes me more manic and anxious. And I need exercise, and I can't do much exercise because I'm not strong enough. At this time of day, my temperature always gets a bit higher and I feel even weaker than usual. Luckily, yesterday I received some important advice from Julia over the phone: for a sore throat, there's nothing better than chewing a bit of raw onion. I argued that onions have the disadvantage of infusing your underarm sweat with their aroma, meaning that after a few hours, the sweat starts smelling quite offensive. Then Julia gave me another key piece of advice: that I should dust my armpits with bicarbonate of soda. Well, before going to sleep I chewed a bit of onion, and today my sore throat is almost completely gone. Now my armpits are dusted with bicarbonate, and I hope the second piece of advice turns out to be as good as the first.

The ID card business has had some interesting after-effects. I thought that when they gave me the new ID, they'd take the old one away; it wasn't a completely unfounded idea, since that had happened before. This time it didn't, which means I still have my old ID. But the day before going to renew it, when I still didn't know the situation, I decided to scan it to avoid losing the photo. Not because it's a particularly special photo, but because I see it as a record of a time in my life from which I don't think I've kept any other pictures; what's more, ID card photos have a particular quality, I don't know what exactly, something it's impossible to find in other kinds of photo. They always reveal features or details that, for better or worse, generally for worse, aren't revealed by other processes.

Once I had a .jpg file of the photo from the old ID, it occurred to me to experiment with the symmetries, taking advantage of the fact the photo is completely face-on, or almost completely. A few years ago, I used to find it fascinating to experiment with a mirror, to see what imaginary characters could be produced by duplicating each half of my head. Some of the results were quite blood-curdling, à la Dr Jekyll and Mr Hyde: a psychopathic murderer coexisting with a benevolent halfwit. The results of my experiment with the out-of-date ID card were less chilling, but they had their moments. And the less said about the results with the new ID card the better.

MONDAY 5, 21:01

Towards the end of an extremely long dream, in a house I don't recognise as any house I know, I encounter a big, black, wolflike dog in one room; and then I realise that a little white dog has also come in, looking a lot like Diana, the dog I was given as a present when I had the measles. For a second I was afraid the big dog would attack the little one, but I soon saw he wasn't showing any interest in her. The big dog was standing by a door that opened onto what I presumed was a garden, and I imagined he wanted to go out. When I went over to the door, I found it was locked, and then the dream shows me a close-up of a big, rusty iron lock, though it wasn't inserted into that dark wooden door, but rather into some bars that looked like part of a prison. I began to walk around in circles endlessly the way you do in dreams, hunting for the key, and when I found it, I tried to open the lock. But it was very rusty, and however hard I tried, almost bending the enormous iron key, the mechanism seemed irreparably jammed. So I went to look for some oil . . . more going round in circles . . . and I amused myself with other things, with people having conversations, etc.; and at one point I found myself pouring a stream of oil into the lock, but by then I'd already lost sight of why I wanted to open it, and indeed of the dogs, although somehow they were still present. Next comes a long and very interesting scene, involving a young man who could have been a doctor or a psychologist; blond, with glasses and a friendly personality. I'd written a whole story for him to read – or for him to look at, because I think I'd actually written it in the form of a cartoon. In it, I described something like the equivalent of a therapy session. Indirectly, this man seemed to be a kind of therapist I had, and whom I'd consulted before, though as a friend, in an unofficial capacity. At that moment, he was getting ready to leave, but I don't know if he was going on holiday (as my doctor has done, in fact) or leaving that place – that city or town, or perhaps seaside resort – for good. When I take my story over to where the man is, I find him in the company of a very attractive young woman I don't recognise. I address her immediately and with great eloquence, and while with my left hand I'm passing the sheets of paper to the doctor, with my right I select some others on which there's a different cartoon I've drawn (and which has some connection to Superman) and give them to the girl, and say something to her. I don't know what I say, but it had the assured, decisive tone of a sexual advance, and, bringing all my seductive abilities to bear, and with considerable energy and confidence, I asked her if she'd like to meet up later.

MONDAY 5, 23:59

I forgot a fragment of the dream. It seems I did manage to open that door to let the dogs out, because at some point I found myself standing by an open door, and on the other side stood a little dog (a different one from before) who was looking at me steadily. She had a funny round face, with wide, eager and rather sad eyes. She seemed to be very fond of me and wanted to come in, but I couldn't let her because it would cause problems with someone else (a dog or a woman, I don't know . . . ) who'd get annoyed, perhaps out of jealousy. So I carried out a complicated manoeuvre to avoid offending the dog by closing the door in her face: I went outside, distracted her somehow to lure her away from the door, and then walked casually back in and shut the door behind me, leaving the little dog outside.

WEDNESDAY 7, 21:47

As I expected, the maid called to say she had low blood pressure and would come on Friday instead. She always finds out right away, the moment I turn my kitchen into an inferno. Since I'd been expecting it, I was already resigned, and eventually I rolled up my sleeves and washed the dishes myself. I washed everything except a Pyrex dish Chl used last night for a concoction involving chopped-up potatoes with the skins on, egg, a little ham and grated cheese. She ate her share and left. I tried to eat a bit later but the potatoes had gone cold and turned rock-hard. I only managed to chew a couple of small pieces, but they were exquisite. Then I put the whole thing in the microwave for a few minutes and the potatoes grew soft enough for me to eat some. When they cooled down again, once again they were rock-hard. Today I didn't wash the dish because it was still very encrusted with food; I left it soaking to soften it.

Chl's visit left me feeling very unsettled. Although a few days ago I'd decided to forget about my sex life once and for all and focus on enjoying the time I have left without getting embroiled in any more difficult relationships, yesterday Chl really shook me up. She radiates sexual attraction, along with other great and extraordinary things. As soon as she left I felt disconcerted and began doing pointless activities. I ruined a lot of things on the computer and had to redo them all painstakingly. I ended up going to sleep very late, and today I got up later than ever. It was after 6 p.m. by the time I had breakfast. Before going to sleep I thought intensively about my yoga teacher, as a kind of cry for help. Then I dreamed about her; all I was able to hang onto from the dream is a fragment in which I was crying and saying to my teacher that I didn't know how to free myself from Chl's influence. She tried to calm me down and stop me making any drastic decisions. This afternoon, my yoga teacher called to say she was back. We didn't manage to arrange a class for today in the end, but we'll try again on Friday.

Although I've overcome the terrible effects of the heat thanks to the air conditioners, I've realised that there's much more to the summer than heat, and, air conditioners or no air conditioners, it still leaves me in a bad way. I'm having a better time this year than in previous years, of course. But there's something storm-like, involving static electricity, a kind of subtropical stickiness and humidity that never goes away. Yesterday's storm affected me a lot; the hours before the storm broke out, I mean. Then things improved. But I was very thirsty, thirstier almost than ever before, and that carried on until, just before going to sleep, I decided to eat a few grains of salt. Although it seems paradoxical, the salt quenched my thirst. My body had been asking for salt, and it took me a long time to listen because I was scared the salt would raise my blood pressure.

But summer has other drawbacks too; carnival, for example. Although for some time the Council has been making sure that – to quote the tango song – 'every day is carnival', and especially weekends; now that we're in official carnival time, which began on the first day of this month and who knows when it will end, Saturdays and Sundays on Avenida 18 de Julio are supremely carnivalesque. On Sunday N and I finally went for our much-postponed walk together. Fortunately N is an excellent companion, so I was able to get over the feeling of alienation, and even terror, that was bubbling up inside me the whole time we were walking down the street. There was a loud-speaker every few yards along the whole length of the avenue, with the volume turned up inexplicably, thunderously high. What's more, not all the loudspeakers were transmitting the same thing; every so often they'd change from *cumbia* to *candombe* and other such atrocities, and in the space between them, the two musical styles would merge and overlap. There were also live acts, including the Bolivians again, and, on the way back, a couple of tango musicians who weren't bad but were amplified to unbearable levels. People had formed a large circle, in the middle of which some ridiculous couples were dancing tango. A few yards further along, tropical music. On the way back, we also passed what looked like the end of who knows what other monstrous recital, in the Plaza Libertad, just in time to hear the farewells and the expressions of thanks to some people or other 'who made it all possible'. Damn them.

These walks through something very similar to Hell fill me with a feeling of unreality, which can be quite alarming. Something is drastically wrong and out of place, and I don't know if it's me or the whole urban milieu of the new millennium. There must be a connection between this mentality and the end – and the beginning – of a century and millennium. If I remember rightly, the passion for noise began around 1995, with advertising and tacky music in some super-markets. I complained to the supermarkets in question, successfully on a few occasions, though they soon stopped taking any notice and I had to give up on going to supermarkets and buy my groceries from smaller shops instead. Then those smaller shops were seized by the same passion, along with all the shops on and around 18 de Julio, and all the bars and restaurants and patisseries, and then the buses (where there is now television as well) and the taxis, and eventually the streets. I should add that I've never heard a single song come out of those loudspeakers that was any good. But even if the songs were all right, imposing them on everyone like that would still be intolerable. It's pure fascism – a kind of fascism associated with an underdeveloped and mentally stunted subculture. The Council not only tolerates but actively participates in the production of this stupidifying racket; and

I can only imagine what this country will be like within a few years . . . the domain of rude remarks and street gangs, and almost certainly of more state terrorism.

THURSDAY 8, 03:59

Rotring.

To my immense surprise, and in a departure from a schedule that's been in operation for years, the Feria del Libro was open on Sunday. I picked up another novel that was missing from my Erle Stanley Gardner collection; this time I had the lists with me, which I'd printed off from the database, showing the names of the books I have and the ones I still need. N found this remarkable; she couldn't believe I was so meticulous. I explained that otherwise I can never be sure I don't have a particular book, because I've read so many, almost all of them, and I always think I own them. This one, for example, looked familiar, based on the names of some characters who appear at the beginning. The list was right, because when I got home I saw that I didn't have it already; but my memory was also right, because I found that I did have it . . . in English. How was I supposed to know that the original title of *The Case of the Sentimental Blackmailer* was *The Case of the Gilded Lily*? What's more, when I read it in Spanish there wasn't a lily anywhere to be seen, and there was a sentimental blackmailer. Maybe in English 'gilded lily' is an expression or idiom with a particular meaning, or perhaps a gilded lily did appear but I didn't spot it; I didn't look up the meaning of the words 'gilded' and 'lily' until I'd finished the book, so I wasn't on the lookout for lily references while I was reading. I also bought a crime thriller, by a more contemporary author, but although it kept me entertained, I didn't think it was anything special.

It's always very interesting to talk to N, both because of the things she tells me and because of the extremely funny way she tells me them. I'm never entirely sure when her humour is intentional; it seems to come about naturally, without her even realising she's telling a funny story, and although she does sometimes laugh, I think it's more out of nervousness than amusement. On our walk, it was torture trying to communicate in the midst of an environment designed to make communication impossible. People who are obliged to walk down the avenue (which, all things considered, and especially now the police have reappeared, is a safer route, or a less unsafe route, than others); these people, as I was saying, if they want to communicate with each other, have to shout, and a conversation can't last very long or be very profound if you're shouting. In the open-air café, we could chat a little more comfortably, but the background noise was still considerable.

MONDAY 12, 01:06

A few days ago, I began reading this diary and correcting the errors. I was surprised to find that now, a few months on, I can read it with interest; it doesn't seem as worthless as it did before. It's hard to know how interesting it would be to a reader who isn't me, but even the fact it's interesting to me means a lot. Yesterday I read a very negative review in a back issue of a weekly paper, written by a Uruguayan journalist, of the diary Bukowski kept when he was even older than I am now. I'd like to be able to read it, despite that review, because it seems to have points in common with this diary, in terms of the trivial things it describes, and the insistent inclusion of stories about a single topic – horse races – which could be similar to my insistence on the topic of the computer. I don't mind having things in common with Bukowski.

But the fact is that after reading and correcting half of August, I stopped writing this diary or anything else, and I also stopped reading it and correcting it. I'd like to know why, although I'm not curious enough to put any mental effort into finding out. I'm still very lazy, very out of sorts from the summer weather and the carnival, and most of all from the absence of Chl (and sometimes from her presence; when she appears, from time to time, it's clear I've built up such resentment and such feelings of abandonment that it's difficult to be with her) (I've even noticed, the past few times I've seen her, that when she hugs me, I move away very quickly and actually push her back a little, with my hands resting on her shoulders) (this topic is a permanent thorn in my side). It should be clear that I have no objections to Chl's behaviour; I try my hardest to make my feelings match my thoughts, but it's no use: there's a stubborn, petulant creature inside me, one of those dogs that won't let go of a bone.

MONDAY 12, 18:59

Memory versus database: I found a Gardner book at the stall on the corner; my printed list from the computer said it was missing from my collection, and my memory said it wasn't. I bought it anyway. When I got home, there it was on the shelf. But the database was right: the book in my library has some pages missing. At the end, no less. So it was both there and not there.

I need to write down today's dream, the one about the 'abyss'. I don't have time now.

TUESDAY 13, 03:12

The dream was very 'realistic', especially in terms of the development of the action in 'real' time; everything was narrated in detail, very meticulously and naturally. It's a shame I've forgotten most of the plot, though I suspect that what I've forgotten was largely filler, or a way of keeping me entertained so I slept peacefully. The place where it all occurred wasn't named, although it could have been Piriapolis, or Colonia, or a combination of the two, especially their qualities as seaside towns. Almost all my family were represented: my father, my mother, my grandmother, I think, and also my friend Ricardito (Tinker), or at least a boy with very similar attitudes or behaviour to him. My family was running a business, like in the days when I had my bookshop and my mother helped out, though I seemed to be fairly disconnected from it all, as in the time after Piriapolis, by which point the bookshop belonged to my mother and I was the one who sometimes helped out. Towards the end of the dream, however, I learn they've made a significant outlay, they've bought a lot of stock, probably entire libraries, and this makes me anxious, or apprehensive, because 'the season's almost over, it's not the right time to buy things'.

But I don't say anything to them and pretend to be happy about the purchase. Which is odd, because in the bookshop days I was the one who always wanted to buy things, and my mother was opposed to all spending.

But before that came the most important part, and the part I remember best: my mother is going down a street with that boy (or Ricardo). Alongside the street (in a very clear, very open landscape; you couldn't see any of the city, or anything at all besides this street or main road); alongside the street, there runs a wall that's more or less the height of a person, or perhaps slightly lower, but the interesting thing is that on the other side of the wall is another street or main road, perhaps going in the opposite direction, and that other street or main road is much lower down than the first. This could correspond to an area on the coast of Colonia where there are various levels. But the climate was very different.

I hide behind that wall, in an operation in the dream-dimension that I can't now explain, since first I'm hiding behind the wall with the intention of listening in on the conversation between my mother and this boy, so as to play a trick on them later by repeating it all back and making them think I know those things by magic; but then, after climbing over the wall to hide, I notice that the only way of hiding is to cling onto the top of the wall with my fingers, because there's a vertical drop on the other side and no footholds of any kind. The other street, as I've said, is a great deal lower down; as a result I find myself suspended directly above an abyss, and falling would probably be fatal. And yet I don't feel dizzy or scared, just slightly concerned that it might be a tricky situation to get out of. There's also a short, almost abstract line of reasoning, more of a feeling, something along the lines of: 'It wasn't worth risking all this just for a joke.' Anyway, when my mother and the boy have already moved on, I manage to pull myself up with my arm muscles, onto the top of the wall, though it's not easy. At the same time there's a slight, very slight, awareness of my real age . . . and the thought, or feeling, that I shouldn't risk such exertions because I'm not as fit as I used to be.

I wasn't hanging by my fingers for very long, but it was long enough for the experience to be imprinted on my memory; long enough and intense enough. It wasn't exactly a nightmare, but it might as well have been.

When I woke up, I wondered what kind of an abyss I'd been about to fall into. Madness, being devoured by the unconscious? Or perhaps it was simply an expression of my fear of finding out about things I've buried, of 'falling' into those unpleasant things.

SATURDAY 17, 19:24

Rotring.

Waiting for M so we can go for a walk.

Perhaps the hypothetical reader, and the no less hypothetical Mr Guggenheim, are convinced – if they're looking at the date at the top of each diary entry – that I've completely abandoned both this diary and the project. Quite the contrary. Last Wednesday I began working set hours, between 4 and 6 p.m., and I've managed to stick fairly closely to this routine. And, as part of me was expecting, by this Wednesday it had become a habit, and, better still, I found myself working enthusiastically and even out of hours, for long stretches of time. Today, Saturday, I decided to have a rest, because I was low on sleep. In order to begin work at 4 p.m., I had to ask for wake-up calls at 1.30 p.m. and 2 p.m.; and on those three days, I got up at two without letting myself stay in bed a minute longer, even though my bedtime hasn't changed and I'm very tired when I wake up. Yesterday I found it harder than ever, because I was dreaming about something erotic, though not very explicit, involving my childhood friend who died a few months ago. This erotic dream about a woman who's not only dead but also living happily and peacefully in a dimension we might call 'the Kingdom of Heaven' strikes me as in rather bad taste; one day I'll have to explain why. But, as theologians and saints unanimously maintain, we're not responsible for the contents of our dreams.

The point is that I'd been sleep-deprived for three days, and so today I decided to have a break. But I made good progress editing August and September of this diary, and some materials that relate to the project, including those few pages that now definitely form part of the project itself. What I found most exciting was that when I read the last page I'd written of the project itself, I spontaneously burst into tears; the tears didn't last long (because I didn't let them) but they were very healthy nonetheless. And this means that at least one passage on that page is written truthfully and with the right spirit.

M called a few minutes ago; she was just setting off in a taxi, so she should be arriving any second.

SATURDAY 17, 20:07

Something must have happened to M, because she said she was setting off in a taxi more than forty minutes ago and she still hasn't arrived. Even if she'd taken a bus, she'd be here by now. Waiting like this has made me very nervous, because I don't feel able to do anything else. I just pace and pace around my apartment like a caged beast. Meanwhile, things are getting more complicated because I'm starting to feel hungry, and if I eat, I won't be able to go for a walk immediately afterwards. I need to calm down, and that's why I've begun this page, still writing by hand because the computer's off and I don't want to turn it on.

It's not that M is a paragon of punctuality, but this is a very strange situation; I can't think what could have happened to her, or at least I can't think of anything good.

Tomorrow it looks like I'm going for a walk with F; we've agreed to go at 7 p.m. F heard that N had taken me for a walk and volunteered to do the same. It's the new fashion, taking the sexagenarian out for an airing. That suits me; the last few times I went out alone, the phobia hit me hard. There goes the doorbell.

SUNDAY 18, 04:35

You'd think I'd understand women better by this point in my life, but no. They always manage to throw me off. M turned up about fifty minutes after telling me she was leaving in a taxi 'right away', and I got worried. But then she arrived as fresh as a daisy, and was very surprised that I'd been so anxious. What happened to her? Nothing – just a couple of phone conversations before she left. She also said the taxi had gone very, very slowly. 'It must have seemed slow to you because you were in a rush,' I observed. 'In a rush?' She raised her eyebrows, amazed. No, she hadn't been in a rush at all. Fifty minutes late is nothing. And meanwhile, things had been getting difficult for me; the hunger, for example. I solved that by eating a minuscule piece of ham and drinking a coffee. Enough to get me to the *boliche* on Calle Ejido without any upsets.

We called in at the Feria del Libro; I was very keen to look at the selection of detective novels, because I hadn't been able to go for a while. To my delight, I found *two* Gardner novels I didn't have; and one of them wasn't even on my list because I didn't know it existed: *The Case of the Fabulous Fake*. I'm halfway through the other one, which I decided to read first because it's shorter: *The Case of the Shapely Shadow*. Brevity is a virtue that came late to Gardner; his first Perry Mason novels were endless sagas.

In the *boliche*, M continued to disconcert me. She told me about a few episodes from her life that seemed extraordinary to me; I had no idea she'd been through those things. I thought I knew her very well, after all these years, and that the story of her life held no more surprises for me, and I was wrong there too. Women are unpredictable, they really are.

Summer, carnival, and yet the avenue was very peaceful. A normal flow of people, not particularly deafening. Most of the population have probably relocated to the beach. But the Council seems to have calmed down as well. Fewer loudspeakers, fewer *cumbia* songs. All very unusual. However, just today M said that this city is very odd, very peculiar. 'For years I've found it a living nightmare,' I replied. Maybe she's noticed my permanent feeling of alienation, because she's sensitive to an almost supersensory degree. But in fact, today the city was more normal than usual, so to speak. I felt a bit dizzy now and then; from the feeling of alienation, from the heat perhaps, from having been shut up indoors for so long, from the ever-thickening cloud of phobias that engulfs me. And M picked up on all that, I'm sure of it. On the way back I ran into a friend; he was sitting at the table of a *boliche*, almost on the pavement. He came over to greet me very cordially, and then, when we were saying goodbye, I insulted him in the most absurd and gratuitous manner. I insulted him directly, and I don't know why, and he didn't even seem to register it. But I was amazed, and frightened. It's not only women I find unpredictable and incomprehensible; it seems I'm unpredictable and incomprehensible as well, even to myself.

Later, back at home, something very satisfying happened. I downloaded an *extremely* important and extremely useful program from the internet, after checking a few details with a friend by email, and best of all I was able to crack the program so it does absolutely everything it can for me without holding back, without adverts or restrictions of any kind. These things always leave me feeling perfectly satisfied.

TUESDAY 20, 19:47

On Sunday F turned up accompanied by P, just as I expected. We went for a walk and a coffee, still following my usual route. At least one of us, i.e. me, had a very nice time, although pandemonium had returned to the avenue, now thanks to some loudspeakers that seemed about to explode, firing out sound waves at an unimaginable decibel level. The loudspeakers belong to some bars, which are fairly close together and which put tables on the pavement and in the street. There was no one sitting at the tables, and I thought nobody could possibly sit at those tables because of the auditory suffering it would entail, but on the way back there were plenty of people sitting there; I expect they're all deaf, and if they aren't yet, they will be soon. F, P and I had to protect our ears when we passed the loudspeakers, either with our hands or by opening our mouths (me) (I learnt this from a relative of mine in the navy, who was advised to open his mouth every time the cannon was fired during military drills). Back at my apartment, P and I got into one of those conversations that I can only ever have with P, since he seems to be of a very similar mindset to me, and similarly well informed about scientific matters, although really he's probably better informed and more up to date. F was scared, since we discussed perfectly naturally, carelessly even, the details of certain phenomenologies that shatter our normal understanding of the universe.

And yesterday, Monday, I went for a walk with N. But we didn't manage to walk much. There was a storm brewing; as we were crossing the Plaza Independencia, the wind was very strong, and we even felt a few stray drops of rain. I was in favour of calling off the walk, but N insisted it wasn't going to rain (and it didn't). The sky was a dark grey, verging on black in places, and when the wind died down it felt unbearably hot; or, more than hot, as if a suffocating electrical charge were enveloping our bodies. Everything suggested there'd be a violent explosion any second, but there was nothing of the sort. My doctor came in the evening, and when I told her about this episode, she couldn't believe it; she says she was on the *rambla* at the same time, not so far away, and the weather was splendid and calm, with no hint of a storm.

As I was saying, N and I didn't go very far; I got tired and my whole body started to ache, and I had trouble breathing normally. We turned back and ended up in a *boliche* a block away from my apartment, where we had a coffee and chatted. The conversation was very interesting, and today I heard via email that N thought the same, and would like to continue it soon.

I felt sure I'd see Chl today, but Chl changed her plans and today she went away on another trip. So we didn't see each other. And I miss her. And she says she misses me too. What a mystery, the whole thing.

THURSDAY 22, 17:39

Right now, the widow, alone on the railings, some distance from the corpse but looking in its direction. Once more, she's in the pose of a broody hen. Sitting there, motionless.

MONDAY 26, 04:53

Rotring.

Depending on the state of my beard, sometimes, when I'm getting ready to clean my teeth before bed, I see a face in the mirror that looks a lot like Salman Rushdie (an author I've never read and have no intention of reading). This resemblance could well be an optical illusion, and besides, there are some obvious differences: much less hair, older, the gaze both less astute and less self-satisfied. But just in case: a warning to all Muslims that Rushdie is not in Montevideo. I repeat: Rushdie is not in Montevideo. Please check the identity very carefully before acting.

MONDAY 26, 16:54

Towards the end of last month, prompted by my reading of Burroughs, I told the story of Chl's 'ghost' in this diary. It left me feeling worried about 'familiars' that possess us, generally at night, whether we're awake or asleep, whether we're conscious or not of being possessed, and I remembered a most unusual dream I'd had about my friend Ginebra not so many years ago, in a very particular period of my life. It was shortly before, very shortly before, meeting Chl in person, and the dream had other ramifications that I'd also like to record. Anyway, at the time I was very keen to tell Ginebra about my dream, but I didn't know if I could do it tactfully – so I sent her a preparatory email, and then I sent her, also by email, my account of the dream, written up rather elliptically. It turns out I've lost both those emails. I keep all my emails, absolutely all of them (except the spam), and I spent hours looking for this material on every single one of my backup disks to no avail. It seems those emails are from a time when a procedure went wrong and I lost some. After it happened I wrote to my email correspondents, asking them to please forward me all my emails from that time. Many did, but it looks like Ginebra wasn't one of them. I have backups of the most inconsequential files, but the rule seems to be that when I lose something, it's something important, like the time when a single terrible manoeuvre made me lose *all* the programs I'd ever made. And some of them were impossible to reconstruct.

To get hold of those emails with the account of the dream and the ensuing saga, then, I had to write to Ginebra and ask her to look for them. She took a while to find them . . . although, as another very telepathic person, she'd been rereading them only the day before, but in the form of some copies she'd kept. In the end she sent them to me, all together, in a single .rtf file, but the headers didn't include the date. I bothered her again, asking her to have a look for the dates, and eventually I learnt that I'd sent the emails between 14 and 18 May 1998. Nothing more precise, but I think that's enough.

Now I must ask the hypothetical reader to be patient a little while longer, because I'm going to copy that series of emails in here and comment on them. For me, for the investigation into myself I'm currently carrying out, it's a very important thing to do. At any rate, the reader has permission to skip whatever they want, even the whole of the rest of this diary.


I write to Ginebra, probably on 14 May 1998.

*Subject:* it turns out that . . .

. . . in a certain therapeutic setting, it's suggested that I (my interior being) should reveal what the obstacles are that stop it doing what it really wants. The next day, I dream about an old boss trying to convince me to take part in a particular business (it's not very clear what, though it seems to relate to toothpaste, and pharmacies; something involving some not very appealing publicity – an overdetermined project with little space for creativity or individuality. It was all sketched out very vaguely in the dream; these are more like a posteriori impressions). Well: my response (or rather, the response I was awaiting from my interior being) consisted of a simple, magnificent pair of words: 'Seduce me,' I said, and then I left that place.

Later, not in the dream any more but once I was awake, I went for a walk in the afternoon, looked at the world and thought, 'Of course, the devil's so stupid. There's nothing REALLY attractive here.' I ran my usual indifferent, daydreaming gaze over the world. Remembering the dream, I said to the world: 'Seduce me,' and opened my eyes wide, but no. Everything was horribly monotonous and even detestable.

But the devil's no fool.

Today . . . (no, no; my pen is holding back).


.    .    .


339

I was too shy to write about the more recent dream. Then, perhaps later the same day or perhaps the day after, I found an elegant way of doing it:

*Subject:* perhaps you recall . . .

 . . . that famous section of a masterpiece, I forget whether it's by Michelangelo or someone else, where the hand of man almost brushes the hand of God. Well, there was a very similar situation in my dream today, though it didn't involve hands, or God the Father exactly.

Blocked once again by shyness, or, more than shyness, by the need to be obscure, since the last thing in the world I wanted was to cause Ginebra problems with her partner, who was naturally jealous. I should clarify that when I met Ginebra, I described her as 'the most beautiful woman in the world'. The third email goes a little further:

*Subject:* gasp

 Of course I had a kind of dwarf assistant with me (Nick Carter's Tinker, if you read my *Nick Carter Enjoys Himself etc.*), and his presence didn't let things go very far, but it was very exciting nonetheless. I seemed to be writing a kind of personal diary, though really it wasn't a diary but a novel, and it was related, very closely related, to Carlos Gardel; it could have been a biography of Carlos Gardel, only in the first person, and including fragments of things I came up with myself; all this is also an impression, nothing was said clearly. But the important thing is that the project was progressing; there was a temporal, cumulative progression. At one point I realise a friend of mine has a similar project, and it occurs to me that we should obviously combine the two. I telephone her, with all the difficulties that sometimes arise in dreams when you try to use a telephone, and set off for her house. I'm made very welcome. (And if it wasn't for that damn dwarf . . . but still, it was all very nice.) Incidentally, the embryonic novel, or whatever it was, had to be called *Gardel, Gardel*. That is, I stuck my tongue out at the devil and the crazy guy hit me with everything he'd got! Do you think I'll lose my soul?

Ginebra, who is neither thick nor lazy, understood perfectly that the friend in the dream was her. I have no way of knowing, now, if she censored this email at all, or if my self-censorship was enough; the main thing is that the most interesting section isn't recounted. Since it sounds like we were due to see each other in person over the coming days, I probably kept the most difficult part to tell her face to face.

In the part of the dream I didn't describe in my email, after reaching Ginebra's house and being 'made very welcome', without further ado I find myself lying down with my back resting on the floor, and Ginebra is squatting on top of me, in the lovemaking position in which the woman is on top of the man. The reference to the hand of man almost brushing the hand of God came about because in the dream there wasn't strictly speaking any insertion; the genitalia were very close together, but they weren't touching, and between them flowed a very strong current of energy. I could feel it flowing quite clearly, like a kind of vibration. I woke up with a very pleasurable sensation, and full of energy. The next emails aren't important at all, except the postscript of the last one, supposedly from the eighteenth.

In the ninth email, something very important appears:

*Subject:* the plot thickens
    The complexity of the universe really is marvellous. Today a friend came to see me . . . but I'll tell you later. I'll tell you later.

That visit from a friend is closely related to my dream, and I'll write about it a little further on.

In the next email, I'm replying to an email from Ginebra (hence the 'Re:' in the subject line), which she asked me to delete after reading, because it discussed the situation with my partner at the time, and contained some very harsh, perceptive analysis. I'll copy the relevant parts:

*Subject: Re: Trash after reading, please!*

The famous scene in the dream involving the 'exchange of energy' could suggest several more interpretations, all perfectly superimposed (since this is one of the great advantages of dreams: they can condense several layers of interpretation without the usual inevitable contradictions) [. . .] All that remains, on that score, is the (theoretical) possibility that a beautiful woman will fall in love with me. I probably wouldn't be able to resist that so heroically, because it would play on my narcissism rather than against it. And therefore it's not up to me, or even, strictly speaking, to the hypothetical beautiful woman, since these things can't be controlled by the will. So I am (and it could never be otherwise) entirely in God's hands. [. . .]

PS: Ha, ha. I just realised that these latest digressions of mine about how the only possibility of salvation is being loved by a beautiful woman not only evoke fairy tales (kissing toads, etc.) but also perfectly reproduce the phrase from the dream: 'Seduce me.'

At least you can't deny I'm coherent in my incoherence.

End of the series of emails on the matter. Later I'll try to write about my friend who visited me, and comment a bit on the whole thing.

MONDAY 26, 18:52

I'm waiting for N so we can go for a walk. Yesterday I went for a walk with M. I didn't find a single detective novel. On the way back, we went into the supermarket on 18 de Julio, which is open until 10 p.m., and when, weighed down with the shopping, we were walking past the Palacio Salvo, heading for my apartment, M swiftly spun forty-five degrees to the right and started crossing over to the opposite pavement. I followed, not understanding what was going on. I asked her. She answered, out of the corner of her mouth: 'Pickpockets.' Women are very quick to notice what's happening around them; all I saw were the backs of two boys who were walking away from us, towards Calle Andes, and only when M pointed them out. She told me the full story: one of them, in blue, came too close and looked at the bag M was carrying (inside: an enormous pack of dog food). Then he sat down on the steps of a building. Meanwhile, the other one, who was shorter and wearing a white shirt, had approached me and looked at my shopping bag (ten packets of salt-free biscuits and two pots of yoghurt). Then he shook his head at the one in blue and went over to where he was; the one in blue had got up by that point, and they walked off together. I don't know what they were hoping to find in those shopping bags, but they evidently decided that salt-free biscuits and dog food weren't worth the risk.

Back at home, M agreed to read the first chapter (August) of this diary. I was sure she'd put it down after a few pages, but no: she read the whole thing, to the end, and very attentively – she even marked a few errors. I asked her if she perhaps found it interesting because of that curiosity we all have, especially women, about the intimate details of other people's lives. She said certainly, but that as far as she could tell, although it's difficult to distinguish, there was also a literary interest. And she mentioned some passages she'd particularly enjoyed, or found moving. Later she called me from her house to make another comment: she says that for the common reader, the diary could perhaps pass for a novel, with a protagonist and various situations invented by me. I liked that comment. It makes me want to keep working.

TUESDAY 27, 17:30

I'll call him 'Rafael', the friend whose story I'm trying to tell, which relates to my 'finger of God' dream.

Rafael doesn't live in Montevideo, and he usually comes to see me on his occasional visits to the city. In a way, he's exactly the opposite sort of person to what my usual sort of person would be, but in another way he isn't quite; the similarities are buried deep down inside him, but they've always been there. As for the differences, I could point to his perseverance with our friendship; he never stopped writing to me, even though I didn't always reply. Other notable differences are his extreme modesty, his great humility and the extreme consistency of his thoughts and actions. For years and years he's remained markedly true to himself, and to other people, including his wife.

A few years ago he began to develop, or perhaps continued developing and making more visible, a state of mind that was gradually revealed as depressive. When, in our irregular correspondence, I began to notice his depression growing dangerously bad, I took the liberty of recommending that he consult a psychiatrist and look into the possibility of being prescribed one of those 'new-generation' antidepressants that have worked so well for so many people I know; not because I'm a supporter of medication, but because I understand that depression usually has various causes, some of which are physical, and perhaps even viral, and that it can, at times, be very dangerous. With every letter – and then, following technological developments, with every email – Rafael showed an increasing detachment from life.

He listened to me. He saw a psychiatrist, was given medication, and it wasn't long before he'd visibly improved. I wouldn't say he turned into someone optimistic, verbose and self-satisfied; nothing about his character changed at all, but his detachment from life rapidly dissolved and his attitude to life and to himself became much more appropriate.

Around the time of my aforementioned dream, Rafael emailed to say he was coming to Montevideo in the next few days. He said that something extraordinary had happened to him and he needed to tell me about it, and that it was somehow related to me. He seemed very worried.

When he arrived, he wasted no time in broaching the subject; I've even come to believe that he travelled to Montevideo exclusively, or at least with his main aim being, to tell me his story.

'I think I've gone mad, or I'm about to go mad,' he said.

WEDNESDAY 28, 16:27

'It all began with a dream . . . ' he told me. 'In the dream, we were sitting around a table like this one.' I had received my friend in a kind of dining room with a long wooden table. 'Renata was facing me.' Needless to say, I've changed the name; I chose Renata, meaning 'reborn', to reflect her sudden reappearance from a past that seemed long buried. 'You've met her.'

I didn't remember her, of course. Then he described the circumstances in which I'd met her with total precision and, as usual, I was able to 'see' the scene quite clearly, but I couldn't be sure if it was a real memory. According to Rafael, I'd been very struck by Renata's beauty and had said something to that effect. I met her, still according to his story, at the house of a mutual friend.

'In the dream,' my friend continued, 'I was facing her, and you were there as well, to one side. The three of us around a table like this one. I was very surprised to see her there so clearly, and very confused, because she'd been extremely important to me, no question about that.'

I don't remember any more details about the dream, if there were any; I can't, however, forget the astonishing finale, which made the hairs on the back of my neck stand on end and sent something like a cold shiver through my body:

'She was asking me for help,' my friend continued; 'she said I was the only one who could help her, and she asked me in a very dramatic, urgent way. I stretched out a hand to touch her, and my hand got very close to her hand but they didn't quite meet. It was like that Michelangelo fresco in the Sistine Chapel, where ___Adam's hand almost brushes the finger of God___.'

Those were almost his exact words; I need to check if it really is a fresco, if it's by Michelangelo and if it's in the Sistine Chapel; they're vague notions I have, in my generally uncultured way, and I always forget details like that. But the words I've underlined and put in bold and italics are unforgettably his.

Now, almost three years later, I couldn't guarantee that my friend's dream was more or less simultaneous with my dream about the 'finger of God', or with my use of that expression to describe it in those emails to Ginebra, the co-protagonist of my dream; but I'm sure the two experiences happened very close together in time – if they really were two experiences, that is, and not a single experience that showed itself to each of us in a different way.


Rafael thought he'd had a relapse with his depression. He told me that ever since the dream he'd been feeling profoundly uneasy, and that he couldn't shake off its influence. To me, he seemed more scared than depressed. And his fear was a fear of madness, because he had begun to experience things that were completely foreign to him. For one thing, he was obsessed with finding Renata in 'real' life and learning how he could help her; he thought the communication in the dream had been real, and that Renata's request was indisputably genuine. The problem was that he didn't have the slightest idea how to find her.

But his fear of madness didn't come only from the obsession that was overpowering him, but also from a series of strange occurrences that had begun taking place in his waking hours. Renata would appear before him, and speak to him. He saw her, he had conversations with her. A few weeks later, when Rafael was in Montevideo again, we went for a drive and I had the privilege of witnessing one of these encounters. Rafael calmly informed me that Renata was there with us, and began to tell me what she was saying to him. He did it perfectly naturally, without seeming alarmed, almost without my even realising he'd changed the subject (and more than the subject, the dimension). Then he carried on with his usual normal behaviour.

During the conversation in which he told me about his dream and its ramifications, I was also feeling nervous, and rather responsible, without really knowing why, though the fact is that I'd been present in that dream of his which gave rise to the situation, and I had reason to believe that the image of the finger of God was more than just a strange coincidence. The first thing I did that day, while we were still sitting at the table that resembled the table in the dream, was try to calm him down. I explained that such experiences normally shake you up a lot the first time they happen, and that, after all, he'd gone his whole life completely oblivious to the existence of other dimensions. That similar things happened to me all the time. That it could all boil down to a telepathic phenomenon. That it could equally be caused by an eruption of the Anima archetype. I talked about Jung. I even lent him a book by Jung. Essentially, I tried in every way possible to draw him out of that frightened state which, in my view, was the only real risk to his mental health. The rest of it, the strange phenomena, could be explained in plenty of ways that had nothing to do with madness, even if they did include a kind of hallucination. Sometimes hallucinations, when they're significant, are a way for the Unconscious to express itself, and more useful than damaging. Finally, I recommended that he call in at a church now and then, of any faith. That he went in and sat down there to rest. I wanted to cover all possible bases.

I also decided to help him with the physical hunt for Renata and suggested a few different ways of making a start, principally with the help of the internet. This, in the weeks and perhaps months that followed, presented me with a series of setbacks of such magnitude that I was forced to abandon the search for health reasons. My friend understood when I emailed to tell him. 'It's my job,' he said, and advised me to look after myself. I don't know what forces were at play, but they gave me very, very clear signals that my intervention in the search was no longer welcome.


The rest of that story, which is still going on to this day, isn't particularly interesting to anyone other than Rafael, and I have no right to go on airing other people's secrets. But I can say that the encounters with Renata continued and things started looking up in all areas of his life, including professionally. And that in the end he found her (on the physical plane, let's say) and communicated with her by email and phone. That he then lost her again, through a strange and almost inexplicable manoeuvre, and that the 'virtual', ideal, imaginary, hallucinatory – or whatever you want to call them – meetings have continued reasonably regularly, and have always kept his quality of life higher than he'd previously known it. He read several things by Jung and other writers, and became convinced that these phenomena are natural and there's no reason to fear them, and he even came to have a most interesting telepathic or precognitive experience. One day, Renata appears to him and says: 'I expect you're very happy.' He answers that he doesn't see any particular reason to be happy. 'What do you mean?' Renata asks, a little teasingly. 'What about the letter?' Soon after that, a letter arrives, bringing him very good news related to his work.

# MARCH 2001

THURSDAY 1, 14:59

When I lift the blind in my bedroom, I see a little snowman on the railings of the flat roof next door, exactly opposite me. It's a white pigeon, completely white, immaculately white; I've never seen another like it. White, fat, with ruffled feathers. It looks at me with one eye, winking.

SATURDAY 3, 16:56

### In which the strange name of 'Chl' is explained

I was looking, in order to complete the story of the finger of God and related matters, for the exact date of my first face-to-face meeting with Chl. As with my dream about Ginebra, I couldn't find any of the necessary emails. I also looked through the letters, but our letters sent as encrypted email attachments came later, when we had things to say to each other that couldn't be read by anyone else. The date of our meeting can be placed with near perfect accuracy in the same month, May '98, almost certainly on Tuesday the twenty-sixth.

But just now, when I was looking through the letters, I opened one at random. It was dated 5 July and contained none other than my clear, concise declaration of love, and the origin of the name 'Chl':

> . . . I'll be brief, then: I love you, I want you, I like you very much and find you terribly impressive. You've thrown me off balance and I'll probably go under once and for all. But at least now there's a smile on my face.

Thank you very much, little *chica lista*.

Chl, then, means '*Chica lista*', or clever girl. And I really did go under once and for all, just as my hyperlucidity in that moment foresaw.

SUNDAY 4, 17:47

I imagine the eventual, hypothetical, long-suffering reader got lost a long time ago; if not entirely, then at least when it comes to this story I've been attempting to tell for some days. What with tracking down material (emails, letters) and editing this diary, which I'm still doing, and which involves various different tasks, there isn't much time left for the diary itself, for continuing to write about minor everyday events. Nothing spectacular has happened, and I hope nothing does, but I've definitely been missing opportunities to make progress with some of the storylines forming the body of the narrative.

Now I'd like to take a few minutes to recapitulate, to give a short summary of the key points of my recent investigations and see if I can record any conclusions or reflections. The events that make up the set are:

1) My original dream, with therapeutic origins, in which I challenge 'the world' to seduce me.
2) My dream in which Ginebra appears, and the mention of the finger of God in my email telling Ginebra about the dream.
3) My rather desperate conviction, in the last of those emails to Ginebra, that only a kiss from a princess can break the curse:

   All that remains, on that score, is the (theoretical) possibility that a beautiful woman will fall in love with me.

4) The sudden arrival of 'Rafael' and him telling me about the dream that's similar to mine in many ways, with the explicit mention from him of the finger of God.
5) The first meeting with Chl in person, during which I'm immediately seduced. And the seduction seems to be mutual. Later on, I'll include a dream Chl had about it.

All this in a period that runs from 6 to 26 May 1998; the sixth is the likely date of the dream in which I challenge the world to seduce me, and the twenty-sixth is the day of my meeting with Chl.

There are, of course, more questions than answers. I wonder, for example, if the 'finger of God' dream involving Ginebra is showing something that really happened; if Ginebra is one of those 'familiars' Burroughs describes. It's obviously not a simple erotic dream; I feel no desire in it whatsoever and there's no build-up, nothing that paves the way for Ginebra's unexpected possession of me as I'm lying on the floor. And then there's that flow of energy from sex to sex, which isn't the same, if you ask me, as a sexual act. It's quite clear that there's contact between two worlds that can't touch, but between which an exchange of energy is possible. It strikes me as natural for the energy to flow down the sexual channels, and there are some precedents for this. There seems to be an indissoluble union, or a single identity, linking the so-called psychic energy and the sexual energy that some people call libido.

I also wonder how that dream could relate to my challenge to the world to seduce me. What happens with Ginebra isn't a seduction, yet something tells me that the scene is part of the process, that it's an early response from the world (or the devil) to my challenge. Perhaps in that scene I'm receiving the energy I need for the changes I'll soon have to face.

I should also emphasise that, in the dream, the person who appears as Ginebra doesn't inevitably or necessarily have to be Ginebra. Nothing in her replies to me suggested that she'd felt anything herself; on the contrary, she was worried about my situation and the state of my relationship with my partner, etc., despite being a woman very given to witchcraft and mystical perceptions. Now it occurs to me that this dream-Ginebra could easily in fact have been Chl, whom I knew over email even though we hadn't met in person, and with whom I'd discussed the possibility of meeting face to face. On that note, in the email where Chl tells me about the dream I promised to copy in here, I've just come across some revealing lines:

The thing is, meeting you wasn't a surprise for me; first of all, I'd seen photos of you in magazines, and then [X], by telling me all those imperceptible details that matter to us women, helped me to put the finishing touches to your portrait, and when you opened the door to your house I knew it was you.

This suggests 'a previous meeting'; and it's very strange, on that note, how although I had no erotic expectations whatsoever before the meeting with Chl – whom I'd imagined very vividly as completely different to how she really is, and not very attractive at all – early in the morning before our meeting I decided to shave off my beard. At precisely four in the morning, in a complicated procedure that took about an hour.

Whatever it was, ever since hearing Rafael describe his dream I've been convinced that somewhere, in some dimension, something happened; an important event took place, which I depicted in my dream as the exchange with Ginebra, and which Rafael depicted in his as the encounter with Renata.

This could have happened to many other people, who could have noticed it in multiple different ways, though maintaining the basic principle of the masculine and the feminine *almost* touching. I wonder what role Chl can have played in it. Whether she noticed it, or indeed whether she created it, and whether she took part. There are no answers, and there never will be.

I'm also convinced that, from the dream about my challenge onwards, I began to live, and lived for a few days, in a state very different to any of my usual states, and that I definitely travelled in time, most of all forwards, which is why I could say to Ginebra that a beautiful woman would fall in love with me, and why I shaved in the early hours of that morning.

SUNDAY 4, 21:56

The punctilious reader may recall that some days ago I mentioned *Red Harvest*, by Hammett, probably the first Spanish edition of it, in the Rastros series. Then I added that *The Dain Curse* also appears in the catalogue. *The Dain Curse* is another Hammett book I've never seen in the Rastros series, even though I've been looking at Rastros books for about half a century. Well, today I found it. For five pesos. Along with eleven more Rastros, although perhaps one or two of them already exist in my library. And another copy, a deliberate extra copy this time, of *Memoirs of Leticia Valle*, by Rosa Chacel; I couldn't resist it at that price, fifteen pesos, and it's a book that could disappear from my library forever at any moment because I'm always lending it to people.

All this during my walk with F, around a city suffering temperatures of thirty-three degrees centigrade, or so I was told; this time without P. I felt extra frightened on leaving the apartment because F was looking ravishing in a very thin, almost transparent white dress, low-cut at the front and the back, as if she wanted the jealous Uruguayans to throw stones at me. But the heat seemed to have made everyone more docile, because I saw no signs of aggression. The books didn't come from the Feria del Libro, but from that other bookshop, which had the good sense to put some second-hand detective novels on its awful sale table.

The air conditioners, each one in turn, are flashing up a message that apparently means there's low voltage. Curiously, when one of the units shows this message, the other one doesn't. I'll have to study the problem further, but right now I don't know what I could do about it. They seem to be working, anyway, because the temperature in my apartment is very tolerable, and I'd even say cool.

MONDAY 5, 00:59

I'm coming to the end of this complicated story. Now for the dream I promised; Chl's dream. This is copied from an email she sent on 21 June, when there was still precisely one month to go before our physical union, but when we both knew well enough where things were headed.

. . . I had a dream last night. I dreamed we were on the flat roofs of two buildings, you on one and me on the other. A narrow street ran between the two buildings, but the buildings were so high, so very high, that we couldn't see it. We were face to face, looking at each other, with the tips of our toes in mid-air. I said: 'You have to turn into a cat; it's very easy and you'll be able to jump over here, and when you get here I'll turn you back into Mario.' So you turned into a big, slightly misshapen cat and jumped onto my roof, and when you were turning back into Mario I woke up.

I evidently found this dream very interesting and asked for more details, because the next day she wrote:

In the dream we were feeling very dizzy (I'm afraid of heights) but we didn't care. I was wearing a long dark-grey overcoat and a neckerchief, and you were in something black but I don't remember what. We swayed a little over the abyss (with the tips of our toes in the air) in silence until I decided to speak to you. I was surprised at how easy it was to persuade you to turn into a cat, and even more so to jump; as soon as I said it you were already doing it, they were two almost simultaneous actions.

An empty line, and then she ends the email with a touching domestic addition:

I bought some coffee cups with matching saucers.

So, I turned into a cat and jumped. In fact, I jumped twice; first, to extricate myself from that living death after several years, and to land in the arms of the wonderful Chl. The second jump was something like the extension of that first jump in material space and time, and it happened when I left the house where I was living for good and spent those six months in my friends' house, looking for an apartment in the painful way I've already described. I spent those months in the air, dizzy from leaping so high, and when I landed . . . Chl was hardly there to catch me, because along came that trip of hers, and in a way

I'm still in mid-air, with vertigo, with the sensation of an endless fall in slow motion, and the feeling of inevitable disaster.

'You know you're choosing solitude,' my therapist said, more as a statement than a question, in a special session, a consultation I requested when she was no longer my therapist. I'd requested that session so she could assess my psychological state before I took the decisive step of moving out of what had once been my home. Her assessment was positive, as was that statement, more statement than question – though really it was a warning.

'Yes,' I answered, firmly and decisively. I knew the affair with Chl couldn't last, because perhaps I myself couldn't last. But I was prepared to take on my final solitude, which is what I'm going through now, though I never imagined it would be like this, filled with such ambiguity.

I felt as if that kind old woman was somehow giving me her blessing, and that she was somehow satisfied with the session, which was the true end of our therapy. My libido had managed to emerge and take notice of 'an external object' (my words, because she rarely used psychoanalytical language).

I spoke to 'the external object' on the phone earlier; tomorrow I'll see her . . . and then she'll go away again for a few days.

But I can't seem to move on from this topic, and I always get distracted and end up drifting through memories and old emails. At one point in the past few days I thought I was mixing the diary with the project, and wondered if these pages might perhaps fit better in the luminous novel. Then I thought that there's no luminosity in this story; there's magic, yes, but not that luminous magic I've sought, and am still seeking, to record in the novel, with no visible success.

There's something dark, perhaps even macabre, about the magic of May 1998. 'Familiars' have more to do with death and demons (incubi and succubi), and one night I saw a ghost in the corridor of my house. I don't mean Chl is a demon, and if there's anything luminous about all this, it's her; luminous, bursting with light, and so full of grace and goodness that I came to worship her as if she were a supernatural being.

My final conclusion, having revived this story, is that Chl was probably the response to my challenge, and that all the strange events were generated by her, from my friend Rafael's dream to the ghost in the corridor of my house. At the beginning of our relationship, in those months with their extremes of heaven and hell, Chl was a completely different being to today. Today she behaves like a perfectly ordinary young woman, almost even vulgar, with vulgar tastes and vulgar activities, or at least perfectly ordinary ones. In a way, she's a healthier person now, and perhaps happier too. When I met her she was suffering from frequent depressions, during which she would be unable to speak. She went through long silent periods, turned in on herself. She also very often had miraculous dreams; every one of those dreams she described to me was practically a novel, and a science-fiction novel at that, in which she and the other people who appeared in it, as well as the scenery, were all part of a different and perhaps archetypal world. Around then, I began to suspect that there were beings from other planets walking this earth, and that Chl was one of them. We were frequently linked by paranormal phenomena, and her understanding of the most complex human problems was instantaneous and natural.

Sometimes when we were in a room together as the evening shadows gathered, in a certain kind of half-light I'd see her face change into a multitude of whitish, ghostly faces. One of them, which was repeated many times, was the face of Julia. But then came others, in quick succession, some very ugly, one a devil, another an indigenous man, and an old woman, and various others that weren't repeated, but just appeared once, and plenty I couldn't make out. It's easy to say I was 'projecting images from my unconscious', but . . . I shook my head, I moved, I did everything I could to get out of a hypothetical trance state, and the ghostly figures didn't go away.

Then all this strange phenomenology began to fade, to disappear, even the archetypal or extraplanetary dreams, and Chl gradually turned into a perfectly ordinary clever girl. Very beautiful, sometimes radiating beauty in that almost supernatural way I've mentioned in some parts of this diary, but perfectly ordinary at the same time.

One personality gave way to another, which was perhaps easier for her to live with. The new personality doesn't love me any more; it's very fond of me, but the passion has gone, and so has the magic.

I think that when love, true love, springs up between a man and a woman, it transforms them both, giving them certain magical qualities. Perhaps they don't realise. Love comes to guide them, to lead them, and they both find themselves able to do things that would normally seem impossible. They live in a reality with more dimensions.

I'm going to end up sounding almost blasphemous, but again, once again, on reaching this point, I can only return to the same thing: in erotic love, in loving sex, in the tension of desire, in the projection of the energies of the man and the woman onto the creation of a new life, there, in that tension and those intimate circumstances, is where whatever they each have within them of God, which is usually hidden, makes its presence felt. Only God can give life, and this and nothing else is the purpose of sex.

In the tension of our desire, Chl and I were, for a brief time, like gods. A supernatural form of magic that's within everyone's reach, but that few people recognise as such.

MONDAY 5, 02:26

I was able to confirm those details online: it is indeed the Sistine Chapel and Michelangelo.

MONDAY 5, 18:07

I should record in this diary that the telepathy with the bookseller round the corner hasn't been working. I went to his stall a few days ago, entirely convinced there would be some major new arrivals, and there was nothing. Today, although I felt I should have another look, because I had to pay the electricity bill and it's more or less part of the routine to stop by the stall on the way home, I was sure I wouldn't find anything. And yet there were several new detective novels. The bookseller was waiting for me, delighted.

Something I forgot to mention about my walk with F yesterday: on the way home, on the *rive gauche* of the Plaza Libertad, we ran into Gérard de Nerval. I did a double take, which is not something I'm used to doing with men, and he noticed and looked at me and there was a kind of recognition in his eyes, as if he knew I'd once been a fairly devoted reader of his work. F hadn't read anything by him; I looked on my shelves when we got home and found *Daughters of Fire*. There's a photo of him in the book, and F was quite astonished that we'd run into him – especially when I informed her that he'd hanged himself from a lamp post many years ago, or had been hanged, because the matter was never cleared up. 'The dead get recycled,' I explained. She took the book home.

TUESDAY 6, 15:03

Last night, Chl read the recent pages of this diary which talk about our meeting. Reading them had the same effect on her as writing them did on me, and her eyes were red and her cheeks damp when she'd finished. I'm not suggesting that other readers will be moved in the same way, but those tears are still an encouraging comment on my work.

WEDNESDAY 7, 22:19

I finished reading *No Business of Mine* by Raymond Marshall, a detective novel that was part of the extremely old El Elefante Blanco series, from the publisher Saturnino Calleja. There's no publication date anywhere in the book. The beginning was impressive, very atmospheric and with a captivating storyline. Something resonated in my mind while I was reading it, something like a sense of déjà vu. Then I thought about Graham Greene, and in particular about the very unique atmosphere of *The Third Man*. Much later I came across a scene that seemed to be straight out of Chandler, and then I thought I understood what was going on. 'Raymond Marshall is a pseudonym of James Hadley Chase,' I said to myself, and I felt as if I'd known that once before. I opened the Vázquez de Parga book, which towards the end has a very handy list of pseudonyms alongside the corresponding real names, and to my disappointment I found that Raymond Marshall is called, or perhaps was called, René Raymond.

I couldn't let the matter rest, so later on I had another look at the list of names and pseudonyms, and there it was: James Hadley Chase is a pseudonym of René Raymond. Chandler once accused Chase of plagiarism, though not because of this book, and he won the lawsuit. My reading today told me that René Raymond is, or was, an accomplished plagiarist; but he was also a skilled craftsman. He knew how to construct an entertaining narrative. At first, I thought: 'It's no bad thing that this pseudonym doesn't write with the same morbid sadism as Chase' – sadism that ultimately made me stop reading him, though not without some regret, because he published plenty of books and, as I said, he's a skilled writer and very entertaining. But I read on, and yes, there were the gratuitous violence and sadism and degrading treatment of women: the fingerprints, I'd almost say, of James Hadley Chase.

THURSDAY 8, 19:55

Yesterday, when I raised the blind in my bedroom, just slightly, to let in a bit of light but no sun, I saw there was someone on the flat roof next door. A man, crouching down with his back to me, or almost, peering through something that looked like a camera. It seemed odd that a person would go up to the flat roof to take photos, but I couldn't investigate further because I was in a hurry, though I'm not entirely sure why. There must have been something I was meant to be doing, perhaps having my breakfast.

I remembered in the evening and tried to see if the pigeon's corpse had been taken away, but it was all very dark and I couldn't be sure.

Today, on raising the blind slightly, I saw there were some men at work; it obviously wasn't a camera that the man yesterday had been holding but a measuring instrument. The men were busy erecting an extremely tall mast with something on top, a kind of small metal box in the shape of a cube. The pigeon's corpse had changed place; now it was closer to the railings on the far side of the roof, next to a little box of tools. I wondered again whether the corpse would eventually be taken away. Now night has fallen and I've just had a look out of the window, and once again it's impossible to see anything on the flat roof. You can see the mast and the sinister device on top of it; probably something electromagnetic that causes brain tumours. The mast is held firmly in place by several tightly stretched wires. The landscape has been ruined, and fingers crossed it's only the landscape.

SATURDAY 10, 02:42

I've just received an email response I'd been waiting for; the response allows me to include in this diary, after some delay, the account of a dream. The dreamer is called Carmen, and she's a new email friend of mine from Mexico. On 21 February this year, she wrote:

I dreamed about you last night: you came to Mexico, you were standing by the wardrobe in my bedroom and I was looking at you, and looking at you, and thinking how wonderful it was that we'd met. Then you started rummaging through my clothes and pulling out different things, which I found funny but at the same time surprising; laughing, I asked: 'What are you looking for, Mario? Do you need anything?' And you said: 'I just want to see your clothes, so I can get to know you.'

SATURDAY 10, 16:27

I'm about fifty pages into *Diplomatic Corpse*, by Phoebe Atwood Taylor (Rastros no. 175), and I wasn't prepared for this lady's sense of humour. I've hardly ever come across such a funny detective novel.

Yesterday I went for a walk with M. It took me a while to realise she was upset, and a little longer to work out the reasons why. Halfway through the walk to the *boliche* on Ejido, in the midst of her usual logorrhoea, which is always chaotic – or, rather than chaotic, not organised by subject area – she blurted out that she'd resigned from a job she recently got and described the dramatic scene that had unfolded; drama that was entirely justified on her part, but also unnecessary. That's when I remembered the episode with the dog and all became clear. The dog, as she'd told me via email a few days ago – and yesterday she re-enacted it very impressively in my apartment – had opened her bag, taken out the plastic container where she keeps her medication and, after munching down part of the plastic, eaten six of the new pills it contained. The vet had to get involved.

'What day did you quit, and what day did the dog eat the pills?' I asked.

She laughed nervously and said my calculations were wrong; that her resignation had come before the episode with the dog. It was true that she'd been feeling rather unstable because of the lack of medication, but this had nothing to do with her quitting. Since I know she's taking two kinds of medication, I asked which kind the dog had eaten; it was the tranquillisers. 'And the antidepressants?' I demanded, inquisitorially, because I realised she was in one of her self-destructive phases. 'Well, the antidepressants ran out a few days earlier.' 'Aha,' I said. 'I didn't buy more because I didn't have any money,' she added. 'Why didn't you ask me?' I said. She came out with some excuse I don't remember, but it was clear that M had been without her main medication for several days, and that, as I'd deduced, her resignation had been a self-destructive act. Not the resignation itself, but the way she'd burnt her boats with that dramatic scene. A couple of months ago she'd done the same thing with a different job, also during a gap in her antidepressants. She thinks, as she's told me before, that the tranquillisers are the medication which really does her good, and the antidepressants aren't very important. When in fact it's the other way around. In the end I made her promise to go and see her psychiatrist that very night – at an unconventional hour – and get prescriptions for both kinds of medication, and start taking them again immediately. We were sitting at a table in the *boliche* by this point, and I picked up a serviette and wrote 'Monitor medication M' on it, along with the date. I said I was going to make sure she didn't end up without medication, and she agreed to this. The reminder is now scheduled in the relevant program.

The end result of all this was that I spent hours glued to the computer screen and went to sleep very late; M had passed her anxiety on to me, along with some of that state which is so difficult to describe, a kind of mental disorganisation and a permanent effort to organise it, leading to disjointed, fragmentary speech whose ultimate meaning is very difficult to make out. Often she slips imperceptibly from one topic to another, and it takes me a while to realise she's changed the subject; I lose the thread, characters and situations get muddled, and I almost always need to ask: 'What are you talking about?'

Today she left a message on my answerphone, announcing the number of pills she'd got hold of. I'm glad to be keeping track. It seems I can't forget the time twenty-five years ago when M decided to commit suicide, stuffed herself with pills, went for a walk and then, as if by chance, ended up ringing my doorbell. Not long afterwards I was in a desperate panic and struggling with the dead weight of her body, which was stretched out on the tiles in the hallway of my old apartment.

SUNDAY 11, 02:43

This afternoon, while I was waiting for F so we could go for our walk, I wrote this down by hand:

> I find it very curious how in translations from English into Spanish, even when the translation isn't bad, you so rarely come across the expression '*tener hambre*'.*

F arrived at that point and I broke off. I didn't have the chance to add – although now I've forgotten everything I'd been planning to say about this, and, worse, how I'd been planning to say it – that the

---

\* *Translator's note*: Spanish commonly uses the construction '*tener hambre*' (literally 'to have hunger') instead of '*estar hambriento*' ('to be hungry').

'*estar hambriento*' that translators use instead of '*tener hambre*' isn't the same thing at all; or at least, I think it sounds much more dramatic. To me, '*tengo hambre*', which would describe a normal state of affairs at lunchtime, is very different to '*estoy hambriento*', which seems to suggests a level of distress, as if lunchtime had come and gone a very long time ago. However, for most translators, '*tener hambre*' might as well not exist.


F came alone today as well. She wasn't in as good a mood as last week, and the reasons for this were revealed during our conversation on the walk. We had to change *boliches* this time; the one on Ejido didn't have any croissants, which happened to be what both F and I felt like eating. The usual waiter wasn't there either; he's a very nice waiter, with something of the natural happiness of Central Americans about him. He doesn't have an accent, admittedly, though there is something Central American about his facial features. He's always smiling, or making a polite gesture or a funny comment. I think he greets me particularly enthusiastically, perhaps because he sees me three times a week, with three different female companions on rotation, though I'm not sure he realises they're different. Whoever the lady is, he greets her as if he'd last seen her the day before. But today's waiter was terse and not very polite. When F and I were exchanging disconcerted glances because there were no croissants, and the offer to give us sandwiches instead didn't cheer us up, he went to attend to some other tables. So we got up and left. It's something I like to do in *boliches* to show my displeasure: sweep out, just like that. We walked a couple of blocks and then went to a *boliche* that had no outdoor tables but did have particularly good croissants. When I went inside, I remembered that I'd swept out of that one, too, a couple of months ago, because a waiter had come over to tell me that Chl and I were sitting in an area reserved for non-smokers. The information about the reserved area was written in tiny letters on a menu that you only saw once you'd sat down. He wanted me to put out my cigarette and move to a different area, but once we'd got up from our chairs, we left. It was brilliant. Today, F told me there was a smoking area at the far end, and that's where we went. I couldn't help noticing that, in contrast to the smoking area, which was packed, the non-smoking area wasn't having much success: it was practically empty, except for a table near the window, with three people at it, one of whom was smoking.

Once we were sitting down, each with a good cup of coffee and a filled croissant in front of us, the conversation flowed much more easily than it had in the street. I learnt various bits and pieces about people I know, and who I didn't realise know each other, or at least see each other from time to time. I was pleased to hear about this, especially because they met, as far as I'm aware, through me.

There was nothing for me on the bookshops' sale tables. In the Feria del Libro, the detective-novel section wasn't even there. I asked a member of staff and he told me they'd taken it down to make room for textbooks. Student season has begun. They could have taken something else down instead. But apparently they'll put it back next month.

MONDAY 12, 20:48

I don't remember a detective novel ever boring me as much as *Double, Double* by Ellery Queen. But the information must have been filed away in my unconscious, because I had a bad feeling about it when I saw the cover. I know that as a teenager, when I was a real E. Q. fan, one of his novels left me furious and disillusioned, and not only me but the whole group of friends with whom I shared the detective novels I bought. At the bookstall a few days ago, I stood looking at that cover and hesitating about whether or not to buy it; I searched my memory, but I didn't find anything specific. Just that bad feeling about the cover.

For years I've had the theory, or the suspicion, that the cousins who sign their books 'Ellery Queen' stopped writing once they became famous. They were the editors of *Ellery Queen's Mystery Magazine*, a periodical that was also very successful, and which published selections of stories and short novels. They must have made pots of money.

They stopped writing, my theory goes, but they didn't stop publishing books under the name Ellery Queen. Perhaps there's someone who knows about this; I should look it up online. *Double, Double* bears no resemblance to the books that came before it. Only the ingenious but rather flimsy detective-novel riddle, which is very much E. Q.'s style but which isn't enough for anything more than a twenty-page short story. This novel has 192 pages in small print (perhaps size eight), and it's boring, boring beyond words, thanks to the parallel plot line of the friendship, and almost romance, between the detective and a girl. I wouldn't be surprised if the bulk of the novel had been written by a woman. The romantic touches and sentimental scenes pile up and make you want to vomit, and they're swathed in prose full of literary pretensions, as if the cousins Dannay and Lee had passed through a Uruguayan creative writing workshop. Quotes from famous authors, cheap philosophy, endless passages of detective-novel clichés, which are repeated over and over again in the guise of deductive reasoning . . . Oh, there are so many pages I skipped, and so many more I should have skipped. Last night I was actually falling asleep, and then carried on reading while I was asleep, without finding the strength to skip anything; I was almost stupefied by that inexhaustible stream of rubbish, by that story that didn't go anywhere, and still didn't go anywhere, and still . . . Compared to that book, this diary is a dynamic, interesting, entertaining and thoroughly enjoyable read.

MONDAY 12, 23:07

A message from Lilí on the answerphone; I hope no one's died. The sing-song tone of her voice suggests not, but . . . She doesn't really leave messages; she talks to see if I pick up.

That was once I'd returned from a quick outing with Chl, who'd called in briefly for a visit. With her usual radiant beauty, so radiant it hurts.

TUESDAY 13, 03:35

Fascinated by the information online. I searched for 'Ellery Queen' and found plenty of results. One was a website with a huge number of pages, describing the life and work of these cousins in exhaustive detail. I also found what I was most interested in:

Since 1950 they started recruiting and training ghostwriters they already had used on some juvenile adaptations of Queen movies and radio shows.

The novel I've just read, and which caused me such irritation, was published in Spanish in 1951; 28 August, to be precise.

This research, which will involve plenty more work because I copied so many pages from the internet and now I have to sort them out ready to print and read, is an homage to the teenage fan I once was. It's strange, clearing up some of these mysteries so easily, fifty years on. The image of myself on a bus on the way back from the market is still fresh in my memory, as if it had happened today. I'm in a seat to the left of the aisle, turning the pages of a book from the Serie Naranja collection with a feeling of awe; it was probably *The New Adventures of Ellery Queen*. In the first few pages, the mystery about their real dual personality – which had been hidden for some years – was revealed, and there were two circular photos, in black and white of course. Manfred B. Lee had a horrible face, particularly because of his tight, cruel lips, and general air of a high-ranking Nazi.

TUESDAY 13, 16:18

A medical practice used as a radical cure for certain illnesses, a practice as common as a surgical procedure, consisted of killing the patient and then bringing them back to life. On being resuscitated, the patient would be completely cured and even rejuvenated.

My doctor had brought me to a clinic and installed me in a bed; she left, and I lay waiting for the doctor from the clinic whose job it would be to kill me and bring me back to life. She was talking on the phone in the next room; she was talking in a very loud voice, so loud it was annoying, but I couldn't make out the words, or perhaps I wasn't very interested in what she was saying. I felt calm, and strangely indifferent about what was going to happen to me. The only thing that bothered me was having to wait for that woman who was nattering away in the next room. On my right was one of those devices used for hanging drips; at the upper end was a little bottle that looked like an old, many-sided vinegar dispenser, and I was connected to that bottle somehow; I was probably receiving oxygen from it, by means of a tube. The bottle also had a metallic device on the front, something like a valve or a little pipe. My doctor had explained that another device was to be connected to it, which would put a gas into circulation that would kill me quickly. The device was within reach. I saw it would be very easy to operate, and I even had the crazy idea that if that doctor went on talking on the phone and delaying things, I could connect it myself to save time.

I spent a long while looking at those things and convincing myself it would be very easy to operate the device; and while I was mulling it over I had a sudden revelation, a flash of understanding. I called my doctor, who must still have been somewhere nearby, and as I was getting out of bed and hurriedly pulling on my clothes, I said I wasn't going through with the procedure. 'If they kill me and I come back to life, I won't be myself any more; I'll be myself plus the experience of having died.' I grew increasingly frantic and vehement as I spoke. My doctor seemed wholly indifferent, neither contradicting nor agreeing with me. Perhaps that's what made me so frantic, as if she didn't understand the overwhelming truth of my words, and I repeated my speech to her, with gestures and gesticulations, but she remained as detached as ever. The other doctor came over, though I couldn't see her clearly, and she seemed equally detached.

'Don't you understand?' I practically shouted. 'If I die and come back to life, I won't be the same person. And I don't want to stop being the same person. I don't care if I carry on being ill. I'd even rather have my legs cut off!'

They nodded, still distant and detached.

TUESDAY 13, 17:56

At the intersection of four of the tiles in my bathroom, there existed, for a time, a special dimensionality. A tangle of hair was lying there, probably made up of strands that had fallen out of a comb and perhaps been collected together by a draught of air; the tangle was of a considerable size, and the amount of hair involved was also considerable. Now, then: at points, this tangle seemed to be submerged in a puddle of water, though it didn't look quite like water. It looked more like a solid transparent entity, like those models suspended in transparent resin I used to make; but that puddle or block of resin didn't have clear limits, it didn't have edges, although instead of stretching out indefinitely, it only just cleared the clump of hair on all sides. I thought there was something wrong with my eyes; but if there had been, the effect would have been visible in other parts of the bathroom when I moved my eyes or head, and it wasn't: it was always in the same place. I approached it with some trepidation, thinking: 'If I put my hand in and pull out the tangle of hair, perhaps my hand will be swallowed up by something and appear in another dimension; who knows what kind of a fold in space-time this is, and if I put my hand in, maybe it will end up in a remote galaxy and some mysterious thing will bite off my fingers,' etc. In the end, I steeled myself and picked up the tangle of hair. And that's all it was: a tangle of hair. The puddle, block of resin or visual effect vanished. Then I put the tangle of hair back, and the strange effect returned. I put it down in other places and there was nothing. Then I put it back in the same place, but by then its configuration was slightly different and it didn't have the same effect; it was just any old tangle of hair.

There are some computer-generated optical illusions that were in fashion a few years ago; books were even published that made use of the effects. You had to look at diagrams in a certain way (I managed it by squinting), and then suddenly, poof, the three-dimensional effect kicked in, and things appeared to be floating in what looked like space. Well, that clump of hair achieved the same effect by chance, and much more successfully than those drawings, since I didn't need to squint or do anything special with my eyes. It was enough to rest my gaze on it.

WEDNESDAY 14, 21:48

Today was a bad day. It began in the early hours of the morning, with what I presume are the effects of some new cystitis medication.

When my doctor found out that nothing had changed after several days of treatment, she put me on a different drug. This one seems very effective: the symptoms quickly cleared up, even though I'd gone back to sleep with the air conditioning on. When I went to bed I turned it off, after taking my temperature twice within the space of an hour, because I felt feverish; the top of my head was very hot and my lips were chapped, and I had that unpleasant sensation in my fingertips that sometimes comes with a fever. But my temperature was perfectly normal. At the same time, although I was very tired, despite it being early for me – three in the morning – I also felt very uneasy, with a strange overexcitement that wouldn't let me sleep. What's more, one of the effects of the new medication was to make me urinate abundantly, which must have contributed to my feeling better, and I had to get up very frequently to go to the bathroom. Things carried on that way until five o'clock and I still couldn't sleep. I realised that as well as feeling feverish, I was too hot; and at five o'clock I turned on the air conditioning and took something like an eighth of a Valium 10 tablet which, strangely enough, gradually soothed my anxieties until at last I fell asleep. But taking Valium at that time always makes waking up very confusing. I woke up at what's currently my usual time, 1.30 p.m., but I couldn't get out of bed right away. I spent over an hour trying to shake off the dregs of sleep and waiting for my mind to clear a little. In the end I got up, but begrudgingly. My body was aching, especially around my waist. I had all the signs of flu, and it was difficult to coordinate my usual movements and get through my routines; I made mistakes, objects fell from my hands, I didn't do things in a logical order, or in the order I normally do them in, logical or not. The afternoon was passing me by. At the last minute I managed to go out and have a look at the bookstall, and buy some cigarettes. Once again, plenty more novels had arrived – detective novels, I mean. I brought home a small batch of new ones, and a list of five or six I wasn't sure I had (and when I got home I found I only had two from the list). Then my yoga teacher came, but I didn't want to have the class. I wasn't feeling well, and what's more I was hungry.

THURSDAY 15, 16:54

Reviewing this diary, I find that in mid-January I was worried about short circuits blowing the fuse in the caretaker's office at an inopportune moment. The capricious Ulises had assured me there was no reason for it to blow. I asked him to cause a short circuit deliberately to see what happened, but he laughed and did nothing. Well, some time after 5 a.m. a few days ago, just as I was falling asleep, I went to the bathroom, turned on the light, and BANG! One of the two bulbs exploded spectacularly and, of course, the fuse in the apartment blew. I thought: 'The fuse downstairs must have blown as well,' and began cursing Ulises in advance whilst tentatively making my way towards the fuse in the little passage that extends from the kitchen. And indeed it had: I flicked the switch over and over in vain. Nothing. Summoning all my patience, I set off slowly through the darkness to get the torch I always keep handy on my bedside table, returned to the kitchen with it, unplugged the fridge, and then went to the pocket of the shirt where I keep the telephone number for Rosa, the caretaker, just in case. I copied the number out onto a piece of paper in big writing, taped the paper to the telephone receiver, and then went back to the bedroom, flicked the switch on the lamp so the bulb wouldn't light up unexpectedly when the power came back, and tried to sleep whilst repeating to myself in my head: 'Call Rosa no later than ten,' because the food in the freezer might start going off. Fortunately I'd already read enough to be feeling sleepy, meaning there was no need for the laborious activity of reading by the light of a torch or a candle.

So, the matter of the electricity supply is back on the table. I'm waiting until we're through the height of summer, because going outside before 5 p.m. is nothing short of suicide at the moment. Meanwhile, every time I switch on a light, I tremble a little. Especially in the early hours of the morning.

THURSDAY 15, 17:23

On the railings of the flat roof next door, exactly opposite my window – the one I look through when I'm dressing to go out – there are two pigeons. On the right, one that looks a lot like the widow; and on the left, a few feet away, one that looks a lot like the husband, or whatever he was, who kept her company while she was looking after her young. They're both scratching themselves like things possessed. This suggests they really are who I suspect they are, but I still have my doubts. The widow, if it is her, is much fatter, unless it's an effect of the scratching and the gusts of wind that mess up her feathers; perhaps that's what's making her look a bit inflated. She has the same white mark on her back where it's always been, and now I can see that it stretches almost all the way down, because in order to scratch herself she sometimes spreads her wings and reveals her back in its entirety. But those wings are a lighter grey than I remember the widow's wings being. It occurs to me that maybe wings are renewed every so often, and that maybe the new ones are paler in colour, at least for a while. The corpse is still on the flat roof, where the workmen left it when they installed that mysterious mast. It's lost all its dignity; it was probably nudged by a foot, or even kicked, to its new location by the railings on the other side, which are always in the shade. And its shape is very confusing now, like an old, worn-out feather duster with no handle.

FRIDAY 16, 15:40

Tola has died. Thirty-one years later. I heard the news at the same time; my yoga teacher left me an answerphone message at eleven in the morning. The message said Tola 'had left his body', meaning that as well as the information, the message contained an ideological element.

It shouldn't be sad news; he lived a good, long and productive life. As for me, although I've become an orphan again, fully this time – or almost, because there's always someone around who can serve as a father or mother – it doesn't feel like that. We hadn't seen each other for a few years, but, as he himself said to my daughter, 'There are many different ways of seeing people'; I never felt disconnected from him, or lacking in his presence or support.

Thirty-one years ago I was told in a dream – three times – that Tola had died. When the telephone rang at eleven that morning, I went to answer it feeling absolutely sure I was going to have the news from the dream confirmed, but no, there was a translation error in the message from the unconscious, and in fact it was my physical father who had died. The figure of Tola had become such a powerful paternal image for me that, when something or someone told me telepathically that my father had died, I read the message as if it had been Tola. And at that moment I would have had reason to weep for him loudly. Now I don't; everything's OK, everything's as it should be.

I got up to listen to the answerphone message, because I'd heard the voice even though I couldn't make out the words, and it sounded like my yoga teacher. I knew it was crucial to listen to the message, because she'd never call at eleven in the morning without a compelling reason to do so. Then I went back to bed, but I didn't sleep, and I spent a while thinking about these things and remembering the story of that message from thirty-one years ago. In doing so, I reached an interesting conclusion: that telepathic messages are transmitted through symbols; primitive, essential and no doubt archetypal symbols. I remembered what I'd read about some experiments carried out on monkeys. They're given a kind of computer keyboard that responds to their wishes, and the monkeys learn how to make themselves understood by combining the limited number of symbols available to them. I particularly remember the case of one monkey who was a real coffee fiend, and who learnt to ask for coffee by pressing the key that made people bring him water and a key that represented the colour black. Black water.

The transmission between one unconscious and another presumably uses similar mechanisms; 'death' and 'father' must of course be two of those universal symbols, and two of the most powerful. I received the death + father package, and when the information reached my consciousness, my consciousness opened the package and translated it as 'Tola has died', because at that time the symbol 'father' was associated more strongly with him than with the figure of my father.

· · ·

371

It's true that sometimes words which don't easily correspond to universal symbols are transmitted telepathically, which suggests that there isn't one single form of telepathic transmission. The form that uses symbols is the most universal and primitive and, as far as we know, it's linked to the emotions. You could say it's an emotional transmission rather than an intellectual one. The messages are clearer and more colourful than when the transmission isn't linked especially closely to emotions or strong affections, and is instead what you might call the intellectual variety. These intellectual messages are more easily lost, or they get confused with the person's own thoughts, or perhaps they only very occasionally reach the consciousness; conversely, the messages that come from that emotional zone, perhaps the most primitive centre of the brain, the 'reptile brain', or perhaps not even from the brain but from some plexus, probably the solar plexus; these messages, I was saying, come with such urgency that they're difficult to ignore; I don't think they ever fail to reach the consciousness, and even when the consciousness is determined not to receive them, they find other, often fairly drastic ways of making themselves heard – like the clock that fell off the wall at the moment of my mother's death.

Well, Tola, we'll be in touch.

FRIDAY 16, 19:52

Typing up my corrections to January, I notice there's a story about the 'new neighbour', the usual bookseller's competitor. Well, he was there for two or three days and then he never came back. I asked the bookseller what happened, and he told me the guy hadn't sold much and it had been a lot of work for him, because he had to come from a long way away carrying all the boards, trestles and books on a trolley. 'It's a shame, because it suited me to have him there,' he added. I was surprised. 'Yes, yes. Think about Calle Bacacay. There used to be one restaurant on that street and it was always empty. Now there are ten, and they're all full.' He's right.

SUNDAY 18, 05:59

Rotring.

Today you can feel the first of the autumn winds. The walk today (or rather yesterday, Saturday) was in the company of M and her daughter – small, captivating, solemn and silent. Amidst the remnants of high summer, brief gusts of air formed whirlwinds, neatly arranging the dry leaves (already!) on the pavement into heaps – heaps of different sizes, because there were several almost simultaneous whirlwinds, some of which were bigger than others. I thought, and said, that it would be wonderful to be able to see the whirlwinds; they should have a colour. Although, actually, I find it hard to imagine their exact shape. You'd need something lighter in substance than the leaves (perhaps, for example, a feather), so its movement could better trace the shape of each whirlwind. Later on we found ourselves right in the middle of one; it wasn't quite a tornado, but it did feel a bit alarming. Everything was spinning around as if it wanted to wrap us up and carry us away; the dry leaves spun at the level of the pavement, with us as their centre.

In exactly a month, the workshops will begin. I need to start organising them.

MONDAY 19, 15:23

The weather is still building on its tendencies from yesterday, and autumn continues apace. Inside my apartment, the ambiguity (a cool breeze coming in through the east-facing windows, and heat, though less intense than in high summer, filtering in through the west-facing ones) is producing a fairly pleasant mixture. I haven't turned the air conditioners on yet today, and nor were they on while I slept; that considerably reduced the irritation from the cystitis, of which the air conditioners seem to be the sole cause. Yes, it was, and still is, an atypical summer, in no way as torturous as all the others have been for as long as I can remember. Even the walks in the company of my guardians, even at temperatures of thirty-three degrees, were, rather than a torment, a relief from the cold I was experiencing at home. The downsides were moderate bronchitis and moderate cystitis, and a deafness that didn't go away as it usually does when summer arrives. Still, I'm glad autumn is here, and with it, crucially, this air containing some amount of oxygen, which is blowing in through the east-facing windows and taking the place of the stale air, the kind you find inside a freezer, in this apartment whose windows have been shut for far too long.

## WEDNESDAY 21, 17:15

I was in charge of a bookshop, and a distributor had given me some books on consignment; among them were at least two substantial volumes which looked very expensive. I don't remember seeing or experiencing any of this, but it's possible to deduce it from what I do remember: two boys appear in the shop, salesmen working for the distributor, and they look at me askance, rather accusingly, though instead of saying anything outright they just drop a few hints. I understand, with some effort, that those two very expensive volumes are not in my bookshop, and that they think I've sold them and kept the money. Then a more important character shows up, the owner or manager of the distribution company, and I tell him resolutely that there are two books which have disappeared; that I haven't sold them, and that they've probably been stolen, but that at any rate it's my responsibility. I'm not sure I have enough money to pay for them, but I imagine I'll be able to do it in instalments. The man, however, doesn't appear to think it's very important, and seems more concerned about some circulars my mother has sent to the press, promoting books written by me, or about me as an author. This is very confusing. I'm annoyed, because I don't like my mother, or anyone else, to do things like that, much less without my knowledge. And it sounds like she's made some mistakes in those circulars, such as using the word 'fumature' instead of 'literature'. Then the dream becomes rapidly more confusing and all I remember is that the action somehow moves to a place that's ambiguously related to both the youth wing of the Uruguayan Communist Party and the Guardia Nueva tango club.

.    .    .

Soon after waking up, I interpret this dream as, essentially, a way of calling my attention to the fact I've 'lost' (I've stopped working on) two books, i.e. this diary and the grant project. I feel like I'm falling behind.

I'll try to start repaying this debt, if only in instalments.

WEDNESDAY 21, 18:08

You can't deny that autumn's been punctual this year; really it began yesterday, with some persistent drizzle, and today it settled in with this blustery weather that's been going on all day. It's terrifying how quickly summer went by; that summer period which has always felt to me like a hell without end, and has seemed to last whole lifetimes. My strategy of air conditioning, detective novels and the computer kept me in an almost constant trance state, and although I wouldn't say that today I've awoken like Sleeping Beauty of the Forest with a kiss from Prince Autumn, or that I'm now functioning at full capacity, I have opened my eyes enough to be terrified by the pulverisation of that summer which, I can say with total certainty, I didn't experience. You can't have everything, and if I manage to get rid of the suffering, I get rid of a lot of other things as well. But the point is that I had an OK time, which at this stage in my life and under the current circumstances is saying a lot. It's just that the almost instantaneous disappearance of a quarter of a year really makes you think.

What I remember of summer are the hallucinatory walks with my loyal guardians, through a Montevideo I didn't recognise; it was strange, ridiculous, arduous, circus-like, hellish in the aesthetic sense of the word and perhaps in other senses too. It's a much more dreamlike memory than the memory of an actual dream or nightmare, more like the memory of a fantasy film. *Blade Runner*, for example. Philip K. Dick would no doubt have found an experience like this very interesting.

When I thought about Sleeping Beauty, I remembered that the most accurate translation probably isn't the one in the stories I read, or had read to me, as a child – 'The Sleeping Beauty of the Forest' – but rather 'The Beauty of the Sleeping Forest', a far more evocative and logical title, because the translation used in those books from my childhood suggested a dull, standard-issue forest, which in fact didn't need to appear in the title at all; not only would 'The Sleeping Beauty' contain all the necessary information, but it's also stronger in a literary sense than 'The Sleeping Beauty of the Forest'. But the image, from the title onwards, of a sleeping forest, which on top of that contains a Beauty, has an unparalleled evocative power. And it's true that in the story the forest was sleeping as well; it seemed almost dead.

As for me, I may have opened my eyes a bit but I haven't woken up, and neither has the forest. And I don't think any prince would be capable of waking this forest up.


Chl's back. I still haven't seen her, but what I mean is that it looks like as of today, we'll fall back into our rhythm from before the summer. I hope I can resist it. What's more, if my guardians are prepared to keep dragging me around, I'd like to continue our walks.

## THURSDAY 22, 18:10

Today I dreamed about Vargas Llosa, the writer. Literature is obviously not quite ready to leave me alone. An initial reflection on the dream ('Why Vargas Llosa specifically?') reminded me of something my friend Ginebra told me via email a couple of weeks ago: according to her, Mario Vargas Llosa is really called Jorge Mario, like me. The dream must have made use of that point we have in common to develop its narrative.

As ever, there's a long, muddled stretch of the dream about which I can't provide any details. I know Elvio Gandolfo was present, and there was a whole storyline about something, perhaps a record that appears in the final part of the dream, which I do remember. My inability to remember this stretch of the dream is particularly frustrating, because I <u>know</u> there were several very interesting aspects.

I was visiting Vargas Llosa at home. He looked just the way he does in photos, and had the elegant presence of aristocratic Peruvians, although at the same time his manner was laid-back, even democratic; he addressed me as an equal, despite the fact that I had a strong sense of being his inferior, as far as social class is concerned.

(I've just been interrupted by a fly, goddamn it. It landed exactly opposite me, on the computer monitor, and looked at me steadily whilst rubbing its front legs together. I had to get up, close the door, open the window, raise the blind, turn off the light and waft it with my hand to get rid of it. I think it's gone, because I can't see it any more, but I didn't notice it leave.)

I was sitting in an armchair and leaning backwards, reclining even, probably because the shape of the chair was forcing me to; I didn't feel very comfortable. He was moving around the room, and he put on a record, which I was supposed to listen to from start to finish. It was an LP, and I estimated it would last about an hour. The truth was that I didn't want to listen to that record at all, let alone from start to finish, but it seemed very important to Vargas that I did, and I got the sense that it contained some secret or truth I ought to hear. When it started playing, I realised I recognised it; it was one of those pretentious, jazzy pieces, like *Rhapsody in Blue*. I tried to tell Vargas something to that effect, but he cut me off and gestured that I should pay attention to the record. A little later in the piece came the whole of an extremely famous operatic fragment, which might be called 'Rustic Cavalry', or perhaps 'Light Cavalry'; the passage that bursts equally unexpectedly into the original work, which I'd listened to a few days before. It imitates a horse's gallop, and in the past it was used in cowboy films to soundtrack the scenes where the cavalry come to the rescue.

The record went on and on, and Vargas, standing a few steps away from me, didn't alter his facial expression. 'Wait and see,' it seemed to be saying, always in relation to that record.

(Now I've been interrupted again, not by the fly but by my old friend Georgette, from Paris, upset by Tola's death; the shock waves have reached as far away as that. Here the laments can still be heard, all around.)

SUNDAY 25, 17:54

I'd finished some paperwork, at the counter in an office; I don't know what the paperwork was about, though I have the strange sensation that I'd enrolled in a club or association for people who do sport, and that there was just one administrative detail left to provide before I could gain access to the social area. I have no idea how big the office was, either; all I could see was the counter and, behind it, the young woman who'd served me. The young woman explains that I have to go to another office to finish the paperwork and receive the document accrediting me as a member. She explains that I need to go down some stairs. I don't understand the explanation very well. She comes out from behind the counter and points, rather impatiently, and a little mockingly, at a door to my right, through which you can see the beginning of a staircase leading down to a lower floor. There's some uncertainty as to whether I should go down that staircase or another one that's out of sight and can be reached via a small corridor. The young woman explains things to me with total clarity, but now I don't remember which of the staircases I went down.

In the office on the floor below, the scene is repeated: a counter, and a woman behind it. This woman looks a little older than the other one. She attends to me and, after a few stages I don't remember, shows me a piece of paper, holding it some distance away from my eyes. She says this is the document she's going to give me, but that for some rather bureaucratic reasons, which I don't understand, she wasn't able to use the right kind of paper, and had to use another, lower-quality kind instead, and as a result the document won't last long. As she speaks, I notice that on the document, where she's holding it with her thumb, a small mark is slightly smudging the letters. She hands me the document, and I go out into the street. As I walk along the pavement, away from the building, I think about that last woman, whom I'd found very pleasant and attractive. I think about how I'd like to see her again, and I know that at that moment she's walking behind me, accompanied by a small boy who's her son.

On Friday evening Chl reappeared, now back in the city for good. She came to visit, and this time her presence made it impossible for me to relax; she was very tense, on the verge of hysteria, and with a series of urgent issues to resolve. She spent the whole time trying to speak on the phone to people who weren't answering her calls, and anxiously chewing gum. An entire pack, twelve pieces of gum.

Yesterday, Saturday, she was a little calmer. I'd dreamed about her that morning, a cornucopia of sex scenes. The dream wasn't very clear and there were no particular emotions associated with it, and it brought me no pleasure either asleep or awake. It didn't seem like a 'familiar'-style 'visit', just a standard wish-fulfilment dream.

We tried to resume our Saturday routine, but, just as she'd predicted when she arrived – an hour and a half before we set off – the moment we stepped outside it began to rain. We've had this experience a few times: going out, walking a block or so and then having to turn back because of the rain.

She brought me *milanesas*. I ate *milanesas*. In two sittings; the last one very late, in the early hours of the morning, a long time after she'd gone home.

It was raining almost constantly for about five days, with the odd brief interruption. Today it's not raining, but it's completely overcast. N will be here soon to join me for a walk; I haven't been out in all this time, except for yesterday's frustrated attempt, and today's attempt may well be frustrated too.

I have some work ahead of me: the article for the magazine, the project, this diary, organising the workshops . . . It's difficult to face it all, especially now autumn's begun. Now autumn's begun I've also felt a few twinges of anxiety, as if the defences I developed for the summer weren't also applicable to the autumn. And the thing is, they're not. I'm still tied to the reading of detective novels and the computer, but I'm starting to find the detective novels boring and exasperating, and as for the computer, generally all I do is play games, carry out pointless tasks and worry about insignificant details.

These sources of anxiety interest me; they must hold the key to some sort of solution.

MONDAY 26, 04:25

The rain didn't start again, which meant I could go for a walk with N. My body was complaining the whole time; every bit of me hurt. And I didn't manage that corporeal harmony I can normally achieve after walking a few blocks, that certain elasticity and coordination. Today my legs and feet seemed to be moving arbitrarily, or at least uncoordinatedly, and at no point did I feel particularly stable. I couldn't devote myself to observing my surroundings; lacking the reflexes to move easily through the streets, I was concentrating hard on the conversation with N and enclosed in a kind of bubble. The only thing keeping me whole, it seemed, was the movement; I felt that if I stopped unexpectedly, my relationship with the rest of the world would be plunged into a sudden chaos, or something like that, as if in fact I were the one maintaining that veneer of order in the world through my own efforts. Later on, at the *boliche*, sitting at one of the outside tables, N made me laugh uproariously a few times. She's always funny. Even when she's also slightly tragic. Her way of recounting what could be described as 'her misfortunes' is funny as well. Although on more than one occasion I sensed her deep sadness, and felt it as if it were my own.

N said goodbye at the entrance to my building and got into her car. When I went inside, the lift was on its way down. A white-haired woman emerged, dressed in a black coat. Her plain attire and humble demeanour made me think she was a maid, and perhaps she was. I was taken aback when, after saying hello, she asked: 'Are you the teacher?' I replied that people often call me a teacher, but they're wrong. Then she asked if I ran writing workshops. When I said I did, she told me that people had recommended she come to them. She said that she wrote, and she said it very shyly, as if she were confessing a sin. She also said that unfortunately she couldn't come to my workshops because she had to work. She knew perfectly well who I was, and seemed to have read some of my books. When we said goodbye, she called me 'teacher' again. I asked her not to give me that title, because I'm just a writer somehow trying to convey his experience to a few students. She shook her head as she walked away, saying: 'The greatest are always the humblest.' This warmed my heart, not because it made me feel like one of the greatest, but because of the goodness of that woman. When a person is truly good, they always find a way to lift other people's spirits.

TUESDAY 27, 18:32

Today my 'invisible friend' died.

WEDNESDAY 28, 16:32

I really don't feel like writing. I don't feel like doing anything else, either. Yesterday was one of my lowest days, at least recently – at least since my move. I was awake in the early hours of the morning, busy with one of my delirious, obsessive tasks: a program I installed not long ago had dared to add a nefarious procedure to my computer; a procedure I won't describe in detail, as per my decision not to try the reader's patience with these things. I knew the intrusion could be removed by means of the famous Windows Registry, but I didn't know how. After working away for a while, I managed to remove one of the intrusive parts of the program, but the other one was stubbornly clinging on, and I had to go to sleep without solving the problem. I only managed to solve it in the early hours of this morning, thanks to a sudden flash of inspiration that took me straight to where the clues to the answer were hidden. However, after getting rid of the problem, I felt none of the happiness I usually feel in such situations, and I think I know why: it seems that the whole sudden obsession, although very legitimate in itself, very mine, I mean, in that I know I'm hypersensitive to intrusions into my computer, was really masking something else. Or indeed, various other things.

One of those things gradually revealed itself when I woke up yesterday around noon; I felt drained, broken and, most extraordinary of all, I had suicidal thoughts – which, as if that weren't enough, came back a second time. They left me rather frightened, I have to admit. Then I felt an overwhelming desire for a very long lie-in. I needed it, I thought; I hadn't let myself lie in for ages, and I was tired of my routines, my computer, my detective novels and myself. The best thing to do in such situations is rest, and, if possible, sleep. But I remembered that a friend was coming over at 5 p.m., as arranged days ago, and later on I was expecting a visit from my doctor, with whom I wanted to discuss, very seriously, once and for all, the problem with my gallbladder, which was still bothering me. And I thought about how the next day, i.e. today, the maid was coming, and after that I had a yoga class, and there were entries in my calendar for the following days as well, and I felt profoundly sorry that I couldn't allow myself any rest. When hunger set in I got up, and when I got up I noticed my abdomen was monstrously swollen; I was sure the problem wasn't simply cystitis, but cancer of the gallbladder or intestine, a cancer that was rapidly spreading. And the worst thing of all was my mood; dispirited, unpleasant, a kind of psychological pain. It wasn't long before the telephone rang: my doctor telling me that Jorge, my 'invisible friend', had died, and although we'd never met face to face, I felt just then that we'd had a very close connection, and that our friendship had been much deeper than you'd expect a friendship between email correspondents to be. You have to bear in mind that my friend was a bit of a wizard himself, and telepathic, too, of course. My doctor was very upset. Although her friendship with Jorge was also fairly recent, in her case it had been a far more intense relationship because she'd become his doctor straight away and had been through many delicate medical situations with him. What's more, my friend had played an essential therapeutic role in her life. He was the one who magically cured my doctor of the pain of our separation when I started living alone, allowing her friendship with me to flourish once more. I realise I've told all this very badly, and I apologise for entangling the presumed reader in these attempts to use writing to organise my mind.

I understood, then, that the sudden obsession which had kept me awake until 7 a.m. had been masking my awareness of the worsening health and indeed the dying moments of my friend, and that my suicidal thoughts on waking up were none other than the message of death he was sending out into the world. With this realisation, the extreme discomfort in my abdomen faded. I noticed it was moving towards my stomach, and it struck me that all my discomfort was due to a kind of hidden anxiety that had made me swallow tons of air.

There was another component of the package that produced this obsession: certain slight differences I'd noticed in the way Chl was talking and acting around me, which I'd let pass without analysing properly. When she was here yesterday evening, she told me that the main topic of her therapy session had been me. But she wouldn't go into detail. She was still anxious; less crazy than on previous days, but very anxious nonetheless, and with a strange look in her eye. Then I had another small revelation – the first of the day, because I still hadn't solved the cybernetic problem – and I asked her to speak clearly. It was obvious there was something she wanted to say, and the best thing to do would be to come out with it once and for all. At the same time I remembered a very unsettling dream I'd had that morning, in which Chl had been unpleasant to me, looking at me with a repugnant cynicism completely unlike her true personality, whilst declaring that she had a whole list of lovers.

'It's that I'm detaching myself . . . ' she said, and her eyes filled with tears. Mine did too; I tried to hold the tears in and they stung my eyes.

'Well,' I said, 'it's natural, and normal, and what I was hoping for all along.'

It felt like I was dying, but I was telling the truth. I'd been recommending she go to therapy from very early on, and she waited two or three years before taking my advice. Now she was reaching the stage of detaching herself from me, and above all, I imagine, of the more important detachment from her father. My darling Chl is growing, or at least she's doing what she can. She'll lose a lot . . . and I'll lose more; but I think what she'll gain will be infinitely more valuable. Recovering her libido, for example. And being able to make that list of lovers she spoke of in my dream.

At this dramatic moment, as we both sat red-eyed and tearful, we were holding hands. I felt the warmth of her hand just like in the old days, and I saw that her face was recovering the glorious colours of her usual good health, and her beauty was beginning to shine once more. I realised that the causes of the anxiety which had been torturing her for days were connected to that process of growth.

I hope the process includes both of us, and that I too can, in the end, detach myself from her and grow a little . . . not much, just the necessary amount.

WEDNESDAY 28, 18:40

This morning I had a dream with two parts; they could have been two separate dreams, but I feel sure that one sequence was a continuation of the other, although I don't know how or why, since I only have a few odd fragments.

I find one of the parts astonishingly cryptic, which must mean it would be perfectly transparent to any expert (latent homosexuality, that sort of thing). It was about a young man who was gay, though he wasn't at all effeminate and behaved completely normally; he was also a very pleasant person. It was more that the topic of homosexuality was there in a few conversations, or as one of those mysterious kinds of information you get in dreams, which said that the man was part of an organisation of homosexuals, and that he'd come to the city to carry out some of his duties as a member of that organisation. One such duty seemed to relate to a restaurant, or rather, to a place that made meals to sell. I caught sight of a selection of cakes or tarts. I even tried a portion of one, a triangle of pastry with something on top, which might have been pieces of ham or something sweet.

The other part of the dream (and now that I think about it, the young homosexual guy in the part I've described could be the same male character who appears in this second part) is obviously linked to the news I had from Chl the night before the dream. She was in a huge underground garage, or something like that, and she was trying to drive out of it in a car. I was outside the car, walking ahead, and I saw that some other cars were parked along Chl's exact route out, with very little room between them; I wasn't sure Chl's car would fit past. At the same time, the place where those cars were parked was an outdoor road, and next to one car there was a gnarled old tree. The underground garage hadn't exactly turned into something else; that stretch of road in the countryside must have begun just after the exit.

Chl's solution was to buy another car. And do to that, we had to go up in a very large service lift. She went up with a man, perhaps the homosexual, and shut herself away with him in what looked like a normal lift, which was attached to part of the service lift. I stayed outside that lift, or whatever it was, very annoyed at how Chl had shut herself away with that man and left me outside; I was jealous and at the same time I felt rejected, out of place. These feelings were heightened by Chl's expression, which was solemn and indifferent, and not at all affectionate towards me. It seemed she had to negotiate with that man and I was getting in the way, but nevertheless, I opened the doors to the lift and joined them inside.

Without a doubt, Chl and her therapist (interpretation A), or Chl and her current or future boyfriend, most likely future (interpretation B), and it's highly plausible that both interpretations are correct (polyvalence of symbols). Chl stopped telling me the specifics of her therapy a while ago, and I noticed how the therapist had made considerable progress when it came to helping his patient recover her libido; I found this extremely annoying, of course, but at the same time, ambiguously, I was happy the therapy seemed to be working. For months I'd been worried about the fact I was still Chl's main focal point, while the therapist was more of a secondary figure; the therapy would never have got anywhere under those conditions.

FRIDAY 30, 17:43

My way of processing all this grief is involuntary, and perhaps not very effective, but it's not something I'm able to choose. Any more than I can choose how to perceive certain things; I found out through my doctor that my 'invisible friend', Jorge, had a noticeably swollen abdomen in his last moments – my doctor explained something about the blood having flooded his liver, horrible things I didn't want to pay too much attention to – and that was how I'd woken up that day, at more or less the time he died. When my doctor called me to pass on the news, I passed on my own news that there was something horrible growing in my stomach, and joked in very bad taste about the possibility I was pregnant, or, more acceptably, that I was rapidly developing cancer.

But of all the grief I've been accumulating lately, the most difficult to deal with is the grief for Chl, or rather, for myself in relation to Chl, especially because it's mixed with a furious wave of paranoid jealousy, which is completely inappropriate. And that's how I've come to be breaking records with my screen time, downloading exotic and almost never useful programs from the internet, making a database to organise everything related to those programs, and other equally trivial things. That's how I've spent the past forty-eight hours. I hope these lines mark the beginning of a change of direction, away from these avoidance techniques.

In a few hours, I'll have a visit from Pablo Casacuberta and his Japanese friend and film-making partner, Yuki.

I don't know how we'll understand one other; the Japanese man doesn't understand Spanish, and I don't speak Japanese. Yuki's English, according to Pablo, isn't up to much, and neither is mine.

Today I was thinking about Burroughs' 'familiars', and I was reminded of the recent rediscovery of a kind of matter, called 'dark' for some reason, even though it's transparent, which coexists with the matter we know about. Apparently it occupies empty spaces or mingles with the matter we know about because of something to do with lower density – I don't know exactly how the theory goes. But it's just a theory, though I read somewhere that some person has found strong evidence to confirm it. I imagine a universe made of this other kind of matter, inhabited by people made of this other kind of matter, and the possibility that under certain conditions, something in one of the universes could be sensed in the other.

FRIDAY 30, 18:12

Heading out for my weekend errands, but I want to make a note of this so I don't forget: topic of distorted perception (insect in hair); topic of today's dream (big rally, photos with my friend [?], loss of camera and other things).

# APRIL 2001

MONDAY 2, 05:21

It's not an appropriate time to begin this diary entry, but I've been feeling very guilty. The guilt isn't specifically about the connection between this diary and the project, although it is slightly about the project; most of all, it's about my inappropriate behaviour. That is, the guilt is caused less by what I haven't been doing than by what I have been doing. And what I have been doing for several days, or, more precisely, since the last deaths, the two most recent, in my group of friends, what I have been doing is devoting myself passionately, with every fibre of my being, to computer-related activities. One such activity is the classic search for programs, large and small, but mostly small – small utilities – on the internet. I've found the address of a web page that contains hundreds of files, and each file contains a few addresses from which you can download various programs for free, and I've downloaded lots, some of which are very handy, though most of them are more like curiosities with very limited usefulness. Some things that I get hold of aren't good for anything, or don't work on my computer, or are programs made fairly clumsily and without taking into account the ways they could go wrong. But among all the things I've downloaded, and no doubt will download, there are a few programs, small or not so small, that really are ingenious, very helpful and very satisfying. Another of my computer-related activities involves a little world that was revealed to me a few days ago: the world of icons. I've always been very fond of using and creating icons, particularly as a way of identifying my own programs, but what I didn't know is that there's a whole world of icon artists out there, and that the creation of icons is a lot like an art; a modest art, if you like, but in my view a very worthwhile one. It's the art of suggesting a lot with very little, of creating an illusion of reality with resources that seem almost magical.

But I began writing with the idea of describing that dream and another one, I forget which. Now I'm going to sleep; tomorrow, tomorrow, tomorrow I'll focus on the diary and catching up with my emails.

## MONDAY 2, 19:41

I'd be lying if I said I went to sleep after writing those last few pages; by the time I finally managed to tear myself away from this blessed machine, it was already nine in the morning. Things are going from bad to worse.

## MONDAY 2, 20:17

I'd completely forgotten about the dream I wanted to write up, and then, a few minutes ago, in the kitchen, while I was cleaning an ashtray, a chain of apparently unrelated thoughts suddenly brought a particular character to mind, and that's when the memory of the dream came back to me – the dream in which this character, tangential as he was, played a role. I'd found the dream odd because it's a while since I've had social dreams like that, involving mass participation. A kind of rally or huge festival was taking place, affecting much of the city; the streets were flooded with people, and there were different meeting points and attractions. It was a kind of national celebration (the sort that doesn't exist any more, where everyone is happy and carefree, moving through the crowds without feeling afraid). In a central area there was a platform and people speaking, though it didn't sound like some dreary political rally, and, what's more, most people weren't paying much attention; almost everyone was on the move, going from street to street and place to place. Against this backdrop, I went into what could have been a museum or a historical building (although equally, the idea of a zoo, which occurs to me now, wouldn't be too far off ). I was with a woman, probably Chl, and a couple of friends who I now sometimes think were F and P, but who may also have been X and Z (X is an old friend, or ex-friend, because ever since he became a million-aire, we haven't spoken). Very near the entrance to this building, on a wall above a wide door, there hung an extremely large, long mirror. I had a camera with me and thought it would be interesting to take a photo of that mirror; since the top of it was tilted slightly forward, it reflected us and a lot of the vast space around the entrance. I suggested to my friend, whoever he was, that he take a photo at the same time, because he had a camera as well, and that way we'd both appear in the photos reflected in different sides of the mirror, photographing each other, only with the cameras pointing at the image of the mirror and not the other person. Once again, my writing is fucking dreadful.

WEDNESDAY 4, 16:40

No one reading these lines will have failed to notice, by this point in my story, that I'm going through a particularly serious phase of galloping looniness. I see that to cap it all I managed to get annoyed with my own narrative style, not without reason of course – because the confusion and clumsiness feel to me like a personal affront, made worse by the fact I'm to blame – and broke off abruptly before I'd finished my account of the dream I was remembering. Worst of all, at that moment I didn't even realise the account of the dream was unfinished, such was the power of the obsession that gripped me and that for the most part is still gripping me today, an obsession linked to the management of various rebellious programs. I know full well that this obsession isn't a cause but a consequence, and I'm very aware of the causes, but being aware of them doesn't help me improve my behaviour in the slightest. A nice package for a therapist, but where, oh where will I find the therapist I need?

In an attempt to impose a bit of order on the chaos, I'll continue my account of the dream:

After the mirror scene – and I don't know if those photographs were actually taken, although I expect they were, but what I mean is that

I don't have the concrete image or the sensation of pressing a button to click the shutter; after that scene, as I was saying, and without being sure what form the transition took, I'm back in the street again, alone this time, still with my camera slung over my left shoulder, and I notice that the party mostly seems to have finished; there aren't many people left moving through the streets, though the loudspeaker system is still transmitting voices, speeches and a certain atmosphere of jubilation. The gathering in front of the main platform is still going on, though the number of people standing around has considerably reduced; still, it's a fairly substantial group, perhaps a few hundred people. I notice that a voice coming out of the loudspeakers is insisting on mentioning the Socialist Party over and over again, and I feel slightly indignant that a political party is trying to take advantage of some local festivities that have attracted a large part of the population. There must, I decide, be a well-known Socialist Party figure behind this manoeuvre. I drift away from that centre of activity, which is still holding out despite the general end-of-party atmosphere, while the evening shadows gradually take possession of the streets. I go round a corner and down a deserted little road, stopping for reasons I don't remember now, and I do something; perhaps I take my jacket off, because I'm hot, which would fit with what comes next in the dream, but I don't know what exactly I do. Then I carry on walking, go round another corner, and after a few yards I realise I don't have my camera with me any more, or my jacket, or another item I now can't remember. I'm missing three things (psychoanalysts, take note). For a moment I'm flustered, but then I feel more confident and retrace my steps, and indeed, a few yards past the corner, on the previous street, I find my things on the ground. The jacket, the camera, and . . . ?

FRIDAY 6, 05:15

Today I saw the widow again, in her usual place on the railings closest to my building; always at a slight distance from her companion, who, according to my calculations, is her third husband. I have to say that I dislike this bird less than his predecessor, the one who helped to raise her children; he doesn't have the same iridescent chest. For some reason

I can't pin down, I have a profound dislike of that iridescence. The chest itself, when it's very pronounced – as it normally is in pigeons with iridescent chests – puts me off; it gives the pigeon a flashy and effeminate air, and makes it look as if it's simultaneously puffing up its chest and revealing a fat old woman's double chin. I took a while to recognise the widow; she's no longer in mourning. Her feathers really have got much lighter, from a dark grey verging on black to a light grey. But it's her; I recognise her style and her white mark. The installation of that horrible mast and the wires that hold it in place probably kept the couple away for a while; but eventually they returned to this place that's so intertwined with her, the widow. The corpse is still there, of course, almost unrecognisable. But in fact, it's a while since I spent much time taking in the view from my bedroom window; during the summer I barely lifted the blinds, so as not to let in too much sun, and now that it's been raining, or drizzling, or cloudy, almost constantly since autumn officially began, my sleeping hours are so unhinged that when I wake up and get out of bed, it's already too late to do anything, and even though I raise the blinds all the way I hardly pause to look out, because I'm very behind with everything and feel pressured by all kinds of urgent matters. Today, or rather yesterday, there was a hint of a recovery; I was less anxious and less obsessed with the computer, and able to take a slightly calmer look at the outside world.

Yesterday evening I had a business meeting. I was visited by a man who moves freely and ably in the corporate world, and he listened attentively to the proposal I had for him. He seemed interested. This might, or might not, but I hope it does, lead to a very interesting project that, if it works out, could provide me with a reasonable monthly income. There's a long way to go before the project's up and running, if it ever is up and running. But I'm feeling confident.

FRIDAY 6, 16:13

I remember making a note a few days ago about recording a particular incident. Now the anecdote doesn't seem worth telling, to say the least, but I thought it was interesting at the time. I'll have a go at writing about it, though later I might decide to remove all references to it from this diary.

The night was stormy, as all days and nights in this city currently seem to be. The atmosphere was very stuffy and the heavens were threatening to open at any moment. On our walk, N and I had reached the usual *boliche*, and we were sitting at a table, drinking coffee and chatting. Suddenly, I felt something land on my head and come to rest in a position above and slightly behind my right ear. I was immediately filled with a kind of frantic desperation, because whatever it was seemed to have the not inconsiderable proportions of a plane-tree leaf, and it was moving, moving and trying to extricate its legs from my hair, which in that region actually exists and is even fairly long. The first image that occurred to me was that of a toad – one of those almost flat, round toads, which don't look very toad-like – and then, swiftly ruling out the toad image because this creature felt too light to be a toad, a spider. A tarantula. What else could be so big? I flapped at it wildly with my hands and emitted some possibly humiliating cries of panic. The creature was still there, entangled, moving laboriously onwards and frightening me. Then N, who hadn't done anything to calm me down and had on the contrary widened her eyes in an expression of horror, reinforcing the idea that I had something really terrifying on my head, reached out an arm and delicately, with one finger or two, flicked the predatory beast onto the ground. When I looked down, ready to jump and squash the tarantula, I found myself looking at an innocent, inoffensive and very, very tiny beetle. How did it create the impression that it was ten or fifteen times larger than it was? Just the other day, an explanation occurred to me: perhaps my long, tangled hair had transmitted to my brain, through movements generated by the movements of the insect, precise information about the spatial location of the foreign object, but since the roots of the hairs touching the insect's legs were nowhere near each other, because my hair is messy and long, the brain had constructed a false and much larger image. If my hair had been neat, the insect would have moved hairs whose roots were close together, and then my brain would have calculated its actual size correctly. It's not a brilliant explanation, and nor am I very convinced it's the right one, but I can't think of anything else.

SATURDAY 7, 17:48

The enigma of Mr Matra:
'This might be a conspiracy, secretly directed at harming Mr Matra,'
I said to the woman.

She was somebody's wife; in fact, everyone there was quite separate
from me, as if I'd found myself in the same place as them quite by
chance. Still, I seemed broadly committed to them and their activities,
which I knew very little about. When I tried to say the name of this
Mr Matra I hesitated, because I wasn't sure he was called exactly that;
I pronounced it with some confusion, as if embarrassed to be uncertain of the name of such an important person. He was something like
the boss, or the employer, of all of us; he wielded enormous power,
not only over us but over many people, a power rooted in money.
He had a huge fortune. We were all there because we were hoping
to get something from him. And after a long wait, he'd eventually
addressed me from some way off, a distance of several yards, saying:
'A hundred and fifty words, font [Tahoma], size [six].' (The square
brackets indicate that I'm not sure if those details are correct.) I asked
for a moment to find a pen and paper and write down what he'd said,
and started looking around, and then the delays and confusions that
are so common in dreams began. I'm not sure if I did write down those
details, though the work I was being assigned by Mr Matra was very
important to me. Then a few things happened, I don't know what,
which made me suspect that some of what was going on might be
directed not so much against me, or against any particular member
of our group, as against Mr Matra.

I don't have much more to say about this very long dream with its
busy, eventful plot; as usual, there's a whole novel there that I couldn't
hold onto.

I've been thinking obsessively about that name, Matra. It obviously
suggests the idea of a mother, and in my particular case it's complicated
by personal events, such as the fact that my maternal grandmother,
who gave me all the affection my mother couldn't provide, was called

Marta. But what do these female figures have to do with that powerful man . . . I thought about other anagrams, but none were very satisfying and some were unpleasant, like '*matar*', meaning 'to kill'. Tram. Arm. Art. Marat: this one is interesting. Thanks to the famous play I immediately associate it with Sade, and that, in relation to a powerful character, is a topic to delight the psychoanalysts.

In the end, I arrived at the not particularly satisfying, though certainly very plausible, conclusion that Mr Matra is none other than Mr Guggenheim, the character I've invented to personify the Guggenheim Foundation. Or rather, Mr Matra is the Foundation itself. Who else has tasked me with writing a certain number of pages? And I can't deny that for months now the Foundation has been feeding me and looking after me like a mother, or like an affectionate grandmother.

WEDNESDAY 25, 17.07

Mysterious disappearance of the pigeon's corpse!
To be continued.

# MAY 2001

THURSDAY 3, 01:07

Today (yesterday) I had a fleeting visit from Chl. We've not been seeing much of each other. I don't know if I was already in an unusual state, because today saw some changes, permanent ones I hope, to my sleeping hours and my relationship with the computer, but if I was, I didn't notice. The fact is that when I saw her I felt strange, dizzy, and little by little I realised I was becoming deeply distressed, almost to the point of shedding a few tears. At the same time, there seemed to be something undefinable and strange about her, almost as if I didn't know her. Maybe the treatment she'd had done at the hairdresser was something to do with it; her hair looked too smooth and limp. As a side point, she's going to the hairdresser too much; something like three times a week, or so she says. I shouldn't care, but I do care, and it bothers me that I do. The expression on her face today, especially in her eyes, which are usually wonderful and frank, open and transparent like a girl's, was rather evasive. I had the feeling she was hiding something. I often have that feeling these days, and I try not to take it seriously, but today my impression seemed entirely true and accurate. She stayed for a few minutes, ate a few slices of my cheese and drank a coffee, then she put her raincoat back on and left. I didn't want to go with her to the bus stop. There have been a few times lately when I haven't wanted to go with her, perhaps because I barely leave the house all day and feel infinitely too lazy to go out at that time. I always offer her money for a taxi, which every now and then she accepts, and then I don't worry so much; but today I didn't offer her anything. Suddenly, looking at her, I was overcome with distress and had a feeling of irreparable loss. That feeling must have been brewing for a while now; not for nothing did I disappear several weeks ago.

A few days back I wrote this about Chl to an invisible email friend, replying to a message she'd sent me:

> . . . today she arrived resplendent; the therapy is setting her more and more on the right path. She said we needed to talk . . . and we all know what women mean by that. She said, 'I think it's time to end what we have.' I laughed uproariously, with thunderous guffaws. 'What we have ended a long time ago. It's dead and buried, six feet underground.' She laughed, too, but she was worried. 'But I don't want to stop seeing you, or going for walks with you, or making you *milanesas*.' I laughed thunderously once again: 'So what will be different?' Well, it seems what will be different is saying it out loud, making the reality of the situation official. It's the strangest break-up I've ever experienced.

Weeks of that; mourning for Chl, and for the dead-dead. A hidden, subterranean sort of mourning, which doesn't show how much it hurts. I think I stopped writing in this diary when my invisible friend died; the final straw. And today that grief has hit me all at once. Chl left hours ago, and I'm still in the same state, as if I'm about to start weeping. I should actually do it. I should relax my control.

The mystery of the disappeared corpse: the day I announced it, I raised the blinds and saw that the dead pigeon was gone from the roof. Near where it used to be there was an empty plastic bottle, and I have no idea how it got there. A family-size soft-drink bottle, which the wind had been blowing from place to place. There was also a small rod a few inches long, which looked like it was made of wood, probably left behind by the men who installed the mast. And a few other pieces of rubbish coming and going in the wind. All that was there, but the corpse was not, which I found deeply surprising. If someone had been intending to clear the flat roof, they wouldn't only have moved the corpse; how hard would it have been to take the bottle and the rod as well? I also thought the corpse had been there

for too long to make appealing prey for a rat; it's now an unrecognisable pile of squashed, congealed feathers. I was surprised, but I didn't
let myself get carried away by the mystery, and decided instead to
see it as a relief. It certainly cheered me up to be able to look out
of the window without immediately seeing the ugly, pathetic and
spine-chilling presence of death.

But the other day, when I raised the blinds, the bottle had disappeared
and the pigeon was back in its place. Rather than speculating about
shadowy machinations, I'd like to think that the bottle had been
blocking my view of the most visible part of the corpse, the pale part,
and that the dark part had merged with the shadows on the floor of
the flat roof, with the help of the cloudy sky. It's the most reasonable
explanation. As for the bottle, it's simple; the wind moves it around,
and it must have blown over to a part of the flat roof I can't see. Today
it was back again, in the same place as before.

TUESDAY 8, 03:41

When I raised the blinds at the beginning of my day, which still
isn't over, I saw the widow for the first time in months, a few feet
away from the corpse. On the railings furthest from my building
was another pigeon, gazing out over the bay. That pigeon flew off.
The widow stood there a while longer, only moving to arrange her
feathers nervously with her beak from time to time. She didn't get
any closer to the corpse. She seemed rather distracted, or confused. Or
as if she were waiting for something to happen. Then she flew onto
the railings and stayed there for a bit, more or less where the other
pigeon had been, also looking out over the bay. I looked out over
the bay myself, but I didn't see anything interesting. Then I stopped
staring through the window because I was very behind; I'd woken up
extremely late, thanks to a mosquito that bit me just as I was dozing
off at 5 a.m. I got up, looked for it, found it – a miserable mosquito,
small and sickly looking, but an effective biter nonetheless – and took
it out with a good wallop. But I couldn't go back to bed right away;

I was overexcited, I'm not sure why. I smoked a cigarette, and then went back to bed and read until 7.30 a.m.

It would be very hard work attempting to fill the gaping expanse of my diary in recent times with anecdotes – I don't know if it's been weeks or months since I stopped writing with any regularity.

I could at least write that around the middle of April my workshops started again. I have a few students; only on Thursdays, in the morning and afternoon. After which I'm a wreck, as always, until Sunday. Then I start trying to piece myself back together.

I'd like to be better at keeping my life, my schedule and my interests on track. But it seems ever more difficult, more unattainable. The control I have over my mind is negligible, almost non-existent. I do everything entirely automatically.

THURSDAY 10, 03:08

I'm drugged, and sleepy, because at 9 p.m. I started taking little pieces of Valium, with the aim of going to sleep early because tomorrow I have workshops from four thirty in the afternoon. I've taken about 4 milligrams, according to my calculations, which is enough to flatten out my mind, though without putting me to sleep too drastically. In a few moments' time, I'll take the final milligram to complete the dose, and go to bed.

Today Chl came with a load of steaks (the butcher in her neighbourhood has much better meat than I can find in the market) and lots of *milanesas* she'd made. The girl's a saint. But this novel is drawing to a close . . .

She brought me a bag of videos I'd lent her; this afternoon, while I was looking for an item of clothing, I found the odd garment of hers in my wardrobe. And when she was here this evening, she found a few more of her things of her own accord, and I remembered the clothes and gave them to her, and I remembered a few more of her possessions that were in the other room and handed them over as well. Concomitantly – a horrible word – I found, after she'd left, that she'd put the comb I kept at her house in the bag with the videos. That made me very sad. I thought: 'The novel is coming to an end.' And this novel is also coming to an end, because it seems that they're one and the same.

Chl was so beautiful today.

SUNDAY 13, 05:56

There they go again with Beethoven; again with the 'Ode to Joy', *Freude, Freude*. It makes me think of Germans doing gymnastics, following orders from a horse-faced instructor. They played the same thing yesterday. It's like a nightmare, only this part of the nightmare is the least abrasive; I wouldn't say I've come to enjoy Beethoven, or at least not his symphonies, though I've heard the odd sonata that's decent enough, but I'm classifying him as a lesser evil. It's a few weeks since I switched from Radio Clarín to SODRE, coinciding more or less with the beginning of SODRE's continuous transmission; instead of playing the national anthem at midnight and then going off to bed the way they used to, they carry on continuously, following the example of Clarín. Clarín has become unbearable; they're always repeating the same things (and I see now that SODRE does it, too, but I'd been listening to Clarín for years and I knew it all off by heart) and they've included a few unbearable, melodramatic adverts, which seem entirely out of place. It's all in terrible taste. But sometimes I need to go back to Clarín; first I give SODRE on FM a go, and sometimes it's fine, but there they do play the national anthem at midnight and then go to bed. They have a slimy announcer with a persuasive voice, the sort I can't stand, though fortunately they don't have many advertisers. But where the real nightmare begins, on both SODRE stations, and especially the AM one, is with opera. Opera seems to be back in fashion at the moment, or perhaps it was never out of fashion; but I'm amazed at how many hours a day they dedicate to those vociferous men and women, whether in an opera proper or in songs butchered by low barreltones, hollow tenors or, worst of all, the most absolutely unbearable, sopranos. All people whose necks I'd gladly wring with my own hands. I can't imagine what kind of perversion, inner demon, abnormality or defect could bring people to come out with those monstrous, repulsive shrieks, to force the voice in that anti-natural, insolent, over-the-top way, as if they were competing in an Olympic event, showing off their physical strength, trying to break some kind of record. Nothing could be further from, more separate from or more opposed to art. How that stupid sport has managed to get mixed up in music is something I'll never understand, and nor do I want it explained to me. It makes me ill. Sometimes I leave the radio on and go to the bathroom, and the people of SODRE take advantage of the situation to slip on a soprano, and there I am, suffering, wondering whether to interrupt the important activities I'm engaged in and turn the radio off, or to put up with even more of it. The same thing happens when I'm concentrating on the computer; I often become disengaged from the world around me and fall into a kind of trance, and then from one moment to the next I notice I'm not feeling good, I'm on edge, all is not right with the world, and finally I realise there's opera on the radio and they've been bombarding me for ages with their disgusting vocal exercises.

Luckily there were no opera fans in my family; I'd almost say I was completely unaware of its existence for many happy years. In contrast, my cousin Pocho's father tortured his son systematically, night after night, during and after dinner, with operas broadcast on the radio (SODRE, no doubt). My cousin Pocho, when he was a boy, covered his ears and yelled for someone to turn off 'those shouting men'. 'Shouting men', shouting men and women, is a perfect description of opera. And the way they shout, too; so enthusiastically.

Operas generally have interesting overtures. They should stick to those. The overture sounds like the only point when the composer feels at liberty to give free rein to his imagination. Then come the dramatic acts, and he's back in the service of some stupid libretto. Inspiration is replaced by manual labour, brick upon brick. Yesterday they played the overture to the third act of *Lohengrin*; I like it, despite all the Wagnerian pomposity. Maybe I like it because I had the record when I was younger, on a 78, and used to listen to it a lot.

.    .    .

Now Beethoven's over and they're playing some fairly outlandish contemporary thing. There are various worthwhile examples of contemporary music, but what they play on SODRE, at least, suffers from the malady that's unfortunately so common in this kind of music: it's too cerebral, with too many calculated effects and a total lack of inspiration, freedom and joy. Strange, disconnected sounds, and long pauses, as if to create a sense of anticipation that's very unlikely to lead anywhere pleasant.

True, they sometimes play something by Bach, Vivaldi or Brahms, or other minor but very interesting geniuses. I've been surprised by Dvořák; I didn't know him well – only his symphony *From the New World*, which I like – and lately I've found myself listening attentively to very peculiar pieces of music whose origins I can't identify, and sometimes I end up standing by the radio in the early hours of the morning, putting off going to bed, listening to that music and waiting for the announcer to reveal what it is, and very often it's Dvořák. And now I'm going to bed, while the radio carries on doling out disjointed and almost meaningless sounds, which are completely unsuitable for this time of night, or morning, when you want something warmer and friendlier, whether you've just got up and are about to have breakfast, or whether, like me, you're on the way to bed.

WEDNESDAY 16, 20:50

As I was saying, my friend, this novel is coming to an end. I saw Chl again fleetingly yesterday; she turned up half asleep, drank a coffee and then left, but it was enough for me to feel how horribly tied to her I am. My sexual urges, which are normally dormant, awaken the moment I see her; and when I say 'sexual urges' I don't just mean desire, but much more besides. She's still the only female presence that can move me to my very core; she's still a part of me, body and soul. Today I woke up feeling a kind of cosmic disorientation that gradually turned into nervousness, and later into fury; I reacted violently to the slightest upsets, and when I spoke to people, even just over the phone,

I did it in a kind of bark. Later, intrigued by the lack of news, I called Chl; I was hoping to see her again today, but she reminded me of something I'd never known; that she'd invited NNN – the individual whom I've thought for some weeks is her current partner – round for dinner, to eat one of her stews. She says she told me yesterday, and it's very likely that she did and I didn't want to take it in, and now an immense sadness has been added to my fury. I want to burst out sobbing. She's revealing her cards very slowly, and I think I'd rather have the truth all together, all in one go. I didn't manage to extract any more information during that phone call, but something in her way of expressing herself, and the way she carefully avoided giving clear, direct responses, makes me 98 per cent sure I'm right.

And it makes me even more furious that it's making me furious at all. I understand the sadness, but not the fury. Or the jealousy.

The same reprehensible part of me has been calling the shots for too long now, and it's time for a coup d'état in my psychological make-up to put someone reasonable in charge. That spoilt child, that primitive reptile, that aching, suffering mass has to be got rid of, pushed under and made to relinquish all power over my behaviour once and for all. What have I been doing over these long months? I've been collecting computer programs, downloading them from the internet. As I learn to use them, I've been writing descriptions of them and organising the descriptions in a database, but there are so many of them; by now I've acquired precisely 394 programs, and I'm still hunting for more. I have programs of all kinds, some dreadful, others brilliant; some free, others paid-for; though I normally trick the paid-for ones so I don't have to pay. I trawl the internet looking for cracks for these programs on pages of cracks. I've even opened programs to examine them in a hexadecimal viewer so I can try to modify them, and sometimes, though not very often, I've succeeded. I'd like to look into this more; how to crack and patch programs. This exhilarating activity has filled hundreds of late nights, or early mornings. Pornography has fallen by the wayside; I no longer have any interest in downloading so much as a single photo, and I even deleted the obscene contents of two or three ZIP disks, which means that all those hours I spent searching, and all that money I spent on the telephone bill, have gone to waste.

I understood this lack of interest in photos, whether soft-core or hardcore, as a positive sign. And so it was, or would have been, were it not for the fact that it cleared the way for a new kind of addiction. I've become hooked on these little robots, their jolly colours and the way they work, often so precisely and elegantly, on tasks I could very easily do without but which have now become essential, such as clearing the hard drive of junk files, cleaning the Windows Registry, defragging the hard drive, manipulating files in programs that are considerably better than the infernal Microsoft programs, swapping icons, creating new icons, retouching old icons, adding sounds, and filling the edges of the screen with toolbars that hide themselves when they're not in use, and which allow me to open any one of the infinite programs I'm accumulating at the click of a mouse.

Admittedly, I don't use them all; not even close. I'd say I end up uninstalling most of them, but while I learn how they work and how useful they might be, I keep them handy in those toolbars.

That's what I've been doing over the past few months, as well as reading detective novels, still at an average rate of one per day, and not much else. I've been going to bed at an average time of around 7 a.m., and getting up at three in the afternoon, though sometimes four, or five, or even six. Tomorrow, Thursday, I have a workshop; I'll need to get up early. That means being on my feet by about 2 p.m., which, given the circumstances, is a heroic act I'm never sure I'll achieve. I've managed until now, and I hope I manage tomorrow.

But the fury is still overwhelming, and the sadness, and I'm groping blindly at the keyboard in search of a way of finishing this novel, of giving it a decent ending, even if it's unlikely to be a happy one.

WEDNESDAY 23, 02:53

I couldn't sleep in the early hours of this morning, though I was dying of exhaustion, with my eyes glued shut and weepy from lack of rest. What's more, I had to get up a lot to go to the bathroom and urinate, which to my surprise I did abundantly. I was cold and covered myself with the thermal duvet; that, combined with the gas heater, soon made my legs horribly uncomfortable, since I can't stand them being too hot or under any weight, and I had to get rid of the duvet and use a thin blanket instead, which left me with cold feet. I got up to fill the hot-water bottle, for the first time this year. When I went back to bed I started coughing and felt short of oxygen, so I got up again and turned off the heater. Then I realised the cough was mainly caused by the gastric reflux, which means I have to sleep practically sitting up, and that always gives me a sore neck and shoulders. Once I had everything more or less sorted and thought I'd finally be able to sleep, I realised I couldn't; I felt strangely uneasy, and was tossing and turning as a result. Then I realised I really did have a stomach ache, or what's known as 'a bad case of indigestion'. I wasn't surprised, because I remembered I'd had dinner quite late, and I'd eaten a spectacular stew Chl had brought round. The stew wasn't made for me, but rather for the person I consider my rival, that young man who's been visiting her a lot lately; the fact she cooks for him makes me uneasy in a way I think I've already mentioned in this diary. According to Chl, the young man stood her up, and so I claimed the stew for myself – a sad victory over the enemy. And because of that, and because of the slightly less psychological matter of the high levels of fried food and red peppers in the stew, it's not surprising it didn't agree with me. However, I think I stayed up for long enough after eating that I would have digested a good deal of it, were it not for the fact that immediately after the stew I had a steak and my classic tomato with garlic and onion. Since I recently cut out bread, I had to accompany this with a huge quantity of biscuits, which didn't really agree with me either, because for a while I haven't been able to find my preferred brand. I can digest my preferred brand of biscuits with no trouble at all. And on top of all that, before going to bed, I had some spoonfuls of peach jam. I don't usually eat jam; it's a rare occurrence for me. But when I'm seized with the urge, I can't resist. And jam, of course, can't be eaten by itself; there's no fun in that. So I had to send a few more biscuits down after it. All this was working its way through me while I was trying to sleep, hence the tossing and turning. It was impossible to get comfortable. My eventration was so swollen I thought it was going to burst. When I woke up at around five in the afternoon, after finally getting to sleep at 7 a.m., I had a horrible taste in my mouth and understood better what the trouble had been. But while I was trying to sleep and imagining I had insomnia, I thought about this diary.

I have a big problem with this diary. Before going to sleep I was thinking that its novelistic structure means it should be coming to an end by now, but its diary-like quality doesn't allow that, for the simple reason that nothing exciting has happened in my life for some time that would make a suitable ending. I can't just write 'The End'; there has to be something, something special, an event that enlightens the reader about all that's been said, something to justify the hard work of reading this mountain of pages. An ending, in other words.

When I woke up today, I carried on thinking. It occurred to me that I should do something; since there's no sign of anything new, or any change or interesting surprise, I should take matters into my own hands and create a suitable topic for the ending. Then I decided that wasn't really allowed. I can't go out into the street dressed as a monkey to generate an interesting and unusual anecdote with which to finish the book; I can't start structuring my life around the diary and the need to finish it. I also thought about how the ideal ending would be something like this:

'I'm tired of this situation, I'm tired of this grey life, I'm tired of the pain caused by this strange relationship with Chl, the knowledge that I've lost her even though she's right there, the sexual tension every time we meet, which doesn't lead to anything except this absurd addiction to the computer; I'm tired of myself, of my inability to live, of my failure. I didn't manage to finish the grant project; it was a bad idea, it can't be done, I didn't realise that time can't go backwards, or that I've become someone else. The writerly role is stuck to my skin but I'm not a writer any more, and I never wanted to be one. I don't want to write, I've said everything I wanted to say, and writing has stopped being fun and giving me an identity. It's not true what my friend Verani says in some essays, particularly in his work on *Empty Words*: that my desperation arises from not being able to write. I can write; look, I'm writing now and I'm doing it well. I can write whatever I like; no one disturbs me, no one interrupts me, I have all the equipment and all the comfort I need; I just don't want to, I don't feel like it. And I'm tired of playing this role. I'm tired of everything. Life is no more than a stupid, unnecessary, painful burden. I don't want to suffer any more, or carry on with this miserable life of routines and addictions. As soon as I close these quotation marks, then, I'm going to shoot myself in the head.'

That would perhaps make the book sell very well; in this country, death whips up an exceptional interest in the work of the person who died. It's the same with people who go into exile. But I'm not interested in selling books. I never have been. And what's more, I'm not actually tired of life. I could carry on living exactly the life I'm living now for all the time the good Lord allows me, indefinitely even. It's true that some of my behaviour annoys me, but it's also true that I don't work very hard to fight it. I'm happy, really, I'm comfortable, I'm content, even within a kind of overarching depression. My emotional dependence on Chl stops me attaching myself to other women, but that could also be a clever move on the part of my unconscious to protect me from further complications and problems. Felipe came today with another load of books. We were chatting, and he said: 'People love you.' And it's true, and I told him that I can't reconcile feeling universally loved with my paranoia, my famous paranoia. I don't think I could ask for more than I have, or feel better than I feel. I hope God grants me many years of health; and in the meantime, nothing could be further from my intentions than picking up a gun and shooting myself in the head – especially considering that I might not even know how to pick up a gun. That ending for the novel, then, will have to be ruled out.

So the problem remains. I don't know what to do to keep hold of the reader, to make them carry on reading. Something had better happen soon, or all this work will have been in vain.

WEDNESDAY 23, 04:32

I'd already turned the computer off and begun my bedtime ritual when I heard the SODRE announcer saying 'soprano', a key word that always has me sprinting furiously for the radio to switch it off, effing and blinding, but then I heard him saying 'Villa-Lobos' and I smiled. As a result, I turned the computer on, because I've lost the habit of writing by hand, and it didn't occur to me that writing by hand would have been much quicker and easier, and now here I am, writing in Word to set down my opinion, which is somewhat radical, and subject to alterations if more information is added to my squalid musical knowledge, that Villa-Lobos is the only musician who has managed to use a soprano – in his *Bachianas Brasileiras* – artfully and elegantly, without damaging the ears or spirits of his listeners, and without giving me homicidal urges. I also share his love of cellos.

SUNDAY 27, 18:16

Worm dream; must write it down.

MONDAY 28, 01:16

The dream, as usual, was long and complex. I'm sure it was full of very interesting and significant situations, but it was erased when I woke up. Only a few images remained, and almost all of them were gone before long. Now the only thing left is the part relating to the worm.

At what I'll call the beginning of the dream, to show that it's quite a distance from the end, I was going into a room, probably a kitchen, though I can't be sure; I could only see part of it. On the floor was an enormous light-coloured wicker basket. There were a few objects inside it, a plate and something else; but most importantly, and this I did see very clearly and remember well, there was a big, fat worm, a greenish yellow in colour. It was disproportionately large – around one and a half feet long or more, and some four inches in diameter – which made it seem more like a toy worm, or a tacky decoration, but it was real. Someone had stabbed it, and the big knife, like the one I use to cut raw meat, was still buried in its body; the body had been cut in two, but not all the way. The part on the left was longer than the part on the right, and on either side of the knife you could see a circle of that sliced flesh, which was lighter in colour than the outside of the body. The worm was completely still, which made me think it was dead, and there was no blood or any kind of bodily fluid in sight that the wound could have secreted. The cut was clean, and what you might call dry. It was a disturbing sight, but I was busy with other things and couldn't hang about; somehow or other the dream went on and on, and a lot took place. Towards the end, I went back to that room, and I saw the sliced-up worm in exactly the same state as before. I felt upset again, and had a sense that this was the wrong way to go about things, that if someone wanted to cut a worm in half they should do it properly and not leave the job unfinished. Then I moved closer, leant over the worm and pushed the blade of the knife down hard. The worm was divided into two entirely separate pieces. At that moment, both pieces of worm started moving, as if the fact of still being joined by a small ligament had immobilised them, and on being cut in half they'd recovered their freedom. The two parts were moving in different directions, both apparently whole, healthy and normal.

When I woke up and remembered the dream, my first thought, of course, was about the castration complex. Then I realised there was another, more important theme, albeit still linked to castration. I saw clearly that this worm had been made up of me and Chl, that someone (Chl) had begun to cut it, to separate the two parts, but hadn't managed to finish the job, and that it was up to me to make the final cut and get us back our freedom. It's like being castrated, yes; more broadly, it's like being mutilated, or without the 'like': it is a mutilation. Necessary, however painful it might be. But in the dream there was no pain.

Now, yes, I am feeling a little pain, but most of all I'm worried: I didn't hear from Chl yesterday, Saturday, or today, Sunday (I know it's now Monday, but my Sunday hasn't finished yet). During the day I didn't feel the need to call her, and that attitude seemed to be in keeping with the separation shown in the dream; the dream, I thought, wasn't advising me to make that cut, but simply demonstrating that I'd already done it, or that I was doing it at that moment. But at 10.20 p.m. I started to worry, after returning home tired from a walk with E. There were no messages on my answerphone. Then I called Chl's house and left a message. At midnight on the dot, very worried indeed, I called her on her mobile; no answer. I called her house again and left another message; I could tell by the number of beeps that no one had listened to the previous one – although perhaps someone had heard me leaving it. In the new message, I asked her to call me as soon as she was able to talk. But she hasn't yet, and I know I won't hear anything until tomorrow now, or rather until this afternoon, when I wake up and call her work, and find out about the horrible things that have happened to her, or, more likely, hear a story I won't believe. But right now I just want to know she's alive and well.

# JUNE 2001

SATURDAY 16, 23:13

It's true that I got a bit distracted from checking up on Mónica (whom I've stupidly been calling M throughout this diary, just as I've been calling Inés N and Fernanda F, as if there were something sinful in my relationship with them that I needed to hide. There isn't; they just take me for walks) (it's different with Chl; there's nothing sinful in my relationship with her either, but it's an important romantic relationship, which she herself wisely decided not to make public). As I was saying, I got a bit distracted, not only from Mónica but from all people and things, with the exception of the computer. This is easy to see from the dates at the tops of the recent pages of this diary. Although I tried to get in touch with Mónica the day the reminder flashed up on my screen telling me it was time to check on her medication, and the day after, and the day after that, the very fact of not being able to contact her should have told me that something unusual was going on. I also dismissed the fact that the last time I did manage to speak to her and check up, I wasn't at all satisfied with what she told me. I thought she was lying, that perhaps she hadn't taken her medication for some days. You can tell; there's something different about her voice and her way of speaking. I said as much, and she assured me emphatically that no, she wasn't lying, that she'd taken her tablets on time and still had two left, and that she'd go to the doctor the next day to request a new prescription. I had no choice but to believe her, because what else could I have done? But that uneasy feeling was still there, under the surface, and it got worse when I couldn't get in touch with her during those days. Nevertheless, it stayed under the surface, and once again I find myself wondering what else I could have done.

Things carried on like that until last Thursday. Thursday is my day of work, the whole day taken up with two writing workshops. I woke up feeling confused, as usual, but this time even more so because I needed to get up earlier and had asked for wake-up calls from the phone company at 1 p.m., one thirty and two – which was in no way over the top, because only after the two o'clock call, knowing it was the last one, did I manage to drag myself out of bed and begin, slowly and laboriously, my working day. So slowly and so laboriously that when the first students rang the doorbell, at 4.30 p.m., I still had to make the finishing touches to my preparations (by cleaning my teeth, among other things). Not long before the doorbell went for the first time, I heard the telephone. I let the answerphone take it, and when I walked past as I was getting things ready I heard Mónica's voice and didn't stop to listen. She seemed to have a cold; she was speaking in a very small voice, with a noticeable lack of energy and what sounded like a blocked nose. It didn't occur to me that she'd been crying, and I didn't pick up; I thought she was just calling to tell me she wouldn't be at the workshop that evening because she'd come down with the flu. She didn't hang around waiting for me to pick up the phone the way she normally does, and I didn't pick it up. I heard a brief goodbye, and then she hung up.

Then, between 5 and 6 p.m., there was another call. I left my students briefly and went over to the answerphone, as usual, to see if it was a call I should take or if I could ignore it. As soon as I heard Mónica's first words I realised what was going on, and the hairs on the back of my neck stood on end. A monotonous voice, slurring the words the way drunk people do, and a faraway tone that was more like a murmur:

'. . . I want to ask you to please look after my files, don't let anyone else touch them, you'll know what to do with them . . . '

I lifted the receiver and said:

'No, I won't look after anything. Please, call someone.'

SATURDAY 16, 23:56

Written by hand.


'The one time I go to mass,' as my grandfather used to say on similar occasions, 'the priest shows up drunk.' Can you believe, reader, that after not touching this diary for so long, when I finally do sit down to write – *bang!* – a blackout? Who knows how much Word managed to save of what I'd written. I hope it was a lot, because the power didn't cut out from one millisecond to the next, but rather it progressively decreased, admittedly very quickly, but if Word was even slightly on the ball it would have realised things were going downhill and saved everything. It had about a second to act.

As usual, first I went to get the torch I keep on my bedside table. From there I went to the kitchen to turn off the fridge, and then back to my bedroom to turn on the heater – so that, as was explained to me once, its resistor would absorb the excess voltage that normally follows the return of the power, thereby saving the bulbs and motors. I peered through each window in turn, and the view was the same from all of them: solid blackness, in what looked like the whole city. I waited a while before lighting a candle, because there are few things I find more irritating than the power coming back just as I've fixed a candle in an ashtray. It feels more like a rude joke than anything else. I carried the candle to the bathroom and cleaned my teeth, mostly to get rid of the remains of the chocolate. Lately, especially since the worm dream, I've been greedily scoffing sugary things. There's barely a night when I don't eat a sweet, which goes against the habits of almost all my life. And sometimes chocolate, too, compulsively (in fact, everything I do, I do compulsively; I'm nothing but a bundle of compulsive behaviours. I don't have a single atom of will left). I gave the electricity a bit of time to come back, and in the end I got tired of waiting and lit two more candles. I was convinced the power would come back the moment I'd stuck the third candle in its ashtray, but no. This time there were no jokes. It seemed serious. I imagine people trapped, on a Saturday evening, in cinemas, theatres, dances, lifts, and the luckiest ones in brothels. Here's the power coming back now; I think I heard the beep of the answerphone.

## SUNDAY 17, 01:51

Word behaved very well; it saved almost all of what I'd been writing before the blackout. Now I'm writing in Word again. First I had a bit of a break; I was feeling a little jumpy after the blackout. I don't like to admit it, because it seems childish, but the truth is I get scared during blackouts. I don't realise at the time, but later I notice myself feeling on edge, more anxious than usual.

On Thursday, then, I told Mónica I wouldn't look after her writing or anything else of hers; that she should call someone right away, preferably her doctor, so they could go and help her; that I was working and couldn't do anything, and I didn't even know her address.

'No, no . . . I've locked the doors and I won't let anyone in. I mean it.'

And she began explaining that she had debts, that her brother had said bad things to her, he'd said this, that and the other, and she went on listing more and more arguments in order to crush me with their weight. Among the arguments was this one: 'And I thought you were annoyed because I stopped going for walks with you.'

'Mónica, please, call someone. You know these things pass and you'll laugh about it afterwards. Think of your daughter . . . '

This argument made me feel perfectly idiotic, because it's the first thing any old oaf would say, not taking all her drama into account and unjustifiably assuming the role of the superego. She went on talking, repeating her reasons, and I went on repeating mine, feeling worse and worse because I could see I wasn't going to convince her; she was waiting for someone to come to the rescue. Just like once before, in a similar, though much worse, situation some twenty-five years ago, she must have thought I wouldn't let her down. I was getting annoyed, though not with her, I realise, but with the thing that had possessed her; a repugnant thing, which made her voice sound vile, like the voice of a demon pretending to be a nice guy. There's something in people suffering from psychosis that's almost repellent in that way; something non-human, or extra-human, something like that archaic reptile, something saccharine and frightening, and the more saccharine it is the more frightening it is, and most of all, that: repellent. This wasn't my friend. I was getting annoyed and I told her I was going to hang up because she was only keeping me talking so time would pass and everything would become irreversible.

'I'm not listening any more,' I said. 'Call someone else.' And I hung up.

If I were a bit more robust I would have gone back to my students and carried on with the workshop as if nothing had happened, confident that on finding herself alone again she'd end up asking for help from her doctor or someone softer than me. But I was in a state of shock. My students, in the main room, were having a whale of a time. They're an exceptional group, and very close-knit despite the short time they've spent together. But I didn't realise how exceptional they were until what happened next.

I walked over to put a stop to the fun, with my arms stretched out in front of me and my palms facing forward, as if to push against a wall I was facing.

'Sorry for abandoning you all. I'm in a state of shock. A friend, and a student in the evening workshop, Mónica, who some of you know, has just taken something and I couldn't persuade her to call a doctor. I don't have her address and now I don't know what to do.'

Horror, frustration and powerlessness on my part. They leapt into action.

'Do you have her phone number?'

'Yes.'

'We need to call directory enquiries; they'll be able to give you the address.'

'I can't do anything right now,' I said, and flopped down into the reading armchair.

SUNDAY 17, 03:06

A witches' Sabbath. Legions of witches on brooms go whistling through the sky, borne along by the gale. I've never heard the wind whistle so piercingly; I don't know what's behind this phenomenon. I had to lower all the blinds and cover a gap in the kitchen window, because the draughts coming in under the doors meant the apartment was getting too cold and, what's more, some of the doors were slamming. I had to turn on the air conditioner, though to warm the place up rather than cool it down. A few days ago, during the late-summer heatwave, I had to use it to cool down. Not because I couldn't put up with the hot weather, but because they'd turned the heating on in the building. Doña Rosa, the caretaker, said she was following the landlady's orders. For me it meant a double expense. And why the landlady wants our veins to explode is a mystery to me.

As for the whistling wind, I have no choice but to listen to it because there's no way of blocking it out; both SODRE and Radio Clarín have stopped working. I know it's pointless even to consider other radio stations, but I still went through them to see what there was, and very few were working. The one that was working the most loudly and energetically was broadcasting a deranged sermon by some minister or guru or whatever you call them, from a sect; he was making his pronouncements in a mixture of languages, including Spanish, and it was very alarming. Clarín might come back, but SODRE definitely won't; its employees are public-sector workers.

Now I see where the blackout came from: this gale, which before arriving here was no doubt overturning posts (and roofs and trees and animals) in other parts of the country. The damage was dealt with very quickly, considering the prevailing conditions.


Returning to Thursday afternoon:

Various mobile phones were immediately produced, and each of their respective owners began a separate investigation; I didn't know what they were doing or how they were doing it. As I gradually came to, I tried to put my thoughts in order. I searched through my mind and found a few important details: for example, there was her friend Beatriz, whose mobile phone number I had because she'd been a student of mine last year (the 'private student' I think I've mentioned in this diary). I got up and from the shelf under the telephone produced a small clear plastic box filled with scraps of paper, all with telephone numbers on them, and then collapsed back down into the armchair and began looking through them slowly, one by one, over and over, without taking in what they said. Finally I found Beatriz's number. I got up again and went to the phone. I dialled, waited, but she didn't answer. I hung up and dialled the number again, carefully, in case I'd made a mistake the first time. No answer.

And I can't go on with this story, which has already been interrupted by a blackout and the subsequent work to recover the Word file. The urge has gone. To sum up: in the end I found the number for Daniel, Mónica's old boss, who answered the phone, listened carefully, and then said: 'Don't worry. I'll take care of everything.' Which is exactly what he did. And so the damsel was rescued once again from the jaws of the cursed dragon.

## SUNDAY 24, 03:45

Thursday, workshop day, was extremely cold, and I felt shaky when I got up, as if my blood pressure was too high. I tried several times to measure it with the electronic device, but it could be that the device is affected by the cold and only works properly between certain temperatures. At the same time, when my blood pressure is higher than usual, the device doesn't measure it right on the first attempt and generally corrects itself. But this time it didn't correct itself, and it said there was an error. At the beginning of the workshop, since I was still feeling fairly dizzy, I called my doctor. She thought for a bit and then told me to take another dose of antihypertensives, and that she'd call round, perhaps interrupting the workshop, to measure my blood pressure using her traditional device. To the second dose of antihypertensives I added a minuscule portion of Valium, and during the first workshop, perhaps because the work kept me entertained, I didn't feel so bad. But my doctor didn't come, and in the interval between the two classes I felt shaky again and called her. She'd received the news that an uncle of hers was in a serious condition, in an intensive care unit, and had to prioritise that. Later, not far off the early hours of the morning, she called to ask how I was feeling; I still wasn't very well, and she advised me to lie horizontally. She'd said the same thing before the second workshop, and I'd been able to obey the order for a good quarter of an hour; I left one very punctual student manning the door and relied on the others to be late, as usual. In the break I slept, and even dreamed.

That day I went to bed earlier than usual. I fell asleep with the heater on, because my bedroom is the coldest room in the apartment. The next day, Friday, I was feeling shaky again when I woke up, and the electronic device was still showing an error message. In the evening I was due to see some ex-students, to discuss a publishing project of mine, which, fortunately, they've taken charge of. My doctor promised to call in and interrupt that meeting, but once again she didn't turn up. I think this time she just forgot, what with all the other things on her mind. I called her after the meeting and in the end she came, quite late, accompanied as always by her dog, Mendieta.

Mendieta is a very strange dog. I think I've already talked about him in this diary, and how he's traumatised by the education he was subjected to by a brutal dog-trainer. We treat one another with mutual respect, keeping our distance. I'm a little afraid of him, because you never know when he might bite; he's bitten people before, though not me. My doctor arrived in a hurry, taking the blood-pressure monitor out of a nylon bag and telling me to remove my jacket. I removed it and threw it onto a little armchair in the living room, and then went to sit in my reading armchair. She put the sleeve around my arm and started to inflate it. Just then, Mendieta the dog, who was standing between the two rooms, looking sideways at the window from some distance away, began to growl. The fur on his neck was standing on end and he even seemed to be shrinking back, as if someone were threatening him. Then he got braver and started barking desperately. It looked like he was barking at something he could see on the balcony. My doctor told me afterwards that at that moment the measuring device leapt to above the maximum of 20. The final reading was 18. Very high indeed, but it made sense considering the damn dog had given me such a fright. We went to have a look and there was no one on the balcony. If the cat had been there, I would have seen it through the window near my reading armchair, walking along the railings. I couldn't think what the dog had seen, but it left me feeling a bit nervous. I lowered the blind all the way. And the other blinds, too, while I was at it, because not only did that keep out all mysterious dangers, but it also kept out the cold; or at least it was another defence against the cold.

The doctor gave me some samples of a new kind of medication and told me to take half a tablet right away, warning me that it contained a diuretic. The diuretic kept me busy until six in the morning, at which point I was able to go to bed with a relatively easy mind, but I put a plastic container by the bed just in case. I didn't need to use it; just once I woke up needing to pee, but I went to the bathroom because I wasn't cold. In fact, I was hot, what with the heater, the duvet, the blanket and the hot-water bottle.

But long before I went to bed, and shortly after my doctor had left, I looked for my jacket to put on and saw I'd left it draped over that little armchair. Then it occurred to me that perhaps Mendieta the dog had been barking at that shape, because the little armchair is the one he uses every time my doctor brings him for a visit; he likes to scratch it with his claws, walk around it a few times and then go to sleep in it. That night, since it was quite late, the dog was obviously tired and wanted to use the armchair; the shape of the jacket must have disconcerted him, making him feel his position had been usurped by some strange unrecognisable thing, and so he started to growl and bark. It's the best explanation I've found; I'm not entirely convinced by it, but it's better than nothing.


A few weeks ago, I noticed there seem to be some white bones showing in the pigeon's corpse on the flat roof next door. I'm too far away to see if there definitely are, or if it's an optical illusion created by the ruffled white feathers. But what I can see appears to be shaped like the skeleton of a bird.

I haven't seen the widow again, or I don't know if I have. To be honest, I don't look out of the window much, and it's always quite dark outside, because of the cloudy sky and how late it is when I get up. These are the shortest days of the year, and it's ages since I last saw the sun. I have, however, seen a number of different pigeons, almost all of whom have a touch of the widow about them. I suppose those children of hers are all grown up by now, and returning to the places they knew in their youth. But it's odd: most of the birds who land on the railings of the flat roof next door look so much like the widow that it takes careful analysis to decide whether or not they're her. With some, I can't make up my mind.

# AUGUST 2001

Above this is a heading that refers to time (the date, the hour), but time has lost almost all meaning for me. I can say 'some time ago', but I'm not at all sure how much time the 'some' might cover: weeks, yes, but perhaps even months. Well, whatever it means, some time ago these words appeared in my head: 'The never-ending small hours', and I thought they should be the title of this book. It's a bit of a pretentious title, and far too poetic; but that's how the words came out, and those words seem very accurate, very true, very fitting and exact. A never-ending series of small hours is what my life is, and what it has been these past years – best not to ask how many.

Saying 'the small hours' isn't the same as saying 'night'; they look similar in the dark, but something about the small hours makes them ill-suited to life – perhaps the inexorable quality of the solitude of whoever is alone at that time. Especially if they're awake.

(Technically, the way to refer to the hours I mean is one, two and three in the morning – but it seems absurd to talk about the morning when the sky is completely black.)

Many things happened in that difficult-to-measure time, and many things are still happening, and I feel too lazy to go into them all one by one. I realise I'm not in a comfortable writing position; my hands are in the wrong place in relation to the keyboard, the angle isn't right; it's tiring me out and I'm making lots of mistakes. At least I've noticed; it's been happening all along, but I hadn't noticed until now. Perhaps my chair should be higher, although this chair is already very high, or perhaps the keyboard should be slightly lower, or perhaps I should lower the armrests on the chair, but that's impossible; they can go higher, but no lower than where they are now.

I just tried raising them a little, and in fact I think this is better, but I can't say I'm positively comfortable. Perhaps this business with my arm position is why I'm feeling too lazy to write, though I'm sure there's a whole host of other factors as well. Sometimes I think about writing and formulate things in my head, but I don't write them down.

On 30 June, the year of the grant ended. Seven days later, as expected, the Foundation sent the request for a report on my activities and spending. I tried to be completely truthful, but someone advised me not to be, especially because they were asking for a short, concise report. In the end I explained that the original project had become much more complicated, and much bigger, and I was still a long way from finishing it. It's true, but vague. Besides, they don't care; they just need me to take responsibility for the grant I received, to show the donors that they haven't thrown their money away. And I can assure them they haven't. On the contrary, I think they've made a stupendous investment.

THURSDAY 2, 03:18

A strange object next to the dead pigeon, seen by the rare light from the sun on a rare afternoon when the sun was shining, and when I was awake to see it — this object, as I was saying, turned out to be the pigeon's head; the skull, I mean. It makes sense, I suppose, but even so, I was amazed to see it was just a little round ball with a large beak-shaped protrusion, or indeed a beak. Without feathers or flesh, the head of a pigeon is almost all beak; the beak is enormous compared with the cranium. No wonder they're so stupid.

THE LUMINOUS NOVEL

# CHAPTER ONE

Fairly often, for some time now, an image has been occurring to me spontaneously in which I'm writing calmly with a pen and India ink on a sheet of very high-quality white paper. And now I'm doing just that, giving in to what seems to be a deep-seated desire, even though all my life I've tended to use a typewriter. Unfortunately, this image that springs itself upon me unannounced on an almost daily basis never includes the words of the text I'm presumably writing. At the same time, however, and completely independently of this image, I have a desire to write about certain experiences of mine. This would become something I've been describing to myself as a 'luminous novel', which is the counterpart to what I've been calling – again, only when I talk to myself – a 'dark novel'. That dark novel exists, though it's unfinished and perhaps unfinishable. I feel imprisoned by it, by its mood, by the shadowy images and even more shadowy emotions that have been pushing me to write it for the past couple of years. There are periods of weeks or months when I wake up almost every day with an over-whelming urge to destroy it. During other periods I forget about it completely. And now and then I reread it, think it sounds more or less acceptable and get ready to carry on with it. Sometimes I manage to work on it for a few days. Not long ago, I burnt the original manuscript.

The luminous novel, however, will never be a novel; I have no way of reshaping the real events in such a way that they become 'literature', any more than I can free them from a line of thinking – not necessarily a philosophy – that inevitably connects them to one other. Will it have to be an essay, then? I resist the idea (I resist the idea of writing an essay, and perhaps at the same time, unconsciously, I meant that I resist the idea, or ideas in general, and especially the possibility of ideas as the driving force of literature).

I look at the first page I've written and it seems acceptable, not because of what it says – which I haven't read – but because of its resemblance to the image that keeps coming back to me.

Initially, I tried to integrate the luminous novel into the dark novel. I thought it might just be possible. But now, before I've even written anything, I realise it's not. The luminous novel, whether it's a novel or something else entirely, needs to have a completely independent existence. Perhaps, I think now, the image has been returning to me again and again as a way of showing me just that. The image expresses something like the pleasure of writing; a pleasure which, I confess, I haven't felt in far too long (the dark novel has turned into something very like an obligation, though I don't have the faintest idea why I imposed it on myself – if I was the one who imposed it).

The most appropriate form for the luminous novel is, of course, autobiography. The most honest form, too. I can't make it a fully fledged autobiography, however, because it would almost certainly turn out to be the dullest book ever written: a succession of grey days stretching from my childhood until the present, plus those two or three sparks or lightning bolts or luminous moments that gave me the idea for the title. But on the other hand, the luminous moments, described in isolation, would be indistinguishable from a life-affirming article in *Selections from Reader's Digest*, and the thoughts that inevitably accompanied them would only make matters worse. This is the first time I've had a problem like this; in fact, I've never had any problem writing before. Normally, I either write, seized by inspiration and at a feverish pace that means I have to use a typewriter, or I don't write at all and that's that. Now I need to write (the dark novel) and I want to write (the luminous novel), but I don't know how to do it. My mischievous spirit, my lost soul, my familiar, or whatever you want to call it, which has always done the work for me, has run away. I'm alone with my duty and my desire. Left to my own devices, I realise I'm not a man of letters, or a writer, or even a hack. What's more, I need false teeth, two new pairs of glasses (to see close-up and to see far away) and a gallbladder operation. And I need to stop smoking, because of my emphysema. It wouldn't surprise me, then, if the *daemon* had moved into newer and more reliable accommodation elsewhere.

Life, for me, hasn't started at forty. Nor has it finished. For the most part I feel quite calm; sometimes – rarely – I'm happy; I don't believe in anything, and I'm filled with a deeply suspicious indifference towards almost everything, or indeed everything.

Perhaps the luminous novel is this thing that I started writing today, just now. Maybe these sheets of paper are a warm-up exercise. Maybe I'm just trying to bring the recurring image to life. I don't know. But it's quite possible that if I go on writing – as I usually do – with no plan, although this time I know very well what I want to say, things will start to take shape, to come together. I can feel the familiar taste of a literary adventure in my throat. This isn't a metaphor; it's a real taste, somewhere between bitter and sickly-sweet, which I vaguely associate with adrenaline.

I'll take that as confirmation, then, and start describing what I think was the beginning of my spiritual awakening – though nobody should expect religious sermons at this point; they'll come later. It all began with some ruminations prompted by a dog. Of course, a string of personal circumstances had already paved the way, and the less said about those the better. But I wonder what would have become of me had it not been for that anonymous dog, sniffing a tuft of grass with real relish one warm afternoon. He was obviously completely transported by his olfactory relish, and you could almost see the life pulsing through his tense little body. The way he was standing made him look partly like a hunter, although not entirely – this was a different kind of tension, with his ears drooping rather than pricked, and his tail too – and partly like someone in a trance. I didn't doubt for a moment that he was on the trail of a female dog. I'd be extremely disappointed to learn it was actually something else. But what sparked my ruminations – the first transcendental ruminations I'd ever had, and by this point I was twenty-five – was noticing that rather than following or sniffing out a trail, the dog seemed to be face to face with the object itself. I remembered reading somewhere that the sense of smell for dogs is similar to the sense of sight for humans. A dog will recognise its owners when it can smell them, even if it's been able to see them for a while – it sees them and recognises them but it's not quite sure, and it needs to smell them for confirmation.

And then I thought: if smell is for dogs what sight is for people, this dog is seeing the female herself and not just her trail. It's like when I spot someone approaching from a distance; in a way, that person is already here. They're the present, not the future – or a kind of present, at least.

This simple rumination – but the reader would have to have been in my place, under that sun and that sky, among the aromas of the trees and the beach, and with all the time in the world to do nothing in . . . Anyway, this simple rumination had a noticeable effect on the wiring – or, to be more up to date, on the chemistry – of my brain. It felt rather like a complicated series of cogs grinding into motion – not heavily, though, but lightly, ever so lightly. I felt the joy that follows an intimate discovery, and the fright, the fear, as if I'd just trespassed on some mysterious land that belonged to someone else, or opened a forbidden door. Not for nothing do I associate the taste of adrenaline with literature, although literature hadn't yet appeared; that soul, demon or spirit, or whatever it was, was still taking shape, and, one year later, it would begin to write.

I should make a brief digression here – within the long digression, you might say, of this handwritten exercise I've so cautiously embarked upon – to say that I became a writer not because it was my calling, but for complicated socio-politico-econo-psychological reasons. At this moment, for example, rather than writing, I'd like to be devising a computer game, making a film, playing some Bach on an organ in a historic (European) cathedral, or simply depositing my seed in a series of women's wombs, lined up one after the other as far as the eye can see. My relationship with literature is all I can allow myself; or, indeed, all I've been allowed – up to a point – by other people. To put it more plainly and more accurately, writing is cheaper and less dangerous, or more comfortable, for me. I'm lazy and cowardly, and poor to boot; I should therefore resign myself to writing, and even be thankful for it. End of brief digression.

I was talking about an open door, some machinery grinding into motion, and the combination of fear and delight that always accompanies forbidden things. Who, then, had forbidden me from thinking? I'll leave that question hanging for now, since the answer is the central theme of this luminous novel and I need to administer it carefully so as not to end up with an article or a polemical pamphlet instead of a book. Notice, by the way, that the *daemon* (the same one or a different one, I don't know) is with me again, leading me onwards by the hand as I write. Notice, too, that I'm writing freely, as freely as a man condemned to death (I'm probably somewhat exaggerating the risks of my imminent gallbladder operation, but an operation is an operation, and besides, exaggerating the risks is what gives me this precious freedom. This is the only way anyone should write, the only way anyone should live: knowing you won't have to answer for any of it, simply enjoying the moment; as freely as the condemned man smokes his last cigarette, with no thought for cancer or emphysema). I'm writing, then, the way I used to write; not expecting there to be any readers, let alone a critic to judge how my games turned out, and most of all without the defining weight of a literary reputation, that 'style' everyone's looking out for, which perhaps exists – but which I'd prefer not to know about, so I can set off once more on the adventure into the unknown.

So, we'd got as far as the unexplained existence of something that was forbidding me from thinking. Thinking in a particular direction, I mean; or not thinking and leaving the mind empty, so that another, autonomous and underlying kind of thought could emerge into the consciousness. For example, after that rumination about the dog and its sense of smell, and sight and its relationship with time, the idea came to me spontaneously – I don't remember if it was the same day, or afterwards – that the Earth wasn't Hell, as it's perfectly possible to believe, but rather Purgatory; that Hell was on Mars and Heaven was on Venus. I don't know if this is true, because later I came across the same idea in an occult publication (one of the lowbrow ones), which would suggest it's an unconscious idea that functions symbolically; in other words, a symbolic truth or reality. The 'thinking ban' would have been directed at that same symbolic reality, or at the reality of the soul, which needs to be expressed through symbols because it's part of a whole world of experiences that are unlike what we experience day to day. The rumination prompted by the dog's olfactory frissons, though in itself simple enough, or even stupid, is nevertheless a basic tenet of philosophical-scientific thought. That other spontaneous idea, about Purgatory, belongs to another path, another order of thinking; or, more precisely, to another mind that coexists with, or forms part of, our 'habitual' mind. All this happened to me long before I became aware of the current theories and experiments involving brain hemispheres, alpha waves, the hypothalamus, etc. What's more, knowing about all that wouldn't have helped with the experience itself – opening the door, the pleasure and fear – any more than it would have helped the researchers themselves, or any more than it helps me now, when I want to carry on down that path (and I can't!). A mistaken belief – the Earth as Purgatory – is worth more, in this field, than the most dazzling, proven scientific truth!

I've left literature behind and written a polemical pamphlet instead. Oh well: I realise what I've done, take a breath, resume (be patient with me, reader; I'm a baby bird testing its wings before its first flight, and my parents aren't here to guide and protect me).

As I resume the narrative, which so far has only described my encounter with that unidentified fateful dog, I notice a problem arising. It's similar to the problem of the recurring image I wanted to explore through this text, and which I only began to see as linked to the luminous novel when I came to write about it. Now, seemingly unrelatedly to the story of the dog and going against the linear progression of the plot, I find myself fixated on another image – a memory, this time – which I'll begin to describe purely out of a blind and completely unfounded faith that it will fit harmoniously into the luminous novel because it forms part of it, even if I don't know it yet. In other words, I have blind faith in the *daemon*. The memory I'm obsessed with relates to what I thought was a fairly unusual sexual experience, though of course it might be standard fare for other people. I need to be constantly aware of my own singularity, so I don't make a fool of myself by reinventing the wheel (just yesterday, in fact, at the age of forty-four, I shyly asked my optician how people normally read, i.e. with both eyes or just one. She said it's usually with both, which seemed implausible to me, and then she added that I only read with one because I'm short-sighted in my right eye and long-sighted in my left, and the glasses I use all the time are no good for reading.

I tell this brief anecdote to show why I've learnt to exercise caution when it comes to generalising about other people based on my own idiosyncrasies, and vice versa). (And while we're on the subject, I have no idea what my left eye gets up to when my right eye is busy reading.)

She (the protagonist of the sexual encounter I mentioned above, I mean; not my optician) was, and I imagine still is, what you'd call an old friend. One day, some years ago now, we ran into each other again and began a very casual relationship that was subject to the whims of fate. By which I mean that she used to come to my house when she was in the mood, although for the most part, in one of those curiosities of nature, it almost always coincided with my being in the mood myself. For a long time, though I couldn't say how long, she made me happy – and I suppose she was made happy in turn. We got on well, especially because we didn't see much of each other outside the bedroom, and when we talked, we tried as far as possible to avoid the topics we knew would lead to arguments. Until, one afternoon . . .

I hope the critics don't see that ellipsis as a childish attempt to build suspense; in fact, remembering what happened that afternoon made me begin to see how it relates to the luminous novel (this novel, the one I'm trying to write), although I still haven't come to the obsessive incident which involved the same woman, only a long time afterwards. The incident I'm working up to didn't happen on the afternoon I left in suspense just now; something else happened that afternoon, something subtler and therefore more difficult to describe. We made love listening to music, as usual, but the music that day turned out to be decisive in many ways. It was an album of beautiful Indian music, with some mind-altering qualities, as I discovered too late (for example, I once played it while a family I was friends with were visiting, and when one of the children heard the first few notes from the other room, where he was playing with his sisters, he came running in and threw himself down on the mattress I had on the floor at that time, especially for listening to music on, and began to do a kind of slow-motion gymnastics that looked a lot like yoga. It wasn't a short piece of music; it filled a whole side of the LP. The boy, who couldn't have been more than four or five – and not trained in yoga, let alone this kind of music – continued until the end in perfect concentration, and perfect coordination, to the unwavering astonishment of his parents and myself. When the piece of music finished, he sprang up and, as wordlessly as he'd come, ran out of the room to carry on playing with his sisters as if nothing had happened).

Well. Oh, how I'd love to call this woman by her name, and just look, reader, at why it's so hard for me to write this, and why I want so badly to avoid autobiographical material! I can't think of another name for her than her own; no other name suits her. I can't say anything here that isn't strictly true, because otherwise everything will come crashing down around me. Remember: I'm writing with the freedom of a man condemned to death – but even a condemned man, if he's a gentleman, doesn't stop being a gentleman for the sake of a freedom that would, in that case, be no freedom at all. There's no way I can name this woman, then, or mention so much as a single detail that might allow people to guess her identity. These prim protestations may seem a bit old-fashioned, since a simple sexual relationship, without the Church's blessing, isn't a scandal for anyone these days, perhaps not even for the Church, but it's important to understand that later I'll have to mention certain intimate details that nobody – I imagine – would want to see published. And this novel is going to be published, no doubt about it; this luminous novel by a writer who's trying to show, by means of it, that he isn't luminous and never has been.

That afternoon, then, the music wrought its mysterious effects on our psyches and we enjoyed a sexual experience that was unusually beautiful, unusually prolonged and unusually spiritual – I couldn't tell you how many times I reached over to move the needle on the record player back to the beginning of the track, and nor could I tell you much of what we said about it. That afternoon sparked plenty of conversation – between her and me, that is, and infused with a nostalgia that must have been nostalgia for a paradise lost. Because, and here I need to slip in a polemical aside, things like that are unrepeatable, and the spirit is never moved twice by the same lever. And the spirit never appears twice in the same way; for example, another spiritual encounter (and how unusual, how wretchedly scarce are these encounters between two spirits! An encounter with one's own spirit is memorable enough); another spiritual encounter, with another unnameable woman (a thousand times holy and blessed be her name, and her person), came about in almost exactly the opposite way to what I've just described. That one was the result of renunciation. I noticed one night that she was letting me have my way with her just to please me, but she wasn't enjoying it; that in fact she wanted to think about other things besides my unwelcome sexual advances, but, because of her saintly character, she couldn't say so. Anyway, I realised this of my own accord a second before what would undoubtedly have been another rape, and I set my jaw and repressed the urge and lay back next to her and took her hand. She smiled, immensely relieved, and nestled her head into my chest. Then it happened.

What I'm going to say next should be taken literally; it's not symbolic, it's not a way of saying something else, and it's not an attempt to be poetic. It's a fact, and anyone who doesn't believe me should please leave immediately and stop besmirching my text with their slippery gaze – and never, ever try reading one of my books again.

What happened, then, was that something began to emerge from us; something psychic, that is, though I don't know what 'psychic' means, and that thing, at the same time as being outside us, never stopped being inside us, although perhaps there wasn't strictly speaking an 'inside' and an 'outside'. You could also say that I felt an expansion of my self, as if I were taking up much more space (and time!), though my body was still taking up the same space as before and I was experiencing it all from my section of the bed. Something was moving outside us and within us, something that wasn't quite me or her but rather both of us, although not entirely, since a part of me needed to speak to a part of her to ask: 'Are you feeling it too?' and the part of her answered, with absolute calm and certainty, that she was. We didn't need to discuss it further, because I could feel without asking that we were intimately connected and knew everything, in some secret language, about one another. I could be more graphic and say that we had a child that night, not a child of the flesh but a child of the renunciation of the flesh – and now and then it makes me shiver to think that this being could still be alive, in its world, doing who knows what; however, I suspect it was an ephemeral being, more ephemeral than the loving I shared with this woman. (Not than my love for this woman; I said my 'loving', or rather, the spatial-sexual-temporal relationship.) We fell asleep aware of this thing, which in turn was aware of us. When we woke up the next day, it was gone.

I see the luminous novel is in motion; not at all the way I would have imagined, but in motion nonetheless. Strangely enough, of everything I've written about so far, I was only planning to write about the dog, and some other things I hope to cover later. These women, and the album of Indian music, didn't feature at all on my mental list of experiences I wanted to record as a kind of testimony before going under the knife (because you never know). And yet they're as significant, or more significant, than the things I had in mind. Thank you, *daemon*.

I'll return to the earlier woman, then, to the one in the obsessive memory; the one I keep trying to get to because I want to see if I can discover her essence, although, as you can see, she's already given me a great deal. But in fact, I've been putting off a small act of fairness for too long, because it's never seemed like the right time for it. It relates to another woman, although in this case there's no sex or romance involved. I don't mention her only out of fairness; the matter has its mysterious side as well, though it's not supernatural or difficult to explain. It's about the high-quality paper over which this pen filled with Indian ink is gliding. A girl I barely know, whom I've only spoken to once, found out a while ago through a mutual friend that I was in such dire economic straits that I didn't even have paper to write on. No one's shocked when I say I don't have anything to eat, and I try not to let it shock me either. But when I realised I didn't have any paper – which never happens – or any money to buy so much as a hundred sheets (which might seem like a lot to the reader, but it isn't; bear in mind that this delicate creature known as inspiration, or the demon, can be very demanding, and it would never let me begin writing something if there was the slightest chance I wouldn't be able to finish it – however long it was – on pieces of paper of the same size, shade of white and thickness). As I was saying, when I noticed that for the first time in sixteen years I didn't have any paper or any means of getting hold of some, I panicked. I'd hit rock bottom this time, I really had; the very depths of destitution.

Anyway, when this girl I barely knew got wind of the situation, she immediately and without hesitation stole a considerable amount of paper from the office where she worked and sent it to me. Admirable sensitivity; an incredible capacity for understanding. (If she'd sent money, my weak flesh would have made me buy food, pay the rent or something like that. Perhaps she couldn't send money, and was only able to help me with what she had to hand, even though it wasn't hers. But I'm sure anyone but her would have done anything but that, which was the best possible thing to do. Because those sheets of paper went far beyond just meeting a need: they made me feel that my writing was more important than I am myself, which, independently of the objective value of my writing, is true. Because whether it's good, average or bad, it transcends me.)

That paper remained untouched, by me, until I began writing this. At one point I gave some of it to a friend of mine who draws, thinking he'd get more use out of it than I would, since it's excellent paper for drawing on, and for writing any paper will do. In fact, until I began writing this, I hadn't felt equal to the quality of this paper; even when I started using it, it wasn't without guilt or misgivings, but simply to match that recurring image. I knew, in some shadowy way, that if I didn't write with Indian ink on this very paper, I'd never write again. Thank you, paper-stealing girl. I can't name you either, but I hope that your theft – along with your other sins, if you have any – has gone unremarked, and that your life is a bed of roses.

I'll return to the story of woman A (to keep things orderly). That afternoon of magical sex had truly disastrous consequences. If there was one thing we couldn't allow ourselves, neither she nor I, each for different reasons which unfortunately I can't explain here, it was having a child. And we didn't have one; that's the tragic part, because there was an abortion involved, which still weighs on me now, though I know God has forgiven it. She's perhaps the person who managed to permeate my soul the most deeply, and who knows more precisely than anyone else the extent of my fragility. In various ways – and preferably by means of silence – she was able to keep me safe from a number of different dangers. It seems almost incredible to me, when I compare this woman to others of her gender, that she never took advantage of this knowledge of hers to compete with me, humiliate me or try to reform me. She accepted me just as I was, and no doubt sensed that any change she attempted to impose, however positive, would mean losing a part of me she thought was important. Anyway, the fact remains that I found out about her abortion when it had already happened. And she mentioned it to me as if in passing, at a bus stop, I think only to explain why she hadn't wanted to sleep with me that afternoon.

When all this happened, I was going through one of my frequent and prolonged depressive crises. At the other end of the scale from the experiences I want to include in this luminous novel is the image I still have of us at the bus stop, on what was probably a chilly autumnal afternoon. I remember my voice, struggling to emerge from the depths of an immense fatigue; I remember my stiff muscles, my clenched jaw, how I couldn't move my head on my neck, how I wanted to sleep for the whole of autumn and winter. I remember feeling fully aware of how utterly powerless I was, and the alarm that ran through my body, adding a moral panic to my depression. Even though it had already happened, hearing about it did me a great deal of harm – or good, I don't know, because without it I might not have realised how seriously ill I was.

We're getting closer, then, to the image that so obsessed me. Woman A disappeared for a while, after that scene at the bus stop. Here, my sense of time becomes completely distorted. I don't know when exactly she returned to bring me God's forgiveness and free me from my guilt. But return she did, one afternoon, to tell me there was milk in her breasts; and she let me drink, and then she left again, this time intending not to come back.

I'd discovered some time ago – long after the business with the dog, and long before woman A – that my depressions corresponded to punishments for certain misdeeds. I'd developed a whole theory about it, and the theory helped me through the crises. I'm not saying it was true; I'm just saying it worked. In simple terms, the theory said that God holds people prisoner within their own selves. You're still free to come and go and stay alive by whatever means you choose, but you remain a prisoner in the area – so to speak – where you made the mistake. In this case, my mistake had been sexual; as a result, I had to serve my punishment, secretly, depriving myself of the pleasure of sex, and even of women's affection. I had an intimate, though vague, sense of how long my punishment would last. And after going through enough of these crises, I learnt to accept them. Trying to swim against the current was the worst thing I could do, because not only would I not escape the punishment, but my life would also start to fall apart all over the place. When I accepted things, everything went on as well as could be expected considering my depression (which, thanks to my trick of acceptance, usually turned into a melancholic state that was almost pleasant) ('Transform Your Depression into Melancholia Through Acceptance and Get Your Life Back!' my *Reader's Digest* article could be called).

In these states, then, I waited peacefully – or tried to, battling my own impatience – for the end of the punishment. I came to see that at particularly difficult moments, when life became quite unbearable – I don't know how to explain it; the pain isn't physical, though it's not dissimilar to being bitten by dogs, constantly, day and night – I had to wait, in that trance, for a sign from God. The sign could take the form of any strange, spontaneous and somehow satisfying occurrence (I'm in two minds, for example, about the time a pigeon flew in through the window; it wasn't satisfying, though it's a classic image of the Holy Spirit and it was certainly a strange occurrence) (there are other signs, however, that I'm quite sure about, such as one involving a bunch of grapes, which I'll explain about later).

That afternoon, as I drank from those breasts, I felt that God was granting me forgiveness and the end of the punishment was near. I'd like to say I was right, but since I want this to be an honest account and not a polemical pamphlet, I should confess that I don't have a clue what happened afterwards. My depression could have gone on for a few more days or a few more months. I suspect it was just a few days, because otherwise I'd have lost confidence in my theory, faced with empirical proof of its failure. But I don't remember anything, so I'll leave it at that.

We haven't yet reached the obsessive image involving woman A. I'm still on the unavoidable preamble, but little by little, and in accordance with the plans of the *daemon* guiding my hand, we're getting there. I can't hide, even from myself, the fact that something significant is holding me back from writing about that event (the relevance of which to this luminous novel I'm still not sure of), but since the image goes on returning to me obsessively day after day, it must have its reasons, and who knows how I'll end up getting on to it in the end. It's annoying, too, to have accidentally built up all this suspense about a scene that appears to bear no relation whatsoever to the theme of the novel. All I can do now – especially now, when it seems the *daemon* has abandoned me – is define my ideas about this theme a little more clearly. Just now I reread part of what I've written so far, and in the passage describing the 'birth' of that ephemeral child not of the flesh, the product of renunciation (a scene involving the woman I'll call B, in the interests of simplicity), I noticed I hadn't used the convenient word 'dimension' – perhaps because it's already been used too much and in many different ways in discussions of these matters. However, if I said that as I was seeing myself in that strange way I had 'another dimension', it might be easier to understand what I meant. I wouldn't presume to talk about a fourth, let alone a fifth, dimension (the fourth dimension had its moment in the sun, before being replaced by the fifth), and I have to admit that I understand very little of the whole argument about whether time is the fourth dimension (of space, according to some; others disagree). Nor were there any noteworthy phenomena while I was seeing myself in that way – which there have been on other occasions, generally accompanied by something fairly objective that's made me all the more aware of the supernatural nature of the phenomenon. However, I think it might help people to understand what I felt (I don't want to say 'what we felt', though I know woman B felt the same thing) if I say that at that moment I felt whole, as if we were beings of more than three dimensions who had been restricted to seeing things only in three, and then, suddenly, a barrier was lifted and we saw what was really there. Alternatively: like suddenly looking at a photograph through special glasses and seeing the same image, only in relief. Or alternatively: like looking at the Velázquez painting *Las Meninas* in a mirror.

But here I encounter another problem, which I very much foresaw when I wrote about what happened with my optician: could it be that the way I usually perceive reality is different, and that if for an instant I perceive things normally, the way other people do all the time, it seems magical to me? I can't dismiss this possibility, though if it were true, I'd be very sad to have to admit that I've lived all my life under a grave misapprehension. I ought to dismiss this possibility for the moment, so my novel doesn't fall to pieces. Perhaps I should never have started writing without the *daemon*. I feel deeply perplexed and vulnerable, with nothing to hold onto; I'm alone, there's no one to ask and I don't think I could even formulate the right question. I've lost confidence in what I'm writing, and I've lost confidence in myself. I'd better stop here, then, and wait for the *daemon* to return.

# CHAPTER TWO

It's pointless. I can't go on with this novel. I woke up today in a terrible rage, eyes bloodshot, fingers trembling with the desire to rip the two copies and the original of the first chapter to shreds. Not because I think what I've written so far is definitively and irredeemably awful, but because I feel certain I won't be able to continue it:

A) Because I'm too young to work on autobiographical material; much as I feel like a total wreck, physically and mentally, morally and spiritually, and will soon have to face, naked, defenceless and with my senses dulled, the surgeon's knife, I am, objectively speaking, a young man – young when it comes to writing something like this, anyway. I should wait at least another thirty years. This sort of text should be written when most people you know have died, or at least deteriorated enough that they either don't understand what you've written, don't recognise themselves in it, recognise themselves but don't feel hurt, or simply don't realise that anyone has written anything at all.

B) Because although I think I'm too young for this sort of work, I'm old enough to forget a lot of things or get them mixed up; for example, the story about the dog that I told so enthusiastically is riddled with errors and accidental lies: it didn't happen in the period I said it did (a year before the *daemon* began to write) but rather a year later, or so I believe; in fact, what I did was mix up the story about the dog with a story about a little girl with green eyes. It's understandable, from a profound, psychological perspective, because both stories had a similar effect on me; but even so, when it comes to reporting the facts, I'm crap.

C) Because, sneaking a peek at the topics I'll have to cover almost immediately if I carry on writing, I realise I can't go on dodging certain ideological positions – positions that would very much annoy some powerful groups: the government, the opposition, the far left, the left, the centre, the right, the far right, and even that anonymous floating mass which appears in keys to surveys as 'undecided' or 'don't know/no response'. They would probably also annoy the Catholic Church, the Masons, the Mormons, the Jehovah's Witnesses, Christian Science, the various occult sects, the Rotary Clubs and the Lions Clubs, and most likely a few social clubs, sports clubs and boules clubs.

D) Because I can't accept my narcissism as brazenly as all that; the whole of the first chapter is nothing but I, my, me, myself, and there's no reason to think that will change as I carry on.

E) Because, and this is the most important point, I know it's a hopeless task; that it will be unpublishable, not only because no publisher will be interested in it, but because I myself will keep it jealously hidden.

Well then: it's a pointless task, and that's exactly why I need to do it. I'm sick of going after things that have points; for too long now I've been cut off from my own spirituality, hemmed in by the demands of this world, and only pointless things, only indifferent things, can give me the freedom I need in order to get back in touch with what I honestly believe is the essence of life, its ultimate meaning, its first and last reason for being. There's one problem: when I do something pointless, I feel guilty, and everyone around me – family and friends – actively colludes to make me feel that way. If I want to continue, I need to be prepared to stand firm against the ghost of that guilt, to attack it on its own turf and beat it to a pulp, armed with nothing more than the wavering conviction that I am entitled to write.

With that matter decided, I'll begin the chapter proper by correcting a few mistakes and filling in some gaps in the previous chapter. First of all: due to the pressing demands of the plot, there was never a good moment to pause and explain that I was no longer writing with Indian ink on very high-quality paper. The time came when, exhausted from reading my own handwriting, I realised I needed to type it all up, and as I did, I made a few corrections, cut some things out and added others in, and then carried on using the typewriter for the final sections. In doing so, I understood why I'd begun writing by hand, which will be revealed later on if I can find a way of doing so without upsetting certain sensibilities. And now, without further ado, I must tell the story of the little girl with green eyes. It's very simple.

I was on a bicycle, not far from the place where, one year later, I was to encounter that fateful dog. Back then, though this may be hard to believe, I used to get up at seven every morning and go out on a bicycle to deliver newspapers. Even in the cold, wind and rain. And I did it for free; I didn't earn a cent. I did it for the same reason I'm writing this now: because it fit with my way of thinking. It's just that I used to think in a very different way to now. It's unfortunate that my current mindset doesn't include an urge to get up at dawn or do any healthy exercise on a bicycle; it's unfortunate that the will to do something can only be developed under the weight of a mistaken belief – as History has made very clear. But I mustn't get carried away by these reflections, or begin explaining how I thought then and how I think now; I have a duty to those green eyes, those enchaining, burning, liberating eyes. The girl, who was very young, was sitting on a fence (it must really have been a wall, since fences aren't very comfortable to sit on, but I remember it as a fence), and there were other people nearby. I got off my bicycle, walked across some grass or down a dirt path, and delivered the newspaper. I don't remember which of the people who lived there I delivered it to. I know I saw the girl, and saw her very clearly, though I don't remember looking at her; it's possible to see things without looking at them and look at things without seeing them. I know I saw her because later I dreamed about her.

I've said there was something inside me that had banned me from thinking (in a particular direction), but I haven't mentioned another ban, which was related to that one but much more terrible: a ban on loving.

I'm getting into a terrible mess. There's no honest way of continuing this story without explaining exactly what my life had been like until that point, but nor is there any way of changing the subject or inter-rupting the narrative without everything falling to bits. What's more, I feel exhausted at the very thought of confronting all that again, even if it's only in my head. Perhaps, while I'm trying to process all this, I could permit myself a few lines on the problem of consciousness.

The way we normally perceive things means they fit easily enough into our daily routine. And yet if we paused to look at anything whatsoever as closely as anything whatsoever deserves, there could be no daily routine, there could be no social contract. Our perception is managed by our consciousness according to its tastes, and the narrower our consciousness, the duller our perception. Perception is a painful act; it's an act of surrender, of psychological disintegration. That's why we're careful about the focus and extent of it. We're blind because we don't want to see, and we don't want to see because we know, or think we know, that we don't have the strength to change everything.

It wasn't convenient for me, it wasn't convenient for my narrow consciousness, to perceive that girl. My eyes were meant to slide off her lovely surface. Perhaps I got as far as thinking: 'She's beautiful,' but that was all. At the same time, a teeming mass of other thoughts, which must at that moment have crashed against the doors of my consciousness, were barbarically suppressed. I returned to my bicycle and pedalled away, completely oblivious to the most important thing that had ever happened to me.

In the early hours of the next morning I woke up with a start, covered in sweat, my teeth chattering, as if I'd had a terrible nightmare. I switched on the lamp and lit a cigarette. I thought back over the dream I'd just had, and when I finally switched the light off and settled down to go back to sleep, I was a different person.

I'd dreamed about the eyes of that girl, nothing more; it was just the perception of what had happened a few short hours ago rising to the surface – it took a while, but it succeeded despite the ruthless system of censorship. Very simply: she had looked at me with love.

In the dream, her eyes seemed to accuse me of something; to pierce me, burn me, destroy me. But her gaze was still there, in spite of those tricks from the censors; the censors who must have woken me up, calling desperately on the resources of my clumsy waking state to put a stop to things. But her gaze was still there. There was nothing accusatory, or piercing, or burning, or destructive about it. There was only love, love that I wasn't ready to accept. Love, what's more, that wasn't necessarily aimed at me, although I was part of what she loved – which was probably everything in the world, because her capacity to love hadn't yet been destroyed. Until that moment I'd never seen love in anyone's eyes. Not even in films. They weren't the shining eyes of a girl in love, but a docile loving gaze. And the gaze was still there. And it was still there. And it is still there. And it's still here now, I promise you it's still living inside me, you glorious girl; it doesn't matter that I never saw you again, it doesn't matter if you've become a plump woman laden with children and your gaze has turned bovine. That girl is alive, I promise you, and she always will be, because there's a dimension of reality in which these things don't die; they don't die because they've never been born and nobody owns them and they're not subject to time and space. Love, the spirit, is an eternal breeze, fluttering down the empty tubes that we are. It's not your photograph I carry in my soul, featureless girl; it's your gaze, the very thing that was never yours, that was never you.

As I smoked that cigarette and waited for my pulse to slow down, I didn't know – I couldn't know – everything that was at stake at that moment. Had I known, I would probably have found the strength to repress, to suppress, the image of those eyes once and for all. Because at that moment the end of my marriage was secretly being decreed, along with my forthcoming marginalisation – to the very edge of society – and what many, including me, see as 'my madness'. Strangely enough, until that moment it hadn't occurred to anyone to say, or presumably to think, that I was mad. And yet I was absolutely out of my tree. My consciousness was narrower than the head of a pin. No one applauded when I ended my marriage, quit my job and began spending my time drifting around and doing 'strange things' – but I'm getting it wrong again: there was a rambunctious and brutally frank Galician man who congratulated me heartily, roaring with laughter, when he heard about my divorce; and I have him to thank for what little oxygen I was able to breathe during that long and difficult time. On the faces of everyone else I knew, both family and friends, was written blame, suspicion or pity, or a combination of all three.

Although I then went back to work, even fairly enthusiastically, albeit with a great deal of freedom and not much responsibility, it was only so I could make up for my isolation by purchasing culture, alcohol and prostitutes. The mention of alcohol, I hasten to add, shouldn't be taken too seriously; it was partly to impress people, most of all myself. I owe a lot to the films I saw during that time, however, and the books I read. As for the prostitutes, they deserve a chapter of their own. One of them does.

All this was decided imperceptibly while I was remembering the dream gaze and the real gaze, which were one and the same, and smoking a cigarette, and accepting that gaze. By the time I turned off the light to go back to sleep, I'd surrendered to it entirely. It extended over my whole being, opening up ever more avenues of sensitivity, preparing me for a new destiny. Afterwards, I did the right things. I didn't look for the girl; in fact, I forgot all about her for a while, and even when I did remember her, it never occurred to me to go looking for her. Certainly not. I did all the right things. I had to destroy everything I'd been, thought, believed and felt. I had to get rid of every trace of that delirious life I'd been dragging along like a clumsy worm behind me for the past twenty-five years. I didn't do it consciously, deliberately; I should have done. Accustomed as I was to my narrow consciousness, I carried on within its limits; but that gaze had injected me with the dimension of love, which everyone knows works of its own accord. My narrow consciousness fought back against the dimension of love; it shouldn't have done. The battle was lost – or rather won – because God didn't allow that dream to go unnoticed. STOP RIGHT THERE! DO YOU EXPECT US TO BELIEVE YOU'RE GOING TO TELL US ABOUT LUMINOUS, MYSTICAL, SPIRITUAL EXPERIENCES, WHEN YOU'VE TALKED ABOUT NOTHING BUT WOMEN, DESTRUCTION, ALCOHOL AND PROSTITUTES? ALL THAT'S MISSING IS DRUGS! GO ON, MINIONS, TAKE THIS MISERABLE WRETCH AND THROW HIM INTO THE MOST PESTILENT DUNGEON! Little old ladies in dark-green shawls are whacking me on the head with their umbrellas. You can hear the beating of a drum. A multitude of mothers with their children in their arms, their eyes full of tears, silently mouth the letters of a curse. The pyre is ready. While my body burns in resignation, I think: 'They weren't patient enough, they weren't curious enough. If only they'd carried on reading . . . ' And I raise my eyes to the heavens, wanting to exclaim piously: 'Forgive them, oh Lord, for they know not what they do,' but a final flicker of consciousness makes me shout instead: 'The bastards! The fucking bastards!'

Excuse this digression, reader; a trivial matter I had to debate with my superego. Now I'm back in the novel. A little agitated and confused, yes, but I think triumphant. Don't forget that in order to survive over the past few years, it's been necessary to look like everyone else, and even – as far as possible – to think like them. So much inner work, destroyed! So much subtle development, demolished! But I'm with you now, although I need to make one small concession to the superego:

Young people, listen closely: there's nothing good about alcohol, cigarettes, prostitutes, pornography or drugs. They destroy you, body and mind. Don't think for a second they could be tools of liberation: on the contrary, they lead to dependency and alienation, they ruin you and, in the end, they kill you. My only tool of liberation was that loving gaze God sent me in the eyes of a woman; the rest of the story was nothing but one long mismatching of my means and my ends: ignorance; solitude; lack of support and affection; an enormous world which that gaze released within me and which I didn't know how to control. I had to destroy myself because I didn't know about the tools I could use to build myself up. It's not a fail-safe method. Don't try to follow in my footsteps. Besides, it was only one liberation, nothing definitive.

In case that wasn't clear – young people, listen once again: there's nothing good about television, newspapers, money, politics, religion and work. They destroy you, body and mind. Don't think for a second they could be tools of liberation: on the contrary, they lead to dependency and alienation, they ruin you and, in the end, they kill you.

Only your soul, young man, can show you the way. Wind it up, set it in motion, and let it be whatever God wants. The sublime, that dimension we never consider, that thing we're missing: it's nowhere and it might be anywhere; here today, there tomorrow, gone completely the day after, and in twenty years it'll be back again, or perhaps it won't; it all depends on the Grace of God – and how you're getting on with yourself. Once, perhaps by chance, Grace brushed against me in a church. I was thirty-six years old, and that experience, which I'll write about in due course, made me take Communion for the first time. Not even churches are off limits to the hand of God.

But I return urgently to the story of A, which I interrupted in the last chapter and absolutely must finish in this one, in order to make way for the rest of the novel, which, what with one thing and another, seems to be escaping from my clutches.

She came back. After a long time, maybe a year, or two, or three. But she came back. She wasn't the same any more. I could see other men had passed through her life, marking her in new ways. Other men, other problems, who knows – I know, in fact, but I'd better not go into it. I'm sure the abortion also played a part, and this was clear from her behaviour in bed: fearful, worried, never fully letting go; she didn't always reach orgasm, and afterwards, of course, she picked fights. She had begun to see flaws in me. We almost, almost ended up behaving like a married couple. I realised what was going on when, on one occasion, she actually pushed me out of her body, afraid of getting pregnant again. Then the day came when I decided to indulge her in one of her whims. It was something she brought up often, hesitantly but with a certain insistence over time. I attributed it to experiences she must have had with a different sort of man, and which I didn't, and don't, find very appealing. She wanted anal sex. Well, if she was that afraid of getting pregnant, I thought, I might as well agree; at least then, perhaps, she'd be able to let go and surrender to the experience. I was able to slide quickly and comfortably inside her; it was a tight squeeze, but not so much that I couldn't make the necessary movements back and forth. There was just a slight problem: three reasons for overexcitement on my part. Namely, the aforementioned extra tightness; the position; and, last but not least, the sadistic brute that's sometimes unleashed in these situations, the feeling of dominating someone completely, the desire to hurt them and make them suffer, mixed with the perverse frisson of transgression, the mockery of nature. In short, I soon realised I was on the brink of an orgasm I couldn't contain, and that if I tried to hold it in through some kind of mental gymnastics, the overexcitement might actually make me beat her to death. I thought it had all been a terrible failure because it was over so quickly. However . . . as soon as the first drop of semen hit her mucous membranes, she was seized by the most extraordinary orgasm imaginable. All the muscles in her body began to shudder as if they were plugged into the mains, subsumed in wave after uncontainable wave, the waves of many turbulent oceans, layer upon layer; and before the electric current had left her body, another jet of sperm set off the exact same effect, with no reduction in voltage, and you could feel the waves colliding as they came and went, those on the way back violently colliding with those just setting out, and all the muscles in her body trembling uncontrollably under her skin, although her body remained perfectly still; like background music, her voice, which I always heard as if it were coming from deep inside me, modulated the deepest, longest amorous moans, full of subtle variations, with notes that rose from Hell itself, the moans of lost souls, up to the songs of birds on branches laden with fruit in the blazing sunshine, and, higher still, the sky a mass of angels with mandolins, intoning sublime canzonettas and canticles, and an orchestra conductor in an immaculate tailcoat with a rose in his lapel, indicating precisely when each voice should come in, each subtle variation, each sigh; and so it went on, until the final drop of sperm had been released; sperm which, I confess with pathetic amazement, had very rarely been put to such good use. Then the waves gradually subsided, and with them the voices, and in the end there was silence and stillness and, on my part, amazement and amazement.

I'm not sure if you can tell, but I've breathed life into a deranged monster that's now pursuing me relentlessly. Of course, of course there was a reason why I resisted and prevaricated so much before writing the first lines of this novel. The most ridiculous episodes of my life are all flooding into my head and they won't leave me alone; I can hardly eat or sleep, I wake up very late and go to bed when the sun's already risen; yesterday I saw serious signs that more biliary colic is on the way; and since even before starting to write, I've been in a constant flu-like state, which is obviously false: an excuse to waste all my time writing. I live for the novel; I think about it all the time; I write up neat versions of the drafts, making additions and cuts, and I think and think and think and think. My life has turned into a speech, an uninterrupted monologue completely beyond my control. I'm in thrall to the delirium, the search for catharsis, the demands of the work I must do, whether I like it or not, with the single vague hope of one day reaching a full stop and finding myself empty, exhausted, cleaned out – and ready for another. Because the point is that none of the luminous experiences and none of the liberating experiences have served to make me say 'Enough now', 'I've made it', 'That was the one'. What's more, although there was a time when I tried – and oh, how I tried – to reach something that would allow me to say 'Enough', 'I've made it', I'm now very aware that we only get to this point when we die, and I recoil from that even more than from the very demon itself. Readers, do not be deceived: I have no great wisdom to pass on, and I hope I never acquire any. The name of wisdom is: arteriosclerosis.

I chase after my thoughts, then, because they're demanding to be set down on paper, and that's the only method I can think of that's guaranteed to get rid of them.

Since I'm very meticulous about my work, the first thing I need to do on returning to it now is clarify something in the second chapter. It's easy to get carried away by the writing at the expense of the truth, or to tell only some of the facts, the ones you want to highlight – and all the more so when it comes to polemical literature like this. So you make countless mistakes and commit countless injustices and, as a result, almost without meaning to, you lead the reader astray. For example, when I read the scene involving the green-eyed girl, I realised I'd written it in such a way that no one would understand it properly. My description of the gaze and its after-effects made it sound reminiscent of certain religious paintings, and the gazes of certain virgins, or apostles or saints. That was certainly part of it, but there was something else as well: sex, desire, sensuality and the physical realm. In other words, the unknown dimension doesn't override the usual dimensions; it completes them. Nothing could be more misleading than the false dichotomy between spirit and matter, which we've had so forcefully pressed upon us. I'll come back to this later, adding a detail that I think should be far more widely known, which involves the number four, the Virgin and the Devil, and is drawn from the work of a distinguished thinker. Now I'd like to explain a bit more about the problems I have with what I call 'dimension'.

Philosophers, scientists, occultists and writers have all given considerable thought to the 'fourth dimension'. Some say this fourth dimension is time; others say that the dimension of time could never be incorporated into space; others still talk about the 'fifth dimension'; and in mathematics, you can end up at infinite dimensions as easily as you can at any other kind of infinity. I understand very little of all this, and when I talk about the 'unknown dimension', for want of more precise terms, I mean something that's part of the natural existence of things, but is only revealed when something special happens deep within us. I don't know of anything that can be done voluntarily to reach this state. There is, however, a certain kind of perception, which has an affinity with the luminous experience, though it's not exactly what I'd call a luminous experience itself, and which supports the theory that time is the fourth dimension of space. I've only experienced it when I've had a need for close communication with someone. On those occasions, what would happen is that I'd begin to see variations of that person's face; generally the face would alter as if it were going back in time, and instead of seeing before me a woman of forty, for example, I'd see a girl of six. Rarely, I managed to confirm that my perception was accurate, that it matched reality, either through photos or through some particular detail – if the person wore her hair in plaits when she was a girl, if she was chubby, etc. Less often, I actually saw the whole spectrum of ages, all the way to the person's maturity, or even old age. I know, in my heart of hearts, that a certain very young girl I met a few years ago is on the way to becoming a plump, stocky matron. And some confirmations or assurances about the truth of these perceptions have come indirectly, since, along with the image from the past or the future, I'm always given an intimate detail about the person; generally something medical, since I'm a frustrated doctor. A painting by Velázquez, *Venus at Her Mirror*, has also given me much food for thought: if you look closely, you can see the temporal variations in her face reflected one after another in the oval mirror; including the open eyes, which suddenly close. Youth, age and death. It's occurred to me that Velázquez must have experienced this kind of perception himself. And don't ask me how he managed to produce a painting that moves.

This allows for the possibility of seeing time as the fourth dimension – not necessarily of space, but certainly of life. The perception I describe has never worked for me with inanimate objects (and to tell the truth, only very rarely with men), but I wouldn't want to say it's impossible. [Revising this in 2002, I notice my memory was deceiving me when I wrote that. There was in fact an extraordinary incident of this sort involving inanimate objects in 1968.] However, based on my experiences alone, I'd say I have a strong sense that human beings are four-dimensional and that, whatever happens, each one of us is a single object, whole and complete, containing its own birth and death; that we see ourselves grow and age because we only see a bit at a time, but that the old person and the child are present in the same being all along. We're like a kind of sausage going by behind a slot, and all we can see of this sausage is what the slot allows. There are countless people who, presumably after similar experiences, think the same way as me, or more or less the same. But I wouldn't bet my life on this way of thinking, and since it doesn't seem to have any practical purpose for the time being, and since for the time being anything without a practical purpose is highly dangerous to a person's sub-existence, I've simply stopped having these perceptions. But take note: since I stopped having these perceptions, and all other perceptions and intuitions of the 'unknown dimension', my depressions have been getting worse, and lasting longer.

Since I've mentioned the girl who's turning into a plump, stocky matron, I should add that she has an important place in this torrent of thoughts that's been unleashed within me. Not in relation to my perceptions, which I only just remembered about, but in relation to the desperate need many people have for a madman. When all else fails, when you've lost your way and feel that nothing and no one can help you, find a madman. I'm unlikely to be remembered as a writer, though for a time I might appear in critical analyses of the period, for reasons, I suspect, of emergency or scarcity. But I'm sure I'll be remembered for a good long while by the people who knew me, and the one thing they'll remember me for is being mad. In other words, my true social function is madness.

Supporting evidence: all kinds of people have come to me for advice on their personal problems, especially 'educated' people – doctors, notaries, psychologists, psychoanalysts, orthodontists and, of course, artists. In fact, it was a psychoanalyst who helped me to understand this mysterious tide which, ever since that rumination about the dog, has been flowing non-stop to my door: 'I come to you for advice on these problems,' he said, 'because you're mad. I couldn't talk about this with anyone else, especially not my friends.' Strangely enough, my daughter said something very similar not long ago. I hadn't found the right way of approaching her until then – until she needed a madman. 'I know you're mad,' she told me, and we've spoken easily and openly together ever since, which makes me very happy. (In parenthesis: this novel, which I promised her, is part of the answer to her questions. And the reader should know that I'm writing it with all the good faith and sense of responsibility of a father writing for his daughter. She needs to know these things so that her life is worth living.)

That girl, then (I mean the plump, stocky matron), showed up one day in the company of some mutual friend or other. I was at the very zenith of my madness. A few days later she reappeared, alone. Or not quite alone: accompanied by an enormous and very beautiful bouquet of roses, which I learnt much later she'd stolen from a park. Observe, reader, how tragically blinkered human consciousness can be: from that moment on, with absurd persistence, I set about trying to rape her. She always rebuffed me, and I'm not a fully fledged sex offender, so things never went too far and she kept, to what end I don't know, her precious hymen intact. Nor did I ever find out what she wanted, though now I have my suspicions. She came, and she sat in silence. Then she left, and, in spite of my shadowy intentions, she came back. Again and again. There's no point deploring my blinkered consciousness; to have avoided acting so stupidly, I'd have to have known then what I know now. This story is painful, unflattering, deeply embarrassing. She needed a madman, not a fool. And yet, and yet, I feel marginally better when I think that she must have found some of what she was looking for in me, since she came back. From time to time, she even brought a new bunch of flowers. Serious, quiet, intent, she always addressed me politely and formally, even while I was trying to remove her clothes. I think what she found in me in the end was laughter. I was quite taken aback when one day I heard her laugh for the first time; tinkling, crystalline peals of laughter. I think that must have cured her a little, because soon afterwards she disappeared.

A few years later, thanks to my reflections on this and other experiences, and above all to the psychotherapeutic help I received, I was able to embark on another acquaintance that was similar to this one in a way, though in other ways almost the complete opposite. I saw a girl, who was also very young, sitting at a table in a bar; she looked so depressed, so sad and alone, that I went into the bar and sat down opposite her. I tried to find out what was wrong, but she wouldn't say. Then I told her to keep me in mind, and to pay me a visit if she ever thought I'd come in useful. One afternoon, she came. And she began to spray me with all the pus that had been festering inside her. Few things have made me feel so ill, or been so painful, so difficult to take. The girl was playing at cynicism, relishing – it seemed – recounting each and every one of her perverse experiences, which included almost all the sexual perversions under the sun. I listened with an outward display of monastic passivity, while inside me, all my moral and emotional fibres trembled and contorted. Then she left. Very soon she came back again with another dose.

I knew that if I showed the slightest disapproval or ventured any sort of moral judgement, that little soul would be lost once and for all in the flames of its hell. What's more, I felt the need to act, to do or say something, though I didn't know what. I was desperate. I consulted a friend who used to be a priest. He said: 'You have to love her, really love her.' Which, incidentally, was what I'd been doing, but the advice reassured me and helped me persevere. Fortunately, my genitalia didn't get in the way. Through therapy, I'd dealt with much of my lack of confidence in my own virility, so I no longer felt the need to sleep with all the women I met. What's more, at that time I was well furnished with intellectual adventures and, what's even more, it was one of the periods when my relationship with A was active – and at the same time, a parallel relationship was developing with a woman who danced and played the castanets. I could give myself over, then, to the genuinely paternal love I needed to show to this 'lost sheep', as my priestly friend and I called the perverse girl. A difficult, harrowing love; the kind of love that requires you to give, give, give, give, give,

give, give until you're utterly drained, and receive nothing in return but those filthy darts of cynicism. One afternoon I suggested she lie next to me in bed. She looked at me with misgivings, but what she saw must have reassured her because she did as I suggested. We stayed there in silence for a long time. Then, spontaneously, she shifted to lie on top of my body – both of us dressed, motionless, silent. The feeling of peace at that moment was tangible; it descended and settled inside us, a peace I remember simply as the colour white filling the whole of my body. The genitals, the mind, the senses: everything seemed dead, and happily so. An impossible-to-measure time passed, then suddenly we felt the moment was over. We got up, and she kissed me on the mouth and then left. She came back another day and we did the same thing; we didn't need words any more. And she came back again. Every now and then she said something, the remains of some sin, some little piece of rubbish I was able to absorb perfectly calmly. One afternoon, during one of these strange sessions, something made me place my left hand on her waist and softly press down. Nothing more. As if I'd pushed a button on a machine, immediately and with no warning, the little sheep began to cry. She cried and cried, and then carried on crying and crying. An ancient, primitive sobbing I knew very well from my own experience. And the more she cried, the happier I felt. She was free at last.

The story should end here in order to be perfect, but nothing is perfect in this world, and there's almost always a less than elegant coda. Still, I've promised to tell the truth, and that's what I need to do. She came to see me one more time. By then I felt completely detached from her. My love had run out, the madman had fulfilled his purpose; what more could she want from me? The lying down didn't work, the peace didn't descend, we were tense and irritable. She said something I didn't like; I don't remember what. In response, I gave her a few resounding slaps on the rear end. She didn't like that much, either; it seemed I'd strayed from my role as an entirely benevolent, indulgent father. She glared at me furiously and shed some tears that were in no way proportionate to what minimal physical pain I could have caused her. The next thing I knew, she'd ripped off all her clothes and, in a voice brimming with spite and contempt, she told me to possess her.

I did so, very unwillingly; it was a real effort and I didn't enjoy it at all. Then she left, and that time she never came back. Years later I saw her in the street. Her face looked healthy and happy, and there was purity and maturity in her eyes. She told me she was doing very well; she was married and had children, and all those things that good therapeutic stories ought to end with. Sometimes I think what happened on the last visit came about simply because she felt a need to pay me for the therapy. Oedipus fulfilled, etc.? I don't deny it; but don't, reader, deny me that other dimension which I'm trying to shed light on by means of this work, and don't deny me the tangibility of that mysterious white peace that descended over our bodies and illuminated us from within.

# CHAPTER THREE

To reach that humble bunch of grapes, and for the grapes to be understood in their capacity as grapes and as something more, or a lot more, I need to make an effort to drag myself (again!) down the same winding, overgrown, treacherous – and sad – path I was dragging myself down at the time. I don't particularly want to. I've returned to the pen with Indian ink and the very high-quality paper – for reasons I won't reveal for the time being – and thrown away plenty of pages which I'd already typed up, but which, in my view, were only hindering the novel's development. I was sorry to do it, but it's time I started taking more control of the plot and the images. I don't think the second chapter was very well put together; there's a lot of ideological rubbish in it and very little substance. But I can't pause to revise it, because for days now I've been subsumed in this part of the story, the part that leads to the grapes, though I haven't had any time to write it. In all honesty, I want to get it over with as quickly as possible. The business with the grapes isn't so bad, but the rest – which I can't avoid, if I want these grapes to have the same significance for the reader as they did for me – is grubby, grey, depressing and even ridiculous. Although I feel fairly content about the role I was called upon to play with the sheep, I can't say the same for my role here. And yet, if I could condense my work into this one story, covering each and every detail of each and every one of its days and nights, the result would perhaps be worth it – because in spite of everything, it was a time rich in situations and characters. However, I would no longer be writing the luminous novel and would be writing a different one instead, with a very different centre of gravity. Here, I need to stick to the basic facts and leave a great deal out, committing many injustices in the process. Which is what always happens when you want to be efficient.

To reach the grapes, then, I need to go via G. Technically, G ought to be C, to keep to the alphabetical order I established in the first chapter. However, although they only appeared fleetingly, the plump, stocky matron and the sheep deserve to be C and D respectively, and I have internal organisational reasons to disregard E and F for now and call the woman I'm about to describe G. If I had to reduce my description of her to a single word, I'd say: goddess. G was a goddess. Imagine a goddess, reader, and you will have the spitting image of G – but with one proviso: this is the image I constructed upon the mystery of what she was really like as a woman. And I use the word 'mystery' because I still haven't fully absorbed the reality that was latent in the image, a reality that is perhaps very inferior, as I could well have understood a long time ago if I'd thought about it.

First sighting: tall, proud, shapely, with very black hair and a white dress; suave, elegant, warm and educated. Accompanied by a tall, proud, athletic, elegant and educated man. They came into the place where I worked, in the period following the episode with the green-eyed girl – the period of films, books, alcohol and prostitutes. We talked for a while, and after they left, my business partner and I fell silent, looking at the place where she'd stood. My business partner was having a mild attack of asthma. As the minutes went by, the invisible pedestal holding her aloft grew higher and higher without us noticing. After a while, my business partner and I dared to exchange a glance. Then we looked up and down but with our chins tilted a little to the right, somewhere between nodding and shaking our heads, our lower lips pushed slightly forward to simulate disappointment. What a shame, we were trying to say to each other, that a woman like that could never be ours. In the days that followed, we began to reminisce about her out loud. My business partner, who was very observant, or had an overactive imagination, always added some new detail I'd overlooked or forgotten: the tasteful patterning on her embossed belt, how well the strip of white wool peeping over the top of her dainty leather boots suited her, or the lock of jet-black hair nestling behind her left ear. And after a few more days we'd forgotten her, at least to a certain extent.

How can we say whether anything's good or bad for us? Are we capable of judging an ordinary event, sure of not being mistaken?

Because the course of the rest of this story was determined, indirectly, by my father – and to this day, after . . . many, many years, I don't know whether to curse him, as I cursed him then, or be thankful to him, as I was thankful then, alternately, switching back and forth between the two. What's more, I'm eligible for some cursing or thanking myself, since, as on other occasions, I could have chosen to do whatever I pleased; and yet, that time, I meekly complied with his verdict. What happened was that after my divorce I wanted to live alone, leading whatever life I chose to lead unobserved and at my own risk. I looked for an apartment, and found the most suitable one imaginable. The owner liked me and agreed to let me rent it – which was crucial, because he lived in the same building and wanted to choose who his neighbours would be. The drawback: as ever, the rent itself, which, whatever your budget, always turns out to be a little – or a lot – higher than you can afford. In that instance, I would have been able to pay it; and although things would have been a little tight at first, two or three months later the inflation that swept through the country would have made it quite manageable. Where is all this leading? It's leading to my father's impassioned opposition to my renting that apartment, and his threat not to give me any help with it whatsoever. He saw it as an unnecessary extravagance. I saw being alone as a matter of life and death. However, I lost my nerve and didn't rent it, instead renting from a friend a kind of, what do you call it, one of those spaces where you normally keep brooms and mops, for a quarter of what I would have paid for the apartment. In that space – which, needless to say, I could barely fit into even if I crouched – what I did was roll a mattress up during the day and keep it there, behind the closed door of said space whose name I don't know. At night, the rent I paid gave me the right to take that mattress out and unroll it onto the floor of a psychiatrist's consulting room (the space I rented was in a large house containing a medical clinic where my friend was the administrator; he lived there as well, with his family). At 8 a.m. my friend would come to wake me, sometimes with the help of a friendly kick or two, and I'd get up, fold the blankets, open the windows to air the room, roll up the mattress and put it, along with the blankets, in the space I was renting. Then I had a coffee next to the clinic and took a bus into the city centre. At nine, the psychiatrist arrived at his consulting room, i.e. my bedroom; at nine, I was raising the shutters of the shop where I worked.

And now there's an unexpected flash of 'luminous' lightning, which obliges me to turn away once again from the main story – if there still is a main story – though I can't let it escape me completely. I have no choice but to describe what happened one night, when I was sleeping on that very rubber mattress on the wooden floor of the consulting room. I was dreaming one of those slow, lumbering, confused dreams, with repetitive toing and froing and silly things getting in the way; the sort of dream it's impossible to remember in detail, that lingers in the memory as something more like a map or a sound. Then the dream abruptly changed course, and I found myself making love to a woman who was just the outline of a woman. I couldn't see her face, but that wasn't a problem because I knew it was very ugly; her body was ugly as well, blackish and scrawny – obviously a concession through gritted teeth on the part of the miserly superego, after my sex drive won out and forced it to permit me a few crumbs of pleasure. And the next thing I know, *clack*, I'm fully awake and feeling the last moments of spontaneous ejaculation. The phenomenon known as 'nocturnal emission' wasn't something I experienced often, but nor was it entirely unfamiliar to me. This, however, was the first time it had been accompanied by that kind of perception. 'I' filled the whole room. Not my body, which I could feel pulsating with pleasure, though very calmly, on the mattress, infinitely savouring every microsecond of an orgasm that shook me with unusual force, that hit every one of my cells and resonated through my whole organism. 'I' – though I wasn't disconnected from my body, or seeing, as happens in experiences other people describe, my body from the outside; 'I' filled all the available space in the large room. I can't say any more than that. It was very like the experience of the 'spiritual son' with B, which happened some six years later; in this case, of course, there was nothing like a spiritual son, and no mutual contemplation – not even a strange exploration of anything. It was simply – simply! – the awareness of myself in all my true dimensions, or at least in one more dimension than I'm usually aware of. Curiously, I didn't feel at all afraid, or do anything to repress what I was feeling and 'return to myself'; everything was just fine as it was and then suddenly, *clack*, I went back to sleep.

In the years that followed I tried to repeat the experience, but to no avail. However much I arranged rubber mattresses on wooden floors and, occasionally, underwent the odd nocturnal emission, it never again led to that wondrous sensation – which did, however, return in different forms, and under different circumstances. 'The spirit is never moved twice by the same lever,' as I've said before, and will say again, 'and the spirit never shows itself twice in the same way.'

To return to the story of G: we'd got as far as me raising the shutters of the shop each day at 9 a.m. Well, early one morning, the goddess reappeared in the shop. I was by myself; my business partner used to come in the afternoons. She reappeared, strangely enough, at a height altogether more appropriate to my own, having swapped the heels she'd been wearing to match the athlete for others that were very much within reach of my five foot nine and three quarter inches. And what's more: she was no longer addressing me formally. And what's more: she asked me to get hold of some books for her, and gave me her phone number. And what's more – know, reader, that tears are stinging my eyes as I write this. And what's more: before she left, she told me she had separated from her husband.

What is there in these tears? I don't know. Perhaps pain, shame, self-pity, humiliation, longing. I don't know, I don't know. Please excuse me, reader; for years now I've been waiting in vain for some tears. Leave me by myself for a few moments, and then I'll carry on with the story.


I'll carry on, saying that my tears were all those things combined, and something else – the memory of having been very happy for a few hours, enormously happy, deliriously happy. They also reveal the chasm stretching between that age and the age I am now; I had mornings, I had work, salaries were high enough that people could buy a thing or two; I could have croissants and *café con leche* for breakfast, not only because of my purchasing power but also because of the digestive power I enjoyed back then. But what I feel most wistful

about, believe it or not, is my ignorance of how the world works –
because then (although *only* then and not before) I was about to begin
finding out. Do I know everything now? No; now I only know that
it's not worth knowing – 'how the world works', that is. You have
to know something so you don't go under, so you can haul yourself
more easily through the mud, so people don't necessarily *always* get
the better of you in *everything*; but what I mean is that knowledge
doesn't bring you any closer to what you need in order to make your
life better, or even to make you feel better. Does anyone know what
I'm talking about? Never mind. I know what I mean.

I got hold of the books she'd asked for – almost immediately, of
course. I telephoned her. She came. And it was all so easy that . . . She
hung around chatting until closing time. I lowered the shutters and
we talked some more, and all along I was thinking: 'She's going to
leave now', 'She'll leave any second', 'Why isn't she leaving?', 'Surely
she's going to leave'. I didn't know how to get rid of her. I asked if she
wanted to go for a walk and she said she did. We walked. We walked
some more. 'Now she's going to get on a bus. Surely now she'll leave.
She has to leave. Why isn't she leaving?' I realise the reader will be
wondering what kind of an idiot I am. Well, you'd be wondering a
lot more than that, I can assure you, and in a lot more detail, too, if
you'd seen those firm legs encased in black fishnet stockings, which
were so generously displayed when she sat down in the bookshop;
if you'd seen the look in her eye, if you'd felt her air of docile avail-
ability. Yes, reader; you have the right to think as you do. I thought
that way myself, and sometimes I still do, especially when I wake up
with liver trouble. But at the time, all I wanted was to be rid of her,
was for her to leave.

The trouble was that I'd put her on a pedestal, and I didn't know
how to take her down. Although really, I wouldn't have wanted to even
if I could. Really, I needed everything to go exactly the way it did.

Or did I? I don't know. I'd have to toss a coin. I don't know how
I wanted things to go. I can only describe what happened.

It happened that in those days I had a creative energy inside me
that was almost completely repressed. If I wrote something, I hid it
and quickly destroyed it – ever since my father, when I was a boy,

found a poem I'd written and made fun of me, informing me that poets were faggots, or at least that one of his colleagues had said they were. It happened that I went years and years without daring to express anything at all. It happens that even now, today, at this very moment, I'm ashamed of my writing and feel a desperate urge to destroy everything I do.

'That's OK,' the reader tells me. 'I understand. But what I don't understand is why the hell you're dumping all this rubbish in your novel rather than talking it through with your therapist. Stop messing me around,' the reader adds, 'and write something that's actually entertaining: images, not sob stories. Like those legs encased in black fishnet stockings.'

'Point taken,' I say, 'point taken. I, too, scrupulously avoid poems written by housewives, and all the sob stories and psychoanalytical material people want me to swallow as if it's literature. But wait a bit longer, be a little more patient and trust me. I promised you a bunch of grapes, and I can't get on to the grapes themselves without crossing this squalid, vulgar terrain.'

'Fine,' the reader responds. 'I'll give you half a page more to masturbate over your delayed adolescence; but I swear, if this goes on much longer I'm ditching this book. You see, I actually have a Chandler on my bedside table that . . . '

'OK, OK, let me do things my way, and stop interrupting. You're not the only one with better things to be doing; I myself have a Beckett on my bedside table . . . '

But my father wasn't a bad person; quite the opposite. He was a much better person than me. What I've just described was merely a slip-up, one of two or three such slip-ups of his, and who's never made a mistake? Anyway: I was trying to say that to me the whole world of culture, of the inner workings of culture, seemed magical, noble and out of my reach. I could read, but not write; listen, but not make music; gaze entranced at a painting, but not paint. And I had a strong artistic calling, just as I had a strong scientific calling, both of which were left undirected and, worse still, repressed from the outside even before they were repressed from within. And what happened, I think, is that I placed that whole world into that woman; I chose her, in the

unknown depths of my soul, as a symbol, but also as a lever or a catapult that could pull me from the shadowy bowels of repression and
propel me over the palisades into the world I so desired. If she turned
out, in practice, to be more like one of those butterflies that flutter
around the beds of intellectuals and the tables of *boliches* – and I think
she was, though I say that not out of disdain but based on my current
knowledge of 'how the world works', which I was talking about today;
if, after all, my goddess was, after all, nothing but a woman, and a
woman, after all, with, after all, a normal woman's needs and, after all,
if she was unable to see anything more in me than a potentially erect
phallus – after all, after all, after all, she's not to blame, and what is
to blame is my distorted understanding of the situation, i.e. what the
reader has just referred to very astutely as my 'delayed adolescence'.
At twenty-six, I'd relapsed into an adolescence which, what's more,
had been quite enough of an ado the first time around.

And we walked here and there, and we called in here and there,
and we went on walking and walking until eventually I managed to
tire her out and she suggested I accompany her home because it was
getting a bit late. Since I hadn't rented that apartment in the end, I had
a sudden hope that I might perhaps be able to join her in hers. It was all
very simple: I needed a suitable place to carry my love and adoration
for her down the paths my soul demanded; and it was inconceivable
that this goddess might sully her divine form by setting foot on the
tiles of a room rented by the hour, let alone sully her divine form
in between those sheets that smelled of freshly ironed sperm. Nor
could I lie her down on that cold rubber mattress on the floor of a
consulting room. In my hypothetical apartment, or rather in hers, I'd
have devised an approach that reconciled her cultural and intellectual
aspects with carnal pursuits. I should clarify, in my defence, that at
the time I wasn't short of carnal pursuits or by-the-hour hotel rooms,
even with shades of tenderness (I'll call the prostitute who deserves
her own chapter H, and I think the chapter she deserves is this one.
My journey with G can be left in suspense for a moment; the two of
us heading towards her apartment on that drab little night bus, with
all the men – and bear in mind the bus was quite full – looking at me
with hate and envy in their eyes. And before discussing H, since this is

the right moment to insert that little homage, I'll turn, for just a few lines, to a brief technical point: there will be Freudian readers – there always are – who would like to see the unfortunate consequences of an Oedipus complex in my story of romantic frustration with G. I'm not entirely against this, considering that my mother, at least within my family unit, was what you might call the cultural cutting-edge: she'd been to some talks, read some books and professed a respectful admiration for artistic expression in all its forms. The Freudians would say I acted the way I did because of the prohibition of incest, and the resulting threat of castration. I don't deny it, but they'll have to agree to let me tell the story my own way.

A diagnosis of sadism, however, would be far less welcome. And so, to avoid keeping the reader needlessly in suspense, I can reveal that G did not want me to come inside when we reached her apartment. And that we therefore didn't sleep in the same bed that night, any more than we did when we went out again another evening; that we never did, in fact, and that by this point in my life I doubt we ever will. The story of G, however, and especially its repercussions, doesn't end there. But since the weft of our existence is subtle and complex, it's impossible to finish the story of G without first discussing H. Unlike G, H didn't feel out of bounds to me, although she, too, had a full, shapely body, and it would have been very easy to see one's mother in her, and I liked squeezing her breasts and sucking on her dark nipples – as much as she let me, since our prostitutes are, or were at the time, I don't know about now, very particular, as I'll soon explain. But there were no issues with incest or threats of castration – a problem I'll leave the Freudian readers to worry about, since they were the ones who butted in to interpret my novel in the first place.

I've already spoken, if I'm not mistaken, about my isolation, my loneliness, the sour faces of my family and friends after the divorce, and my blind search for something, though I didn't know what; and about the feelings of inferiority that were gradually becoming overwhelming, and my doubts about my wisdom and virility, and how I went around enveloped in a kind of atmosphere of failure. To be honest, the problem with G shouldn't surprise me too much, since I didn't dare try anything with other women either. I felt I had nothing to offer them. A friend, the owner of the clinic and the only person to whom I'd stuttered my brief confession, told me: 'You have your body.'

Well, I may have had my body, but I saw it as worthless. For a start, I thought I was short, despite my five feet nine and three quarter inches; it's amazing what an inferiority complex can do. From my height I looked down at a fairly respectable portion of the population, and yet I felt everyone was looking down at me. There are reasons for all this, but I don't want to go on criticising my parents, especially now I'm a parent myself and my children aren't exactly lacking in reasons to criticise me. Put simply, my sexual needs, and my need for something resembling affection, made me seek out prostitutes as an emergency solution, while I waited to see what on earth would become of that life of mine which had suddenly, ever since the gaze of the green-eyed girl, transformed into unsteady flailing and going round in circles and bumping into invisible walls. I was like a fly that's flown into a bottle and got stuck and can feel itself running out of air (ricocheting off G, in the end, was what helped me escape).

And so I began to sample those cold, cruel, hard women, who are always so rushed and so frightened. I didn't find it particularly satisfying, until one night, on a street corner not far from my apartment, I came across H. And would you believe that she smiled at me, an effortless, genuine smile? I didn't notice her body at first; I liked her eyes, I liked her smile, and soon I liked her voice and her easy-going manner. She wasn't the usual wide-eyed bundle of nerves, constantly on the lookout for men to proposition or policemen to dodge; leaning mellowly against a wall, she looked more like she was waiting for a bus, and for a moment I was worried I'd made a mistake – so much so that I didn't say anything when I approached, not wanting to offend her if she wasn't what I thought she was. But she was. She didn't say anything coarse or dirty ('Out for a walk?' she asked, by way of a greeting), and we agreed the price and set off together, unhurriedly, to a by-the-hour hotel. For the first time, I wasn't worried about bumping into anyone I knew. I treated all these women, without exception, like ladies: walking on the side closest to the street, opening doors and then standing aside slightly reverently to let them through, that sort of thing; and I was surprised to find that in this case she responded, as far as she could, like a lady.

I gave her the money in advance, which is standard practice, and that was the only time she accepted it; from then on she'd reply, 'No, please, friends trust each other.' She asked me to unzip her dress at the back. Fully clothed, she gave away nothing of what her body was really like; a vision of full, firm flesh. She whipped off her underwear with the speed of a prestidigitator, as all those women do, and then lay down on the bed. 'Do whatever you want,' she said, 'but don't touch my hair' – which was elaborately styled and covered in hairspray. She was drenched in a sickly-sweet perfume that clung to my clothes for days afterwards, and I even wore that shirt to bed so I could drift off to sleep in a state of infinite bliss. Did I ever fall in love with her? Perhaps.

She didn't let me play much with her body; like the others, she wanted a swift penetration, to get things over with as soon as possible. I told her I'd pay more if she didn't rush me; and she never rushed me again during the act itself, and almost always, after a brief rest, there'd be another. Still, playing with her body was out of the question, and nor did she let me – none of them did, because it was reserved for their men – kiss her on the mouth. One day she suggested, joking, that I marry her. Later I wondered if it had really been a joke. With time I came to learn something, though not much, about her life, and I began to suspect she hadn't had a man around for a while – he was probably in prison, I thought. One day she showed me a photo of him, which she kept in her wallet: a fierce, insolent criminal's face that could have been straight out of a film. He was even wearing a typical criminal's hat. But it seemed she carried his photo with her because she no longer had him. If the same situation arose now, perhaps I would marry her, or at least try to determine whether it was a genuine proposal; at the time I just smiled idiotically. Perhaps I hurt her with that idiotic smile. But while I still hadn't begun to get my youth back, she, conversely, was ageing in plain sight. It's a cruel line of work, very cruel. Five or six years later, when I saw her again because of another series of events that aren't relevant here, she was a wreck.

I had a good time with her. Oh, such a good time! I'd leave the hotel a new man, and then work away contentedly to save up more money and sperm for her. The story of H is interrupted by the appearance, or rather the disappearance, of G; it's interrupted, but it doesn't end, although it ends as far as this novel is concerned.

It ends on a night of slight, steady, stubborn drizzle. It was the night I hit rock bottom, when I drank the very dregs of my adolescent madness.

However, I can't move on quite so easily from H. All of this chapter until now was written last night, and last night I was completely absorbed in the story of G; I passed poor H by without seeing her, without feeling her, as if she were no more than necessary filler for my narrative, a mere plot device. No, I can't move on from H as easily as all that. Only today, when I was waking up, did I begin to realise how important she'd been in my life; and this delay, I confess, has a lot to do with the prejudice, social hierarchies and established norms that weigh heavily upon us and shape our actions, however free we think we are. Free me, oh Lord, from believing I'm free! But I do believe it, far too often. This prejudice has held firm for – yes, why not give the dates – for almost twenty years. Only today – and when I say today, I mean 27–28 April 1984 – only today can I say to myself: yes, I loved that good woman. See, reader, how my narrow consciousness behaves, how it saves me – or seems to – from irresolvable problems. A young man, a shopkeeper, plagued by intellectual and spiritual anxieties, falls in love with a prostitute, and a streetwalker at that – the lowest rung of the trade. Not only does he fall in love with her, but he loves her. He eagerly seeks her out, two or three times a week, and when he doesn't find her he feels an odd sort of pain. He doesn't think, he doesn't want to think that she must be in the by-the-hour hotel, hard at work. By night he wanders and wanders through the city, which some short time ago he started to see more clearly in all its ugliness and beauty – and even feel the beauty of its ugliness.

Before that, I moved through the city like a sleepwalker; although my eyes were open, I saw no more than the bare minimum I needed in order to get where I had to go. But then, in the time opened up by the green-eyed gaze, the city filled all three, or four, of its dimensions; I lived in it, breathed in it and breathed it in, coming to know its pleasant and not-so-pleasant smells. I began to pick up on the slight sadness of particular neon lights glimmering on particular pavements, or the fleeting joy of an unexpected reflection – the red of a car in a torrent of water, traffic lights on rainy nights (the jubilation of the brilliant red or the gentle purity of the green, wet from the rain and bouncing off the asphalt; marble walls or the shiny surfaces of cars, which contrasted with the sweet, infinite sadness of those meek, tireless March and April showers that fell endlessly onto a city carpeted by the plane trees' yellowish-brown leaves). Yes, there are happy autumns, just as there is happiness in sadness and even in despair: the point is to be alive and to know it, to feel it – and I curse and curse the dull fear of these long years, when all our lives are gradually drying out, dwindling, reducing, with never any place for sadness: nothing but fear, nothing but hatred, nothing but that long-lost, oft-hidden morsel of hope, worn out from so much manhandling, from our longing to squeeze just a few more drops from it, a few more drops to get us through the present with its shrinking horizons and impenetrable lead roof; and oh, how I also came to hate this city, which was falling to pieces, which was burying us under ever-higher walls and rubble and dust and noise and silence and shame.

But I often hated the city before all that as well; and it was, although I didn't know how to explain it, a different kind of hatred. Perhaps it was the hatred or bitterness of unrequited love; the city had no space for me, it was beautiful and distant. It wasn't this city that has until recently been rounding us up like a desperate beast, covered in wounds and scratches, egged on and torn asunder by malevolent forces; or today's city, which we look at fondly, the way you might look at a sick woman, an injured woman, perhaps even a woman suffering the pain of childbirth. It was a hatred that gave me life, obliging me to cling on in a desperate effort to carve out a space for myself; it's a hatred I've felt more than once towards a woman who turned me down.

All these things have to do with H. 'Whore' is the wrong word for her; it occurs to me now, and I can see it doesn't fit. 'Prostitute' is more technical, less offensive, and completely inadequate. I find it impossible to unravel her mystery; there's something shared by all the women in her trade, something particular and different, ineffable, and it was missing in her. Still, she knew her trade and did a good job;

she was an honest, conscientious professional, and I'd even say she was a skilled worker. All the others I encountered, and there were a fair few, had that ineffable quality in common – which I should try to explain fully, thorny and elusive as it may be. I can pin down a few of its components, although others escape me. There's scorn for the customer, deceit, and moral, spiritual and emotional baseness; fear, as I've said elsewhere; pretence – behaving one way outside the hotel and the opposite way inside it, much like a dishonest salesman: chasing easy money and prepared to cheat to get it. (H, conversely, wanted the customer to come back. 'I was hoping to see you yesterday, but I didn't have the money,' I said to her once, and she seemed almost affronted. Who did I take her for?) (Outside, she went practically unnoticed. Her clothes didn't show off her figure; she didn't call out to men, or even look at them – she didn't have a whore's eyes, those slightly bulging eyes, with their permanent expression of feigned lust which, after a while, is fixed there forever like a mask.)

However, in her work, in what was strictly speaking her work, H gave more than the others, and in a way also less. I'll try to explain: prostitutes (at least the street prostitutes I knew, all of them), when they're inside the bedroom, turn into a kind of inflatable doll. They give nothing but the surface, the skin, including the skin of the vagina, but only the skin. Technically, sleeping with a whore isn't so very different to masturbating – except, of course, for the three-dimensionality of the woman. But if the man's mind doesn't help him out a bit somehow, it's a painful act, like sliding your penis into a rocky cave (the image I actually have is of a fish, the toothy jaws of a fish, the inside of the body of a fish full of bones); that is, until the male's lubricants begin to work, if they ever do. Then the pain goes away. But pleasure doesn't come in its place, or at least it didn't for me, unless I used my imagination to force things along a bit. They know this and, very cleverly, even use words that stimulate the imagination – because after all, they need the client to orgasm quickly, so they can move on to the next. Some don't use this technique, presumably because their contempt for the customer is so great that they don't want to give him *anything*, anything at all. H didn't use it, but – also presumably – for other reasons: she respected herself, as much as was possible. And there was no talking to her about any more perverse variations. 'What kind of women have you been with? What do you think I am?' she once retorted, enraged, when I made a suggestion.

And H gave no more than skin, like the others. She lacked excitement and therefore lubricants, which made penetration painful. She was a blow-up doll who chewed gum and stared at the ceiling as if in a trance, like the others, waiting for the ordeal to be over. The difference? Well, I think I've discovered it at last, after writing all these rather unpleasant and non-literary details, which are nevertheless essential for reaching an understanding. The difference between H and the others of her trade was that she didn't look down on the customer – or rather, she didn't look down on me. She took pity on me, which is something very different, if the reader understands the exact meaning of the word 'pity'. I could read it in her eyes: 'Why do you come to me? You're young, you have money, you could find yourself a real woman. Why are you coming to me?' Her pity included patience and tolerance. True, I paid her, and always more than she asked. But even with that incentive, not one of the others changed her attitude in the slightest. I don't know if she'd come to realise that I needed her presence, her company, her gaze, and that I was paying a much higher price for it than I was paying in money. Although I often needed the first orgasm, the second was always too much; it was the secret ploy – secret even to me – that let me spend more time with her. The pause to smoke a cigarette – me – and talk about whatever occurred to us (which was how I came to learn a few things about her life, though very few) and feel at peace with myself and the world for a few minutes, lying next to her. How could I answer 'perhaps' so cynically when, just a few pages ago, I asked myself if I loved her? My God, I love her so much!!

And might this not be the real reason for what happened with G? If my heart belonged to someone else . . . Even now, there are nights when I return to that part of the city, and I feel, of course I do (fool that I am, unable to connect to my feelings unless I sit down and write like a man possessed), I feel a sweet ache; and I glance, of course I do, I glance around, and I don't dare look any more closely or approach that figure huddling in a doorway, because it might be her, what's left of her, destroyed like the city by the same cruel, miserable force, the same stupid meanness, the infinite blindness of man. I'm afraid of seeing you defeated, and far more afraid that you'll recognise me and feel a surge of hope that I've come back to you; I wouldn't dare insult you by throwing you some change, you, who were once whole; and nothing in the world, nothing in the world could make me return with you to that room, to the smell of freshly ironed sperm, to the bells on the doors and the staff listening to tangos by Canaro or Roberto Firpo or football matches on the radio.

I'm sorry, literature, you who also have something of a guileless and pitying prostitute about you, I've abandoned you too in this reverie of self-absorption, reminiscing behind your back. I'm losing you, too, but it had to be done. I hope you understand: I'm trying to put my own jigsaw together, calling out in a voice that has to travel down tunnels that are fifteen, eighteen, twenty years long, calling to my scattered pieces, to the unburied corpses of myself, grotesque spectres that never rest, images that never had a mirror to reflect them, broken glass crushed under the wheels of a thousand cars travelling down the road in the same direction, all going to the same place.

## CHAPTER THREE-TO-FOUR

At times, my current existence feels like travelling in an enormous bus at full speed; it's crammed full of people, it never stops, I can't see the driver and I don't have a clue where he's taking us; I'm panicking and want to get off, but when I reach the door I see through the dirty glass that there's no road beneath the vehicle and no landscape on either side; nothing. I'd like to be able to reflect on this problem, try to remember how I got here, imagine some end point for the journey or think up some clever argument that will let me alight in a safe place without getting hurt; but the other passengers, who don't seem to realise or care what's going on, keep annoying me, demanding things from me, making noise and distracting me with topics that seem extremely interesting at first, but which I later discover are worthless. And if I attempt to explain to anyone what I'm seeing and feeling, they look at me in alarm and change the subject, or move as far away from me as possible down the bus.

This image reminds me, in some ways at least, of my theory from a couple of years ago about 'the trains'. According to this theory, we spend our time taking trains that go to different places and travel at different speeds – and we often take several at once, including some that travel in opposite directions. For example: I take a train towards a future date, a date on which I'm meant to be paid a certain amount of money. The train's so slow and sluggish it hardly seems to be moving. At the same time, around that date I have to pay some money to another person; I take that train, too, and it's travelling at the speed of light. But at the same time as that, I take the train of the gripping detective novel whose ending I'm desperate to find out, and another, much faster train, that whisks me far too quickly through the colourful scenes and aesthetic pleasures of the same book; simultaneously, I'm on the train of some problems that my daughter is facing, and this one crawls along at a snail's pace towards some vague resolution, and only very rarely stops for a few moments in a station, when I get a letter from her; and I've taken the train (which goes like the clappers) towards the removal of my gallbladder, and the train that's almost entirely motionless, which is my hypothetical move from this apartment – I'd like to change it for a decent house in a decent neighbourhood – and a train for every letter I send, every publishing project, every friend I'd like to see. And then there are the small trains, which remain almost unnoticed on the tracks, or carry on and arrive at their destinations without my realising; like the train I took yesterday, for example, when I exchanged some rather meaningful looks with a girl of around fourteen in a doctor's waiting room (she was with her mother, of course, and besides, I wasn't about to embark on any erotic adventures. Still, it was a train I took, and in a certain mysterious way I'm still on it). Or the train I boarded the day I was developing this very theory, whilst looking out of my window – and this is how I described it in a letter to a friend: I see the postman come walking down the opposite pavement; he crosses the road and enters the building where I live, perhaps with a letter for me; he's out again in a flash, and I'm tempted to go down and check the letter box on the ground floor, but instead, not realising what I'm letting myself in for, I get on the postman train. I continue watching his progress, out of mere idle curiosity, or the desire to see a cycle completed; since he first appeared in my field of vision from the right, something makes me want to wait for him to disappear off to the left, so I can leave the window feeling satisfied and go back to whatever I was doing. Soon the man crosses the street again, and probably drops a letter off in the pasta shop opposite my apartment; then he comes out and goes into another shop nearby, comes out again, and rings the intercom on an apartment building (yes, the same building where the dry-cleaner is). Someone lets him in, and the postman disappears from sight. And I'm still, to this day, waiting for him to reappear. Would you believe that I never saw him come out of that building, and some two or three years have gone by since then? I wasted much of the morning waiting for that postman, making ever more elaborate conjectures about what had become of him (he got stuck in the lift; he dropped dead just like that and his corpse is still lying in a dark corner somewhere; he'd recently moved to an apartment in that building, and when he finished his rounds there he went home to bed; he was kidnapped; he slipped out through a secret door onto Calle San José; he wasn't a postman at all but a hallucination; he came out in disguise and I didn't recognise him) until eventually – maybe because I was hungry or thirsty, or something else, I don't remember – I gave in, admitted defeat, and began to write the letter to my friend, with the idea of passing some of my frustration on to him. What became of that train? If you ask me, it'll carry on going forever, whether or not I pay it any attention. But that train, like all the ones I take, travels at the expense of my psychological energy. And that, my dear friend, is no way to live.

I'll have to adapt the initial image of the bus, then, to arrive at a synthesis of my Universal Theory of My Life: the bus, as well as being a bus, is a large mobile railway station, and trains are constantly departing from it which may or may not reach their destinations, and which may or may not return to the station, each one carrying a tiny anxious version of me, wide-eyed and with his yellowish face glued to the window; he has a gigantic bag of sea biscuits on the luggage rack for the journey. This novel has turned into one of those trains, one of the most important; in it rides a version of me that's larger than practically all the others put together, though his destination is no less uncertain. At the same time, and from another point of view, the version of me on that train is sending out a multitude of other small trains, in which other tiny versions of me are travelling – and I hope a few versions of the reader have also jumped aboard. Knowing how to combine the journeys of all the trains is the art of writing, just as the art of living would be knowing how to combine them all in real life. I know so little about this second art that I find it altogether over-whelming; I hope, however, though I can't be sure, that the literary arts will make up for it. And so I begin this chapter with renewed enthusiasm, on the ashes, or rather the confetti, of a previous attempt that I've just reduced to countless tiny bits of paper (two typed copies, nineteen double-spaced A4 pages, more or less an entire week's work). The chapter three I envisaged – and indeed wrote – discussed G and

H with the aim of arriving at a humble bunch of grapes, the story of which I'd promised to tell. But it was a total failure, because as I was writing, the nature of G and H was changing; I was coming to see the real importance of each of them for the first time; in the process I cried tears of love and frustration over both of them, discovered a few things about them and myself, and saw how wrong a number of my judgements had been; I had my small catharses and felt empty at first, then a little freer – but all the while I was fighting tooth and nail against literature and even good taste, until I ultimately managed to defeat them both. Only a couple of passages were salvageable, the ones about the city, and since I kept the original, maybe I'll find somewhere to put them; as for the rest, it was pure rubbish. I suspected as much while I was writing, because I'd completely lost sight of the luminous experiences that were meant to be guiding my hand, and I felt myself wallowing in the very bog where the dark novel is now mired. But I had to carry on, because it was vital for me to examine the truths I was uncovering. Today, a few days after the whole adventure, I was able to reread everything and discard, with no regrets, that useless version of the current chapter. I hope the work I do this time around is *also* useful for the novel.

In the pages I threw away, I described my encounter with G (and half explained this alphabetical system: we've met A and B already; the plump, stocky matron and the sheep, because of their importance and despite only appearing briefly, would be C and D; and I've set aside the letters E and F for reasons of internal organisation) and how I'd put G on a pedestal from which, alas, I didn't know how to lift her down in order to lay her on a mattress. I explained my problematic living situation; how my father had stopped me from renting a wonderful apartment, and how instead I rented the right to sleep on the floor of a psychiatrist's consulting room and the right to keep a rolled-up mattress and some blankets in a cramped little cupboard under some stairs, which I shared with a broom and a mop. Then I turned my hand to pornography, or to a treatise on prostitution, which paved the way for the appearance of H, the prostitute who deserved a chapter of her own. In fact, she deserved much more than I thought: as I wrote about her, it gradually dawned on me that I loved her, and that social prejudice had kept me from realising it at the time. I wrote about G with tears of rage and humiliation, and with tears of affection about H. My idea was to prepare the ground for the bunch of grapes; to do that, I would have needed to pass through the night when a delicate thread joined the stories of G and H in the midst of the drizzle and my feverish madness, but I didn't get as far as that night, let alone the grapes. The chapter ended long before; I began going round in circles and getting lost in minor details, though in the end I rescued that howl of love for H which I'd suppressed since 1966, and it was worth it. Only now do I see them both, G and H, as the women they really were; and on those terms, H is streets ahead in every respect. I always treated prostitutes with the respect owing to ladies, and H, incredibly, made an effort to live up to this. G, conversely, made no effort to live up to her status as a goddess. Maybe I'll return to them both in the undiscovered course of this novel.

But I can't continue discussing this now, because my erratic spirit or capricious *daemon* appears to have moved on to something else, and I need to pass the pen over to him. And what's he up to now? He's examining some ants. Which is, I agree, a fascinating pursuit, and one to which I'd like to have dedicated, if not my entire life, then at least a more significant portion of it. What little time I have dedicated to it, however, has borne some fruit. I'll begin with the last occasion, which was fairly recent. A couple of months ago, on a summer holiday in a seaside town, and thanks to the relative immobility imposed on me by my gallbladder troubles, I had a chance to observe the activities of two of the various kinds of ant in the vicinity. One kind were black with large whitish, or sometimes brownish, abdomens. They usually lived inside wood, although I never saw them destroy any – to give just one example, they had completely filled a hollowed-out door to the house with their minuscule bodies, slipping in via the keyhole. Anyway, these ants, which didn't look very nice, and in fact seemed quite nervous and aggressive, when they weren't inside the door, could often be found on a patch of concrete surrounding a barbecue and a room at the back of the house. I was surprised to see that some of them were always busy with what looked like a patrol, on an area of the concrete bordered by grass. They paced determinedly back and forth from a point that seemed to be their guard post. On most journeys, the patrolling ant would come across an identical ant engaged in the same task; each time, the two would collide fairly violently, apparently in an act of mutual recognition, and then quickly let go of one another and continue on their way. They reminded me of magnets, because of the apparent attraction and the force of the collision.

In the days that followed I came across some strange black balls, which on closer inspection turned out to be pairs of these ants, dead and mysteriously entwined. Everything suggested a fight to the death, or a sexual encounter. I found it hard to take this last hypothesis seriously, however, since although we have examples like the black widow spider, who eats the male after copulation, or the murder of the drones by the worker bees once one of them has impregnated the queen, I see no reason why Nature would want to bring about the death of both the male and the female, considering how careful she is – too careful, you might say – when it comes the preservation of species. It must have been a fight, then. But did it always result in the death of both ants, or were those little black balls the exception? A few days later I came across two fighters who had only just interlocked, or at least who hadn't yet died. The ants' behaviour made it quite clear that one of them was the guard, and the other was a civilian who'd been in the wrong place at the wrong time; the guard had the body language of someone on the offensive, and the civilian of someone who wants only to escape – purely defensive. Since I didn't have a good view of what was going on down there on the ground, I used a twig to lift them onto the table. I moved my short-sighted eye closer and saw that the guard was gripping one of the civilian's legs determinedly, decisively and very tightly indeed in his powerful jaws. The civilian was simply trying to free his leg, tugging as hard as he could. His adversary did nothing but cling on. Needless to say, I took the civilian's side – it was easy to put myself in his place. When I saw his movements were slowing down, and he seemed resigned, or stunned, I picked up a knife and cut off that leg, hoping to see him make a break for it, lame but alive. And yet he couldn't. The other ant must have injected him with some kind of poison – probably formaldehyde – by means of the bite, and been holding on while waiting for it to take effect. The strange thing was that the guard, who seemed unhurt, had also been poisoned. I couldn't tell whether the civilian had managed to bite him back, or if, on injecting the other ant with poison, the guard inevitably poisoned himself as well. Either way, this second explanation is correct on one plane of existence, and I remembered that part of Ecclesiastes – 'He that leadeth into captivity shall go into captivity' – and its slightly mocking continuation: 'And he that hath ears to hear, let him hear.'

The other kind of ant – which I came to think the first kind were part of, as a sub-variety specialised in defence – were black as well, but more svelte, with abdomens in proportion to their thoraxes and a graceful way of moving. These ants provided me with another topic of investigation after a child spat a sweet out onto the same concrete floor where the barbecue was, this time near the middle of the area under a sink. By noon the next day, the sweet was a seething black mass, completely covered in ants. There was a line of ants coming and going from the sweet, stretching all the way across the concrete and disappearing into the grass. Since I didn't like the idea of killing ants as I walked, and I often had to go that way, I brought about an artificial rain shower with a kettle of water, and the ants scuttled off at full speed. Then I gave them back the sweet, putting it somewhere more appropriate, not far from where the others had their guard post. When they found where it was and got back to work on it, I was able to watch them carefully. They were in ecstasy, or in a trance, on the surface of the sweet; they didn't take anything back to their nest and instead seemed to be eating the sugar right then and there. Oddly, several of the passing ants didn't take the slightest interest in the sweet. And so I tried a new experiment: a little further away, near the path of another group of these ants, who were busy collecting up some kind of plant, I placed a new sweet, along with a spoonful of sugar and a little piece of quince jelly. I wondered if they'd be able to abandon their work and surrender to ecstasy. And *quelle surprise*: as with human beings, there were some that could and some that couldn't. Some, when they realised the true nature of the object Providence had placed in their path, dropped their leaves with comical speed, climbed onto the sweet and immediately fell into a trance. Others, however, went on a diversion that took them a considerable distance away from the tempting object, as if they knew their own weakness and wanted to take precautions; others – though without letting go of their loads – even examined the bait carefully, only to conclude that it was more important to carry on with their work. And there was more than one whose load got stuck, whether to the warm sugar or the quince jelly. They did whatever was necessary to unstick and go on with their journey; one particularly determined and stubborn ant was struggling for an extraordinary length of time to rescue his piece of plant, which would come unstuck in one place only to reattach itself elsewhere. I would have given up long, long before.

I was pleased to see such a high incidence of individualism; although limited, that capacity for transgression made me feel hopeful about the future of ants, a domain of Nature whose societal model had seemed as perfect, absolute and mechanical as that of bees; a model in which the individual counts for nothing. And what became of the individualist transgressors? If you ask me, they got drunk on sugar and had a wild night of hedonism and sexual excess. That's my opinion. But in fact, what I saw that night by artificial light was a group of ants forming more little black balls. When man, i.e. me, intervened with his twig, they separated with some difficulty, moving slowly and clumsily and never straying too far from the centre of the gathering; not a single ant took hold of another ant's leg; and at the centre of the gathering was invariably an ant of the same type but with a slightly smaller body. Man went further; he separated two ants from the group and put them on the table. They stayed there for some time, walking around in rather listless circles, looking disoriented and not showing much flight reflex when man goaded them with a stick. The next day, there were no ant corpses to be seen; and neither, oddly, did a single ant take any notice of my bait. They were all busy with their usual tasks.

As will have become clear during the course of all this, I myself am highly individualistic. It's because of my upbringing – an only child, sickly and overprotected, etc. – but also by conviction (and what can we do but convince ourselves of the virtues of what we have to endure?); although not, of course, without effort or guilt, or without paying a terrible price.

Mario Levrero

Now and then I feel, or think – via the superego – that these laid-back ants and I are like the respective cancer cells of our respective socially minded individuals. If I fight hard against the superego, however, I sometimes manage to think the opposite: that these ants and I are the salubrious cells of our societies. As far as I can tell, the anthill is a wholly sick individual, decaying and useless, and capable only of looking after itself (sub-existence); and I see contemporary human society – that crazy bus I was talking about at the beginning – in the same way. If I were God, I'd pardon it solely on the basis of the few 'just men and women' in the Bible, or, from my own point of view, on the basis of those magnificent individuals, those all-round great people who have either gone down in history as such or are personally known to us. And the ones I know personally are great regardless of their apparent social function and way of thinking; I've found them in the ranks of communists, Nazis, Catholics, occultists, Masons, etc., or simply as unaffiliated lunatics. What they have in common is that, one way or another, consciously or unconsciously, they participate, and make you participate, in what I've called the 'unknown dimension'; and I should point out that the 'events', if we can call them that, which occur in or form part of that dimension, don't always look like 'luminous' experiences; these great people may have their sinister side, or even be entirely sinister, and yet, because of their disproportionate sinister side, they're worthwhile.

I'm not dismissing the herd instinct or human society; I'm trying to find a way of synthesising the different doctrines so as to glimpse the possibility, if only in theory, of reconciling the individual with the species. But I won't try to construct an ideology, with all the sad, narrow connotations and echoes that word has; I'll stay within my social role – the role of a madman – which, ironically, consists of sticking resolutely to an individualistic stance, come what may.

I've digressed a little from the ants I have in mind in order to touch on this topic which, as I've said, stops me writing my novel freely because I think the world will be against me; later, further on, I'll unfortunately have to come back to it. Now I'll turn to some earlier ants, from the same period as the dog sniffing with olfactory relish (and as the bunch of grapes, for crying out loud), around a year after the green-eyed gaze, and not long at all after the collapse brought on by G, and the love for H that I was completely unaware of; it was as a result of the collapse that, once again, I abandoned everything and went away to die, or so I thought – although I didn't know by what means – in the house in the seaside town where, one year before, I'd been delivering newspapers and my marriage had come to an end. Luckily, when I got off the bus, I was spotted by a friend, a friend who was the very model of the all-round great people I've been talking about. He must have seen something in my face, because from that point on he took personal charge of not letting me die. I don't know exactly how many days went by before I managed to emerge from my depression and begin taking a tentative interest in my surroundings. The nearest thing to me – always a good place to start – was the house where I was living, which, as usual, I occupied without ever really seeing. Of course, before I started taking what I'd say was a positive interest in the ants, grapes and other such life forms, I found it useful to have to take a more immediate interest, which I'd describe as negative, in other kinds of life, namely spiders and fleas. The spiders presumably slipped in through the gaps in the zinc sheeting which served as the roof of that tiny house – a house with such thin walls that hitting them with your hand made them shake, creating the worrying impression that they might collapse at any moment. The spiders were big and black, with rather thick legs, and although they seemed docile enough and didn't do much, the thought of them still sent shivers down my spine. I knew killing them would be very unpleasant, as indeed it was, but at the same time, I couldn't stand the idea that one might crawl under the covers while I was asleep. The daily nightmare, just before going to bed, involved hunting them down and murdering them one by one. They were mostly in full view on the walls, and in the end I decided that killing those ones was enough. I let any that might be lurking out of sight stay alive as long as they didn't show themselves, and once I'd turned the lights off I tried to banish all images of them from my mind. There was nothing luminous about that experience, needless to say, but along with the ant that I'll soon introduce, and the dog, of course, they helped to develop my awareness of an unknown dimension, or at least one I hadn't previously taken into account: the spiders had – and have – such a strong psychic presence that when I came home in the evenings, I often knew where I'd find them even before turning on the light.

As for the fleas, they had taken over the mattresses and blankets, along with the damp. Every night, before going to bed, I had to dry the blankets and sheets, and also, as far as possible, the mattress and the pillows, with infinite patience, using the flame of a Primus – my only source of heat. And still, when I got into bed, I would feel the damp rising from the depths of the mattress, and with it the fleas; countless tiny fleas, seeking the warmth of my body, and there was nothing I could do but let them come and go as they pleased. Curiously enough, they never bit me; I didn't feel any biting, and nor did I see any of the little specks of blood they normally leave on your clothes. What's more, once they'd climbed out of the mattress and settled on my body, they stopped moving around and, I imagine, slept peacefully; it was only warmth they were after, or perhaps company. By the time I woke up each morning, they'd disappeared. They never bothered me during the day. I didn't even see them, however meticulously I examined my clothes and my body.

The damp went away, or at least considerably reduced, when the wind set in. It was a constant wind that began around July, or August, I don't remember, and lasted about a month – or that's what I think now; I might be exaggerating, and I don't want to lie. What I am sure about, though, is its insistent, exhausting permanence. It was very strong, forcing people to walk through the streets at a consistent and considerable angle to the ground, whether they were facing into the wind or against it; it blew at all hours, without pause, without respite. The sheets of zinc on my roof clattered incessantly, day and night – and at night, the sound replaced the furtive scurrying of mice and cats. After a while, everyone looked exhausted, with suffering in their eyes, and they spoke very little, as if saving the last of their energies for the battle against the wind. The sea was always choppy, but the furious crashing of the waves now produced large flecks of foam; the same wind then distributed these along the promenade and a few neighbouring streets, making it look as if it had been snowing. But I'm getting carried away by my memories of what was, unquestionably, the happiest time of my life, despite the spiders, fleas, mice, damp, cats, wind and a few other things I won't go into so as not to wear the reader out. I was at my happiest because I was at my most free; I'd cut absolutely all ties with my recent and less recent past, and even, or so I thought, with human society as a whole, which I'd discovered was to blame for all my troubles – not realising that it was also the source of all the good things in my life, including that freedom I enjoyed thanks to the protection of the wonderful family who had, in their way, adopted me, on the day my friend saw me getting off the bus. Not realising, in other words, that this family also constituted human society. Anyway, I should add that I sometimes woke up depressed, or angry, and cured myself by staying in bed and muttering complaints about human society, and repeating over and over: 'I don't have *anything* to do; they can all get along perfectly well without me; I don't have to do *anything*,' a formula I had unconsciously adopted as a mantra, prayer or method of relaxation. Incidentally, I was unaware of relaxation techniques at the time, but I later learnt that they're very similar; not doing anything, thinking about not doing anything, repeating the same formula again and again. My mood soon improved considerably, and it went on getting better by the day. Why did I lose that freedom? As always, because of a woman. But that story isn't part of this novel.

Right: now I'm coming to the ant. There turned out to be ants all over the place in that house; the same pleasing, svelte black kind that took part in the hedonistic orgy all those years ago. They had various holes, even one in the bedroom, I don't know to what end. But the ant hole I liked the most, because of the exceptional conditions for observation, was in the hallway by the front door, almost directly under the electric light bulb. Partly as an experiment, and partly so they didn't get too interested in the hole in the bedroom, I started leaving food at the entrance to their cave. I tried different things and gradually learnt their preferences: lemon or orange peel, pieces of meat, and even, on one occasion, some soap. And cake, bread, sweets. I don't remember exactly what they chose and what they refused (the soap was only accepted once; they carried off a small amount, but after that they never touched it again). I do remember that they weren't always interested in a second or third helping of substances they'd been interested in before; with some things, it seemed, they only needed to fill a certain quota.

I observed them though a magnifying glass, which later I also used to take close-up photos of small objects – scraps of tree bark, tiny spiderwebs, peeling patches of wall – and that was what helped me out of the cesspit G had pushed me into (and I'm thankful to God for having made it out, but also for having fallen in). Once, in my phase of all-out experimentation, I saw there was a lone explorer in the area around the hole. I went to find something to offer it, hoping to learn how it alerted the others, which was something I'd never seen before. I brought over the bait and put it down near the ant, a yard or slightly more from the hole. And I waited. When the ant came across the bait, it scrutinised it from all angles and seemed to like what it saw. Then it did the last thing I expected: it stood on its hind legs, and its body, precariously balanced with the help of movements of what were now its arms, began to sway gently, as if a wave were passing over it; and at the same time it made rhythmical movements with its antennae. It looked like a Watusi warrior doing a ritual dance.

But if I found the behaviour of this ant disconcerting, it was nothing compared to the response from the nest: in almost no time, one by one, the other individuals began to appear, marching in perfect formation towards the bait. I couldn't believe my eyes. At the same time, the scene filled me with a strange sort of elation, as if it resonated with something in my own spirit. And, more incredibly still, these individuals didn't even approach the ant that was still transmitting its message and instead headed straight for the bait, getting to work on it as if the whole thing were a well-rehearsed routine and each ant knew in advance where to go and what to do. I observed the broadcasting ant through a magnifying glass and saw all the details I've described here, not a single one of which is invented.

Well, when some time later I told this story to my friends, especially the doctors among them, whom I'd have expected to be familiar with the phenomenon – I'd simply been wondering what the ant had used to send its message, whether it was sound waves, smell waves, electromagnetic waves or something else – those doctors almost packed me off to an asylum. Since they didn't approve of shock therapy, and I couldn't afford psychoanalysis, they opted instead for some good-natured teasing. Life later proved me right about a few things, including this; and nowadays one of those doctors admits to having 'read a description of the process somewhere' but doesn't consider it very important, 'since it's a well-known phenomenon'. The bastards. Damn them to hell. Why didn't they believe me at the time? Why did they make me doubt myself, with the constant doubt that plagues me in so many of my perceptions, opinions and ruminations? They're such imbeciles. And so am I, of course: who am I meant to trust, if not myself?

And so the ant joined the dog – and the green-eyed girl! – and many other things that had begun happening to me, and that was how, around the same time, I was able to write a novel (not without first reading *America* and *The Castle*; I saw Kafka as a kind of older brother, who had arrived before me at a very similar world view to the one I was developing. But most of all, he convinced me it wasn't necessary to *write well*). (I didn't say '*¡Mierda!*', like García Márquez's famous colonel, but I did say something more Uruguayan, like '*¡Carajo!*'.) It was in the midst of that spiritual ferment, surrounded by an aggressive but wholesome nature, and with the terrible – and painful, and difficult – freedom I'd won that, yet again, one morning I woke up depressed. When I glanced out of the window I saw a grey sky, and when I looked into my own head there was a grey sky there too. I don't know why, but I'd relapsed into a rather nasty sadness; a combination of fatigue, faint anxiety and low spirits. I got up glumly and drifted around my room; I don't know what else I could have done in that grey mood, until it occurred to me, for the first time since I'd arrived, to rest my elbows on the windowsill and look out. It probably hadn't occurred to me before because generally I either stayed in bed, repeating my antisocial mantra, or got up and went out immediately, and stayed out all day – since at that time in my life I used to spend all day out of the house. So I looked through the window for a bit, and then suddenly, to my immense surprise, I thought I spotted a familiar shape among the vine leaves that formed a roof over the garden. When I looked more closely, a great happiness flooded through me: hanging there was a bunch of grapes, miraculously forgotten by the people who'd lived in the house during the season, and overlooked by the local children. I hurried outside, with a genuine prayer to the Lord on my lips for the first time in years, a prayer of gratitude and joy; I picked the bunch, which was moderately sized and dense with very fat black grapes; I washed it under the tap at the sink where I washed my clothes, and began eating the grapes, savouring each one. It was July by then, or the end of June; the grapes had turned to wine, and I, who had drunk alcohol self-destructively in the past and now avoided it like the plague, received that alcohol for breakfast like a real blessing, a gift from God. As indeed it was, since God had marked out all the steps that led me to that carefully prepared sign; he had made the bunch of grapes invisible to many other people, with the sole aim of my receiving it in the form of some wine that, He knew, I was still in no fit state to request in a mass. The sky was still grey, but to me it seemed full of light. And I got drunk on that tiny amount of holy wine and began to sing at the top of my lungs. I was singing when I went to bed and I was singing when I fell asleep, and I woke up fully aware that God existed and loved me; and that a dimension of reality exists that we're always trying to hide; and that never again would I lose sight of that dimension, however many times I relapsed into depressions and felt that God was absent from my life – as I do now, for example. Never again would the existence of God be up for debate, much as He often changes shape, sign, place and even gender.

I've been suspecting for some time that however I told the story of the grapes, the reader would feel a little hard done by. There's nothing magical about it, nothing inexplicable, and my conclusions, which I've just recorded, don't flow logically and rationally from the events. That's exactly why I found it so difficult to reach the part about the grapes, and arrived there via a route I wasn't expecting, i.e. by discussing the ants, though at least they're the same dark colour. Besides, it's not about conclusions. The existence of God doesn't flow naturally from the story; rather, it took shape within me at the same time as I noticed the bunch of grapes among the vine leaves. It's not that I was converted by the evidence of a miracle; the occurrence was made into a miracle by revealing the presence of God, simultaneously, in me. The same thing could have happened without any grapes. The grapes are like an aide-memoire, fixing what I felt at that moment in my mind, and what I felt can't be explained, or even described in words. A mute feeling of wonder, which in a thousand other dramatic stories, stories far more dramatic than this one, simply wasn't there; and which often, afterwards, was there without the need for a story to jog my memory.

The story of the grapes marks the transition, the axis, the point of no return, between one way of living, being and thinking and another that was completely different, and that had to clear a path for itself by destroying the first, like a pendulum swinging back the other way. The green-eyed girl gave me a push; dizzily, dangling from a rope, I crossed an abyss that yawned endlessly beneath me. When I reached the other side, the hand of God was there to receive me and, as with the biblical rainbow, to seal the deal with that wine, which for me was sacred.

## CHAPTER FOUR-TO-FIVE

I was sitting down, reading a book, under a tree I remember as a peach tree that produced sickly and inedible peaches, but which I now think was too big to have been a peach tree. Never mind. There I was, reading away, when all of a sudden something made me stop and look upwards. It's a good thing I did: a spider was making its way down from the top of the tree, moving at a steady and fairly rapid pace in the very direction of my head. It wasn't as large as the spiders that got into that little house, but with its legs stretched out it looked quite formidable. And, as will become clear, it wasn't light. Even though at the time – and I forget whether it was the time of the green-eyed gaze or of the dog and the ant, though I think it must have been the former because I was wearing espadrilles; the post-G period, which takes up much of the previous chapter, covered the end of autumn and the winter, and I don't think I would have spent any of it reading, or wearing espadrilles, in the garden outside the house. Perhaps it was even later . . . But as I was saying, even though at the time I was surprised to have looked up at exactly the right moment, that's not why I'm telling this story. I'm telling it because of what happened next. I sprang up and leapt to safety, then took off my espadrilles, held them one in each hand with their soles facing inwards, and waited intently for the moment to strike. I could have reached out and caught the spider then and there, but I decided to hold off, less out of laziness than to give it a chance to repent, since I don't like killing anyone if I can help it. I decided to hold off until the spider, continuing its downward journey, had entered the space between my jute-soled shoes of its own accord. And yet my plan was foiled, not because the spider repented – on the contrary, it continued its descent at the same slightly manic speed – but because, in the second big surprise in a short space of time, my prey was snatched from my clutches.

Later, when I was taking evening classes to get a high-school diploma in medicine, I had to study this in books: there's a particular kind of wasp, whose name I won't be able to remember now no matter how hard I try, which is an expert spider-hunter. These wasps paralyse their prey and then stab it with their rear stinger, injecting fertilised eggs into its body – while the spider is still alive and paralysed – and then leave it there. When the larvae hatch from the eggs, they feed on the spider's body until it's completely destroyed, in the most diabolical torture technique Nature has ever invented. Because the spider needs to stay alive for as long as possible to give the larvae something fresh, healthy and nutritious to eat, Nature has made it so the vital organs are attacked last, when the baby wasps are ready to face the world themselves. I'm telling this exactly as I heard it. But at the time, I didn't know any of that, and all I saw was a furious form come hurtling towards us from a long way off and slam straight into the spider, which was so, so close to ending up between my shoes. The two creatures thrashed about on the ground in a frenzy; it was a horrific battle, though brief, and it ended a small distance from my feet. When I got over the shock, I saw quite clearly that the attacker was a wasp and the spider was almost completely paralysed. It could just about move a few of its legs, but that was all. I thought it was dying.

I edged closer, and the wasp didn't seem at all perturbed by my presence; it was very busy, even though the battle was over. When I drew near enough to see what was going on, I was amazed: the wasp had a kind of saw attached to its nose, which it was using to cut the spider's legs off one by one. The body was left completely bare, and then the wasp somehow lifted it onto its back – always with nervous little movements, like a housewife who's expecting people for dinner and has a thousand details to attend to – and tried to fly away. But the spider was too heavy and the wasp couldn't stay airborne for long; it seemed more like it was jumping, covering a few yards each time; the wasp would get a little way off the ground and then almost immediately land again. Well, somehow or other, it carried the spider off to who knows where; I lost sight of it when I reached the corner, half a block from the house, because after all, I wasn't especially interested in finding out where the wasp lived. And why am I describing all this, when any textbook would provide more, and better, information? I'm describing it because it was one of the experiences that have, somehow or other, helped me to think, or perhaps not to think. I'll try to explain what I mean.

Have you ever been looking at an insect, or a flower, or a tree, and found that for a moment your values, or your sense of what's important, have completely changed? I don't know when I first experienced this – perhaps as a child, though the predatory wasp seems like the first time – but I know it's happened to me on several occasions. It's as if I'm seeing the universe from the point of view of the wasp – or the ant, or the dog, or the flower – and finding it more valid than when I saw it from my own point of view. Civilisation becomes meaningless, as do History, cars, cans of beer, neighbours, thoughts, words, and even mankind itself and its undisputed place at the top of the pyramid of living beings. In that moment, all forms of life seem equivalent. And, as I'll now try to show, inanimate things are no longer inanimate, and there's no place for any kind of non-life.

In other words: engrossed in observing the wasp's feverish work, I suddenly understand how immensely significant this work is, and how necessary, and what the species has gone through to arrive at it. And although my mind at the time is empty of thoughts, I feel an awareness that it's not a pointless, contemptible or secondary activity; that newspapers are full of news which perhaps doesn't have the same informative weight as the events I've just described. Or, seen another way, that the wasp doesn't care about the value of the dollar or the double murder on such-and-such a street, and instead is important to itself the way I'm important to myself, and is important full stop, important to Something. Or, seen yet another way, that if I were a wasp I wouldn't have any sort of inferiority complex towards humans. There are trees that have made me feel the same. And rocks.

I don't know how better to explain it. Probably because it scares me a bit and I've always hung back from deepening and developing this almost secret feeling, which is secret even from myself. I can sense that it contains a tremendous truth; that it contains, quite simply, the truth. But to understand it fully, enough to be able to explain it better, would be too dangerous. I don't know why. Or rather, I do know.

Where, for God's sake, does life really take place? Do people reproduce by means of the sperm and the egg, or do the sperm and the egg reproduce by means of people, using them as a kind of luxury carrying-case? Should our focus be on the chicken or the egg? Everything essential and important, everything that's going to last, everything that really exists, once all appearances have faded: is it micro or macro, or some other unknown category? Who are we working for? And why? Etc.

(I notice that all the psychotherapy, all my efforts to adapt, this life I'm leading on Earth and my decent or at least vaguely normal appearance in recent years, are merely a veneer or a kind of simulation, which disappears as if by magic the moment I begin to write, or think, or try to rescue myself from my depressions, or confront the idea of death as I approach my operation – when I seek out the mainsprings of life and hope, I run into these things, always the same beloved things.)

Yes, I know; even good old Jung thought *participation mystique* involved a kind of regressive perception, corresponding to a time before the 'self' is formed in the child. But this 'self' – has it not hypertrophied within us, has it not grown at the expense of a psychological formation that would be a source of health for humanity? In other words: is there anyone, for God's sake, who is satisfied with this thing called 'reality'? Is there a single imbecile out there who thinks the world is inhabitable? Yes, I know, I know; there is. There is, there is, there is. Anyway.

It was a paranoid patient who half convinced Freud of the existence of an ancient language, of which the language of dreams would be one of the last surviving traces. Freud thinks this dream-language is so rich in sexual symbols because sex was humanity's main pursuit before certain (unexplained) conditions made it necessary to repress sex in favour of *work*; the 'pleasure principle' superseded by the 'reality principle'. Why is work 'reality', and not sex? But take note, psychologists, philosophers, workers and the general public: I have at my side a miniature marvel of modern technology, which cost me just thirty dollars, and which I'm paying for in modest instalments of Uruguayan pesos (I'm referring to a calculator-diary-watch). For just a few dollars more, you could make, and indeed people should be making, or perhaps have already made, a little device not much more complicated, or much bigger or heavier, than this, which could, for example, keep a factory running with only one or two employees working shifts, or even just checking up on things from time to time. Modern technology is almost the triumph of spirit over matter, and for that very reason it is – it can't help but be – the beginning of another bite of the cherry, another swing of the pendulum. Do you know, reader, why there are still workers and employees in this world? Because they are, at the same time, consumers. Do you know what would happen if these workers and employees stopped consuming? Think about it. What happened to the Charrúa tribe here in Uruguay? What always happens when someone with strong muscles, or the technological equivalent thereof, finds someone weaker or slower in their path? Well, workers and employees, you are condemned; in the best-case scenario, to a slow and gradual extinction; and in the best best-case scenario, to a move up to a higher level of education and life. (Meanwhile, please, don't stop consuming! Because when it comes to production, they really don't need you any more.)

What I was trying to say was that nowadays, since people are free from the need to work, and if we pay attention to the theories of Freud and his paranoid patient, we could easily return to the 'pleasure principle', spitting in the face of the 'reality principle' once and for all. Let's see what the psychologists think of the *participation mystique* then, and what their standards of mental health are, if there are any standards left (or any psychologists, for that matter).

The reader, I fear, won't have followed me through that series of polemical and rather tenuous digressions. I'll give a summary just in case: I think that everything's going to shit, for better or worse (but what's better and what's worse?). And that with all the knowledge we've acquired, we can't go on being imbeciles forever. No one's going to pay monthly salaries to a hundred workers if they can manage their affairs with a tiny, almost non-existent gadget costing 1.95 Uruguayan pesos. A whole society based on alienation from work, and physical, intellectual, moral and spiritual slavery, will inexorably collapse, because of itself and its vices and, at the same time, because of the introduction of a real reality, namely the power of the spirit. Contemporary society will give way to either a nuclear nothingness or a society founded on *pleasure*. And pleasure centres around the possibility of *participation mystique*, that is, the crumbling of a hypertrophied self in favour of the perception of reality *in all its dimensions*, or at least, in all the dimensions that we're qualified to perceive, although we don't make use of this birthright, to say the least.

I realise there's a risk involved in saying these things, but I'm sick of keeping them quiet as if they were crimes. I once heard about the case of a boy who discovered he liked going to the zoo. He felt good among the animals, even though they were in cages. He felt so good that gradually he realised he was able to communicate with some of them. One day, he made the mistake of mentioning this to his psychoanalyst. And believe me, reader, he was never the same again. No one is, after a hefty dose of electroshocks. Knowing this, I refrained from mentioning that I once encountered some enormous rocks, which protruded from the beach like the backs of whales and with which it was possible to hold a friendly conversation. I refrained from mentioning that a traffic light once informed me that I – and it, of course – was alive. It didn't say so in words, because traffic lights don't speak our language any more than rocks do; I simply understood theirs. For years, I refrained from mentioning that a woman's hand once stroked my face from some two or three miles away, and that another woman, at a distance of around sixty miles, once bit me on the back. And that another woman, similarly far away, said my name and I heard it. For years, I refrained from mentioning that I have reason to believe there's a – dimension? – superimposed on the world we know, inhabited by large, invisible and intangible beings which appear to have no interest in us. For years, I refrained from mentioning that a plant once produced a very strange seed under the influence of my love for a woman; that I communicated telepathically with a dog, and that, years later, on the night when the same dog was poisoned, I dreamed about it, from many miles away – I dreamed the weather was very cold, and snowy, and that I found the dog in the street and took him in my arms, as the snow fell and fell upon us. For years, I refrained from mentioning my discovery that flowers can travel without moving from where they are, and that they dream. For years, I refrained from mentioning that I once saw the colours in a landscape – in a dream – with the mind of a friend of mine who's a painter; and that I once heard a song with the mind of somebody else. And I refrained from mentioning lots of other things, too, which I'm still refraining from mentioning now.

When it comes to the rocks, there's no denying that C – the eighteen-year-old whose hymen, as far as I'm concerned, is intact – played a decisive role. She persuaded me to go on a particular walk, to a place whose whereabouts I can only vaguely guess at, given my limited, fragmentary and extremely vague knowledge of the city where I live. She'd often spoken to me, in that cryptic way of hers, between long and meditative silences, of 'her' place; a place she had found for herself and which, if there was any justice in the world, would belong to her: it was her refuge and her peace, her escape valve, her myth. And so, after all this advertising – and besides, I was young, and my spirit of adventure wasn't entirely dead – I finally agreed to go. We were due to meet on such-and-such a day (chosen by her, naturally) at such-and-such a time, in a little square. She explained which bus I had to take, where to take it from, and how I'd know when to get off. I did as I was told. The bus drove on and on down streets I didn't know, for so long that we almost went beyond the city limits. I got off in exactly the right place – a little square I'd never seen before, and have never seen since – and she appeared as if we'd synchronised our watches in advance. Then she broke the news: we had to take another bus. Don't ask me which. So we took another bus, and it drove on and on and on – for even longer than the first, or so it felt to my backside. This time we almost went beyond the limits of the country, or the planet. The buildings grew further and further apart, and we got off somewhere that could very well have been the infinite Pampa. Then we had to walk. A lot. I forget whether it was on the way there or the way back that we went through what looked like some small farms, or orchards, where there were fruit trees laden with, well, fruit. I don't remember any other signs of human life beyond those well-maintained trees or the wire fences meant to protect them; C, I should add, was as good at stealing fruit as she was at stealing flowers. I don't recall whether she stole any then or simply told me about previous thefts, but I do remember we were eating something as we walked. Her eyes were shining, full of life and enthusiasm; she was pleased to be sharing her secret place with me, and most of all, I think, she enjoyed seeing me so vulnerable and ignorant of where we were, with her taking the lead and me surrendering meekly to her plans. Something else I remember clearly is the approach, after plenty of walking, to the place in question. A wild, rugged landscape and hard ground covered in rocks, with a few tufts of prickly grass and the odd gnarled bush or tree. The effect was enhanced by the afternoon itself: in keeping with the foul breath of tragedy that enveloped us whenever we were together, even if we were feeling perfectly fine or enjoying ourselves, the sunny weather turned stormy. As if they'd appeared from nowhere, or as if we'd walked so far that the weather had changed, huge, heavy clouds coloured everything grey. They heightened the contrast between light and shadow, drawing out the hidden meanings of simple things – the grass, the bushes, the stones and then the rocks. Fields surrounded by wire fences. A sign: private property, no entry. Clothes snagging in barbed wire. 'Are you sure we can go this way?' She laughed happily in response. 'Sometimes they shoot at intruders.' I looked around and didn't see anyone, but I certainly wouldn't have said no to turning back and making a run for it. I tried to suggest something along those lines; that the walk had been very nice, but that the weather seemed to be getting worse; it was about to start pouring with rain. Gleeful, tinkling laughter from her, like the sound of a rattlesnake, perverse in a childish and captivating way. And we arrived at the beach – a place where a sea came into view, who knows where from, creating a kind of bay or cove. One of those locations that's perfect for smugglers, and I think she told me some story or other about that. A beach with no sand, or with sparse, thick grains of it, and most of all pebbles, and bigger stones – and those smooth, black rocks, like the bodies of beached whales, prisoners of the land, hoping in vain for liberation.

The wind blew. She used to seek out places like that, with strong winds and salt water. Sometimes she took me to the area around the port, where there were other magical spots she saw as her own, and I had to wait as she carried out her ritual of standing with her face to the wind, as if she needed to breathe it in, filling up with tears, sometimes for a very long time. She seemed to be praying, and it would have been pointless to say anything to her. She'd know when she was done. There, on the little beach, she did the same thing. She took off her shoes and socks, rolled up her trousers and stood in the water with her face to the wind, which was now bringing with it some small drops of rain. I raised my jacket collar and sheltered by one of the big whalebacks, in a mood that wasn't entirely unfamiliar; it reminded me of the headachy fatigue that invariably followed my attempts at sexual assault, or, worse still, the minor concessions – when she occasionally allowed me, or at least only very half-heartedly resisted my attempts, to reveal her breasts and fondle them and kiss them and suck them and breathe them in, and when I then fondled and kissed and sucked and breathed them in some more until the successive erections left my penis a slimy mess, all shrivelled and damp, and the inflammation spread from my testicles to my kidneys, and from there to my neck and my temples; oh, it was a heroic time, no doubt about it. Well, that's how I was feeling, only without the pain, that afternoon. The stupid victim of the stupid whim of a stupid girl – just wait till we're alone in my apartment later . . . She was facing into the wind. I sat on a rock, rested one hand on it and felt it pulsating. But what's pulsating? My hand or the rock? My hand, of course. But this rock is so warm, so lovely and warm. It's like it's alive. It's like it's the back of a half-buried animal, so warm and so smooth . . . And why is my hand pulsating, if it really is my hand pulsating? This is strange, very strange indeed.

And my mood changed. I don't know what kind of psychic work she was doing, some thirty yards away from me and my rock, but the fact is, my mood changed completely, and yes, there it was, that dimension I'd been missing, am always missing, and I felt such peace, such beautiful warmth. I felt safe, and everything felt good. Thank you, C; thank you, thank you, C, for your walk and your beach and your secret. Let them come and chase us away with their guns. Let them set their dogs on us. Who'd be foolish enough to waste their time on fear? Shoot, shoot your gun once and for all, you cardboard barbarian: kill me if you like, but I'm eternal. This rock loves me. This girl loves me. This beach loves me. This sky, this wind, these seagulls, these pebbles. My God! Blessed are you, and blessed is your Creation, forever and ever, amen. And blessed be your law of love.

Don't expect me to tell you what the rock and I discussed, because I don't know. But I'm sure we both learnt secrets of life that then gradually rose to the surface, little by little, in times of need. That's what real learning means. Not knowing you know something, then suddenly finding you do.

The end of the story isn't worth telling. Communication was abruptly cut off. Hunger, cold, night, an endless journey. She completed her cycle with her face to the wind and I finished mine on those rocks, and we returned in silence. I don't remember if she came home with me afterwards, or, if she did, what happened with her breasts. Perhaps she got off the bus in that little square. I don't know, it doesn't matter.

The experience with the traffic light was briefer, but similarly intense. There were no enchantresses that time, or any other kind of intermediary. Just the traffic light and me. An old, familiar traffic light near my house. I was waiting for it to change so I could cross the road. It was in the early evening, probably around sunset; not that we ever see sunsets in this city. The sky was tinged with countless gloomy colours, oranges and purples, and there was a strong sense of gathering darkness. The buildings here spoil everything, because they block out so much of the sky – one day, incidentally, I was walking along in a kind of daze, transfixed by a layer of pink clouds carpeting the evening sky; autumn clouds that said cold weather was on the way. I ran into someone I knew who lived nearby, and whom I often used to see around. 'Wonderful sky, isn't it?' I said. The look he gave me is impossible to describe. 'Yeah, sure,' he said, but I could tell what he was thinking; something about damn halfwits who walk around with their mouths hanging open, gawping at the sky. Such is life, my dear reader.

So, that evening, instead of looking at the traffic light straight ahead, I looked at the one to the side. I don't know why. I saw it change from green to amber, and it didn't say any more to me than 'Get ready'; and from amber to red, and then yes, *blop*, a rush of blood, of life, of love, a 'Hello, my darling, and how are you doing?', a 'God exists and he remembers you' – in short, the most perfect message of love and solidarity, the fullest and most complete. Laughter and tears, the bitter-sweet pleasure of the living, the pulsating current of life. The Spirit passed through that red light, as it can pass through anywhere – and only once. In the following years, and I've been keeping an eye on it, that traffic light has never been anything other than an old traffic light. That afternoon, however, it gave me life, encouragement, warmth; it helped me to go on living, and it taught me something good – something that, afterwards, would have been rising to the surface little by little, in times of need, as I was saying today.

Anyway, carrying on. A woman, let's call her J, why not, said to me one afternoon: 'Last night, before going to sleep, I was thinking about you. I was thinking about stroking your face.' And yes, I'd felt that soft pressure, almost like a breath of air, and I'd known, somehow, that it was her (probably because, along with the caress, I'd caught the aroma of some perfume, and perhaps recognised it; it was the same one she was wearing when I saw her later and she told me about the caress). And so this example was confirmed, which is why I'm writing about it. Similar things have happened on other occasions, but I haven't been able to confirm them. I'll keep those ones to myself.

I have an annoying insect bite on my back, and it's quite painful. I scratch it. The next day I feel the same thing again, and it doesn't go away. I have to travel to a place that's about sixty miles from where I live. When I leave the house, I glance at the letterbox: there's a letter for me, but I don't pick it up – I don't know why not, perhaps because I recognise the handwriting and know it won't be urgent, and because I think I'll see the person within the next few hours, in that very place I'm getting ready to go to. I go to the place. On arrival, since I still have that annoying bite, I ask someone I trust completely to have a look at my back. I lift up my shirt. The person says: 'What you have is an actual bite, not an insect bite. Who bit you?' 'No one bit me,' I say. 'You can see the tooth marks perfectly, the top ones and the bottom ones. Human teeth.' And the person I trust completely who's inspecting my back, and who happens to be my mother, gives me her usual smug look. 'I know you're not about to tell your old mother what you get up to in the bedroom,' she's obviously thinking, 'but I'll have you know that I wasn't born yesterday.' She applied some lotion, because it looked like it was beginning to get infected.

I return home, and I return without visiting the person who sent me that letter, simply because 'I didn't feel like visiting her'. I pass the letterbox and open the letter. 'The other night I dreamed I bit you on the back . . . ' Signed, my friend O. Think what you like; I won't say another word on the subject.

I'm tired of going through all the points I jotted down above one by one. The matter of the voice I heard was duly confirmed, even down to the time of day. The dog had indeed died, poisoned on the night I dreamed about him and the snow. Perhaps I'll discuss the rest later on, along with a few things I haven't mentioned, if they're relevant. I'm not making any promises. Now I have to go looking for the *daemon*, which, truth be told, was with me until it made its excuses at the whaleback-like rocks and vanished into thin air. Well, I suppose it's not difficult to guess where I'll find it – and there it is, hanging on delightedly to those breasts I spoke of a few lines ago. It paws, sucks, ogles, fondles, licks, admires. What a pig. 'Come on, *daemon*,' I say, 'or the novel will go down the drain, if it hasn't already. You remember, *daemon*, that this is the luminous novel? We want to write something that echoes like a hymn, that awakens sleeping minds, that makes the unknown dimension vibrate in uncontainable waves, for the greater glory of God.' By way of response, he cups those breasts lightly as if feeling their weight, and gives me a look that says: 'What greater hymn could there be than this? What greater glory? Idiot!' and he carries on fondling them. Personally, I haven't yet worked out what I think about the relationship, or the relationships – since there are various – between religion and sex. There's a great deal of philosophising to be done on the subject. For now, however, I'll merely describe an image, suggested of course by the *daemon*, an image worth more than a thousand words, which refers to that difficult, though essential, connection between religion and sex. It's about Q (I skipped P, to avoid suspicions and snide remarks; previously, I'd called the woman who bit me on the back O, because K, L, M and N have other connotations, and the Ñ doesn't seem very elegant). Q was a friend of mine who was also very well furnished in the breast department (the other woman, O, perhaps wins the prize – but I have no valid excuse to involve her breasts in this novel, at least not for the time being. Which is a shame, because they deserve a novel all to themselves). Although our friendship (my friendship with Q, that is) has been very long, our romance was fairly short, for many reasons, and fundamentally, I think, for one: because before making love she took off all her clothes except for an enormous crucifix, with Jesus on it and everything, which she left hanging around her neck; and a particularly tormented Jesus, too, all writhing and anguished-looking – for which you can't blame him, of course, given the circumstances. If I suggested that it would all be much easier and more comfortable if she took off her crucifix as well, she'd say: 'Isn't He the God of love?' – and that was that. You just try, sir – and for once, the female reader will forgive me the obligatory exclusion – you just try, sir, to maintain a good erection face to face with the image of the suffering Redeemer, however well appointed he might be between a pair of magnificent tits. Perhaps you – as a good atheist – could do it. But I could not. It was hard work, believe me. The girl was lovely, sweet, gentle, warm, fragrant – a real delight. I'd close my eyes and get lost in the moment and for a while I could forget everything, but then, *crack*, the crucifix would end up in my mouth, or in my eye, or give me a scratch on the cheek. Or I'd open my eyes – since you have to open them, of course, and open them wide – and there they'd all be, parading past: the Sacred History, Death and the Resurrection, Good Friday, Holy Saturday and Easter Sunday; the three denials of Peter, the Sermon on the Mount, the wedding at Canaan, the raising of Lazarus . . . and the Apocalypse. The image of the Redeemer, which demands, even if you're not exactly a saint, a kind of supernatural respect that pushes you to examine your conscience and confess your sins, set against those erect nipples wet with saliva and . . . anyway: I generally managed to bring things to a satisfying conclusion, but afterwards my head, spine and kidneys were a mess. I don't think these things should mix, despite the fact that 'He's the God of love', which He certainly is, and despite the intimate, profound connection there is between religion and sex. Goodbye, Q. Sometimes I worry my luminous novel will turn into a similar mixture. I want to believe it won't. I want to believe I've been able to balance the two poles of what is, I think, a unique phenomenon. I'm also afraid people will consider me a cynic, a liar or a heretic. I might be a heretic, but I have a theory in my defence (it's very simple, too: if Christianity was imposed through blood and fire and money and the Inquisition and other things like that, and now here we are, brought up with no alternative and within the cage of dogma – and, worse, of popular superstition deriving from badly digested dogma – we surely have the right to make all the adjustments we need in order to carry on believing – and, at the same time, to be free). But whether I like it or not, I seem to be arriving – via some erect nipples – at my conversion. Or 'conversion', since this is something I'm not very clear about either. I don't know what my exact relationship with the Church is nowadays – and I'm also writing this, partly, in an attempt to find out. Nor do I know what my relationship with the Church will be in the future: I'm in the dark, or the half-light. But did a conversion take place? Yes, it did. And was it luminous? It was.

## FIRST COMMUNION

When I moved into this apartment a couple of years ago, it was a nice surprise to spot a little tile above the door with an image of the Virgin on it, which is visible from the landing. Underneath, screwed into the lintel, was a plaque that read '*Ave María Purísima*'. I imagined a scene on a farm: someone claps their hands and shouts, '*¡Ave María Purísima!*' and I answer from inside in traditional Spanish style, shouting as well, over the barking of the dogs: 'Conceived without sin!'

That little tile helped me to feel protected as I embarked on the adventure of living alone, which was something I hadn't done for years. Not long ago, a student leaving my apartment after a workshop turned around when she reached the lift and pointed at the tile.

'Are you Catholic?' she asked.

I looked at her for several seconds, thoroughly perplexed. It was an unanswerable question.

'I don't know what to tell you,' I said. I carried on pondering the matter long after the students had all gone home, and it kept returning to me in the days that followed. One afternoon, in the kitchen, while I was washing the dishes – an excellent opportunity for reflection – the answer came to me. I formulated it slowly and clearly: 'Yes, I'm a Catholic in the same way that I'm Uruguayan.' Not by choice, but by birth.

My entry into this nation was, needless to say, due to my mother; and, less obviously, it was also through her that I had my first contact with the Church. Something that in other countries would have been perfectly normal was, here, entirely down to chance. Whether because of staunch adherence to the ideas of Don Pepe Batlle, or because he was an anarchist, or simply because he was stubborn and ignorant, my maternal grandfather was a fanatical atheist, or, more precisely, he was virulently anti-religious, anticlerical and blasphemous, and it was rare for anything he said, however brief, not to contain a few wholly gratuitous and indecent epithets directed at a member of the Holy Family, particularly God the Father. The social sphere, it's safe to say, was (and is) happily separate from religion; Don Pepe had fought and roundly beaten the powers of the Church, but the fight didn't stop there: he finished up by exterminating all religious feeling from the majority of the population, or at least the outward signs of it. An ex-priest friend of mine told me that, around the middle or the end of the thirties, priests even had stones thrown at them in the street.

Nowadays, for better or worse, all that repressed, latent religiosity has broken out in the appearance of dozens, perhaps even hundreds, of sects, and the churches of these different groups are sprouting up like mushrooms all over the city.

When I was eight years old I voluntarily agreed to be baptised, and my mother took advantage of this to get baptised as well. In the years before that, I only remember occasional strange visits to some church or other on Good Friday; and a priest who stood in a kind of sentry box with his back to everyone, speaking in Latin; and my mother looking as serious as a dog in a boat, the corners of her lips turned downwards in a very sour expression and a black shawl covering her head. And my uneasiness, a feeling somewhere between guilt and fear, though I didn't know the reason for either.

There was also a brief period during which I was taken to a place called 'Sunday school'. I don't remember much about it, but I think it looked like an Evangelist temple; instead of the uncomfortable pews you get in Catholic churches, it had wooden chairs, which were far more comfortable and varnished to a deep shine. I can't have looked up very much, because the chairs are all I remember; everything else is shrouded in mystery. I think I was taken to this place with other children, because I vaguely remember there being a group of us, but I don't have a clue who they were, any more than I can imagine who would have taken us, though I think it was a very young woman. If my current experiences are anything to go by, I probably fell into a trance as soon as I was left in that person's care and noticed almost nothing about my surroundings, as often happens to me these days when I leave the house. If there's someone with me, after a few blocks I might begin to look up and take some interest in the world around me, but I always begin with my gaze fixed on my shoes. How I manage to cross roads or avoid walking into pedestrians or pillars I'll never know. I probably have peripheral vision that I'm largely unaware of, or perhaps I emit ultrasound waves like a bat.

I've retained one very clear image of that Sunday school, and only one: my right shoe – and who knows what unnatural material it was made of, or what fiendishly pointy shape it had – tracing random shapes on the back of the seat in front of me, or, in other words, scratching the impeccable varnish. It made a very soft, very satisfying scraping sound, which I thought only I could hear, while the room echoed with the voice of a figure a long way in front of me, out of my sight. I have a feeling I didn't hear a single word properly, and if I did, either I didn't understand or I wasn't interested. The truth is, I learnt absolutely nothing at that Sunday school, and I couldn't even say what they were trying to teach us. Along with the pleasing image of the little picture I was drawing with my shoe, another much less pleasing image occurs to me: the frowning face of someone, perhaps the same young woman who was in charge of us, looking at me sternly and gesturing for me to stop what I was doing. The telling-off made me feel self-conscious and I must have withdrawn into myself even further, enveloped in an infinite boredom.

The simultaneous baptisms came about once we'd moved to the city centre, thanks to a man we used to call Don Tomás. I don't know how he came into our lives, and I've never, even now, been able to pin down exactly what sort of a person he was. He was an accountant by trade, if I'm not mistaken. And his hobby – or perhaps his second profession, since I often saw my mother surreptitiously slipping him a roll of banknotes – his hobby, let's say, was being a healer. But he was no ordinary, run-of-the-mill healer. Born in Majorca, he was what you'd call an educated man, or at least educated enough to give that impression; he was well spoken, although he didn't say much, and he knew a vast amount about a wide range of topics. The strangest thing about him was his relationship with various members of the Catholic Church. It's no secret that Catholics, especially priests, have no time for healers, spiritualists or charlatans of any kind; and yet Don Tomás was friends with several high-ranking clergymen. So much so that, if I remember rightly, our baptism, which was orchestrated by him, took place in the Cathedral itself.

He maintained, and in this he was energetically backed up by his wife, that he could see dead people. He was often running into them and saying hello, and he told us that for him it was an everyday occurrence. His therapeutic approach was quite mysterious: with no warning, and when no one was expecting it, he'd fall into a trance (he called it 'concentration'). He screwed his eyes shut and stayed perfectly still, while around him a respectful silence fell. Sometimes nobody noticed and the conversation continued for a few moments, until whoever was talking broke off suddenly in embarrassment, even though Don Tomás had explained more than once that when he was 'concentrating' you could fire a cannon and he wouldn't hear. Nevertheless, we fell into a deep silence, if only out of a kind of fearful respect. What strange things were happening around us, under the influence of that concentration? I hardly breathed. We were all waiting for him to wake up, and sometimes we were waiting a long time. I never worked out whether it was all an act. My mother was once bold enough to ask him what happened during those concentrations. His answer, like all his answers, was very vague, or rather indirect, but it included something about how 'he could see inside the human body with perfect clarity, and even move around inside it'. He didn't say this was what he was doing; he just said he could do it. From then on I used to wonder, during his trances, whether he was looking inside me, and what he might find.

At first, our sessions with Don Tomás were held in the house of some well-to-do Galicians, a couple I'd never seen before then and never saw since. In the scene from these sessions that's most clearly recorded in my memory, the owner of the house was diagnosed by Don Tomás as having a broken or cracked rib. The treatment struck me as particularly strange: he had to stand on a chair and jump off it backwards. He was made to repeat this several times. I don't know what came of it.

Nor do I know what my father thought of all this. My father was a shop assistant, an outwardly unpretentious man. And yet with time I discovered a wisdom in him that was probably innate, and which allowed him to behave in the most correct and appropriate way no matter what situation he found himself in. One of his most firmly held principles, I believe, was his respect for things he knew nothing about, combined with a frank and natural recognition of his own limitations. When it came to those sessions with Don Tomás, he did what he had to do: he came along, he was respectful, he almost certainly paid, because my mother didn't have her own income in those days, and he sat through each and every session with no apparent difficulty, even though some of them went on for a very long time. But I never found out what he thought of it all. Maybe he didn't think anything.

The Galicians soon found a way of passing the buck; we inherited Don Tomás and the sessions began taking place in our house, and that went on for a good while – certainly months, and perhaps more than a year. The Galician man's technique must have been very simple and effective, since he was always the one who put an end to the sessions in his house, with the words: 'Well, this is all very interesting, but tomorrow we have to work.' He stood up and we all immediately did the same, and then we went home.

In our house, things were different. One of Don Tomás's skills was sending his wife ahead to infiltrate long before he arrived, which put us in a very awkward position. As far as I know, this was never explicitly agreed; but one fine day, the day of a session, his wife rang the doorbell, we opened the door, she came in and sat down, and there she stayed, with my grandmother and mother taking it in turns to keep her company. She was a very fat, ugly woman, seemingly lacking in any particular talent. She had nothing to talk about and sat in her chair like a vegetable, dozing off every now and then. Who knows what her husband was up to in the meantime; sometimes he didn't arrive until much later. With time, even my grandmother and mother left her alone and went back to whatever they were doing. She didn't mind; her face was completely expressionless, almost shapeless.

It must, I realise now, have been my father who discreetly put an end to those sessions. I've just remembered how, at one point, he began to wonder out loud about the man's powers.

'If he has the power to cure people,' I can hear him saying, 'why doesn't he cure that stuff in his eyes?'

And indeed, as well as wearing glasses, Don Tomás had trouble with a whitish secretion at the outer corners of his eyelids, perhaps caused by tiredness or some kind of infection. I think the seeds of my father's rebellion were sown when Don Tomás said one day that 'you can catch dandruff from hairdressers'. My father's doctor had told him that dandruff was the result of stomach problems, and for my father, his doctor's word was the word of God. In fact, as I understand it now there are various possible causes of dandruff; like almost everything else, it doesn't come from just one thing but from a combination of factors. And besides, Don Tomás's explanation strikes me as more plausible than the explanation of my father's doctor, but neither of them is completely right. Still, I heard my father repeat this argument more than once, and it's quite possible that from then on Don Tomás's days in our house were numbered. Like me, my father wasn't a violent man, but he was very persistent.

The person I can't find anywhere in these reminiscences is my grandfather; it's as if he were already dead by this point. But I don't think he died until some time afterwards. It could well be, however, that when one of the sessions was taking place in the house, he made himself scarce, presumably retiring to a different room, since by then he'd stopped going out. If he was still alive, it seems strange that I can't remember a single story about him in which the healer makes an appearance; there should be plenty, and juicy ones at that, or at least with bursts of very colourful language.

The story of Don Tomás began with me and that famous heart murmur I had to put up with from the age of three. Around the time of the sessions, the doctors announced that the murmur 'was cured'. My mother was convinced Don Tomás had worked a miracle. But my theory is that the murmur never existed; when I was about thirty, a doctor told me that the doctors who diagnosed the heart murmur had most likely been hearing the sound of the apex of one of my lungs. What's more, the doctors who said it had been cured were from the city centre, and very different to the ones who treated me in that obscure polyclinic in the back of beyond, and who gave me a check-up every so often to see if the murmur was still there. They had obviously read my medical records and weren't about to disagree with the initial diagnosis, because, as everyone knows, the medical profession is one big mafia whose members look out for one another. The nurses in that public health dispensary were gangsters as well. At the end of each visit, they'd ask my mother if she 'needed anything'. My mother always needed a litre of alcohol, or something like that, which she acquired for the price of a modest tip. Corruption is nothing new in Uruguay, contrary to what people believe today. I remember my aunt the teacher, whose house was stuffed with industrial quantities of exercise books, pencils and other equipment she stole from the local school where she worked. And all the other public-sector workers were as much thieves as she was. Stealing from the State was the natural, logical thing to do, and nobody disapproved. Not even the State, since as far as I know it never did anything to stop it. And don't tell me no one knew about the vox populi, or about whatever the Latin is for 'the sight of the people'. The point is that it wasn't just rumour: everything was plainly, flagrantly on show.

Anyway, what I wanted to say before I merrily embarked on this digression was that Don Tomás was the man behind my baptism and the simultaneous baptism of my mother, and I'm grateful to him for that, in spite of his horrible fat wife and the boredom of those interminable sessions.

The selectiveness of memory never ceases to amaze me. I imagine the unconscious has its reasons for fixing some scenes in the mind more firmly than others, but my conscious self has no idea why, for example, of everything I experienced during the baptism, all I remember is happily descending the steps when it was over – and that it was sunny. They could well have been the Cathedral steps; there were several of them, and they were very large. That patch of stone and sun; my only memory of an act that's meant to be transcendental, and that I must have found interesting and affecting. As for the inside of the church, the priest, the holy water on my head, my mother . . . all I have is a dark, hazy impression, with no clearly defined images, which seems more like a product of logical necessity than anything else.

The only more or less fair criticism I could make of my father, of the many I secretly or overtly made of him when I was young, is that he was absent. I've often described, in different places, my most pressing concern, my insistent question when I could still barely speak: where's my father? And the answers never made sense to me, and nor, of course, did they fill the gap. Where was he? He was working, in a shop, standing behind a counter for eight hours a day to support us. And later, when the eight hours were over, he spent his evenings teaching English. Even when he was physically present in the house, he didn't have time for me.

Saying he worked in a shop to support us is a rather dramatic way of putting it; he could have done other, less apparently demanding things if he'd wanted. But the fact is, he liked that work, or, more than liking it, he found that it fulfilled a deep internal need. He had always got on very badly with his own father, about whom all I know is that he was extremely strict, even brutal. My father once mentioned, in passing, when we were talking about other things, that as a boy he only had one place in his house that belonged to him: a little wooden box with a padlock, where he kept his most treasured possessions – and I could never imagine what they might have been. From time to time, his father would use a tool to open the padlock and look inside the box, saying that his son could have no secrets from him. So my father left home as soon as possible, and to make it possible he decided to get a job. You don't need to be a certified psychoanalyst to unravel the secret of his love for his work; the first shop that employed him was called Paternostro, and that was also the surname of the owner. When Paternostro closed down, my father moved to the London-Paris shop, and he was there until he retired. He talked about the owner of that shop as reverently as he used to talk about Paternostro. They were both obvious father figures, and to him they were almost like gods. In those shops he found the home he'd never had, and, although they were his bosses, father figures who were kinder to him than his real father had ever been. The owner of the London-Paris shop had the surname Tapié, and I never heard my father call him anything other than 'Mr Tapié'. At one point, Mr Tapié fell seriously ill, and when my father came home for lunch he'd always update us on the medical situation, deeply concerned. And when Mr Tapié died, my father went through a period of genuine mourning.

I mention these things to explain the gap in my childhood where a father figure should have been, and my lifelong difficulties with exerting even a tiny amount of self-discipline. The thing is, I could never identify with a figure who had any real authority. My mother was the one with the authority, but because it wasn't real authority, she always exercised it in that ambiguous way women do, ambiguous and arbitrary, and exaggerated, over-the-top, hysterical, when a bit of love and intelligence would have sufficed. And this authoritarianism has evidently become a part of me, judging by how I treat myself when I want to be more disciplined; as some of my friends have pointed out, I turn into a kind of fascist sergeant. Without achieving a great deal, of course, which is always the way with illegitimate authority.

That being the case, there came a time, dangerously close to when I hit puberty, in which my mother apparently found me quite impossible to control. I don't remember a single incident that backs up this claim – no particularly bad behaviour on my part, that is – because, after all, I was fairly easy-going; I was fussy, certainly, and certainly almost always with good reason, but not the type to cause a scene or go in for any antisocial or abnormal activities. Still, one day my mother was at her wits' end, and she tried something completely disproportionate: she threw a Bible at me. She threw it at me, literally, and told me to read it, saying I'd learn a thing or two and see what kind of future I had in store.


I picked up the Bible with great interest; at last, I thought, I was going to get to grips with the famous business of God, about whom I'd heard so many one-sided and contradictory things – from my grandfather, for example. I soon established a relationship with Jehovah, the early God of the Jews, and it wasn't long before that terrifying figure became part of my life – and in a way, I think he still is. Many years later, before she died, my mother asked for forgiveness for all the harm she'd caused me. I told her not to be silly and said I had nothing to forgive her for, but in those fraught moments it was hard to be objective. I had plenty of things to forgive her for, in fact, and I hope I've managed to do so; and that business with the Bible was surely among the most serious. After my first reading of it, which I found overwhelming, because at the end of the day I didn't understand much of what I was reading, and I still don't think I'm capable of understanding much of that mixture of texts which some people see as the 'word of God', but after my first reading, as I was saying, for a considerable time I lived in fear. I'd already spent a considerable time living in fear, especially at night, ever since they dropped those atomic bombs on Hiroshima and Nagasaki and everyone started talking about atomic danger and chain reactions. Once, when I was about eight, I heard that the way to protect yourself from radiation was to cover yourself with a white sheet from top to toe, and so every night before going to sleep I pulled the sheet up over my head. I still wasn't sure if the blankets on top of the sheet covering the rest of my body would stop it working. Night after night, interminably, waiting for the explosion of the bomb and the complete destruction of everything around me, and probably also myself, because to be honest I didn't have much faith in the white-sheet method; I'd seen documentaries that showed experiments involving atomic bombs exploding on islands, and I wondered what a piece of cloth could possibly do in the face of all that. The image of Jehovah didn't help matters; in fact, it made things worse, because now I had someone inside me checking up on my thoughts, and I had bad thoughts, which I tried to hide even from myself. I couldn't say how long this terror lasted, but it's certainly never entirely gone away; it's still there now, more or less hidden, more or less buried – especially since I found out, many years later, that it's completely true that God knows all our thoughts. But since God is no longer the Jehovah of the Jews, it doesn't bother me so much that he knows them, although my thoughts continue to be pretty bad.

What made my mother's act of throwing a Bible at me so serious was that, in doing so, she put me in direct contact with God, or what I thought was God, without the mediation of a priest. This is too much for anyone, especially a child. Perhaps, at the time, a good priest could have sorted things out.


My relationship with God continued to change after that first encounter in the Bible. When I was around twenty-five, a door opened up inside me that led to the spiritual world. Extraordinary things gradually began to happen, showing me that reality had far more dimensions than I'd realised; and I set about investigating this, haphazardly and not very systematically but with great determination, using a wide range of sources and not discounting personal adventures. I got into a few scrapes – and got out of them with psychotherapeutic assistance – but I gained things as well, not least literature. I investigated, as I said, in a disorderly and haphazard way, consulting spiritualist, occultist, psychoanalytical, religious and scientific materials, and I managed to find out that something really did exist, and that you could call it God if you wanted, although it also answered to other names. At any rate, it was something beyond my capacity for perception and understanding; but there was, yes, something alive and transcendental, involving the multidimensionality of the universe. I found, too, that you could communicate with this something in strange ways, and that these ways were never the same twice and I couldn't simply use them whenever I pleased.

An ex-priest, who at the time practised parapsychology, supplemented my psychological therapy with some parapsychological therapy which saved me, to an extent, from that dangerous world of uncertainties. He may not have provided any certainties, but he gave me some simple guidelines to ensure I didn't get carried away by paranormal phenomenology, or irrevocably overpowered by it. I was still in contact with this paranormal therapist when Cándido appeared at a birthday party.


To my surprise, he was introduced to me as a priest. He didn't look like a priest. He had coarse but pleasant features, like a European peasant, and at first I thought he was Catalan, because of his proud expression. He was probably a few years older than me – I was around thirty-five or thirty-six – but his thick hair was already grey, almost white. His cheeks were the kind of pink that makes you think of health and apples, but that's not to say he was one of those chubby-faced priests: he was a thin man, with a peasant's sharp and slightly suspicious gaze. He didn't so much speak as mumble through gritted teeth, wrestling with a language he hadn't mastered. It took me a while to recognise his Spanish as distorted by Italian, because it was nothing like the usual Spanish spoken by Italian immigrants; he must have been from the countryside and had a dialect as his first language. To complete the picture, which is making me sweat, because describing people has never been my forte, I'll simply add that he was dressed in very simple, rough clothes, especially his trousers, which were baggy at the knees. Oh, yes: and that his whole being exuded an air of resolute frankness. The moment I saw him, I thought: 'Now, here's a person you can trust.'


I didn't realise it at the time, but when we left the birthday party and set off down the street, we were already friends. We walked to my apartment, which wasn't far away, and I invited him up. The moment he set foot in my study, he saw the chessboard on a table. Without further ado, he emptied the box of pieces onto the board, sat down and started to arrange half of them. The whites, of course. I sat down, arranged the black pieces, and selected two pawns, one of each colour, which I mixed up with my hands behind my back; I then presented him with my two closed fists to choose from. I don't know which of us ended up with white, or which of us won. And I didn't realise that at that moment we were establishing a ritual, or at least a powerful shared addiction. Cándido came over a lot from then on. He always headed straight for the chessboard, and generally didn't leave until we'd decided on a winner after the usual two or three games. We didn't speak much, if at all. Sometimes we'd carry on until late: one, two, or even three in the morning. This was bad for him because he invariably had to give mass at 8 a.m.; a mass that he didn't enjoy. 'For those old ladies . . . ' he'd say, his jaws clenched. He hated pious old ladies, especially the ones who got up early.

The priestly office, in any religion, has always inspired respect in me. I assume there's a permanent link between God and the priest, and that this link is a form of divine presence. Faced with a priest, my best qualities make themselves known to me and my worst qualities try to hide. In a way, I find being close to a priest therapeutic, because when your better qualities rise to the surface, you feel better yourself somehow; you treat yourself better, and you treat other people better as well. The divine presence could be real or imaginary; if it's imaginary, the priest simply serves as a reminder that there are higher powers in the universe. And even that means a great deal, in a world that's constantly pelting us with low, vile, ordinary things.

However, the day came when I had no choice but to separate my friend Cándido into two personalities: the priest and the friend, or, more precisely, the priest and the chess adversary. The first time this happened I was very surprised, by both his behaviour and my own. During a game, he got distracted and left his queen vulnerable to one of my pieces.

'Cándido,' I said. 'I don't know if you saw, but you're about to lose your queen.'

He looked at the board and quickly moved the piece back.

'Ah, yes,' he said. He didn't say thank you. A little later, I accidentally left my queen exposed to one of his pieces. Cándido, impassive, snatched my queen off the board, and put his piece on that square. At first I thought it was a funny way of pointing out my mistake, and I waited for him to give back my queen. But he didn't. He carried on looking serenely at the board, waiting for my move. I exploded with rage.

'Jesus fucking Christ, Cándido!' I burst out, forgetting his priestly status. 'You're not a gentleman,' I added, a little calmer now, though still furious, 'you're a lout.'

He looked at me nonplussed, and didn't give back my queen.

'Cándido,' I tried again, summoning all my patience. 'You handed your queen over just now without realising, and I told you and let you go back. Why should you play with an advantage, like a child?'

Then he mumbled more incomprehensible things in an unrecognisable language, returned the queen to its place and waited for me to make another move.

I think he picked up that ruthless style, more appropriate to sport than to an intellectual puzzle, from his games against the boys in the student residence he ran. That style of play, which involves exploiting your opponent's distraction, makes me lose all interest in the game. It turns it from an intellectual confrontation into a matter of old-fashioned street cunning. But he also played football with those boys, and his ankles were always covered in bruises. I could never get him out of the habit of playing chess that way, and that wasn't the only time I had to swear at him; every time I pointed out something he'd missed, he moved the piece back; but any distraction on my part, *bam*, before I knew it Cándido had seized the piece like a falcon swooping down on an unsuspecting baby animal.

As long as he wasn't doing things like that, I always felt very aware that he was a priest, and I treated him with the requisite respect. He didn't seem to notice, and I'm sure it didn't matter to him at all.

Once, I brought up the topic of religion, in relation to one of my many anxieties on the matter. And I brought it up again several times after that, and he never did once. His answers to my questions weren't exactly brilliant, though he took me very seriously, forgetting about the chess game for a moment and giving me his full attention. He provided me with formulaic, even childlike explanations; dogma expressed in its simplest form. It was completely useless trying to dig deeper; that was how things were, because it was; although he didn't say this in an authoritarian way, but simply with total conviction. It was what he'd been taught, and because he believed what he'd been taught he repeated it honestly – indeed, if I can allow myself a pun on his name, I'd say he repeated it candidly. It took me a long time to begin to tell the difference between his faith and his credulity, or, to put it another way, his simple-mindedness.

I once invited him to a lecture on parapsychology, to be given by my therapist friend. At first he said no and launched into a rant about parapsychology and parapsychologists. I said that this particular para-psychologist was a serious person, that he used to be a priest like him and had left the cloth to get married; and that proof of his seriousness was the fact that the lecture would take place in a Catholic school. He carried on stubbornly refusing. I knew that if he went, he'd love it; and by then I knew him well enough to play on his weaknesses.

'Besides,' I said, 'the speaker is going to levitate, and he'll come into the lecture hall through the window. The lecture hall is on the second floor.'

He said no more about it, and neither did I. I didn't really think he believed me, but when it was time to leave for the lecture, there he was in my apartment; he'd come without my needing to repeat the invitation. We went together, then, and he did indeed love it. On the way back we were walking along, looking for a bus stop, and talking about different parts of the lecture. I'd forgotten my tactic for luring him along, but when we saw the bus approaching, Cándido turned to me accusingly and said:

'He didn't come in through the window.' And he went on looking at me, waiting for me to explain. I burst out laughing. He was in a bad mood for a while.

But hand in hand with his gullibility came his faith; and that faith gave him all of his strength. That faith is the only thing I'll consciously let myself envy about him. Thanks to that faith, he could install himself anywhere, in any part of the world, in any situation, and feel at home. I, on the other hand, am permanently on edge, even in my own home, as if I didn't want to get in the way, or as if I might be moved on at any moment, even when I'm living alone.

.    .    .

One day, Cándido gruffly expressed a desire for me to watch him giving mass. 'On a Sunday evening,' he said. There was a good crowd on Sundays, among them my friends from the birthday party and lots of young people, and Cándido wanted me to see him at work in this congenial atmosphere. 'Not the other days because those old ladies will be there. Sundays.' I said I would, and the following Sunday I walked the few blocks to the church feeling quite expectant. I couldn't imagine him delivering mass, let alone the sermon – or the homily, as he called it, using the more correct term. I sat in a pew in one of the back rows, as I always did on the rare occasions I went to a church. A little out of humility, a little out of shyness, and a little to keep my distance from a religion that, despite many approaches over the years, has always felt alien to me.

I was surprised to see Juan José, my friend from the birthday party, step onto the little podium or whatever it's called – priests must have some technical name for it – which was a kind of platform protected by a backrest and fitted with a microphone, from which laypeople sometimes speak and sometimes sing. My friend began to sing, in his beautiful, powerful, full-bodied voice, the hymn that precedes the entrance of the priest. And there was Cándido, dressed in some unbelievable violet robes that didn't look bad on him, and which he wore quite naturally and with dignity. I don't remember the exact order of the stages of the mass, though I experienced them again countless times after that. There was a reading, and then came the homily, and Cándido expressed himself with notable clarity and good sense. Then, when it was time for the celebration, or whatever you call it – the mass itself – as he handed out the bread and wine, he really was transfigured, and it was no longer Cándido standing there. He was evidently in a trance, or a kind of ecstasy, if you like; concentrating hard, serene, detached from his surroundings for a long while, his eyes closed. The faithful formed a queue – spurred on by the soaring voice of my friend, who was back in position – all singing at full volume (one woman, probably not very young and clearly very histrionic, always stood out for her piercing high notes, like a soprano in an opera. I don't remember seeing her face; her voice was coming from somewhere outside my field of vision). When he began to distribute the wafers, Cándido, or whoever it was that had taken his place, remained distant and deep in concentration; he'd opened his eyes again, but only slightly. It was interesting to see the different ways the faithful had of receiving the host; some simply opened their mouth so the priest could place it inside, which has always struck me as slightly obscene. Others took it in their hand, which is what I'd do, I said to myself, if I had to take Communion.

I sat down and stood up many times that evening, following the orders I heard or the actions of everyone else. The main thing, in my view, is to respect the customs of the places you go. But I didn't kneel, because it didn't seem right, and because there were other people who didn't kneel either.

'And now we'll say goodbye, as usual, by singing to our mother, the Virgin Mary,' said my friend Juan José, up on the podium again, and during another chorus, the procession towards the exit began, with the priest himself at the head. Then Cándido stationed himself at the door, and he was Cándido again, but an exultant, rejuvenated Cándido, rosy-cheeked and beaming like a happy child.

From then on, I don't think I missed a single Sunday. Sometimes, on Saturday nights, Cándido would interrupt the chess to ask my advice. 'Tomorrow I have to do a homily on . . . ' – and he'd mention a topic. 'Can you think of anything?' he'd ask. I could always think of something. As a layperson with all the freedom in the world to say whatever I liked, I unleashed upon him every more or less secret line of reasoning that had accompanied me throughout my life; curiously, he accepted them without further discussion, because, of course, he'd asked and I'd answered. To my amazement, the next day, during the homily, I'd usually find that Cándido had appropriated my ideas and was calmly dispensing them to the congregation. He didn't use my words or my concepts; instead he developed them, or rather digested them, processed them and made them his own. It wasn't that he smoothed out the rough edges or adapted my thoughts into dogma; he simplified them without distorting them, and in that simplification they lost all intellectual malevolence, and sometimes he went further, much further than I had. On one occasion I was completely horror-struck, expecting nothing less than Cándido's excommunication, when, based on some of my arguments from that Saturday night, he declared from the pulpit: 'Baptism is completely unnecessary.'


One Sunday, the date of which I could calculate with total precision, I went to Cándido's mass, just like on any other Sunday. The mass took place as usual, with no special details that would make it stick in the memory, until the very end. Cándido pronounced his '*Ite, missa est*' according to the formula in Spanish that I now don't remember, and Juan José, up on the podium, reminded us that 'As usual, we'll say goodbye by singing to our Mother, the Holy Virgin' and, as usual, my face twisted with distaste, because of all the parts of the dogma I found hard to swallow, the Virgin was the most difficult. I'm a man of the Holy Spirit; unlike Borges, it's all I understand, all I know, all I believe in. The rest of the figures seem rather vague; I don't have an exact image of the Father, and in the image I have of the Son, he's been manhandled so much that he doesn't seem very appealing. Like the poet Machado, I prefer the one who walked on the sea, though I always picture the one on the cross, and I don't like that. But back then the idea of the Mother of God, and a virgin on top of everything else, struck me as more than unpleasant; it rubbed me up the wrong way, and I found her popularity particularly galling. So I twisted my mouth into a grimace, as usual, and stayed in my seat, waiting for the end of the procession, which was moving slowly towards the exit, its members singing at the top of their lungs. That was when it started to rain; a drop fell onto my shirt, in the region of my chest, on the left side, where we think the heart is. I was very surprised. How could it rain inside a church? Was there a hole in the roof? I looked up and, of course, all I saw was the drawings (if there were in fact drawings; in my imagination, the ceiling of that church looks like the ceiling of the Sistine Chapel, but there probably weren't any 'drawings'). Another droplet landed on me, symmetrical to the last, and I began to feel nervous; I hadn't brought anything waterproof, or a coat, and my apartment was a few blocks away. I thought that if rain was dripping through a leak in a building as solid as the church seemed to be, there was surely a torrential downpour. But in the end I realised it wasn't raining. Instead, my eyes were crying. I say my eyes because I myself still hadn't started to cry; I was completely removed from what was happening inside me, or wherever it was – in that place where emotions are created. And, filled with confusion as I felt those tears sliding down my cheeks and wetting my shirt, for a moment I was utterly disconcerted, and also rather afraid, because I wasn't used to the schizophrenia that meant I could have someone inside me crying and only find out by means of deduction. But that schizophrenia ended abruptly, and I saw, I saw, don't ask me with what eyes, but I saw inside me the face of a woman I knew and loved, and then another, and another, a whole legion of women I loved, which included my mother, and in such numbers and at such speed that I couldn't recognise them individually, but there they all were, parading along, coming towards me, and they all seemed to say the same thing, a 'Why don't you love me?', and I realised that what was addressing me, this pure essence of femininity, this common denominator of all the women and all the loves of my life, was Her, Mary herself, in all her power and all her presence. She looked nothing like she does on the prayer cards. She wasn't one woman; she was all women. A living abstraction, living and present. I shuffled leftwards along the pew, half sitting, half crouching, looking for a pathway free of people, and I escaped in distress, ashamed of my crying, which not only hadn't finished but in fact seemed to be just getting started; the famous lump in the throat, the unbearable angst that only sobbing can release, rising up from the chest. I crept along, hiding behind pillars and pressing myself against walls, until I found a discreet way out and went down the steps furthest from the entrance, where Cándido and my friends must have been waiting for me, and shrunken, hunched, made my way through the shadows of the evening and the street until I arrived home, without stopping my crying for a single moment. When I was back in my apartment, without having run into anyone I knew on the way, I threw myself down onto my bed, just as I was, and carried on crying, and I was crying when I fell asleep, and the next day when I woke up I was still crying.

.     .     .

I find it very hard to believe that I went out that morning without having breakfast, but I also can't imagine having breakfast and crying at the same time. I know I called Cándido the second I got up, telling him I had an urgent problem and needed to ask his advice as soon as possible. He told me to come and see him in his office, in the student residence he ran, which was in the same block as the church. And so, with or without breakfast, off I went. Cándido showed me to a comfortable armchair. He sat behind his desk. I briefly explained what was happening to me, crying and blowing my nose the whole time. He was silent for a few moments, and then reached for a Bible he had on one side of his desk. He opened it at random. 'Let's see what the word of God says,' he mumbled, and fixed his gaze on the page in front of him. As if it were the I Ching, the response fit the question perfectly. Cándido read aloud a few paragraphs of that strange story from the Gospels in which Jesus cried.

> Then when Mary was come where Jesus was, and saw him, she fell down at his feet, saying unto him, Lord, if thou hadst been here, my brother had not died. When Jesus therefore saw her weeping, and the Jews also weeping which came with her, he groaned in the spirit, and was troubled. And said, Where have ye laid him? They said unto him, Lord, come and see. Jesus wept.

Martha and Mary were Lazarus' sisters. Cándido explained that the function of women is to encourage men to do their work; without women's encouragement, men would do nothing. Martha and Mary push Jesus to resuscitate the dead man, just as the other Mary, the mother, had pushed him to turn water into wine. (Jesus got annoyed and objected, but in the end he did as he was told.)

'I think you're ready to take Communion,' Cándido added. And I agreed, and the crying stopped.

'I understand there's a lot of preparation to do first,' I said. 'You're more than prepared,' he replied. 'You can take it directly next Sunday.' When I said I could calculate the date with total precision if necessary, it was because the day of my First Communion was the Feast of Corpus Christi, the festival in honour of the Eucharist; the sacrament, that is, which, in the form of bread and wine – according to Catholic doctrine – contains the true presence of Jesus Christ.

That Corpus Sunday I joined the queue to receive the host. Cándido fully respected my request for anonymity, but that didn't stop him telling a few of my close friends; after the ceremony there was a small gathering, even with cake and savoury snacks, in a room next to the nave of the church. The parapsychologist and his wife were there, and Alicia and Juan José, of course. And Elisa, my childhood and lifelong friend. But during mass I'd sat alone a long way away, as usual, and I'd gone up alone to receive the First Communion. No one had the right to take anything away from me of that moment that was totally mine.

That night, Cándido came round to play chess as usual, with his baggy trousers and peasant's expression; as ever, there was no sign of the transfiguration he'd undergone during mass. This time, I stopped him abruptly when he went into my study, and before he'd sat down at the chessboard, I stood up as tall as I could and pointed an accusatory finger at him:

'What do they put in the wafers?' I demanded.

He seemed momentarily taken aback, then responded very naturally:
'Flour and water.'

'I know that, Cándido. I'm not stupid. But what do they put in with the flour and water? I mean: what kind of drug?'

He looked at me for some time, bewildered. Then he clenched his teeth and repeated:

'Flour and water. Just flour and water.'

'That's as may be. But for mine in particular, because today was a special occasion, you added something extra.'

Cándido was alarmed now.

'I didn't even see you,' he confessed.

And I realised it was true: he gave out the wafers in a state of beatitude or trance, with his eyes half-closed, repeating mechanically 'the body of Christ'. He hadn't seen me, and he couldn't have selected a spiked wafer especially for me.

.    .    .

I'd taken the wafer from his hand and put it in my mouth, and then, without chewing, returned slowly to my place in the pew. I closed my eyes to explore what I was feeling as the wafer gradually dissolved, now with the help of a little work from my teeth. I swallowed it and went on meditating, or trying to meditate, but my whole mind had become cloudy, filled with something cotton-like though not entirely white, but with a few greyish patches. That was when the wing of an angel brushed against me. Against my chest. From the inside. On the solar plexus, perhaps. And not even the wing; a single feather of the wing. The most delicate physical contact imaginable; or indeed less than physical, as if it involved a material vastly more delicate than the most delicate material we know. At that moment, I described it as the wing of an angel, and I never found a better way of expressing it. And then it was over.

The following Sunday, I went to receive my wafer with an antici-patory longing to feel that gentle flutter once again. Everything was repeated exactly, except for the flutter. This time, in my pew, when I closed my eyes and swallowed the wafer, my mind wasn't filled with that cottony substance, and instead, suddenly, with no prior warning, I saw myself nailed to a cross. The vertical part of the cross was made of wood that looked thin and flexible, like a rod, because of the distance; it was several miles high, and from up there the Earth looked tiny, almost like a dot far below. The vertical part of the cross was bending with my weight, or because of the curvature of space. I felt dizzy and panicked. It lasted a few moments, then it was gone.

And never again did a wafer have any noticeable effect on me.

So I'm a Catholic, then, although it's many years since I last set foot in a church. I don't think it's necessary. Once that symbol of something unnameable, which is named Christ, has become part of you, it will be part of you forever, and the Church will be inside you; the real Church, not the earthly, political one.

When Cándido was transferred to the interior of the country and after a while escaped to Italy – having promised to write to me often, though he never sent a single letter – I felt bereft for a while. I drifted from one church to another, but it all sounded completely hollow, and the wafers were made of lower-quality flour and water.

Many years later, I was living in Colonia. One afternoon, Cándido called me on the phone: he was in Montevideo.

'I'll be right there,' he said. Someone had told him how to find me. And he came; a few hours later he was ringing the doorbell to my house.

There he was at the front door, the same as ever. I later found out that he'd come from Australia. And I don't think he was in Colonia just to see me; a film was being shot there starring Marcello Mastroianni, and the next day Cándido set about tracking him down. Eventually he found him and was able to ask the actor, in Italian, how he was. '*Bene*,' Marcello answered, and Cándido was satisfied.

But that night, standing at my front door, very serious, with his teeth clenched, he didn't even say hello, or ask how I was doing. He simply said:

'Where's the chessboard?'

# EPILOGUE TO THE DIARY

27.10.2002/23:31

> I'm finished with this. Or, rather, it's finished with me. Fundamentally, my mind has always balked at any kind of ending.
>
> J. D. SALINGER, *SEYMOUR: AN INTRODUCTION*

A diary is not a novel; storylines often begin which then go nowhere, and it's unlikely any of them will reach a neat conclusion. I find it fascinating, and more than a little mysterious, how I almost never have a precise memory of the things and people who come and go from my life. I hardly ever know when I met someone, or under what circumstances, and I frequently find that someone has disappeared from my life without me realising. Some disappearances last a few years and then the person shows up again; others seem to be permanent, and in some cases the person is even erased from my memory, apparently leaving no trace.

I would have liked it to be possible to read the diary of the grant as a novel; my vague hope was that all the unfinished storylines would somehow or other be resolved. But of course, that wasn't what happened, and this book, taken as a whole, is a display or even a museum of unfinished stories.

The aim of this epilogue is not to tie up all the loose ends, but simply to show how things currently stand with some of them.

*Antidepressants*. On Sunday, 13 August 2000, at 5.35 a.m., I wrote: 'I think the antidepressants are poisoning me.' A few months later, in the period no longer covered by the diary, this first impression was proved entirely correct. One afternoon, when I was in the kitchen, I had an attack of vertigo. This happened again on other days, always in the kitchen. I thought it might be an optical phenomenon, related to the pattern on the tiles. Then I began to have similar attacks elsewhere in the apartment, and out in the street. Especially in the street, and especially when I stopped at a red light before crossing the road; sometimes I had to hold onto whoever was with me and, if there was no one with me, to the pole of the traffic light itself. I began to suspect that this vertigo was a consequence of the antidepressants and stopped taking them, and tried to clean out my body by drinking lots of water. Little by little, the vertigo went away; it took about a month to disappear. It's funny how the immediate reaction faded as my organism adapted, only to return much more forcefully after some time.

*Yoghurt with vitamin C.* These days I'm drinking that marvellous, exquisite yoghurt I couldn't drink before because it gave me haemorrhoids – which, according to my theory, was due to the use of ascorbic acid as a preservative. I discovered that the acid, or whatever it was, was floating on the surface of the liquid in concentrated form, probably contained in a small amount of cream, because even though it's fat-free yoghurt there's always a bit of cream. Now I spoon some of this substance off the top and throw it away, and the yoghurt has stopped causing me problems.

*Rosa Chacel trilogy.* On Saturday, 16 September, I wrote: 'it seems to be the first volume of a trilogy, meaning that when I get hold of the other two I'll have to choke them down as well. I hope they're more appetising than this one.' Well, they're not. I got hold of another volume and it was unreadable. Then Chl gave me another book by Doña Rosa, which wasn't part of the trilogy, and it was unreadable as well. This doesn't take away from my admiration for her, but I think it's a shame.

*The poor-quality monitor.* No change.

*Defrag.* I found a program online that fixes the problems with the Windows 98 DEFRAG, and now a procedure that used to take some four hours can be wrapped up in less than twenty minutes.

*Ghosts.* This year, a few months ago, my doctor came to see me, and as always her dog, Mendieta, came too. My doctor sat down in one of the armchairs and I asked if she'd like some coffee. She said yes. The air conditioning was on, so I had the door to the corridor I needed to go down to reach the kitchen closed. The corridor was dark, and when I opened the door, the only light came from the room where the armchairs are; in the gloom I saw Mendieta the dog trot briskly past in the direction of my bedroom, which was also in darkness. 'How strange,' I thought, because Mendieta the dog always comes over to wherever we are to beg for treats, or, if he's not hungry, he heads for the little chair by the balcony where he can curl up and sleep. I turned and asked my doctor if she knew where Mendieta the dog was. 'He must have gone to sit in his chair,' she said. 'But I just saw him go past. How did he get into the corridor?' I was sure the door between the living room and the corridor had been shut. Then I began to doubt myself, because although I'd seen a shape that more or less resembled Mendieta, really it had just been a fairly compact, three-dimensional shadow, and not a properly defined figure. And the thing is, this is what ghosts usually look like: more of a sketch, a projection, than a finished form. I stepped into the corridor and saw that the door was indeed shut. Had he slipped out between my legs without my noticing? I went into the bedroom and turned on the light, and I didn't see any dogs. There was no sign of him in the kitchen either. I continued with my exclamations and questions; my doctor got up from her armchair and went to investigate. Strangely, she found Mendieta the dog lying in a corner where he never normally goes, to the left of the double doors into the living room. When he saw his owner, he perked up and went back to his usual normal behaviour. 'Now Mendieta the dog has started splitting in two,' I said. 'He's learnt how to do it.' It was the first time in my life I'd encountered the astral body of a dog. And it was the second time in my life I'd seen a ghost.

My doctor was unmoved; she's always been convinced that I'm mad, or at least that I have an overactive imagination. But the next day she called me on the phone. 'My mother says she saw Mendieta the dog's shadow while Mendieta the dog was somewhere else,' she said. 'I thought she was confusing it with the maid's shadow.' I laughed at that, because the maid is about six feet tall. And the following day, my doctor's mother saw the shadow of Mendieta the dog a second time.

There have been no further apparitions of this ghost, at least not that any of us have seen.

*Telepathy with the bookseller.* It hasn't worked since.

*Walks.* It was an extremely cold winter. And a few months ago the country hit the sharp end of an economic crisis, meaning that most of my guardians are busy with extra hours of paid work, though they don't always get paid for them. As a result I haven't done much walking at all, and I'm even more worried about the health consequences of my sedentary existence.

*Love.* Ever since the worm dream, I've been able to see Chl without feeling torn in half when she leaves. We don't see each other much, but we see each other. Sometimes she takes me out for a walk. She's still a saint.

And ever since that dream I've felt free enough to begin the odd romance, but now isn't the time to go into those.

*Electricians.* Ulises has gone back to Colonia, leaving me with plenty of unresolved electrical problems. My doctor recommended another electrician who she says is very good, but it looks like my waking hours don't suit him, and so far he hasn't come to do any of the work I've requested.

*Stealing software.* I've given it up, so now no one needs to worry about coming after me. I uninstalled most of the programs I had, because they take up a lot of space on the hard drive and I never use them. My computer's still a bit slow, though. I've kept some of the free programs, and with some of the ones that aren't free, instead of cracking them, I install them again when the trial period's over, which is normally every thirty days. With others, I don't change the programs themselves but I do alter certain modifications they effect in the Registry, which I'm well within my rights to do; these programs surreptitiously place, on *my* hard drive, information about the date on which they were installed, and if I find where this information is saved I feel perfectly entitled to remove or replace it.

*Mónica*. She's fine at the moment, working very hard, like all the women I know. I regret not having the strength to finish that dramatic story in the diary; it was very careless of me.

*Chl*. I was able to confirm her paranormal faculties. A few months ago she recounted, without my having mentioned anything to her, a dream she'd had; this dream contained a very strange scene involving me. I was quite shocked when I heard her account of it, because, give or take a few details, it was an accurate description of a scene I'd experienced in what we usually call 'real life'. The dream took place simultaneously with the 'real' scene, or perhaps a little later. And the scene itself was so preposterous that it would be foolish to see it as a coincidence.

*Bad language censored by Word*. With the help of some special programs, I carried out a careful investigation and found that the censorship of terms like 'penis' in Word is the work of a file called MSSP3ES. DLL. I was able to open that file in a special editor and modify it so it stopped getting in my way. It's quite educational to look through the file and see the words it censors; I didn't even know some of them existed.

*Body clock*. On 5 September of this year I took the radical step of giving up coffee, probably for the wrong reasons (although maybe not entirely; I thought it was responsible for a rash I was getting around the time I went to bed. After I'd experimented with all the foods that could have been causing it, coffee was the only thing left. I stopped drinking it, and the rash came back again after a few days). The immediate, unexpected effect of cutting out coffee was that I began to wake up at 11 a.m. This is still going on now, even though I don't always go to bed at a sensible hour. I found it hard work adapting to the new rhythm and I still haven't completely managed; often I get irresistibly sleepy after meals, in a more pronounced way than before, and doze off in the reading armchair. Still, I've made it out for a few walks during daylight hours, and today (30.10.2002), for the first time in ages, I crossed the Plaza Independencia in the sunshine, at four in the afternoon. I walked home using one hand as a visor, protecting my eyes, which are still very sensitive to natural light.

My theory is that the coffee was altering my sleeping hours by suppressing the production of melatonin, rather than by increasing my nervous excitement; I say this in case anyone is interested in investigating.

*Pigeons.* On 3 March of this year, no sooner had I lifted the bedroom blinds than I saw a sizeable delegation of pigeons arrive and distribute themselves over the flat roof next door. Strangely enough, most if not all of them looked very similar to the widow – or to the widow's children, because these were young pigeons. It wasn't easy to count them because they wouldn't stop moving, coming to rest and then changing position on the railings and ledges. In the end I arrived at an estimate: there were around forty-five of them.

*Aerial.* The aerial is gone from the flat roof next door. I have no idea when it was taken away; a few days ago I was looking out of the window for a bit, which I haven't done in a while, and suddenly I saw that the aerial, or whatever it was – that post with something on top of it – had vanished without a trace. The landscape is as clear as it was before. The pigeon's skull doesn't seem to have moved. I can't see the bones of the body, but perhaps, even now, they're still there.

# TRANSLATOR'S AFTERWORD

In the year 2000, in Montevideo, Uruguay, Mario Levrero was awarded a Guggenheim grant to complete his 'luminous novel', a project he had abandoned some fifteen years before. Thanks to 'Mr Guggenheim's dollars', he was preparing to spend the next twelve months living a life of 'full-time leisure', released from his usual money-making commitments and able to turn his whole attention to writing. But first, he thinks, he'd better fix the shutters in his apartment. And buy a couple of armchairs. And maybe a lamp. So begins his 'diary of the grant' – and so it goes on, for 400 pages, recording everything Levrero does *except* finishing his book: the detective novels he reads, the computer programs he writes, the pigeons he watches through the window and the portable air-conditioning units he makes endless ill-fated attempts to purchase. This diary becomes the prologue to the unfinished manuscript, and the two together form Levrero's masterpiece: *The Luminous Novel*.

In January 2018, in south London, I was preparing to translate this beguiling, preposterous, uncategorisable book. I had a grant from English PEN, a year to finish the project, and more leisure than I'd had in a long time, having recently left an office job. And, as the year went on, I found my life overlapping with Levrero's in ever more ways. Soon I, too, was keeping a diary, in which I recorded my own dreams, run-ins with bureaucracy and attempts to get out of bed at a civilised hour. After a few months, when the file containing my translation grew too unwieldy, I tried my hand at Levrero's beloved Visual Basic, using a macro to split the text into six exactly equal parts. Meanwhile, my dabbling in computer card games – for research purposes – became an addiction that encroached alarmingly on my translation time, and I, like Levrero, began keeping a guilty eye on whether my most-used program was Word or Solitaire. In the summer, inspired by Levrero's musings on the activities of some ants, I decided to investigate the insects in my garden, and ended up gripped for weeks on end by the drama unfolding among the spiders on the patio. And when, in August, my boyfriend announced that he was considering buying a portable air-conditioning unit, I fixed him with a thousand-yard stare and told him he didn't know what he was getting into.

The translator Robin Myers has said that translating a text is like going to live in it for a while, and this felt particularly true with *The Luminous Novel*. The book is a world unto itself, existing half in real life – I corresponded with and even met several of the characters – and half in Levrero's own inner universe of dreams, visions, supernatural presences and telepathic communication with booksellers. Levrero, however, would have bristled at such a distinction: he was adamant that what took place in his imagination was no less real than what took place in 'so-called objective reality', just as he maintained that instead of saying that something was 'only a dream', we ought to say it was 'no less than a dream'. Marcial Souto, Levrero's first publisher, describes him as 'a realistic novelist who lives on another planet', and he's right: Levrero treats the fantastical as if it were perfectly ordinary, and makes the mundane shimmer with bizarre possibility. As he becomes increasingly reclusive and nocturnal, drifting through the 'never-ending small hours' in his Montevideo apartment, exploring the inner reaches of the computer and his subconscious mind, though rarely venturing further afield than the supermarket or the dentist, he records his experiences with the care and curiosity of a traveller through uncharted terrain.

Only Levrero would devote pages to an account of finding an automatic dial-up program in the early days of the internet, being 'annoyed beyond words' by a particular dialogue box that appeared whenever the program opened, and writing 'a very interesting, entertaining, agreeable email' to the program's manufacturer, a man from Texas, offering to 'send him some amusing stories in exchange for the codes that would get rid of that damn box'. Only Levrero would make it so funny – 'But I couldn't soften his hard Texan heart' – or describe, with no shift in tone whatsoever, how he took a siesta one 'warm, muggy summer evening', dreamed about visiting the programmer's house and being given a cup of coffee by his wife, and then woke up knowing exactly how to solve the problem. And only he would move from this to a discussion of ownership and artistic creation – 'A text I've written isn't "mine" because I own it; it's "mine" in the way a child might be "mine".'

*The Luminous Novel* was published in 2005, a year after Levrero's death from a heart attack at sixty-four, and it is often compared to another posthumous novel that changed the face of Latin American literature at the turn of the millennium. While Levrero was wrestling with Word 2000 and refining his home-made yoghurt recipe in his Montevideo apartment, thousands of miles away, in Spain, the Chilean writer Roberto Bolaño was racing to finish his continent-hopping, genre-defying magnum opus, *2666*. First published in 2004, a year after Bolaño's death from liver failure at the age of fifty, *2666* takes in Nazi Germany, the Black Panthers, Dracula's castle, European academia and the maquiladora factories on the US-Mexico border, and couldn't be further from the cloistered, inward-looking *Luminous Novel*. Nonetheless, these two literary epics thrust together by circumstance make a fascinating pair, one full to the brim and the other empty – but empty to the brim. In the words of the Argentinian author Mauro Libertella: 'If Roberto Bolaño showed us it was still possible to write the great Latin American novel, Levrero told us it wasn't necessary.' *2666* is a book about everything, but *The Luminous Novel* is a book about everything else: about how writing, imagination and the human soul behave in the downtime, in the 'never-ending small hours' when most people are asleep.

ANNIE MCDERMOTT, HASTINGS, DECEMBER 2020

Dear readers,

As well as relying on bookshop sales, And Other Stories relies on subscriptions from people like you for many of our books, whose stories other publishers often consider too risky to take on.

Our subscribers don't just make the books physically happen. They also help us approach booksellers, because we can demonstrate that our books already have readers and fans. And they give us the security to publish in line with our values, which are collaborative, imaginative and 'shamelessly literary'.

All of our subscribers:

- receive a first-edition copy of each of the books they subscribe to
- are thanked by name at the end of our subscriber-supported books
- receive little extras from us by way of thank you, for example: postcards created by our authors

## BECOME A SUBSCRIBER, OR GIVE A SUBSCRIPTION TO A FRIEND

Visit andotherstories.org/subscriptions to help make our books happen. You can subscribe to books we're in the process of making. To purchase books we have already published, we urge you to support your local or favourite bookshop and order directly from them – the often unsung heroes of publishing.

## OTHER WAYS TO GET INVOLVED

If you'd like to know about upcoming events and reading groups (our foreign-language reading groups help us choose books to publish, for example) you can:

- join our mailing list at: andotherstories.org
- follow us on Twitter: @andothertweets
- join us on Facebook: facebook.com/AndOtherStoriesBooks
- admire our books on Instagram: @andotherpics
- follow our blog: andotherstories.org/ampersand

# CURRENT & UPCOMING BOOKS

Translated by Annie McDermott

# Empty Words

MARIO LEVRERO.

'One of the funniest and most influential writers of recent times. This book might change your life, or at least your handwriting.' ALEJANDRO ZAMBRA

# EMPTY WORDS

*Translated by Annie McDermott*

An eccentric novelist decides to go back to basics on his journey of self-improvement: he will strip out the literary aspect of his writing and simply improve his handwriting. The novelist begins to keep a notebook of handwriting exercises, hoping that if he is able to improve his penmanship, his personal character will also improve. What begins as a mere physical exercise becomes involuntarily coloured by humorous reflections and tender anecdotes about living, writing, and the sense – and nonsense – of existence. The first book by Mario Levrero to be translated into English, *Empty Words* is the perfect introduction to a major author.

'*Empty Words* looks like a novel about handwriting, but really it's a book about the self. It shows the fragile, magical work that can be done by the novel as a form.'
Adam Thirlwell, *London Review of Books*

'Levrero relishes the mundane comedy of household dynamics as much as more cosmic jokes of existence. It's enticing.'
Anthony Cummins, *The Guardian*

'Levrero is an author who challenges the canonical idea of Latin American literature. If you want to complete the puzzle of our tradition, you must read him.'
Juan Pablo Villalobos, *Granta*

'A lighthearted wisdom beats in every sentence of *Empty Words*, a little masterpiece by Mario Levrero, one of the funniest and most influential writers of recent times. This book might change your life, or at least your handwriting.'
Alejandro Zambra

# I DON'T EXPECT ANYONE TO BELIEVE ME

JUAN PABLO VILLALOBOS

**TRANSLATED BY**
**DANIEL HAHN**

# I DON'T EXPECT ANYONE TO BELIEVE ME

by Kirkus Prize Finalist

## Juan Pablo Villalobos

*Translated by Daniel Hahn*

'I don't expect anyone to believe me,' warns the narrator of this novel, a Mexican student called Juan Pablo Villalobos. He is about to fly to Barcelona on a scholarship, when he's kidnapped in a bookshop and whisked away by thugs to a basement. The pistol-toting gangsters are threatening his cousin – a wannabe entrepreneur known to some as 'Projects' and to others as 'dickhead' – who is gagged and tied to a chair. The thugs say Juan Pablo must work for them in Barcelona. He accepts, albeit unwillingly, and albeit after the crime boss has forced him at gunpoint into a discussion on the limits of humour in literature.

Part campus novel, part gangster thriller, *I Don't Expect Anyone to Believe Me* is Villalobos at his best, exuberantly foul-mouthed and intellectually agile.

'An eccentric hybrid, combining pulpy crime fiction . . . with avant-garde archness. Villalobos's take is refreshingly exuberant.'
Houman Barekat, *The Guardian*

'A testament to the vibrancy of the Latin American novel.'
Nick Burns, *Literary Review*

'Villalobos's chaotic, feverish narrative works – it is a challenging, but rewarding read.'
Lucy Popescu, *Financial Times*

MARIO LEVRERO was born in Montevideo, Uruguay, in 1940 and died there in 2004. He wrote twelve novels and several short story collections and it was not long before he gained cult status amongst readers in Uruguay and Argentina, despite keeping a low profile. He has inspired Latin American writers such as Rodolfo Fogwill, César Aira and Alejandro Zambra. In 2000 he was awarded the Guggenheim grant that allowed him to complete work on *The Luminous Novel*, which was published posthumously.

ANNIE MCDERMOTT's translations include Mario Levrero's *Empty Words* and *The Luminous Novel* for And Other Stories, as well as *Loop* by Brenda Lozano, *Feebleminded* by Ariana Harwicz (co-translation with Carolina Orloff) and *City of Ulysses* by Teolinda Gersão (co-translation with Jethro Soutar). She has previously lived in Mexico City and São Paulo, and is now based in London.